THE WORLD'S CLASSICS

ALEXANDRE DUMAS

Louise de la Vallière

Edited with an Introduction by
DAVID COWARD

Oxford   New York
OXFORD UNIVERSITY PRESS
1995

Oxford University Press, Walton Street, Oxford OX2 6DP

Oxford New York
Athens Auckland Bangkok Bombay
Calcutta Cape Town Dar es Salaam Delhi
Florence Hong Kong Istanbul Karachi
Kuala Lumpur Madras Madrid Melbourne
Mexico City Nairobi Paris Singapore
Taipei Tokyo Toronto
and associated companies in
Berlin Ibadan

Oxford is a trade mark of Oxford University Press

British Library Cataloguing in Publication Data

Data available

Library of Congress Cataloging-in-Publication Data
Dumas, Alexandre, 1802–1870.
[Louise de la Vallière. English]
Louise de la Vallière / Alexandre Dumas; edited with an
introduction by David Coward.
Includes bibliographical references.
1. La Vallière, Françoise-Louise de La Baume Le Blanc, duchesse
de, 1644–1710—Fiction. 2. France—History—Louis XIV, 1643–1715—
Fiction. I. Coward, David. II. Title. III. Series.
PQ2227.L78E5 1995 94–45612
ISBN 0–19–282389–2

1 3 5 7 9 10 8 6 4 2

Typeset by Graphicraft Typesetters Ltd., Hong Kong
Printed in Great Britain by
BPC Paperbacks Ltd.
Aylesbury, Bucks

CONTENTS

CONTENTS

INTRODUCTION

THE Romantic Age in France was a period of extravagance and
excess when feelings replaced thought and heroes died young.
But it was also an Age of Money. After 1789, France had run
through successive regimes of different political hues, from the
rabid republicanism of the *sans culottes* to Napoleonic imperial-
ism and, after 1815, the entrenched conservativism of the newly
restored monarchy. The Revolution of July 1830 carried the
hopes of a new generation eager to see the establishment of the
rule of liberal values. In the event, it did not, as is the way with
Revolutions, devour its children. Instead, it encouraged them to
grow rich. The cautious reign of Louis-Philippe offered little to
idealists. It refused to extend the suffrage, did nothing to improve the life of the poor, and, as J. S. Mill remarked, operated
'almost exclusively through the meaner and more selfish impulses of mankind'.

For France now at last embarked upon its long delayed industrial revolution. Manufacturers began to be a power in the land.
Railways put out tentacles everywhere. Lawyers and money-
men became the new élite. Books, hitherto a privilege of the
leisured classes, became a product and were now put within the
reach of shallower pockets, not in the cause of enlightenment,
but of profit. The artisanal publishing trade of the eighteenth
century had been transformed by better inks, improved papers,
and mechanized presses. Small and medium-sized publishing
houses learned new methods and by the 1860s publishing would
represent 10 per cent of France's industrial output. Thus the
phenomenal abbé Migne, who cornered the market for sacred
texts, was in 1842 employing 300 typesetters, printers, book-
binders, and clerks, a work-force exceeded only by the larger
ironmasters and textile barons. But the competition for the hearts,
minds, and money of the French was nowhere keener than in
the fledgling newspaper industry.

The July Monarchy relaxed the rules controlling the press,
which had contributed significantly to bringing down the previous regime. Anyone who could afford to put up a modest surety

could now start a newspaper. The result was an explosion of newsprint. There were satirical and literary reviews, magazines for women, children, socialists, and catholics, and dailies which carried news and comment. The newspaper columnist was born: Jules Janin and Sainte-Beuve emerged as arbiters of literary taste and Mme de Girardin, author of popular novels, invented the gossip column with her weekly contributions to *La Presse*, founded by her husband, Émile, in 1836. Girardin was one of the new breed of press lords. He halved his cover price by carrying advertisements. Armand Dutacq, founder of *Le Siècle*, responded immediately, and their more conservative colleagues had no option but to follow. When it was launched in 1829, annual subscription rates for the highly respected intellectual *Revue des Deux Mondes* were fixed at 80 francs: it was read by few manual workers, who were paid an average of 3 francs a day. In 1835 there were about 70,000 subscribers to periodicals published in Paris. In 1836, after the opening salvos of the press war, 200,000 Parisians were subscribing to a daily newspaper and the figure continued to rise. *Le Siècle*, aimed at manual workers and the lower middle classes, quickly got into its stride with an unprecedented circulation of 36,000 copies. The battle for readers, who meant economic survival, was joined.

Newspapers may have followed different editorial policies and catered for different audiences, but on one thing they agreed: running a novel in episodes could mean the difference between success and failure. The *roman feuilleton* became an indispensable factor in the expansion of the cheap press. So strong was the belief that fiction sold papers that until the end of the century nearly all novels were first published in serial parts. Girardin, Dutacq, and Dr Varon (who acquired *Le Constitutionnel* in 1844) now commissioned writers to provide gripping copy to tight deadlines. Stories which proved popular were extended indefinitely; those which did not were terminated abruptly. Balzac and George Sand failed to demonstrate the popular touch which, however, was possessed in abundance by Frédéric Soulié and Eugène Sue, who specialized in vast, sensational novels of low life. Sue's *Les Mystères de Paris* (*Le Journal des Débats*, June 1842–October 1843) set new cliff-hanging standards and *Le Juif errant* (1844–5) had an immediate impact on the circulation of

Le Constitutionnel in which it appeared: the number of subscribers rose from 3,600 to 24,000 almost overnight. Serialized fiction, condemned by Sainte-Beuve as 'industrial literature', acquired a vast readership which in 1847 the historian Michelet estimated at 1.5 million. To newspaper editors, *feuilletonistes* had become indispensable and they were prepared to pay them huge fees. The situation was made for Alexandre Dumas, who was to overtake even Sue and become the 'King of Romance'.

Born with no social advantages in 1802 at Villers-Cotterêts, he had taken Paris by storm in 1829 with a play which catapulted him into the front ranks of the young Romantics. But this first success had not been bought easily, nor was it easy to sustain. His mother was an innkeeper's daughter. His father was the illegitimate son of a minor French noble, the Marquis Davy de la Pailleterie, who had emigrated to Saint-Domingo (Haiti) in the middle of the eighteenth century. In 1762 a son, Thomas-Alexandre, was born of his liaison with Marie-Cessette Dumas, a slave. After the Marquis returned to France in 1780, Thomas-Alexandre took his mother's name, enlisted, and during the Revolution rose rapidly through the ranks where, for his impetuous bravura, enormous physical strength, and the colour of his skin, he was known as 'the Black Devil', an inspiring cavalry commander but a general of erratic judgement. He took part in the Egyptian campaign in 1798 and proved to be Napoleon's most uninhibited critic. Though Bonaparte once threatened to stand him in front of a firing squad, General Dumas was tolerated for his qualities of military leadership. But when he applied for sick leave at the end of 1798, it was immediately granted. The captain of his ship, unaware that Nelson's friend, King Ferdinand, was now at war with France, ill-advisedly put into southern Italy and General Dumas was detained in a pestilential prison, returning to France, broken in health, in 1801. He died in 1806, when Alexandre was only 4 but already old enough to register the tales his father told. Indeed, the General's career could have been a novel written by his son. His headstrong courage and outspoken individualism belong to d'Artagnan and his giant strength to Porthos (who Dumas said was 'perhaps the best' of the Musketeers), while the relationship between Athos and Raoul has seemed to some critics to reflect both Dumas's love for his lost father and his paternal affection for his own son, the author of *The Lady of the Camellias*. In the same way, the triumph of the Count of Monte Cristo, one of the most famous examples of the Romantic fascination with prisons, may be seen as retribution for the Italian privations of the father he had known only briefly.

The General bequeathed him the swarthy skin and tight curls which were later to prove a boon to cartoonists, but little else. His mother had no money and when Dumas was later to seek patrons, his father's former colleagues, with their feet comfortably under the restored Bourbon table, were not anxious to be reminded of their Napoleonic past. Dumas received an education of sorts, was put to work in a lawyer's office at 14 but quickly decided that he would be a writer. By the time he was 16, he was writing plays with a friend. In 1823 he moved permanently to Paris where he was employed as a copyist by the Duc d'Orléans. In 1825, already a father (Alexandre *fils* was born in 1824), he staged a play, written in collaboration with two other young hopefuls, which went unremarked. The following year he published, at his own expense, a volume of short stories which sold only four copies. But he managed to get his poems into respectable periodicals and slowly gained a foothold in literary circles. In 1829 *Henri III and his Court*, a rousing melodrama which not only broke all the accepted dramatic rules but was highly critical of the prevailing regime, made his name famous. At 27, Dumas was one of the acknowledged leaders of the Romantic movement in literature and, in his own terms, a General.

Romanticism, said Victor Hugo, meant 'liberalism in literature'. But before literature could become liberal, France had to be made free of the stranglehold of the reactionary right. When unrest turned into revolution in July 1830, Dumas put down his pen and picked up a gun, though he never fired it in anger. He toured the streets, stood on a barricade or two, and rushed off to Soissons where, much to the surprise of the bemused and most co-operative garrison commander, he captured a gunpowder depot single-handed. Fresh from this triumph, which he was to describe with self-disparaging irony in his *Memoirs*, he persuaded General La Fayette, commander of the insurgents, to send him on a mission to the Vendée, where Bourbon loyalties were strongest, to attract recruits to the National Guard which would serve the new Orleanist regime. The Vendéens surrendered to his charm but not to his cause and Dumas soon returned to Paris, laden less with political glory than with vivid memories of La Rochelle, Tours, and Blois which he would later use as settings for tales of the Musketeers.

The July Revolution proved to be as grave a disappointment to Dumas as it was to progressive opinion generally. The new government, he said, was arbitrary in its actions and no friend to freedom, and it was staffed by hangers-on who put preferment above justice. But if Dumas's political opinions were sincere, his political indignations were short-lived. Besides, his extravagant lifestyle had to be financed, and writing was his only resource. *Henri III* was followed by a stream of explosive melodramas with plots drawn from historical sources and contemporary manners. In the preface to *Napoleon*, he stated his creed. 'I do not recognize any literary system; I belong to no school; I march under no banner. To entertain and intrigue are the only rules, which I do not say I succeed in observing, but which I acknowledge.' Fortunately, his notion of what 'entertained and intrigued' coincided exactly with that of his audiences who thrilled to inflamed passions, poetic retribution, heroic self-sacrifice, and gore. These, Dumas furnished in generous measure. He was quite aware that in terms of poetry and subtlety his plays were inferior to those of Hugo, whom he greatly admired. But he also knew that his crudeness was his strength. He had a greater feel for theatre which he rooted in the principle of brutal conflicts between strong characters in strong situations. To the dissection of motive and feeling and the introspective monologue, he preferred action. Audiences loved Dumas.

But the public palate becomes easily jaded and by 1835 tastes were changing. Dumas remained committed to the theatre—he liked the immediacy of contact with an audience—and *Kean* was staged with great success in 1836. But the vogue for Romantic drama was fading and he turned increasingly to prose. He published short fictions and accounts of his travels in magazines, but they consolidated rather than enhanced his reputation. He was generous to budding authors who asked his opinion of plays and tales which he would revise and sometimes rewrite. Dumas was not entirely disinterested in this. For all his creative energies, he was not blessed with the kind of imagination which conjures narratives out of nothing. He needed a spark—an incident, a climax, a character—to ignite his invention and he regularly begged, borrowed, and even stole plots which appealed to him. It was a habit, no doubt exacerbated by the tight deadlines to which he worked, which created considerable misunderstanding. Few authors rely entirely on their imaginations and most depend on real memories, live 'models', and written 'sources'. Dumas was no plagiarist and was never successfully sued for theft of literary property. But he did use 'collaborators' in ways which anticipate the use made by cinema and television of 'researchers', 'script editors', and 'story consultants'. His long collaboration with Auguste Maquet, whom he met in 1838, is instructive.

In 1838 Maquet, a former history teacher who had hopes of a literary career, brought Dumas a play and asked for an opinion. Dumas revised it extensively and it was performed the following year, as *Bathilde*, under Maquet's name. But Dumas so transformed a short novel, *Le Bonhomme Buvat*, which Maquet had set in the early eighteenth century, that it was entirely reasonable that the result, expanded into four volumes, *Le Chevalier d'Harmental*, should have been credited to Dumas alone. From these beginnings developed a ten-year association which coincided with Dumas's most productive and brilliant period. It continued until 1851 when Maquet, tired of waiting for Dumas (then in straitened circumstances and, as always, far too impatient to attend to such dull matters) to pay him the money he owed under the terms of the formal written agreement they had drawn up. He never complained that he was exploited. He did not take the opportunity to protest when, in 1845, a journalist publicly accused Dumas of being the capitalist director of a 'fiction factory' which employed ill-paid hacks to churn out tales which he then sold at a large profit. Dumas sued and won his case. Much later, in 1858, Maquet asked the courts to recognize him as Dumas's 'co-author', not to establish plagiarism, but rather to give him a legal entitlement to his unpaid royalties. He lost the argument.

If Dumas came to count on Maquet's help, Maquet was not

indispensable and, left to his own devices after their association ended, his attempts to make an independent career came to nothing. Nor did any other of Dumas's collaborators achieve great things alone. But Dumas was always grateful to Maquet and acknowledged his role whenever his publishers agreed: the plain commercial fact was that a book signed by Dumas sold more copies than a book for which he shared the credit. But the exact nature of their collaboration is still mysterious. It is certain that they worked together adapting the novels, once written, for the stage. But it is clear too that Maquet had a hand in planning the novels, discussing plots with Dumas and helping to develop story-lines. But between the drafting of a plan and the writing of the book, considerable changes were made by Dumas, as the draft outline of the opening of *Louise de la Vallière* will make clear: the original order of events has been changed (the corresponding chapter numbers appear in square brackets) and the published text contains additional material:

[...] The request to the King—the King's reply [1]. Madame's co-quettish behaviour towards the King [20]. The King's love for Madame. Monsieur's jealousy—Anne of Austria torn between her 2 children. Monsieur's jealousy—he goes to see his mother [17]. Anne of Austria warns the King [18]. The King in love with Madame [19]. Madame accepts his love. Plan agreed between the King and Madame to make it appear that H. M. loves somebody else. Madame says it should be somebody unimportant. They choose La Vallière [20].

The fête at Fontainebleau [21]. La Vallière confessing to Montalais that she cannot understand how anyone who has seen the King could fall in love with any other man [23].

Fouquet—the King asks him for another 2 millions to pay for the fête at Fontainebleau; he is convinced that no finer fête had ever been staged. Ah, says Colbert, who has skimped on the festivities, M. Fouquet ought to lay on a fête for the King at his splendid mansion at Vaux. Agreed, replies Fouquet [28].

Athos, d'Artagnan walking the staircase. Baisemeaux at the foot. His little difficulty. What he tells d'Artagnan about deferring his debt to Aramis [3] . . .

But Maquet also supplied what would now be called 'treatments' which Dumas would then expand beyond recognition. Some of Maquet's outline chapters for *The Three Musketeers* have survived and they show how drastically Dumas altered them, turning flat descriptions into dramatic action, adding new twists, and injecting suspense and humour. But there is no doubt that on odd occasions, when Dumas ran out of time, Maquet's copy was sent directly to the printer without being changed (or probably even read) by Dumas.

But in one area, Maquet was invaluable. As a trained historian, he filled the gaps in Dumas's knowledge and suggested books where he might find authentic background details. Now, Dumas's taste for history was no personal idiosyncrasy, but a professional necessity. The novels of Walter Scott and Fenimore Cooper had thrilled French readers in the 1820s and Romantic writers sought and found inspiration in their own history. It was a source of local colour and a stick with which to beat the present. It furnished playwrights like Dumas, Vigny, and Musset with subjects and it fed the imagination of novelists: Hugo set *Notre Dame de Paris* (1831) in the fifteenth century and even Balzac, the chronicler of contemporary manners, revisited the French Revolution in *Les Chouans* (1829). Historians like Michelet and Guizot adopted a strongly narrative style, but readers who wished to explore their past in the original texts were spoiled for choice. Memoirs, journals, and letters were published, some for the first time, in huge collections, often running to hundreds of volumes, and demand seemed inexhaustible. But the general public was not interested in the causes of the French Revolution or the clauses of the Treaty which ended the Thirty Years War. It clamoured for the dramas of history, the anguish of victims, and the triumph of heroes. As his career as a dramatist began at last to wane, Dumas decided to give them, through the columns of newspapers which paid so well, what they wanted.

He had been commissioned to write a history of *The Century of Louis XIV* (1843), and during the course of his researches had wandered down many byways littered with tales waiting to be told. It was thus, quite by chance, that he found his four heroes. In the preface to *The Three Musketeers*, he tells how he stumbled across the pseudo-*Mémoires de M. d'Artagnan* (1700) by Courtilz de Sandras, which he promptly 'devoured'. He was much taken by the central character, a resourceful Gascon, who steps gaily from one adventure to another and, in one episode, roguishly gets the better of a steely Englishwoman referred to only as 'Milédi'. He was also struck by the names of d'Artagnan's three companions which he thought might be assumed. Though they make only a brief appearance in the pseudo-*Mémoires*, they were enough to set his imagination to work.

Dumas claimed that history was a 'peg' on which he hung his stories. But if his musketeers rub shoulders with real kings and queens and involve themselves in events which decided the fate of nations, they are heroes who sprang fully grown from Dumas's imagination. Even so, they had distant links with history. For behind Courtilz's d'Artagnan, a picaresque adventurer who might have stepped out of a sub-Defoe novel, lay a rather dull and unattractive career soldier, Charles de Batz-Castelmore, born near Tarbes in about 1615, a d'Artagnan on his mother's side and a distant ancestor of Robert de Montesquiou, Proust's model for the homosexual Charlus. Charles de Batz joined Richelieu's Guards in 1635, took part in the King's wars and may have fought at the side of the royalists at the battle of Newbury in 1643. He became a Musketeer the following year and made a friend of a fellow officer, François de Montlézun, future governor of the Bastille (the Baisemeaux of *Louise de la Vallière*). When the company was disbanded in 1646 he became, as Colbert later put it, a 'creature of Mazarin' for whom he undertook many missions which may have included drowning an English spy. He saw further active service in the 1650s and rose to be Captain of Mazarin's Guards. When the Musketeers were re-formed in 1657, he was given effective command, though the absentee Duc de Nevers, a nephew of Mazarin, was officially the company's Captain-Lieutenant. He married in 1659 but the marriage, which produced two sons, ended in separation in 1665. After the death of Mazarin in 1661, he transferred his loyalties to Colbert whose orders he followed without question. It was he who arrested Fouquet, Louis XIV's disgraced finance minister, in 1661, and Lauzun, the King's rival for the affections of the Duchesse de Montpensier, a decade later. Doubtless as a reward for such loyal services, he was appointed Captain-Lieutenant of the Musketeers in 1667 and, in 1672, acting governor of Lille. A few official letters survive, the spelling of which is atrocious even by seventeenth-century standards, and they suggest that he exercised his authority rather uneasily. He was shot in the throat by a stray bullet at the siege of Maastricht in March 1673.

Much less is known about Athos, Aramis, and Porthos, though Dumas was wrong in suspecting that their names were assumed and perhaps concealed the identities of 'illustrious persons'. All three were Gascons and, like many of their compatriots whose fathers had loyally served Henri IV, 'King of France and Navarre', they sought to make their way in the King's armies. All three were distantly related to each other and to the Comte de Tréville who was appointed Captain-Lieutenant of Musketeers in 1634. Armand de Sillègue d'Athos d'Autevielle was born in the valley of the Oloron in about 1615, became a Musketeer in about 1640, and died in Paris in 1643. Henri d'Aramitz, born in the Béarn, joined the Musketeers in 1640, married in 1654, produced four children, and died perhaps in 1674. Isaac de Portau was born at Pau in 1617, was a member of Richelieu's regiment of Guards in 1640, transferred to the Musketeers in 1643, and thereafter disappeared without trace. Behind the larger-than-life characters invented by Dumas lay shadowy, unremarkable men.

When he began work, Dumas did not possess even these meagre facts. But it scarcely mattered: those names had started wheels turning in his mind. He approached Maquet who, to begin with, was unenthusiastic but was won over when Dumas showed the way. He began by rewriting and amplifying Courtilz's account of the first encounter of d'Artagnan, a raw youth from the Midi, and Athos, Aramis, and Porthos, veteran Musketeers and seasoned campaigners. But soon his doughty quartet came to life under his pen and thereafter Courtilz was largely abandoned. Taking a hint here and borrowing an anecdote there, he supplied his champions with adventures which immediately thrilled the readers of Le Siècle and, within a few years, had conquered all parts of the known world.

The Three Musketeers was written quickly and appeared in episodes in Le Siècle between 14 March and 14 July 1844. Covering a three-year period (1626–8), it tells how the champions of right confront evil in the delicious shape of the wicked Milady and counter the realpolitik of the ruthless Richelieu, the cunning Red Duke. Dumas inserted his heroes into the chronicles of France—they are present at the siege of La Rochelle and had a secret hand in the events which made history—but their instant popularity did not stem from Dumas's ambition 'to raise the novel to the dignity of history'. What boosted the circulation of *Le Siècle* was their unconquerable spirit, a mix of nonchalant bravado, selfless comradeship, and an unflagging zeal for just causes. On 30 June 1844, before the last episode appeared, readers were informed that a sequel was already in hand. In reality, Dumas was committed elsewhere: among other obligations was *The Count of Monte Cristo*, promised to *Le Journal des Débats*, which began appearing on 28 August 1844. It was not until the end of the year that he began work on *Twenty Years After*, which was serialized, again in *Le Siècle*, between 21 January and 2 August 1845.

Lesser authors would have been only too happy to produce further adventures cast in the same heroic, youthful mould. Not so Dumas. The novel opens in 1648 and time has taken its toll. D'Artagnan is still a musketeer but is bitter because he has not been given the rank to which his past services and undoubted qualities entitle him. Aramis has joined a religious order and sees his future in the Church. Athos has retired to a small estate near Blois, far from the sordid jostling for power which passes for life at Court. Porthos married a rich widow, now dead, and has become a gentleman who would dearly love to grace his absurd new name of Monsieur du Vallon de Bracieux de Pierrefonds with the title of Baron. But when the call comes they sink their differences, unsheathe their swords, and sally forth to save kings from their enemies. They travel to England and make a desperate attempt to rescue Charles I from the axe of the puritan executioner, confront evil once more in the guise of Mordaunt, son of Milady, and finally end the civil war in France in such a way that the French throne is made secure for the young Louis XIV.

In the issue carrying the final instalment of *Twenty Years After*, *Le Siècle* announced that the first episode of a further sequel, to be called *Ten Years After, or the Vicomte de Bragelonne*, would appear within three months. Dumas had decided that on their third outing his heroes would be not young, nor even mature, but on the threshold of old age. Unfortunately, he had over-committed himself again and would not settle down to work until September 1847. By then, he was at the height of his powers and success. He was living in his splendidly ornate Château de Monte Cristo at Marly and the Théâtre Historique which he had created and managed was doing excellent business. *The Vicomte de Bragelonne* (the subtitle *Or, Ten Years After* was added when the novel began appearing in volume form in 1848) was published in *Le Siècle* between 20 October 1847 and 12 January 1850. It is 1660. D'Artagnan has still not been given the promotion he believes he has earned. Athos has retired and is writing his memoirs, having raised his son, Raoul, to believe that a gentleman's honour lies in serving kings. Aramis has become a bishop but has even greater ambitions. And Porthos, now a baron and hoping for a dukedom, is still busy being a gentleman. Time has barnacled them and while they are all still committed to the principles of honour and monarchy, they no longer trust each other. Athos and d'Artagnan follow different paths in their efforts to restore Charles II to his throne. But if they have changed, so have the times: the new political undergrowth cannot be cleared with a swift thrust of a rapier. Their views are too honest and straightforward to allow them to enter the labyrinthine struggle for power between Fouquet and Colbert and understand the King's decision to become an absolute monarch. Only Aramis, always a master of intrigue, finds himself at home in the new age of political manœuvring. Porthos, chasing his dukedom, is a pawn to be used by whoever gets to him first. Yet in the end, they unite once more to uncover the mystery of the prisoner in the Iron Mask . . .

Dumas had been concerned that *Twenty Years After* had been weak in one respect: it had no love interest. The whole saga is, of course, an unashamed celebration of male clubbability which reduces women to stereotyped roles. In the first instalment, Milady, the tigress, not only wounded Athos to the point that he never loves again, but she murdered Constance, the only woman who ever touches d'Artagnan's heart. Aramis has always avoided commitments and known only scheming coquettes, while Porthos embarked on marriage with at least half an eye to the widow Coquenard's money. Dumas, always alert to the demands of the market, clearly decided that *The Vicomte de Bragelonne* would be different. For long periods, the Musketeers disappear from the

story, which makes a great deal of room for the amorous intrigues of the court. Guiche, Buckingham, and Louis are all drawn
to the pert and pretty Duchesse d'Orléans, while Raoul, a character conjured out of a stray reference in a memoir of the period,
is doomed to love Louise without return, for she loves and is
loved by the King.

Louise de la Vallière is the middle section of *The Vicomte de
Bragelonne*, the final instalment of the Musketeer saga. It is also
the least swashbuckling and most talkative stretch of Dumas's
epic narrative. For this reason, many readers have preferred the
earlier adventures of the Musketeers, a choice which 'pained
and puzzled' Robert Louis Stevenson, who confessed to having
read *The Vicomte de Bragelonne* at least five times with increasing
admiration. He accepted that Raoul, 'so well-conducted, so fine-
spoken, and withal so dreary' makes a poor hero, and conceded
that Louise, who is 'well-meant, not ill-designed, and sometimes has a word that rings out true', is an uninspiring heroine.
But he was greatly taken with the Duchesse d'Orléans and was
prepared 'to forgive that royal minx her most serious offences'.
But Dumas, so inventive, spreads a 'feast' before us: 'the love
adventures at Fontainebleau, with St Aignan's story of the dryad
and the business of de Guiche, de Wardes, and Manicamp;
Aramis made general of the Jesuits; Aramis at the Bastille . . .':

What other novel has such epic variety and nobility of incident? often,
if you will, impossible; often of the order of an Arabian story; and yet
all based in human nature. For if you come to that, what novel has
more human nature? not studied with the microscope, but seen largely,
in plain daylight, with the natural eye? What novel has more good
sense, and gaiety, and wit, and unflagging, admirable literary skill? . . .
what novel is inspired with a more unstrained or a more wholesome
morality? (*Works*, London, 1889, ix. 131)

Stevenson, like many of his generation, was convinced that
'there is no quite good book without a good morality' and would
not have exchanged a chapter of 'bracing old Dumas' 'for the
whole boiling of Zola'. It was a view echoed by Dumas's son in
1893 when he tried to explain why nearly three million copies of
his father's books had been sold and 600 of his titles re-serialized
in newspapers in the 23 years since his death. 'Man surrenders

completely only to those things which strike a deep chord, engage and move him to the core, exalt and elevate his inner being; those things which make him aware of his own worth, his dignity and that better part of himself which every serious writer is duty-bound to awaken or enhance. Man will never take lasting pleasure from the recital of human turpitude and vileness.'

It is not necessary to believe to quite such an extent in the moral influence of literature to surrender to the charm of Dumas. Written at high speed over six years—during which time Dumas also published *The Count of Monte Cristo*, *Marguerite de Valois*, *The Chevalier de Maison Rouge*, *The Memoirs of a Physician*, *The Forty-Five Guardsmen*, and others too numerous to list—the Musketeer cycle is a marvel of sustained pace and suspense. But the thrills and adventures do not alone account for Dumas's universal appeal. The tale is rooted in the principle of a conflict between primary values—good and evil, right and wrong, love and hate, success and failure—and Dumas always ensures that, whoever we are, we always know where we stand: on the side of the angels, shoulder to shoulder with dashing cavaliers who do not fear life, and with our faces set resolutely against the mean-spirited roundheads who impose their cramped will on others. Dumas is the champion of youth and comradeship which, in spite of the passing years and hardening arteries, remain always green. Raoul and Louise do not bear comparison with the young d'Artagnan and his Constance; Guiche is unworthy of the Buckingham who in 1626 would have given his life for a smile from Anne of Austria; and, as a villain, de Wardes never approaches the diamond-hard wickedness of Milady or Mordaunt who lived and breathed only to vent their hate on their enemies. *Louise de la Vallière* is, in this sense, an autumnal book, a comment by Dumas on the weakling generation who had grown up under Louis-Philippe, the bourgeois king, and showed none of the fire and idealism of the revolutionaries of 1830 who took up arms for their ideals.

But in a more specific sense, *Louise* is a politically charged novel. Dumas had almost reached the point in his tale where Athos makes his request to the king (ch. 1) when revolution broke out in February 1848. He had clear hopes for the outcome. In July 1830, he had fought for freedom; in 1831, he was one of the few to speak out in favour of the strike of the silk-workers in Lyons, victims of capitalist exploitation; in 1833, his liberal opinions became suspect and he thought it wise to remove himself for a time to Switzerland. But though he was committed to the people, he despised the ignorant populace, and his own extravagant lifestyle—Dumas was neither frugal nor chaste, nor could he resist the flattery of the great—brought accusations that he was a champagne socialist. In February 1848 he decided to stand as a parliamentary candidate. To prove his good faith to the voters of the Seine-et-Oise, he drew up a document setting out his credentials as a worker. 'Leaving aside my education which lasted six years, the four years spent working for a lawyer and the seven in an office, I have toiled 10 hours a day for 20 years, a total of 73,000 hours. In those 20 years, I have written 400 volumes and composed 35 plays.' He calculated that the 400 volumes had grossed 11,853,600 francs which, assuming an average daily wage of 3 francs, had provided work for 692 persons in the book and allied trades. His plays had realized 6,360,000 francs, and had given employment to 2,150 men and women in the theatres of Paris. His statement provides an interesting view of his industry but it failed to impress his audience. In any case, as an orator, he was sincere, but underinformed and maybe a trifle forceful: 'A parliamentary candidate, however eloquent,' wrote Albert Vandam, an Englishman who knew him at this time, 'who flings his constituents into the river whenever they happened to annoy him, must have been a novelty even in those days.'

Dumas was not elected but regretted his own defeats much less than the fact, which became clear almost immediately, that the Revolution of 1848 had failed to create a just society based on liberal values. It is not surprising, therefore, if *Louise de la Vallière*, written in the aftermath of a missed opportunity for France and serialized in *Le Siècle* between October 1848 and April 1849, should show the Musketeers in an unusually sombre mood. Athos's request to Louis is turned down and he retires from public life; d'Artagnan is reduced to groping in the dark; Porthos is deprived of any opportunity to use his strength to despatch the enemies of freedom. Aramis's dark subversion seems the only option left to opponents of the regime. Personal happiness seems unreachable: the love of Raoul for Louise is as doomed as hers for the King will be short-lived. On the political level, Louis XIV serves notice that he will be an autocrat and the clash between Colbert and Fouquet involves more than a difference of styles or temperaments. Fouquet stands for spontaneity and generosity, while Colbert is a cipher for the materialism, creeping bureaucracy, and official attempts to control the lives of ordinary people which Dumas was not alone in abominating. Stendhal deplored the grubby morality of the times and preferred Italy. Flaubert and Baudelaire used the word 'bourgeois' as an insult. Hugo would soon go into exile for opposing Louis-Napoleon. Dumas's answer was to castigate the political expediency, secrecy, and underlying authoritarianism of Richelieu, Mazarin, and Colbert, and contrast their shabby values with an idealized view of a pre-Colbertian, still chivalrous France which allowed a man to be honest and honourable and free to make his own decisions. It was a creed which Dumas never abandoned and the attractiveness of his champions is attributable in part to the sense of liberation they communicate to the reader: they simplify the world for us and remind us how good it feels to smite Philistines.

But 1848 was to bring Dumas other difficulties. The Revolution was followed by an economic recession and the newspaper industry was subjected to severe controls. Dumas's income dropped alarmingly. He was forced to sell his château at Marly, close the Théâtre Historique, and become a slave to his pen. At the end of 1851 he took himself off to Belgium to escape his creditors. He loved new mistresses, wrote other novels and plays, and launched more newspapers. His public stayed faithful and he was still lionized in Paris where he was regarded as excellent company and a brilliant conversationalist. Dumas had many friends and, perhaps uniquely for so famous a man, no enemies. His personality, which is responsible for the sunshine in his books, was irresistible to men and women alike, none of whom seemed able to stay cross with him for long.

In 1858 he toured Russia where, to his delight, he found that his fame had preceded him. In 1860, still faithful to liberal causes, he ran guns for Garibaldi and stayed on in Italy where Louise Colet, Flaubert's former mistress, glimpsed him one day sitting on a beach under a canopy, writing. He could still impress and his last novel, *The Prussian Terror* (1867), recaptured something of his old flourish. In it, he warned that Germany was no friend to France. But Dumas's brand of flamboyant individualism had grown unfashionable and his public at last abandoned him. His health declined and he kept restlessly on the move, floating ideas for more books, plays, and newspapers which came to nothing or failed. He lived long enough to see his talent desert him and his prophecy fulfilled: the Franco-Prussian war was declared in July 1870. By then he was seriously ill and in September he moved into his son's villa at Puys, near Dieppe. He who once had lifted the spirits of millions of readers grew depressed and sat listlessly staring out to sea. After a series of minor strokes, he died on 5 December 1870. The next day, Prussian soldiers marched into Dieppe. Paris, besieged and bombarded by German guns, scarcely marked his passing. In life, Dumas had never been afraid to walk boldly. In death, he was upstaged by history. But it hardly mattered: the King of Romance had left giant footprints in the earth.

SELECT BIBLIOGRAPHY

The Vicomte de Bragelonne was serialized in *Le Siècle* between 20 October 1847 and, with a few breaks, 12 January 1850. The middle section, comprising *Louise de la Vallière*, appeared between October 1848 and April 1849. The full text, in 276 chapters, was published in France in book form by Michel Lévy (Paris, 26 vols., 1848–50). The standard French edition fills volumes 2 and 3 of the complete Musketeer cycle edited by Claude Schopp (Paris, Laffont, 1991, 3 vols.). A full version was published in English by Thomas Pederson (Philadelphia, T. E. Pederson) in 1850–1. Subsequently, nearly all 'new' translations published in the USA and in Great Britain, either in full or, more frequently, as three distinct parts (*The Vicomte de Bragelonne, Louise de la Vallière*, and *The Man in the Iron Mask*), have been adaptations of this first American translation. The present edition is no exception. It reproduces the text, many times reprinted, of the classic translation issued by Routledge in 1857 (London, 6 vols.). It has been lightly revised and corrected against the French original.

Readers wishing to follow the complex printing history of Dumas's voluminous writings in French may usefully consult Frank W. Reed's *A Bibliography of Dumas Père* (London, 1933) and Douglas Munro's *Dumas: A Bibliography of Works Published in French, 1825–1900* (New York and London, 1981). *Alexandre Dumas Père: A Bibliography of Works Translated into English to 1910* (New York and London, 1978), also by Douglas Munro, is the best guide to British and American editions.

Courtilz de Sandras's *Mémoires de M. d'Artagnan* (1700) has been edited by Gilbert Sigaux (Paris, 1965); the English translation by Ralph Nevill (London, 1899) still makes lively reading. The *Histoire de Madame Henriette d'Angleterre* (1720), which first revealed Raoul to Dumas, is included in Mme de La Fayette's *Œuvres complètes* (ed. Roger Duchêne, Paris, 1990). The most detailed account of the historical Musketeer, Charles de Batz-Castelmore, is still Charles Samaran's *D'Artagnan* (Paris, 1912).

Dumas's autobiography, *Mes mémoires* (1852–5) (ed. Claude

Schopp, Paris, 1989; English translation, London, 1907–9) is an
entertaining but highly romanced account of his life to 1832.
The best French biographies are by Henri Clouard, *Alexandre
Dumas* (Paris, 1955); André Maurois, *Les Trois Dumas* (Paris,
1957; English translation, London, 1958); Claude Schopp, *Dumas,
le génie de la vie* (Paris, 1985; trans., New York and Toronto, 1988);
and Daniel Zimmerman, *Alexandre Dumas le Grand* (Paris, 1993).
Dumas enthusiasts will not wish to be without the *Dictionnaire
Dumas* (Montréal, 1990) by Réginald Hémel and Pierrette Méthé,
an encyclopedia of characters and situations.

For a spirited defence of the Musketeers' final adventure, see
Robert Louis Stevenson's 'A Gossip on a Novel of Dumas's'
(*Scribner's Magazine*, July 1888; repr. in *Works*, London, 1891,
ix. 124–33). Among the many books in English devoted to Dumas,
very readable introductions are provided by Ruthven Todd, *The
Laughing Mulatto* (London, 1940), A. Craig Bell, *Alexandre Dumas*
(London, 1950), and Richard Stowe, *Dumas* (Boston, 1976).
Michael Ross's *Alexandre Dumas* (Newton Abbot, 1981) gives a
sympathetic account of Dumas's life. The most balanced and
comprehensive guide, however, is F. W. J. Hemmings's excellent *The King of Romance* (London, 1979).

A CHRONOLOGY OF
ALEXANDRE DUMAS

1762   25 March: Birth at Saint-Domingo of Thomas-Alexandre, son of the French-born Marquis Davy de la Pailleterie and Marie-Cessette Dumas, a slave. After returning to France in 1780, he enlists in 1786 and rises rapidly through the ranks during the Revolution.

1802   24 July: Birth at Villers-Cotterêts of Alexandre Dumas, second child of General Dumas and Marie-Louise-Elizabeth Labouret, an innkeeper's daughter.

1806   26 February: Death of General Dumas. Alexandre is brought up in straitened circumstances by his mother. He attends local schools and has a happy childhood.

1819   Dumas, now a lawyer's office-boy, falls in love with Adèle Dalvin who rejects him. Meets Adolphe de Leuven, with whom he collaborates in writing unsuccessful plays.

1822   Visits Leuven in Paris, meets Talma, the leading actor of the day, and is confirmed in his ambition to become a playwright.

1823   Moves to Paris. Enters the service of the Duc d'Orléans. Falls in love with a seamstress, Catherine Labay.

1824   27 July: Birth of Alexandre Dumas *fils*, author of *La Dame aux Camélias*.

1825   22 September: Dumas's first performed play, written in collaboration with Leuven and Rousseau, makes no impact.

1826   Publication of a collection of short stories, Dumas's first solo composition, which sells four copies.

1827   A company of English actors, which includes Kean, Kemble, and Mrs Smithson, performs Shakespeare in English to enthusiastic Paris audiences: Dumas is deeply impressed. Liaison with Mélanie Waldor.

1828–9 Dumas enters Parisian literary circles through Charles Nodier.

1829   11 February: First of about 50 performances of *Henri III and his Court* which makes Dumas famous and thrusts him into the front ranks of the Romantic revolution in literature. Dumas meets Victor Hugo. He consolidates his reputation as a dramatist with *Antony* (1831), *La Tour de Nesle* (1832), and *Kean*

(1836), which are all landmarks in the history of Romantic drama.

1830   May: Start of an affair with the actress Belle Krelsamer.
        Active in the July Revolution: Dumas single-handedly captures a gunpowder magazine at Soissons. Sent by La Fayette to promote the National Guard in the Vendée, he visits Blois and locations in Brittany which will figure in *Le Vicomte de Bragelonne*.

1831   5 March: Birth of Marie, his daughter by Belle Krelsamer.
        17 March: Dumas acknowledges Alexandre, his son by Catherine Labay.

1832   6 February: Start of his affair with the actress Ida Ferrier.
        15 April: Dumas succumbs to the cholera which kills 20,000 Parisians.
        29 May: First performance of *La Tour de Nesle*: Gaillardet accuses Dumas of plagiarism.
        July: Suspected of republican sympathies, Dumas leaves Paris for Switzerland. After the spectacular failure of his next play, he begins to take a systematic interest in the literary possibilities of French history.

1833   Serialization of a book of impressions of Switzerland, the first of his travelogues.

1834–5 October: Dumas travels in the Midi. From the Riviera, he embarks on the first of many journeys to Italy.

1836   31 August: Dumas returns triumphantly to the theatre with *Kean*.

1838   Death of Dumas's mother. Travels along the Rhine with Gérard de Nerval who introduces him to Auguste Maquet in December.

1840   1 February: Dumas marries Ida Ferrier, travels to Italy, and publishes *Le Capitaine Pamphile*, the best of his children's books.

1840–2 Dividing his time between Paris and Italy, Dumas increasingly abandons the theatre for the novel.

1842   June: Publication of *The Chevalier d'Harmental*, the first of many romances written in association with Maquet.

1844   March–July: Serialization of *The Three Musketeers* in *Le Siècle*.
        August: First episode of *The Count of Monte Cristo* published in *Le Journal des Débats*.
        15 October: amicable separation from Ida Ferrier.
        Publication of *Louis XIV and his Century*.

1845   21 January–2 August: Serialization of the second d'Artagnan story, *Twenty Years After*, in *Le Siècle*.

February: He wins his libel suit against the journalist Jacquot, author of *A Fiction Factory: The Firm of Alexandre Dumas and Company*, in which he was accused of publishing other men's work under his own name.

2 August: Publication of the last episode of *Twenty Years After* in *Le Siècle* which announces an imminent sequel: *Ten Years After, or The Vicomte de Bragelonne*, in six volumes, to begin appearing within three months. However Dumas, who had signed a contract for it in March, was over-committed elsewhere and was forced to postpone work on it.

27 October: First performance of *Les Mousquetaires*, an adaptation of *Twenty Years After*.

1846   Formal separation from Ida Ferrier. Brief liaison with Lola Montès.

November–January: Travels with his son to Spain and North Africa.

1847   30 January: Loses a lawsuit brought by newspaper proprietors for failure to deliver copy for which he had accepted large advances.

11 February: Questions are asked in the National Assembly about Dumas's appropriation of the Navy vessel, *Le Véloce*, during his visit to North Africa.

20 February: Opening of the 'Théâtre Historique'.

7 March: Completion of the 'Château de Monte Cristo' at Marly-le-Roi.

August: Dumas begins work on the final Musketeer adventure.

20 October–12 January 1850: Serialization of *The Vicomte de Bragelonne*, in *Le Siècle*.

1848   Dumas stands unsuccessfully as a parliamentary candidate and votes for Louis-Napoleon in the December elections.

1849   17 February: First performance at the Théâtre Historique of *La Jeunesse des Mousquetaires*, based on *The Three Musketeers*.

1850   20 March: The Théâtre Historique is declared bankrupt. The Château de Monte Cristo is sold off for 30,000 francs.

1851   Michel Lévy begins to bring out the first volumes of Dumas's complete works.

7 December: Dumas flees to Belgium to avoid his creditors.

1852   Publication of the first volumes of *My Memoirs*. Dumas declared bankrupt with debts of 100,000 francs.

1853   November: Returns to Paris and founds a periodical, *Le Mousquetaire* (last issue 7 February 1857), for which he writes most of the copy himself.

1857   23 April: Founds a literary weekly, *Le Monte Cristo*, which, with one break, survives until 1862.

1858   20–21 January: Hearing of Macquet's application to have the right to call himself Dumas's co-author.
3 February: Macquet loses his case.
15 June: Dumas leaves for a tour of Russia and returns in March 1859.

1859   11 March: Death of Ida Ferrier. Beginning of a liaison with Emilie Cordier which lasts until 1864.

1860   Meets Garibaldi at Turin and just misses the taking of Sicily (June). He returns to Marseilles where he buys guns for the Italian cause and is in Naples just after the city falls in September. Garibaldi stands, by proxy, as godfather to Dumas's daughter by Emilie Cordier.
11 October: Founds *L'Indipendente*, a literary and political periodical published half in French and half in Italian.

1864   April: Dumas returns to Paris.

1865   Further travels through Italy, Germany, and Austria.

1867   Publishes *The Prussian Terror*, a novel intended to warn France against the coming Prussian threat. Begins a last liaison, with Adah Menken, an American actress (d. 1868).

1869   10 March: Dumas's last play, *The Whites and the Blues*.

1870   5 December: Dumas dies at Puys, near Dieppe, after suffering a stroke in September.

1872   Dumas's remains transferred to Villers-Cotterêts.

1883   Unveiling of a statue to Dumas by Gustave Doré in the Place Malesherbes.

LOUISE DE LA VALLIÈRE

CONTENTS

CONTENTS

I

KING LOUIS XIV DOES NOT THINK MADEMOISELLE DE LA VALLIÈRE EITHER RICH ENOUGH OR PRETTY ENOUGH FOR A GENTLEMAN OF THE RANK OF THE VICOMTE DE BRAGELONNE

RAOUL and the Comte de la Fère* reached Paris the evening of the same day on which Buckingham had had the conversation with the Queen-Mother.* The Comte had scarcely arrived, when, through Raoul, he solicited an audience of the King. His Majesty had passed a portion of the morning in looking over, with Madame and the ladies of the court, various goods of Lyons manufacture, of which he had made his sister-in-law a present.* A court dinner had succeeded, then cards, and afterwards, according to his usual custom, the King, leaving the card-tables at eight o'clock, passed into his cabinet in order to work with M. Colbert and M. Fouquet.* Raoul entered the antechamber at the very moment the two ministers quitted it, and the King, perceiving him through the half-closed door, said, 'What do you want, M. de Bragelonne?'

The young man approached: 'An audience, sire,' he replied, 'for the Comte de la Fère, who has just arrived from Blois,* and is most anxious to have an interview with your Majesty.'

'I have an hour to spare between cards and my supper,' said the King. 'Is the Comte de la Fère ready?'

'He is below, and waits your Majesty's commands.'

'Let him come at once,' said the King, and five minutes afterwards Athos entered the presence of Louis XIV. He was received by the King with that gracious kindness of manner which Louis, with a tact beyond his years, reserved for the purpose of gaining those who were not to be conquered by ordinary favours. 'Let me hope, Comte,' said the King, 'that you have come to ask me for something.'*

'I will not conceal from your Majesty,' replied the Comte, 'that I am indeed come for that purpose.'

'That is well, then,' said the King joyously.

'It is not for myself, sire.'

'So much the worse; but, at least, I will do for your protégé what you refuse to permit me to do for you.'

'Your Majesty encourages me. I have come to speak on behalf of the Vicomte de Bragelonne.'

'It is the same as if you spoke on your own behalf, Comte.'

'Not altogether so, sire. I am desirous of obtaining from your Majesty what I cannot do for myself. The Vicomte thinks of marrying.'

'He is still very young; but that does not matter. He is an eminently distinguished man. I will choose a wife for him.'

'He has already chosen one, sire, and only awaits your Majesty's consent.'

'It is only a question, then, of signing the marriage contract?' Athos bowed. 'Has he chosen a wife whose fortune and position accord with your own views?'

Athos hesitated for a moment. 'His affianced bride is of good birth, but has no fortune.'

'That is a misfortune which we can remedy.'

'You overwhelm me with gratitude, sire; but your Majesty will permit me to offer a remark.'

'Do so, Comte.'

'Your Majesty seems to intimate an intention of giving a marriage-portion to this young girl.'

'Certainly.'

'I should regret, sire, if the step I have taken towards your Majesty should be attended by this result.'

'No false delicacy, Comte; what is the bride's name?'

'Mademoiselle La Baume Le Blanc de la Vallière,'* said Athos coldly.

'I seem to know that name,' said the King, as if reflecting; 'there was a Marquis de la Vallière.'

'Yes, sire, it is his daughter.'

'But he died, and his widow married again M. de St Rémy, I think, steward of the dowager Madame's household.'*

'Your Majesty is correctly informed.'

'More than that, the young lady has lately become one of the Princess's maids of honour.'*

'Your Majesty is better acquainted with her history than I am.'

The King again reflected, and glancing at the Comte's anxious countenance, said: 'This young lady does not seem to me to be very pretty, Comte.'*

'I am not quite sure,' replied Athos.

'I have seen her, but she did not strike me as being so.'

'She seems to be a good and modest girl, but has little beauty, sire.'

'Beautiful fair hair, however?'

'I think so.'

'And her blue eyes are tolerably good.'

'Yes, sire.'

'With regard to beauty, then, the match is but an ordinary one. Now for the money side of the question.'

'Fifteen to twenty thousand francs dowry at the very outside, sire; the lovers are disinterested enough; for myself, I care little for money.'

'For superfluity, you mean; but a needful amount is of importance. With fifteen thousand francs, without landed property, a woman cannot live at court. We will make up the deficiency; I will do it for de Bragelonne.' The King again remarked the coldness with which Athos received his remark.

'Let us pass from the question of money to that of rank,' said Louis XIV; 'the daughter of the Marquis de la Vallière, that is well enough; but there is that excellent St Rémy, who somewhat damages the credit of the family;* and you, Comte, are rather particular, I believe, about your own family.'

'Sire, I no longer hold to anything but my devotion to your Majesty.'*

The King again paused. 'A moment, Comte. You have surprised me in no little degree from the beginning of your conversation. You came to ask me to authorise a marriage, and you seem greatly disturbed in having to make the request. Nay, pardon me, Comte, but I am rarely deceived, young as I am;* for while with some persons I place my friendship at the disposal of my understanding, with others I call my distrust to my aid, by which my discernment is increased. I repeat that you do not prefer your request as though you wished its success.'

'Well, sire, that is true.'

'I do not understand you, then; refuse.'

'Nay, sire; I love de Bragelonne with my whole heart; he is smitten with Mademoiselle de la Vallière, he weaves dreams of bliss for the future; I am not one who is willing to destroy the illusions of youth. This marriage is objectionable to me, but I implore your Majesty to consent to it forthwith, and thus make Raoul happy.'

'Tell me, Comte, is she in love with him?'

'If your Majesty requires me to speak candidly, I do not believe in Mademoiselle de la Vallière's affection, the delight at being at court, the honour of being in the service of Madame, counteract in her head whatever affection she may happen to have in her heart; it is a marriage similar to many others which already exist at court; but de Bragelonne wishes it, and let it be so.'

'And yet you do not resemble those easy-tempered fathers who make slaves of themselves for their children,' said the King.

'I am determined enough against the viciously disposed, but not so against men of upright character. Raoul is suffering, and is in great distress of mind; his disposition, naturally light and cheerful, has become gloomy and melancholy.* I do not wish to deprive your Majesty of the services he may be able to render.'

'I understand you,' said the King; 'and what is more, I understand your heart, too, Comte.'

'There is no occasion, therefore,' replied the Comte, 'to tell your Majesty, that my object is to make these children, or rather Raoul, happy.'

'And I, too, as much as yourself, Comte, wish to secure M. de Bragelonne's happiness.'

'I only await your Majesty's signature. Raoul will have the honour of presenting himself before your Majesty to receive your consent.'

'You are mistaken, Comte,' said the King firmly; 'I have just said that I desire to secure M. de Bragelonne's happiness, and from the present moment, therefore, I oppose his marriage.'

'But, sire,' exclaimed Athos, 'your Majesty has promised!'

'Not so, Comte, I did not promise you, for it is opposed to my own views.'

'I appreciate all your Majesty's considerate and generous intentions in my behalf; but I take the liberty of recalling to you that I undertook to approach your Majesty as an ambassador.'

'An ambassador, Comte, frequently asks, but does not always obtain what he asks.'

'But, sire, it will be such a blow for de Bragelonne.'

'My hand shall deal the blow; I will speak to the Vicomte.'

'Love, sire, is overwhelming in its might.'

'Love can be resisted, Comte, I can assure you of that.'

'When one has the soul of a King,—your own, for instance, sire.'

'Do not make yourself uneasy on the subject. I have certain views for de Bragelonne; I do not say that he shall not marry Mademoiselle de la Vallière, but I do not wish him to marry so young; I do not wish him to marry her, until she has acquired a fortune; and he, on his side, no less deserves my favour, such as I wish to confer upon him. In a word, Comte, I wish them to wait.'

'Yet once more, sire.'

'Comte, you told me you came to request a favour.'

'Assuredly, sire.'

'Grant me one, then, instead; let us speak no longer upon this matter. It is probable that, before long, war may be declared; I require men about me who are unfettered. I should hesitate to send under fire a married man, or a father of a family; I should hesitate also, on de Bragelonne's account, to endow with a fortune without some sound reason for it, a young girl, a perfect stranger; such an act would sow jealousy among my nobility.'

Athos bowed, and remained silent.

'Is that all you had to ask me?' added Louis XIV.

'Absolutely all, sire; and I take my leave of your Majesty. Is it, however, necessary that I should inform Raoul?'

'Spare yourself the trouble and annoyance. Tell the Vicomte that at my levée to-morrow morning I will speak to him: I shall expect you this evening, Comte, to join my card-table.'

'I am in travelling costume, sire.'

'A day will come, I hope, when you leave me no more. Before long, Comte, the monarchy will be established in such a manner as to enable me to offer a worthy hospitality to all men of your merit.'

'Provided sire, a monarch reigns truly great in the hearts of his subjects, the palace he inhabits matters little, since he is worshipped in a temple.' With these words Athos left the cabinet, and found de Bragelonne, who awaited his return.

'Well, monsieur?' said the young man.

'The King, Raoul, is well disposed towards us both; not, perhaps, in the sense you suppose, but he is kind, and generously disposed for our house.'

'You have bad news to communicate to me, monsieur,' said the young man, turning very pale.

'The King will himself inform you to-morrow morning that it is not bad news.'

'The King has not signed, however?'

'The King wishes himself to settle the terms of the contract, and he desires to make it so grand that he requires time for it. Throw the blame rather on your own impatience, than on the King's good feeling towards you.'

Raoul, in utter consternation, both on account of his knowledge of the Comte's frankness as well of his tact, remained plunged in a dull heavy stupor.

'Will you not go with me to my lodgings?' said Athos.

'I beg your pardon, monsieur; I will follow you,' he stammered out, following Athos down the staircase.

'Since I am here,' said Athos suddenly, 'may I see M. d'Artagnan?'*

'Shall I show you his apartment,' said de Bragelonne.

'Do so.'

'It is on the other staircase.'

They altered their course, but as they reached the landing of the grand staircase, Raoul perceived a servant in the Comte de Guiche's livery,* who ran towards him as soon as he heard his voice.

'What is it?' said Raoul.

'This note, monsieur. My master heard of your return, and wrote to you without delay; I have been seeking you for the last hour.'

Raoul approached Athos as he unsealed the letter, saying, 'With your permission, monsieur.'

'Certainly.'

'DEAR RAOUL,'—said the Comte de Guiche, 'I have an affair in hand which requires immediate attention; I know you have returned, come to me as soon as possible.'

Hardly had he finished reading it, when a servant in the livery of the Duke of Buckingham, turning out of the gallery, recognised Raoul, and approached him respectfully, saying, 'From His Grace, monsieur.'

'Well, Raoul, as I see you are already as busy as a general of an army, I shall leave you, and will find M. d'Artagnan myself.'

'You will excuse me, I trust,' said Raoul.

'Yes, yes, I excuse you; adieu, Raoul; you will find me at my apartments until to-morrow; during the day I may set out for Blois, unless I have orders to the contrary.'

'I shall present my respects to you to-morrow, monsieur.'

When Athos had left, Raoul opened Buckingham's letter.

'MONSIEUR DE BRAGELONNE,' said the Duke, 'you are, of all the Frenchmen I have known, the one with whom I am most pleased; I am about to put your friendship to the proof. I have received a certain message, written in very good French. As I am an Englishman, I am afraid of not comprehending it very clearly. The letter has a good name attached to it, and that is all I can tell you. Will you be good enough to come and see me, for I am told you have arrived from Blois. Your devoted,

'VILLIERS, Duke of Buckingham.'

'I am going now to see your master,' said Raoul to de Guiche's servant, as he dismissed him; and 'I shall be with the Duke of Buckingham in an hour,' he added, dismissing with these words the Duke's messenger.

II

D'ARTAGNAN CALLS DE WARDES TO ACCOUNT

RAOUL, on betaking himself to de Guiche, found him conversing with de Wardes* and Manicamp.* De Wardes, since the affair of the barricade,* had treated Raoul as a stranger. It might have been imagined that nothing at all had passed between them; only they behaved as if they were not acquainted. As Raoul entered, de Guiche walked up to him, and Raoul, as he grasped his friend's hand, glanced rapidly at his two young companions, hoping to be able to read on their faces what was passing in their minds. De Wardes was cold and impenetrable, and Manicamp seemed absorbed in the contemplation of some trimming to his dress. De Guiche led Raoul to an adjoining cabinet, and made him sit down, saying, 'How well you look?'

'That is singular,' replied Raoul, 'for I am far from being in good spirits.'

'It is your case, then, Raoul, as it is my own, that your love affair does not progress satisfactorily.'

'So much the better, Comte, as far as you are concerned; the worst news, that indeed which would distress me most of all, would be good news.'

'In that case do not distress yourself, for, not only am I very unhappy, but what is more, I see others about me who are happy.'

'Really, I do not understand you,' replied Raoul; 'explain yourself.'

'You will soon learn. I have tried, but in vain, to overcome the feeling which you saw dawn in me, increase in me, and take such entire possession of my whole being.* I have summoned all your advice and all my own strength to my aid. I have well weighed the unfortunate affair in which I have embarked; I have sounded its depths; that it is an abyss, I am well aware, but it matters little, for *I* shall pursue my own course.'

'This is madness, de Guiche, you cannot advance another step without risking your own ruin to-day, perhaps your life to-morrow.'

'Whatever may happen, I have done with reflection: listen.'

'And you hope to succeed; you believe that Madame will love you?'

'Raoul, I believe nothing; I hope, because hope exists in man, and never abandons him till he dies.'

'But admitting that you obtain the happiness you covet, even then, you are more certainly lost than if you had failed in obtaining it.'

'I beseech you, Raoul, not to interrupt me any more; you could never convince me, for I tell you beforehand, I do not wish to be convinced; I have gone so far that I cannot turn back; I have suffered so much, that death itself would be a boon. I no longer love to madness, Raoul, I am in a perfect rage of jealousy.'

Raoul struck both his hands together with an expression resembling anger. 'Well?' said he.

'Well or ill, matters little. This is what I claim from you, my friend, my almost brother. During the last three days, Madame has been living in a perfect intoxication of gaiety. On the first day, I dared not look at her; I hated her for not having been as unhappy as myself. The next day I could not bear her out of my sight; and she, Raoul—at least I thought I remarked it—she looked at me, if not with pity, at least with gentleness. But between her looks and mine, a shadow intervened; another's smile invited her smile. Beside her horse another's always gallops, which is not mine; in her ear another's caressing voice, not mine, unceasingly vibrates. Raoul, for three days past my brain has been on fire; fire courses through my veins. That shadow must be driven away, that smile must be quenched; that voice must be silenced.'

'You wish Monsieur's death,' exclaimed Raoul.

'No, no, I am not jealous of the husband: I am jealous of the lover.'

'Of the lover?' said Raoul.

'Have you not observed it, you, who were formerly so keen-sighted?'

'Are you jealous of the Duke of Buckingham?'*

'To the very death.'

'Hopelessly jealous?'

'This time the affair will be easy to arrange between us; I have taken the initiative, and have sent him a letter.'

'It was you, then, who wrote to him?'

'How do you know that?'

'I know it because he told me so. Look at this,' and he handed to de Guiche the letter which he had received nearly at the same moment as his own. De Guiche read it eagerly, and said, 'He is a brave man, and more than that, a gallant man.'

'Most certainly the Duke is a gallant man; I need not ask if you wrote to him in a similar style.'

'I will show you my letter when you call on him on my behalf.'

'But that is almost out of the question.'

'What is?'

'That I should call on him for that purpose.'

'Why so?'

'The Duke consults me as you do.'

'I suppose you will give me the preference. Listen to me, Raoul, I wish you to tell his Grace—it is a very simple matter—that to-day, to-morrow, the following day, or any other day he may choose, I wish to meet him at Vincennes.'*

'Reflect, de Guiche.'

'I thought I had already said that I had reflected.'

'The Duke is a stranger here; he is on a mission* which renders his person inviolable. . . . Vincennes is close to the Bastille.'*

'The consequences concern me.'

'But the motive for this meeting? What motive do you wish me to assign?'

'Be perfectly easy on that score, he will not ask any. The Duke must be as sick of me as I am of him. I implore you, therefore, to seek the Duke, and if it is necessary to entreat him to accept my offer, I will do so.'

'That is useless. The Duke has already informed me that he wishes to speak to me. The Duke is now playing cards with the King. Let us both go there. I will draw him aside in the gallery; you will remain aloof. Two words will be sufficient.'

'That is well arranged. I shall take de Wardes to keep me in countenance.'

'Why not Manicamp? De Wardes can rejoin us at any time; we can leave him here.'

'Yes, that is true.'

'He knows nothing?'

'Positively nothing. You continue still on an unfriendly footing then?'

'Has he not told you anything?'

'Nothing.'

'I do not like the man, and, as I never liked him, the result is, that I am on no worse terms with him to-day than I was yesterday.'

'Let us go, then.'

The four descended the stairs. De Guiche's carriage was waiting at the door, and took them to the Palais Royal.* As they were going along, Raoul was engaged in framing some scheme. The sole depositary of two secrets he did not despair of concluding some arrangement between the two parties. He knew the influence he exercised over Buckingham, and the ascendancy he had acquired over de Guiche, and affairs did not look utterly despairing to him. On their arrival in the gallery, dazzling with the blaze of light, where the most beautiful and illustrious women of the court moved to and fro, like stars in their atmosphere of light, Raoul could not prevent himself for a moment forgetting de Guiche in order to seek out Louise, who, amidst her companions, like a dove completely fascinated, gazed long and fixedly upon the Royal circle, which glittered with jewels and gold. All the members of it were standing, the King alone being seated. Raoul perceived Buckingham, who was standing a few paces from Monsieur, in a group of French and English, who were admiring his haughty carriage, and the incomparable magnificence of his costume. Some few of the older courtiers remembered having seen the father,* and their remembrance was in no way prejudicial to the son.

Buckingham was conversing with Fouquet, who was talking with him aloud of Belle-Isle.* 'I cannot speak to him at present,' said Raoul.

'Wait then, and choose your opportunity, but finish everything speedily. I am on thorns.'

'See our deliverer approaches,' said Raoul, perceiving d'Artagnan, who, magnificently dressed in his new uniform of captain of the musketeers,* had just made his victorious entry in the gallery; and he advanced towards d'Artagnan.

'The Comte de la Fère has been looking for you, chevalier,' said Raoul.

'Yes,' replied d'Artagnan, 'I have just left him.'

'I thought you would have passed a portion of the evening together.'

'We have arranged to meet again.'

As he answered Raoul, his absent looks were directed on all sides, as if seeking some one in the crowd or looking for something in the room. Suddenly his gaze became fixed, like that of an eagle on its prey. Raoul followed the direction of his glance, and noticed that de Guiche and d'Artagnan saluted each other, but he could not distinguish at whom the captain's inquiring and haughty glance was directed.

'Chevalier,' said Raoul, 'there is no one here but yourself who can render me a service.'

'What is it, my dear Vicomte?'

'It is simply to go and interrupt the Duke of Buckingham to whom I wish to say two words, and, as the Duke is conversing with M. Fouquet, you understand that it would not do for me to throw myself into the middle of the conversation.'

'Ah, ah, is M. Fouquet there?' inquired d'Artagnan.

'Do you not see him?'

'Yes, now I do. But do you think I have a greater right than you have?'

'You are a far more important personage.'

'Yes, you're right; I am captain of the musketeers; I have had the post promised me so long, and have enjoyed its dignity for so brief a period, that I am always forgetting my dignity.'

'You will do me this service, will you not?'

'M. Fouquet—the deuce!'

'Are you not on good terms with him.'

'It is rather he who may not be on good terms with me;* however, since it must be done some day or another——'

'Stay; I think he is looking at you; or is it likely that it might be——'

'No, no; don't deceive yourself, it is indeed me for whom this honour is intended.'

'The opportunity is a good one, then.'

'Well, I will go.'

De Guiche had not removed his eyes from Raoul, who made a sign to him that all was arranged. D'Artagnan walked straight up to the group, and civilly saluted M. Fouquet as well as the others.

'Good-evening, M. D'Artagnan; we were speaking of Belle-Isle,' said Fouquet, with that usage of society, and that perfect knowledge of the language of looks, which require half a lifetime thoroughly to acquire, and which some persons, notwithstanding all their study, never attain.

'Of Belle-Isle-en-Mer! Ah, ah!' said d'Artagnan. 'It belongs to you, I believe, M. Fouquet?'

'M. Fouquet has just told me that he had presented it to the King,' said Buckingham.

'Do you know Belle-Isle, chevalier?' inquired Fouquet.

'I have only been there once,' replied d'Artagnan with readiness and good humour.

'Did you remain there long?'

'Scarcely a day.'

'Did you see much of it while you were there?'

'All that could be seen in a day.'

'A great deal can be seen with observation as keen as yours,' said Fouquet; at which d'Artagnan bowed.

During this, Raoul made a sign to Buckingham. 'M. Fouquet,' said Buckingham, 'I leave the captain with you, he is more learned than I am in bastions, and scarps, and counter-scarps, and I will join one of my friends, who has just beckoned to me.' Saying this, Buckingham disengaged himself from the group, and advanced towards Raoul, stopping for a moment at the table where the Queen-Mother, the young Queen,* and the King were playing together. 'Now, Raoul,' said de Guiche, 'there he is; be firm and quick.'

Buckingham having made some complimentary remark to Madame, continued his way towards Raoul, who advanced to meet him while de Guiche remained in his place, though he followed him with his eyes. The manœuvre was so arranged that the young men met in an open space which was left vacant, between the group of players and the gallery, where they walked, stopping now and then for the purpose of saying a few words to some of the graver courtiers who were walking there. At the moment when the two lines were about to unite, they were broken by a third. It was Monsieur who advanced towards the Duke of Buckingham. Monsieur had his most engaging smile on his red and perfumed lips.*

'My dear Duke,' said he with the most affectionate politeness; 'is it really true what I have just been told?'

Buckingham turned round, he had not noticed Monsieur approach, but had merely heard his voice. He started, in spite of his command over himself, and a slight pallor overspread his face. 'Monseigneur,' he asked, 'what has been told you that surprises you so much?'

'Something that throws me into despair, and will, in truth, be a real cause of mourning for the whole court.'

'Your Highness is very kind, for I perceive that you allude to my departure.'*

'Precisely.'

Guiche had overheard the conversation from where he was standing, and started in his turn. 'His departure,' he murmured. 'What does he say?'

Philip continued with the same gracious air, 'I can easily conceive, monsieur, why the King of Great Britain recalls you; we all know that King Charles II, who appreciates true gentlemen,* cannot dispense with you. But it cannot be supposed we can let you go without great regret; and I beg you to receive the expression of my own.'

'Believe me, monseigneur,' said the Duke, 'that if I quit the court of France——'

'It is because you are recalled; but, if you should suppose that the expression of my own wish on the subject might possibly have some influence with the King, I will gladly volunteer to entreat his majesty Charles II to leave you with us a little while longer.'

'I am overwhelmed, monseigneur, by so much kindness,' replied Buckingham; 'but I have received positive commands. My residence in France was limited, I have prolonged it at the risk of displeasing my gracious sovereign. It is only this very day that I recollected I ought to have set off four days ago.'

'Indeed,' said Monsieur.

'Yes; but,' added Buckingham, raising his voice in such a manner that the Princess could hear him,—'but I resemble that dweller in the East,* who turned mad, and remained so for several days, owing to a delightful dream that he had had, and who one day awoke, if not completely cured, in some respects rational at least. The court of France has its intoxicating properties, which are not unlike this dream, my lord; but at last I wake and leave it. I shall be unable, therefore, to prolong my residence, as your Highness has so kindly invited me.'

'When do you leave?' inquired Philip, with an expression full of interest.

'To-morrow, monseigneur. My carriages have been ready for three days past.'

The Duc d'Orléans made a movement of the head, which seemed to signify, 'Since you are determined, Duke, there is nothing to be said.' Buckingham returned the gesture, concealing under a smile a contraction of his heart, and then Monsieur moved away in the same direction by which he had approached. At the same moment, however, de Guiche advanced from the opposite direction. Raoul feared that the impatient young man might possibly make the proposition himself, and hurried forward before him.

'No, no, Raoul, all is useless now,' said Guiche, holding both his hands towards the Duke, and leading him himself behind a column. 'Forgive me, Duke, for what I wrote to you, I was mad; give me back my letter.'

'It is true,' said the Duke, 'you cannot owe me a grudge any longer now.'

'Forgive me, Duke; my friendship, my lasting friendship is yours.'

'There is certainly no reason why you should bear me any ill will from the moment I leave her never to see her again.'

Raoul heard these words, and comprehending that his presence was now useless between the two young men, who had now only friendly words to exchange, withdrew a few paces; a movement which brought him closer to de Wardes, who was conversing with the Chevalier de Lorraine* respecting the departure of Buckingham. 'A wise retreat,' said de Wardes.

'Why so?'

'Because the dear Duke saves a sword-thrust by it.' At which reply both began to laugh.

Raoul, indignant, turned round frowningly, flushed with anger, and his lip curling with disdain. The Chevalier de Lorraine turned away upon his heel, but de Wardes remained firm and waited. 'You will not break yourself of the habit,' said Raoul to de Wardes, 'of insulting the absent; yesterday it was M. d'Artagnan, to-day it is the Duke of Buckingham.'

'You know very well, monsieur,' returned de Wardes, 'that I sometimes insult those who are present.'

De Wardes touched Raoul, their shoulders met, their faces were bent towards each other, as if mutually to inflame each other by the fire of their breath and of their anger. It could be seen that the one was at the height of his anger, the other at the end of his patience. Suddenly a voice was heard behind them full of grace and courtesy, saying, 'I believe I heard my name pronounced.'

They turned round and saw d'Artagnan, who, with a smiling eye and a cheerful face, had just placed his hand on de Wardes's shoulder. Raoul stepped back to make room for the musketeer. De Wardes trembled from head to foot, turned pale, but did not move. D'Artagnan, still with the same smile, took the place which Raoul abandoned to him. 'Thank you, my dear Raoul,' he said. 'M. de Wardes, I wish to talk with you. Do not leave us, Raoul; every one can hear what I have to say to M. de Wardes.' His smile immediately faded away, and his glance became cold and sharp as a sword.

'I am at your orders, monsieur,' said de Wardes.

'For a very long time,' resumed d'Artagnan, 'I have sought an opportunity of conversing with you; to-day is the first time I have found it. The place is badly chosen, I admit; but you will perhaps have the goodness to accompany me to my apartments, which are on the staircase at the end of this gallery.'

'I follow you, monsieur,' said de Wardes.

'Are you alone here?' said d'Artagnan.

'No; I have M. Manicamp and M. de Guiche, two of my friends.'

'That's well,' said d'Artagnan; 'but two persons are not sufficient; you will be able to find a few others, I trust.'

'Certainly,' said the young man, who did not know the object d'Artagnan had in view. 'As many as you please.'

'Very well, get a good supply, then. Do you come too, Raoul; bring M. de Guiche and the Duke of Buckingham.'

'What a disturbance,' replied de Wardes, attempting to smile. The captain slightly signed to him with his hand, as though to recommend him to be patient, and then led the way to his apartments. D'Artagnan's apartment was not unoccupied; for the Comte de la Fère, seated in the recess of a window, awaited him. 'Well,' said he to d'Artagnan, as he saw him enter.

'Well,' said the latter, 'M. de Wardes has done me the honour to pay me a visit, in company with some of his own friends, as well as of ours.' In fact, behind the musketeer appeared de

Wardes and Manicamp, followed by de Guiche and Buckingham, who looked surprised, not knowing what was expected of
them. Raoul was accompanied by two or three gentlemen; and,
as he entered, glanced round the room, and, perceiving the
Comte, he went and placed himself by his side. D'Artagnan
received his visitors with all the courtesy he was capable of; he
preserved his unmoved and unconcerned look. All the persons
present were men of distinction, occupying posts of honour and
credit at the court. After he had apologised to each of them for
any inconvenience he might have put them to, he turned towards de Wardes, who, in spite of his great self-command,
could not prevent his face betraying some surprise mingled with
not a little uneasiness. 'Now, monsieur,' said d'Artagnan, 'since
we are no longer within the precincts of the King's palace, and
since we can speak out without failing in respect to propriety, I
will inform you why I have taken the liberty to request you to
visit me here, and why I have invited these gentlemen to be
present at the same time. My friend, the Comte de la Fère, has
acquainted me with the injurious reports you are spreading about
myself. You have stated that you regard me as your mortal
enemy, because I was, so you affirm, that of your father.'*

'Perfectly true, monsieur, I have said so,' replied de Wardes,
whose pallid face became slightly tinged with colour.

'You accuse me, therefore, of a crime, or a fault, or of some
mean and cowardly act. Have the goodness to state your charge
against me in precise terms.'

'In the presence of witnesses?'

'Most certainly in the presence of witnesses; and you see I
have selected them as being experienced in affairs of honour.'

'You do not appreciate my delicacy, monsieur. I have accused
you, it is true; but I have kept the nature of the accusation a
perfect secret. I have not entered into any details; but have
rested satisfied by expressing my hatred in the presence of
those on whom a duty was almost imposed to acquaint you with
it. You have not taken the discreetness I have shown into consideration, although you were interested in remaining silent. I
can hardly recognise your habitual prudence in that M.
d'Artagnan.'

D'Artagnan, who was quietly biting the corner of his moustache, said, 'I have already had the honour to beg you to state the particulars of the grievances you say you have against me.'

'Aloud?'

'Certainly, aloud.'

'In that case, I will speak.'

'Speak, monsieur,' said d'Artagnan, bowing; 'we are all listening to you.'

Those who were present at this scene had, at first, looked at each other with a good deal of uneasiness. They were reassured, however, when they saw that d'Artagnan manifested no emotion whatever. De Wardes still maintained the same unbroken silence. 'Speak, monsieur,' said the musketeer; 'you see you are keeping us waiting.'

'Listen then:—My father loved a woman of noble birth, and this woman loved my father.' D'Artagnan and Athos exchanged looks. De Wardes continued: 'M. d'Artagnan found some letters which indicated a rendezvous, substituted himself, under a disguise, for the person who was expected, and took advantage of the darkness.'*

'That is perfectly true,' said d'Artagnan.

A slight murmur was heard from those present. 'Yes, I was guilty of that dishonourable action. You should have added, monsieur, since you are so impartial, that, at the period when the circumstance which you have just related, happened, I was not one-and-twenty years of age.'

'The action is not the less shameful on that account,' said de Wardes; 'and it is quite sufficient for a gentleman to have attained the age of reason, to avoid committing any act of indelicacy.'

A renewed murmur was heard, but this time of astonishment, and almost of doubt.

'It was a most shameful deception, I admit,' said d'Artagnan, 'and I have not waited for M. de Wardes's reproaches to reproach myself for it, and very bitterly too. Age has, however, made me more reasonable, and, above all, more upright: and this injury has been atoned for by a long and lasting regret. But I appeal to you gentlemen, this affair took place in 1626, at a period, happily for yourselves, known to you by tradition only, at a period when love was not over-scrupulous, when consciences did not distil, as in the present day, poison and bitterness. We were young soldiers, always fighting, or being attacked, our swords always in our hands, or at least ready to be drawn from their sheaths. Death then always stared us in the face, war hardened us, and the Cardinal pressed us sorely. I have repented of it, and more than that—I still repent it, M. de Wardes.'

'I can well understand that, monsieur, for the action itself needed repentance; but you were not the less the cause of that lady's disgrace. She of whom you have been speaking, covered with shame, borne down by the affront she had had wrought upon her, fled, quitted France, and no one ever knew what became of her.'

'Stay,' said the Comte de la Fère, stretching his hand towards de Wardes, with a peculiar smile upon his face, 'you are mistaken, she was seen; and there are persons even now present, who, having often heard her spoken of, will easily recognise her by the description I am about to give. She was about five-and-twenty years of age, slender in form, of a pale complexion, and fair-haired; she was married in England.'*

'Married?' exclaimed de Wardes.

'So, you were not aware she was married? You see we are far better informed than yourself. Do you happen to know she was usually styled "my lady," without the addition of any name to that description?'

'Yes, I know that.'

'Good heavens!' murmured Buckingham.

'Very well, monsieur. That woman who came from England returned to England after having thrice attempted M. d'Artagnan's life. That was but just, you will say, since M. d'Artagnan had insulted her. But what was not just was, that, when in England, this woman, by her seductions, completely enslaved a young man in the service of Lord Winter, by name Felton. You change colour, my lord,' said Athos, turning to the Duke of Buckingham, 'and your eyes kindle with anger and sorrow. Let your grace finish the recital, then, and tell M. de Wardes who this woman was who placed the knife in the hand of your father's murderer.'*

A cry escaped from the lips of all present. The young Duke passed his handkerchief across his forehead, which was covered with perspiration. A dead silence ensued among the spectators.

'You see, M. de Wardes,' said d'Artagnan, whom this recital had impressed more and more, as his own recollection revived as Athos spoke, 'you see, that my crime did not cause the destruction of any one's soul, and that the soul in question may fairly be considered to have been altogether lost before my regret. It is, however, an act of conscience on my part. Now this matter is settled, therefore, it remains for me to ask, with the greatest humility, your forgiveness for this shameless action, as most certainly I should have asked it of your father, if he were still alive, and if I had met him after my return to France, subsequent to the death of King Charles I.'*

'That is too much, M. d'Artagnan,' exclaimed many voices, with animation.

'No, gentlemen,' said the captain. 'And now, M. de Wardes, I hope all is finished between us, and that you will have no further occasion to speak ill of me again. Do you consider it completely settled?'

De Wardes bowed, and muttered to himself inarticulately.

'I trust also,' said d'Artagnan, approaching the young man closely, 'that you will no longer speak ill of any one as it seems you have the unfortunate habit of doing; for a man so puritanically conscientious as you are, who can reproach an old soldier for a youthful indiscretion five-and-thirty years after it has happened, will allow me to ask whether you, who advocate such excessive purity of conscience, will undertake on your side to do nothing contrary either to conscience or a principle of honour. And now, listen attentively to what I am going to say, M. de Wardes, in conclusion. Take care that no tale, with which your name may be associated, reaches my ear.'

'Monsieur,' said de Wardes, 'it is useless threatening to no purpose.'

'I have not yet finished, M. de Wardes, and you must listen to me still further.' The circle of listeners, full of eager curiosity, drew closer together. 'You spoke just now of the honour of a woman and of the honour of your father. We were glad to hear you speak in that manner; for it is pleasing to think that such a sentiment of delicacy and rectitude, and which did not exist it seems in our minds, lives in our children; and it is delightful, too, to see a young man, at an age when men from habit become the destroyers of the honour of women, respect and defend it.'

De Wardes bit his lips and clenched his hands, evidently much disturbed to learn how this discourse, the commencement of which was announced in so threatening a manner, would terminate.

'How did it happen then, that you allowed yourself to say to M. Bragelonne that he did not know who his mother was?'

Raoul's eye flashed, as, darting forward, he exclaimed,— 'Chevalier, this is a personal affair of my own!' at which exclamation, a smile, full of malice, passed across de Wardes's face. D'Artagnan put Raoul aside, saying,—'Do not interrupt me, young man.' And looking at de Wardes, in an authoritative manner, he continued,—'I am now dealing with a matter which cannot be settled by means of the sword, I discuss it before men of honour, all of whom have more than once had their swords in their hands in affairs of honour. I selected them expressly. These gentlemen well know that every secret for which men fight, ceases to be a secret. I again put my question to M. de Wardes. What was the subject of conversation when you offended this young man, in offending his father and mother at the same time?'

'It seems to me,' returned de Wardes, 'that liberty of speech is allowed, when it is ready to be supported by every means which a man of courage has at his disposal.'

'Tell me what the means are by which a man of courage can sustain a slanderous expression.'

'The sword.'

'You fail, not only in logic, in your argument, but in religion and honour. You expose the life of many others, without referring to your own, which seems to be full of hazard. Besides, fashions pass away, monsieur, and the fashion of duelling has passed away, without referring in any way to the edicts of His Majesty, which forbid it.* Therefore, in order to be consistent with your own chivalrous notions, you will at once apologise to M. de Bragelonne; you will tell him how much you regret having spoken so lightly, and that the nobility and purity of his race are inscribed, not in his heart alone, but, still more, in every action of his life. You will do and say this, M. de Wardes, as I, an old officer, did and said just now to your boy's moustache.'

'And if I refuse?' inquired de Wardes.

'In that case the result will be——'

'The very thing you are hoping to prevent,' said de Wardes, laughing; 'the result will be that your conciliatory address will end in a violation of the King's prohibition.'

'Not so,' said the captain, 'you are quite mistaken.'

'What will be the result, then?'

'The result will be that I shall go to the King, with whom I am on tolerably good terms, to whom I have been happy enough to render certain services, dating from a period when you were not born, and who, at my request, has just sent me an order in blank for M. Baisemeaux de Montlezun,* governor of the Bastille; and I shall say to the King,—"Sire, a man has cowardly insulted M. de Bragelonne in insulting his mother; I have written this man's name upon the order which your Majesty has been kind enough to give me, so that M. de Wardes is in the Bastille for three years."' And d'Artagnan, drawing the order signed by the King from his pocket, held it towards de Wardes. Remarking that the young man was not quite convinced, and received the warning as an idle threat, he shrugged his shoulders, and walked leisurely towards the table, upon which lay a writing case and a pen. De Wardes then saw that nothing could well be more seriously intended than the threat in question, for the Bastille, even at that period, was already held in dread. He advanced a step towards Raoul, and, in an almost unintelligible voice, said,— 'I offer my apologies in the terms which M. d'Artagnan just now dictated, and which I am forced to make to you.'

'One moment, monsieur,' said the musketeer, with the greatest tranquillity, 'you mistake the terms of the apology. I did not say, "and which I am forced to make," I said, "and which my conscience induces me to make." This latter expression, believe me, is better than the former, and it will be far preferable, since it will be the most truthful expression of your own sentiments.'

'I subscribe to it,' said de Wardes, 'but admit gentlemen, that a thrust of a sword through the body, as was the custom formerly, was far better than tyranny like this.'

'No, monsieur,' replied Buckingham; 'for the sword-thrust, when received, was no indication that a particular person was right or wrong; it only showed that he was more or less skilful in the use of the weapon.'

'Monsieur,' exclaimed de Wardes.

'There now,' interrupted d'Artagnan, 'you are going to say something very rude, and I am rendering you a service in stopping you in time.'

'Is that all, monsieur?' inquired de Wardes.

'Absolutely everything,' replied d'Artagnan, 'and these gentlemen, as well as myself, are quite satisfied with you.'

'Believe me, monsieur, that your reconciliations are not successful.'

'In what way?'

'Because, as we are now about to separate, I would wager that M. de Bragelonne and myself are greater enemies than ever.'

'You are deceived, monsieur, as far as I am concerned,' returned Raoul; 'for I do not retain the slightest animosity in my heart against you.'

This last blow overwhelmed de Wardes; he cast his eyes around him like a man utterly bewildered. D'Artagnan saluted most courteously the gentlemen who had been present at the explanation; and every one, on leaving the room, shook hands with him; but not one hand was held out towards de Wardes. 'Oh!' exclaimed the young man, abandoning himself to the rage which consumed him, 'can I not find some one on whom to wreak my vengeance?'

'You can, monsieur, for I am here,' whispered a voice full of menace in his ear.

De Wardes turned round, and saw the Duke of Buckingham, who, having probably remained behind with that intention, had just approached him. 'You, monsieur?' exclaimed de Wardes.

'Yes, I! I am no subject of the King of France; I am not going to remain on the territory, since I am about setting off for England. I have accumulated in my heart such a mass of despair and rage, that I too, like yourself, need to revenge myself upon some one. I approve M. d'Artagnan's principles extremely, but I am not bound to apply them to you. I am an Englishman, and, in my turn, I propose to you that you proposed to others to no purpose. Since you, therefore, are so terribly incensed, take me as a remedy. In thirty-four hours' time I shall be at Calais. Come with me; the journey will appear shorter if together than if alone. We will fight, when we get there, upon the sands which are covered by the rising tide, and which form part of the French territory during six hours of the day, but belong to the territory of Heaven during the other six.'

'I accept willingly,' said de Wardes.

'I assure you,' said the Duke, 'that if you kill me, you will be rendering me an infinite service.'

'I will do my utmost to be agreeable to you, Duke,' said de Wardes.

'It is agreed then, that I carry you off with me?'

'I shall be at your commands. I required some real danger, and some mortal risk to run, to tranquillise me.'

'In that case, I think you have met with what you are looking for. Farewell, M. de Wardes; to-morrow morning my valet will tell you the exact hour of departure; we will travel together like two excellent friends. I generally travel as fast as I can. Adieu.'

Buckingham saluted de Wardes, and returned towards the King's apartments; de Wardes, irritated beyond measure, left the Palais Royal, and hurried through the streets homeward to the house where he lodged.

III

BAISEMEAUX DE MONTLEZUN

AFTER the rather severe lesson administered to de Wardes, Athos and d'Artagnan together descended the staircase which led to the courtyard of the Palais Royal. 'You perceive,' said Athos to d'Artagnan, 'that Raoul cannot, sooner or later, avoid a duel with de Wardes, for de Wardes is as brave as he is vicious and wicked.'

'I know these fellows well,' replied d'Artagnan, 'I have had an affair with the father. I assure you that, although at that time I had good muscles and a sort of brute courage, I assure you the father did me some mischief. But you should have seen how I fought it out with him. Ah! Athos, such encounters never take place in these times! I had a hand which could never remain at rest, a hand like quicksilver—you knew its quality, for you have seen me at work. My sword was no longer a piece of steel, it was a serpent which assumed every form and every length, seeking where it might thrust its head; in other words, where it might fix its bite. I advanced half a dozen paces, then three, and then, body to body, I pressed my antagonist closely, then I darted back again ten paces. No human power could resist such ferocious ardour. Well, de Wardes, the father, with the bravery of his race, with his dogged courage, occupied a good deal of my time; and my fingers, at the end of the engagement, were, I well remember, tired enough.'*

'It is, then, as I said,' resumed Athos, 'the son will always be looking out for Raoul, and will end by meeting him; and Raoul can easily be found when he is sought for.'

'Agreed; but Raoul calculates well; he bears no grudge against de Wardes,—he has said so; he will wait until he is provoked, and in that case his position is a good one. The King will not be able to get out of temper about the matter; besides we shall know how to pacify His Majesty. But why so full of these fears and anxieties; you don't easily get alarmed?'

'I will tell you what makes me anxious: Raoul is to see the King to-morrow, when His Majesty will inform him of his wishes respecting a certain marriage. Raoul, loving as he does, will get out of temper, and once in an angry mood, if he were to meet de Wardes, the shell will explode.'

'We will prevent the explosion.'

'Not I,' said Athos, 'for I must return to Blois. All this gilded elegance of the court, all these intrigues, disgust me. I am no longer a young man who can make his terms with the meannesses of the present day. I have read in the great Book of God many things too beautiful and too comprehensive to take any interest in the little trifling phrases which these men whisper among themselves when they wish to deceive others. In one word, I am sick of Paris wherever and whenever you are not with me; and as I cannot have you always, I wish to return to Blois.'

'How wrong you are, Athos; how you gainsay your origin and the destiny of your noble nature. Men of your stamp are created to continue, to the very last moment, in full possession of their great faculties. Look at my sword, a Spanish blade, the one I wore at La Rochelle;* it served me for thirty years without fail; one day in the winter it fell upon the marble floor of the Louvre and was broken. I had a hunting-knife made of it which will last a hundred years yet. You, Athos, with your loyalty, your frankness, your cool courage, and your sound information, are the very man kings need to warn and direct them. Remain here; Monsieur Fouquet will not last so long as my Spanish blade.'

'Is it possible,' said Athos smilingly, 'that my friend d'Artagnan, who, after having raised me to the skies, making me an object of worship, casts me down from the top of Olympus, and hurls me to the ground? I have more exalted ambition, d'Artagnan. To be a minister—to be a slave, never! Am I not still greater? I am nothing. I remember having heard you occasionally call me "the great Athos"; I defy you, therefore, if I were minister, to continue to bestow that title upon me. No, no; I do not yield myself in this manner.'

'We will not speak of it any more, then;—renounce everything, even the brotherly feeling which unites us.'

'It is almost cruel what you say.'

D'Artagnan pressed Athos's hand warmly. 'No, no; renounce everything without fear. Raoul can get on without you; I am at Paris.'

'In that case I shall return to Blois. We will take leave of each other to-night; to-morrow at daybreak I shall be on my horse again.'

'You cannot return to your hotel alone; why did you not bring Grimaud* with you?'

'Grimaud takes his rest now; he goes to bed early, for my poor old servant gets easily fatigued. He came from Blois with me, and I compelled him to remain within doors; for if, in retracing the forty leagues which separate us from Blois, he needed to draw breath even, he would die without a murmur. But I don't want to lose Grimaud.'

'You shall have one of my musketeers to carry a torch for you. Hallo! some one there,' called out d'Artagnan, leaning over the gilded balustrade—the heads of seven or eight musketeers appeared—'I wish some gentleman who is so disposed, to escort the Comte de la Fère,' cried d'Artagnan.

'Thank you for your readiness, gentlemen,' said Athos; 'I regret to have occasion to trouble you in this manner.'

'I would willingly escort the Comte de la Fère,' said some one, 'if I had not to speak to Monsieur d'Artagnan.'

'Who is that?' said d'Artagnan, looking into the darkness.

'I, Monsieur d'Artagnan.'

'Heaven forgive me, if that is Monsieur Baisemeaux's voice.'

'It is, monsieur.'

'What are you doing in the courtyard, my dear Baisemeaux?'

'I am waiting your orders, my dear Monsieur d'Artagnan.'

'Wretch that I am,' thought d'Artagnan; 'true, you have been told, I suppose, that some one was to be arrested, and have come yourself, instead of sending an officer?'

'I came because I had occasion to speak to you.'

'You did not send to me?'

'I waited until you were disengaged,' said Monsieur Baisemeaux timidly.

'I leave you, d'Artagnan,' said Athos.

'Not before I have presented Monsieur Baisemeaux de Montlezun, the governor of the Bastille.'

Baisemeaux and Athos saluted each other.

'Surely you must know each other,' added d'Artagnan.

'I have an indistinct recollection of Monsieur Baisemeaux,' said Athos.

'You remember, my dear Baisemeaux, that king's guardsman with whom we used formerly to have such delightful meetings in the Cardinal's time.'*

'Perfectly,' said Athos, taking leave of him with affability.

'Monsieur le Comte de la Fère, whose *nom de guerre* was Athos,' whispered d'Artagnan to Baisemeaux.

'Yes, yes; a brave man, one of the celebrated four.'

'Precisely so. But, my dear Baisemeaux, shall we talk now?'

'If you please.'

'In the first place, as for the orders—there are none. The King does not intend to arrest the person in question.'

'So much the worse,' said Baisemeaux, with a sigh.

'What do you mean by so much the worse?' exclaimed d'Artagnan, laughing.

'No doubt of it,' returned the governor, 'my prisoners are my income.'*

'I beg your pardon, I did not see it in that light.'

'And so there are no orders,' repeated Baisemeaux, with a sigh. 'What an admirable situation yours is, captain,' he continued after a pause, 'captain-lieutenant of the musketeers.'

'Oh, it is good enough; but I don't see why you should envy me; you, governor of the Bastille, the first castle in France.'

'I am well aware of that,' said Baisemeaux, in a sorrowful tone of voice.

'You say that like a man confessing his sins. I would willingly exchange my profits for yours.'

'Don't speak of profits to me, if you wish to save me the bitterest anguish of mind.'

'Why do you look first on one side and then on the other, as if you were afraid of being arrested yourself, you whose business it is to arrest others?'

'I was looking to see whether any one could see or listen to us; it would be safer to confer more in private, if you would grant me such a favour.'

'Baisemeaux, you seem to forget we are acquaintances of five-and-thirty years' standing. Don't assume such sanctified airs; make yourself quite comfortable; I don't eat governors of the Bastille raw.'

'Heaven be praised!'

'Come into the courtyard with me; it's a beautiful moonlight night; we will walk up and down, arm in arm, under the trees, while you tell me your pitiful tale.' He drew the doleful governor into the courtyard, took him by the arm as he had said, and, in his rough, good-humoured way, cried:—'Out with it, rattle away, Baisemeaux; what have you got to say?'

'It's a long story.'

'You prefer your own lamentations, then; my opinion is, it will be longer than ever. I'll wager you are making fifty thousand francs out of your pigeons in the Bastille.'

'Would to Heaven that were the case, M. d'Artagnan.'

'You surprise me, Baisemeaux; just look at yourself. I should like to show you your face in a glass, and you would see how plump and florid looking you are, as fat and round as a cheese, with eyes like lighted coals; and if it were not for that ugly wrinkle you try to cultivate on your forehead, you would hardly look fifty years old, and you are sixty,* if I am not mistaken.'

'All quite true.'

'Of course I knew it was true, as true as the fifty thousand francs profit you make;' at which remark Baisemeaux stamped on the ground.

'Well, well,' said d'Artagnan, 'I will run up your account for you: you were captain of M. Mazarin's guards; and 12,000 francs a year* would in twelve years amount to 140,000 francs.'

'Twelve thousand francs! Are you mad!' cried Baisemeaux; 'the old miser gave me no more than 6,000, and the expenses of the post amounted to 6,500. M. Colbert, who deducted the other 6,000 francs, condescended to allow me to take fifty pistoles as a gratification; so that, if it were not for my little estate at Montlezun,* which brings me in 12,000 francs a year, I could not have met my engagements.'

'Well, then, how about the 50,000 francs from the Bastille? There, I trust, you are boarded and lodged, and get your 6,000 francs salary besides.'

'Admitted!'

'Whether the year be good or bad, there are fifty prisoners, who, on an average, bring you in a thousand francs a year each.'

'I don't deny it.'

'Well, there is at once an income of 50,000 francs; you have held the post three years, and must have received in that time, 150,000 francs.'

'You forget one circumstance, dear M. d'Artagnan.'

'What is that?'

'That while you received appointment as captain from the King himself,* I received mine as governor from Messrs Tremblay and Louvière.'*

'Quite right, and Tremblay was not a man to let you have the post for nothing.'

'Nor was Louvière either; the result was, that I gave 75,000 francs to Tremblay as his share.'

'Very agreeable that! and to Louvière?'

'The same.'

'Money down?'

'No; that would have been impossible. The King did not wish, or rather M. Mazarin did not wish, to have the appearance of removing those two gentlemen, who had sprung from the barricades;* he permitted them, therefore, to make certain extravagant conditions for their retirement.'

'What were those conditions?'

'Tremble . . . three years' income for the goodwill.'

'The deuce! so that the 150,000 francs have passed into their hands.'

'Precisely so.'

'And beyond that?'

'A sum of 50,000 francs, or 15,000 pistoles, whichever you please, in three payments.'

'Exorbitant enough.'

'Yes, but that is not all.'

'What besides?'

'In default of the fulfilment by me of any one of those conditions, those gentlemen enter upon their functions again. The King has been induced to sign a document to that effect.'

'It is enormous, incredible!'

'Such is the fact, however.'

'I do indeed pity you, Baisemeaux. But why, in the name of fortune, did M. Mazarin grant you this pretended favour? It would have been far better to have refused you altogether?'

'Certainly, but he was strongly persuaded to do so by my protector.'

'Who is he?'

'One of your own friends, indeed; M. d'Herblay.'

'M. d'Herblay! Aramis!'*

'Just so; he has been very kind towards me.'

'Kind! to make you enter into such a bargain.'

'Listen! I wished to leave the Cardinal's service. M. d'Herblay spoke on my behalf to Louvière and Tremblay—they objected; I wished to have the appointment very much, for I knew that it could be made to produce; in my distress I confided in M. d'Herblay, and he offered to become my surety for the different payments.'

'You astound me! Aramis become your surety?'

'Like a man of honour; he procured the signature; Tremblay and Louvière resigned their appointments; I have paid every year 25,000 francs to these two gentlemen; on the 31st of May, every year, M. d'Herblay himself comes to the Bastille, and brings me 5,000 pistoles to distribute between my crocodiles.'

'You owe Aramis 150,000 francs, then?'*

'That is the very thing which is the cause of my despair, for I only owe him 100,000.'

'I don't quite understand you.'

'He has been only two years. To-day, however, is the 31st of May, and he has not been yet, and to-morrow, at midday, the payment falls due; if, therefore, I don't pay to-morrow, those gentlemen can, by the terms of the contract, break off the bargain; I shall be stripped of everything; I shall have worked for three years, and given 250,000 francs for nothing, absolutely for nothing at all, dear M. d'Artagnan.'

'This is very strange,' murmured d'Artagnan.

'You can now imagine that I may well have wrinkles on my forehead; can you not?'

'Yes, indeed!'

'And you can imagine, too, that notwithstanding I may be as round as a cheese, with a complexion like an apple, and my eyes like coals on fire, I may almost be afraid that I shall not have a cheese or an apple left me to eat, and that I shall only have my eyes left me to weep with.'

'This is really a very grievous business.'

'I have come to you, M. d'Artagnan, for you are the only one who can get me out of my trouble. You are acquainted with the Abbé d'Herblay, and you know that he is somewhat mysterious. Well, you can, perhaps, give me the address of his presbytery, for I have been to Noisy-le-Sec,* and he is no longer there.'

'I should think not, indeed. He is Bishop of Vannes.'

'What! Vannes in Bretagne?'

The little man began to tear his hair, saying, 'How can I get to Vannes from here by midday to-morrow? I am a lost man.'

'But, listen; a bishop is not always a resident. M. d'Herblay may not possibly be so far away as you fear.'

'Pray tell me his address.'

'I really don't know it.'

'In that case, I am utterly lost. I will go and throw myself at the King's feet.'

'But, Baisemeaux, I can hardly believe what you tell me; besides, since the Bastille is capable of producing 50,000 francs a year, why have you not tried to screw 100,000 out of it?'

'Because I am an honest man, M. d'Artagnan, and because my prisoners are fed like potentates.'

'Well, you're in a fair way to get out of your difficulties; give yourself a good attack of indigestion with your excellent living, and put yourself out of the way between this and midday to-morrow.'

'How can you be hard-hearted enough to laugh?'

'Nay, you really afflict me. Come, Baisemeaux, if you can pledge me your word of honour, do so, that you will not open your lips to any one about what I am going to say to you.'

'Never, never!'

'You wish to find Aramis?'

'At any cost!'

'Well, go and see where M. Fouquet is.'

'Why, what connection can there be——'

'How stupid you are. Don't you know that Vannes is in the diocese of Belle-Isle, or Belle-Isle is in the diocese of Vannes? Belle-Isle belongs to M. Fouquet, and M. Fouquet nominated M. d'Herblay to that bishopric!'

'I see, I see; you restore me to life again.'

'So much the better; go and tell M. Fouquet very simply that you wish to speak to M. d'Herblay.'

'Of course, of course,' exclaimed Baisemeaux delightedly.

'But,' said d'Artagnan, checking him by a severe look, 'your word of honour?'

'I give you my sacred word of honour,' replied the little man, about to set off running.

'Where are you going?'

'To M. Fouquet's house.'

'It is useless doing that; M. Fouquet is playing at cards with the King. All you can do is to pay M. Fouquet a visit early to-morrow morning.'

'I will do so. Thank you.'

'This is a strange affair,' murmured d'Artagnan, as he slowly ascended the staircase after he had left Baisemeaux. 'What possible interest can Aramis have in obliging Baisemeaux in this manner? Well, I suppose we shall learn some day or another.'

IV

THE KING'S CARD-TABLE

FOUQUET was present, as d'Artagnan had said, at the King's card-table. It seemed as if Buckingham's departure had shed a balm upon all the ulcerated hearts of the previous evening. Monsieur, radiant with delight, made a thousand affectionate signs to his mother. The Comte de Guiche could not separate himself from Buckingham, and while playing, conversed with him upon the circumstance of his projected voyage. Buckingham, thoughtful, and kind in his manner, like a man who has adopted a resolution, listened to the count, and from time to time, cast a look full of regret and hopeless affliction at Madame. The Princess, in the midst of her elation of spirits, divided her attention between the King, who was playing with her, Monsieur, who quietly joked her about her enormous winnings, and de Guiche, who exhibited an extravagant delight. Of Buckingham she took but little notice, for her, this fugitive, this exile, was now simply a remembrance, and no longer a man. The Duke could not conceal this change, and his heart was cruelly hurt at it. Of a sensitive character, proud, and susceptible of deep attachment, he cursed the day on which the passion had entered his heart. The looks which he cast, from time to time, at Madame, became colder by degrees at the chilling complexion of his thoughts. He could hardly yet despair, but he was strong enough to impose silence upon the tumultuous outcries of his heart. In exact proportion, however, as Madame suspected this change of feeling, she redoubled her activity to regain the ray of light which she was about to lose; her timid and indecisive mind was first displayed in brilliant flashes of wit and humour. At any cost, she felt that she must be remarked above everything and every one, even above the King himself. And she was so, for the

Queens,* notwithstanding their dignity, and the King, despite the respect which etiquette required, were all eclipsed by her. The Queens, stately and ceremonious, were softened, and could not restrain their laughter. Madame Henrietta, the Queen-Mother, was dazzled by the brilliancy which cast distinction upon her family, thanks to the wit of the grand-daughter of Henry IV. The King, so jealous, as a young man and as a monarch, of the superiority of those who surrounded him, could not resist admitting himself vanquished by that petulance so thoroughly French in its nature, and whose energy was more than ever increased by its English humour. Like a child, he was captivated by her radiant beauty, which her wit made still more so. Madame's eyes flashed like lightning. Wit and humour escaped from her ruby lips like persuasion from the lips of Nestor* of old. The whole court subdued by her enchanting grace, noticed for the first time that laughter could be indulged in before the greatest monarch in the world, like people who merited their appellation of the wittiest and most polished people in the world.

Madame, from that evening, achieved and enjoyed a success capable of bewildering whomsoever it might be, who had not been born in these elevated regions termed a throne, and which, in spite of their elevation, are sheltered from similar vertigoes. From that very moment Louis XIV acknowledged Madame as a person who might be recognised. Buckingham regarded her as a coquette deserving the cruellest tortures, and de Guiche looked upon her as a divinity; the courtiers as a star whose light might become the focus of all favour and power. And yet, Louis XIV a few years previously had not even condescended to offer his hand to that 'ugly girl' for a ballet;* and yet Buckingham had worshipped this coquette in the humblest attitude; and yet de Guiche had looked upon this divinity as a mere woman; and yet the courtiers had not dared to extol this star in her upward progress, fearful to displease the monarch whom this star had formerly displeased.

Let us see what was taking place during this memorable evening at the King's card-table. The young Queen, although Spanish by birth, and the niece of Anne of Austria, loved the King, and could not conceal her affection. Anne of Austria, a keen observer, like all women, and imperious, like every Queen, was sensible of Madame's power, and acquiesced in it immediately, a circumstance which induced the young Queen to raise the siege and retire to her apartments. The King hardly paid any attention to her departure, notwithstanding the pretended symptoms of indisposition by which it was accompanied. Encouraged by the rules of etiquette, which he had begun to introduce at the court as an element of every position and relation of life, Louis XIV did not disturb himself; he offered his hand to Madame without looking at Monsieur his brother, and led the young Princess to the door of her apartments. It was remarked, that at the threshold of the door, His Majesty, freed from every restraint, or less strong than the situation, sighed very deeply. The ladies present—for nothing escapes a woman's observation— Mademoiselle Montalais,* for instance—did not fail to say to each other, 'the King sighed,' and 'Madame sighed, too.' This had been indeed the case. Madame had sighed very noiselessly, but with an accompaniment very far more dangerous for the King's repose. Madame had sighed, first closing her beautiful black eyes, next opening them, and then, laden, as they were, with an indescribable mournfulness of expression, she had raised them towards the King, whose face at that moment had visibly heightened in colour. The consequence of these blushes, of these interchanged sighs, and of this royal agitation, was, that Montalais had committed an indiscretion, which had certainly affected her companion, for Mademoiselle de la Vallière, less clear-sighted, perhaps, turned pale when the King blushed; and her attendance being required upon Madame, she tremblingly followed the Princess without thinking of taking the gloves, which court etiquette required her to do. True it is that this country girl might allege as her excuse the agitation into which the King seemed to be thrown, for Mademoiselle de la Vallière, busily engaged in closing the door, had involuntarily fixed her eyes upon the King, who, as he retired backwards, had his face towards it. The King returned to the room where the card-tables were set out. He wished to speak to the different persons there, but it could easily be seen that his mind was absent. He jumbled different accounts together, which was taken advantage of by some of the noblemen who had retained those habits since the time of Monsieur Mazarin who, though a good mathematician,

had a bad memory. In this way, Monsieur Manicamp, with a
thoughtless and absent air,—for Monsieur Manicamp was the
honestest man in the world,—appropriated simply 20,000 francs,
which were littering the table, and the ownership of which did
not seem legitimately to belong to any person in particular. In
the same way, Monsieur de Wardes, whose head was doubtless
a little bewildered by the occurrences of the evening, somehow
forgot to leave the sixty double-louis which he had won for the
Duke of Buckingham, and which the Duke, incapable, like his
father, of soiling his hands with coin of any sort, had left lying
on the table before him. The King only recovered his attention
in some degree at the moment that Monsieur Colbert, who had
been narrowly observant for some minutes, approached, and,
doubtless, with great respect, yet with much perseverance, whispered a counsel of some sort into the still tingling ears of the
King. The King, at the suggestion, listened with renewed attention, and immediately looking around him said, 'Is Monsieur
Fouquet no longer here?'

'Yes, sire, I am here,' replied the Minister, who was engaged
with Buckingham, and approached the King, who advanced a
step or two towards him with a smiling yet negligent air. 'Forgive
me,' said Louis, 'if I interrupt your conversation; but I claim
your attention wherever I may require your services.'

'I am always at the King's service,' replied Fouquet.

'And your cash-box too,' said the King, laughing with a false
smile.

'My cash-box more than anything else,' said Fouquet coldly.

'The fact is I wish to give a fête at Fontainbleau, to keep open
house for fifteen days, and I shall require——' and he stopped,
glancing at Colbert. Fouquet waited without showing discom-
posure; and the King resumed, answering Colbert's cruel smile,
'Four million francs.'

'Four millions,' repeated Fouquet, bowing profoundly. And
his nails, buried in his bosom, were thrust into his flesh, the
tranquil expression of his face remaining unaltered. 'When will
they be required, sire?'

'Take your time,—I mean—no, no; as soon as possible.'

'A certain time will be necessary, sire.'

Colbert looked triumphant.

'The time, monsieur,' said the Minister of Finance, with the haughtiest disdain, 'simply to count the money; a million only can be drawn and weighed in a day.'

'Four days then,' said Colbert.

'My clerks,' replied Fouquet, addressing himself to the King, 'will perform wonders for His Majesty's service, and the sum shall be ready in three days.'

It was for Colbert now to turn pale. Louis looked at him astonished. Fouquet withdrew without any parade or weakness, smiling at his numerous friends, in whose countenances alone he read the sincerity of their friendship—an interest partaking of compassion. Fouquet, however, should not be judged by his smile, for, in reality he felt as if he had been stricken by death. Drops of blood beneath his coat stained the fine linen which covered his chest. His dress concealed the blood, and his smile the rage which consumed him. His domestics perceived, by the manner in which he approached his carriage, that their master was not in the best of humours; the result of their discernment was, that his orders were executed with that exactitude of manœuvre which is found on board a man-of-war, commanded during a storm, by a passionate captain. The carriage, therefore, did not simply roll along, but flew. Fouquet had hardly had time to recover himself during the drive; on his arrival he went at once to Aramis, who had not yet retired for the night. As for Porthos,* he had supped very agreeably from a roast leg of mutton, two pheasants, and a great mound of crayfish; he then directed his body to be anointed with perfumed oils, in the manner of the wrestlers of old; and when the anointment was completed, he was wrapped in flannels and placed in a warm bed. Aramis, as we have already said, had not retired. Seated at his ease in a velvet dressing-gown, he wrote letter after letter in that fine and hurried hand-writing, a page of which contained a quarter of a volume. The door was thrown hurriedly open, and the Minister of Finance appeared, pale, agitated, and anxious. Aramis looked up: 'Good evening,' said he, and his searching look detected his host's sadness, and disordered state of mind. 'Was the play good at His Majesty's?' asked Aramis, as a way of beginning the conversation.

Fouquet threw himself upon a couch, and then pointed to the

door to the servant who had followed him; when the servant had left he said, 'Excellent.'

Aramis, who had followed every movement with his eyes, noticed that he stretched himself upon the cushions with a sort of feverish impatience. 'You have lost, as usual?' inquired Aramis, his pen still in his hand.

'Better than usual,' replied Fouquet.

'You know how to support losses.'

'Sometimes.'

'What, Monsieur Fouquet a bad player!'

'There is play and play, Monsieur d'Herblay.'

'How much have you lost?' inquired Aramis, with a slight uneasiness.

Fouquet collected himself a moment, and then, without the slightest emotion, said, 'The evening has cost me four millions,' and a bitter laugh drowned the last vibration of these words.

Aramis, who did not expect such an amount, dropped his pen. 'Four millions!' he said; 'you have lost four millions— impossible!'

'Monsieur Colbert held my cards for me,' replied the Minister, with a similar bitter laugh.

'Ah, now I understand; so, so, a new application for funds?'*

'Yes, and from the King's own lips. It is impossible to destroy a man with a more charming smile. What do you think of it?'

'It is clear that your ruin is the object in view.'

'That is still your opinion?'

'Still. Besides there is nothing in it which should astonish you, for we have foreseen it all along.'

'Yes; but I did not expect four millions.'

'No doubt the amount is large; but, after all, four millions are not quite the death of a man, especially when the man in question is Monsieur Fouquet.'

'My dear d'Herblay, if you knew the contents of my coffers, you would be less easy.'

'And you promised?'

'What could I do? The very day when I refuse, Colbert will procure it; whence I know not, but he will procure the money and I shall be lost.'

'There is no doubt of that. In how many days hence have you promised these four millions?'

'In three days; the King seemed exceedingly pressed. And it is very uncertain whether I have the money. Everything must be exhausted: Belle-Isle is paid for; the pension has been paid; and money, since the investigation of the accounts* of those who farm the revenue, is rare. Besides, admitting that I pay this time, how can I do so on another occasion? When kings have tasted money, they are like tigers who have tasted flesh, they devour everything. The day will arrive—must arrive—when I shall have to say, "Impossible sire," and on that very day I am a lost man.'

Aramis raised his shoulders slightly, saying, 'A man in your position, my lord, is only lost when he wishes to be so.'

'A man, whatever his position may be, cannot hope to struggle against a king.'

'Nonsense; when I was young I struggled successfully with the Cardinal Richelieu who was King of France—nay more— Cardinal.'*

'Where are my armies, my troops, my treasures? I have not even Belle-Isle.'*

'Bah! necessity is the mother of invention, and when you think all is lost, something will be discovered which shall save everything.'

'Who will discover this wonderful something?'

'Yourself.'

'I! I resign my office of inventor.'

'Then I will.'

'Be it so. But then, set to work without delay.'

'Oh! we have time enough.'

'You kill me, d'Herblay, with your calmness,' said the Minister, passing his handkerchief over his face.

'Do you remember that I one day told you not to make yourself uneasy, if you possess but courage. Have you any?'

'I believe so.'

'Then don't make yourself uneasy.'

'It is decided then, that, at the last moment, you will come to my assistance.'

'It will only be the repayment of a debt I owe you.'

'It is the vocation of financiers to anticipate the wants of men such as yourself, d'Herblay.'

'If obligingness is the vocation of financiers, charity is the virtue of the clergy. Only on this occasion do you act, monsieur. You are not yet sufficiently reduced, and at the last moment we shall see what is to be done.'

'We shall see, then, in a very short time.'

'Very well. However, permit me to tell you that, personally, I regret exceedingly that you are at present so short of money, because I was about to ask you for some.'

'For yourself?'

'For myself, or some of my people; for mine or for ours.'

'How much do you want?'

'Be easy on that score; a roundish sum it is true, but not too exorbitant.'

'Tell me the amount.'

'Fifty thousand francs.'

'Oh! a mere nothing. Of course, one has always 50,000 francs. Why the deuce cannot that knave Colbert be as easily satisfied as you are; and I should give myself far less trouble than I do. When do you need this sum?'

'To-morrow morning; but you require to know its destination?'

'Nay, nay, Chevalier, I need no explanation.'

'To-morrow is the first of June.'

'Well?'

'One of our bonds becomes due.'

'I did not know we had any bonds.'

'Certainly, to-morrow we pay our last third instalment.'

'What third?'

'Of the 150,000 to Baisemeaux.'

'Baisemeaux—who is he?'

'The governor of the Bastille.'

'Yes, I remember; on what grounds am I to pay 150,000 for that man?'

'On account of the appointment which he, or rather, we, purchased from Louvière and Tremblay.'

'I have a very vague recollection of the whole matter.'

'That is likely enough, for you have so many affairs to attend to. However, I do not believe you have any affair of greater importance than this one.'

'Tell me, then, why we purchased this appointment.'

'Why, in order to render him a service in the first place and afterwards ourselves.'

'Ourselves, you are joking?'

'Monsiegneur, the time may come when the governor of the Bastille may prove a very excellent acquaintance.'

'I have not the good fortune to understand you, d'Herblay.'

'Monseigneur, we have our own poets, our own engineer, our own architect, our own musicians, our own printer, and our own painters; we needed our own governor of the Bastille.'

'Do you think so?'

'Let us not deceive ourselves, monseigneur; we are very much exposed to paying the Bastille a visit,' added the prelate, displaying, beneath his pale lips, teeth which were still the same beautiful teeth so admired thirty years previously by Marie Michon.*

'And you think it is not too much to pay 150,000 for that? I assure you that you generally put out your money at better interest than that.'

'The day will come when you will admit your mistake.'

'My dear d'Herblay, the very day on which a man enters the Bastille he is no longer protected by the past.'

'Yes he is, if the bonds are perfectly regular; besides, that good fellow Baisemeaux has not a courtier's heart. I am certain, my lord, that he will not remain ungrateful for that money, without taking into account, I repeat, that I retain the deeds and titles.'*

'It is a strange affair! usury in a matter of benevolence.'

'Do not mix yourself up with it monseigneur; if there be usury, it is I who practise it, and both of us reap the advantages of it—that is all.'

'Some intrigue, d'Herblay?'

'I do not deny it.'

'And Baisemeaux an accomplice in it?'

'Why not? there are worse accomplices than he. May I depend, then, upon the 5,000 pistoles to-morrow?'

'Do you want them this evening?'

'It would be better, for I wish to start early; poor Baisemeaux will not be able to imagine what has become of me, and must be upon thorns.'

'You shall have the amount in an hour. Ah, d'Herblay, the interest of your 150,000 francs will never pay my four millions for me. Good-night, I have business to transact with my clerks before I retire.'

V

M. BAISEMEAUX DE MONTLEZUN'S ACCOUNTS

THE clock of St Paul's was striking seven as Aramis, on horseback, dressed as a simple citizen, that is to say, in a plain suit, with no distinctive mark about him except a kind of hunting-knife by his side, passed before the Rue Petit-Musc, and stopped opposite the Rue des Tournelles at the gate of the Bastille.* Two sentinels were on duty at the gate; they raised no difficulty about admitting Aramis, who entered without dismounting, and they pointed out the way he was to go by a long passage with buildings on both sides. This passage led to the drawbridge, or, in other words, to the real entrance. The drawbridge was down, and the duty of the day was about being entered upon. The sentinel on duty at the outer guard-house stopped Aramis's further progress, asking him in a rough tone of voice what had brought him there. Aramis explained, with his usual politeness, that a wish to speak to M. Baisemeaux de Montlezun had occasioned his visit. The first sentinel then summoned a second sentinel, stationed within an inner lodge, who showed his face at the grating and inspected the new arrival very attentively. Aramis reiterated the expression of his wish to see the governor, whereupon the sentinel called to an officer of lower grade who was walking about in a tolerably spacious courtyard, and who, in his turn, on being informed of the object ran to seek one of the officers of the governor's staff. The latter, after having listened to Aramis's request, begged him to wait a moment, then went away a short distance, but returned to ask his name. 'I cannot tell it you monsieur,' said Aramis; 'I would only mention that I have matters of such importance to communicate to the governor that I can only rely beforehand upon one thing, that M. de Baisemeaux will be delighted to see me; nay, more than that, when you shall have told him that it is the person he expected on the 1st of June, I am convinced he will hasten here himself.' The officer could not possibly believe that a man of the governor's importance should put himself out for a man of so little importance as the citizen-looking person on horseback. 'It happens, most fortunately, monsieur,' he said, 'that the governor is just going out, and you can see his carriage, with the horses already harnessed, in the courtyard yonder; there will be no occasion for him to come to meet you, as he will see you as he passes by.' Aramis bowed to signify his assent; he did not wish to inspire others with too exalted an opinion of himself, and therefore waited patiently, and in silence, leaning upon the saddle-bow of his horse. Ten minutes had hardly elapsed when the governor's carriage was observed to move. The governor appeared at the door, got into the carriage, which immediately prepared to start. The same ceremony was observed for the governor himself as had been the case with a suspected stranger; the sentinel at the lodge advanced as the carriage was about to pass under the arch, and the governor opened the carriage door, himself setting the example of obedience to orders; so that, in this way, the sentinel could convince himself that no one left the Bastille improperly. The carriage rolled along under the archway, but, at the moment the iron gate was opened, the officer approached the carriage, which had been again stopped, and said something to the governor, who immediately put his head out of the doorway, and perceived Aramis on horseback at the end of the drawbridge. He immediately uttered almost a shout of delight, and got out, or rather darted out of his carriage, running towards Aramis, whose hands he seized, making a thousand apologies. He almost kissed him. 'What a difficult matter to enter the Bastille,' said Aramis. 'Is it the same for those who are sent here against their wills as for those who come of their own accord?'

'A thousand pardons, my lord. How delighted I am to see your grace.'

'Hush! What are you thinking of, my dear M. Baisemeaux; what do you suppose would be thought of a bishop in my present costume?'

'Pray excuse me, I had forgotten. Take this gentleman's horse to the stables,' cried Baisemeaux.

'No, no,' said Aramis, 'I have 5,000 pistoles in the portmanteau.'

The governor's countenance became so radiant, that if the prisoners had seen him they would have imagined some prince of the blood royal had arrived. 'Yes, you are right the horse shall be taken to the governor's residence. Will you get into the carriage, my dear M. d'Herblay, and it will take us back to my house.'

'Get into a carriage to cross a courtyard; do you believe I am so great an invalid? No, no, we will go on foot.'

Baisemeaux then offered his arm as a support, but the prelate did not accept it. They arrived in this manner at the governor's house, Baisemeaux rubbing his hands and glancing at the horse from time to time, while Aramis was looking at the black and bare walls. A tolerably handsome vestibule, a straight staircase of white stone, led to the governor's apartments, who crossed the ante-chamber, the dining-room, where breakfast was being prepared, opened a small side door, and closeted himself with his guest in a large cabinet, the windows of which opened obliquely upon the courtyard and the stables. Baisemeaux installed the prelate with that obsequious politeness of which a good man, or a grateful man, alone possesses the secret. An armchair, a footstool, a small table beside him, on which to rest his hand, everything was prepared by the governor himself. With his own hands too, he placed upon the table, with almost religious solicitude, the bag containing the gold, which one of the soldiers had brought up with the most respectful devotion; and the soldier having left the room, Baisemeaux himself closed the door after him, drew aside one of the window-curtains, and looked steadfastly at Aramis to see if the prelate required anything further. 'Well, my lord,' he said, still standing up, 'of all men of their word, you still continue to be the most punctual.'

'In matters of business, dear M. de Baisemeaux, exactitude is not a virtue only, but a duty as well.'

'Yes, in matters of business, certainly; but what you have with me is not of that character, it is a service you are rendering me.'

'Come, confess, dear M. de Baisemeaux, that, notwithstanding this exactitude, you have not been without a little uneasiness.'

'About your health, I certainly have,' stammered out Baisemeaux.

'I wished to come here yesterday, but I was not able, as I was too fatigued,' continued Aramis. Baisemeaux anxiously slipped another cushion behind his guest's back. 'But,' continued Aramis, 'I promised myself to come and pay you a visit to-day, early in the morning.'

'You are really very kind, my lord. And it was a good thing for me that I was punctual, I think.'

'What do you mean?'

'Yes, you were going out.' At which latter remark Baisemeaux coloured, and said, 'Yes, it is true I was going out.'

'Then I prevent you,' said Aramis; whereupon the embarrassment of Baisemeaux became visibly greater. 'I am putting you to inconvenience,' he continued, fixing a keen glance upon the poor governor; 'If I had known that I should not have come.'

'How can your lordship imagine that you could ever inconvenience me?'

'Confess you were going in search of money.'

'No,' stammered out Baisemeaux, 'no! I assure you I was going to——'

'Does the governor still intend to go to M. Fouquet,' suddenly called out the major from below. Baisemeaux ran to the window like a madman. 'No, no,' he exclaimed in a state of desperation, 'who the deuce is speaking of M. Fouquet? are you drunk below there? why am I interrupted when I am engaged on business?'

'You were going to M. Fouquet's,' said Aramis, biting his lips, 'to M. Fouquet, the abbé, or the superintendant?'

Baisemeaux almost made up his mind to tell an untruth, but he could not summon courage to do so. 'To the superintendant,' he said.

'It is true, then, that you were in want of money, since you were going to the person who gives it away?'

'I assure you, my lord——'

'You are suspicious of me.'

'My dear lord, it was the uncertainty and ignorance in which I was as to where you were to be found.'

'You would have found the money you require at M. Fouquet's, for he is a man whose hand is always open.'

'I swear that I should never have ventured to ask M. Fouquet for money. I only wished to ask him for your address.'

'To ask M. Fouquet for my address?' exclaimed Aramis, opening his eyes in real astonishment.

'Yes,' said Baisemeaux, greatly disturbed by the glance which the prelate fixed upon him; 'at M. Fouquet's certainly.'

'There is no harm in that, dear M. Baisemeaux, only I would ask, why ask my address of M. Fouquet?'

'That I might write to you.'

'I understand,' said Aramis, smiling, 'but that is not what I meant. I do not ask you what you required my address for; I only ask why you should go to M. Fouquet for it?'

'Oh!' said Baisemeaux, 'as Belle-Isle is the property of M. Fouquet, and as Belle-Isle is in the diocese of Vannes, and as you are bishop of Vannes——'

'But my dear Baisemeaux, since you knew I was bishop of Vannes, you had no occasion to ask M. Fouquet for my address.'

'Well, monsieur,' said Baisemeaux, completely at bay, 'if I have acted indiscreetly, I beg your pardon most sincerely.'

'Nonsense,' observed Aramis, calmly, 'how can you possibly have acted indiscreetly?' And while he composed his face and continued to smile cheerfully on the governor, he was considering how Baisemeaux, who was not aware of his address, knew, however, that Vannes was his residence. 'I will clear all this up,' he said to himself, and then speaking aloud, added, 'Well, my dear governor, shall we now arrange our little accounts?'

'I am at your orders, my lord; but tell me beforehand, my lord, whether you will do me the honour to breakfast with me as usual?'

'Very willingly indeed.'

'That's well,' said Baisemeaux, as he struck the bell before him three times.

'What does that mean?' inquired Aramis.

'That I have some one to breakfast with me, and that preparations are to be made accordingly.'

'And you rang thrice. Really, my dear governor, I begin to think you are acting ceremoniously with me.'

'No, indeed. Besides, the least I can do is to receive you in the best way I can.'

'But why so?'

'Because not a prince even could have done what you have done for me.'

'Nonsense! nonsense!'

'Nay, I assure you——'

'Let us speak of other matters,' said Aramis. 'Or rather, tell me how your affairs here are getting on.'

'Not over well.'

'The deuce!'

'M. de Mazarin was not hard enough.'

'Yes, I see; you require a Government full of suspicion—like that of the old Cardinal, for instance.'

'Yes; matters went on better under him. The brother of His "Grey Eminence,"* made his fortune in it.'

'Believe me, my dear governor,' said Aramis, drawing closer to Baisemeaux, 'a young king is well worth an old cardinal. Youth has its suspicions, its fits of anger, its prejudices, as old age has its hatreds, its precautions, and its fears. Have you paid your three years' profits to Louvière and to Tremblay?'

'Most certainly I have.'

'So that you have nothing more to give them than the fifty thousand francs which I have brought with me? Have you not saved anything?'

'My lord, in giving the fifty thousand francs of my own to these gentlemen, I assure you that I give them everything I earn. I told M. d'Artagnan so yesterday evening.'

'Ah!' said Aramis, whose eyes sparkled for a moment, but became immediately afterwards as unmoved as before; 'so you have seen my old friend d'Artagnan; how was he?'

'Wonderfully well.'

'And what did you say to him, M. de Baisemeaux?'

'I told him,' said the governor, not perceiving his own thoughtlessness; 'I told him that I fed my prisoners too well.'

'How many have you?' inquired Aramis, in an indifferent tone.

'Sixty.'*

'Well, that is a tolerably round number.'

'In former times, my lord, there were, during certain years, as many as two hundred.'

'Still a minimum of sixty is not to be grumbled at.'

'Perhaps not; for, to anybody but myself, each prisoner would bring in two hundred and fifty pistoles: for instance, for a prince of the blood I have fifty francs a day.'

'Only you have no prince of the blood; at least, I suppose so,' said Aramis, with a slight tremor in his voice.

'No, thank Heaven—I mean, no, unfortunately.'

'What do you mean by unfortunately?'

'Because my appointment would be improved by it. So, fifty francs per day for a prince of the blood, thirty-six for a marshal of France——'

'But you have as many marshals of France, I suppose, as you have princes of the blood?'

'Alas! yes; it is true that lieutenant-generals and brigadiers pay twenty-six francs, and I have two of them. After that come the councillors of the Parliament, who bring me fifteen francs, and I have six of them.'

'I did not know,' said Aramis, 'that councillors were so productive.'

'Yes; but from fifteen francs I sink at once to ten francs; namely, for an ordinary judge, and for an ecclesiastic.'

'And you have seven, you say; an excellent affair.'

'Nay, a bad one, and for this reason. How can I possibly treat these poor fellows, who are of some good, at all events, otherwise than as a councillor of the Parliament?'

'Yes, you are right; I do not see five francs' difference between them.'

'You understand; if I have a fine fish, I pay four or five francs for it; if I get a fine fowl, it costs me a franc and a half. I fatten a good deal of poultry, but I have to buy grain, and you cannot imagine the multitude of rats which infest this place.'

'Why not get half a dozen cats to deal with them?'

'Cats indeed; yes, they eat them, but I was obliged to give up the idea because of the way in which they treated my grain. I have been obliged to have some terrier dogs sent me from England to kill the rats. The dogs have tremendous appetites; they eat as much as a prisoner of the fifth order, without taking into account the rabbits and fowls they kill.'—Was Aramis really listening or not? No one could have told; his downcast eyes showed the attentive man, but the restless hand betrayed the man absorbed in thought—Aramis was meditating.—'I was saying,' continued Baisemeaux, 'that a tolerably-sized fowl costs me a franc and a half, and that a good-sized fish costs me four or five francs. Three meals are served at the Bastille, and as the prisoners, having nothing to do, are always eating, a ten-franc man costs me seven francs and a half.'

'But did not you say that you treated those at ten francs like those at fifteen?'

'Yes, certainly.'

'Very well! Then you gain seven and a half francs upon those who pay you fifteen francs?'

'I must compensate myself somehow,' said Baisemeaux, who saw how he had been caught.

'You are quite right, my dear governor; but have you no prisoners below ten francs?'

'Oh, yes! we have citizens and barristers at five francs.'

'And do they eat too?'

'Not a doubt about it; only you understand they do not get fish or poultry, nor rich wines at every meal; but at all events thrice a week they have a good dish at their dinner.'

'Really, you are a philanthropist, my dear governor, and you will ruin yourself.'

'No; understand me; when the fifteen francs has not eaten his fowl, or the ten francs has left his dish unfinished, I send it to the five-franc prisoner; it is a feast for the poor devil, and one must be charitable, you know.'

'And what do you make out of your five-franc prisoners?'

'A franc and a half.'

'Baisemeaux, you're an honest fellow; in honest truth, I say so.'

'Thank you, my lord. But I feel most for the small tradesmen and bailiffs' clerks, who are rated at three francs. Those do not often see Rhine carp or Channel sturgeon.'

'But do not the five-franc gentlemen sometimes leave some scraps?'

'Oh! my lord, do not believe I am so stingy as that. I delight the heart of some poor little tradesman or clerk by sending him a wing of a red partridge, a slice of venison, or a slice of a truffled pasty, dishes which he never tasted except in his dreams;

these are the leavings of the twenty-four franc prisoners; and he eats and drinks, at dessert he cries "Long live the King," and blesses the Bastille; with a couple of bottles of champagne, which cost me five sous, I make him tipsy every Sunday. That class of people call down blessings upon me, and are sorry to leave the prison. Do you know that I have remarked, and it does me infinite honour, that certain prisoners, who have been set at liberty, have, almost immediately afterwards, got imprisoned again? Why should this be the case, unless it be to enjoy the pleasures of my kitchen? It is really the fact.' Aramis smiled with an expression of incredulity.

'You smile,' said Baisemeaux.

'I do,' returned Aramis.

'I tell you that we have names which have been inscribed on our books thrice in the space of two years.'

'I must see it before I believe it,' said Aramis.

'Well, I can show it you, although it is forbidden to communicate the registers to strangers; and if you really wish to see it with your own eyes——'

'I should be delighted, I confess.'

'Very well,' said Baisemeaux, and he took out of a cupboard a large register. Aramis followed him most anxiously with his eyes, and Baisemeaux returned, placed the register upon the table, turned over the leaves for a minute, and stayed at the letter M.

'Look here,' said he, 'Martinier, January, 1659; Martinier, June, 1660; Martinier, March, 1661. Mazarinades,* etc.; you understand it was only a pretext; people were not sent to the Bastille for jokes against M. Mazarin; the fellow denounced himself in order to get imprisoned here.'

'And what was his object?'

'None other than to return to my kitchen at three francs the head.'

'Three francs—poor devil!'

'The poet, my lord, belongs to the lowest scale, the same style of board as the small tradesman and bailiff's clerk; but I repeat it is to these people only that I give those little surprises.'

Aramis mechanically turned over the leaves of the register, continuing to read the names, but without appearing to take any interest in the names he read.

'In 1661, you perceive,' said Baisemeaux, 'eighty entries; and in 1659, eighty also.'

'Ah!' said Aramis. 'Seldon;* I seem to know that name. Was it not you who spoke to me about a certain young man?'

'Yes, a poor devil of a student, who made——What do you call that where two Latin verses rhyme together?'

'A distich.'

'Yes; that is it.'

'Poor fellow; for a distich.'

'Do you not know that he made this distich against the Jesuits?'

'That makes no difference; the punishment seems very severe.'

'Do not pity him; last year you seemed to interest yourself in him.'

'Yes, I did so.'

'Well, as your interest is all-powerful here, my lord, I have treated him since that time as a prisoner at fifteen francs.'

'The same as this one, then,' said Aramis, who had continued turning over the leaves, and who had stopped at one of the names which followed Martinier.

'Yes, the same as that one.'

'Is that Marchiali* an Italian?' said Aramis, pointing with his finger to the name which had attracted his attention.

'Hush!' said Baisemeaux.

'Why hush,' said Aramis, involuntarily clenching his white hand.

'I thought I had already spoken to you about that Marchiali?'

'No; it is the first time I ever heard his name pronounced.'

'That may be; but I may have spoken to you about him without naming him.'

'Is he an old offender?' said Aramis, attempting to smile.

'On the contrary, he is quite young.'

'Is his crime then, very heinous?'

'Unpardonable. It is he who——' and Baisemeaux approached Aramis's ear, making a sort of ear-trumpet of his hands, and whispered, 'It is he who has the audacity to resemble the——'

'Yes, yes,' said Aramis, 'I now remember you already spoke about it last year to me; but the crime appeared to me so slight.'

'Slight, do you say?'

'Or rather, so involuntary.'

'My lord, it is not involuntarily that such a resemblance is detected.'

'Well, the fact is, I had forgotten it. But, my dear host,' said Aramis, closing the register, 'if I am not mistaken, we are summoned.'

Baisemeaux took the register, hastily restored it to its place in the closet, which he closed, and put the key in his pocket. 'Will it be agreeable to your lordship to breakfast now?' said he; 'for you are right in supposing that breakfast was announced.'

'Assuredly, my dear governor,' and they passed into the dining-room.

VI

THE BREAKFAST OF MONSIEUR DE BAISEMEAUX

ARAMIS was generally temperate; but, on this occasion, while taking every care with regard to himself, he did ample justice to Baisemeaux's breakfast, which, in every respect, was most excellent. The latter, on his side, was animated with the wildest gaiety; the sight of the five thousand pistoles, which he glanced at from time to time, seemed to open his heart. Every now and then he looked at Aramis with an expression of the deepest gratitude, while the latter, leaning back in his chair, sipped a few drops of wine from his glass, with the air of a connoisseur. 'Let me never hear an ill word against the fare of the Bastille,' said he, half-closing his eyes; 'happy are the prisoners who can get only half a bottle of this Burgundy every day.'

'All those at fifteen francs drink it,' said Baisemeaux. 'It is very old Volnay.'*

'Does that poor student, Seldon, drink such good wine?'

'Oh, no!'

'I thought I heard you say he was boarded at fifteen francs.'

'He! no, indeed; a man who makes districts—distichs, I mean —at fifteen francs. No, no! it is his neighbour who is at fifteen francs.'

'Which neighbour?'

'The other, the second Bertaudière.'

'Excuse me, my dear governor; but you speak a language which requires an apprenticeship to understand.'

'Very true,' said the governor. 'Allow me to explain:—the second Bertaudière is the person who occupies the second floor of the tower of La Bertaudière.'

'So that Bertaudière is the name of one of the towers of the Bastille?* The fact is, I think I recollect hearing that each tower has a name of its own. Whereabouts is the one you are speaking of?'

'Look,' said Baisemeaux, going to the window. 'It is that tower to the left—the second one.'

'Is the prisoner at fifteen francs there?'

'Yes.'

'Since when?'

'Seven or eight years, nearly.'*

'What do you mean by nearly? Do you not know the dates more precisely?'

'It was not in my time, dear M. d'Herblay.'

'But I should have thought that Louvière or Tremblay would have told you.'

'The secrets of the Bastille are never handed over with the keys of the governorship of it.'

'Indeed! Then the cause of his imprisonment is a mystery—a State secret?'

'Oh, no! I do not suppose it is a State secret, but a secret like everything else that happens at the Bastille.'

'But,' said Aramis, 'why do you speak more freely of Seldon than of the second Bertaudière?'

'Because, in my opinion, the crime of the man who writes a distich is not so great as that of the man who resembles——'

'Yes, yes: I understand you. Still, do not the turnkeys talk with your prisoners?'

'Of course.'

'The prisoners, I suppose, tell them they are not guilty?'

'They are always telling them that; it is a matter of course; the same song over and over again.'

'But does not the resemblance you were speaking about just now strike the turnkeys?'

'My dear M. d'Herblay, it is only for men attached to the court, as you are, to take any trouble about such matters.'

'You're right, you're right, my dear M. Baisemeaux. Let me give you another taste of this Volnay.'

'Not a taste merely, a full glass; fill yours, too.'

'Nay, nay! A taste for me; a glass for yourself.'

'As you please.' And Aramis and the governor nodded to each other as they drank their wine. 'But,' said Aramis, looking with fixed attention at the ruby-coloured wine, as if he wished to enjoy it with all his senses, 'but what you might call a resemblance, another would not, perhaps, take any notice of.'

'Most certainly he would, though, if it were any one who knew the person he resembles.'

'I really think, dear M. de Baisemeaux, that it can be nothing more than a resemblance of your own creation.'

'Upon my honour, it is not so.'

'Stay,' continued Aramis, 'I have seen many persons very like the one we are speaking of; but, out of respect, no one ever said anything about it.'

'Very likely; because there is resemblance and resemblance. This is a striking one, and, if you were to see him, you would admit it to be so.'

'If I were to see him indeed,' said Aramis in an indifferent tone; 'but in all probability I never shall.'

'Why not?'

'Because if I were even to put my foot inside one of those horrible dungeons, I should fancy I was buried there for ever.'

'No, no; the cells are very good as places to live in.'

'I really do not, and cannot, believe it, and that is a fact.'

'Pray, don't speak ill of the second Bertaudière. It is really a good room, very nicely furnished and carpeted. The young fellow has by no means been unhappy there; the best lodging the Bastille affords has been his. There is a chance for you.'

'Nay, nay,' said Aramis coldly; 'you will never make me believe there are any good rooms in the Bastille; and, as for your carpets, they exist only in your own imagination. I should find nothing but spiders, rats, and perhaps toads, too.'

'Toads?' said Baisemeaux.

'Yes, in the dungeons.'

'Ah! I don't say there are not toads in the dungeons,' said

Baisemeaux. 'But—will you be convinced by your own eyes?' he continued, with sudden impulse.

'No, certainly not.'

'Not even to satisfy yourself of the resemblance which you deny, as you do the carpets?'

'Some spectral-looking person, a mere shadow; an unhappy dying man.'

'Nothing of the kind—as brisk and vigorous a young fellow as ever lived.'

'Melancholy and ill-tempered, then?'

'Not at all; very gay and lively.'

'Nonsense; you are joking.'

'Will you follow me?' said Baisemeaux.

'Why?'

'You will then see for yourself—see with your eyes.'

'But the regulations?'

'Never mind them. To-day my major has leave of absence; the lieutenant is visiting the posts on the bastions; we have the run of the place.'

'No, no, my dear governor; why, the very idea of the sound of the bolts makes me shudder. You will only have to forget me in the second or fourth Bertaudière, and then——'

'You are refusing an opportunity that may never present itself again. Do you know that, to obtain the favour I propose to you gratis, some of the princes of the blood have offered me as much as fifty thousand francs.'

'Really! he must be worth seeing then?'

'Forbidden fruit, my lord; forbidden fruit. You who belong to the Church ought to know that.'

'Well, if I had any curiosity, it would be to see the poor author of the distich.'

'Very well, we will see him too; but if I were at all curious, it would be about the beautiful carpeted room and its lodger.'

'Furniture is very commonplace, and a face with no expression in it offers little or no interest.'

'But a boarder at fifteen francs is always interesting.'

'By the bye, I forgot to ask you about that. Why fifteen francs for him, and only three francs for poor Seldon?'

'The distinction made in that instance was a truly noble act, and one which displayed the King's goodness of heart to great advantage.'

'The King's, you say?'

'The Cardinal's, I mean; "this unhappy man," said M. Mazarin, "is destined to remain in prison for ever."'

'Why so?'

'Why, it seems that his crime is a lasting one; and, consequently, his punishment ought to be so.'

'Lasting?'

'No doubt of it, unless he is fortunate enough to catch the small-pox, and even that is difficult, for we never get any impure air here.'

'Nothing can be more ingenious than your train of reasoning, my dear M. de Baisemeaux. Do you, however, mean to say that this unfortunate man must suffer without interruption or termination?'

'I did not say that he was to suffer, my lord; a fifteen-francs boarder does not suffer.'

'He suffers imprisonment, at all events.'

'No doubt, there is no help for it; but this suffering is sweetened for him. You must admit that this young fellow was not born to eat all the good things he does eat; for instance, such things as we have on the table now; this pasty that has not been touched, these crawfish from the river Marne, of which we have hardly taken any, and which are almost as large as lobsters; all these things will at once be taken to the second Bertaudière, with a bottle of that Volnay which you think so excellent. After you have seen it, you will believe it, I hope.'

'Yes, my dear governor, certainly; but all this time you are thinking only of your very happy fifteen-francs prisoner, and you forget poor Seldon, my protégé.'

'Well, out of consideration for you, it shall be gala day for him; he shall have some biscuits and preserves with this small bottle of port.'

'You are a good-hearted fellow; I have said so already, and I repeat it, my dear Baisemeaux.'

'Well, let us set off, then,' said the governor, a little dazed, partly from the wine he had drunk, and partly from Aramis's praises.

'Do not forget that I only go to oblige you,' said the prelate.

'Very well; but you will thank me when you get there.'

'Let us go, then.'

'Wait until I have summoned the jailer,' said Baisemeaux, as he struck the bell twice; at which summons a man appeared. 'I am going to visit the towers,' said the governor. 'No guards, no drums, no noise at all.'

'If I were not to leave my cloak here,' said Aramis, pretending to be alarmed, 'I should really think I was going to prison on my own account.' The jailer preceded the governor, Aramis walking on his right hand; some of the soldiers who happened to be in the courtyard drew themselves up in line, as stiff as posts, as the governor passed along. Baisemeaux led the way down several steps which conducted to a sort of esplanade; thence they arrived at the drawbridge, where the sentinels on duty received the governor with the proper honours. The governor turned towards Aramis, and, speaking in such a tone that the sentinels could not lose a word he said, observed—'I hope you have a good memory, monsieur?'

'Why?' inquired Aramis.

'On account of your plans and your measurements, for you know that no one is allowed, not architects even, to enter where the prisoners are, with paper, pens, or pencil.'

'Good,' said Aramis to himself, 'it seems I am an architect, then? It sounds like one of d'Artagnan's jokes, who saw me acting as an engineer at Belle-Isle.'* Then he added aloud, 'Be easy on that score, monsieur; in our profession a mere glance and a good memory are quite sufficient.'

Baisemeaux did not change countenance, and the soldiers took Aramis for what he seemed to be. 'Very well; we will first visit La Bertaudière,' said Baisemeaux, still intending the sentinels to hear him. Then, turning to the jailer, he added, 'you will take the opportunity of carrying to No. 2 the few dainties I pointed out.'

'Dear M. de Baisemeaux,' said Aramis, 'you are always forgetting No. 3.'

'So I am,' said the governor; and, upon that, they began to ascend. The number of bolts, gratings, and locks, for this single courtyard, would have sufficed for the safety of an entire city.

Aramis was neither an imaginative nor a sensitive man; he had been somewhat of a poet in his youth, but his heart was hard and indifferent, as the heart of every man of fifty-five years of age is who has been frequently and passionately attached to women in his lifetime, or rather who has been passionately loved by them.* But when he placed his foot upon the worn stone steps, along which so many unhappy wretches had passed, when he felt himself impregnated, as it were, with the atmosphere of those gloomy dungeons, moistened with tears, there could be but little doubt he was overcome by his feelings, for his head was bowed and his eyes became dim, as he followed Baisemeaux without uttering a syllable.

VII

THE SECOND FLOOR OF LA BERTAUDIÈRE

ON the second flight of stairs, whether from fatigue or emotion, the breathing of the visitor began to fail him, and he leaned against the wall. 'Will you begin by this one?' said Baisemeaux; 'for since we are going to both it matters very little whether we ascend from the second to the third story, or descend from the third to the second.'

'No, no,' exclaimed Aramis eagerly, 'higher, if you please; the one above is the more urgent.' They continued their ascent. 'Ask the jailer for the keys,' whispered Aramis. Baisemeaux did so, took the keys, and, himself, opened the door of the third room. The jailer was the first to enter; he placed upon the table the provisions, which the kind-hearted governor called dainties, and then left the room. The prisoner had not stirred; Baisemeaux then entered, while Aramis remained at the threshold, from which place he saw a youth about eighteen years of age, who raising his head at the unusual noise, jumped off the bed as he perceived the governor, and clasping his hands together, began to cry out, 'My mother, my mother,' in tones which betrayed such deep distress, that Aramis, despite his command over himself, felt a shudder pass through his frame. 'My dear boy,' said Baisemeaux, endeavouring to smile, 'I have brought you a diversion and an extra,—the one for the mind, the other for the body; this gentleman has come to take your measure, and here are some preserves for your dessert.'

'Oh, monsieur,' exclaimed the young man, 'keep me in solitude for a year, let me have nothing but bread and water for a year, but tell me that at the end of a year I shall leave this place, tell me that at the end of a year I shall then see my mother again.'

'But I have heard you say that your mother was very poor, and that you were very badly lodged when you were living with her, while here—upon my word!'

'If she were poor, monsieur, the greater reason to restore her only means of support to her. Badly lodged with her! oh, monsieur, every one is always well lodged when he is free.'

'At all events, since you yourself admit you have done nothing but write that unhappy distich——'

'But without any intention, I swear. Let me be punished,— cut off the hand which wrote it, I will work with the other—but restore my mother to me.'

'My boy,' said Baisemeaux, 'you know very well that it is not up to me; all I can do for you is to increase your rations, give you a glass of port wine now and then, slip in a biscuit for you between a couple of plates.'

'Great Heaven!' exclaimed the young man, falling backward and rolling on the ground.

Aramis, unable to bear this scene any longer, withdrew as far as the landing. 'Unhappy, wretched man,' he murmured.

'Yes, monsieur, he is indeed very wretched,' said the jailer; 'but it is his parents' fault.'

'In what way?'

'No doubt. Why did they let him learn Latin? Too much knowledge, you see; it is that which does harm. Now I, for instance, can't read or write, and therefore I am not in prison.' Aramis looked at the man, who seemed to think that being a jailer in the Bastille was not being in prison. As for Baisemeaux, noticing the little effect produced by his advice and his port wine, he left the dungeon quite upset. 'You have forgotten to close the door,' said the jailer.

'So I have,' said Baisemeaux; 'there are the keys, you do it.'

'I will solicit the pardon of that poor boy,' said Aramis.

'And if you do not succeed,' said Baisemeaux, 'at least beg that he may be transferred to the ten-franc list, by which both he and I shall be gainers.'

'If the other prisoner calls out for his mother in a similar manner,' said Aramis, 'I prefer not to enter at all, but will take my measure from outside.'

'No fear of that, monsieur architect, the one we are now going to see is as gentle as a lamb, before he could call after his mother he must open his lips, and he never says a word.'

'Let us go in, then,' said Aramis gloomily.

'Are you the architect of the prison, monsieur?' said the jailer.

'I am.'

'It is odd, then, that you are not more accustomed to all this.'

Aramis perceived that, to avoid giving rise to any suspicions, he must summon all his strength of mind to his assistance. Baisemeaux, who carried the keys, opened the door. 'Stay outside,' he said to the jailer, 'and wait for us at the bottom of the steps.' The jailer obeyed and withdrew.

Baisemeaux entered the first, and opened the second door himself. By the light which filtered through the iron-barred window, could be seen a handsome young man, short in stature, with closely-cut hair, and a beard beginning to grow; he was sitting on a stool, his elbow resting on an arm-chair, and all the upper part of his body reclining against it. His dress, thrown upon the bed, was of rich black velvet, and he inhaled the fresh air which blew in upon his breast through a shirt of the very finest cambric. As the governor entered, the young man turned his head with a look full of indifference; and on recognising Baisemeaux, he arose and saluted him courteously. But when his eyes fell upon Aramis, who remained in the background, the latter trembled, turned pale, and his hat, which he held in his hand, fell upon the ground, as if all his muscles had become relaxed at once. Baisemeaux, accustomed to the presence of the prisoner, did not seem to share any of the sensations which Aramis experienced, but, with all the zeal of a good servant, he busied himself in arranging on the table the pasty and crawfish he had brought with him. Occupied in this manner, he did not remark how disturbed his guest had become. When he had finished, however, he turned to the young prisoner and said, 'You are looking very well,—are you so?'

'Quite well, I thank you, monsieur,' replied the young man.

The effect of the voice was such as almost to overpower Aramis, and, notwithstanding his command over himself, he advanced a few steps towards him, with his eyes wide open, and his lips trembling. The movement he made was so marked that Baisemeaux, notwithstanding his occupation, observed it. 'This gentleman is an architect who has come to examine your chimney,' said Baisemeaux; 'does it smoke?'

'Never, monsieur.'

'You were saying just now,' said the governor, rubbing his hands together, 'that it was not possible for a man to be happy in prison; here, however, is one who is so. You have nothing to complain of, I hope?'

'Nothing.'

'Do you ever feel wearied?' said Aramis.

'Never.'

'Ha, ha,' said Baisemeaux, in a low tone of voice; 'was I not right?'

'Well, my dear governor, it is impossible not to yield to evidence. Is it allowed to put any questions to him?'

'As many as you like.'

'Very well; be good enough to ask him if he knows why he is here.'

'This gentleman requests me to ask you,' said Baisemeaux, 'if you are aware of the cause of your imprisonment?'

'No, monsieur,' said the young man unaffectedly, 'I am not.'

'That is hardly possible,' said Aramis, carried away by his feelings in spite of himself; 'if you were really ignorant of the cause of your detention, you would be furious.'

'I was so during the earlier days of my imprisonment.'

'Why are you not so now?'

'Because I have reflected.'

'May one venture to ask you, monsieur, on what you have reflected?'

'I felt that as I had committed no crime, Heaven could not punish me.'

'What is a prison, then,' inquired Aramis, 'if it be not a punishment?'

'Alas! I cannot tell,' said the young man; 'all that I can tell you now is the very opposite of what I felt seven years ago.'

'To hear you converse, to witness your resignation, one might almost believe that you liked your imprisonment?'

'I endure it.'

'In the certainty of recovering your freedom some day, I suppose?'

'I have no certainty; hope I have, and that is all: and yet I acknowledge that this hope becomes less every day.'

'Still, why should you not again be free, since you have already been so?'

'That is precisely the reason,' replied the young man, 'which prevents me expecting liberty; why should I have been imprisoned at all if it had been intended to release me afterwards?'

'How old are you?'

'I do not know.'

'What is your name?'

'I have forgotten the name by which I was called.'

'Who are your parents?'

'I never knew them.'

'But those who brought you up?'

'They did not call me their son.'

'Did you ever love any one before coming here?'

'I loved my nurse and my flowers.'

'Was that all?'

'I also loved my valet!'

'Do you regret your nurse and your valet?'

'I wept very much when they died.'

'Did they die since you have been here, or before you came?'

'They died the evening before I was carried off.'

'Both at the same time?'

'Yes, both at the same time.'

'In what manner were you carried off?'

'A man came for me, directed me to get into a carriage, which was closed and locked, and brought me here.'

'Would you be able to recognise that man again?'

'He was masked.'

'Is not this an extraordinary tale?' said Baisemeaux, in a low tone of voice to Aramis, who could hardly breathe.

'It is indeed extraordinary,' he murmured.

'But what is still more extraordinary is, that he has never told me so much as he has just told you.'

'Perhaps the reason may be that you have never questioned him,' said Aramis.

'It's possible,' replied Baisemeaux; 'I have no curiosity. Have you looked at the room; it's a fine one, is it not?'

'Very much so.'

'I'll wager he had nothing like it before he came here.'

'I think so, too.' And then, turning again towards the young man, he said, 'Do you not remember to have been visited at some time or another by a strange lady or gentleman.'

'Yes, indeed; thrice by a woman, who each time came to the door in a carriage, and entered covered with a veil, which she raised when we were together and alone.'

'What did she say to you?'

The young man smiled mournfully, and then replied, 'She inquired, as you have just done, if I were happy, and if I were getting weary.'

'And what did she do on arriving and on leaving you?'

'She pressed me in her arms, held me in her embrace, and kissed me.'

'Do you recall her features distinctly?'

'Yes.'

'You would recognise her then, if accident brought her before you, or led you into her presence?'

'Most certainly.'

A flush of fleeting satisfaction passed across Aramis's face. At this moment Baisemeaux heard the jailer approaching. 'Shall we leave?' he said hastily, to Aramis.

Aramis, who probably had learnt all that he cared to know, replied, 'When you like.'

The young man saw them prepare to leave, and saluted them politely. Baisemeaux replied merely by a nod of the head, while Aramis, with a respect, arising perhaps from the sight of such misfortune, saluted the prisoner profoundly. They left the room, Baisemeaux closing the door behind them.

'Well,' said Baisemeaux, as they descended the staircase, 'what do you think of it all?'

'I have discovered the secret, my dear governor,' he said.

'Bah! what is the secret then?'

'A murder was committed in that house.'

'Nonsense.'

'But attend; the valet and the nurse died the same day.'

'Well.'

'And by poison. What do you think?'

'That it is very likely to be true.'

'What! that that young man is an assassin?'

'Who said that? What makes you think that poor fellow could be an assassin?'

'The very thing I was saying. A crime was committed in his house,' said Aramis, 'and that was quite sufficient; perhaps he saw the criminals, and it was feared he might say something. Has he any books?'

'None; they are strictly prohibited, and under M. de Mazarin's own hand.'

'Have you the writing still?'

'Yes, my lord; would you like to look at it as you return to take your cloak?'

'I should, for I like to look at autographs.'

'Well, then, this one is of the most unquestionable authenticity; there is only one erasure.'

'Ah, ah! an erasure; and in what respect?'

'With respect to a figure. At first there was written "To be boarded at 50 francs."'

'As princes of the blood in fact?'

'But the Cardinal must have seen his mistake, you understand; for he cancelled the zero, and has added a 1 before the 5. But, by the bye, you do not speak of the resemblance.'

'I do not speak of it, dear M. de Baisemeaux, for a very simple reason—because it does not exist.'

'The deuce it doesn't.'

'Or if it does exist, it is only in your own imagination; but supposing it were to exist elsewhere, I think it would be better for you not to speak about it.'

'Really.'

'The King, Louis XIV—you understand—would be excessively angry with you, if he were to learn that you contributed, in any way, to spread the report that one of his subjects has the effrontery to resemble him.'*

'It is true, quite true,' said Baisemeaux, thoroughly alarmed; 'but I have not spoken of the circumstance to any one but yourself, and you understand, monseigneur, that I perfectly rely on your being discreet. Do you still wish to see the note?'

'Certainly.'

While engaged in this manner in conversation, they had returned to the governor's apartments; Baisemeaux took from the cupboard a private register, like the one he had already shown Aramis, but fastened by a lock, the key which opened it being one of a small bunch of keys which Baisemeaux always carried with him. Then, placing the book upon the table, he opened it at the letter 'M,'* and showed Aramis the following note in the column of observations:—'No books at any time, all linen and clothes of the finest and best quality to be procured; no exercise; always the same jailer; no communications with any one. Musical instruments; every liberty and every indulgence which his welfare may require; to be boarded at fifteen francs. M. de Baisemeaux can claim more, if the fifteen francs be not sufficient.'

'Ah,' said Baisemeaux, 'now I think of it, I shall claim it.'

Aramis shut the book. 'Yes,' he said, 'it is indeed M. de Mazarin's handwriting; I recognise it well. Now, my dear governor,' he continued, as if this last communication had exhausted his interest, 'let us now turn to our own little affairs.'

'Well, what time for payment do you wish me to take? Fix it yourself.'

'There need not be any particular period fixed; give me a simple acknowledgement for 150,000 francs.'

'When to be made payable?'

'When I require it. But you understand, I shall only wish it when you yourself do so.'

'Oh, I am quite easy on that score,' said Baisemeaux, smiling; 'But I have already given you two receipts.'

'Which I now destroy,' said Aramis; and, after having shown the two receipts to Baisemeaux, he destroyed them. Overcome by so great a mark of confidence, Baisemeaux unhesitatingly wrote out an acknowledgement of a debt of 150,000 francs, payable at the pleasure of the prelate. Aramis, who had, by glancing over the governor's shoulder, followed the pen as he wrote, put the acknowledgment into his pocket, without seeming to have read it, which made Baisemeaux perfectly easy. 'Now,' said Aramis, 'you will not be angry with me if I were to carry off one of your prisoners?'

'What do you mean?'

'In obtaining his pardon, of course. Have I not already told you that I took a great interest in poor Seldon?'

'Yes, quite true, you did so.'

'Well?'

'That is your affair; do as you think proper. I see you have an open hand, and an arm that can reach a great way.'

'Adieu, adieu.' And Aramis left, carrying with him the governor's blessings.

VIII

THE TWO FRIENDS

AT the very time M. de Baisemeaux was showing Aramis the prisoners in the Bastille, a carriage drew up at Madame de Bellière's door,* and, at that still early hour, a young woman alighted, her head muffled in a silk hood. At the moment the servants announced Madame Vanel* to Madame de Bellière, the latter was engaged or rather was absorbed, in reading a letter, which she hurriedly concealed. She had hardly finished her morning toilette, her woman being still in the next room. At the name—at the footsteps of Marguerite Vanel, Madame de Bellière ran to meet her. She fancied she could detect in her friend's eyes a brightness which was neither that of health nor of pleasure. Marguerite embraced her, pressed her hands, and hardly allowed her time to speak. 'Dearest,' she said, 'are you forgetting me? Have you quite given yourself up to the pleasures of the court?'

'I have not even seen the marriage fêtes.'

'What are you doing with yourself then?'

'I am getting ready to leave for Bellière.'*

'You are becoming rustic in your tastes, then; I delight to see you so disposed. But you are pale.'

'No, I am perfectly well.'

'So much the better; I was becoming uneasy about you. You do not know what I have been told.'

'People say so many things.'

'Yes, but this is very singular.'

'How well you know how to excite curiosity, Marguerite.'

'Well, I was afraid of vexing you.'

'Never; you have yourself always admired me for my evenness of temper.'

'Well, then, it is said that—no, I shall never be able to tell you.'

'Do not let us talk about it then,' said Madame de Bellière, who detected the ill-nature which was concealed by all these prefaces, yet felt the most anxious curiosity on the subject.

'Well, then, my dear Marquise, it is said that, for some time past, you no longer continue to regret Monsieur de Bellière as you used to do.'

'It is an ill-natured report, Marguerite. I do regret, and shall always regret, my husband; but it is now two years since he died. I am only twenty-eight years old,* and my grief at his loss ought not always to control every action and thought of my life. You, Marguerite, who are the model of a wife, would not believe me if I were to say so.'

'Why not? Your heart is so soft and yielding,' she said spitefully.

'Yours is so, too, Marguerite, and yet I do not perceive that you have allowed yourself to be overcome by grief when your heart was wounded.' These words were in direct allusion to Marguerite's rupture with the Minister of Finance, and were also a veiled but direct reproach made against her friend's heart.

As if she only awaited this signal to discharge her shaft, Marguerite exclaimed, 'Well, Eliza, it is said that you are in love.' And she looked fixedly at Madame de Bellière, who blushed without being able to prevent it.

'Women never escape slander,' replied the Marquise, after a moment's pause.

'No one slanders you, Eliza.'

'What!—people say that I am in love, and yet they do not slander me!'

'In the first place, if it be true, there is no slander, but simply a scandal-loving report. In the next place—for you did not allow me to finish what I was saying,—the public does not assert that you have abandoned yourself to this passion. It represents you, on the contrary, as a virtuous but loving woman, defending herself with claws and teeth, shutting yourself up in your own house, as in a fortress, and in a fortress in other respects as impenetrable as that of Danaë, notwithstanding Danaë's tower* was made of brass.'

'You are witty, Marguerite,' said Madame de Bellière tremblingly.

'You always flatter me, Eliza. To be brief, however, you are reported to be incorruptible and unapproachable. You can decide whether people slander you or not;—but what is it you are musing about while I am speaking to you? You are blushing and quite silent.'

'I was trying,' said the Marquise, raising her beautiful eyes, brightened with an indication of approaching anger; 'I was trying to discover to what you could possibly have alluded, you who are so learned in mythological subjects, in comparing me to Danaë.'

'You were trying to guess that,' said Marguerite, laughing.

'Yes; do you not remember that at the convent, when we were solving our problems in arithmetic—ah! what I have to tell you is learned also—but it is my turn—do you not remember, that, if one of the terms were given, we were to find out the other? Therefore, can you guess now?'

'I cannot imagine what you mean.'

'And yet nothing is more simple.'

'You pretend that I am in love, do you not?'

'So it is said.'

'Very well; it is not said, I suppose, that I am in love with an abstraction. There must surely be a name mentioned in this report.'

'Certainly, a name is mentioned.'

'Very well; it is not surprising, then, that I should try to guess this name, since you do not tell it me.'

'My dear Marquise, when I saw you blush, I did not think you would have to spend much time in conjectures.'

'It was the word Danaë which you used that surprised me. Danaë means a shower of gold, does it not?'

'That is to say that the Jupiter* of Danaë changed himself into a shower of gold for her.'

'My lover, then, he whom you assign me——'

'I beg your pardon; I am your friend, and assign you no one.'

'That may be; but those who are evilly disposed towards me.'

'Do you wish to hear the name?'

'I have been waiting this half-hour for it.'

'Well, then, you shall hear it. Do not be shocked; he is a man high in power.'

'Good,' said the Marquise, as she clenched her hands like a patient at the approach of the knife.

'He is a very wealthy man,' continued Marguerite; 'the wealthiest, it may be. In a word it is——'

The Marquise closed her eyes for a moment.

'It is the Duke of Buckingham,'* said Marguerite, bursting into laughter. The perfidiousness had been calculated with extreme ability; the name that was pronounced, instead of the name which the Marquise awaited, had precisely the same effect upon her as the badly-sharpened axes, which had hacked, without destroying, Messieurs de Chalais and de Thou* on their scaffolds, had upon them. She recovered herself, however, and said, 'I was perfectly right in saying you were a witty woman, for you are making the time pass away most agreeably. The joke is a most amusing one, for I have never seen the Duke of Buckingham.'

'Never!' said Marguerite, restraining her laughter.

'I have never even left my own house since the Duke has been at Paris.'

'Oh!' resumed Madame Vanel, stretching out her foot towards a paper which was lying on the carpet near the window; 'it is not necessary for people to see each other, since they can write.' The Marquise trembled, for this paper was the envelope of the letter she was reading as her friend had entered, and was sealed with M. Fouquet's arms. As she leaned back on the sofa on which she was sitting, Madame de Bellière covered the paper with the thick folds of her large silk dress, and so concealed it. 'Come, Marguerite, tell me, is it to tell me all these foolish reports that you have come to see me so early in the day?'

'No; I came to see you in the first place, and to remind you of those habits of our earlier days, so delightful to remember, when we used to wander about together at Vincennes, and, sitting beneath an oak or in some sylvan shade, used to talk of those we loved, and who loved us.'

'Do you propose that we should go out together now?'

'My carriage is here, and I have three hours at my disposal.'

'I am not dressed yet, Marguerite; but if you wish that we should talk together, we can, without going to the woods of Vincennes, find in my own garden here, beautiful trees, shady groves, a green sward covered with daisies and violets, the perfume of which can be perceived from where we are sitting.'

'I regret your refusal, my dear Marquise, for I wanted to pour out my whole heart into yours.'

'I repeat again, Marguerite, my heart is yours just as much in this room, or beneath the lime-trees in the garden here, as it is under the oaks in the wood yonder.'

'It is not the same thing for me. In approaching nearer to Vincennes, Marquise, my ardent aspirations approach nearer to that object towards which they have for some days been directed.' The Marquise suddenly raised her head. 'Are you surprised, then, that I am still thinking of St Mandé?'*

'Of St Mandé,' exclaimed Madame de Bellière; and the looks of both women met.

'You, so proud, too!' said the Marquise disdainfully.

'I, so proud!' replied Madame Vanel. 'Such is my nature. I do not forgive neglect,—I cannot endure infidelity. When I leave any one who weeps at my abandonment, I feel induced still to love him; but when others forsake me and laugh at their infidelity, it makes me desperate.'

Madame de Bellière could not restrain an involuntary movement.

'She is jealous,' said Marguerite to herself.

'Then,' continued the Marquise, 'you are quite enamoured of the Duke of Buckingham. I mean of M. Fouquet. And you wished to go to Vincennes,—to St Mandé even?'

'I hardly know what I wished: you would have advised me, perhaps.'

'Most certainly I should not have done so in the present

instance, for I do not forgive as you do. I am less loving, perhaps; but when my heart has been once wounded, it remains so always.'

'But M. Fouquet has not wounded you,' said Marguerite Vanel, with the most perfect simplicity.

'You perfectly understand what I mean. M. Fouquet has not wounded me; I do not know him either from any obligation or any injury received at his hands, but you have reason to complain of him. You are my friend, and I am afraid I should not advise you as you would like.'

'Ah! you are prejudging the case.'

'The sighs you spoke of just now are more than indications.'

'You overwhelm me,' said the young woman suddenly, as if collecting her whole strength, like a wrestler preparing for a last struggle; 'you take only my evil dispositions and my weaknesses into calculation, and do not speak of the pure and generous feelings that I have. If, at this moment, I feel instinctively attracted towards the Minister of Finance, if I even make an advance to him, and which I confess is very probable, my motive for it is that M. Fouquet's fate deeply affects me, and because he is, in my opinion, one of the most unfortunate men living.'

'Ah!' said the Marquise, placing her hand upon her heart, 'something new, then, has occurred.'

'Do you not know it?'

'I am utterly ignorant of everything about him,' said Madame de Bellière, with that palpitation of anguish which suspends thought and speech, and even life itself.

'In the first place, then, the King's favour is entirely withdrawn from M. Fouquet, and conferred on M. Colbert.'*

'So it is stated.'

'It is very clear, since the discovery of the plot at Belle-Isle.'

'I was told that the discovery of the fortifications there had turned out to M. Fouquet's honour.'*

Marguerite began to laugh in so cruel a manner, that Madame de Bellière could at that moment have delightedly plunged a dagger in her bosom. 'Dearest,' continued Marguerite, 'there is no longer any question of M. Fouquet's honour; his safety is at stake. Before three days are past the ruin of the Minister of Finance will be complete.'

'Stay,' said the Marquise, in her turn smiling, 'that is going a little too fast.'

'I said three days, because I wish to deceive myself with a hope; but most certainly the catastrophe will not extend beyond twenty-four hours.'

'Why so?'

'For the simplest of all reasons, that M. Fouquet has no more money.'

'In matters of finance, my dear Marguerite, some are without money to-day, who to-morrow can procure millions.'

'That might be M. Fouquet's case when he had two wealthy and clever friends who amassed money for him, and wrung it from every source; but these friends are dead.'*

'Money does not die, Marguerite; it may be concealed; but it can be looked for, bought, and found.'

'You see things on the bright side, and so much the better for you. It is really very unfortunate that you are not the Egeria* of M. Fouquet, you might show him the source whence he could obtain the millions which the King asked him for yesterday.'

'Millions!' said the Marquise, in terror.

'Four,—an even number.'

'Infamous!' murmured Madame de Bellière, tortured by her friend's merciless delight.

'M. Fouquet, I should think, must certainly have four millions,' she replied courageously.

'If he has those which the King requires to-day,' said Marguerite, 'he will not perhaps possess those which the King will require in a month.'

'The King will require money from him again then?'

'No doubt, and that is my reason for saying that the ruin of this poor M. Fouquet is inevitable. Pride will induce him to furnish the money, and when he has no more, he will fall.'

'It is true,' said the Marquise tremblingly; 'the plan is a bold one; but tell me, does M. Colbert hate M. Fouquet so very much?'

'I think he does not like him. M. Colbert is powerful; he improves on close acquaintance; he has gigantic ideas, a strong will, and discretion; he will make great strides.'*

'He will be Minister of Finance?'

'It is probable. Such is the reason, my dear Marquise, why I felt myself impressed in favour of that poor man, who once loved, nay even adored, me; and why, when I see him so unfortunate, I forgive his infidelity, which I have reason to believe he also regrets; and why, moreover, I should not have been disinclined to afford him some consolation, or some good advice; he would have understood the step I had taken, and would have thought kindly of me for it. It is gratifying to be loved, you know. Men value love highly when they are no longer blinded by its influence.'

The Marquise, bewildered, and overcome by these cruel attacks, which had been calculated with the greatest correctness and precision of aim, hardly knew what answer to return; she even seemed to have lost all power of thought. Her perfidious friend's voice had assumed the most affectionate tone: she spoke as a woman, but concealed the instincts of a panther. 'Well,' said Madame de Bellière, who had a vague hope that Marguerite would cease to overwhelm a vanquished enemy, 'why do you not go and see M. Fouquet?'

'Decidedly, Marquise, you have made me reflect. No it would be unbecoming for me to make the first advance. M. Fouquet no doubt loves me, but he is too proud. I cannot expose myself to an affront . . . besides, I have my husband to consider. You say nothing to me. Very well, I shall consult M. Colbert on the subject.' Marguerite rose smilingly, as though to take leave, but the Marquise had not the strength to imitate her. Marguerite advanced a few paces, in order that she might continue to enjoy the humiliating grief in which her rival was plunged, and then said suddenly, 'You do not accompany me to the door, then?' The Marquise rose, pale and almost lifeless, without thinking of the envelope, which had occupied her attention so greatly at the commencement of the conversation, and which was revealed at the first step she took. She then opened the door of her oratory, and without even turning her head towards Marguerite Vanel, entered it, closing the door after her. Marguerite said, or rather muttered, a few words, which Madame de Bellière did not even hear. As soon, however, as the Marquise had disappeared, her envious enemy, not being able to resist the desire to satisfy herself that her suspicions were really founded, advanced stealthily towards it like a panther, and seized the envelope. 'Ah!' she said, gnashing her teeth, 'it was indeed a letter from M. Fouquet she was reading when I arrived,' and then darted out of the room. During this interval, the Marquise, having arrived behind the rampart, as it were, of her door, felt that her strength was failing her; for a moment she remained rigid, pale, and motionless as a statue; and then, like a statue shaken on its base by a storm of wind, she tottered and fell inanimate on the carpet. The noise of the fall resounded at the same moment as the rolling of Marguerite's carriage leaving the hotel was heard.

IX

MADAME DE BELLIÈRE'S PLATE

THE blow had been the more painful on account of its being unexpected. It was sometime before the Marquise recovered herself; but, once recovered, she began to reflect upon the events which had been announced to her. She therefore returned, at the risk even of losing her life on the way, to that train of ideas which her relentless friend had forced her to pursue. Treason, then—dark menaces concealed under the semblance of public interest—such were Colbert's manœuvres. A detestable delight at an approaching downfall, untiring efforts to attain this object, means of seduction no less wicked than the crime itself—such were the means which Marguerite employed. The tentacled atoms of Descartes triumphed; to the man without compassion was united a woman without a heart.* The Marquise perceived, with sorrow rather than with indignation, that the King was an accomplice in a plot which equalled the duplicity of Louis XIII in his advanced age, and the avarice of Mazarin at a period of life when he had not had the opportunity of gorging himself with French gold.* The spirit of this courageous woman soon resumed its energy, and was no longer interrupted by a mere indulgence in compassionate lamentations. The Marquise was not one to weep when action was necessary, nor to waste time in bewailing a misfortune when means still existed of relieving it. For some minutes she buried her face in her icy hands, and then, raising her head, rang for her attendants with a steady hand, and with a gesture betraying a fixed determination of purpose. Her resolution was taken.

'Is everything prepared for my departure?' she inquired of one of her female attendants who entered.

'Yes, madame; but it was not expected that your ladyship would leave for Bellière for the next few days.'

'All my jewels and articles of value, then, are locked up?'

'Yes, madame, but hitherto we have been in the habit of leaving them in Paris. Your ladyship does not generally take your jewels with you into the country.'

'But they are all in order, you say?'

'Yes, in your ladyship's own room.'

The Marquise remained silent for a few moments and then said calmly, 'Let my goldsmith be sent for.'

Her attendants quitted the room to execute the order. The Marquise, however, had entered her own room, and inspected her casket of jewels with the greatest attention. Never, until now, had she bestowed so much attention upon riches in which women take so much pride; never until now had she looked at her jewels, except for the purpose of making a selection according to their settings or their colours. On this occasion, however, she admired the size of the rubies and the brilliancy of the diamonds; she grieved over every blemish and every defect; she thought the gold light, and the stones wretched. The goldsmith, as he entered, found her thus occupied. 'M. Faucheux,'* she said, 'I believe you supplied me with my gold service?'

'I did, your ladyship.'

'I do not now remember the amount of the account.'

'Of the new service, madame, or of that which M. de Bellière presented you on your marriage? for I furnished both.'

'First of all, the new one?'

'The ewers, the goblets, and the dishes, with their covers, the wrought centre-piece, the ice-pails, the dishes for the preserves, and the tea and coffee urns, cost your ladyship sixty thousand francs.'

'No more?'

'Your ladyship thought the account very high.'

'Yes, yes, I remember, in fact that it was dear; but it was the workmanship, I suppose?'

'Yes, madame; the designs, the chasings, and new patterns.'

'What proportion of the cost does the workmanship form? Do not hesitate to tell me.'

'A third of its value, madame.'

'There is the other service, the old one, that which belonged to my husband.'

'Yes, madame; there is less workmanship in that than in the other. Its intrinsic value does not exceed thirty thousand francs.'

'Thirty thousand,' murmured the Marquise. 'But, M. Faucheux, there is also the service which belonged to my mother; all that massive plate which I did not wish to part with, on account of the associations connected with it.'

'Ah! madame, that would indeed be an excellent resource for those, who, unlike your ladyship, might not be in a position to keep their plate. In working that, one worked in solid metal. But that service is no longer in fashion. Its weight is its only advantage.'

'That is all I care about. How much does it weigh?'

'Fifty thousand livres at the very least. I do not allude to the enormous vases for the side board, which alone weigh five thousand livres, or ten thousand the two.'

'One hundred and thirty,' murmured the Marquise. 'You are quite sure of your figures, M. Faucheux?'

'Positive, madame. Besides there is no difficulty in weighing them.'

'The amount is entered in my books.'

'Your ladyship is exceedingly methodical, I am aware.'

'Let us now turn to another subject,' said Madame de Bellière; and she opened one of her jewel-boxes.

'I recognise these emeralds,' said M. Faucheux; 'for it was I who had the setting of them. They are the most beautiful in the whole court. No, I am mistaken; Madame de Châtillon has the most beautiful set; she had them from Messieurs de Guise;* but your set, madame, are next.'

'What are they worth?'

'Mounted?'

'No; supposing I wished to sell them.'

'I know very well who would buy them,' exclaimed M. Faucheux.

'That is the very thing I ask. They could be purchased then?'

'All your jewels could be bought. It is well known that you possess the most beautiful jewels in Paris. You are not changeable in your tastes; when you make a purchase, it is of the very best.'

'What could these emeralds be sold for, then?'

'A hundred and thirty thousand francs.'

The Marquise wrote upon her tablets the amount the jeweller mentioned. 'This ruby necklace?' she said.

'Are they balas rubies,* madame?'

'Here they are.'

'They are beautiful—magnificent. I did not know that your ladyship had these stones.'

'What is their value?'

'Two hundred thousand francs. The centre one alone is worth a hundred.'

'I thought so,' said the Marquise. 'As for diamonds, I have them in numbers; rings, necklaces, studs, earrings, clasps. Tell me their value, M. Faucheux.'

The jeweller took his magnifying glass and scales, weighed and inspected them. 'These stones,' he said, 'would give your ladyship an income of forty thousand francs.'

'You value them at eight hundred thousand francs?'

'Nearly so.'

'It is about what I imagined—but the settings are not included?'

'No, madame; but if I were called upon to sell or to buy, I should be satisfied with the gold of the settings alone, as my profit upon the transaction. I should make a good twenty-five thousand francs.'

'Will you accept that profit, then, on condition of converting the jewels into money?'

'But you do not intend to sell your diamonds, madame?' exclaimed the bewildered jeweller.

'Silence, M. Faucheux, do not trouble yourself about that; give me an answer simply. You are an honourable man, with whom my family has dealt for thirty years; you have known my father and mother,* whom your own father and mother had served. I address you as a friend—will you accept the gold of the settings in return for a sum of ready money to be placed in my hands?'

'Eight hundred thousand francs! it is enormous. Reflect, madame, upon the effect which will be produced by the sale of your jewels.'

'No one need know it. You can get sets of false jewels made for me similar to the real. Do not answer a word; I insist upon it. Sell them separately, sell the stones only.'

'In that way it is easy. Monsieur is looking out for some sets of jewels as well as single stones for Madame's toilette. There will be a competition for them. I can easily dispose of 600,000 francs' worth to Monsieur. I am certain yours are the most beautiful.'

'When can you do so?'

'In less than three days' time.'

'Very well, the remainder you will dispose of among private individuals. For the present, make me out a contract of sale, payment to be made in four days.'

'I entreat you to reflect, madame; for if you force the sale, you will lose a hundred thousand francs.'

'If necessary, I will lose two hundred; I wish everything to be settled this evening. Do you accept?'

'I do, your ladyship. I will not conceal from you that I shall make fifty thousand francs by the transaction.'

'So much the better. In what way shall I have the money?'

'Either in gold, or in bills of the bank of Lyons, payable at M. Colbert's.'

'I agree,' said the Marquise eagerly; 'return home and bring the sum in question in notes, as soon as possible.'

'Yes, madame, but for Heaven's sake——'

'Not a word, M. Faucheux. By the bye, I was forgetting the silver plate. What is the value of that which I have?'

'Fifty thousand francs, madame.'

'That makes a million,' said the Marquise to herself. 'M. Faucheux, you will take away with you both the gold and silver plate. I can assign as a pretext, that I wish it remodelled for patterns more in accordance with my own taste. Melt it down, and return me its value in money, at once.'

'It shall be done, your ladyship.'

'You will be good enough to place the money in a chest, and direct one of your clerks to accompany the chest, and without my servants seeing him; and direct him also to wait for me in a carriage.'

'In Madame de Faucheux's carriage?' said the jeweller.

'If you will allow it, and I will call for it at your house.'

'Certainly, your ladyship.'

'I will direct some of my servants to convey the plate to your house.' The Marquise rang. 'Let the small coach be placed at M. Faucheux's disposal,' she said. The jeweller bowed and left the house, directing that the van should follow him closely, saying aloud, that the Marquise was about to have her plate melted down in order to have other plate manufactured of a more modern style. Three hours afterwards she went to M. Faucheux's house and received from him eight hundred thousand francs in gold enclosed in a chest, which one of the clerks could hardly carry towards Madame Faucheux's carriage—for Madame Faucheux kept her carriage. The Marquise entered this vehicle, sitting opposite the clerk, who endeavoured to put his knees out of the way, afraid even of touching the Marquise's dress. It was the clerk, too, who told the coachman, who was very proud of having a Marquise to drive, to take the road to St Mandé.

X

THE DOWRY

MONSIEUR FAUCHEUX'S horses were serviceable animals, but they were not as fleet as the English horses of M. Fouquet, and consequently, took two hours* to get to St Mandé. The Marquise stopped the carriage at a door well known to her, although she had only seen it once, in a circumstance, it will be remembered,* no less painful than that which brought her to it again on the present occasion. She drew a key from her pocket and inserted it in the lock, pushed open the door, which noiselessly yielded to her touch, and directed the clerk to carry the chest upstairs to the first floor. The weight of the chest was so great that the clerk was obliged to get the coachman to assist him with it. They placed it in a small cabinet, ante-room, or boudoir rather, adjoining the saloon where we once saw M. Fouquet at the Marquise's feet. Madame de Bellière gave the coachman a louis, smiled gracefully at the clerk, and dismissed them both. She closed the door after them, and waited in the room, alone and barricaded. There was no servant to be seen about the rooms, but everything was prepared as though some invisible genius had divined the wishes and desires of the guest who was expected. The fire was laid, the candles in the candelabra, refreshments upon the table, books scattered about, fresh-cut flowers in the vases. One might almost have declared it to be an enchanted house. The Marquise lighted the candles, inhaled the perfume of the flowers, sat down, and was soon plunged in profound thought. Her deep musings, melancholy though they were, were not untinged with a certain sweetness. Spread out before her was a treasure, a million wrung from her fortune as a gleaner plucks the blue cornflower from her crown of flowers. She conjured up the sweetest dreams. Her principal thought, and one that took precedence of all others, was to devise means of leaving this money for M. Fouquet without his possibly learning from whom the gift had come. This idea, naturally enough, was the first to present itself to her mind. But although, on reflection, it appeared difficult to carry out, she did not despair of success. She would ring then to summon M. Fouquet and make her escape, happier if, instead of having given a million, she had herself found one. But, being there, and having seen the boudoir so coquettishly decorated, that it might almost be said the least particle of dust had but the moment before been removed by the servants; having observed the drawing room so perfectly arranged that it might almost be said her presence there had driven away the fairies who were its occupants, she asked herself if the glance or gaze of those whom she had driven away, whether spirits, fairies, elves, or human creatures, had not already recognised her. To secure success, it was necessary that some steps should be taken seriously, and it was necessary also that the Minister should comprehend the serious position in which he was placed, in order to yield compliance with the generous fancies of a woman; all the fascinations of an eloquent friendship would be required to persuade him, and should this be insufficient, the maddening influence of a devoted passion which, in its resolute determination to carry conviction, would not be turned aside. Was not the Minister, indeed, known for his delicacy and dignity of feeling? Would he allow himself to accept from any woman that of which she had stripped herself? No! He would resist, and if any voice in the world could overcome his resistance, it would be the voice of the woman he loved. Another doubt, and that a cruel one, suggested itself to Madame de Bellière with a sharp, acute pain, like a dagger-thrust. 'Did he really love her? Would that volatile mind, that inconstant heart, be likely to be fixed for a moment, even were it to gaze upon an angel? Was it not the same with Fouquet, notwithstanding his genius and his uprightness of conduct, as with those conquerors on the field of battle who shed tears when they have gained a victory?* I must learn if it be so, and must judge of that for myself,' said the Marquise. 'Who can tell whether that heart, so coveted, is not common in its impulses, and full of alloy? Who can tell if that mind, when the touchstone is applied to it, will be found of a mean and vulgar character? Come, come,' she said, 'this is doubting and hesitating too much—to the proof.' She looked at the timepiece. 'It is now seven o'clock,' she said, 'he must have arrived; it is the hour for signing his papers.' With a feverish impatience she rose and walked towards the mirror, in which she smiled with a resolute smile of devotedness; she touched the spring and drew out the handle of the bell. Then, as if exhausted, beforehand, by the struggle she had just undergone, she threw herself on her knees in utter abandonment, before a large couch, in which she buried her face in her trembling hands. Ten minutes afterwards she heard the spring of the door sound. The door moved upon invisible hinges, and Fouquet appeared. He looked pale, and seemed bowed down by the weight of some bitter reflection. He did not hurry, but simply came at the summons. The preoccupation of his mind must indeed have been very great, that a man, so devoted to pleasure, for whom, indeed, pleasure was everything, should obey such a summons so listlessly. The previous night, in fact, fertile in melancholy ideas, had sharpened his features, generally so noble in their indifference of expression, and traced dark lines of anxiety around his eyes. Handsome and noble he still was, and the melancholy expression of his mouth, a rare expression with men, gave a new

character to his features, by which his youth seemed to be renewed. Dressed in black, the lace in front of his chest much
disarranged by his feverishly restless hand, the looks of the
Minister, full of dreamy reflection, were fixed upon the threshold
of the room which he had so frequently approached in search
of expected happiness. This gloomy gentleness of manner, this
smiling sadness of expression, which had replaced his former
excessive joy, produced an indescribable effect upon Madame
de Bellière, who was regarding him at a distance. A woman's eye
can read the face of the man she loves, its every feeling of pride,
its every expression of suffering; it might almost be said that
Heaven has graciously granted to women, on account of their
very weakness, more than it has accorded to other creatures.*
They can conceal their own feelings from a man, but from them
no man can conceal his. The Marquise divined in a single glance
the whole weight of the unhappiness of the Minister. She divined
a night passed without sleep, a day passed in deceptions. From
that moment she was firm in her own strength, and she felt that
she loved Fouquet beyond everything else. She rose and approached him, saying, 'You wrote to me this morning to say that
you were beginning to forget me, and that I, whom you have not
seen lately, had no doubt ceased to think of you. I have come to
undeceive you, monsieur, and the more completely so, because
there is one thing I can read in your eyes.'

'What is that, madame?' said Fouquet, astonished.

'That you have never loved me so much as at this moment. In
the same manner you can read in my present step toward you,
that I have not forgotten you.'

'Oh! madame,' said Fouquet, whose face was for a moment
lighted up by a sudden gleam of joy, 'you are indeed an angel,
and no man can suspect you. All he can do is to humble himself
before you, and entreat forgiveness.'

'Your forgiveness is granted, then,' said the Marquise. Fouquet
was about to throw himself upon his knees. 'No, no,' she said;
'sit here, by my side. Ah! that is an evil thought which has just
crossed your mind.'

'How do you detect it, madame?'

'By a smile which has just injured the expression of your

countenance. Be candid, and tell me what your thought was—
no secrets between friends.'

'Tell me, then, madame, why have you been so harsh for
these three or four months past?'

'Harsh?'

'Yes; did you not forbid me to visit you?'

'Alas!' said Madame de Bellière, sighing deeply, 'because your
visit to me was the cause of your being visited with a great
misfortune; because my house is watched; because the same eyes
which have already seen you might see you again; because I
think it less dangerous for you that I should come here than that
you should come to my house; and, lastly, because I know you
to be already unhappy enough not to wish to increase your
unhappiness further.'

Fouquet started, for these words recalled all the anxieties
connected with his office of Minister of Finance,—he who, for
the last few minutes, had indulged in all the wild aspirations of
the lover. 'I unhappy?' he said, endeavouring to smile; 'indeed,
Marquise, you will almost make me believe that I am so, judging
from your own sadness. Are your beautiful eyes raised upon me
merely in pity?—I look for another expression from them.'

'It is not I who am sad, monsieur; look in the mirror, there—
it is you who are so.'

'It is true I am somewhat pale, Marquise; but it is from over-
work; the King yesterday required a supply of money from me.'

'Yes, four millions; I am aware of it.'

'You know it?' exclaimed Fouquet, in a tone of surprise; 'how
can you have learned it? It was after the departure of the Queen
and in presence of one person only, that the King——'

'You perceive that I do know it; is not that sufficient?
Well go on, monsieur, the money the King has required you to
supply——'

'You understand, Marquise, that I have been obliged to procure it, then to get it counted, afterwards registered,—altogether a long affair. Since Monsieur de Mazarin's death, financial
affairs occasion some little fatigue and embarrassment. My administration is somewhat overtaxed, and this is the reason why
I have not slept during the past night.'

'So that you have the amount?' inquired the Marquise, with some anxiety.

'It would indeed be strange, Marquise,' replied Fouquet, cheerfully, 'if a Minister of Finance were not to have a paltry four millions in his coffers.'

'Yes, yes, I believe you have, or will have, them.'

'What do you mean by saying that I shall have them?'

'It is not so very long since you were required to furnish two millions.'

'On the contrary, to me it seems almost an age, but do not let us talk of money matters any longer.'

'On the contrary, we will continue to speak of them, for that is my only reason for coming to see you.'

'I am at a loss to know your meaning,' said the Minister, whose eyes began to express an anxious curiosity.

'Tell me, monsieur, is the office of Finance Minister an irremovable one?'

'You surprise me, Marquise, for you speak as if you had some motive or interest in putting the question.'

'My reason is simple enough; I am desirous of placing some money in your hands, and naturally I wish to know if you are certain of your post.'

'Really, Marquise, I am at a loss what to reply, and I cannot conceive your meaning.'

'Seriously, then, dear M. Fouquet. I have certain funds which somewhat embarrass me. I am tired of investing my money in land, and am anxious to entrust a friend to turn it to account.'

'Surely it does not press?' said M. Fouquet.

'On the contrary, it is very pressing.'

'Very well, we will talk of that by-and-by.'

'By-and-by will not do, for my money is there,' returned the Marquise, pointing out the coffer to the Minister, and showing him, as she opened it, the bundles of notes and heaps of gold. Fouquet, who had risen from his seat at the same moment as Madame de Bellière, remained for a moment plunged in thought; then, suddenly starting back, he turned pale, and sank down in his chair, concealing his face in his hands. 'Madame, madame,' he murmured, 'what opinion can you have of me when you make me such an offer?'

'Of you!' returned the Marquise. 'Tell me, rather, what you yourself think of the step I have taken.'

'You bring me this money for myself, and you bring it because you know me to be embarrassed. Nay, do not deny it, for I am sure of it. Do I not know your heart?'

'If you know my heart then, can you not see that it is my heart which I offer you?'

'I have guessed rightly then,' exclaimed Fouquet. 'In truth, madame, I have never yet given you the right to insult me in this manner.'

'Insult you,' she said, turning pale, 'what singular delicacy of feeling. You tell me you love me; in the name of that affection you wished me to sacrifice my reputation and my honour, and yet, when I offer you money, which is my own, you refuse me.'

'Madame, you are at liberty to preserve what you term your reputation and your honour. Permit me to preserve mine. Leave me to my ruin, leave me to sink beneath the weight of the hatreds which surround me, beneath the faults I have committed, beneath the load even of my remorse; but, for Heaven's sake, madame, do not overwhelm me under this last infliction.'

'A short while since, M. Fouquet, you were wanting in judgment, now you are wanting in feeling.'

Fouquet pressed his clenched hand upon his breast, heaving with emotion, saying, 'Overwhelm me, madame, for I have nothing to reply.'

'I offered you my friendship, M. Fouquet.'

'Yes, madame, and you limited yourself to that.'

'And what I am now doing is the act of a friend.'

'No doubt it is.'

'And you reject this mark of my friendship?'

'I do reject it.'

'Monsieur Fouquet, look at me,' said the Marquise with glistening eyes, 'I now offer you my love.'

'Oh! madame,' exclaimed Fouquet.

'I have loved you for a long while past; women, like men, have a false delicacy at times. For a long time past I have loved you, but would not confess it. Well then, you have implored this love on your knees, and I have refused you; I was blind, as you were a little while since; but as it was my love that you sought, it is my love that I now offer you.'

'Oh! madame, you overwhelm me beneath the weight of my happiness.'

'Will you be happy, then, if I am yours—yours entirely?'

'It will be the supremest happiness for me.'

'Take me then. If, however, for your sake I sacrifice a prejudice, do you, for mine, sacrifice a scruple.'

'Do not tempt me.'

'Do not refuse me.'

'Think seriously of what you are proposing.'

'Fouquet, but one word. Let it be No, and I open this door,' and she pointed to the door which led into the street, 'and you will never see me again. Let that word be Yes, and I am yours entirely.'

'Elise! Elise! But this coffer?'

'It contains my dowry.'

'It is your ruin,' exclaimed Fouquet, turning over the gold and papers, 'there must be a million here.'

'Yes, my jewels, for which I care no longer if you do not love me, and for which, equally, I care no longer if you love me as I love you.'

'This is too much,' exclaimed Fouquet. 'I yield, I yield, even were it only to consecrate so much devotion. I accept the dowry.'

'And take the woman with it,' said the Marquise, throwing herself into his arms.

XI

ON THE SANDS AT CALAIS

During the progress of these events, Buckingham and de Wardes travelled in excellent companionship, and made the journey from Paris to Calais in undisturbed harmony together. Buckingham had hurried his departure,* so that the best part of his adieux were very hastily made. His visit to Monsieur and Madame, to the young Queen, and to the Queen-Dowager, had been paid collectively—a precaution on the part of the Queen-Mother,* which saved him the distress of any private conversation with Monsieur, and saved him also from the danger of seeing Madame again. The carriages containing the luggage had already been sent on beforehand, and, in the evening, he set off in his travelling carriage with his attendants.

De Wardes, irritated at finding himself dragged away, in so abrupt a manner, by this Englishman, had sought in his subtle mind for some means of escaping from his fetters; but no one having rendered him any assistance in this respect, he was absolutely obliged, therefore, to submit to the burden of his own evil thoughts, and of his own caustic spirit. Such of his friends in whom he had been able to confide, had, in their character of wits, rallied him upon the Duke's superiority. Others, less brilliant, but more sensible, had reminded him of the King's orders which prohibited duelling. Others, again, and they the larger number, who, from Christian charity, or national vanity, might have rendered him assistance, did not care to run the risk of incurring disgrace, and would, at the best, have informed the ministers of a departure which might end in a massacre on a small scale. The result was, that, after having fully deliberated upon the matter, de Wardes packed up his luggage, took a couple of horses, and, followed only by one servant, made his way towards the barrier, where Buckingham's carriage was to await him.

The Duke received his adversary as he would have done an intimate acquaintance, made room beside him on the same seat with himself, offered him refreshments, and spread over his knees the sable cloak which had been thrown upon the front seat. They then conversed of the court, without alluding to Madame; of Monsieur, without speaking of domestic affairs; of the King, without speaking of his brother's wife; of the Queen-Mother, without alluding to her daughter-in-law; of the King of England, without alluding to his sister; of the state of the affections of either of the travellers, without pronouncing any name that might be dangerous. In this way the journey, which was performed by short stages, was most agreeable, and Buckingham, almost a Frenchman,* from his wit and education, was delighted at having so admirably selected his travelling companion. Elegant repasts were served, of which they partook but lightly; trials of horses in the beautiful meadows which skirted the road; coursing, for Buckingham had his greyhounds with him; and in such and other various ways did they pass away the time. The Duke somewhat resembled the beautiful river Seine, which encloses France a thousand times in its loving embraces, before deciding upon joining its waters with the ocean. In quitting France, it was her recently adopted daughter* he had brought to Paris, whom he chiefly regretted; his every thought was a remembrance of her, and, consequently, a regret. Therefore, whenever, now and then, despite his command over himself, he was lost in thought, de Wardes left him entirely to his musings. This delicacy might have touched Buckingham, and changed his feelings towards de Wardes, if the latter, while preserving silence, had shown a glance less full of malice, and a smile less false. Instinctive dislikes, however, are relentless; nothing appeases them; a few ashes may sometimes, apparently, extinguish them; but, beneath those ashes, the smothered flames rage more furiously. Having exhausted all the means of amusement which the route offered, they arrived, as we have said, at Calais, towards the end of the sixth day. The Duke's attendants had already, since the previous evening, been in advance, and had chartered a boat, for the purpose of joining the yacht, which had been tacking about in sight, or bore broadside on, whenever it felt its white wings wearied, within two or three cannon-shots from the jetty.

The boat was destined for the transport of the Duke's equipages from the shore to the yacht. The horses had been embarked, having been hoisted from the boat upon the deck in baskets, expressly made for the purpose, and wadded in such a manner that their limbs, even in the most violent fits of terror or impatience, always protected by the soft support which the sides afforded, and their coats were not even turned. Eight of these baskets, placed side by side, filled the ship's hold. It is well known that, in short voyages, horses refuse to eat, but remain trembling all the while, with the best of food before them, such as they would have greatly coveted on land. By degrees, the Duke's entire equipage was transported on board the yacht; he was then informed that everything was in readiness, and that they only waited for him, whenever he would be disposed to embark with the French gentleman. For no one could possibly imagine that the French gentleman would have any other accounts to settle with His Grace than those of friendship. Buckingham desired the captain to be told to hold himself in readiness, but that, as the sea was beautiful, and as the day promised a splendid sunset, he did not intend to go on board until nightfall, and would avail himself of the evening to enjoy a walk on the strand. He added also, that, finding himself in such excellent company he had not the least desire to hasten his embarkation.

The Duke's attendants had received directions to have a boat in readiness at the jetty-head, and to watch the embarkation of their master, without approaching him until either he or his friend should summon them. 'Whatever may happen,' he had added, laying a stress upon these words, so that they might not be misunderstood. Having walked a few paces upon the strand, Buckingham said to de Wardes, 'I think it is now time to take leave of each other. The tide, you perceive, is rising; ten minutes hence it will have soaked the sands where we are now walking in such a manner that we shall not be able to keep our footing.'

'I await your orders, my lord, but——'

'But you mean, we are still upon soil which is part of the King's territory.'

'Exactly.'

'Well, do you see yonder a kind of little island surrounded by a circular pool of water; the pool is increasing every minute, and the isle is gradually disappearing. This island, indeed, belongs to Heaven, for it is situated between two seas, and is not shown on the King's maps. Do you observe it?'

'Yes; but we can hardly reach it now, without getting our feet wet.'

'Yes; but observe that it forms an eminence tolerably high, and that the tide rises on every side, leaving the top free. We shall be admirably placed upon that little theatre. What do you think of it?'

'I shall be perfectly happy wherever I may have the honour of crossing my sword with your lordship's.'

'Very well, then, I am distressed to be the cause of your wetting your feet, M. de Wardes, but it is most essential you should be able to say to the King, "Sire, I did not fight upon your Majesty's territory." Perhaps the distinction is somewhat subtle, but, since Port-Royal,* you abound in subtleties of expression. Do not let us complain of this, however, for it makes your wit very brilliant, and of a style peculiarly your own. If you do not object, we will hurry ourselves, for the sea, I perceive, is rising fast, and night is setting in.'

'My reason for not walking faster was, that I did not wish to precede your Grace. Are you still on dry land, my lord?'

'Yes, at present I am. Look yonder, my servants are afraid we should be drowned, and have converted the boat into a cruiser. Do you remark how curiously it dances upon the crests of the waves? But as it makes me feel sea-sick, would you permit me to turn my back towards them?'

'You will observe, my lord, that in turning your back to them, you will have the sun full in your face.'

'Oh, its rays are very feeble at this hour, and it will soon disappear; do not be uneasy at that.'

'As you please, my lord; it was out of consideration for your lordship that I made the remark.'

'I am aware of that, M. de Wardes, and I fully appreciate your kindness. Shall we take off our doublets?'

'As you please, my lord.'

'Do not hesitate to tell me, M. de Wardes, if you do not feel comfortable upon the wet sand, or if you think yourself a little too close to the French territory. We could fight in England, or else upon my yacht.'

'We are exceedingly well placed here, my lord; only I have the honour to remark that as the sea is rising fast, we have hardly time——'

Buckingham made a sign of assent, took off his doublet and threw it on the ground, a proceeding which de Wardes imitated. Both their bodies, which seemed like two phantoms to those who were looking at them from the shore, were thrown strongly into relief by a dark red violet-coloured shadow with which the sky became overspread.

'Upon my word, your Grace,' said de Wardes, 'we shall hardly have time to begin. Do you not perceive how our feet are sinking into the sand?'

'I have sunk up to the ankles,' said Buckingham, 'without reckoning that the water even is now breaking in upon us.'

'It has already reached me. As soon as you please, therefore, your Grace,' said de Wardes, who drew his sword, a movement imitated by the Duke.

'M. de Wardes,' said Buckingham, 'one final word. I am about to fight you because I do not like you,—because you have wounded me in ridiculing a certain devotional regard I have entertained, and one which I acknowledge that at this moment I still retain, and for which I would very willingly die. You are a bad and heartless man, M. de Wardes, and I will do my utmost to take your life; for I feel assured that, if you survive this engagement, you will, in the future, work great mischief towards my friends. That is all I have to remark, M. de Wardes,' continued Buckingham, as he saluted him.

'And I, my lord, have only this to reply to you: I have not disliked you hitherto, but since you have divined my character, I hate you, and will do all I possibly can to kill you,' and de Wardes saluted Buckingham.

Their swords crossed at the same moment, like two flashes of lightning in a dark night. The swords seemed to seek each other, guessed their position, and met. Both were practised swordsmen, and the earlier passes were without any result. The night was fast closing in, and it was so dark that they attacked and defended themselves almost instinctively. Suddenly de Wardes felt his sword arrested,—he had just touched Buckingham's shoulder. The Duke's sword sunk as his arm was lowered.

'You are touched, my lord?' said de Wardes, drawing back a step or two.

'Yes, monsieur, but only slightly.'

'Yet you quitted your guard.'

'Only from the first effect of the cold steel, but I have recovered.'

'Let us go on, if you please.' And disengaging his sword with a sinister clashing of the blade, the Duke wounded the Marquis in the breast.

'Touched also,' he said.

'No,' said de Wardes, not moving from his place.

'I beg your pardon, but observing that your shirt was stained—' said Buckingham.

'Well,' said de Wardes furiously, 'it is now your turn.'

And with a terrible lunge he pierced Buckingham's arm

through, the sword passing between the two bones. Buckingham, feeling his right arm paralysed, stretched out his left arm, seized his sword, which was about falling from his nerveless grasp, and before de Wardes could resume his guard, he thrust him through the breast. De Wardes tottered, his knees gave way beneath him, and leaving his sword still fixed in the Duke's arm, he fell into the water. De Wardes was not dead; he felt the terrible danger which menaced him, for the sea rose fast. The Duke, too, perceived the danger also. With an effort and an exclamation of pain, he tore out the blade which remained in his arm, and turning towards de Wardes said, 'Are you mortally wounded?'

'No,' replied de Wardes, in a voice choked by the blood which rushed from his lungs to his throat; 'but very near it.'

'Well, what is to be done; can you walk?' said Buckingham, supporting him on his knee.

'Impossible,' he replied. Then falling down again, said, 'Call to your people, or I shall be drowned.'

'Hallo! boat there! quick! quick!'

The boat flew over the waves, but the sea rose faster than the boat could approach. Buckingham saw that de Wardes was on the point of being again covered by a wave; he passed his left arm, safe and unwounded, round his body and raised him up. The wave ascended to his middle, but could not move him. The Duke immediately began to walk towards the shore. He had hardly gone ten paces when a second wave, rushing onwards higher, more furious, more menacing than the former, struck him at the height of his chest, threw him over, and buried him beneath the water. At the reflux, however, the Duke and de Wardes were discovered lying on the strand. De Wardes had fainted. At this moment, four of the Duke's sailors, who comprehended the danger, threw themselves into the sea, and in a moment were close beside him. Their terror was extreme when they observed how their master became covered with blood, in proportion as the water, with which it was impregnated, flowed towards his knees and feet;—they wished to carry him away.

'No, no,' exclaimed the Duke, 'take the Marquis on shore first.'

'Death to the Frenchman,' cried the English sullenly.

'Wretched knaves,' exclaimed the Duke, drawing himself up with a haughty gesture, which sprinkled them with blood, 'obey directly!—M. de Wardes on shore! M. de Wardes's safety to be looked to first or I will have you all hanged.'

The boat had by this time reached them, and the secretary and steward leapt into the sea, and approached the Marquis, who no longer showed any sign of life.

'I commit him to your care, as you value your lives,' said the Duke. 'Take M. de Wardes on shore.' They took him in their arms, and carried him to the dry sand, where the tide never rose so high. A few idlers and five or six fishermen had gathered on the shore, attracted by the strange spectacle of two men fighting with the water up to their knees. The fishermen, observing a group of men approaching carrying a wounded man, entered the sea until the water was up to the middle of their bodies. The English transferred the wounded man to them, at the very moment the latter began to open his eyes again. The salt water and the fine sand had got into his wounds and caused him the acutest pain. The Duke's secretary drew out a purse filled with gold from his pocket, and handed it to the one among those present who appeared of most importance, saying:—'From my master, His Grace the Duke of Buckingham, in order that every conceivable care may be taken of the Marquis de Wardes.'

Then, followed by those who had accompanied him, he returned to the boat, which Buckingham had been enabled to reach with the greatest difficulty, but only after he had seen de Wardes out of danger. By this time it was high tide: the embroidered coats and silk sashes were lost; many hats, too, had been carried away by the waves. The flow of the tide had borne the Duke's and de Wardes' clothes to the shore, and de Wardes was wrapped in the Duke's doublet, under the belief that it was his own, and they carried him in their arms towards the town.

XII

MADAME AMUSES HERSELF

As soon as Buckingham had gone, Guiche imagined that the coast would be perfectly clear for him without any interference.* Monsieur, who no longer retained the slightest feeling of jealousy, and who, besides, permitted himself to be monopolised by the Chevalier de Lorraine, allowed as much liberty and freedom in his house as the most exacting persons could desire. The King, on his side, who had conceived a strong predilection for Madame's society,* invented a variety of amusements, in quick succession, in order to render her residence in Paris as cheerful as possible, so that, in fact, not a day passed without a ball at the Palais Royal, or a reception in Monsieur's apartments. The King had directed that Fontainebleau* should be prepared for the reception of the court, and every one was using his utmost interest to get invited. Madame led a life of incessant occupation, neither her voice nor her pen were idle for a moment. The conversations with de Guiche were gradually assuming a tone of interest which might unmistakably be recognised as the preludes of a deep-seated attachment. When eyes look languishingly while the subject under discussion happens to be the colours of materials for dresses; when a whole hour is occupied in analysing the merits and the perfume of a *sachet* or a flower; there are words in this style of conversation, which every one might listen to, but there are gestures or sighs which every one cannot perceive. After Madame had talked for some time with de Guiche, she conversed with the King, who paid her a visit regularly every day. They played, wrote verses, or selected mottoes or emblematical devices; the spring was not only the spring-time of seasons, it was the youth of an entire people, of which those at court were the head. The King was handsome, young, and of unequalled gallantry. All women were passionately loved by him, even the Queen, his wife. This great King was, however, more timid and more reserved than any other person in the kingdom, to such a degree, indeed, that he had not confessed his sentiments even to himself. This timidity of bearing restrained him within the limits of ordinary politeness, and no woman could boast of having had any preference shown her beyond that shown to others. It might be foretold that the day when his real character would be displayed would be the dawn of a new sovereignty; but as yet he had not declared himself. M. de Guiche took advantage of this, and constituted himself the sovereign prince of the whole amorous court. It had been reported that he was on the best of terms with Mademoiselle de Montalais; that he had been assiduously attentive to Mademoiselle de Châtillon;* but now, he was not even barely civil to any of the court beauties. He had eyes and ears but for one person alone. In this manner, and, as it were, without design, he devoted himself to Monsieur, who had a great regard for him, and kept him as much as possible in his own apartments. Unsociable from natural disposition, he estranged himself too much previous to the arrival of Madame, but, after her arrival, he did not estrange himself sufficiently. This conduct, which every one had observed, had been particularly remarked by the evil genius of the house, the Chevalier de Lorraine, for whom Monsieur exhibited the warmest attachment, because he was of a very cheerful disposition even in his remarks most full of malice, and because he was never at a loss how to make the time pass away. The Chevalier de Lorraine, therefore, having noticed that he was threatened with being supplanted by de Guiche, resorted to strong measures. He disappeared from the court, leaving Monsieur much embarrassed. The first day of his disappearance, Monsieur hardly inquired about him, for he had de Guiche with him, and except the time devoted to conversation with Madame, his days and nights were rigorously devoted to the Prince. On the second day, however, Monsieur, finding no one near him, inquired where the Chevalier was. He was told that no one knew.

De Guiche, after having spent the morning in selecting embroideries and fringes with Madame, went to console the Prince. But, after dinner, as there were tulips and amethysts to look at, de Guiche returned to Madame's cabinet. Monsieur was left quite to himself during all the time he devoted to dressing and decorating himself; he felt that he was the most miserable of men, and again inquired whether there was any news of the Chevalier, in reply to which he was told, that no one knew where the Chevalier was to be found. Monsieur, hardly knowing in what direction to inflict his weariness, went to Madame's apartments dressed in his morning-gown. He found a large assemblage of people there, laughing and whispering in every part of the room; at one end, a group of women around one of the courtiers talking together, amid smothered bursts of laughter; at the other end, Manicamp and Malicorne were being pillaged by Montalais and Mademoiselle de Tonnay-Charente,* while two others were standing by, laughing. In another part were Madame seated upon some cushions on the floor, and de Guiche, on his knees beside her, spreading out a handful of pearls and precious stones, while the Princess, with her white and slender finger, pointed out such among them as pleased her the most. Again, in another corner of the room, a guitar-player was playing some of the Spanish seguedillas,* to which Madame had taken the greatest fancy ever since she had heard them sung by the young Queen with a melancholy expression of voice. But the songs which the Spanish Princess had sung with tears in her eyes, the young English-woman was humming with a smile which displayed her beautiful, pearl-like teeth. The cabinet presented, in fact, the most perfect representation of unrestrained pleasure and amusement. As he entered, Monsieur was struck at beholding so many persons enjoying themselves without him. He was so jealous at the sight that he could not resist saying, like a child, 'What! you are amusing yourselves here, while I am sick and tired of being alone!'

The sound of his voice was like a clap of thunder which interrupts the warbling of birds under the leafy covert of the trees; a dead silence ensued. De Guiche was on his feet in a moment. Malicorne tried to hide himself behind Montalais's dress. Manicamp stood bolt upright, and assumed a very ceremonious demeanour. The guitar-player thrust his guitar under a table, covering it with a piece of carpet to conceal it from the Prince's observation. Madame was the only one who did not move, and, smiling at her husband, said, 'Is not this the hour you usually devote to your toilet?'

'An hour which others select it seems for amusing themselves,' replied the Prince grumblingly.

This untoward remark was the signal for a general rout; the women fled like a flight of terrified birds, the guitar-player vanished like a shadow; Malicorne, still protected by Montalais, who purposely widened out her dress, glided behind the hanging tapestry. As for Manicamp, he went to the assistance of de Guiche, who naturally remained near Madame, and both of them, with the Princess herself, courageously sustained the attack. The Comte was too happy to bear malice against the husband; but Monsieur bore a grudge against his wife. Nothing was wanting but a quarrel; he sought it, and the hurried departure of the crowd, which had been so joyous before he arrived, and was so disturbed by his entrance, furnished him with a pretext.

'Why do they run away at the sight of me?' he inquired, in a supercilious tone; to which remark Madame replied, 'that whenever the master of the house made his appearance, the family kept aloof out of respect.' As she said this, she made so funny and so pretty a grimace, that de Guiche and Manicamp could not control themselves; they burst into a peal of laughter; Madame followed their example, and even Monsieur himself could not resist it, and he was obliged to sit down, as for laughing he could scarcely keep his equilibrium. However, he very soon left off, but his anger had increased. He was still more furious from having allowed himself to laugh, than from having seen others laugh. He looked at Manicamp steadily, not venturing to show his anger towards de Guiche; but, at a sign which displayed no little amount of annoyance, Manicamp and de Guiche left the room, so that Madame, left alone, began sadly to pick up her pearls, no longer laughing, and speaking still less.

'I am very happy,' said the Duke, 'to find myself treated as a stranger here, Madame,' and he left the room in a passion. On his way out he met Montalais, who was in attendance in the ante-room. 'It is very agreeable to pay you a visit here, but outside the door.'

Montalais made a very low obeisance. 'I do not quite understand what your Royal Highness does me the honour to say.'

'I say that when you are all laughing together in Madame's apartment, he is an unwelcome visitor who does not remain outside.'

'Your Royal Highness does not think, and does not speak so, of yourself.'

'On the contrary, it is on my own account that I do speak and think. I have no reason, certainly, to flatter myself about the receptions I meet with here at any time. How is it that, on the very day there is music and a little society in Madame's apartments—in my own apartments, indeed, for they are mine—on the very day that I wish to amuse myself a little in my turn, every one runs away? Are they afraid to see me that they all took to flight as soon as I appeared? Is there anything wrong, then, going on in my absence?'

'Yet nothing has been done to-day, monseigneur, which is not done every day.'

'What! do they laugh like that every day?'

'Why, yes, monseigneur.'

'The same group of people, and the same scraping, going on every day?'

'The guitar, monseigneur, was introduced to-day; but when we have no guitars we have violins and flutes; women get wearied without music.'

'The deuce!—and the men?'

'What men, monseigneur?'

'M. de Guiche, M. de Manicamp, and the others.'

'They all belong to your Highness's household.'

'Yes, yes, you are right,' said the Prince, as he returned to his own apartments full of thought. He threw himself into the largest of his arm-chairs, without looking at himself in the glass. 'Where can the Chevalier be?' said he. One of the Prince's attendants happened to be near him, overheard his remark, and replied,—

'No one knows, your Highness.'

'Still the same answer. The first one who answers me again "I do not know," I will discharge.' Every one at this remark hurried out of his apartments, in the same manner as the others had fled from Madame's apartments. The Prince then flew into the wildest rage. He kicked over a chiffonier, which tumbled upon the carpet, broken into pieces. He next went into the galleries, and with the greatest coolness threw down, one after another, an enamelled vase, a porphyry ewer, and a bronze chandelier. The noise summoned every one to the various doors.

'What is your Highness's pleasure?' said the Captain of the Guards, timidly.

'I am treating myself to some music,' replied the Prince, gnashing his teeth.

The Captain of the Guards desired His Royal Highness's physician to be sent for. But before he came, Malicorne arrived, saying to the Prince, 'Monseigneur, the Chevalier de Lorraine is here.'

The Duke looked at Malicorne, and smiled graciously at him, just as the Chevalier entered in fact.

XIII

LORRAINE IS JEALOUS

THE Duc d'Orléans uttered a cry of delight on perceiving the Chevalier de Lorraine. 'This is fortunate indeed,' he said; 'by what happy chance do I see you? Had you indeed disappeared, as every one assured me?'

'Yes, monseigneur.'

'Some caprice?'

'I to venture upon caprices with your Highness! The respect——'

'Put respect out of the way, for you fail in it every day. I absolve you; but why did you leave me?'

'Because I felt that I was of no use to you.'

'Explain yourself.'

'Your Highness has people about you who are far more amusing than I can ever be. I felt that I was not strong enough to enter into a contest with them, and I therefore withdrew.'

'This extreme diffidence shows a want of common sense. Who are those with whom you cannot contend? De Guiche?'

'I name no one.'

'This is absurd. Does de Guiche annoy you?'

'I do not say he does; do not force me to speak, however; you know very well that de Guiche is one of our best friends.'

'Who is it then?'

'Excuse me, monseigneur, let us say no more about it.' The Chevalier knew perfectly well that curiosity is excited in the same way as thirst—by removing that which quenches it; or, in other words, by delaying the explanation.*

'No, no,' said the Prince, 'I wish to know why you went away.'

'In that case, monseigneur, I will tell you; but do not be angry. I remarked that my presence was disagreeable.'

'To whom?'

'To Madame.'

'What do you mean?' said the Duke in astonishment.

'It is simple enough; Madame is very probably jealous of the regard you are good enough to testify for me.'

'Has she shown it to you?'

'Madame never addresses a syllable to me, particularly since a certain time.'

'Since what time?'

'Since the time when, M. de Guiche having made himself more agreeable to her than I could, she receives him at every and any hour.'

The Duke coloured. 'At any hour, Chevalier; what do you mean by that?'

'You see, your Highness, I have already displeased you; I was quite sure I should.'

'I am not displeased; but you put things a little strongly. In what respect does Madame prefer de Guiche to you?'

'I shall say no more,' said the Chevalier, saluting the Prince ceremoniously.

'On the contrary, I require you to speak. If you withdraw on that account, you must indeed be very jealous.'

'One cannot help being jealous, monseigneur, when one loves. Is not your Royal Highness jealous of Madame? Would not your Royal Highness, if you saw some one always near Madame, and always treated with great favour, take umbrage at it? One's friends are as one's lovers. Your Royal Highness has sometimes conferred the distinguished honour upon me of calling me your friend.'

'Yes, yes; but you used a phrase which has a very equivocal signification; you are unfortunate in your remarks.'

'What phrase, monseigneur?'

'You said, "treated with great favour." What do you mean by favour?'

'Nothing can be more simple,' said the Chevalier, with an expression of great frankness; 'for instance, whenever a husband remarks that his wife summons such and such a man near her—whenever this man is always to be found by her side, or in attendance at the door of her carriage; whenever the bouquet of the one is always the same colour as the ribbons of the other—

when music and supper parties are held in the private apartments—whenever a dead silence takes place immediately the
husband makes his appearance in his wife's rooms—and when
the husband suddenly finds that he has, as a companion, the
most devoted and the kindest of men, who, a week before, was
with him as little as possible; why, then——'

'Well, finish.'

'Why, then, I say, monseigneur, one possibly may get jealous.
But all these details hardly apply; for our conversation had nothing to do with them.'

The Duke was evidently much agitated, and seemed to struggle within himself a good deal. 'You have not told me,' he then
remarked, 'why you absented yourself. A little while ago you
said it was from a fear of intruding; you added, even, that you
had observed a disposition on Madame's part to encourage de
Guiche.'

'Pardon me, monseigneur, I did not say that.'

'You did indeed.'

'Well, if I did say so, I noticed nothing but what was very
inoffensive.'

'At all events you remarked something.'

'You embarrass me, monseigneur.'

'What does that matter? Answer me. If you speak the truth,
why should you feel embarrassed?'

'I always speak the truth, monseigneur; but I also always
hesitate when it is a question of repeating what others say.'

'Ah! ah! you repeat? It appears that it is talked about, then?'

'I acknowledge that others have spoken to me on the subject.'

'Who?' said the Prince.

The Chevalier assumed almost an angry air, as he replied,
'Monseigneur, you are subjecting me to the question; you treat
me as a criminal at the bar; and the rumours which idly pass by
a gentleman's ears, do not remain there. Your Highness wishes
me to magnify the rumour until it attains the importance of an
event.'

'However,' said the Duke, in great displeasure, 'the fact remains that you withdrew on account of this report.'

'To speak the truth, others have talked to me of the attentions
of M. de Guiche to Madame, nothing more; perfectly harmless,

I repeat, and more than that, permissible. But do not be unjust, monseigneur, and do not attach an undue importance to it. It does not concern you.'

'M. de Guiche's attentions to Madame do not concern me?'

'No, monseigneur; and what I say to you I would say to de Guiche himself, so little do I think of the attentions he pays Madame. Nay, I would say it even to Madame herself. Only, you understand what I am afraid of—I am afraid of being thought jealous of the favour shown, when I am only jealous as far as friendship is concerned. I know your disposition; I know that when you bestow your affections, you become exclusively attached. You love Madame—and who, indeed, would not love her? Follow me attentively as I proceed:—Madame has noticed among your friends the handsomest and most fascinating of them all; she will begin to influence you on his behalf, in such a way that you will neglect the others. Your indifference would kill me; it is already bad enough to have to support Madame's indifference. I have, therefore, made up my mind to give way to the favourite whose happiness I envy, even while I acknowledge my sincere friendship and sincere admiration for him. Well, monseigneur, do you see anything to object to in this reasoning? Is it not that of a man of honour? Is my conduct that of a sincere friend? Answer me at least, after having so closely questioned me.'

The Duke had seated himself, with his head buried in his hands. After a silence, long enough to enable the Chevalier to judge of the effect of his oratorical display, the Duke rose, saying, 'Come, be candid.'

'As I always am.'

'Very well. You know that we already observed something respecting that mad fellow, Buckingham.'

'Do not say anything against Madame, monseigneur, or I shall take my leave. Is it possible you can be suspicious of Madame?'

'No, no, Chevalier; I do not suspect Madame; but, in fact, I observe—I compare——'

'Buckingham was a madman, monseigneur.'

'A madman about whom, however, you opened my eyes thoroughly.'

'No, no,' said the Chevalier quickly; 'It was not I who opened your eyes. It was de Guiche. Do not confuse us, I beg.' And he began to laugh in so harsh a manner that it sounded like the hiss of a serpent.

'Yes, yes, I remember. You said a few words, but de Guiche showed the most jealousy.'

'I should think so,' continued the Chevalier, in the same tone. 'He was fighting for home and altar.'

'What did you say?' said the Duke haughtily, thoroughly roused by this insidious jest.

'Am I not right? for does not M. de Guiche hold the chief post of honour in your household?'

'Well,' replied the Duke somewhat calmed, 'had this passion of Buckingham been remarked?'

'Certainly.'

'Very well. Do people say that M. de Guiche's is remarked as much?'

'Pardon me, monseigneur, you are again mistaken; no one says that M. de Guiche entertains anything of the sort.'

'Very good.'

'You see, monseigneur, that it would have been better, a hundred times better, to have left me in my retirement, than to have allowed you to conjure up, by the aid of any scruples I may have had, suspicions which Madame will regard as crimes, and she will be right, too.'

'What would you do?'

'I should not pay the slightest attention to the society of these new Epicurean philosophers;* and, in that way, the rumours will cease.'

'Well, I shall see; I shall think over it.'

'Oh, you have time enough; the danger is not great; and then, besides, it is not a question either of danger or of passion. It all arose from a fear I had to see your friendship for me decrease. From the very moment you restore it me, with so kind an assurance of its existence, I have no longer any other idea in my head.'

The Duke shook his head, as if he meant to say: 'If you have no more ideas, I have though.' It being now the dinner-hour, the Prince sent to inform Madame of it, who returned a message to the effect that she could not be present, but would dine in her own apartment.

'That is not my fault,' said the Duke. 'This morning, having taken them by surprise, in the midst of a musical party, I got jealous; and so they are in the sulks with me.'

'We will dine alone,' said the Chevalier, with a sigh; 'I regret de Guiche is not here.'

'Oh! de Guiche will not remain long in the sulks; he is a very good-natured fellow.'

'Monseigneur,' said the Chevalier, suddenly, 'an excellent idea has struck me, in our conversation just now. I may have exasperated your Highness, and caused you some dissatisfaction. It is but fitting that I should be the mediator. I will go and look for the Comte, and bring him back with me.'

'Ah! Chevalier, you are really a very good-natured fellow.'

'You say that as if you were surprised.'

'Well, you are not so tender-hearted every day.'

'That may be; but confess that I know how to repair a wrong I may have done.'

'I confess that.'

'Will your Highness do me the favour to wait here a few minutes?'

'Willingly; be off, and I will try on my Fontainebleau costume.'

The Chevalier left the room, called his different attendants with the greatest care, as if he was giving them different orders. All went off in various directions; but he retained his *valet-de-chambre*. 'Ascertain, and immediately too, if M. de Guiche is not in Madame's apartments. How can one learn it?'

'Very easily, monsieur. I will ask Malicorne, who will learn it from Mlle. de Montalais. I may as well tell you, however, that the inquiry will be useless; for all M. de Guiche's attendants are gone, and he must have left with them.'

'Try to find out, nevertheless.'

Ten minutes had hardly passed when the valet returned. He beckoned his master mysteriously towards the servants' staircase, and showed him into a small room with a window looking out upon the garden. 'What is the matter,' said the Chevalier. 'Why so many precautions?'

'Look, monsieur,' said the valet, 'look yonder, under the walnut-tree.'

'Ah!' said the Chevalier, 'I see Manicamp waiting there. What is he waiting for?'

'You will see in a moment, monsieur, if you wait patiently. There, do you see now?'

'I see one, two, four musicians with their instruments, and behind them, urging them on, de Guiche himself. What is he doing there though?'

'He is waiting until the little door of the staircase, belonging to the ladies of honour, is opened; by that staircase he will ascend to Madame's apartments, where some new pieces of music are going to be performed during dinner.'

'Was it M. de Malicorne who told you this?'

'Yes, monsieur.'

'He likes you, then?'

'No, monsieur, it is Monsieur whom he likes. He wishes to belong to his household.'

'And most certainly he shall. How much did he give you for that?'

'The secret which I now dispose of to you, monsieur.'

'And which I buy for a hundred pistoles. Take them.'

'Thank you, monsieur. Look, look, the little door opens, a woman admits the musicians.'

'It is Montalais.'

'Hush, monseigneur; do not call out her name; whoever says Montalais says Malicorne. If you quarrel with the one, you will be on bad terms with the other.'

'Very well; I have seen nothing.'

'And I,' said the valet, pocketing the purse, 'have received nothing.'

The Chevalier, being now certain that de Guiche had entered, returned to the Prince, whom he found splendidly dressed, and radiant with joy as with good looks. 'I am told,' he exclaimed, 'that the King has taken the sun as his emblem;* really, monseigneur, it is you whom this device would best suit.'

'Where is de Guiche?'

'He cannot be found. He has fled, has evaporated entirely. Your scolding of this morning terrified him. He could not be found in his apartments.'

'Bah! the hare-brained fellow is capable of setting off post-haste to his own estates. Poor fellow! we will recall him. Come, let us dine now.'

'Monseigneur, to-day is a day of ideas; I have another.'

'What is it?'

'Madame is angry with you, and she has reason to be so. You owe her her revenge; go and dine with her.'

'Oh! that would be acting like a weak husband.'

'It is the duty of a good husband to do so. The Princess is no doubt wearied enough; she will be weeping in her plate, and her eyes will get quite red. A husband who is the cause of his wife's eyes getting red is an odious creature. Come, monseigneur, come.'

'I cannot; for I have directed dinner to be served here.'

'You see, monseigneur, how dull we shall be; I shall be low-spirited because I know that Madame will be alone; you, hard and savage as you wish to appear, will be sighing all the while. Take me with you to Madame's dinner, and that will be a delightful surprise. I am sure we shall be very merry; you were wrong this morning.'

'Well, perhaps I was.'

'There is no perhaps at all, for it is a fact you were so.'

'Chevalier, your advice is not good.'

'Nay, my advice is good; all the advantages are on your own side. Your violet-coloured suit, embroidered with gold, becomes you admirably. Madame will be as much vanquished by the man as by the step. Come, monseigneur.'

'You decide me; let us go.'

The Duke left his room, accompanied by the Chevalier, and went towards Madame's apartments. The Chevalier hastily whispered to his valet, 'Be sure that there are some people posted at the little door, so that no one can escape in that direction. Run, run.' And he followed the Duke towards the antechambers of Madame's suite of apartments, and when the ushers were about to announce them, the Chevalier said, laughing, 'His Highness wishes to surprise Madame.'

XIV

MONSIEUR entered the room abruptly,* as those persons do who mean well and think they confer pleasure, or as those who hope to surprise some secret, the melancholy reward of jealous people. Madame, almost out of her senses at the first bars of music, was dancing in the most unrestrained manner, leaving the dinner, which had been already begun, unfinished. Her partner was M. de Guiche, who, with his arms raised and his eyes half closed, was kneeling on one knee, like the Spanish dancers, with looks full of passion, and gestures of the most caressing character. The Princess was dancing round him with a responsive smile, and the same air of alluring seductiveness. Montalais stood by admiringly; La Vallière, seated in a corner of the room, looked on thoughtfully. It is impossible to describe the effect which the presence of the Prince produced upon this happy company, and it would be just as impossible to describe the effect which the sight of their happiness produced upon Philip. The Comte de Guiche had no power to move; Madame remained in the middle of one of the figures and of an attitude, unable to utter a word. The Chevalier de Lorraine, leaning his back against the doorway, smiled like a man in the very height of the frankest admiration. The pallor of the Prince, and the convulsive trembling of his hands and limbs, were the first symptoms that struck those present. A dead silence succeeded the sound of the dance. The Chevalier de Lorraine took advantage of this interval to salute Madame and de Guiche most respectfully, affecting to join them together in his reverences as though they were the master and mistress of the house. Monsieur then approached them, saying, in a hoarse tone of voice, 'I am delighted; I came here expecting to find you ill and low-spirited, and I find you abandoning yourself to new amusements; really, it is most fortunate. My house is the merriest in the whole kingdom.' Then, turning towards de Guiche, 'Comte,' he said, 'I did not know you were so good a dancer.' And, again addressing his wife, he said, 'Show a little more consideration for me,

Madame; whenever you intend to amuse yourselves here, invite me. I am a Prince, alas, very much neglected.'

Guiche had now recovered his self-possession, and with the spirited boldness which was natural to him, and which so well became him, he said, 'Your Highness knows very well that my very life is at your service, and whenever there is a question of its being needed, I am ready; but to-day, as it is only a question of dancing to music, I dance.'

'And you are perfectly right,' said the Prince coldly. 'But, Madame,' he continued, 'you do not remark that your ladies deprive me of my friends; M. de Guiche does not belong to you, Madame, but to me. If you wish to dine without me, you have your ladies. When I dine alone, I have my gentlemen; do not strip me of everything.'

Madame felt the reproach and the lesson, and the colour rushed to her face. 'Monsieur,' she replied, 'I was not aware, when I came to the Court of France, that Princesses of my rank were to be regarded as the women in Turkey are. I was not aware that we were not allowed to be seen; but, since such is your desire, I will conform myself to it; pray do not hesitate, if you should wish it, to have my windows barred even.'

This repartee, which made Montalais and de Guiche smile, rekindled the Prince's anger, no inconsiderable portion of which had already evaporated in words.

'Very well,' he said, in a concentrated tone of voice,—'this is the way in which I am respected in my own house.'

'Monseigneur, monseigneur,' murmured the Chevalier in the Duke's ear, in such a manner that every one could observe he was endeavouring to calm him.

'Come,' replied the Prince, as his only answer to the remark, hurrying him away, and turning round with so hasty a movement that he almost ran against Madame. The Chevalier followed him to his own apartment, where the Prince had no sooner seated himself than he gave free rein to his fury. The Chevalier raised his eyes towards the ceiling, joined his hands together, and said not a word.

'Give me your opinion,' exclaimed the Prince.

'Oh, monseigneur, it is a very serious matter.'

'It is abominable! I cannot live in this manner.'

'How unhappy all this is,' said the Chevalier. 'We hoped to enjoy tranquillity, after that madman Buckingham had left.'

'And this is worse.'

'I do not say that, monseigneur.'

'Yes, but I say it, for Buckingham would never have ventured upon a fourth part of what we have just now seen.'

'What do you mean?'

'To conceal oneself for the purpose of dancing, and to feign indisposition, in order to dine *tête à tête*.'

'No, no, monseigneur.'

'Yes, yes,' exclaimed the Prince, exciting himself like a self-willed child; 'but I will not endure it any longer, I must learn what is really going on.'

'Oh, monseigneur, an exposure——'

'By Heaven, monsieur, am I to put myself out of the way when people show so little consideration for me? Wait for me here, Chevalier, wait for me here.' The Prince disappeared into the neighbouring apartment, and inquired of the gentlemen in attendance if the Queen-Mother had returned from chapel. Anne of Austria felt that her happiness was now complete; peace restored to her family, a nation delighted with the presence of a young monarch who had shown an aptitude for affairs of great importance; the revenues of the state increased; external peace assured; everything seemed to promise a tranquil future for her.* Her thoughts recurred, now and then, to that poor young man,* whom she had received as a mother, and had driven away as a hard-hearted step-mother, and she sighed as she thought of him.'

Suddenly the Duc d'Orléans entered her room. 'Dear Mother,' he exclaimed hurriedly, closing the door, 'things cannot go on as they now are.'

Anne of Austria raised her beautiful eyes towards him, and with an unmoved gentleness of manner, said, 'What things do you allude to?'

'I wish to speak of Madame.'

'Your wife?'

'Yes, madame.'

'I suppose that silly fellow Buckingham has been writing a farewell letter to her.'

'Oh! yes, madame, of course, it is a question of Buckingham.'

'Of whom else could it be, then? for that poor fellow was, wrongly enough, the object of your jealousy, and I thought——'

'My wife, madame, has already replaced the Duke of Buckingham.'

'Philip, what are you saying? You are speaking very heedlessly.'

'No, no.—Madame has so managed matters, that I am still jealous.'

'Of whom, in Heaven's name?'

'Is it possible you have not remarked it? Have you not noticed the M. de Guiche is always in her apartments—always with her?'

The Queen clapped her hands together, and began to laugh. 'Philip,' she said, 'your jealousy is not merely a defect, it is a positive disease.'

'Whether a defect, or a disease, madame, I am the sufferer from it.'

'And do you imagine, that a complaint which exists only in your own imagination can be cured. You wish it to be said, you are right in being jealous, when there is no ground whatever for your jealousy.'

'Of course, you will begin to say for this one, what you already said on behalf of the other.'

'Because, Philip,' said the Queen dryly, 'what you did for the other, you are going to do for this one.'

The Prince bowed, slightly annoyed. 'If I were to give you facts,' he said, 'will you believe me?'

'If it regarded anything else but jealousy, I would believe you without your bringing facts forward; but, as jealousy is in the case, I promise nothing.'

'It is just the same as if your Majesty were to desire me to hold my tongue, and sent me away unheard.'

'Far from it; as you are my son, I owe you a mother's indulgence.'

'Oh, say what you think; you owe me as much indulgence as a madman deserves.'

'Do not exaggerate, Philip, and take care how you represent your wife to me as a woman of a depraved mind.'

'But facts, Mother, facts.'

'Well, I am listening.'

'This morning, at ten o'clock, they were playing music in Madame's apartments.'

'No harm in that surely.'

'M. de Guiche was talking with her alone——Ah! I forgot to tell you that, during the last ten days, he has never left her side.'

'If they were doing any harm they would hide themselves.'

'Very good,' exclaimed the Duke, 'I expected you to say that. Pray do not forget what you have just said. This morning I took them by surprise, and showed my dissatisfaction in a very marked manner.'

'Rely upon it, that is quite sufficient; it was, perhaps, even a little too much. These young women easily take offence. To reproach them for an error they have not committed is, sometimes, almost the same as telling them they might do it.'

'Very good, very good; but wait a minute. Do not forget that you have just this minute said, that this morning's lesson ought to have been sufficient, and that if they had been doing what was wrong, they would have concealed themselves.'

'Yes, I said so.'

'Well, just now, repenting of my hastiness of this morning, and knowing that Guiche was sulking in his own apartments, I went to pay Madame a visit. Can you guess what, or whom, I found there?—Another set of musicians, more dancing, and Guiche himself—he was concealed there.'

Anne of Austria frowned. 'It was imprudent,' she said. 'What did Madame say?'

'Nothing.'

'And Guiche?'

'As much—oh, no! he muttered some impertinent remark or another.'

'Well, what is your opinion, Philip?'

'That I have been made a fool of; that Buckingham was only a pretext, and that Guiche is the one who is really guilty.'

Anne shrugged her shoulders. 'Well,' she said, 'what else?'

'I wish de Guiche to be dismissed from my household, as Buckingham was, and I shall ask the King, unless——'

'Unless what?'

'Unless you, my dear mother, who are so clever and so kind, will execute the commission yourself.'

'I shall not do it, Philip.'

'What, madame?'

'Listen, Philip; I am not disposed to pay people ill compliments every day; I have some influence over young people, but I cannot take advantage of it, without running the chance of losing it altogether. Besides, there is nothing to prove that M. de Guiche is guilty.'

'He has displeased me.'

'That is your own affair.'

'Very well, I know what I shall do,' said the Prince impetuously.

Anne looked at him with some uneasiness. 'What do you intend to do?' she said.

'I will have him drowned in my reservoir, the next time I find him in my apartments again.' Having launched this terrible threat, the Prince expected his mother would be frightened out of her senses; but the Queen was unmoved by it.

'Do so,' she said.

Philip was as weak as a woman, and began to cry out, 'Every one betrays me,—no one cares for me; my mother even joins my enemies.'

'Your mother, Philip, sees further in the matter than you do, and does not care about advising you, since you do not listen to her.'

'I will go to the King.'

'I was about to propose that to you. I am now expecting His Majesty; it is the hour he usually pays me a visit; explain the matter to him yourself.'

She had hardly finished when Philip heard the door of the ante-room open with some noise. He began to feel nervous. At the sound of the King's footsteps, which could be heard upon the carpet, the Duke hurriedly made his escape out of the room. Anne of Austria could not resist laughing, and was laughing still when the King entered. He came very affectionately to inquire after the even now uncertain health of the Queen-Mother, and to announce to her that the preparations for the journey to Fontainebleau were complete. Seeing her laugh, his uneasiness on her account diminished, and he addressed her in a laughing tone himself. Anne of Austria took him by the hand, and, in a voice full of playfulness, said, 'Do you know, sire, that I am proud of being a Spanish woman?'

'Why, madame?'

'Because Spanish women are worth more than English women
at least.'

'Explain yourself.'

'Since your marriage, you have not, I believe, had a single
reproach to make against the Queen?'

'Certainly not.'

'And you, too, have been married some time. Your brother,
on the contrary, has been married only a fortnight.'*

'Well?'

'He is now finding fault with Madame a second time.'

'What, Buckingham still?'

'No, another—Guiche.'

'Really, Madame is a coquette, then?'

'I fear so.'

'My poor brother,' said the King, laughing.

'You do not mind coquetting, it seems?'

'In Madame, certainly I do; but Madame is not a coquette at
heart.'

'That may be, but your brother is excessively angry about it.'

'What does he want?'

'He wishes to drown Guiche.'

'That is a violent measure to resort to.'

'Do not laugh, he is extremely irritated. Think of what can be
done.'

'To save Guiche—certainly.'

'Oh, if your brother heard you, he would conspire against
you, as your uncle Monsieur did against your father.'

'No; Philip has too much affection for me for that, and I, on
my side, have too great a regard for him; we shall live together
on very good terms. But what is the substance of his request?'

'That you will prevent Madame from being a coquette, and
Guiche from being amiable.'

'Is that all? My brother has an exalted idea of sovereign power.
To reform a woman! not to say a word about reforming a man!'

'How will you set about it?'

'With a word to Guiche, who is a clever fellow, I will undertake to convince him.'

'But Madame?'

'That is more difficult; a word will not be enough. I will compose a homily and read it to her.'

'There is no time to lose.'

'Oh, I will use the utmost diligence. There is a rehearsal of the ballet this afternoon.'

'You will read her a lecture while you are dancing?'

'Yes, madame.'

'You promise to convert her?'

'I will root out the heresy altogether, either by convincing her or by extreme measures.'

'That is all right, then. Do not mix me up in the affair; Madame would never forgive me in her life, and, as her mother-in-law, I ought to try and live on good terms with my daughter-in-law.'

'The King, madame, will take all upon himself. But let me reflect.'

'What about?'

'It would be better, perhaps, if I were to go and see Madame in her own apartment.'

'Would not that seem a somewhat serious step to take?'

'Yes; but seriousness is not unbecoming in preachers, and the music of the ballet would drown one half of my arguments. Besides the object is to prevent any violent measures on my brother's part, so that a little precipitation may be advisable. Is Madame in her own apartment?'

'I believe so.'

'What is my statement of grievances to consist of?'

'In a few words, of the following: music uninterruptedly; Guiche's assiduity; suspicions of treasonable plots and practices.'

'And the proofs?'

'There are none.'

'Very well; I shall go at once to see Madame.' The King turned to look in the mirrors at his costume, which was very rich, and his face, which was as radiant and sparkling as diamonds. 'I suppose my brother is kept a little at a distance,' said the King.

'Fire and water cannot possibly be more opposite.'

'That will do. Permit me, madame, to kiss your hands, the most beautiful hands in France.'

'May you be successful, sire,—be the family peacemaker.'

'I do not employ an ambassador,' said Louis; 'which is as much as to say that I shall succeed.' He laughed as he left the room, and carefully dusted his dress as he went along.

XV

THE MEDIATOR

WHEN the King made his appearance in Madame's apartments, the courtiers, whom the news of a conjugal misunderstanding had dispersed in the various apartments, began to entertain the most serious apprehensions. A storm, too, was brewing in that direction, the elements of which the Chevalier de Lorraine, in the midst of the different groups, was analysing with delight, contributing to the weaker, and acting according to his own wicked designs in such a manner with regard to the stronger, as to produce the most disastrous consequences possible. As Anne of Austria had herself said, the presence of the King gave a solemn and serious character to the event. Indeed, in the year 1662,* the dissatisfaction of Monsieur with Madame, and the King's intervention in the private affairs of Monsieur, was a matter of no inconsiderable moment.

The boldest, even, who had been the associates of the Comte de Guiche, had, from the first moment, held aloof from him with a sort of nervous apprehension; and the Comte himself, infected by the general panic, retired to his own apartments alone. The King entered Madame's private apartments, acknow-ledging and returning the salutations, as he was always in the habit of doing. The ladies of honour were ranged in a line on his passage along the gallery. Although His Majesty was very much preoccupied, he gave the glance of a master at the two rows of young and beautiful girls, who modestly cast down their eyes, blushing as they felt the King's gaze upon them. One only of the number, whose long hair fell in silken masses upon the most beautiful skin imaginable, was pale, and could hardly sustain herself, notwithstanding the knocks which her companion gave her with her elbow. It was La Vallière, whom Montalais supported in that manner, by whispering some of that courage to her with which she herself was so abundantly provided. The King could not resist turning round to look at them again. Their faces, which had already been raised, were again lowered, but the only fair head among them remained motionless, as if all the strength and intelligence she had left had abandoned her. When he entered Madame's room, Louis found his sister-in-law reclining upon the cushions of her cabinet. She rose and made a profound reverence, murmuring some words of thanks for the honour she was receiving. She then resumed her seat, overcome by a sudden weakness, which was no doubt assumed, for a delightful colour animated her cheeks, and her eyes, still red from the tears she had recently shed, never had more fire in them. When the King was seated, and as soon as he had remarked, with that accuracy of observation which characterised him, the disorder of the apartment, and the no less great disorder of Madame's countenance, he assumed a playful manner, saying, 'My dear sister, at what hour to-day would you wish the rehearsal for the ballet to take place?'

Madame, shaking her charming head, slowly and languishingly said: 'Ah! sire, will you graciously excuse my appearance at the rehearsal; I was about to send to inform your Majesty that I could not attend to-day.'

'Indeed,' said the King, in apparent surprise; 'are you not well?'

'No, sire.'

'I will summon your medical attendants, then.'

'No, for they can do nothing for my indisposition.'

'You alarm me.'

'Sire, I wish to ask your Majesty's permission to return to England.'

The King started. 'Return to England,' he said, 'do you really say what you mean?'

'I say it reluctantly, sire,' replied the granddaughter of Henry IV firmly, her beautiful black eyes flashing. 'I regret to have to confide such matters to your Majesty, but I feel myself too unhappy at your Majesty's court; and I wish to return to my own family.'

'Madame, madame,' exclaimed the King, as he approached her.

'Listen to me, sire,' continued the young woman, acquiring by degrees that ascendancy over her interrogator which her beauty and her highly strung temperament conferred; 'young as I am, I have already suffered humiliation, and have endured disdain here. Oh! do not contradict me, sire,' she said, with a smile. The King coloured. 'Then,' she continued, 'I have reasoned myself into the belief that Heaven had called me into existence with that object, I, the daughter of a powerful monarch; that since my father* had been deprived of life, Heaven could well smite my pride. I have suffered greatly; I have been the cause, too, of my mother suffering much; but I have sworn that if Providence had ever placed me in a position of independence, even were it that of a workwoman of the lower classes, who gains her bread by her labour, I would never suffer humiliation again. That day has now arrived; I have been restored to the fortune due to my rank and to my birth; I have even ascended again the steps of a throne, and I thought that in allying myself with a French prince I should find in him a relation, a friend, an equal; but I perceive I have found only a master, and I rebel. My mother shall know nothing of it; you whom I respect, and whom I—love——'. The King started; never had any voice so gratified his ear.

'You, sire, who know all, since you have come here; you will, perhaps, understand me. If you had not come I should have gone to you. I wish for permission to pass freely. I leave it to your delicacy of feeling to exculpate and to protect me.'

'My dear sister,' murmured the King, overpowered by this bold attack, 'have you reflected upon the enormous difficulty of the project you have conceived?'

'Sire, I do not reflect, I feel. Attacked, I instinctively repel the attack, nothing more.'

'Come, tell me what have they done to you?' said the King.

The Princess, it will have been seen, by this peculiarly feminine manœuvre, had escaped every reproach, and advanced on her side a far more serious one; from an accused she became the accuser.

It is an infallible sign of guilt; but notwithstanding that all women, even the least clever of the sex, invariably know how to derive some means of attaining success. The King had forgotten that he had paid her a visit in order to say to her, 'What have you done to my brother?' and that he was reduced to saying to her, 'What have they done to you?'

'What have they done to me?' replied Madame; 'one must be a woman to understand it, sire,—they have made me weep'; and, with one of her fingers, whose slenderness and perfect whiteness were unequalled, she pointed to her brilliant eyes swimming in tears, and again began to weep.

'I implore you, my dear sister,' said the King, advancing to take her warm and throbbing hand, which she abandoned to him.

'In the first place, sire, I was deprived of the presence of my brother's friend. The Duke of Buckingham was an agreeable, cheerful visitor, my own countryman, who knew my habits; I will say almost a companion, so accustomed had we been to pass our days together with our other friends upon the beautiful lake at St James's.'

'But Villiers was in love with you.'

'A pretext! What does it matter,' she said seriously, 'whether the Duke was in love with me or not? Is a man in love so very dangerous for me? Ah! sire, it is not sufficient for a man to love a woman.' And she smiled so tenderly, and with so much archness, that the King felt his heart beat and throb within his breast.

'At all events, if my brother were jealous?' interrupted the King.

'Very well, I admit that is a reason; and the Duke was sent away accordingly.'

'No, not sent away.'

'Driven away, expelled, dismissed then, if you prefer it, sire. One of the first gentlemen of Europe was obliged to leave the court of the King of France, of Louis XIV, like a beggar, on account of a glance or a bouquet. It was unworthy of the most gallant court; but forgive me, sire, I forgot, that, in speaking thus, I am attacking your sovereign power.'

'I assure you, my dear sister, it was not I who dismissed the Duke of Buckingham; I was very charmed with him.'

'It was not you?' said Madame; 'ah! so much the better;' and she emphasised the 'so much the better,' as if she had instead said, 'so much the worse.'

A few minutes' silence ensued. She then resumed: 'The Duke

of Buckingham having left, I now know why and by whose means. I thought I should have recovered my tranquillity; but, not at all, for all at once, Monsieur finds another pretext; all at once——'

'All at once,' said the King playfully, 'some one else presents himself. It is but natural; you are beautiful, and will always meet with those who will love you.'

'In that case,' exclaimed the Princess, 'I shall create a solitude around me, which indeed seems to be what is wished, and what is being prepared for me; but no, I prefer to return to London. There I am known and appreciated. I shall have friends, without fearing they may be regarded as my lovers. Shame! it is a disgraceful suspicion, and unworthy of a gentleman. Monsieur has lost everything in my estimation, since he has shown me he can be the tyrant of a woman.'

'Nay, nay, my brother's only fault is that of loving you.'

'Love me! Monsieur love me! Ah! sire,' and she burst out laughing. 'Monsieur will never love any woman,'* she said, 'Monsieur loves himself too much; no, unhappily for me, Monsieur's jealousy is of the worst kind, he is jealous without love.'

'Confess, however,' said the King, who began to be excited by this varied and animated conversation; 'confess that Guiche loves you.'

'Ah! sire, I know nothing about that.'

'You must have perceived it. A man who loves readily betrays himself.'

'M. de Guiche has not betrayed himself.'

'My dear sister, you are defending M. de Guiche.'

'I, indeed. Ah! sire, I only needed a suspicion from yourself to complete my wretchedness.'

'No, madame, no,' returned the King hurriedly; 'do not distress yourself. Nay, you are weeping, I implore you to calm yourself.'

She wept, however, and large tears fell upon her hands; the King took one of her hands in his, and kissed the tears away. She looked at him so sadly and with so much tenderness that he felt his heart throb under her gaze.

'You have no kind of feeling, then, for Guiche?' he said, more disturbed than became his character of mediator.

'None—absolutely none.'

'Then I can reassure my brother in that respect?'

'Nothing will satisfy him, sire. Do not believe he is jealous. Monsieur has been badly advised by some one, and he is of an anxious disposition.'

'He may well be so when you are concerned,' said the King.

Madame cast down her eyes and was silent; the King did so likewise, still holding her hand all the while. His momentary silence seemed to last an age. Madame gently withdrew her hand, and, from that moment, she felt her triumph was certain, and that the field of battle was her own.

'Monsieur complains,' said the King, 'that you prefer the society of private individuals to his own conversation and society.'

'But Monsieur passes his life in looking at his face in the glass, and in plotting all sorts of spiteful things against women, with the Chevalier de Lorraine.'

'Oh, you are going somewhat too far.'

'I only say what is fact. Do you observe for yourself, sire, and you will see that I am right.'

'I will observe; but, in the meantime, what satisfaction can I give my brother?'

'My departure.'

'You repeat that word,' exclaimed the King, imprudently, as if, during the last ten minutes, such a change had been produced that Madame would have had all her ideas on the subject thoroughly changed.

'Sire, I cannot be happy here any longer,' she said. 'M. de Guiche annoys Monsieur. Will he be sent away too?'

'If it be necessary, why not?' replied the King, smiling.

'Well; and after M. de Guiche—whom, by the bye, I shall regret—I warn you, sire.'

'Ah, you will regret him?'

'Certainly; he is amiable, he has a great friendship for me, and he amuses me.'

'If Monsieur were only to hear you,' said the King, slightly annoyed, 'do you know I would not undertake to make it up again between you; nay, I would not even attempt it.'

'Sire, can you, even now, prevent Monsieur from being jealous of the first person who may approach? I know very well that M. de Guiche is not the first.'

'Again; I warn you that as a good brother I shall take a dislike to de Guiche.'

'Ah, sire, do not, I entreat you, adopt either the sympathies or the dislikes of Monsieur. Remain the King; far better for yourself and for every one else.'

'You jest most charmingly, madame; and I can well understand how those whom you attack must adore you.'

'And is that the reason why you, sire, whom I had regarded as my defender, are about to join those who persecute me?' said Madame.

'I your persecutor! Heaven forbid!'

'Then,' she continued languishingly, 'grant me a favour.'

'Whatever you wish.'

'Let me return to England.'

'Never, never,' exclaimed Louis XIV.

'I am a prisoner then?'

'In France, yes.'

'What must I do, then?'

'I will tell you. Instead of devoting yourself to friendships which are somewhat unsuitable, instead of alarming us by your retirement, remain always in our society, do not leave us, let us live as a united family. M. de Guiche is certainly very amiable; but if, at least, we do not possess his wit——'

'Ah, sire, you know very well that you are pretending to be modest.'

'No, I swear to you. One may be a king, and yet feel that he possesses fewer chances of pleasing than many other gentlemen.'

'I am sure, sire, that you do not believe a single word you are saying.'

The King looked at Madame tenderly, and said, 'Will you promise me one thing?'

'What is it?'

'That you will no longer waste upon strangers, in your own apartments, the time which you owe us. Shall we make an offensive and defensive alliance against the common enemy?'

'An alliance with you, sire?'

'Why not? Are you not a sovereign power?'

'But are you, sire, a very faithful ally?'

'You shall see, madame.'

'And when shall this alliance commence?'

'This very day.'

'Then, sire, I promise you wonders: you are the star of the court, and when you make your appearance, everything will be resplendent.'

'Oh, madame, madame,' said Louis XIV, 'you know well that there is no brilliancy which does not proceed from yourself, and that if I assume the sun as my device, it is only an emblem.'

'Sire, you flatter your ally, and you wish to deceive her,' said Madame, threatening the King with her finger raised menacingly.

'What makes you so suspicious?'

'One thing.'

'What is it? I shall indeed be unhappy if I do not overcome it.'

'That one thing in question, sire, is not in your power, not even in the power of Heaven.'

'Tell me what it is.'

'The past.'

'I do not understand, madame,' said the King, precisely because he had understood her but too well.

The Princess took his hand in hers. 'Sire,' she said, 'I have had the misfortune to displease you* for so long a period, that I have almost the right to ask myself to-day why you were able to accept me as a sister-in-law.'

'Displease me! You have displeased me?'

'Nay, do not deny it, for I remember it well.'

'Our alliance shall date from to-day,' exclaimed the King, with a warmth that was not assumed. 'You will not think any more of the past, will you? I myself am resolved that I will not. I shall always remember the present; I have it before my eyes; look.' And he led the Princess before a mirror, in which she saw herself reflected, blushing and beautiful enough to overcome a saint.

'It is all the same,' she murmured, 'it will not be a very worthy alliance.'

'Must I swear?' inquired the King, intoxicated by the voluptuous turn the whole conversation had taken.

'Oh, I do not refuse a good oath,' said Madame; 'it has always the semblance of security.'

The King knelt upon a footstool, and took hold of Madame's

hand. She, with a smile that a painter could not succeed in depicting, and which a poet only could imagine, gave him both her hands, in which he hid his burning face. Neither of them could utter a syllable. The King felt Madame withdraw her hands, caressing his face while she did so. He rose immediately and left the apartment. The courtiers remarked his heightened colour, and concluded that the scene had been a stormy one. The Chevalier de Lorraine, however, hastened to say 'Nay, be comforted, gentlemen, His Majesty is always pale when he is angry.'

XVI

THE ADVISERS

THE King left Madame in a state of agitation which it would have been difficult even for himself to have explained. Why had Louis formerly distained, almost hated Madame? Why did he now find the same woman so beautiful, so captivating? And why, not only were his thoughts full of her, but still more, why were they so full of her? Why, in fact, had Madame, whose eyes and mind were sought for in another direction, shown during the last week towards the King a semblance of favour, which encouraged the belief of still greater regard. But on the downward path of those passions in which the heart rejoices, towards which youth impels us, no one can decide where to stop, not even he who has in advance calculated all the chances of his own success or of another's submission. As far as Madame was concerned, her regard for the King may easily be explained; she was young, a coquette, and ardently fond of admiration. Hers was one of those buoyant, impetuous natures, which upon a theatre would leap over the greatest obstacles to obtain an acknowledgement of applause from the spectators. It was not surprising, then, that, after having been adored by Buckingham, by de Guiche, who was superior to Buckingham, even if it were only from that great merit, so much appreciated by woman, that is to say, novelty—it was not surprising, we say, that the Princess should raise her ambition to being admired by the King, who, not only was the first person in the kingdom, but was one of the handsomest and wittiest men in it. As for the sudden passion with which Louis was inspired for his sister-in-law, physiology would perhaps supply the explanation of it by some hackneyed, commonplace reasons, and nature from some of her mysterious affinity of characters. Madame had the most beautiful black eyes in the world; Louis, eyes as beautiful, but blue. Madame was laughter-loving and unreserved in her manners: Louis melancholy and diffident. Summoned to meet each other, for the first time, upon the grounds of interest and common curiosity, these two opposite natures were mutally influenced by the contact of their reciprocal contradictions of character. Louis, when he returned to his own rooms, acknowledged to himself that Madame was the most attractive woman of his court. Madame, left alone, delightedly thought that she had made a great impression on the King. This feeling with her must remain passive, whilst the King could not but act with all the natural vehemence of the heated fancies of a young man, and of a young man who has but to express a wish to see his wishes executed.

The first thing the King did was to announce to Monsieur that everything was quietly arranged; that Madame had the greatest respect, the sincerest affection for him; but that she was of a proud, impetuous character, and that her susceptibilities were so acute as to require a very careful management.

Monsieur replied in the sour tone of voice he generally adopted with his brother, that he could not very well understand the susceptibilities of a woman whose conduct might, in his opinion, expose her to censorious remarks, and that if any one had a right to feel wounded, it was he, Monsieur himself. To this the King replied in a quick tone of voice, which showed the interest he took in his sister-in-law, 'Thank Heaven, Madame is above censure.'

'The censure of others, certainly, I admit,' said Monsieur; 'but not above mine, I presume.'

'Well,' said the King, 'all I have to say, Philip, is, that Madame's conduct does not deserve your censure. She certainly is heedless and singular, but professes the best feelings. The English character is not always well understood in France, and the liberty of English manners sometimes surprises those who do not know the extent to which this liberty is enriched by innocence.'

'Ah!' said Monsieur, more and more piqued, 'from the very moment that your Majesty absolves my wife, whom I accuse, my wife is not guilty, and I have nothing more to say.'

'Philip,' replied the King hastily, for he felt the voice of conscience murmuring softly in his heart that Monsieur was not altogether wrong; 'what I have done, and what I have said, was only for your happiness. I was told that you complained of a want of confidence or attention on Madame's part, and I did not wish your uneasiness to be prolonged any further. It is part of my duty to watch over your household, as over that of the humblest of my subjects. I have seen, therefore, with the sincerest pleasure that your apprehensions have no foundation.'

'And,' continued Monsieur, in an interrogative tone of voice, and fixing his eyes upon his brother, 'what your Majesty has discovered for Madame—and I bow myself to your Majesty's superior judgment—have you also verified it for those who have been the cause of the scandal of which I complain?'

'You are right, Philip,' said the King. 'I will consider that point.'

These words comprised an order as well as a consolation; the Prince felt it to be so, and withdrew. As for Louis, he went to seek his mother, for he felt that he had need of a more complete absolution than that he had just received from his brother. Anne of Austria did not entertain for M. de Guiche the same reasons for indulgence she had had for Buckingham.* She perceived, at the very first words he pronounced, that Louis was not disposed to be severe, as she was indeed. It was one of the stratagems of the good Queen, in order to succeed in ascertaining the truth. But Louis was no longer in his apprenticeship; already for more than a year past* he had been King, and during that year he had learned how to dissemble. Listening to Anne of Austria, in order to permit her to disclose her own thoughts, testifying his approval only by look and by gestures, he became convinced, from certain profound glances, and from certain skilful insinuations, that the Queen, so clear-sighted in matters of gallantry, had, if not guessed, at least suspected, his weakness for Madame. Of all his auxiliaries, Anne of Austria would be the most important to secure; of all his enemies, Anne of Austria would have been the most dangerous. Louis therefore changed his tactics. He complained of

Madame, absolved Monsieur, listened to what his mother had to say of de Guiche, as he had previously listened to what she had had to say of Buckingham, and then, when he saw that she thought she had gained a complete victory over him, he left her. The whole of the court, that is to say all the favourites and more intimate associates, and they were numerous, since there were already five masters, were assembled in the evening for the rehearsal of the ballet. This interval had been occupied by poor de Guiche in receiving visits. Among the number was one which he hoped and feared almost to an equal extent. It was that of the Chevalier de Lorraine. About three o'clock in the afternoon the Chevalier entered de Guiche's rooms. His looks were of the most assuring character. 'Monsieur,' said he to de Guiche, 'was in an excellent humour, and no one could say that the slightest cloud had passed across the conjugal sky. Besides, Monsieur was not one to bear ill feeling.'

For a very long time past, during his residence at the court, the Chevalier de Lorraine had decided, that of Louis XIII's two sons, Monsieur was the one who had inherited the father's character—an uncertain, irresolute character; impulsively good, evilly disposed at bottom; but certainly a cipher for his friends. He had especially cheered de Guiche by pointing out to him that Madame would, before long, succeed in governing her husband, and that, consequently, that man would govern Monsieur who should succeed in influencing Madame. To this de Guiche, full of mistrust and presence of mind, had replied; 'Yes, Chevalier, but I believe Madame to be a very dangerous person.'

'In what respect?'

'She has perceived that Monsieur is not very passionately inclined towards women.'

'Quite true,' said the Chevalier de Lorraine, laughing.

'In that case Madame will choose the first one who approaches in order to make him the object of her preference, and to bring back her husband by jealousy.'

'Deep! deep!' exclaimed the Chevalier.

'But true,' replied de Guiche. But neither the one nor the other expressed his real thought. De Guiche, at the very moment he thus attacked Madame's character, mentally asked her forgiveness from the bottom of his heart. The Chevalier, while admiring de Guiche's perceptiveness, led him blindfolded to the brink of the precipice. De Guiche then questioned him more directly upon the effect produced by the scene of that morning, and upon the still more serious effect produced by the scene at dinner.

'But I have already told you that they are all laughing at it,' replied the Chevalier de Lorraine, 'and Monsieur himself at the head of them.'

'Yet,' hazarded de Guiche, 'I have heard that the King paid Madame a visit.'

'Yes, precisely so. Madame was the only one who did not laugh, and the King went to her in order to make her laugh too. Nothing is altered in the arrangements of the day,' said the Chevalier.

'And is there a rehearsal of the ballet this evening?'

'Certainly.'

'Are you sure?'

'Quite so,' returned the Chevalier.

At this moment of the conversation between the two young men, Raoul entered, looking full of anxiety. As soon as the Chevalier, who had a secret dislike for him, as for every other noble character, perceived him enter, he rose from his seat.

'What do you advise me to do then?' inquired de Guiche of the Chevalier.

'I advise you to go to sleep with perfect tranquillity, my dear Comte.'

'And my advice, de Guiche,' said Raoul, 'is the very opposite.'

'What is that?'

'To mount your horse and set off at once for one of your estates; on your arrival, follow the Chevalier's advice, if you like; and, what is more, you can sleep there as long and tranquilly as you please.'

'What! go away?' exclaimed the Chevalier, feigning surprise; 'why should de Guiche go away?'

'Because, and you cannot be ignorant of it—you particularly so—because every one is talking about the scene which has passed between Monsieur and de Guiche.' De Guiche turned pale.

'Not at all,' replied the Chevalier, 'not at all, and you have been wrongly informed, M. de Bragelonne.'

'I have been perfectly well informed, on the contrary, mon-sieur,' replied Raoul, 'and the advice I give de Guiche is that of a friend.'

During this discussion, de Guiche, somewhat shaken, looked alternately first at one and then at the other of his advisers. He inwardly felt that a game, important in all its consequences for the rest of his life, was being played at that moment.

'Is it not the fact,' said the Chevalier, putting the question to the Comte himself, 'is it not the fact, de Guiche, the scene was not so tempestuous as the Vicomte de Bragelonne seems to think, and who, moreover, was not himself there?'

'Whether tempestuous or not,' persisted Raoul, 'it is not pre-cisely of the scene itself that I am speaking, but of the conse-quences that may ensue. I know that Monsieur has threatened, and I know that Madame has been in tears.'

'Madame in tears!' exclaimed de Guiche, imprudently clasp-ing his hands.

'Ah!' said the Chevalier laughing, 'that is indeed a cir-cumstance I was not acquainted with. You are decidedly better informed than I am, Monsieur de Bragelonne.'

'And it is because I am better informed than yourself, Cheva-lier, that I insist upon de Guiche leaving.'

'No, no; I regret to differ from you, Vicomte; but his depar-ture is unnecessary. Why, indeed, should he leave? tell us why.'

'The King has taken up the affair.'

'Bah!' said the Chevalier, 'the King likes de Guiche, and particularly his father; reflect, that, if the Comte were to leave it would be an admission that he had done something which merited rebuke.'

'Why so?'

'No doubt of it; when one runs away it is either from guilt or from fear.'

'Or because a man is offended; because he is wrongfully accused,' said Bragelonne. 'We will assign as a reason for his departure that he feels hurt and injured—nothing will be easier; we will say that we both did our utmost to keep him, and you, at least, will not be speaking otherwise than the truth. Come, de Guiche, you are innocent, and, being so, the scene of to-day must have wounded you. So leave.'

'No, de Guiche, remain where you are,' said the Chevalier; 'precisely as M. de Bragelonne has put it, because you are innocent. Once more, forgive me, Vicomte; but my opinion is the very opposite to your own.'

'And you are at perfect liberty to maintain it, monsieur; but be assured that the exile which de Guiche will voluntarily impose upon himself will be of short duration. He can terminate it whenever he pleases, and, returning from his voluntary exile, he will meet with smiles from all lips; while, on the contrary, the anger of the King may draw down a storm upon his head, the end of which no one can foresee.'

The Chevalier smiled, and murmured to himself, 'That is the very thing I wish.' And at the same time he shrugged his shoulders, a movement which did not escape the Comte, who dreaded, if he quitted the court, to seem to yield to a feeling of fear.

'No, no; I have decided, Bragelonne; I stay.'

'I prophesy, then,' said Raoul sadly, 'that misfortune will befall you, de Guiche.'

'I too, am a prophet, but not a prophet of evil; on the contrary, Comte, I say to you remain.'

'Are you sure,' inquired de Guiche, 'that the rehearsal of the ballet will still take place?'

'Quite sure.'

'Well, you see, Raoul,' continued de Guiche, endeavouring to smile, 'you see the court is not so very sorrowful, or so readily disposed for internal dissensions, when dancing is carried on with such assiduity. Come, acknowledge that,' said the Comte to Raoul, who shook his head, saying, 'I have nothing to add.'

'But,' inquired the Chevalier, curious to learn whence Raoul had obtained his information, the exactitude of which he was inwardly forced to admit, 'since you say you are well informed, Vicomte, how can you be better informed than myself, who am one of the Prince's most intimate companions?'

'To such a declaration I submit. You certainly ought to be perfectly well informed, I admit; and, as a man of honour is incapable of saying anything but what he knows to be true, or of speaking otherwise than what he thinks, I shall say no more, but confess myself defeated, and leave you in possession of the field of battle.'

Whereupon Raoul, who now seemed only to care to be left quiet, threw himself upon a large couch, whilst the Comte summoned his servants to aid him in dressing. The Chevalier, finding that time was passing away, wished to leave; but he feared, too, that Raoul, left alone with de Guiche, might yet influence him to change his resolution. He therefore made use of his last resource.

'Madame,' he said, 'will be brilliant! she appears to-day in her costume of Pomona.'*

'Yes, that is so,' exclaimed the Comte.

'And she has just given directions in consequence,' continued the Chevalier. 'You know, Monsieur de Bragelonne, that the King is to appear as Spring.'

'It will be admirable,' said de Guiche; 'and that is a better reason for me to remain than any you have yet given, because I am to appear as Autumn, and shall have to dance with Madame. I cannot absent myself without the King's orders, since my departure would interrupt the ballet.'

'I,' said the Chevalier, 'am to be only a simple *Egypan*;* true it is, I am a bad dancer, and my legs are not well made. Gentlemen, adieu. Do not forget the basket of fruit, which you are to offer to Pomona, Comte.'

'Be assured,' said de Guiche delightedly, 'I shall forget nothing.'

'I am now quite certain that he will remain,' murmured the Chevalier de Lorraine to himself.

Raoul, when the Chevalier had left, did not even attempt to dissuade his friend, for he felt that it would be trouble thrown away; he merely observed to the Comte, in his melancholy and melodious voice, 'You are embarking in a most dangerous enterprise. I know you well; you go to extremes in everything, and she whom you love does so too. Admitting for an instant that she should at last love you——'

'Oh, never!' exclaimed de Guiche. 'It would be a great misfortune for both of us.'

'In that case, instead of regarding you as simply imprudent, I cannot but consider you absolutely mad.'

'Why?'

'Are you perfectly sure, mind, answer me frankly, that you do not wish her whom you love to make any sacrifice for you?'

'Yes, yes, quite sure.'

'Love her, then, at a distance.'

'What! at a distance!'

'Certainly; what matters being present or absent, since you expect nothing from her. Love a portrait, a remembrance.'

'Raoul!'

'Love a shadow, an illusion, a chimera; be devoted to the affection itself, in giving a name to your ideality.'

'Ah!'

'You turn away; your servants approach; I shall say no more. In good or bad fortune, de Guiche, depend upon me.'

'Indeed I shall do so.'

'Very well; that is all I had to say to you. Spare no pains in your person, de Guiche, and look your very best. Adieu.'

'You will not be present then, at the rehearsal, Vicomte.'

'No; I shall have a visit to pay in town. Farewell, de Guiche.'

The reception was to take place in the King's apartments. In the first place there were the Queens, then Madame, and a few ladies of the court who had been selected. A great number of courtiers, also carefully selected, occupied the time, before the dancing commenced, in conversing as people knew how to converse in those days. None of the ladies, who had received invitations, appeared in the costumes of the fête as the Chevalier de Lorraine had predicted, but many conversations took place about the rich and ingenious toilets designed by different painters for the ballet of 'The Demi-Gods,' for thus were termed the Kings and Queens, of which Fontainebleau was about to become the Pantheon. Monsieur arrived, holding in his hand a drawing representing his character; he looked somewhat anxious; he bowed courteously to the young Queen and his mother, but saluted Madame almost cavalierly. His notice of her and his coldness of manner were observed by all. M. de Guiche indemnified the Princess with a look of passionate devotion, and it must be admitted that Madame, as she raised her eyes, returned it to him with interest. It is unquestionable that de Guiche had never looked so handsome, for Madame's glance had had the effect of lighting up the features of the son of the Marshal de Gramont.* The King's sister-in-law felt a storm mustering above her head; she felt, too, that, during the whole of the day, so fruitful in future events, she had acted unjustly, if not treasonably, towards one who loved her with such a depth of devotion. In her eyes the moment seemed to have arrived for an acknowledgment to the poor victim of the injustice of the morning. Her heart spoke and murmured the name of de Guiche; the Comte was sincerely pitied; and accordingly gained the victory over all others. Neither Monsieur, nor the King, nor the Duke of Buckingham was any longer thought of; and de Guiche at the moment reigned without a rival. But although Monsieur also looked very handsome, still he could be not compared to the Comte—it is well known—indeed all women say so—that a very wide difference invariably exists between the good looks of a lover and those of a husband. Besides, in the present case, after Monsieur had left, and after the courteous and affectionate recognition of the young Queen and of the Queen-Mother, and the careless and indifferent notice of Madame, which all the courtiers had remarked; all these motives gave the lover the advantage over the husband. Monsieur was too great a personage to notice these details. Nothing is so certain as a well settled idea of superiority to prove the inferiority of the man who has that opinion of himself. The King arrived. Louis had none of his brother's gloominess, but was perfectly radiant. Having examined a greater part of the drawings which were displayed for his inspection on every side, he gave his opinion, or made his remarks upon them, and in this manner rendered some happy and others unhappy by a single word. Suddenly, his glance, which was smilingly directed towards Madame, detected the silent correspondence which was established between the Princess and the Comte. He bit his lip, but when he opened his lips again to utter a few commonplace remarks, he said, advancing towards the Queens:—

'I have just been informed that everything is now prepared at Fontainebleau, in accordance with my directions.' A murmur of satisfaction arose from the different groups, and the King perceived on every face the greatest anxiety to receive an invitation for the fêtes. 'I shall leave to-morrow,' he added. Whereupon the profoundest silence immediately ensued. 'And I invite,' said the King, finishing, 'all those who are now present to get ready to accompany me.'

Smiling faces were now everywhere visible, with the exception of Monsieur, who seemed to retain his ill humour. The different noblemen and ladies of the court thereupon defiled before the King, one after the other, in order to thank His Majesty for the great honour which had been conferred upon them by the invitation. When it came to de Guiche's turn, the King said, 'Ah! M. de Guiche, I did not see you.'

The Comte bowed, and Madame turned pale. De Guiche was about to open his lips to express his thanks, when the King said, 'Comte, this is the season for farming purposes in the country; I am sure your tenants in Normandy will be glad to see you.'*

The King, after this frontal attack, turned his back to the poor Comte, whose turn it was now to become pale; he advanced a few steps towards the King, forgetting that the King is never spoken to except in reply to questions addressed. 'I have perhaps misunderstood your Majesty,' he stammered out. The King turned his head slightly, and with a cold and stern glance, which plunged like a sword relentlessly into the hearts of those under disgrace, repeated, 'I said retire to your estates,' and allowing every syllable to fall slowly one by one. A cold perspiration bedewed the Comte's face, his hands convulsively opened, and his hat, which he held between his trembling fingers, fell to the ground. Louis sought his mother's glance, as though to show her that he was master; he sought his brother's triumphant look, as if to ask him if he were satisfied with the vengeance taken; and lastly his eyes fell upon Madame; but the Princess was laughing and smiling with Madame de Noailles.* She had heard nothing, or, rather, had pretended not to hear at all. The Chevalier de Lorraine looked on also with looks of settled hostility. M. de Guiche was left alone in the King's cabinet, the whole of the company having departed. Shadows seemed to dance before his eyes. He suddenly broke through the fixed despair which overwhelmed him and flew to hide himself in his own rooms, where Raoul awaited him, confident in his own sad presentiments.

'Well?' he murmured, seeing his friend enter, bareheaded, with a wild gaze and tottering gait.

'Yes, yes, it is true,' said de Guiche, unable to utter more, and falling exhausted upon the couch.

'And she?' inquired Raoul.

'She,' exclaimed his unhappy friend, as he raised his hand, clenched in anger towards Heaven. 'She!——'

'What did she say and do?'

'She said that her dress suited her admirably, and then she laughed.' A fit of hysteric laughter seemed to shatter his nerves, for he fell backwards, completely overcome.

XVII

FONTAINEBLEAU

FOR four days every kind of enchantment brought together in the magnificent gardens of Fontainebleau had converted this spot into a place of the most perfect enjoyment. M. Colbert seemed gifted with ubiquity. In the morning there were the accounts of the previous night's expenses to settle; during the day, programmes, essays, enlistments, payments. M. Colbert had amassed four million francs, and dispersed them with a prudent economy. He was horrified at the expenses which mythology involved; every wood-nymph, every dryad, did not cost less than a hundred francs a day. Each costume alone amounted to three hundred francs. The expense of powder and sulphur for fireworks amounted, every night, to a hundred thousand francs. In addition to these, the illuminations on the borders of the lake cost thirty thousand francs every evening. The fêtes had been magnificent; and Colbert could not restrain his delight. From time to time he noticed Madame and the King setting forth on hunting expeditions, or preparing for the reception of different fantastic personages, solemn ceremonials, which had been extemporised a fortnight before, and in which Madame's sparkling wit and the King's magnificence were equally displayed.

For Madame, the heroine of the fête, replied to the addresses of deputations from unknown races—Garamanths, Scythians, Hyperboreans, Caucasians, and Patagonians,* who seemed to issue from the ground for the purpose of approaching her with their congratulations, and upon every representative of these races the King bestowed a diamond or some other article of great value. Then the deputies, in verses more or less amusing, compared the King to the sun, Madame to Phœbe the sun's sister, and the Queen and Monsieur were no more spoken of than if the King had married Madame Henrietta of England, and not Maria Theresa of Austria. The happy pair, hand in hand, imperceptibly pressing each other's fingers, drank in deep draughts the sweet beverage of adulation, by which the attractions of youth, beauty, power, and love are enhanced. Every one at Fontainebleau was amazed at the extent of the influence which Madame had so rapidly acquired over the King, and whispered among themselves that Madame was, in point of fact, the true Queen; and, in effect, the King himself proclaimed its truth by his every thought, word, and look. He formed his wishes, he drew his inspirations from Madame's eyes, and his delight was unbounded when Madame deigned to smile upon him. And was Madame, on her side, intoxicated with the power she wielded, as she beheld every one at her feet?—This was a question she herself could hardly answer; but what she did know was, that she could frame no wish, and that she felt herself to be perfectly happy. The result of all these changes, the source of which emanated from the royal will, was that Monsieur, instead of being the second person in the kingdom, had, in reality, become the third. And it was now far worse than in the time when de Guiche's guitars were heard in Madame's apartments; for, then, at least, Monsieur had the satisfaction of frightening those who annoyed him. Since the departure, however, of the enemy, who had been driven away by means of his alliance with the King, Monsieur had to submit to a burden, heavier, but in a very different sense, to his former one. Every evening, Madame returned home quite exhausted. Horse-riding, bathing in the Seine, spectacles, dinners under the leafy covert of the trees, balls on the banks of the grand canal, concerts, etc., etc.; all this would have been sufficient to have killed, not a slight and delicate woman, but the strongest porter in the château. It is perfectly true, that, with regard to dancing, concerts, and promenades, and such matters, a woman is far stronger than the most robust porter of the château. But, however great a woman's strength may be, there is a limit to it, and she cannot hold out long under such a system. As for Monsieur, he had not even the satisfaction of witnessing Madame's abdication of her royalty in the evening, for she lived in the royal pavilion with the young Queen and the Queen-Mother. As a matter of course the Chevalier de Lorraine did not quit Monsieur, and did not fail to distil his drops of gall into every wound the latter received. The result was, that Monsieur—who had, at first, been in the highest spirits, and completely restored since Guiche's departure—subsided into his melancholy state three days after the court was installed at Fontainebleau.* It happened, however, that one day, about two o'clock in the afternoon, Monsieur, who had risen late, and had bestowed upon his toilet more than his usual attention, it happened, we repeat, that Monsieur, who had not heard of any plans having been arranged for the day, formed the project of collecting his own court, and of carrying Madame off with him to Moret,* where he possessed a charming country house. He, accordingly, went to the Queen's pavilion, and was astonished, on entering, to find none of the royal servants in attendance. Quite alone, therefore, he entered the rooms, a door on the left opening to Madame's apartment, the one on the right to the young Queen's. In his wife's apartments Monsieur was informed, by a seamstress, who was working there, that every one had left at eleven o'clock for the purpose of bathing in the Seine,* that a grand fête was to be made of the expedition, that all the carriages had been placed at the park gates, and that they had all set out more than an hour ago.

'Very good,' said Monsieur, 'the idea is a good one, the heat is very oppressive, and I have no objection to bathe too.'

He summoned his servants, but no one came. He summoned those in attendance on Madame, but everybody had gone out. He then went to the stables, where he was informed by a groom that there were no carriages of any description. He then desired that a couple of horses should be saddled, one for himself and the other for his valet. The groom told him that all the horses had been sent away. Monsieur, pale with anger, again ascended towards the Queen's apartments, and penetrated as far as Anne of Austria's oratory, where he perceived, through the half-opened tapestry hangings, his young and beautiful sister on her knees before the Queen-Mother, who appeared weeping bitterly. He had not been either seen or heard. He cautiously approached the opening, and listened—the sight of so much grief having aroused his curiosity. Not only was the young Queen weeping, but she was complaining also. 'Yes,' she said, 'the King neglects me, the King devotes himself to pleasures and amusements only in which I have no share.'

'Patience, patience, my daughter,' said Anne of Austria, in Spanish; and then, also in Spanish, added some words of advice which Monsieur did not understand. The Queen replied by accusations, mingled with sighs and sobs, among which Monsieur often distinguished the word *baños*, which Maria Theresa accentuated with spiteful anger.

'The baths,' said Monsieur to himself, 'it seems it is the baths that have put her out.' And he endeavoured to put together the disconnected phrases which he had been able to understand. It was easy to guess that the Queen complained bitterly, and that, if Anne of Austria did not console her, she at least endeavoured to do so. Monsieur was afraid to be detected listening at the door, and he therefore made up his mind to cough; the two Queens turned round at the sound, and Monsieur entered. At the sight of the Prince, the young Queen rose precipitately, and dried her tears. Monsieur, however, knew the people he had to deal with too well, and was naturally too polite to remain silent, and he accordingly saluted them. The Queen-Mother smiled pleasantly at him, saying, 'What do you want, Philip?'

'I?—nothing,' stammered Monsieur. 'I was looking for——'

'Whom?'

'I was looking for Madame.'

'Madame is at the baths.'

'And the King?' said Monsieur, in a tone which made the Queen tremble.

'The King also, and the whole court as well,' replied Anne of Austria.

'Except you, madame,' said Monsieur.

'Oh! I,' said the young Queen, 'I seem to terrify all those who amuse themselves.' Anne of Austria made a sign to her daughter-in-law, who withdrew, weeping.

Monsieur's brows contracted, as he remarked aloud, 'What a cheerless house. What do you think of it, mother?'

'Why, no—everybody here is pleasure-hunting.'

'Yes, indeed, that is the very thing that makes those dull who do not care for pleasure.'

'In what a tone you say that, Philip.'

'Upon my word, madame, I speak as I think.'

'Explain yourself; what is the matter?'

'Ask my sister-in-law, rather, who, just now, was detailing all her grievances to you.'

'Her grievances, what——'

'Yes, I was listening, accidentally, I confess, but still I listened so that I heard only too well my sister complain of those famous baths of Madame——'

'What folly.'

'No, no, no; people are not always foolish when they weep. The Queen said *baños*, which means baths.'

'I repeat, Philip,' said Anne of Austria, 'that your sister is most childishly jealous.'

'In that case, madame,' replied the Prince, 'I too, must, with great humility, accuse myself of possessing the same defect as she has.'

'Are you really jealous of these baths?'

'And why not, madame, when the King goes to the baths with my wife, and does not take the Queen? Why not, when madame goes to the baths with the King, and does not do me the honour to tell me of it? And you require my sister-in-law to be satisfied, and require me to be satisfied, too.'

'You are raving, my dear Philip,' said Anne of Austria, 'You have driven the Duke of Buckingham away; you have been the cause of Monsieur de Guiche's exile; do you now wish to send the King away from Fontainebleau?'

'I do not pretend to anything of the kind, madame,' said Monsieur bitterly; 'but, at least, I can withdraw, and I shall do so.'

'Jealous of the King—jealous of your brother?'

'Yes, madame, I am jealous of the King,—of my own brother, and very jealous, too.'

'Really, Monsieur,' exclaimed Anne of Austria, affecting to be indignant and angry, 'I begin to believe you are mad, and a sworn enemy to my repose. I therefore abandon the place to you, for I have no means of defending myself against such wild conceptions.'

She arose and left Monsieur a prey to the most extravagant transport of passion. He remained for a moment completely bewildered; then, recovering himself, he again went to the stables, found the groom, once more asked him for a carriage or a horse, and upon his replying that there was neither the one nor the other, Monsieur snatched a long whip from the hand of a stable-boy, and began to pursue the poor devil of a groom all round the servants' courtyard, whipping him all the while, in spite of his cries and his excuses; then, quite out of breath, covered with perspiration, and trembling in every limb, he returned to his own apartments, broke in pieces some beautiful specimens of porce-lain, and then got into bed, booted and spurred as he was, crying out for some one to come to him.

XVIII

THE BATH

AT Vulaines,* beneath the impenetrable shade of flowering osiers and willows, which, as they bent down their green heads, dipped the extremities of their branches in the blue waters, a long and flat-bottomed boat, with ladders covered with long blue curtains, served as a refuge for the bathing Dianas,* who, as they left the water, were watched by twenty plumed Acteons, who, eagerly, and full of desire, galloped up and down the moss-grown and perfumed banks of the river. But Diana herself, even the chaste Diana, clothed in her long chlamys, was less beauti-ful, less impenetrable, than Madame, as young and beautiful as that goddess herself. For, notwithstanding the fine tunic of the huntress, her round and delicate knee can be seen; and notwith-standing the sonorous quiver, her brown shoulders can be de-tected, whereas, in Madame's case, a long white veil enveloped her, wrapping her round and round, a hundred times, as she resigned herself into the hands of her female attendants, and thus was rendered inaccessible to the most indiscreet, as well as to the most penetrating gaze. When she ascended the ladder, the poets who were present—and all were poets when Madame was the subject of discussion—the twenty poets who were galloping about, stopped, and with one voice exclaimed, that pearls, and not drops of water, were falling from her person, to be lost again in the happy river. The King, the centre of these effusions, and of such respectful homage, imposed silence upon all the honeyed tongues, for whom it seemed impossible to exhaust their raptures, and he rode away, from fear of offending, even under the silken curtains, the modesty of the woman, and the dignity of the Princess. A great blank thereupon ensued in the scene, and a perfect silence in the boat. From the movements on board,—from the flutterings and agitations of the curtains,—the goings to and fro of the female attendants engaged in their duties, could be guessed.

The King smilingly listened to the conversation of the courtiers around him, but it could be easily perceived that he gave but little if any attention to their remarks. In fact, hardly had the sound of the rings drawn along the curtain-rods announced that Madame was dressed, and that the goddess was about to make her appearance, than the King, returning to his former post immediately, and running quite close to the river bank, gave the signal for all those to approach whose attendance or pleasure summoned them to Madame's side. The pages hurried forward, conducting the led horses; the carriages, which had remained sheltered under the trees, advanced towards the tent, followed by a crowd of servants, bearers, and female attendants. A crowd of people swarming upon the banks of the river, without reckoning the groups of peasants drawn together by their anxiety to see the King, and the Princess, was, for many minutes, the most disorderly, but the most agreeable, pell-mell imaginable. The King dismounted from his horse, a movement which was imitated by all the courtiers, and offered his hand to Madame, whose rich riding-habit displayed her fine figure, which was set off to great advantage by that garment, made of fine woollen cloth, embroidered with silver. Her hair, still damp and blacker than jet, hung in heavy masses upon her white and delicate neck. Joy and health sparkled in her beautiful eyes; composed, and yet full of energy, she inhaled the air in deep draughts under the embroidered parasol, which was borne by one of her pages. Nothing could be more charming, more graceful, more poetical, than these two figures buried under the rose-coloured shade of the parasol; the King, whose white teeth were displayed in continual smiles, and Madame, whose black eyes sparkled like

two carbuncles in the glittering reflection of the changing hues
of the silk. When Madame had approached her horse, a magnificent animal of Andalusian breed, of spotless white, somewhat
heavy, perhaps, but with a spirited and slender head, in which
the mixture so happily combined of Arabian and Spanish blood
could be readily traced, and whose long tail swept the ground;
and as the Princess affected difficulty in mounting, the King
took her in his arms in such a manner that Madame's arm was
clasped like a circlet of fire around the King's neck; Louis, as he
withdrew, involuntarily touched with his lips the arm, which
was not withheld, and the Princess, having thanked her royal
equerry, every one sprang to his saddle at the same moment.
The King and Madame drew aside to allow the carriages, the
outriders, and runners, to pass by. A fair proportion of the
cavaliers, released from the restraint which etiquette had imposed upon them, gave the rein to their horses, and darted after
the carriages which bore the maids of honour, as blooming as so
many Oreades* around Diana, and the whirlwind, laughing,
chattering, and noisy, passed onward.

The King and Madame, however, kept their horses in hand at
a foot-pace. Behind his Majesty and his sister-in-law, certain of
the courtiers—those, at least, who were seriously disposed, or
were anxious to be within reach or under the eyes of the King—
followed at a respectful distance, restraining their impatient
horses, regulating their pace by that of the King and Madame,
and abandoned themselves to all the delight and gratification
which is to be found in the conversation of clever people who
can, with perfect courtesy, make a thousand of the most atrocious remarks about their neighbours. In their stifled laughter,
and in the little reticences of their sardonic humour, Monsieur,
the poor absentee, was not spared. But they pitied, and bewailed
greatly, the fate of de Guiche; and it must be confessed that
their compassion, as far as he was concerned, was not misplaced.
The King and Madame having breathed their horses, and repeated a hundred times over such remarks as the courtiers, who
made them talk, had suggested to them, set off at a hand-gallop,
and the shady coverts of the forest resounded to the heavy
footfall of the mounted party. To the conversations beneath the
shade of trees,—to the remarks made in the shape of confidential

communications, and to the observations which had been mysteriously exchanged, succeeded the noisiest bursts of laughter;—from the very outriders to royalty itself, merriment seemed
to spread. Every one began to laugh and to cry out. The magpies
and the jays flew away, uttering their guttural cries beneath the
waving avenues of the oaks; the cuckoo stayed his monotonous
cry in the recesses of the forest; the chaffinch and tomtit flew
away in clouds; while the terrified fawn and other deer bounded
forwards from the midst of the thickets. This crowd, spreading
wildly joy, confusion, and light wherever it passed, was preceded, it may be said, to the château by its own clamour. As the
King and Madame entered the village, they were both received
by the general acclamations of the crowd. Madame hastened to
look for Monsieur, for she instinctively understood that he had
been far too long kept from sharing in this joy. The King went
to rejoin the Queens; he knew he owed them, one especially, a
compensation for his long absence. But Madame was not admitted to Monsieur's apartments, and she was informed that
Monsieur was asleep. The King, instead of being met by Maria
Theresa smiling, as was usual with her, found Anne of Austria
in the gallery, watching for his return, who advanced to meet
him, and, taking him by the hand, led him to her own apartment. No one ever knew what was the nature of the conversation which took place between them; or, rather, what it was that
the Queen-Mother had said to Louis XIV; but it certainly might
easily be guessed from the annoyed expression of the King's face
as he left her after the interview.

But we, whose mission it is to interpret all things, as it is also
to communicate our interpretations to our readers,—we should
fail in our duty, if we were to leave them in ignorance of the
result of this interview. It will be found sufficiently detailed, at
least we hope so, in the following chapter.

XIX

THE BUTTERFLY-CHASE

THE King, on returning to his apartments to give some directions and to arrange his ideas, found on his toilet-glass a small note, the handwriting of which seemed disguised. He opened it and read—'Come quickly, I have a thousand things to say to you.' The King and Madame had not been separated a sufficiently long time for these thousand things to be the result of the three thousand which they had been saying to each other during the road which separated Vulaines from Fontainebleau. The confused and hurried character of the note gave the King a great deal to reflect upon. He occupied himself but slightly with his toilet, and set off to pay his visit to Madame. The Princess, who did not wish to have the appearance of expecting him, had gone into the gardens with the ladies of her suite. When the King was informed that Madame had left her apartments, and had gone for a walk in the gardens, he collected all the gentlemen he could find, and invited them to follow him. He found Madame engaged in chasing butterflies, on a large lawn bordered with heliotrope and flowering broom. She was looking on as the most adventurous and youngest of her ladies ran to and fro, and with her back turned to a high hedge, very impatiently awaited the arrival of the King, to whom she had given the rendezvous. The sound of many feet upon the gravel walk made her turn round. Louis XIV was bareheaded; he had struck down with his cane a peacock butterfly, which Monsieur de Saint-Aignan* had picked up from the ground quite stunned.

'You see, madame,' said the King, as he approached her, 'that I, too, am hunting for you,' and then, turning towards those who had accompanied him, said, 'Gentlemen, see if each of you cannot obtain as much for these ladies,' a remark which was the signal for all to retire. And thereupon a curious spectacle might be observed; old and corpulent courtiers were seen running after butterflies, losing their hats as they ran, and with their raised canes, cutting down the myrtles and the furze as they would have done the Spaniards.

The King offered Madame his hand, and they both selected, as the centre of observation, a bench with a roofing of moss, a kind of hut roughly designed by the modest genius of one of the gardeners who had inaugurated the picturesque and the fanciful amid the formal style of gardening* of that period. This sheltered retreat, covered with nasturtiums and climbing roses, screened a bench, as it were, so that those sitting there, insulated in the middle of the lawn, saw and were seen on every side, but could not be heard without perceiving those who might approach for the purpose of listening. Seated thus, the King made a sign of encouragement to those who were running about; and then, as if he were engaged with Madame in a dissertation upon the butterfly, which he had thrust through with a gold pin and fastened on his hat, said to her, 'How admirably we are placed here for conversation.'

'Yes, sire, for I wished to be heard by you alone, and yet to be seen by every one.'

'And I also,' said Louis.

'My note surprised you?'

'Terrified me rather. But what I have to tell you is more important.'

'It cannot be, sire. Do you know that Monsieur refuses to receive me?'

'Ah, Madame! in that case we have both the same thing to say to each other.'

'What has happened to you, then?'

'Well, as soon as I returned, I found my mother waiting for me, and she led me away to her own apartments.'

'The Queen-Mother,' said Madame, with some anxiety, 'the matter is serious then.'

'Indeed it is, for she told me . . . but, in the first place, allow me to preface what I have to say with one remark. Has Monsieur ever spoken to you about me?'

'Often.'

'Has he ever spoken to you about his jealousy.'

'More frequently still.'

'Of his jealousy of me?'

'No, but of the Duke of Buckingham and de Guiche.'

'Well, Madame, Monsieur's present idea is a jealousy of myself.'

'Really,' replied the Princess, smiling archly.

'And it really seems to me,' continued the King, 'that we have never given any ground——'

'Never! at least I have not. But who told you that Monsieur was jealous?'

'My mother represented to me that Monsieur entered her apartments like a madman, that he had uttered a thousand complaints against you, and—forgive me for saying it—against your coquetry. It appears that Monsieur indulges in injustice, too.'

'You are very kind, sire.'

'My mother reassured him; but he pretended that people reassure him too often, and that he had had quite enough of it.'

'Would it not be better for him not to make himself uneasy in any way?'

'The very thing I said.'

'Confess, sire, that the world is very wicked. Is it possible that a brother and sister cannot converse together, or take pleasure in each other's society, without giving rise to remarks and suspicions? For, indeed, sire, we are doing no harm, and have no intention of doing any.' And she looked at the King with that proud and provoking glance which kindles desire in the coldest and wisest of men.

'No!' sighed the King, 'that is true.'

'You know very well, sire, that if it were to continue, I should be obliged to make a disturbance. Do you decide upon our conduct, and say whether it has, or has not, been perfectly correct.'

'Oh, certainly, perfectly correct.'

'Often alone together,—for we delight in the same things, we might possibly be led away into error, but have we done so? I regard you as a brother, and nothing more.' The King frowned. She continued:—

'Your hand, which often meets my own, does not excite in me that agitation and emotion which is the case with those who love each other, for instance——'

'Enough,' said the King, 'enough, I entreat you. You have no pity—you are killing me.'

'What is the matter?'

'In fact, then, you distinctly say you experience nothing when near me.'

'Oh, sire! I do not say that—my affection——'

'Enough, Henrietta, I again entreat you. If you believe me to be marble, as you are, undeceive yourself.'

'I do not understand you, sire.'

'Very well,' sighed the King, casting down his eyes. 'And so our meetings, the pressure of each other's hands, the looks we have exchanged——Yes, yes; you are right, and I understand your meaning,' and he buried his face in his hands.

'Take care, sire,' said Madame hurriedly, 'Monsieur de Saint-Aignan is looking at you.'

'Of course,' said Louis angrily; 'never even the shadow of liberty! never any sincerity in my intercourse with any one! I imagine I have found a friend, who is nothing but a spy;—a dearer friend, who is only a—sister.'

Madame was silent and cast down her eyes. 'My husband is jealous,' she murmured in a tone of which nothing could equal its sweetness and its charm.

'You are right,' exclaimed the King suddenly.

'You see,' she said, looking at him in a manner that set his heart on fire, 'you are free, you are not suspected, the peace of your house is not disturbed.'

'Alas!' said the King, 'as yet you know nothing, for the Queen is jealous.'

'Maria Theresa!'

'Perfectly mad with jealousy! Monsieur's jealousy arises from hers; she was weeping and complaining to my mother, and was reproaching us for those bathing parties, which have made me so happy.'

'And me too,' answered Madame by a look.

'When suddenly,' continued the King, 'Monsieur, who was listening heard the word *baños*, which the Queen pronounced with some degree of bitterness, that awakened his attention; he entered the room, looking quite wild, broke into the conversation, and began to quarrel with my mother so bitterly, that she was obliged to leave him; so that, while you have a jealous husband to deal with, I shall have perpetually present before me a spectre of jealousy with swollen eyes, a cadaverous face, and sinister looks.'

'Poor King,' murmured Madame, as she lightly touched the King's hand. He retained her hand in his, and, in order to pass it without exciting suspicion in the spectators, who were not so much taken up with the butterflies that they could not occupy themselves about other matters, and who perceived clearly enough that there was some mystery in the King's and Madame's conversation, Louis placed the dying butterfly before his sister-in-law, and both bent over it as if to count the thousand eyes of its wings, or the particles of golden dust which covered it. Neither of them spoke; however, their hair mingled, their breath united, and their hands feverishly throbbed in each other's grasp. Five minutes passed by in the manner.

XX

WHAT WAS CAUGHT IN THE HAND AFTER THE BUTTERFLIES

THE two young people remained for a moment with their heads bent down, bowed, as it were, beneath the double thought of the love which was springing up in their hearts, and which gives birth to so many happy fancies in the imaginations of twenty years of age. Madame Henrietta gave a side glance from time to time at the King. Hers was one of those finely organised natures capable of looking inwardly at itself, as well as at others at the same moment. She perceived love lying at the bottom of Louis's heart, as a skilful diver sees a pearl at the bottom of the sea. She knew Louis was hesitating, if not in doubt, and that his indolent or timid heart required aid and encouragement. 'Consequently?' she said interrogatively, breaking the silence.

'What do you mean?' inquired Louis, after a moment's pause.

'I mean, that I shall be obliged to return to the resolution which I have already submitted to your Majesty.'

'When?'

'On the very day we had a certain explanation about Monsieur's jealousies.'

'What did you say to me then?' inquired Louis, with some anxiety.

'Do you not remember, sire?'

'Alas! if it be another cause of unhappiness, I shall recollect it soon enough.'

'A cause of unhappiness for myself alone, sire,' replied Madame Henrietta; 'but as it is necessary, I must submit to it.'

'At least tell me what it is,' said the King.

'Absence.'

'Still that unkind resolve?'

'Believe me, sire, I have not formed it without a violent struggle with myself; it is absolutely necessary I should return to England.'

'Never, never will I permit you to leave France,' exclaimed the King.

'And yet, sire,' said Madame, affecting a gentle yet sorrowful determination, 'nothing is more urgently necessary; nay, more than that, I am persuaded it is your mother's desire I should do so.'

'Desire!' exclaimed the King; 'that is a very strange expression to use to me.'

'Still,' replied Madame Henrietta smilingly, 'are you not happy in submitting to the wishes of so good a mother?'

'Enough, I implore you; you rend my very soul, for you speak of your departure with tranquillity.'

'I was not born for happiness, sire,' replied the Princess dejectedly; 'and I acquired, in very early life, the habit of seeing my dearest thoughts disappointed.'

'Do you speak truly?' said the King. 'Would your departure gainsay any one of your cherished thoughts?'

'If I were to say "yes" would you begin to take your misfortune patiently?'

'How cruel you are!'

'Take care, sire; some one is coming.'

The King looked all round him and said, 'No, there is no one,' and then continued, 'Come, Henrietta, instead of trying to contend against Monsieur's jealousy, by a departure which would kill me——'

Henrietta slightly shrugged her shoulders, like a woman

unconvinced. 'Yes,' repeated Louis, 'which would kill me, I say. Instead of fixing your mind on this departure, does not your imagination—or rather, does not your heart—suggest some expedient?'

'What is it you wish my heart to suggest?'

'Tell me, how can one prove to another, that it is wrong to be jealous?'

'In the first place, sire, by giving no motive for jealousy; in other words, in loving no one but the one in question.'

'Oh! I expected better than that.'

'What did you expect?'

'That you would simply tell me that jealous people are pacified by concealing the affection which is entertained for the object of their jealousy.'

'Dissimulation is difficult, sire.'

'Yet, it is only by means of conquering difficulties that any happiness is attained. As far as I am concerned, I swear I will give the lie to those who are jealous of me, by pretending to treat you like any other woman.'

'A bad, as well as an unsafe means,' said the young Princess, shaking her pretty head.

'You seem to think everything bad, dear Henrietta,' said Louis discontentedly. 'You reject everything I propose. Suggest at least something else in its stead. Come, try and think. I trust implicitly to a woman's invention. Do you have any ideas?'

'Well, sire, I have hit upon something. I judge by my own case. If my husband intended to put me on the wrong scent with regard to another woman, one thing would reassure me more than anything else.'

'What would that be?'

'In the first place, to see that he never took any notice of the woman in question.'

'Exactly. That is precisely what I said just now.'

'Very well; but in order to be perfectly reassured on the subject, I should like to see him occupy himself with some one else.'*

'Ah! I understand you,' replied Louis, smiling. 'But confess dear Henrietta, if the means is at least ingenious, it is hardly charitable.'

'Why so?'

'In curing the dread of a wound in a jealous person's mind, you inflict one upon his heart. His fear ceases, it is true; but the evil still exists; and that seems to me to be far worse.'

'Agreed; but he does not detect, he does not suspect the real enemy; he does no prejudice to love itself; he concentrates all his strength on the side where his strength will do no injury to anything or any one. In a word, sire, my plan, which I confess I am surprised to find you dispute, is mischievous to jealous people, it is true; but to lovers it is full of advantage. Besides, let me ask, sire, who, except yourself, has ever thought of pitying jealous people? Are they not a melancholy set of creatures, always equally unhappy, whether with or without a cause? You may remove that cause, but you do not remove their sufferings. It is a disease which lies in the imagination, and, like all imaginary disorders, it is incurable. By the bye, I remember an aphorism upon this subject, of poor Dr Dawley,* a clever and amusing man, who, had it not been for my brother, who could not do without him, I should have with me now. He used to say, "Whenever you are likely to suffer from two affections, choose that which will give you the least trouble, and I will allow you to retain it; for it is positive," he said, "that that very one is of the greatest service to me in order to enable me to get rid of the other."'

'Well and judiciously remarked, dear Henrietta,' replied the King, smiling.

'Oh! we have some clever people in London, sire.'

'And those clever people produce adorable pupils. I will grant this Daley, Darley, Dawley, or whatever you call him, a pension for his aphorism, but I entreat you, Henrietta, to begin by choosing the least of your evils. You do not answer—you smile. I guess that the least of your evils is your stay in France. I will allow you to retain this misfortune; and, in order to begin with the cure of the other, I will this very day begin to look out for a subject which shall divert the attention of the jealous members of either sex who persecute us both.'

'Hush! this time some one is really coming,' said Madame, and she stooped down to gather a flower from the thick grass at her feet. Some one, in fact, was approaching; for, suddenly, a bevy of young girls ran down from the top of the little hillock, following the cavaliers—the cause of this irruption being a magnificent hawk-moth, with wings like rose-leaves. The prey in question had fallen into the net of Mademoiselle de Tonnay-Charente, who displayed it with some pride to her less successful rival. The Queen of the chase had seated herself some twenty paces from the bank on which Louis and Madame Henrietta were reclining; and leaned her back against a magnificent oak-tree entwined with ivy, and stuck the butterfly on the long cane she carried in her hand. Mademoiselle de Tonnay-Charente was very beautiful, and the gentlemen, accordingly, deserted her companions, and, under the pretext of complimenting her upon her success, pressed in a circle around her. The King and the Princess looked gloomily at this scene, as spectators of maturer age look on at the games of little children. 'They seem to be amusing themselves, there,' said the King.

'Greatly, sire; I have always found that people are amused wherever youth and beauty are to be found.'

'What do you think of Mademoiselle de Tonnay-Charente, Henrietta?' inquired the King.

'I think she is rather fair in complexion,' replied Madame, fixing in a moment upon the only fault it was possible to find in the almost perfect beauty of the future Madame de Montespan.*

'Rather fair, yes; but beautiful, I think, in spite of that.'

'Is that your opinion, sire?'

'Yes, really.'

'Very well; and it is mine, too.'

'And she seems to be much sought after too.'

'Oh, that is a matter of course. Lovers flutter from one to another. If we had hunted for lovers instead of butterflies, you can see, from those who surround her, what successful sport we should have had.'

'Tell me, Henrietta, what would be said, if the King were to make himself one of those lovers, and let his glance fall in that direction? Would some one else be jealous in such a case?'

'Oh! sire, Mademoiselle de Tonnay-Charente is a very efficacious remedy,' said Madame, with a sigh. 'She would cure a jealous man, certainly; but she might possibly make a woman jealous too.'

'Henrietta,' exclaimed Louis, 'you fill my heart with joy. Yes, yes; Mademoiselle de Tonnay-Charente is far too beautiful to serve as a cloak.'

'A King's cloak,' said Madame Henrietta, smiling, 'ought to be beautiful.'

'Do you advise me to do it, then?' inquired Louis.

'I! what should I say, sire, except that to give such an advice would be to supply arms against myself. It would be folly or pride to advise you to take, for the heroine of an assumed affection, a woman more beautiful than the one for whom you pretend to feel real regard.'

The King tried to take Madame's hand in his own; his eyes sought hers; and then he murmured a few words so full of tenderness, but pronounced in so low a tone, that the historian, who ought to hear everything, could not hear them. Then, speaking aloud, he said, 'Do you yourself choose for me the one who is to cure our jealous friend. To her, then, all my devotion, all my attention, all the time that I can spare from my occupations, shall be devoted. For her shall be the flower that I may pluck for you, the fond thoughts with which you have inspired me. Towards her, the glance that I dare not bestow upon you, and which ought to be able to arouse you from your indifference. But, be careful in your selection, lest, in offering her the rose which I may have plucked, I should find myself conquered by yourself; and lest my looks, my hand, my lips, should not turn immediately towards you, even were the whole world to guess my secret.'

While these words escaped from the King's lips, in a stream of wild affection, Madame blushed, breathless, happy, proud, almost intoxicated with delight. She could find nothing to say in reply; her pride and her thirst for homage were satisfied. 'I shall fail,' she said, raising her beautiful black eyes, 'but not as you beg me, for all this incense which you wish to burn on the altar of another divinity. Ah! sire, I too shall be jealous of it, and want it to be restored to me; and would not wish that a particle of it should be lost in the way. Therefore, sire, with your royal permission, I will choose one who shall appear to me the least likely to distract your attention, and who will leave my image pure and unsullied in your heart.'

'Happily for me,' said the King, 'your heart is not hard and unfeeling. If it were so, I should be alarmed at the threat you hold out; our precautions have been taken on this point, and around you, as around myself, it would be difficult to meet with a disagreeable-looking face.'

Whilst the King was speaking, Madame had risen from her seat, looked around the green sward, and after a careful and silent examination, she called the King to her side, and said, 'See yonder, sire, upon the declivity of that little hill, near that group of Guelder roses, that beautiful girl walking alone, her head down, her arms hanging by her side, with her eyes fixed upon the flowers which she crushes beneath her feet, like one who is lost in thought.'

'Mademoiselle de Vallière, do you mean?' remarked the King.

'Yes; will she not suit you, sire?'

'Why, look how thin the poor child is. She has hardly any flesh upon her bones.'

'Nay; am I stout then?'

'She is so melancholy.'

'The greater contrast to myself, who am accused of being too lively.'

'She is lame.'*

'Do you think so?'

'No doubt of it. Look; she has allowed every one to pass by her, from the fear of her defect being remarked.'

'Well, she will not run so fast as Daphné, and will not be able to escape Apollo.'*

'Henrietta,' said the King, out of temper: 'of all your maids of honour, you have really selected for me the one most full of defects.'

'Still she is one of my maids of honour.'

'Of course; but what do you mean?'

'I mean that, in order to visit this new divinity, you will not be able to do so without paying a visit to my apartments, and that, as propriety will forbid your conversing with her in private, you will be compelled to see her in my circle, to speak to me while speaking to her. I mean, in fact, that those who may be jealous, will be wrong if they suppose you come to my apartments for my sake, since you will come there for Mademoiselle de la Vallière.'

'Who happens to be lame.'

'Hardly that.'

'Who never opens her lips.'

'But who, when she does open them, displays a beautiful set of teeth.'

'Who may serve as a model for an osteologist.'

'Your favour will change her appearance.'

'Henrietta!'

'At all events you have allowed me to be the mistress.'

'Alas! yes.'

'Well, my choice is made; I impose her upon you, and you must submit.'

'Oh! I would accept one of the furies, if you were to insist upon it.'

'La Vallière is as gentle as a lamb; do not fear she will ever contradict you when you tell her you love her,' said Madame laughing.

'You are not afraid, are you, that I shall say too much to her?'

'It would be for my sake.'

'The treaty is agreed to, then?'

'And signed.'

'You will continue to show me the friendship of a brother, the attention of a brother, the gallantry of a monarch, will you not?'

'I will preserve for you a heart which has already become accustomed to beat only at your command.'

'Very well, do you not see how we have guaranteed the future by this means?'

'I hope so.'

'Will your mother cease to regard me as an enemy?'

'Yes.'

'Will Maria Theresa leave off speaking in Spanish before Monsieur, who has a horror of conversations held in foreign languages, because he always thinks he is being ill spoken of? and lastly,' continued the Princess, 'will people persist in attributing a wrongful affection to the King, when the truth is, we can be nothing to each other, except such as may arise from sympathy, free from all mental reservation?'

'Yes, yes,' said the King hesitatingly. 'But yet other things may still be said of us.'

'What can be said, sire? shall we never be left in tranquillity?'

'People will say I am deficient in taste; but what is my self-respect in comparison with your tranquillity?'

'In comparison with my honour, sire, and that of our family, you mean. Besides, believe me, do not be so hastily prejudiced against La Vallière. She is lame, it is true, but she is not deficient in good sense. Moreover, all that the King touches is converted into gold.'

'Well, Madame, be assured of one thing, namely, that I am still grateful to you; you might even yet make me pay dearer for your stay in France.'

'Sire, some one approaches.'

'Well!'

'One last word.'

'Say it.'

'You are prudent and judicious, sire; but in the present instance you will be obliged to summon to your aid all your prudence, and all your judgment.'

'Oh!' exclaimed Louis, laughing, 'from this very evening I shall begin to act my part, and you shall see whether I am not quite fit to represent the character of a tender swain. After luncheon, there will be a promenade in the forest, and then there is supper and the ballet at ten o'clock.'

'I know it.'

'The ardour of my passion shall blaze more brilliantly than the fireworks, shall shine more steadily than the lamps of our friend Colbert; it shall shine so dazzlingly that the Queens and Monsieur shall be almost blinded by it.'

'Take care, sire, take care.'

'In Heaven's name what have I done, then?'

'I shall begin to recall the compliments I paid you just now. You prudent! you wise! did I say? why you begin by the most reckless inconsistencies. Can a passion be kindled in this manner, like a torch, in a moment? Can a monarch, such as you are, without any preparation, fall at the feet of a girl like La Vallière?'

'Ah! Henrietta, now I understand you. We have not yet begun the campaign, and you are plundering me already.'

'No; I am only recalling you to common-sense ideas. Let your passion be kindled gradually, instead of allowing it to burst forth so suddenly. Jove's thunders and lightnings are heard and seen before the palace is set on fire. Everything has its commencement. If you are so easily excited, no one will believe you are really captivated, and every one will think you out of your senses—unless, indeed, the truth itself be not guessed. People are not always so foolish as they seem.'

The King was obliged to admit that Madame was an angel for good sense, and the very reverse for cleverness. He bowed, and said: 'Agreed, Madame, I will think over my plan of attack; great military men—my cousin de Condé* for instance—grow pale in meditation upon their strategic plans, before they move one of the pawns, which people call armies; I therefore wish to draw up a complete plan of attack, for, you know, that the tender passion is subdivided in a variety of ways. Well, then, I shall stop at the village of Little Attentions, at the hamlet of Love-Letters, before I follow the road of Visible affection; the way is clear enough you know, and poor Madame de Scudéry would never forgive me for passing through a halting-place without stopping.'*

'Oh! now we have returned to our proper senses, shall we say adieu, sire?'

'Alas! it must be so, for, see, we are interrupted.'

'Yes, indeed,' said Madame Henrietta, 'they are bringing Mademoiselle de Tonnay-Charente and her sphinx butterfly in grand procession this way.'

'It is perfectly well understood, then, that this evening during the promenade, I am to make my escape into the forest, and finding La Vallière without you.'

'I will take care to send her away.'

'Very well! I will speak to her when she is with her companions, and I will then discharge my first arrow at her.'

'Be skilful,' said Madame, laughing, 'and do not miss the heart.'

And the Princess took leave of the King, and went forward to meet the merry troop, which was advancing with much ceremony, and a great many pretended flourishes of trumpets, which they imitated with their mouths.

XXI

THE BALLET OF THE SEASONS

AT the conclusion of the banquet, which had been served at five o'clock, the King entered his cabinet, where his tailors were awaiting him, for the purpose of trying on the celebrated costume* representing Spring, which was the result of so much imagination, and had cost so many efforts of thought to the designers and ornament-workers of the court. As for the ballet itself, every person knew the part he had to take in it, and how to perform that part. The King had resolved to make it a matter of surprise. Hardly, therefore, had he finished his conference, and entered his own apartment, than he desired his two masters of the ceremonies, Villeroy* and Saint-Aignan to be sent for. Both replied that they only awaited his orders, and that everything was ready to begin, but that it was necessary to ensure fine weather and a favourable night before those orders could be carried out. The King opened his window; the golden hues of evening could be seen in the horizon through the vistas of the wood, and the moon, white as snow, was already visible in the heavens. Not a ripple could be noticed on the surface of the green waters; the swans themselves even, reposing with folded wings like ships at anchor, seemed penetrated by the warmth of the air, the freshness of the water and the silence of the beautiful evening. The King, having observed all these things, and contemplated the magnificent picture before him, gave the order which de Villeroy and de Saint-Aignan awaited; but, with the view of ensuring the execution of this order in a royal manner, one last question was necessary, and Louis XIV put it to the two gentlemen, in the following manner:—'Have you any money?'

'Sire,' replied Saint-Aignan, 'we have arranged everything with M. Colbert.'

'Ah! very well!'

'Yes, sire, and M. Colbert said he would wait upon your Majesty, as soon as your Majesty should manifest an intention of carrying out the fêtes, of which he has furnished the programme.'

'Let him come in, then,' said the King; and as if Colbert had been listening at the door for the purpose of keeping himself *au courant* of the conversation, he entered as soon as the King had pronounced his name before the two courtiers.

'Ah! M. Colbert,' said the King. 'Gentlemen, to your posts;' whereupon Saint-Aignan and Villeroy took their leave. The King seated himself in an easy-chair near the window, saying: 'The ballet will take place this evening, M. Colbert.'

'In that case, sire, I settle the accounts to-morrow.'

'Why so?'

'I promised the tradespeople to pay their bills the following day to that on which the ballet should take place.'

'Very well, M. Colbert, pay them, since you have promised to do so.'

'Certainly, sire; but I must have money to do that.'

'What! have not the four millions, which M. Fouquet promised, been sent? I had forgot then to ask you about it.'

'Sire, they were sent at the hour promised.'

'Well?'

'Well, sire, the coloured lamps, the fireworks, the musicians, and the cooks have swallowed up four millions in eight days.'

'Entirely?'

'To the last penny. Every time your Majesty directed the banks of the grand canal to be illuminated, as much oil was consumed as there was water in the basins.'

'Well, well, M. Colbert; the fact is, then, you have no more money?'

'I have no more, sire, but M. Fouquet has,' Colbert replied, his face darkening with a sinister expression of pleasure.

'What do you mean?' inquired Louis.

'We have already made M. Fouquet advance six millions. He has given them with too much grace, not to have others still to give, if they are required, which is the case at the present moment. It is necessary, therefore, that he should comply.'

The King frowned. 'M. Colbert,' said he, accentuating the financier's name, 'that is not the way I understood the matter; I do not wish to make use, against any of my servants, of a means of pressure which may oppress him and fetter his services. In eight days M. Fouquet has furnished six millions, that is a good sum.'

Colbert turned pale. 'And yet,' he said, 'your Majesty did not use this language some time ago, when the news about Belle-Isle arrived, for instance.'

'You are right, M. Colbert.'

'Nothing, however, has changed since then; on the contrary, indeed.'

'In my thoughts, monsieur, everything is changed.'

'Does your Majesty, then, no longer believe the machinations?'

'My own affairs concern me alone, monsieur; and I have already told you I transact them myself.'

'Then I perceive,' said Colbert, trembling from anger and from fear, 'that I have had the misfortune to fall into disgrace with your Majesty.'

'Not at all; you are, on the contrary, most agreeable to me.'

'Yet, sire,' said the minister, with a certain affected bluntness, so successful when it was a question of flattering Louis's self-esteem, 'what use is there in being agreeable to your Majesty if one can no longer be of any use to you?'

'I reserve your services for a better occasion; and, believe me, they will only be the better appreciated.'

'Your Majesty's plan, then, in this affair, is——'

'You want money, M. Colbert?'

'Seven hundred thousand francs, sire.'

'You will take them from my private treasure.' Colbert bowed. 'And,' added Louis, 'as it seems a difficult matter for you, notwithstanding your economy, to defray, with so limited a sum, the expenses which I intend to incur, I will at once sign an order for three millions.'

The King took a pen and signed an order immediately, then handed it to Colbert. 'Be satisfied, M. Colbert, the plan I have adopted is one worthy of a King,' said Louis XIV, who pronounced these words with all the majesty he knew how to assume in such circumstances; and he dismissed Colbert for the purpose of giving an audience to his tailors.

The order issued by the King was known in the whole of Fontainebleau; it was already known, too, that the King was trying on his costume, and that the ballet would be danced in the evening. The news circulated with the rapidity of lightning; during its progress it kindled every variety of coquetry, desire,

and wild ambition. At the same moment, and as if by enchantment, every one who knew how to hold a needle, every one who
could distinguish a coat from a pair of trousers, was summoned
to the assistance of those who had received invitation. The King
had completed his toilet at nine o'clock; he appeared in an open
carriage decorated with branches of trees and flowers. The Queens
had taken their seats upon a magnificent dais or platform, erected
upon the borders of the lake, in a theatre of wonderful elegance
of construction. In the space of five hours the carpenters had put
together all the different parts connected with the theatre; the
upholsterers had laid down the carpets, erected the seats; and,
as if at the signal of an enchanter's wand, a thousand arms,
aiding instead of interfering with each other, had constructed
the building on this spot amidst the sound of music; whilst, at
the same time, other workmen illuminated the theatre and the
shores of the lake with an incalculable number of lamps. As the
heavens, set with stars, were perfectly unclouded, as not even a
breath of air could be heard in the woods, and as if Nature
herself had yielded complaisantly to the King's fancies, the back
of the theatre had been left open, so that, behind the foreground
of the scenes, could be seen as a background the beautiful sky,
glittering with stars; the sheet of water, illumined by the lights
which were reflected in it; and the bluish outline of the grand
masses of woods, with their rounded tops. When the King made
his appearance, the whole theatre was full, and presented to the
view one vast group, dazzling with gold and precious stones; in
which, however, at the first glance, no one single face could be
distinguished. By degrees, as the sight became accustomed to so
much brilliancy, the rarest beauties appeared to the view, as in
the evening sky the stars appear one by one to him who closes
his eyes and then opens them again.

The theatre represented a grove of trees;* a few fauns lifting
up their cloven feet were jumping about; a dryad made her
appearance on the scene, and was immediately pursued by them;
others gathered round her for her defence, and they quarrelled
as they danced. Suddenly, for the purpose of restoring peace
and order, Spring, accompanied by his whole court, made his
appearance. The Elements, the subaltern powers of mythology,
together with their attributes, precipitated themselves upon the

trace of their gracious sovereign. The Seasons, the allies of Spring, followed him closely to form a quadrille, which, after many words of more or less flattering import, was the commencement of the dance. The music, oboes, flutes, and viols were descriptive of the rural delights. The King had already made his appearance, amid thunders of applause. He was dressed in a tunic of flowers, which set off his easy and well-formed figure to advantage. His legs, the best-shaped at the court, were also displayed to great advantage in flesh-coloured silken hose, of silk so fine and so transparent that it seemed almost like flesh itself. The most beautiful pale-lilac satin shoes, with bows of flowers and leaves, imprisoned his small feet. The bust of the figure was in harmonious keeping with the base; the waving hair was floating on his shoulders, the freshness of his complexion was enhanced by the brilliancy of his beautiful blue eyes, which softly kindled all hearts; a mouth with tempting lips which deigned to open in smiles.—Such was the prince of the period, who had that evening been justly named 'The King of all the Loves'. There was something in his carriage which resembled the buoyant movements of an immortal, and he did not dance so much as seem to soar along. His entrance had produced, therefore, the most brilliant effect. Suddenly the Comte de Saint-Aignan was observed, endeavouring to approach either the King or Madame.

The Princess—who was clothed in a long dress, diaphanous and light as the finest network tissue from the hands of the skilful Mechlin* workers, her knee occasionally revealed beneath the folds of the tunic, and her little feet encased in silken shoes—advanced, radiant with beauty, accompanied by a laughing group of Bacchantes, and had already reached the spot which had been assigned to her in the dance. The applause continued so long that the Comte had ample leisure to join the King.

'What is the matter, Saint-Aignan?' said Spring.

'Nothing whatever,' replied the courtier, as pale as death; 'but your Majesty has not thought of the Fruits.'

'Yes; it is suppressed.'

'Far from it, sire; your Majesty having given no directions about it, the musicians have retained it.'

'How excessively annoying,' said the King. 'This figure cannot be performed, since M. de Guiche is absent. It must be suppressed.'

'Oh, sire, a quarter of an hour's music without any dancing, will produce an effect so chilling as to ruin the success of the ballet.'

'But, Comte, since——'

'Oh, sire, that is not the greatest misfortune; for, after all, the orchestra could still just as well cut it out, if it were necessary; but——'

'But what?'

'Why, M. de Guiche is here.'*

'Here?' replied the King, frowning, 'here? Are you sure?'

'Yes, sire; and ready dressed for the ballet.'

The King felt himself colour deeply, and said, 'You are probably mistaken.'

'So little is that the case, sire, that if your Majesty will look to the right, you will see that the Comte is waiting.'

Louis turned hastily towards the side, and, in fact, on his right, brilliant in his character of Autumn, de Guiche awaited until the King should look at him, in order that he might address him. To describe the stupefaction of the King, that of Monsieur, who was moving about restlessly in his box,—to describe also the agitated movement of the heads in the theatre, and the strange emotion of Madame, at the sight of her partner,—is a task we must leave to more able hands. The King stood almost gaping with astonishment as he looked at the Comte, who, bowing lowly, approached His Majesty with the profoundest respect.

'Sire,' he said, 'your Majesty's most devoted servant approaches to perform a service on this occasion with similar zeal to that he has already shown on the field of battle. Your Majesty, in omitting the dance of the Fruits, would be losing the most beautiful scene in the ballet. I did not wish to be the cause of so great a prejudice to your Majesty's elegance, skill, and graceful address; and I have left my tenants in order to place my services at your Majesty's commands.'

Every word fell distinctly, in perfect harmony and eloquence, upon Louis XIV's ears. Their flattery pleased, as much as de

Guiche's courage had astonished him, and he simply replied, 'I did not tell you to return, Comte.'

'Certainly not, sire, but your Majesty did not tell me to remain.'

The King perceived that time was passing away, that if the scene were prolonged it might complicate everything, and that a single cloud upon the picture would effectually spoil the whole. Besides, the King's heart was filled with two or three new ideas: he had just derived fresh inspiration from the eloquent glances of Madame. Her look had said to him, 'Since they are jealous of you, divide their suspicions, for the man who distrusts two rivals does not distrust either in particular.' So that Madame, by this clever diversion, decided him. The King smiled upon de Guiche, who did not comprehend a word of Madame's dumb language, but only remarked that she pretended not to look at him; and he attributed the pardon which had been conferred upon him to the Princess's kindness of heart. The King seemed pleased with every one present. Monsieur was the only one who did not understand anything about the matter. The ballet began; the effect was more than beautiful. When the music, by its bursts of melody, carried away these illustrious dancers, when the simple, untutored pantomime of that period (made cruder still by the very indifferent acting of the august actors) had reached its culminating point of triumph, the theatre almost shook with the tumultuous applause.

De Guiche shone like a sun, but like a courtly sun, which is resigned to fill a subordinate part. Disdainful of a success of which Madame showed no acknowledgement, he thought of nothing but of boldly regaining the marked preference of the Princess. She, however, did not bestow a single glance upon him. By degrees all his happiness, all his brilliancy subsided into regret and uneasiness; so that his limbs lost their power, his arms hung heavily by his side, and his head seemed stupefied. The King, who had from this moment become in reality the principal dancer in the quadrille, cast a look upon his vanquished rival. De Guiche soon ceased to sustain even the character of the courtier; without applause, he danced indifferently, and very soon could not dance at all, by which means the triumph of the King and of Madame was assured.

XXII

THE NYMPHS OF THE PARK OF FONTAINEBLEAU

THE King remained for a moment to enjoy a triumph which was as complete as it could possibly be. He then turned towards Madame, for the purpose of admiring her also, a little, in her turn. Young persons love with more vivacity, perhaps with greater ardour and deeper passion, than others more advanced in years; but all the other feelings are at the same time developed in proportion to their youth and vigour; so that vanity being with them almost always the equivalent of love, the latter feeling, according to the laws of equipoise, never attains that degree of perfection which it acquires in men and women from thirty to five-and-thirty years of age.* Louis thought of Madame, but only after he had carefully thought of himself; and Madame carefully thought of herself, without bestowing a single thought upon the King. The victim, however, of all these royal affections and vanities was poor de Guiche. Every one could observe his agitation and prostration—a prostration which was, indeed, the more remarkable since people were not accustomed to see him with his arms hanging listlessly by his side, his head bewildered, and his eyes with their bright intelligence gone. It rarely happened that any uneasiness was excited on his account, whenever a question of elegance or taste was under discussion, and de Guiche's defeat was accordingly attributed by the greater number present to his courtier-like tact and ability. But there were others —keen-sighted observers are always to be met with at court— who remarked his paleness and his altered looks, which he could neither feign nor conceal, and their conclusion was that de Guiche was not acting the part of a flatterer. All these sufferings, successes, and remarks, were blended, confounded, and lost in the uproar of applause. When, however, the Queens had expressed their satisfaction and the spectators their enthusiasm, when the King had retired to his dressing-room to change his costume, and whilst Monsieur, dressed as a woman, as he delighted to be, was, in his turn, dancing about, de Guiche, who had now recovered himself, approached Madame, who, seated at the back of the theatre, was waiting for the second part, and had quitted the others for the purpose of creating a sort of solitude for herself in the midst of the crowd, to meditate, as it were, beforehand, upon choreographic effects; and it will be perfectly understood that, absorbed in deep meditation, she did not see, or rather she pretended not to see, anything that was passing around her. De Guiche, observing that she was alone, near a thicket constructed of painted cloth, approached her. Two of her maids of honour, dressed as hamadryads,* seeing de Guiche advance, drew back out of respect, whereupon de Guiche proceeded towards the middle of the circle and saluted Her Royal Highness; but, whether she did or did not observe his salutation, the Princess did not even turn her head. A cold shiver passed through poor de Guiche; he was unprepared for so utter an indifference, for he had neither seen nor been told of anything that had taken place, and consequently could guess nothing. Remarking, therefore, that his obeisance obtained him no acknowledgement, he advanced one step farther, and in a voice which he tried, though uselessly, to render calm, said, 'I have the honour to present my most humble respects to your Royal Highness.'

Upon this Madame deigned to turn her eyes languishingly towards the Comte, observing, 'Ah! M. de Guiche, is that you; good-day to you!'

The Comte's patience almost forsook him, as he continued,—'Your Royal Highness danced just now most charmingly.'

'Do you think so?' she replied, with indifference.

'Yes; the character which your Royal Highness assumed is in perfect harmony with your own.'

Madame again turned round and, looking de Guiche full in the face with a bright and steady gaze, said,—'Why so?'

'You represent a divinity, beautiful, disdainful, and inconstant.'

'You mean Pomona,* Comte?'

'I allude to the goddess you represent.'

Madame remained silent for a moment, with her lips compressed, and then observed,—'But, Comte, you, too, are an excellent dancer.'

'Nay, madame, I am only one of those who are never noticed, or who are soon forgotten if they ever happen to be noticed.'

With this remark, accompanied by one of those deep sighs which affect the remotest fibres of one's being, he bowed breathlessly, and withdrew behind a thicket. The only reply Madame condescended to make was by slightly raising her shoulders, and, as her ladies of honour had retired while the conversation lasted, she recalled them by a look. The ladies were Mademoiselle de Tonnay-Charente and Mademoiselle de Montalais.

'Did you hear what the Comte de Guiche said?' the Princess inquired.

'No.'

'It really is very singular,' she continued, 'how exile has affected poor M. de Guiche's wit.' And then, in a louder voice, fearful lest her unhappy victim might miss a syllable, she said,—'In the first place, he danced badly, and then afterwards his remarks were very silly.'

She then stood up, humming the air to which she was presently going to dance. De Guiche had overheard everything. The arrow had pieced his heart and wounded him mortally. Then, at the risk of interrupting the progress of the fête by his confusion, he fled from the scene, tearing his beautiful costume of Autumn in pieces, and scattering, as he went along, the branches of vines, mulberry, and almond trees, with all the other artificial attributes of his divinity. A quarter of an hour afterwards he had returned to the theatre; but it will be readily believed, that it was only a powerful effort of reason over his emotions that had enabled him to return; or perhaps, for the heart is so constituted, he found it impossible even to remain much longer separated from the presence of one who had broken that heart. Madame was finishing her figure. She saw, but did not look at, de Guiche, who, heated and furious, turned his back upon her as she passed him, escorted by her nymphs, and followed by a hundred flatterers. During this time, at the other end of the theatre, near the lake, a young woman was seated, with her eyes fixed upon one of the windows of the theatre, from which were issuing streams of light, the window in question being that of the royal box. As de Guiche left the theatre for the purpose of getting into the fresh air he so much needed, he passed close to this figure and saluted her. When she perceived the young man, she rose, like a woman surprised in the midst of ideas she was desirous of concealing from herself. De Guiche stopped as he recognised her, and said hurriedly,—'Good evening, Mademoiselle de la Vallière; I am indeed fortunate in meeting you.'

'I, also, M. de Guiche, am glad of this accidental meeting,' said the young girl, as she was about to withdraw.

'Pray do not leave me,' said de Guiche, stretching out his hand towards her, 'for you would be contradicting the kind words you have just pronounced. Remain, I implore you; the evening is most lovely. You wish to escape from this tumult, and prefer your own society. Well, I can understand it; all women possessed of any feeling do, and you will never find them dull or lonely when removed from the giddy vortex of these exciting amusements. Oh! heavens!' he exclaimed suddenly.

'What is the matter, Monsieur le Comte?' inquired La Vallière, with some anxiety. 'You seem agitated.'

'I! oh, no!'

'Will you allow me, M. de Guiche, to return you the thanks I proposed to offer you on the very first opportunity. It is to your recommendation, I am aware, that I owe my admission among the number of Madame's maids of honour.'

'Indeed! Ah! I remember now, and I congratulate myself. Do you love any one?'

'I!' exclaimed La Vallière.

'Forgive me, I hardly know what I am saying; a thousand times forgive me; Madame was right, quite right, this brutal exile has completely turned my brain.'

'And yet it seemed to me that the King received you with kindness.'

'Do you think so? Received me with kindness—perhaps so—yes——'

'There cannot be a doubt he received you kindly; for in fact, you have returned without his permission.'

'Quite true, and I believe you are right. But have you not seen M. Bragelonne here?'

La Vallière started at the name. 'Why do you ask?' she inquired.

'Have I offended you again?' said de Guiche. 'In that case, I am indeed unhappy, and greatly to be pitied.'

'Yes, very unhappy and very much to be pitied, Monsieur de Guiche, for you seem to be suffering terribly.'

'Oh! mademoiselle, why have I not a devoted sister,* or a true friend, such as yourself?'

'You have friends, Monsieur de Guiche, and the Vicomte de Bragelonne, of whom you spoke just now, is, I believe, one of them.'

'Yes, yes, you are right. He is one of my best friends. Farewell, Mademoiselle de la Vallière, farewell.' And he fled, like one possessed, along the banks of the lake. His dark shadow glided, lengthening, as it disappeared among the illumined yews and glittering undulations of the water. La Vallière looked after him, saying,—'Yes, yes, he, too, is suffering, and I begin to understand why.'

She had hardly finished when her companions, Mademoiselle de Montalais and Mademoiselle de Tonnay-Charente, ran forward. They were released from their attendance, and had changed their costumes of nymphs; delighted with the beautiful night, and the success of the evening, they returned to look after their companion.

'What, already here!' they said to her. 'We thought we should be the first at the rendezvous.'

'I have been here this quarter of an hour,' replied La Vallière.

'Did not the dancing amuse you?'

'No.'

'But surely the whole spectacle?'

'No more than the dancing. As far as a spectacle is concerned, I much prefer that which these dark woods present, in whose depths can be seen now in one direction, and now in another, a light passing by, as though it were an eye, bright red in colour, sometimes open at others closed.'

'La Vallière is quite a poet,' said Tonnay-Charente.

'In other words,' said Montalais, 'she is insupportable. Whenever there is a question of laughing a little, or of amusing ourselves with anything, La Vallière starts to cry; whenever we girls have reason to cry, because, perhaps we have mislaid our dresses, or because our vanity has been wounded or our costume fails to produce any effect, La Vallière laughs.'

'As far as I am concerned, that is not my character,' said Mademoiselle de Tonnay-Charente. 'I am a woman, there are few like me; whoever loves me, flatters me; whoever flatters me, pleases me; and whoever pleases—'

'Well!' said Montalais, 'you do not finish.'

'It is too difficult,' replied Mademoiselle de Tonnay-Charente, laughing loudly. 'Do you, who are so clever, finish for me.'

'And you, Louise?' said Montalais, 'does any one please you?'

'That is a matter which concerns no one but myself,' replied the young girl rising from the mossy bank on which she had been reclining during the whole time the ballet had lasted. 'Now, mesdemoiselles, we have agreed to amuse ourselves to-night without any one to overlook us, and without any escort. We are three in number, we like one another, and the night is lovely; look yonder, do you not see the moon slowly rising, silvering the topmost branches of the chestnuts and the oaks. Oh! beautiful walk! dear liberty! the beautiful soft turf of the woods, the happiness which your friendship confers upon me! let us walk arm-in-arm towards those large trees. Out yonder all are at this moment seated at table or fully occupied, or preparing to adorn themselves for a set and formal promenade; horses are being saddled, or harnessed to the carriages—the Queen's mules or Madame's four white ponies. As for ourselves, we shall soon reach some retired spot where no eye can see us and no step follow ours. Do you not remember, Montalais, the woods of Cheverney and of Chambord, the numberless poplars of Blois, where we exchanged some of our mutual hopes?'*

'And many confidences also?'

'Yes.'

'Well,' said Mademoiselle de Tonnay-Charente, 'I also think a good deal; but I take care——'

'To say nothing,' said Montalais, 'so that when Mademoiselle de Tonnay-Charente thinks, Athenaïs is the only one who knows it.'

'Hush!' said Mademoiselle de Tonnay-Charente, 'I hear steps approaching from this side.'

'Quick, quick, then, among the high reed-grass,' said Montalais; 'stoop, Athenaïs, you are so tall.'

Mademoiselle de Tonnay-Charente stooped as she was told, and almost at the same moment, they saw two gentlemen approaching, their heads bent down, walking arm-in-arm, on the fine gravel walk running parallel with the bank. The young girls had, indeed, made themselves small, for nothing was to be seen of them.

'It is Monsieur de Guiche,' whispered Montalais in Mademoiselle de Tonnay-Charente's ear.

'It is Monsieur de Bragelonne,' whispered the latter to La Vallière.

The two young men approached still closer, conversing in animated voices. 'She was here just now,' said the Count. 'If I had only seen her, I should have declared it to be a vision, but I spoke to her.'

'You are positive, then?'

'Yes; but perhaps I frightened her.'

'In what way?'

'Oh! I was still half mad, at what you know, so that she could hardly have understood what I was saying, and must have become alarmed.'

'Oh!' said Bragelonne, 'do not make yourself uneasy; she is all kindness and will excuse you; she is clearsighted, and will understand.'

'Yes, but if she should have understood, and understood too well, she may talk.'

'You do not know Louise, Count,' said Raoul. 'Louise possesses every virtue and has not a single fault.' And the two young men passed on, and, as they proceeded their voices were soon lost in the distance.

'How is it, La Vallière,' said Mademoiselle de Tonnay-Charente, 'that the Vicomte de Bragelonne spoke of you as Louise?'

'We were brought up together,' replied Louise, blushing; 'M. de Bragelonne has honoured me by asking my hand in marriage, but——'

'Well?'

'It seems the King will not consent to the marriage.'

'Eh! Why the King? and what has the King to do with it?' exclaimed Aure sharply. 'Good gracious! has the King right to interfere in matters of that kind? Politics are politics, as M. de Mazarin used to say; but love is love. If, therefore, you love M. de Bragelonne, marry him; I give my consent.'

Athenaïs began to laugh.

'Oh! I speak seriously,' replied Montalais, 'and my opinion in this case is quite as good as the King's, I suppose, is it not, Louise?'

'Come,' said La Vallière, 'those gentlemen have passed. Let us take advantage of our being alone to cross the open ground, and so take refuge in the wood.'

'So much the better,' said Athenaïs, 'because I see the torches setting out from the château and the theatre, which seem as if they were preceding some persons of distinction.'

'Let us run, then,' said all three, and, gracefully lifting up the long skirts of their silk dresses, they lightly ran across the open space between the lake and the thickest covert of the park. Montalais agile as a deer, Athenaïs eager as a young wolf, bounded through the dry grass, and now and then, some bold Acteon,* might, by the aid of the faint light, have perceived their straight and well-formed limbs somewhat beneath the heavy folds of their satin petticoats. La Vallière, more refined and less bashful, allowed her dress to flow around her; retarded also by the lameness of her foot, it was not long before she called out to her companions to halt, and, left behind, she obliged them both to wait for her. At this moment, a man, concealed in a dry ditch full of willow saplings, scrambled quickly up its shelving side, and ran off in the direction of the château. The three young girls, on their side, reached the outskirts of the park, every path of which they well knew. The ditches were bordered by high hedges full of flowers, which on that side protected the foot-passengers from being intruded upon by the horses and carriages. In fact, the sound of Madame's and of the Queen's carriages could be heard in the distance upon the hard dry ground of the roads, followed by the mounted cavaliers. Distant music was heard in response, and when the soft notes died away, the nightingale, with his song full of pride, poured forth his melodious chants, and his most complicated, learned, and sweetest compositions to those who he perceived had met beneath the thick covert of the woods. Near the songster, in the dark background of the large trees, could be seen the glistening eyes of an owl, attracted by the harmony. In this way, the fête for the whole court was a fête also for the mysterious inhabitants of the forest; for certainly the deer from the brake, the pheasant on the branch, the fox in its hole, were all listening. One could realise the life led by this nocturnal and invisible population from the restless movements which suddenly took place among the leaves. Our sylvan nymphs uttered a slight cry, but, reassured immediately afterwards, they laughed, and resumed their walk. In this manner they reached the royal oak, the venerable relic of an oak which in its earlier days had listened to the sighs of Henry II for the beautiful Diana of Poitiers, and later still to those of Henry IV for the lovely Gabrielle d'Estrées.* Beneath this oak the gardeners had piled up the moss and turf in such a manner that never had a seat more luxuriously reposed the wearied limbs of any monarch. The trunk of the tree, somewhat rough to recline against, was sufficiently large to accommodate the three young girls, whose voices were lost among the branches, which stretched downwards towards the trunk.

XXIII

UNDER THE ROYAL OAK

THE softness of the air, the stillness of the foliage, tacitly imposed upon these young girls an engagement to change immediately their giddy conversation for one of a more serious character. She, indeed, whose disposition was the most lively—Montalais, for instance—was the first to yield to its influence; and she began by heaving a deep sigh, and saying:—'What happiness to be here alone, and at liberty, with every right to be frank, especially towards each other.'

'Yes,' said Mademoiselle de Tonnay-Charente; 'for the court, however brilliant it may be, has always some falsehood concealed beneath the folds of its velvet robes, or beneath the blaze of its diamonds.'

'I,' replied La Vallière, 'I never tell a falsehood; when I cannot speak the truth, I remain silent.'

'You will not remain long in favour,' said Montalais; 'it is not here, as it was at Blois, where we told the dowager Madame all our little annoyances, and all our longings. There were certain days when Madame remembered that she herself had been young, and, on those days, whoever talked with her found in her a sincere friend. She related to us her flirtations with Monsieur, and we told her of the flirtations she had had with others, or, at least, the rumours of them which had been spread abroad. Poor woman, so simple-minded! she laughed at them, as we did. Where is she now?'

'Oh, Montalais,—laughter-loving Montalais!' cried La Vallière; 'you see you are sighing again; the woods inspire you, and you are almost reasonable this evening.'

'You ought not, either of you,' said Athenaïs, 'to regret the court at Blois so much, unless you do not feel happy with us. A court is a place where men and women resort to talk of matter which mothers, guardians, and especially confessors, so severely denounce.'

'Oh, Athenaïs!' said Louise, blushing.

'Athenaïs is frank to-night,' said Montalais; 'let us avail ourselves of it.'

'Yes, let us take advantage of it, for this evening I could divulge the dearest secrets of my heart.'

'Ah, if M. de Montespan* were here!' said Montalais.

'Do you think that I care for M. de Montespan?' murmured the beautiful young girl.

'He is handsome, I believe?'

'Yes. And that is no small advantage in my eyes.'

'There now, you see——'

'I will go further, and say, that of all the men whom one sees here, he is the handsomest, and the most——'

'What was that?' said La Vallière, starting suddenly from the mossy bank.

'A deer which hurried by, perhaps.'

'I am only afraid of men,' said Athenaïs.

'When they do not resemble M. de Montespan.'

'A truce to this raillery. M. de Montespan is attentive to me, but that does not commit me in any way. Is not M. de Guiche here, he who is so devoted to Madame?'

'Poor fellow!' said La Vallière.

'Why poor? Madame is sufficiently beautiful, and of sufficiently high rank, is she not?'

La Vallière shook her head sorrowfully, saying, 'When one loves, it is neither beauty nor rank;—when one loves, it should be the heart, or the eyes only, of him, or of her, whom one loves.'

Montalais began to laugh loudly. 'Heart, eyes,' she said; 'oh, sugar-plums!'

'I speak for myself,' replied La Vallière.

'Noble sentiments,' said Athenaïs, with an air of protection, but with indifference.

'Are they not your own?' said Louise.

'Perfectly so; but to continue; how can one pity a man who bestows his attentions upon such a woman as Madame? If any disproportion exists, it is on the Count's side.'

'Oh! no, no,' returned La Vallière; 'it is on Madame's side.'

'Explain yourself.'

'I will. Madame has not even a wish to know what love is. She diverts herself with the feeling, as children do with fireworks, of which a spark might set a palace on fire. It makes a display, and that is all she cares about. Besides, pleasure and love form the tissue of which she wishes her life to be woven. M. de Guiche will love this illustrious personage, but she will never love him.'

Athenaïs laughed disdainfully. 'Do people really love?' she said. 'Where are the noble sentiments you just now uttered? Does not a woman's virtue consist in the courageous refusal of every intrigue which might compromise her? A properly regulated woman, endowed with a generous heart, ought to look at men, make herself loved—adored, even, by them, and say, at the very utmost, but once in her life, "I begin to think that I ought not to have been what I am,—I should have detested this one less than the others."'

'Therefore,' exclaimed La Vallière, 'that is what M. de Montespan has to expect.'

'Certainly; he, as well as every one else. What! have I not said that I admit he possesses a certain superiority, and would not that be enough? My dear child, a woman is a queen during the whole period nature permits her to enjoy sovereign power,—from fifteen to thirty-five years of age. After that, we are free to have a heart, when we only have that left——'

'Oh, oh!' murmured La Vallière.

'Excellent,' cried Montalais; 'a wife and mistress combined in one. Athenaïs, you will make your way in the world.'

'Do you not approve of what I say?'

'Completely,' replied her laughing companion.

'You are not serious, Montalais?' said Louise.

'Yes, yes; I approve everything Athenaïs has just said; only——'

'Only what?'

'Well, I cannot carry it out. I have the firmest principles; I form resolutions beside which the laws of the Stadtholder* and of the King of Spain are child's play; but, when the moment arrives to put them into execution, nothing comes of them.'

'Your courage fails,' said Athenaïs scornfully.

'Miserably so.'

'Great weakness of nature,' returned Athenaïs. 'But at least you make a choice.'

'Why, no. It pleases fate to disappoint me in everything; I dream of emperors, and I find only——'

'Aure, Aure!' exclaimed La Vallière, 'for pity's sake, do not, for the pleasure of saying something witty, sacrifice those who love you with such devoted affection.'

'Oh, I do not trouble myself much about that; those who love me are sufficiently happy that I do not dismiss them altogether. So much the worse for myself if I have a weakness for any one, but so much the worse for others if I revenge myself upon them for it.'

'You are right,' said Athenaïs, 'and, perhaps, you too will reach the same goal. In other words, young ladies, that is termed being a coquette. Men, who are very silly in most things, are particularly so in confounding, under the term coquetry, a woman's pride, and her contrariness. I, for instance, am proud; that is to say, impregnable. I treat my admirers harshly, but without any pretension to retain them. Men call me a coquette, because they are vain enough to think I care for them. Other women—Montalais, for instance—have allowed themselves to be influenced by flattery; they would be lost were it not for that most fortunate principle of instinct which urges them to change suddenly, and punish the man whose devotion they had so recently accepted.'

'A very learned dissertation,' said Montalais, in the tone of thorough enjoyment.

'It is odious!' murmured Louise.

'Thanks to this sort of coquetry, for, indeed, that is genuine coquetry,' continued Mademoiselle de Tonnay-Charente; 'the lover who, a little while since, was puffed up with pride, a moment later is suffering at every pore of his vanity and self-esteem. He was, perhaps, already beginning to assume the airs of a conqueror, but now he retreats; he was about to assume an air of protection towards us, but he is obliged to prostrate himself once more. The result of all which is, that, instead of having a husband who is jealous and troublesome, from restraint in his conduct towards us, we have a lover always trembling in our presence, always fascinated by our attractions, and always submissive; and for this simple reason, that he finds the same woman never the same. Be convinced, therefore, of the advantage of coquetry. Possessing that, one reigns a queen among women in cases where Providence has withheld that precious faculty of holding one's heart and mind in check.'

'How clever you are,' said Montalais, 'and how well you understand the duty women owe themselves.'

'I am only settling a case of individual happiness,' said Athenaïs modestly; 'and defend myself, like all weak, loving dispositions, against the oppression of the stronger.' La Vallière did not say a word.

'Does she not approve of what we are saying?'

'Nay; only I do not understand it,' said Louise. 'You talk like those who would not be called upon to live in this world of ours.'

'And very pretty your world is,' said Montalais.

'A world,' returned Athenaïs, 'in which men worship a woman until she has fallen,—or insult her when she has fallen.'

'Who spoke to you of falling?' said Louise.

'Yours is a new theory, then; will you tell us how you intend to resist yielding to temptation, if you allow yourself to be hurried away by feelings of affection?'

'Oh!' exclaimed the young girl, raising towards the dark heavens her beautiful eyes filled with tears, 'if you did but know what a heart was, I would explain, and would convince you a loving heart is stronger than all your coquetry, and more powerful than all your pride. A woman is never truly loved, I believe; a man never loves with idolatry, except he feels himself loved in return. Let old men, whom we read of in comedies,* fancy themselves adored by coquettes. A young man is conscious of, and knows, them; if he has a fancy, or a strong desire, or an absorbing passion, for a coquette, he cannot mistake her; a coquette may drive him out of his senses, but will never make him fall in love. Love, such as I conceive it to be, is an incessant, complete, and perfect sacrifice; but it is not the sacrifice of one only of the two persons who are united. It is the perfect abnegation of two who are desirous of blending their beings into one. If I ever love, I shall implore my lover to leave me free and pure; I will tell him, what he will understand, that my heart was torn by my refusal, and he, in his love for me, aware of the magnitude of my sacrifice,—he, in his turn, I say, will show his devotion for me,—will respect me, and will not seek my ruin, to insult me when I shall have fallen, as you said just now, when uttering your blasphemies against love, such as I understand it. That is my idea of love.* And now you will tell me, perhaps, that my lover will depise me; I defy him to do so, unless he be the vilest of men, and my heart assures me that it is not such a man I should choose. A look from me will repay him for the sacrifices he makes, or it will inspire him with virtues which he would never think he possessed.'

'But, Louise,' exclaimed Montalais, 'You tell us this, and do not carry it into practice.'

'What do you mean?'

'You are adored by Raoul de Bragelonne, who worships you on both his knees. The poor fellow is made the victim of your virtue, just as he would be—nay, more than he would be even, of my coquetry, or of Athenaïs's pride.'

'This is simply a different shade of coquetry,' said Athenaïs; 'and Louise, I perceive, is a coquette without knowing it.'

'Oh!' said La Vallière.

'Yes, you may call it instinct, if you please, keenest sensibility, exquisite refinement of feeling, perpetual display of unrestrained outbreaks of affection which end in nothing. It is very artful too, and very effective. I should even, now that I reflect on it, have preferred this system of tactics to my own pride, for waging war with members of the other sex, because it offers the advantage sometimes of thoroughly convincing them; but, at the present moment, without utterly condemning myself, I declare it to be superior to the simple coquetry of Montalais.' And the two young girls began to laugh.

La Vallière alone preserved a silence, and quietly shook her head. Then, a moment after, she added, 'If you were to tell me, in the presence of a man, but a fourth part of what you have just said, or even if I were assured that you think it, I should die of shame and grief where I am now.'

'Very well; die, poor tender little darling,' replied Mademoiselle de Tonnay-Charente; 'for, if there are no men here, there are at least two women, your own friends, who declare you to be attainted and convicted of being a coquette from instinct; in other words, the most dangerous kind of coquette which the world possesses.'

'Oh! mesdemoiselles,' replied La Vallière, blushing, and almost ready to weep. Her two companions again burst out laughing.

'Very well! I shall ask Bragelonne to tell me.'

'Bragelonne?' said Athenaïs.

'Yes! Bragelonne, who is as courageous as Cæsar, and as clever and witty as M. Fouquet. Poor fellow! for twelve years* he has known you, loved you, and yet—one can hardly believe it—he has never even kissed the tips of your fingers.'

'Tell us the reason of this cruelty, you who are all heart,' said Athenaïs to La Vallière.

'I will explain it by a single word—virtue. You will perhaps deny the existence of virtue?'

'Come, Louise, tell us the truth,' said Aure, taking her by the hand.

'What do you wish me to tell you?' cried La Vallière.

'Whatever you like; but it will be useless for you to say anything, for I persist in my opinion of you. A coquette from instinct; in other words, as I have already said, and I say it again, the most dangerous of all coquettes.'

'Oh! no, no; for pity's sake do not believe that!'

'What! twelve years of extreme severity.'

'How can that be, since twelve years ago I was only five years old. The freedom of the child cannot surely be added to the young girl's account.'

'Well! you are now seventeen; three years instead of twelve. During those three years you have remained constantly and unchangeably cruel. Against you are arrayed the silent shades of Blois, the meetings when you diligently watched the stars together, the evening wanderings beneath the plantain trees, his impassioned twenty years speaking to your fourteen summers,* the fire of his glances addressed to yourself.'

'Yes, yes; but so it is!'

'Impossible!'

'But why impossible?'

'Tell us something credible and we will believe you.'

'Yet, if you were to suppose one thing.'

'What is that?'

'Suppose that I thought I was in love, and that I am not.'

'What! not in love!'

'If I have acted in a different manner to what others do when they are in love, it is because I do not love; and because my hour has not yet come.'

'Louise, Louise,' said Montalais, 'take care, or I will remind you of the remark you made just now. Raoul is not here; do not overwhelm him while he is absent; be charitable, and if, on closer inspection, you think you do not love him, tell him so, poor fellow!' and she began to laugh.

'Louise pitied M. de Guiche, just now,' said Athenaïs; 'would it be possible to detect the explanation of the indifference for the one in this compassion for the other?'

'Say what you please,' said La Vallière sadly; 'upbraid me as you like since you do not understand me.'

'Oh! oh!' replied Montalais, 'temper, sorrow, and tears. We are laughing, Louise, and are not, I assure you, quite the monsters you suppose. Look at the proud Athenaïs, as she is called; she does not love M. de Montespan, it is true, but she would be in despair if M. de Montespan were not to love her. Look at me; I laugh at M. Malicorne, but the poor fellow whom I laugh at knows very well when he may be permitted to press his lips upon my hand. And yet the eldest of us is not twenty yet! What a future before us!'

'Silly, silly girls!' murmured Louise.

'You are quite right,' said Montalais, 'and you alone have spoken words of wisdom.'

'Certainly.'

'I do not dispute it,' replied Athenaïs. 'And so it is positive you do not love poor M. de Bragelonne?'

'Perhaps she does,' said Montalais; 'she is not yet quite sure of it. But in any case, listen, Athenaïs: if M. de Bragelonne becomes free, I will give you a little friendly advice.'

'What is that?'

'To look at him well before you decide in favour of M. de Montespan.'

'Oh! in that way of considering the subject, M. de Bragelonne is not the only one whom one could look at with pleasure; M. de Guiche, for instance, has his value also.'

'He did not distinguish himself this evening,' said Montalais; 'and I know from very good authority that Madame thought him unbearable.'

'M. de Saint-Aignan produced a most brilliant effect, and I am sure that more than one person who saw him dance this evening will not soon forget him. Do you not think so, La Vallière?'

'Why do you ask me? I did not see him, nor do I know him.'

'Come, come, this must be affectation on your part; you have eyes, I imagine?'

'Excellent.'

'Then you must have seen all those who danced this evening.'

'Yes, nearly all.'

'That is a very impertinent "nearly all" for some.'

'You must take it for what it is worth.'

'Very well; now, among all those gentlemen whom you saw, which do you prefer?'

'Yes,' said Montalais, 'is it M. de Saint-Aignan, or M. de Guiche, or M.——'

'I prefer no one; I thought them all about the same.'

'Do you mean, then, that among that brilliant assembly, the first court in the world, no one pleased you?'

'I do not say that.'

'Tell us, then who your ideal is.'

'It is not an ideal being.'

'He exists, then?'

'In very truth,' exclaimed La Vallière, aroused and excited, 'I cannot understand you at all. What! you who have a heart as

I have, eyes as I have, and yet you speak of M. de Guiche, of M. de Saint-Aignan, when the King was there.' These words uttered in a precipitate manner, and in an agitated, fervid tone of voice, made her two companions, between whom she was seated, exclaim in a manner which terrified her, 'The King!'

La Vallière buried her face in her hands. 'Yes,' she murmured; 'the King! the King! Have you ever seen any one to be compared to the King?'

'You were right just now in saying you had excellent eyes, Louise, for you see a great distance; too far indeed. Alas! the King is not one upon whom our poor eyes have a right to be fixed.'

'That is too true,' cried La Vallière; 'it is not the privilege of all eyes to gaze upon the sun; but I will look upon him, even were I to be blinded in doing so.' At this moment, and as though caused by the words which had just escaped La Vallière's lips, a rustling of leaves, and of that which sounded like some silken material, was heard behind the adjoining bush. The young girls hastily rose, almost terrified out of their senses. They distinctly saw the leaves move, without observing what it was that stirred them.

'It is a wolf or a wild boar,' cried Montalais; 'fly! fly!' The three girls in the very extremity of terror, fled by the first path which presented itself, and did not stop until they had reached the verge of the wood. There, breathless, leaning against each other, feeling their hearts throb wildly, they endeavoured to collect their senses, but could only succeed in doing so after the lapse of some minutes. Perceiving, at last, the lights from the windows of the château, they decided to walk towards them. La Vallière was exhausted with fatigue, and Aure and Athenaïs were obliged to support her.

'We have escaped well,' said Montalais.

'I am greatly afraid,' said La Vallière, 'that it was something worse than a wolf. For my part, and I speak as I think, I should have preferred to have run the risk of being devoured alive by some wild animal than to have been listened to and overheard. Fool, fool, that I am! How could I have thought, how could I have said what I did.' And saying this her head bowed like the head of a reed; she felt her limbs fail, and, all her strength abandoning her, she glided almost inanimate from the arms of her companions, and sank down upon the grass.

XXIV

THE KING'S UNEASINESS

LET us leave poor La Vallière, who had fainted in the arms of her two companions, and return to the precincts of the royal oak. The young girls had hardly run twenty paces, when the sound which had so much alarmed them was renewed among the branches. A man's figure might indistinctly be perceived and putting the branches of the bushes aside, he appeared upon the verge of the wood, and perceiving that the place was empty, burst out into a peal of laughter. It is useless to say that the form in question was that of a young and handsome man, who immediately made a sign to another, who thereupon made his appearance.

'Well, sire,' said the second figure, advancing timidly, 'has your Majesty put our young sentimentalists to flight?'

'It seems so,' said the King, 'and you can show yourself without fear.'

'Take care, sire; you will be recognised.'

'But I tell you they have gone.'

'This is a most fortunate meeting, sire; and if I dared offer an opinion to your Majesty, we ought to follow them.'

'They are far away by this time.'

'They would easily allow themselves to be overtaken, especially if they knew who were following them.'

'What do you mean by that, coxcomb that you are?'

'Why, one of them seems to have taken a fancy to me, and another compared you to the sun.'

'The greater reason why we should not show ourselves, Saint-Aignan. The sun does not show himself in the night-time.'

'Upon my word, sire, your Majesty seems to have very little curiosity. In your place, I should like to know who are the two nymphs, the two dryads, the two hamadryads, who have so good an opinion of us.'

'I shall know them again very well, I assure you, without running after them.'

'By what means?'

'By their voices, of course. They belong to the court, and the one who spoke of me had a very sweet voice.'

'Ah! your Majesty permits himself to be influenced by flattery.'

'No one will ever say it is a means you make use of.'

'Forgive my stupidity, sire.'

'Come; let us go and look where I told you.'

'Is the passion, then, which your Majesty confided to me, already forgotten.'

'Oh! no, indeed. How is it possible to forget such beautiful eyes as Mademoiselle de la Vallière has?'

'Yet the other had so sweet a voice.'

'Which one?'

'She who has fallen in love with the sun.'

'M. de Saint-Aignan!'

'Forgive me, sire.'

'Well, I am not sorry you should believe me to be an admirer of sweet voices, as well as of beautiful eyes. I know you to be a terrible talker, and to-morrow I shall have to pay for the confidence I have shown you.'

'What do you mean, sire?'

'That to-morrow every one will know that I have designs upon this little La Vallière; but be careful, de Saint-Aignan. I have confided my secret to no one but you, and, if any one should speak to me about it I shall know who has betrayed my secret.'

'You are angry, sire.'

'No; but you understand, I do not wish to compromise the poor girl.'

'Do not be afraid sire.'

'You promise me, then?'

'I give you my word of honour.'

'Excellent,' thought the King, laughing to himself, 'now every one will know to-morrow that I have been running about after La Vallière to-night.'

Then, endeavouring to see where he was, he said, 'Why, we have lost ourselves.'

'Not quite so bad as that, sire.'

'Where does that gate lead to?'

'To the great Rond-Point,* sire.'

'Where we were going, when we heard the sound of women's voices.'

'Yes, sire, and the termination of a conversation in which I had the honour of hearing my own name pronounced by the side of your Majesty's.'

'You return to that subject very frequently, Saint-Aignan.'

'Your Majesty will forgive me, but I am delighted to know that a woman exists whose thoughts are occupied about me without my knowledge, and without having done anything to deserve it. Your Majesty cannot comprehend this satisfaction, for your rank and merit attract attention and compel regard.'

'No, no, Saint-Aignan, believe me or not as you like,' said the King, leaning familiarly upon Saint-Aignan's arm, and taking the path which he thought would lead him to the château; 'but this candid confession, this perfectly disinterested preference of one who will, perhaps, never attract my attention—in one word, the mystery of this adventure excites me, and the truth is, that if I were not so taken up with La Vallière——'

'Do not let that interfere with your Majesty's intentions; you have time enough before you.'

'What do you mean?'

'La Vallière is said to be very strict in her ideas.'

'You excite my curiosity, and I am anxious to find her again. Come, let us walk on.'

The King spoke untruly, for nothing, on the contrary, could make him less anxious, but he had a part to play, and so he walked on hurriedly. Saint-Aignan followed him at a short distance. Suddenly the King stopped; the courtier followed his example.

'Saint-Aignan,' he said, 'do you not hear some one moaning?'

'Yes, sire, and crying too, it seems.'

'It is in this direction,' said the King. 'It sounds like the tears and sobs of a woman.'

'Run,' said the King; and, following a bypath, they ran across the grass. As they approached, the cries were more distinctly heard.

'Help! help!' exclaimed two voices. The King and his companion redoubled their speed, and, as they approached nearer, the sighs they had heard were changed into loud sobs. The cry of 'Help! help!' was again repeated; at the sound of which the King and Saint-Aignan increased the rapidity of their pace. Suddenly, at the other side of a ditch, under the branches of a willow, they perceived a woman on her knees, holding another in her arms, who seemed to have fainted. A few paces from them, a third, standing in the middle of the path, was calling for assistance. Perceiving two gentlemen, whose rank she could not tell, her cries for assistance were redoubled. The King, who was in advance of his companion, leaped across the ditch, and reached the group at the very moment when, from the end of the path which led to the château, a dozen persons were approaching, who had been drawn to the spot by the same cries which had attracted the attention of the King and M. de Saint-Aignan.

'What is the matter, young ladies?' said Louis.

'The King!' exclaimed Mademoiselle de Montalais, in her astonishment, letting La Vallière's head fall upon the ground.

'Yes, it is the King; but that is no reason why you should abandon your companion. Who is she?'

'It is Mademoiselle de la Vallière, sire.'

'Mademoiselle de la Vallière!'

'Yes, sire, she has just fainted.'

'Poor child!' said the King. 'Quick! quick! fetch a surgeon.' But however great the anxiety with which the King had pronounced these words may have seemed to others, he had not so carefully watched over himself, that they appeared, as well as the gesture which accompanied them, somewhat cold to Saint-Aignan, to whom the King had confided the great affection with which she had inspired him.

'Saint-Aignan,' continued the King, 'watch over Mademoiselle de la Vallière, I beg. Send for a surgeon. I will hasten forward and inform Madame of the accident which has befallen one of her maids of honour.' And, in fact, while M. de Saint-Aignan was busily engaged in making preparations for carrying Mademoiselle de la Vallière to the château, the King hurried forward, happy to have an opportunity of approaching Madame, and of speaking to her under some colourable pretext. Fortunately, a carriage was passing; the coachman was told to stop, and the persons who were inside, having been informed of the accident, eagerly gave up their seats to Mademoiselle de la Vallière. The current of fresh air produced by the rapid motion of the carriage, soon recalled her to her senses. Having reached the château, she was able, though very weak, to alight from the carriage; and, with the assistance of Athenaïs and of Montalais, to reach the inner apartments. They made her sit down in one of the rooms on the ground-floor. After a while, as the accident had not produced much effect upon those who had been walking, the promenade was resumed. During this time the King had found Madame beneath a tree with overhanging branches, and had seated himself by her side.

'Take care, sire,' said Henrietta to him, in a low tone, 'you do not show yourself as indifferent as you should be.'

'Alas!' replied the King, in the same tone, 'I much fear we have entered into an agreement above our strength to keep.' He then added aloud, 'You have heard of the accident, I suppose.'

'What accident?'

'Oh! in seeing you I forgot that I had come expressly to tell you of it. I am, however, painfully affected by it; one of your maids of honour, Mademoiselle de la Vallière, has just fainted.'

'Indeed! poor girl,' said the Princess quietly, 'what was the cause of it?'

She then added in an undertone, 'You forget, sire, that you wish others to believe in your passion for this girl, and yet you remain here while she is almost dying, perhaps, elsewhere.'

'Ah! Madame,' said the King, sighing, 'how much more perfect you are in your part than I am, and how well you think of everything.'

He then rose, saying loud enough for every one to hear him, 'Permit me to leave you madame. My uneasiness is great, and I wish to be quite certain, myself, that proper attention has been given to Mademoiselle de la Vallière.' And the King left again to return to La Vallière, whilst those who had been present commented upon the King's remark—'My uneasiness is very great.'

XXV

THE KING'S SECRET

ON his way, Louis met the Comte de Saint-Aignan. 'Well, Saint-Aignan,' he inquired, with affected interest; 'how is the invalid?'

'Really, sire,' stammered Saint-Aignan, 'to my shame I confess I do not know.'

'What! you do not know?' said the King, pretending to take in a serious manner this want of attention for the object of his predilection.

'Will your Majesty pardon me; but I have just met one of our three loquacious wood-nymphs, and I confess that my attention has been taken away from other matters.'

'Ah!' said the King eagerly, 'you have found, then——'

'The one who deigned to speak of me in such advantageous terms; and, having found mine, I was searching for yours, sire, when I had the happiness to meet your Majesty.'

'Very well; but Mademoiselle de la Vallière before everything else,' said the King, faithful to the character he had assumed.

'Oh! our charming invalid!' said Saint-Aignan; 'how fortunately her fainting came on, since your Majesty had already interested yourself on her account.'

'What is the name of your fair lady, Saint-Aignan? Is it a secret?'

'It ought to be a secret, and a very great one, even; but your Majesty is well aware that no secret can possibly exist for you.'

'Well, what is her name?'

'Mademoiselle de Tonnay-Charente.'

'Is she pretty?'

'Exceedingly so, sire; and I recognised the voice which pronounced my name in such tender accents. I then accosted her, questioning her as well as I was able to do in the midst of the crowd; and she told me, without suspecting anything, that a little while ago she was under the great oak with her two friends, when the appearance of a wolf or a robber had terrified them, and made them run away.'

'But,' inquired the King anxiously, 'what are the names of these two friends?'

'Sire,' said Saint-Aignan, 'will your Majesty send me forthwith to the Bastille?'

'What for?'

'Because I am an egotist and a fool. My surprise was so great at such a conquest, and at so fortunate a discovery that I went no further in my inquiries. Beside, I did not think that your Majesty would attach any very great importance to what you heard, knowing how much your attention was taken up by Mademoiselle de la Vallière; and then, Mademoiselle de Tonnay-Charente left me precipitately to return to Mademoiselle de la Vallière.'

'Let us hope, then, that I shall be as fortunate as yourself. Come, Saint-Aignan.'

'Your Majesty is ambitious, I perceive, and does not wish to allow any conquest to escape you. Well, I assure you that I will conscientiously set about my inquiries; and, moreover, from one of the three Graces, we shall learn the names of the others, and, by the name, the secret.'

'I, too,' said the King, 'only require to hear her voice to know it again. Come, let us say no more about it, but show me where poor La Vallière is.'

'Well,' thought Saint-Aignan, 'the King's regard is beginning to display itself, and for that girl, too. It is extraordinary; I should never have believed it.' And with this thought passing through his mind, he showed the King the room where La Vallière had been taken; the King entered, followed by Saint-Aignan. In a low room, near a large window, looking out upon the gardens, La Vallière, reclining in a large arm-chair, inhaled in deep draughts the perfumed evening breeze. From the loosened body of her dress, the lace fell in tumbled folds, mingling with the tresses of her beautiful fair hair, which lay scattered upon her shoulders. Her languishing eyes were filled with tears; she seemed as lifeless as those beautiful visions of our dreams, which pass before the closed eyes of the sleeper, half opening their wings without moving them, unclosing their lips without a sound escaping them. The pearl-like pallor of La Vallière possessed a charm which it would be impossible to describe. Mental and bodily suffering had produced upon her features a soft and noble expression of grief; from the perfect passiveness of her arms and bust, she more resembled one whose soul had passed away, than a living being; she seemed not to hear either the whisperings of her companions, or the distant murmurs which arose around her. She seemed to be communing within herself; and her beautiful, slender, and delicate hands trembled from time to time as though from the contact of some invisible touch. She was so completely absorbed in her reverie, that the King entered without her perceiving him. At a distance he gazed upon her lovely face, upon which the moon shed its pure, silvery light.

'Good heavens!' he exclaimed, with a terror he could not control; 'she is dead.'

'No, sire,' said Montalais, in a low voice; 'on the contrary, she is better. Are you not better, Louise?'

But Louise did not answer. 'Louise,' continued Montalais, 'the King has deigned to express his uneasiness on your account.'

'The King!' exclaimed Louise, starting up abruptly, as if a stream of fire had darted through her frame to her heart; 'the King uneasy about me?'

'Yes,' said Montalais.

'The King is here, then?' said La Vallière, not venturing to look round her.

'That voice! that voice!' whispered Louis eagerly, to Saint-Aignan.

'Yes, it is so,' replied Saint-Aignan; 'your Majesty is right; it is she who declared her love for the sun.'

'Hush!' said the King. And then approaching La Vallière, he said, 'You are not well, Mademoiselle de la Vallière? Just now, indeed, in the park, I saw that you had fainted. How were you attacked?'

'Sire,' stammered out the poor child, pale and trembling, 'I really do not know.'

'You have been walking too much,' said the King, 'and fatigue, perhaps——'

'No, sire,' said Montalais eagerly, answering for her friend, 'it could not be from fatigue, for we passed part of the evening seated beneath the royal oak.'

'Under the royal oak?' returned the King, starting. 'I was not deceived; it is as I thought.' And he directed a look of intelligence at the Comte.

'Yes,' said Saint-Aignan, 'under the royal oak, with Mademoiselle de Tonnay-Charente.'

'How do you know that?' inquired Montalais.

'In a very simple way. Mademoiselle de Tonnay-Charente told me so.'

'In that case, she probably told you the cause of Mademoiselle de la Vallière fainting?'

'Why, yes; she told me something about a wolf or a robber, I forget precisely which.' La Vallière listened, her eyes fixed, her bosom heaving, as if gifted with an acuteness of perception, she foresaw a portion of the truth. Louis imagined this attitude and agitation to be the consequences of a terror but partially removed. 'Nay, fear nothing,' he said, with a rising emotion which he could not conceal; 'the wolf which terrified you so much was simply a wolf with two legs.'

'It was a man, then,' said Louise; 'it was a man who was listening.'

'Suppose it were, mademoiselle, what great evil was there in his having listened? Is it likely that, even in your own opinion, you would have said anything which could not have been listened to?'

La Vallière wrung her hands, and hid her face in them, as if to hide her blushes. 'In Heaven's name,' she said, 'who was concealed there? who was listening?'

The King advanced towards her, to take hold of one of her hands. 'It was I,' he said, bowing with marked respect. 'Is it likely I could have frightened you?' La Vallière uttered a loud cry; for the second time her strength forsook her; and, cold, moaning, and in utter despair, she again fell apparently lifeless in her chair. The King had just time to hold out his arm; so that she was partially supported by him. Mademoiselle de Tonnay-Charente and Montalais, who stood a few paces from the King and La Vallière, motionless and almost petrified at the recollection of their conversation with La Vallière, did not think even of offering their assistance to her, feeling restrained by the presence of the King, who, with one knee on the ground, held La Vallière round the waist with his arm.

'You heard, sire?' murmured Athenaïs. But the King did not reply; he remained with his eyes fixed upon La Vallière's half-closed eyes, and held her drooping hand in his own.

'Of course,' replied Saint-Aignan, who, on his side, hoping that Mademoiselle de Tonnay-Charente would faint, advanced towards her, holding his arms extended, 'of course; we did not miss a word.' But the haughty Athenaïs was not a woman to faint easily; she darted a terrible look at Saint-Aignan, and fled. Montalais, with more courage, advanced hurriedly towards Louise, and received her from the King's hands, who was already fast losing his presence of mind, as he felt his face covered by the perfumed tresses of the seemingly dying girl. 'Excellent,' said Saint-Aignan. 'This is indeed an adventure; and it will be my own fault if I am not the first to relate it.'

The King approached him, and, with a trembling voice, and a passionate gesture, said, 'Not a syllable, Comte.'

The poor King forgot that, only an hour before, he had given him a similar recommendation, but with a very opposite intention; namely, that the Comte should be indiscreet. It was a matter, of course, that the latter recommendation was quite as unnecessary as the former. Half an hour afterwards, everybody in Fontainebleau knew that Mademoiselle de la Vallière had had a conversation under the royal oak with Montalais and Tonnay-Charente, and that in this conversation she had confessed her affection for the King. It was known, also, that the King, after having manifested the uneasiness with which Mademoiselle de la Vallière's health had inspired him, had turned pale, and trembled very much as he received the beautiful girl fainting in his arms; so that it was quite agreed among the courtiers, that the greatest event of the period had just been revealed; that His Majesty loved Mademoiselle de la Vallière, and that, consequently, Monsieur could now sleep in perfect tranquillity. It was this, even, that the Queen-Mother, as surprised as the others by this sudden change, hastened to tell the young Queen and Philip d'Orléans. Only she set to work in a different manner, by attacking them in the following way:—To her daughter-in-law she said, 'See, now, Thérèse, how very wrong you were to accuse the King; now it is said he is devoted to some other person; why should there be any greater truth in the report of to-day than in that of yesterday, or in that of yesterday than in that of to-day?' To Monsieur, in relating to him the adventure of the royal oak, she said, 'Are you not very absurd in your jealousies, my dear Philip? It is asserted that the King is madly in love with that little La Vallière. Say nothing of it to your wife; for the Queen will know all about it very soon.' This latter confidential communication had an immediate result. Monsieur, who had regained his composure, went triumphantly to look after his wife, and, as it was not yet midnight, and the fête was to continue until two in the morning, he offered her his hand for a promenade. At the end of a few paces, however, the first thing he did was to disobey his mother's injunctions.

'Do not go and tell any one, the Queen least of all,' he said mysteriously, 'what people say about the King.'

'What do they say about him?' inquired Madame.

'That my brother has fallen suddenly in love.'

'With whom?'

'With Mademoiselle de la Vallière.' As it was dark, Madame could smile at her ease.

'Ah!' she said, 'and how long is it since this has been the case?'

'For some days, so it seems. But that was nothing but pure nonsense, but it is only this evening that he has revealed his passion.'

'The King shows his good taste,' said Madame; 'and in my opinion she is a very charming girl.'

'I verily believe you are jesting.'

'I! in what way?'

'In any case this passion will make some one very happy, even if it be only La Vallière herself.'

'Really,' continued the Princess, 'you speak as if you had read into the inmost recesses of La Vallière's heart. Who has told you that she agrees to return the King's affection?'

'And who has told you that she will not return it?'

'She loves the Vicomte de Bragelonne.'

'You think so.'

'She is even affianced to him.'

'She was so.'

'What do you mean?'

'When they went to ask the King's permission to arrange the marriage, he refused his permission.'

'Refused?'

'Yes, although the request was preferred by the Comte de la Fère himself, for whom the King has the greatest regard, on account of the part he took in your brother's restoration, and in other events also, which happened a long time ago.'*

'Well! the poor lovers must wait until the King is pleased to change his opinion; they are young, and there is time enough.'

'But, dear me,' said Philip, laughing, 'I perceive that you do not know the best part of the affair.'

'No.'

'That by which the King was most deeply touched.'

'The King, do you say, has been deeply touched?'

'To the very heart.'

'But how—in what manner?—tell me directly.'

'By an adventure, the romance of which cannot be equalled.'

'You know how I love such adventures, and yet you keep me waiting,' said the Princess impatiently.

'Well, then——' and Monsieur paused.

'I am listening.'

'Under the royal oak—you know where the royal oak is?'

'What can that matter? Under the royal oak you were saying.'

'Well! Mademoiselle de la Vallière, fancying herself alone with her two friends, revealed to them her affection for the King.'

'Ah!' said Madame, beginning to feel uneasy, 'her affection for the King?'

'Yes.'

'When was this?'

'About an hour ago.'

Madame started, and then said, 'And no one knew of this affection?'

'No one.'

'Not even His Majesty?'

'Not even His Majesty. The little creature kept her secret most strictly to herself, when suddenly it proved stronger than herself, and so escaped her.'

'And from whom did you get this absurd tale?'

'Why, as everybody else did, from La Vallière herself, who confessed her love to Montalais and Tonnay-Charente, who were her companions.'

Madame stopped suddenly, and by a hasty movement let go her husband's hand.

'Did you say it was an hour ago she made this confession?' Madame inquired.

'About that time.'

'Is the King aware of it?'

'Why, that is the very thing which constitutes the whole romance of the affair, for the King was behind the royal oak with Saint-Aignan, and he heard the whole of the interesting conversation without losing a single word of it.'

Madame felt struck to the heart, saying incautiously, 'But I have seen the King since, and he never told me a word about it.'

'Of course,' said Monsieur; 'he took care not to speak of it to you himself, since he recommended every one not to say a word about it to you.'

'What do you mean?' said Madame, irritated.

'From the fear that your friendship for the young Queen might induce you to say something about it to her, nothing more.'

Madame hung down her head, her feelings were grievously wounded. She could not enjoy a moment's repose until she had met the King. As a King is most naturally, the very last person in his kingdom who knows what is said about him, in the same way that a lover is the only one who is kept in ignorance of what is said about his mistress, therefore, when the King perceived Madame, who was looking for him, he approached her somewhat disturbed, but still gracious and attentive in his manner. Madame waited for him to speak about La Vallière first; but as he did not speak of her, she said, 'And the poor girl?'

'What poor girl?' said the King.

'La Vallière. Did you not tell me, sire, that she had fainted?'

'She is still very ill,' said the King, affecting indifference.

'But surely that will prejudicially affect the rumour you were going to spread, sire?'

'What rumour?'

'That your attention was taken up by her.'

'Oh?' said the King carelessly, 'I trust it will be reported all the same.'

Madame still waited; she wished to know if the King would speak to her of the adventure of the royal oak. But the King did not say a word about it. Madame, on her side, did not open her lips about the adventure, so that the King took leave of her without having reposed the slightest confidence in her. Hardly had she seen the King move away, than she set out in search of Saint-Aignan. Saint-Aignan was never very difficult to find; he was like the smaller vessels which always follow in the wake of, and as tenders to, the larger ships. Saint-Aignan was the very man whom Madame needed in her then state of mind. And as for him, he only looked for worthier ears than others he had found, to have an opportunity of recounting the event with all its details. And therefore he did not spare Madame a single word of the whole affair. When he had finished, Madame said to him, 'Confess, now, that it is all a charming invention.'

'Invention, no; a true story, yes.'

'Confess, whether invention or true story, that it was told to you as you have told it to me, but that you were not there.'

'Upon my honour, Madame, I was there.'

'And you think that these confessions may have made an impression upon the King.'

'Certainly, as those of Mademoiselle de Tonnay-Charente did upon me,' replied Saint-Aignan; 'do not forget, Madame, that Mademoiselle de la Vallière compared the King to the sun; that was flattering enough.'

'The King does not permit himself to be influenced by such flatteries.'

'Madame, the King is just as much man as sun, and I saw that plain enough just now when La Vallière fell into his arms.'

'La Vallière fell into the King's arms!'

'Oh! it was the most graceful picture possible; just imagine, La Vallière had fallen back fainting, and——'

'Well! what did you see?—tell me—speak!'

'I saw what ten other people saw at the same time as myself; I saw that when La Vallière fell into his arms, the King almost fainted himself.'

Madame uttered a subdued cry, the only indication of her

smothered anger. 'Thank you,' she said, laughing in a convulsive manner, 'you relate stories delightfully, M. de Saint-Aignan.' And she hurried away, alone and almost suffocated by her feelings, towards the château.

XXVI

MIDNIGHT RAMBLES

MONSIEUR had left the Princess in the best possible humour, and, feeling very fatigued, had retired to his apartments. When in his room, Monsieur began to dress for the night with careful attention, which displayed itself from time to time in paroxysms of satisfaction. While his attendants were engaged in dressing him, he sang the principal airs of the ballet, which the violins had played, and to which the King had danced. He then summoned his tailors, inspected his costumes for the next day, and, in token of his extreme satisfaction, distributed various presents among them. As, however, the Chevalier de Lorraine, who had seen the Prince return to the château, entered the room, Monsieur overwhelmed him with kindness. The former remained silent for a moment, like a sharp-shooter who deliberates before deciding in what direction he will renew his fire; then, he said, 'Have you remarked a very singular circumstance, monseigneur?'

'No; what is it?'

'The bad reception which His Majesty, in appearance, gave the Comte de Guiche.'

'In appearance?'

'Yes, certainly, since in reality, he has restored him to favour.'

'I did not notice it,' said the Prince.

'What? did you not remark, that, instead of ordering him to return to exile, as would have been natural, he encouraged him in his opposition by permitting him to resume his place in the ballet.'

'And you think the King was wrong, Chevalier?' said the Prince.

'Are not you of my opinion, Prince?'

'Not altogether so, my dear Chevalier; and I think the King

was quite right not to have made any kind of outburst against a poor fellow whose want of judgement is more to be complained of than his intention.'

'Really,' said the Chevalier, 'as far as I am concerned, I confess that this magnanimity astonishes me to the highest degree.'

'Why so?' inquired Philip.

'Because I should have thought the King had been more jealous,' replied the Chevalier spitefully. During the last few minutes Monsieur had felt there was something of an irritating nature concealed under his favourite's remarks; this last word, however, had ignited the powder.

'Jealous!' exclaimed the Prince. 'Jealous!—what do you mean? Jealous of what, if you please—or jealous of whom?'

The Chevalier perceived that he had allowed one of those mischievous remarks to escape him, as he was sometimes in the habit of doing. He endeavoured, therefore, to recall it while it was still possible to do so. 'Jealous of his authority,' he said with an assumed frankness; 'of what else would you have the King be jealous?'

'Ah!' said the Prince, 'that's very proper.'

'Did your Royal Highness,' continued the Chevalier, 'solicit dear de Guiche's pardon?'

'No, indeed,' said Monsieur. 'De Guiche is an excellent fellow, and full of courage; but as I do not approve of his conduct with Madame, I wish him neither harm nor good.'

The Chevalier had assumed a bitterness with regard to de Guiche, as he had attempted to do with the King; but he thought that he perceived that the time for indulgence, and even for the utmost indifference, had arrived, and that, in order to throw some light on the question, it might be necessary for him to put the lamp, as the saying is, under the husband's nose even.

'Very well, very well,' said the Chevalier to himself, 'I shall wait for de Wardes; he will do more in one day than I in a month; for I verily believe that he is still more jealous than I am. Then, again, it is not de Wardes even whom I require so much as that some event or another should happen; and in the whole of this affair I see none. That de Guiche returned after he had been sent away is certainly serious enough, but all its seriousness disappears when I learn that de Guiche has returned at the very moment Madame troubles herself no longer about him. Madame, in fact, is occupied with the King, that is clear; but she will not be so much longer if, as it is asserted, the King has ceased to be interested in her. The result of the whole matter is to remain perfectly quiet, and await the arrival of some new caprice, and let that decide the whole affair.' And the Chevalier thereupon settled himself resignedly in the arm-chair in which Monsieur permitted him to seat himself in his presence; and having no more spiteful or malicious remarks to make, the consequence was that the Chevalier's wit seemed to have deserted him. Most fortunately Monsieur was endowed with great good humour, and he had enough for two, until the time arrived for dismissing his servants and gentlemen of the chamber, and he passed into his sleeping apartment. As he withdrew he desired the Chevalier to present his compliments to Madame, and say that, as the night was cool, Monsieur, who was afraid of the toothache, would not venture out again into the park during the remainder of the evening. The Chevalier entered the Princess's apartments at the very moment she entered them herself. He acquitted himself faithfully of the commission which had been entrusted to him, and, in the first place, remarked the indifference and annoyance with which Madame received her husband's communication—a circumstance which appeared to him fraught with something quite fresh. If Madame had been about to leave her apartments with that strangeness of manner about her, he would have followed her; but Madame was returning to them; there was nothing to be done, therefore he turned upon his heel like an unemployed heron, seemed to question earth, air, and water about it, shook his head, and walked away mechanically in the direction of the gardens. He had hardly gone a hundred paces when he met two young men, walking arm-in-arm, with their heads bent down, and idly kicking the small stones out of their path as they walked on, plunged in thought. It was de Guiche and de Bragelonne, the sight of whom, as it always did, produced upon the Chevalier, instinctively, a feeling of great repugnance. He did not, however, the less, on that account, salute them with a very low bow, and which they returned with interest. Then, observing that the park was becoming thinner, that the illuminations began to burn out, and that the morning breeze was setting in, he turned to the left and entered the château again, by one of the smaller courtyards. The others turned aside to the right, and continued on their way towards the main park. As the Chevalier was ascending the side staircase, which led to the private entrance, he saw a woman, followed by another, make her appearance under the arcade which led from the small to the large court-yard. The two women walked so fast that the rustling of their dresses could be distinguished in the darkness of the night. The style of their mantlets, their graceful figures, a mysterious yet haughty carriage which distinguished them both, especially the one who walked first, struck the Chevalier.

'I certainly know those two persons,' said he to himself, paus-ing upon the top step of the small staircase. Then, as with the instinct of a bloodhound he was about to follow them, one of his servants who had been running after him, arrested his attention.

'Monsieur,' he said, 'the courier has arrived.'

'Very well,' said the Chevalier, 'there is time enough; to-morrow will do.'

'There are some urgent letters which you would be glad to see, perhaps.'

'Where from?' inquired the Chevalier.

'One from England, and the other from Calais; the latter arrived by express and seems of great importance.'

'From Calais! Who the deuce can have to write to me from Calais?'

'I think I can recognise the handwriting of your friend the Comte de Wardes.'

'Oh!' cried the Chevalier, forgetting his intention of acting the spy, 'in that case I will come up at once.' This he did, while the two unknown ladies disappeared at the end of the court opposite to the one by which they had just entered. We shall now follow them, and leave the Chevalier undisturbed to his correspondence. When they had arrived at the grove of trees, the foremost of the two halted, somewhat out of breath, and, cautiously raising her hood, said, 'Are we still far from the tree?'

'Yes, madame, more than five hundred paces; but pray rest awhile, you will not be able to walk much longer at this pace.'

'You are right,' said the Princess, for it was she; and she leaned against a tree. 'And now,' she resumed, after having recovered her breath, 'tell me the whole truth, and conceal nothing from me.'

'Oh, madame,' said the young girl, 'you are already angry with me.'

'No, my dear Athenaïs; reassure yourself, I am in no way angry with you. After all, these things do not concern me personally. You are anxious about what you may have said under the oak; you are afraid of having offended the King, and I wish to tranquillise you by ascertaining myself if it were possible you could have been overheard.'

'Oh, yes, madame, the King was so close to us.'

'Still, you were not speaking so loud that some of your remarks may not have been lost.'

'We thought we were quite alone, madame.'

'There were three of you, you say?'

'Yes; La Vallière, Montalais, and myself.'

'And you, individually, spoke in a light manner of the King?'

'I am afraid so. Should such be the case, will your Highness have the kindness to make my peace with His Majesty.'

'If there should be any occasion for it, I promise to do so. However, as I have already told you, it will be better not to anticipate evil, and to be quite sure that evil has been committed. The night is now very dark, and the darkness is still greater under those large trees. It is not likely you were recognised by the King. To inform him of it, by being the first to speak, is to denounce yourself.'

'Oh, madame, madame! if Mademoiselle de la Vallière were recognised, I must have been recognised also. Besides, M. de Saint-Aignan did not leave a doubt on the subject.'

'Did you, then, say anything very disrespectful of the King?'

'Not at all so; it was one of the others who made some very flattering remarks about the King; and my remarks will have been so much in contrast with hers.'

'That Montalais is such a giddy girl,' said Madame.

'It was not Montalais. Montalais said nothing; it was La Vallière.'

Madame started as if she had not known it perfectly already. 'No, no,' she said, 'the King cannot have heard. Besides, we will now try the experiment for which we came out. Show me the oak. Do you know where it is?' she continued.

'Alas! madame, yes.'

'And you can find it again?'

'With my eyes shut.'

'Very well; sit down on the bank where you were, where La Vallière was, and speak in the tone and to the same effect as you did before; I will conceal myself in the thicket, and if I can hear you, I will tell you so.'

'Yes, madame.'

'If, therefore, you really spoke sufficiently loud for the King to have heard you, in that case——'

Athenaïs seemed to await the conclusion of the phrase with some anxiety.

'In that case,' said Madame, in a suffocated voice, arising doubtless from her hurried progress; 'in that case I forbid you——' And Madame again increased her pace. Suddenly, however, she stopped. 'An idea occurs to me,' she said.

'A good idea, no doubt, madame,' replied Mademoiselle de Tonnay-Charente.

'Montalais must be as much embarrassed as La Vallière and yourself.'

'Less so, for she is less compromised, having said less.'

'That does not matter; she will help you, I dare say, by deviating a little from the exact truth.'

'Especially if she knows that your Highness is kind enough to interest yourself in me.'

'Very well; I think I have discovered what we want.'

'How delightful.'

'You will say that all three of you were perfectly well aware that the King was behind the tree, or behind the thicket, which ever it might have been; and that you knew M. de Saint-Aignan was there too!'

'Yes, madame.'

'For you cannot disguise it from yourself, Athenaïs, Saint-Aignan has made the most of some very flattering remarks which you made about him.'

'Well, Madame, you see very well that one can be overheard,' cried Athenaïs, 'since M. de Saint-Aignan overheard us.'

Madame bit her lips, for she had thoughtlessly committed herself. 'Oh, you know Saint-Aignan's character very well,' she said; 'the favour the King shows him almost turns his brain, and he talks at random; not only that, he very often invents. That is not the question; the fact remains, Did or did not the King overhear?'

'Oh yes, madame, he did hear,' said Athenaïs, in despair.

'In that case, do what I said; maintain boldly that all three of you knew—mind, all three of you, for if there is a doubt about any one of you there will be a doubt about all,—persist, I say, that you all three knew that the King and M. de Saint-Aignan were there, and that you wished to amuse yourselves at the expense of those who were listening.'

'Oh, madame, at the King's expense; we never dare say that.'

'It is a simple jest; an innocent deception readily permitted in young girls whom men wish to take by surprise. In this manner everything is explained. What Montalais said of Malicorne, a mere jest; what you said of M. de Saint-Aignan, a mere jest too; and what La Vallière might have said of——'

'And which she would have given anything to have not said.'

'Are you sure of that?'

'Perfectly so.'

'Very well, an additional reason, therefore. Say the whole affair was a mere joke. M. de Malicorne will have no occasion to get out of temper; M. de Saint-Aignan will be completely put out of countenance, he will be laughed at instead of you; and, lastly, the King will be punished for a curiosity which was unworthy of his rank. Let people laugh a little at the King in this affair, and I do not think he will complain of it.'

'Oh, madame, you are indeed an angel of goodness and sense!'

'It is to my own advantage.'

'In what way?'

'Do you ask me why it is to my advantage to spare my maids of honour the remarks, annoyances, and perhaps even calumnies, which might follow? Alas! you well know that the court has no indulgence for this sort of peccadillo. But we have now been walking for some time, shall we be long before we reach it?'

'About fifty or sixty paces further; turn to the left, madame, if you please.'

'And so you are sure of Montalais?' said Madame.

'Oh, certainly.'

'Will she do what you ask her?'

'Everything. She will be delighted.'

'As for La Vallière——' ventured the Princess.

'Ah, there will be some difficulty with her, madame; she would scorn to tell a falsehood.'

'Yet, when it is in her interest to do so——'

'I am afraid that that would not make the slightest difference in her ideas.'

'Yes, yes,' said Madame, 'I have been already told that; she is one of those over-nice and affectedly-particular persons who place heaven in the foreground to conceal themselves behind it. But if she refuse to tell a falsehood—as she will expose herself to the jestings of the whole court,—as she will have annoyed the King by a confession as ridiculous as it was immodest,—Mademoiselle La Baume Le Blanc de la Vallière will think it but proper that I should send her back again to her pigeons in the country, in order that, in Touraine yonder, or in the Blaisois*— I know not where it may be—she may at her ease study sentiment and a pastoral life together.' These words were uttered with a vehemence and harshness which terrified Mademoiselle de Tonnay-Charente; and the consequence was, that, as far as she was concerned, she promised to tell as many falsehoods as might be necessary. It was in this amiable frame of mind, respectively, that Madame and her companion reached the precincts of the royal oak.

'Here we are,' said Tonnay-Charente.

'We shall soon learn if one can overhear,' replied Madame.

'Hush!' said the young girl, holding Madame back with a hurried gesture, entirely forgetful of her companion's rank. Madame stopped.

'You see that you can hear,' said Athenaïs.

'How?'

'Listen.'

Madame held her breath, and, in fact, the following words, pronounced by a gentle and melancholy voice, floated towards them:—

'I tell you, Vicomte, I tell you I love her madly; I tell you I love her to distraction.'

Madame started at the voice, and, beneath her hood a bright

joyous smile illumined her features. It was she who now stayed her companion, and with a light footstep leading her some twenty paces back, that is to say, out of reach of the voice, she said, 'Remain there, my dear Athenaïs, and let no one surprise us. I think it may be you they are conversing about.'

'Me, madame?'

'Yes, you; or rather your adventure. I will go and listen; if we were both there, we should be discovered. Go and fetch Montalais, and then return and wait for me with her at the entrance of the forest.' And then, as Athenaïs hesitated, she again said, 'Go!' in a voice which did not admit of reply. Athenaïs thereupon arranged her dress so as to prevent its rustling being heard, and, by a path which crossed the group of trees, she regained the flower garden. As for Madame, she concealed herself in the thicket, leaning her back against a gigantic chestnut-tree, one of the branches of which had been cut in a manner to form a seat, and waited there full of anxiety and apprehension. 'Now,' she said, 'since one can hear from this place, let us listen to what M. de Bragelonne and that other madly-in-love fool, the Comte de Guiche, have to say about me.'

XXVII

MADAME ACQUIRES A PROOF THAT LISTENERS CAN HEAR WHAT IS SAID

THERE was a moment's silence, as if all the mysterious sounds of night were hushed to listen, at the same time as Madame, to the youthful and passionate disclosure of de Guiche.

It was Raoul who was about to speak. He leaned indolently against the trunk of the large oak, and replied in his sweet and musical voice, 'Alas, my dear Guiche, it is a great misfortune.'

'Yes,' cried the latter, 'great indeed.'

'You do not understand me, Guiche. I say that it is a great misfortune for you, not that of loving, but that of not knowing how to conceal your love.'

'What do you mean?' said Guiche.

'Yes, you do not perceive one thing; namely, that it is no

longer to the only friend you have,—in other words to a man who would rather die than betray you; you do not perceive, I say, that it is no longer to your only friend that you confide your passion, but to the first one who approaches you.'

'Are you mad, Bragelonne,' exclaimed Guiche, 'to say such a thing to me?'

'The fact is so, however.'

'Impossible! How, in what manner could I have become indiscreet to such an extent.'

'I mean, that your eyes, your looks, your sighs, speak in spite of yourself; that every exaggerated feeling leads and hurries a man beyond his own control. In such a case he ceases to be master of himself; he is a prey to a mad passion, which makes him confide his grief to the trees, or to the air, from the very moment he has no longer any living being within reach of his voice. Besides, remember this, it very rarely happens that there is not always some one present to hear, especially those very things which ought not to be heard.' Guiche uttered a deep sigh. 'Nay,' continued Bragelonne, 'you distress me; since your return here, you have a thousand times, and in a thousand different ways, confessed your love for her; and yet, had you not said anything, your return would alone have been a terrible indiscretion. I persist, then, in drawing this conclusion; that if you do not place a greater watch over yourself than you have hitherto done, one day or another something will happen which will cause an explosion. Who will save you then? Answer me. Who will save her? for, innocent as she will be of your affection, your affection will be an accusation against her in the hands of her enemies.'

'Alas!' murmured Guiche; and a deep sigh accompanied the exclamation.

'Well, what reply have you to make?'

'This, that when the day arrives I shall not be less a living being than I feel myself to be now.'

'I do not understand you.'

'So many vicissitudes have worn me out. At present, I am no more a thinking, acting being; at present, the most worthless of men is better than I am; therefore, my remaining strength is now exhausted, my latest-formed resolutions have vanished, and

I abandon myself to my fate. When a man is out campaigning, as we have been together,* and he sets off alone and unaccompanied for a skirmish, it sometimes happens that he may meet with a party of five or six foragers, and although alone, he defends himself; afterwards, five or six others arrive, unexpectedly, his anger is aroused and he persists; but if six, eight, or ten others should still be met with, he either sets spurs to his horse, if he should still happen to retain it, or lets himself be slain to save an ignominious flight. Such, indeed, is my own case; first, I had to struggle against myself; afterwards against Buckingham; now, since the King is in the field, I will not contend against the King, nor even, I wish you to understand, will the King retire; nor even against the nature of that woman. Still I do not deceive myself; having devoted myself to the service of that affection, I will lose my life in it.'

'It is not her you ought to reproach,' replied Raoul; 'it is yourself. You know the Princess's character,—somewhat giddy, easily captivated by novelty, susceptible to flattery, whether it come from a blind person or a child, and yet you allow your passion for her to eat your very life away. Look at her,—love her if you will,—for no one whose heart is not engaged elsewhere can see her without loving her. Yet, while you love her, respect, in the first place, her husband's rank, then himself, and lastly, your own safety.'

'Thanks, Raoul.'

'For what?'

'Because, seeing how much I suffer from this woman, you endeavour to console me, because you tell me all the good of her you think, and perhaps even that which you do not think.'

'Oh,' said Raoul, 'there you are wrong, Guiche; what I think I do not always say, but in that case I say nothing; but when I speak, I know not either how to feign or to deceive; and whoever listens to me may believe me.'

During this conversation, Madame, her head stretched forward with eager ear and dilated glance, endeavouring to penetrate the obscurity, thirstily drank in the faintest sound of their voices.

'Oh, I know her better than you do, then!' exclaimed Guiche. 'She is not giddy, but frivolous; she is not attracted by novelty, she is utterly oblivious, and is without faith; she is not simply susceptible to flattery, she is a practised and cruel coquette. A thorough coquette! yes, yes, I am sure of it. Believe me, Bragelonne, I am suffering all the torments of hell; brave, passionately fond of danger, I meet a danger greater than my strength and my courage. But, believe me, Raoul, I reserve for myself a victory which shall cost her floods of tears.'

'A victory,' he asked, 'of what kind?'

'One day I will accost her, and will address her thus: "I was young—madly in love; I possessed, however, sufficient respect to throw myself at your feet, and to prostrate myself with my forehead buried in the dust, if your looks had not raised me to your hand. I fancied I understood your looks, I arose, and then, without having done anything towards you than love you yet more devotedly, if that were possible—you, a woman without heart, faith, or love, in very wantonness of disposition, dashed me down again from mere caprice. You are unworthy, princess of royal blood though you may be, of the love of a man of honour; I offer my life as a sacrifice for having loved you too tenderly, and I die hating you."'

'Oh!' cried Raoul, terrified at the accents of profound truth which Guiche's words betrayed, 'I was right in saying you were mad, Guiche.'

'Yes, yes,' exclaimed de Guiche, following out his own idea; 'since there are no wars here now, I will flee yonder, to the north, seek service in the Empire,* where some Hungarian, or Croat, or Turk, will perhaps kindly put me out of my misery at once.' De Guiche did not finish, or rather as he finished, a sound made him start, and at the same moment made Raoul leap to his feet. As for de Guiche, buried in his own thoughts, he remained seated, with his head tightly pressed between his hands. The branches of the trees were pushed aside, and a woman, pale and much agitated, appeared before the two young men. With one hand she held back the branches, which would have struck her face, and with the other, she raised the hood of the mantle which covered her shoulders. By her clear and lustrous glance, by her lofty carriage, by her haughty attitude, and, more than all, by the throbbing of his own heart, de Guiche recognised Madame, and uttering a loud cry, he removed his hands from his temples, and covered his eyes with them. Raoul, trembling, and out of countenance, merely muttered a few formal words of respect.

'Monsieur de Bragelonne,' said the Princess, 'have the goodness, I beg, to see if my attendants are not somewhere yonder, either in the walks or in the groves; and you, M. de Guiche, remain here; I am tired, and you will perhaps give me your arm.'

Had a thunderbolt fallen at the feet of the unhappy young man, he would have been less terrified than by her cold and severe tone. However, as he himself had just said, he was brave; and as in the depths of his own heart he had just decisively made up his mind, de Guiche arose, and, observing Bragelonne's hesitation, he turned towards him a glance full of resignation and of grateful acknowledgement. Instead of immediately answering Madame, he even advanced a step towards the Vicomte, and holding out towards him the hand which the Princess had just desired him to give her, he pressed his friend's hand in his own with a sigh, in which he seemed to give to friendship all life that was left in the depths of his heart. Madame, who, in her pride, had never known what it was to wait, now waited, until this mute colloquy was ended. Her royal hand remained suspended in the air, and, when Raoul had left, it sank without anger, but not without emotion, in that of de Guiche. They were alone in the depths of the dark and silent forest, and nothing could be heard but Raoul's hastily retreating footsteps along the obscure paths. Over their heads was extended the thick and fragrant vault of branches, through the occasional openings of which the stars could be seen glittering in their beauty. Madame softly drew de Guiche about a hundred paces away from that indiscreet tree which had heard, and had allowed so many things to be heard during that evening, and, leading him to a neighbouring glade, so that they could see a certain distance around them, she said, in a trembling voice, 'I have brought you here, because yonder where you were everything can be overheard.'

'Everything can be overheard, did you say, madame,' replied the young man mechanically.

'I have heard every syllable you have said.'

'Oh, Heaven! it lacked only this to destroy me,' stammered de Guiche; and he bent down his head, like an exhausted swimmer beneath the wave which engulfs him.

'And so,' she said, 'you judge me as you have said?' Guiche grew pale, turned his head aside, and was silent; he felt almost on the point of fainting.

'I do not complain,' continued the Princess in a tone of voice full of gentleness; 'I prefer a frankness which wounds me to flattery which would deceive me. And so, according to your opinion, M. de Guiche, I am a coquette and a worthless creature.'

'Worthless,' cried the young man; 'you worthless! No, no; most certainly I did not say, I could not have said that that which was the most precious object in life for me could be worthless. No, no; I did not say that.'

'A woman who sees a man perish, consumed by the fire she has kindled, and who does not allay that fire, is, in my opinion, a worthless woman.'

'What can it matter to you what I said?' returned the Comte. 'What am I compared to you, and why should you even trouble yourself to know whether I exist or not?'

'Monsieur de Guiche, both you and I are human beings, and, knowing you as I do, I do not wish you to risk your life; with you I will change my conduct and character. I will be, not frank, for I am always so, but truthful. I implore you, therefore, to love me no more, and to forget utterly that I have ever addressed a word or a glance towards you.'

De Guiche turned round, bending a look full of passionate devotion upon her. 'You,' he said; 'you excuse yourself; you implore me!'

'Certainly; since I have done the evil, I ought to repair the evil I have done. And so, Comte, this is what we have agreed to. You will forgive my frivolity and my coquetry. Nay, do not interrupt me. I will forgive you for having said I was frivolous and a coquette, or something worse, perhaps; and you will renounce your idea of dying, and will preserve for your family, for the King, and for our sex, a cavalier whom every one esteems, and whom many hold dear.' Madame pronounced this last word in such an accent of frankness, and even of tenderness, that poor de Guiche's heart felt almost bursting.

'Oh! madame, madame!' he stammered out.

'Nay, listen further,' she continued. 'When you shall have renounced all thought of me for ever, from necessity in the first place, and, afterwards, because you will yield to my entreaty, then you will judge me more favourably, and I am convinced you will replace this love—forgive the folly of the expression—by a sincere friendship, which you will be ready to offer me, and which I promise you shall be cordially accepted.'

De Guiche, his forehead bedewed with perspiration, a feeling of death in his heart, and a trembling agitation through his whole frame, bit his lip, stamped his foot on the ground, and, in a word, devoured the bitterness of his grief. 'Madame,' he said, 'what you offer is impossible, and I cannot accept such conditions.'

'What!' said Madame, 'do you refuse my friendship, then?'

'No, no; I need not your friendship, madame; I prefer to die from love, than to live for friendship.'

'Comte!'

'Oh! madame,' cried de Guiche, 'the present is a moment for me, in which no other consideration and no other respect exist, than the consideration and respect of a man of honour towards the woman he worships. Drive me away, curse me, denounce me, you will be perfectly right; I have uttered complaints against you, but their bitterness has been owing to my passion for you; I have said that I would die, and die I shall. If I lived, you would forget me; but dead, you would never forget me, I am sure.'

And yet she, who was standing buried in thought, and as agitated as de Guiche himself, turned aside her head as he but a minute before had turned aside his. Then, after a moment's pause, she said, 'And you love me, then, very much?'

'Madly; madly enough to die from it, whether you drive me from you, or whether you listen to me still.'

'It is, therefore, a hopeless case,' she said, in a playful manner; 'a case which must be treated with soothing applications. Give me your hand. It is as cold as ice.' De Guiche knelt down, and pressed to his lips, not one, but both of Madame's hands.

'Love me, then,' said the Princess, 'since it cannot be otherwise.' And almost imperceptibly she pressed his fingers, raising him thus, partly in the manner of a queen, and partly as a fond and affectionate woman would have done. De Guiche trembled throughout, from head to foot, and Madame, who felt how passion coursed through every fibre of his being, knew that he indeed loved truly. 'Give me your arm, Comte,' she said, 'and let us return.'

'Ah! madame,' said the Comte, trembling and bewildered; 'you have discovered a third way of killing me.'

'But, happily, it is the longest, is it not?' she replied, as she led him towards the grove of trees she had left.

XXVIII

ARAMIS'S CORRESPONDENCE

WHILST de Guiche's affairs which had been suddenly set to rights without his having been able to guess the cause of their improvement, assumed that unexpected change which we have seen, Raoul, in obedience to the request of Madame, had withdrawn in order not to interrupt a frank exchange of views, and he had joined the ladies of honour who were walking in the flower gardens. During this time, the Chevalier de Lorraine, who had returned to his own room, read de Wardes's letter with surprise, for it informed him, by the hand of his valet, of the sword-thrust received at Calais, and of all the details of the adventure, and invited him to communicate to de Guiche and to Monsieur, whatever there might be in the affair likely to be most disagreeable to both of them. De Wardes particularly endeavoured to prove to the Chevalier the violence of Madame's affection for Buckingham, and he finished his letter by declaring that he thought this feeling was returned. The Chevalier shrugged his shoulders at the latter paragraph, and, in fact, de Wardes was very much behindhand as may have been seen.

The Chevalier threw the letter over his shoulder upon an adjoining table, and said in a disdainful tone: 'It is really incredible; and yet poor de Wardes is not deficient in ability, though it doesn't show, so easy is it to grow rusty in the country. The deuce take the simpleton, who ought to have written to me about matters of importance, and who writes such silly stuff as that. If it had not been for that miserable letter, which has no meaning at all in it, I should have detected in the grove yonder a charming little intrigue, which would have compromised a woman, would have perhaps been as good as a sword-thrust for a man, and have diverted Monsieur for some days to come.'

He looked at his watch. 'It is now too late,' he said. 'One o'clock in the morning; every one must have returned to the King's apartments where the night is to be finished; well, the scent is lost, and unless some extraordinary chance——' And, thus saying, as if to appeal to his good star, the Chevalier, much out of temper, approached the window, which looked out upon a somewhat solitary part of the garden. Immediately, and as if some evil genius had been at his orders, he perceived returning towards the château, accompanied by a man, a silk mantle of a dark colour, and recognised the figure which had struck his attention half an hour previously.

'Admirable!' he thought, striking his hands together, 'this is my mysterious affair.' And he started out precipitately, along the staircase, hoping to reach the courtyard in time to recognise the woman in the mantle, and her companion. But, as he arrived at the door in the little court, he nearly knocked against Madame, whose radiant face seemed full of charming revelations beneath the mantle which protected without concealing her. Unfortunately, Madame was alone. The Chevalier knew that since he had seen her, not five minutes before, with a gentleman, the gentleman in question could not be far off. Consequently he hardly took time to salute the Princess as he drew up, to allow her to pass; then, when she had advanced a few steps, with the rapidity of a woman who fears recognition; and when the Chevalier perceived that she was too much occupied with her own thoughts to trouble herself about him, he darted into the garden, looked hastily round, on every side, and embraced within his glance as much of the horizon as he possibly could. He was just in time; the gentleman who had accompanied Madame was still in sight; only he was rapidly hurrying towards one of the wings of the château, behind which he was just on the point of disappearing. There was not a minute to lose; the Chevalier darted in pursuit of him, prepared to slacken his pace as he approached the unknown; but, in spite of the diligence he used, the unknown had disappeared behind the flight of steps before he approached.

It was evident, however, that as he whom the Chevalier pursued was walking quietly, in a very pensive manner, with his head bent down, either beneath the weight of grief or of happiness; when once the angle was passed, unless, indeed, he were to enter by some door or another, the Chevalier could not fail to overtake him. And this certainly would have happened, if, at the very moment he turned the angle, the Chevalier had not run against two persons, who were themselves turning it in the opposite direction. The Chevalier was quite ready to seek a quarrel with these two troublesome intruders, when looking up he recognised the Minister of Finance. Fouquet was accompanied by a person whom the Chevalier now saw for the first time. This stranger was His Grace the Bishop of Vannes. Checked by the important character of the individual, and obliged from politeness to make his own excuses when he expected to receive them, the Chevalier stepped back a few paces; and as Monsieur Fouquet possessed, if not the friendship, at least the respect of every one; as the King himself, although he was rather his enemy than his friend, treated M. Fouquet as a man of great consideration, the Chevalier did what the King would have done, namely, he bowed to M. Fouquet, who returned his salutation with kindly politeness, perceiving that the gentleman had run against him by mistake and without any intention of being rude. Then, almost immediately afterwards, having recognised the Chevalier de Lorraine, he made a few civil remarks, to which the Chevalier was obliged to reply. Brief as the conversation was, the Chevalier de Lorraine saw, with the most unfeigned displeasure, the figure of his unknown becoming smaller and smaller in the distance, and fast disappearing in the darkness. The Chevalier resigned himself, and once resigned, gave his entire attention to Fouquet:—'You arrive late, monsieur,' he said. 'Your absence has occasioned great surprise, and I heard Monsieur express himself as much astonished, that, having been invited by the King, you had not come.'

'It was impossible for me to do so; but I came as soon as I was free.'

'Is Paris quiet?'

'Perfectly so. Paris has received the last tax very well.'

'Ah! I understand, you wished to assure yourself of this good feeling before you came to participate in our fêtes.'

'I have arrived, however, somewhat late to enjoy them. I will ask you, therefore, to inform me, if the King is within the château or not, if I shall be able to see him this evening, or if I am to wait until to-morrow.'

'We have lost sight of His Majesty during the last half-hour or so,' said the Chevalier.

'Perhaps he is in Madame's apartments,' inquired Fouquet.

'Not in Madame's apartments, I should think, for I have just met Madame as she was entering by the small staircase; and unless the gentleman whom you just now passed was the King himself——' and the Chevalier paused, hoping that, in this manner, he might learn who it was he had been hurrying after. But Fouquet, whether he had or had not recognised de Guiche, simply replied, 'No, monsieur, it was not he.'

The Chevalier, disappointed in his expectation, saluted them; but, as he did so, casting a parting glance around him, and perceiving M. Colbert in the centre of a group, he said to the Minister: 'Stay, monsieur, there is some one under the trees yonder, who will be able to inform you better than myself.'

'Who?' asked Fouquet, whose nearsightedness prevented his seeing through the darkness.

'M. Colbert,' returned the Chevalier.

'Indeed! That person, then, who is speaking yonder to those men with torches in their hands, is M. Colbert.'

'M. Colbert himself. He is giving his orders personally to the workmen who are arranging the lamps for the illuminations.'

'Thank you,' said Fouquet, with an inclination of the head, which indicated that he had obtained all the information he wished. The Chevalier, on his side, having on the contrary learnt nothing at all, withdrew with a profound salutation.

He had scarcely left, when Fouquet, knitting his brows, fell into a deep reverie. Aramis looked at him for a moment with a mingled feeling of compassion and sadness. 'What!' he said to him, 'that man's name alone seems to affect you. Is it possible that, full of triumph and delight as you were just now, the sight merely of that man is capable of dispiriting you? Tell me, have you faith in your good star?'

'No,' replied Fouquet dejectedly.

'Why not?'

'Because I am too full of happiness at this present moment,' he replied in a trembling voice. 'You, my dear d'Herblay, who are so learned, will remember the history of a certain tyrant of Samos.* What can I throw into the sea to avert approaching evil? Yes, I repeat it once more; I am too full of happiness! so happy that I wish for nothing beyond what I have. . . . I have risen so high. . . . You know my motto, "*Quo non ascendam*"?* I have risen so high that nothing is left me but to descend from my elevation. I cannot believe in the progress of a success which is already more than human.'

Aramis smiled as he fixed his kind and penetrating glance upon him. 'If I were aware of the cause of your happiness,' he said, 'I should probably fear for your disgrace; but you regard me in the light of a true friend; I mean you turn to me in misfortune, nothing more. Even that is an immense and precious boon, I know; but the truth is, I have a just right to beg you to confide in me, from time to time, any fortunate circumstances which may befall you, and in which I should rejoice, you know, more than if they had befallen myself.'

'My dear prelate,' said Fouquet, laughing, 'my secrets are of too profane a character to confide them to a bishop, however great a worldling he may be.'

'Bah! in confession . . .'

'Oh! I should blush too much if you were my confessor.' And Fouquet began to sigh. Aramis again looked at him without any other betrayal of his thoughts than a quiet smile.

'Well,' he said, 'discretion is a great virtue.'

'Silence,' said Fouquet, 'that venomous beast has recognised us, and is coming this way.'

'Colbert?'

'Yes; leave me, d'Herblay; I do not wish that fellow to see you with me, or he will take an aversion to you.'

Aramis pressed his hand, saying, 'What need have I of his friendship while you are here?'

'Yes, but I may not be always here,' replied Fouquet dejectedly.

'On that day, then, if that day should ever come,' said Aramis tranquilly, 'we will think over a means of dispensing with friendship, or of braving the dislike of M. Colbert. But tell me, my dear Fouquet, instead of conversing with this fellow, as you did him the honour to style him, a conversation, the utility of which I do not perceive, why do you not pay a visit, if not to the King, at least to Madame?'

'To Madame!' said the Minister, his mind occupied by his souvenirs.

'Yes, certainly, to Madame.'

'You remember,' continued Aramis, 'that we have been told that Madame stands high in favour during the last two or three days. It enters into your policy, and forms part of our plans, that you should assiduously devote yourself to His Majesty's friends. It is a means of counteracting the growing influence of M. Colbert. Present yourself, therefore, as soon as possible to Madame, and, for our sakes, treat this ally with consideration.'

'But,' said Fouquet, 'are you quite sure that it is upon her the King has his eyes fixed at the present moment?'

'If the needle has turned, it must have done so since this morning. You know I have my police.'

'Very well! I shall go at once, and at all events I shall have a means of introduction, in the shape of a magnificent pair of antique cameos set round with diamonds.'

'I have seen them, and nothing could be more costly and regal.'

At this moment they were interrupted by a servant followed by a courier. 'For you monsiegneur,' said the courier aloud, presenting a letter to Fouquet.

'For your grace,' said the lackey in a low tone, handing Aramis a letter. And as the lackey carried a torch in his hand, he placed himself between the Minister and the Bishop of Vannes, so that both of them could read at the same time. As Fouquet looked at the fine and delicate writing on the envelope, he started with delight; they who love, or who are beloved, will understand his anxiety in the first place, and his happiness in the next. He hastily tore open the letter, which, however, contained only these words: 'It is but an hour since I quitted you, it is an age since I told you that I love you.' And that was all. Madame de Bellière had, in fact, left Fouquet about an hour previously, after having passed two days with him; and, apprehensive lest his remembrance of her might not be effaced for too long a period from the heart she regretted, she despatched a courier to him as the bearer of this important communication. Fouquet kissed the letter, and rewarded the bearer with a handful of gold. As for Aramis, he on his side was engaged in reading, but with more coolness and reflection, the following letter:—

'The King has this evening been struck with a strange fancy; a woman loves him. He learnt it accidentally, as he was listening to the conversation of this young girl, with her companions; and His Majesty has entirely abandoned himself to this new caprice. The girl's name is Mademoiselle de la Vallière, and she is sufficiently pretty to warrant this caprice becoming a strong attachment. Beware of Mademoiselle de la Vallière.'

There was not a word about Madame. Aramis slowly folded the letter and put it in his pocket. Fouquet was still engaged in inhaling the perfume of his epistle.

'Monseigneur,' said Aramis, touching Fouquet's arm.

'Yes; what is it?' he asked.

'An idea has just occurred to me. Are you acquainted with a young girl of the name of La Vallière?'

'Not at all.'

'Reflect a little.'

'Ah! yes, I believe so, one of Madame's maids of honour.'

'That must be the one.'

'Well, what then?'

'Well, monseigneur, it is to that young girl that you must pay your visit this evening.'

'Bah! why so?'

'Nay, more than that, it is to her you must present your cameos.'

'Nonsense.'

'You know, monseigneur, that my advice is not to be regarded lightly.'

'Yet this unforeseen——'

'That is my affair. Pay your court in due form, and without loss of time to Mademoiselle de la Vallière. I will be your guarantee with Madame de Bellière that your devotion is altogether politic.'

'What do you mean, my dear d'Herblay, and whose name have you just pronounced?'

'A name which ought to convince you that, as I am so well

informed about yourself, I may possibly be as well informed about others. Pay your court, therefore, to La Vallière.'

'I will pay my court to whomsoever you like,' replied Fouquet, his heart filled with happiness.

'Come, come, descend again to the earth, traveller of the seventh heaven,' said Aramis, 'M. de Colbert is approaching. He has been recruiting while we were reading; see, how he is surrounded, praised, congratulated; he is decidedly becoming powerful.' In fact, Colbert was advancing, escorted by all the courtiers who remained in the gardens, every one of whom complimented him upon the arrangements of the fête, and which so puffed him up that he could hardly contain himself.

'If La Fontaine were here,' said Fouquet, smiling, 'what an admirable opportunity for him to recite his fable of "The Frog that wished to make itself as big as the Ox."'*

Colbert arrived, in the centre of a circle blazing with light; Fouquet awaited his approach, unmoved, and with a slight mocking smile. Colbert smiled too; he had been observing his enemy during the last quarter of an hour, and had been approaching him gradually. Colbert's smile was a presage of hostility.

'Oh! oh!' said Aramis, in a low tone to the Finance Minister; 'the scoundrel is going to ask you again for a few more millions to pay for his fireworks and his coloured lamps.' Colbert was the first to salute them, and with an air which he endeavoured to render respectful. Fouquet hardly moved his head.

'Well, monseigneur, what do your eyes say? Have we shown our good taste?'

'Perfect taste,' replied Fouquet, without permitting the slightest tone of raillery to be remarked in his words.

'Oh!' said Colbert maliciously, 'you are treating us with indulgence. We are poor, we other servants of the King, and Fontainebleau is no way to be compared as a residence with Vaux.'*

'Quite true,' replied Fouquet coolly.

'But what can we do, monseigneur?' continued Colbert; 'we have done our best with our slender resources.' Fouquet made a gesture of assent.

'But,' pursued Colbert, 'it would be only a proper display of your magnificence, monseigneur, if you were to offer to His

Majesty a fête in your wonderful gardens—in those gardens which have cost you sixty millions of francs.'

'Seventy-two,' said Fouquet.

'An additional reason,' returned Colbert; 'it would, indeed, be truly magnificent.'

'But do you suppose, monsieur, that His Majesty would deign to accept my invitation?'

'I have no doubt whatever of it,' cried Colbert hastily; 'I will guarantee that he does.'

'You are exceedingly kind,' said Fouquet. 'I may depend on it then?'

'Yes, monseigneur, yes, certainly.'

'Then I will consider of it,' said Fouquet.

'Accept, accept,' whispered Aramis eagerly.

'You will consider of it?' repeated Colbert.

'Yes,' replied Fouquet; 'in order to know what day I shall submit my invitation to the King.'

'This very evening, monseigneur, this very evening.'

'Agreed,' said the Minister. 'Gentlemen, I should wish to issue my invitations; but you know, that, wherever the King goes, the King is in his own palace; it is by His Majesty, therefore, that you must be invited.' A murmur of delight immediately arose. Fouquet bowed and left.

'Proud and haughty man,' said Colbert, 'you accept, and you know it will cost you ten millions.'

'You have ruined me,' said Fouquet, in a low tone to Aramis.

'I have saved you,' replied the latter, whilst Fouquet ascended the flight of steps and inquired whether the King was still visible.

XXIX

THE ORDERLY CLERK

THE King, anxious to be again quite alone, in order to reflect well upon what was passing in his heart, had withdrawn to his own apartments, where M. de Saint-Aignan had, after his conversation with Madame, gone to meet him. This conversation has already been related. The favourite, vain of his twofold importance, and feeling that he had become during the last two hours, the confidant of the King, began to treat the affairs of the court in a somewhat offhanded way; and, from the position in which he had placed himself, or, rather, where chance had placed him, he saw nothing but love and garlands of flowers around him. The King's love for Madame, that of Madame for the King, that of Guiche for Madame, that of La Vallière for the King, that of Malicorne for Montalais, that of Mademoiselle de Tonnay-Charente for himself, was not all this truly more than enough to turn the head of any courtier? Besides, Saint-Aignan was the model of all courtiers, past, present and future, and, moreover, Saint-Aignan showed himself such an excellent narrator, and so discerningly appreciative, that the King listened to him with an appearance of great interest, particularly when he described the excited manner with which Madame had sought for him to converse about the affair of Mademoiselle de la Vallière. When the King no longer experienced for Madame any remains of the passion he had once felt for her, there was, in the same eagerness of Madame, to procure information about him, such a gratification for his vanity, from which he could not free himself. He experienced this gratification then, but nothing more; and his heart was not, for a single moment, alarmed at what Madame might, or might not think of this adventure. When, however, Saint-Aignan had finished, the King, while preparing to retire to rest, asked, 'Now, Saint-Aignan, you know what Mademoiselle de la Vallière is, do you not?'

'Not only what she is, but what she will be.'

'What do you mean?'

'I mean that she is everything that a woman can wish to be, that is to say, beloved by your Majesty; I mean, that she will be everything that your Majesty may wish her to be.'

'That is not what I am asking. I do not wish to know what she is to-day, or what she will be to-morrow; as you have remarked, that is my affair. But tell me what others say of her.'

'They say that her conduct is beyond reproach.'

'Oh!' said the King, smiling, 'that is but report.'

'But rare enough at court, sire, to believe it when it is spread.'

'Perhaps you are right. Is she well born?'

'Excellently so; the daughter of the Marquis de la Vallière,* and step-daughter of that good M. de Saint-Remy.'

'Ah! yes, my aunt's major-domo; I remember it; and I remember now, that I saw her as I passed through Blois. She was presented to the Queens. I have even to reproach myself, that I did not, on that occasion, pay her all the attention she deserved.'

'Oh! sire, I trust that your Majesty will repair the time you have lost.'

'And the report—you tell me—is, that Mademoiselle de la Vallière never had a lover.'

'In any case I do not think your Majesty would be much alarmed at the rivalry.'

'Yet, stay,' said the King, in a very serious tone of voice.

'Your Majesty?'

'I remember.'

'Ah!'

'If she has no lover, she has, at least, a betrothed.'

'A betrothed!'

'What! Comte, do not you know that?'

'No.'

'You, the man who knows all the news?'

'Your Majesty will excuse me. Your Majesty knows this betrothed, then?'

'Assuredly! his father came to ask me to sign the marriage contract; it is—' The King was about to pronounce the Vicomte de Bragelonne's name, when he stopped, and knitted his brows.

'It is——,' repeated Saint-Aignan inquiringly.

'I don't remember now,' replied Louis XIV, endeavouring to conceal an annoyance which he had some trouble to disguise.

'Can I try to jog your Majesty's memory?' inquired the Comte de Saint-Aignan.

'No; for I no longer remember to whom I intended to refer; indeed, I only remember very indistinctly, that one of the maids of honour was to marry——, the name, however, has escaped me.'

'Was it Mademoiselle de Tonnay-Charente he was going to marry?' inquired Saint-Aignan.

'Very likely,' said the King.

'In that case the intended was M. de Montespan; but Mademoiselle de Tonnay-Charente did not speak of it, it seemed to me, in such a manner as would frighten suitors away.'

'At all events,' said the King, 'I know nothing, or almost nothing, about Mademoiselle de la Vallière. Saint-Aignan, I rely upon you to procure me some information about her.'

'Yes, sire, and when shall I have the honour of seeing your Majesty again to give you the information?'

'Whenever you shall have procured it.'

'I shall obtain it speedily, then, if the information can be as quickly obtained as my wish to see your Majesty again.'

'Well said, Count! By the bye, has Madame displayed any ill-feeling against this poor girl?'

'None, sire.'

'Madame did not get angry, then?'

'I do not know; I only know that she laughed continually.'

'That's well; but I think I hear voices in the ante-rooms—no doubt a courier has just arrived. Inquire, Saint-Aignan.' The Count ran to the door and exchanged a few words with the usher; he returned to the King, saying, 'Sire, it is M. Fouquet, who has this moment arrived, by your Majesty's orders, he says. He presented himself, but, because of the advanced hour, he does not press for an audience this evening, and is satisfied to have his presence here formally announced.'

'M. Fouquet; I wrote to him at three o'clock, inviting him to be at Fontainebleau the following morning, and he arrives at Fontainebleau at two o'clock. This is indeed zeal!' exclaimed the King, delighted to see himself so promptly obeyed. 'On the contrary, M. Fouquet shall have his audience. I summoned him, and will receive him. Let him be introduced. As for you, Count, pursue your inquiries, and be here to-morrow.'

The King placed his finger upon his lips; and Saint-Aignan, his heart brimful of happiness, hastily withdrew, telling the usher to introduce M. Fouquet, who, thereupon entered the King's apartment. Louis rose to receive him.

'Good evening, M. Fouquet,' he said, smiling graciously; 'I congratulate you on your punctuality; and yet my message must have reached you late.'

'At nine in the evening, sire.'

'You have been working very hard, lately, M. Fouquet, for I have been informed that you have not left your rooms at Saint-Mandé* during the last three or four days.'

'It is perfectly true, your Majesty, that I have kept myself shut up for the past three days,' replied Fouquet.

'Do you know, M. Fouquet, that I had a great many things to say to you?' continued the King, with a most gracious air.

'Your Majesty overwhelms me, and since you are so graciously disposed towards me, will your Majesty permit me to remind you of the promise your Majesty made to grant me an audience?'

'Ah! yes; some Church dignitary, who thinks he has to thank me for something, is it not?'

'Precisely so, sire. The hour is, perhaps, badly chosen, but the time of the companion whom I have brought with me is valuable, and as Fontainebleau is on the way to his diocese.'

'Who is it, then?'

'The last Bishop of Vannes, whose appointment your Majesty, at my recommendation, deigned, three months since,* to sign.'

'That is very possible,' said the King, who had signed without reading; 'and is he here?'

'Yes, sire; Vannes is an important diocese; the flock belonging to this pastor need his religious consolation; they are savages,* whom it is necessary to polish, at the same time that he instructs them, and M. d'Herblay is unequalled in such kinds of missions.'

'M. d'Herblay!' said the King, musingly, as if his name, heard long since, was not, however, unknown to him.

'Oh!' said Fouquet promptly, 'your Majesty is not acquainted with the obscure name of one of your most faithful and most valuable servants?'

'No, I confess I am not. And so he wishes to set off again?'

'He has this very day received letters which will, perhaps, compel him to leave; so that, before setting off for that unknown region called Brittany, he is desirous of paying his respects to your Majesty.'

'Let him enter.'

Fouquet made a sign to the usher in attendance, who was waiting behind the tapestry. The door opened and Aramis entered.

The King allowed him to finish the compliments which he addressed to him, and fixed a long look upon a countenance which no one could forget after having once beheld it.

'Vannes!' he said; 'you are Bishop of Vannes, I believe?'

'Yes, sire.'

'Vannes is in Brittany, I think?' Aramis bowed.

'Near the coast?' Aramis again bowed.

'A few leagues from Belle-Isle, is it not?'

'Yes, sire,' replied Aramis; 'six leagues, I believe.'

'Six leagues; a mere step, then,' said Louis XIV.

'Not for us poor Bretons, sire,' replied Aramis; 'six leagues, on the contrary, is a great distance, if it be six leagues on land; and an immense distance, if it be leagues on the sea. Besides I have the honour to mention to your Majesty that there are six leagues of sea from the river to Belle-Isle.'*

'It is said that M. Fouquet has a very beautiful house there?' inquired the King.

'Yes, it is said so,' replied Aramis, looking quietly at Fouquet.

'What do you mean by "it is said so"?' exclaimed the King.

'He has, sire.'

'Really, M. Fouquet, I must confess that one circumstance surprises me.'

'What may that be, sire?'

'That you should have at the head of your parishes a man like M. d'Herblay, and yet should not have shown him Belle-Isle.'

'Oh, sire,' replied the Bishop, without giving Fouquet time to answer, 'we poor Breton prelates seldom leave our residences.'

'M. de Vannes,' said the King, 'I will punish M. Fouquet for his indifference. I will change your bishopric.'

Fouquet bit his lips, but Aramis only smiled.

'What income does Vannes bring you in?' continued the King.

'Sixty thousand livres, sire,' said Aramis.

'So trifling an amount as that; but you possess other property, Monsieur de Vannes?'

'I have nothing else, sire; only M. Fouquet pays me one thousand two hundred livres a year for his pew in the church.'

'Well, M. d'Herblay, I promise you something better than that.'

Aramis bowed, and the King also bowed to him in a respectful manner, as he was always accustomed to do towards women and members of the Church. Aramis gathered that his audience was at an end; he took his leave of the King in the simple unpretending language of a country pastor, and disappeared.

'His is, indeed a remarkable face,' said the King, following him with his eyes as long as he could see him, and even to a certain degree when he was no longer to be seen.

'Sire,' replied Fouquet, 'if that Bishop had been educated early in life, no prelate in the kingdom would deserve the highest distinctions better than he.'

'His learning is not extensive, then?'

'He changed the sword for the priest's garments, and that rather late in life.* But it matters little, if your Majesty will permit me to speak of M. de Vannes again on another occasion——'

'I beg you to do so. But before speaking of him, let us speak of yourself, M. Fouquet.'

'Of me, sire?'

'Yes, I have to pay you a thousand compliments.'

'I cannot express to your Majesty the delight with which you overwhelm me.'

'I understand you, M. Fouquet. I confess, however, to have had certain prejudices against you.'

'In that case I was indeed unhappy, sire.'

'But they exist no longer. Did you not perceive——'

'I did, indeed, sire; but I awaited with resignation the day when truth would prevail; and it seems that that day has now arrived.'

'Ah! you knew, then, you were in disgrace with me?'

'Alas! sire, I perceived it.'

'And do you know the reason?'

'Perfectly well; your Majesty thought that I had been wastefully lavish in expenditure.'

'Not so; far from that.'

'Or rather, an indifferent administrator. In a word, your Majesty thought that, as the people had no money, there would be none for your Majesty either.'

'Yes, I thought so; but I was deceived.' Fouquet bowed.

'And no disturbances, no complaints?'

'And money enough,' said Fouquet.

'The fact is that you have been profuse with it during the last month.'

'I have more still, not only for all your Majesty's require-
ments, but for all your caprices.'

'I thank you, M. Fouquet,' replied the King seriously. 'I will
not put you to the proof. For the next two months I do not
intend to ask you for anything.'

'I will avail myself of the interval to amass five or six millions,
which will be serviceable as money in hand in case of war.'

'Five or six millions!'

'For the expenses of your Majesty's household only, be it
understood.'

'You think war is probable,* M. Fouquet?'

'I think that if Heaven has bestowed on the eagle a beak and
claws, it is to enable him to show his royal character.' The King
blushed with pleasure.

'We have spent a great deal of money these few days past,
Monsieur Fouquet; will you not scold me for it?'

'Sire, your Majesty has still twenty years of youth to enjoy, and
a thousand millions of francs to spend in those twenty years.'

'That is a great deal of money, M. Fouquet,' said the King.

'I will economise, sire. Besides, your Majesty has two valuable men in M. Colbert and myself. The one will encourage you
to be prodigal with your treasures—and this shall be myself, if
my services should continue to be agreeable to your Majesty;
and the other will economise money for you, and this will be
M. Colbert's province.'

'M. Colbert?' returned the King, astonished.

'Certainly, sire, M. Colbert is an excellent accountant.'

At this commendation, bestowed by the enemy upon the enemy himself, the King felt himself penetrated with confidence
and admiration. There was not, moreover, either in Fouquet's
voice or look, anything which injuriously affected a single syllable
of the remark he had made; he did not pass one eulogium, as it
were, in order to acquire the right of making two reproaches.
The King comprehended him, and yielding to so much generosity and address, he said, 'You praise M. Colbert, then?'

'Yes, sire, I praise him; for, besides being a man of merit, I
believe him to be devoted to your Majesty's interests.'

'Is that because he has so often interfered with your own
views?' said the King smiling.

'Exactly, sire.'

'Explain yourself.'

'It is simple enough. I am the man who is needed to make the money come in; he the man who is needed to prevent it leaving.'

'Nay, nay, Monsieur le Surintendant, you will presently say something which will correct this good opinion.'

'Upon my honour, sire, I do not know throughout France a better clerk than M. Colbert.'

This word 'clerk' did not possess, in 1661, the somewhat subservient signification which is attached to it in the present day; but as spoken by Fouquet, whom the King had addressed as the surintendent, it seemed to acquire an insignificant and petty character, which served admirably to restore Fouquet to his place, and Colbert to his own.

'And yet,' said Louis XIV, 'it was he, however, who, notwithstanding his economy, had the arrangement of my fêtes here at Fontainebleau; and I assure you, Monsieur Fouquet, that in no way has he interfered with the expenditure of money.' Fouquet bowed, but did not reply.

'Is it not your opinion, too!' said the King.

'I think, sire,' he replied, 'that M. Colbert has done what he had to do in an excellently orderly manner, and that he deserves in this respect, all the praise your Majesty may bestow upon him.'

The word 'orderly' was a proper accompaniment for the word 'clerk'. The King possessed that extreme sensitiveness of organisation, and delicacy of perception, which pierced through and detected the regular order of feelings and sensations, before the actual sensations themselves, and he, therefore, comprehended that the clerk had, in Fouquet's opinion, been too full of method and order in his arrangements; in other words, that the magnificent fêtes of Fontainebleau might have been rendered more magnificent still. The King consequently felt that there was something in the amusements he had provided with which some person or another might be able to find fault; he experienced a little of the annoyance felt by a person coming from the provinces to Paris, dressed out in the very best clothes which his wardrobe can furnish, and finds that the fashionably-dressed man there looks at him either too much or not enough. This part of the conversation, which Fouquet had carried on with so much moderation, yet with such extreme tact, inspired the King with the highest esteem for the character of the man, and the capacity of the minister. Fouquet took his leave at two o'clock in the morning, and the King went to bed a little uneasy and confused at the indirect lesson he had just received; and two good quarters of an hour were employed by him in going over again in his memory the embroideries, the tapestries, the bills of fare of the various banquets, the architecture of the triumphal arches, the arrangements for the illuminations and fireworks, all the offspring of the 'clerk Colbert's' invention. The result was that the King passed in review before him everything that had taken place during the last week, and decided that faults could be found in his fêtes. But Fouquet by his politeness, his thoughtful consideration and his generosity, had injured Colbert more deeply than the latter by his artifice, his ill-will, and his persevering hatred, had ever succeeded in injuring Fouquet.

XXX

FONTAINEBLEAU AT TWO O'CLOCK IN THE MORNING

As we have seen, Saint-Aignan had quitted the King's apartment at the very moment the Finance Minister entered it. Saint-Aignan was charged with a mission which required despatch, and he was going to do his utmost to turn his time to the best possible advantage. He whom we have introduced as the King's friend was indeed an uncommon personage; he was one of those valuable courtiers whose vigilance and acuteness of perception threw all past and future favourites into the shade, and counter-balanced, by his close attention, the servility of Dangeau, who was not the favourite, but the toady of the King.* M. de Saint-Aignan began to think what was to be done in the present position of affairs. He reflected that his first information ought to come from de Guiche. He therefore set out in search of him, but de Guiche, whom we saw disappear behind one of the wings of the château, and who seemed to have returned to his own apartments, had not entered the château. Saint-Aignan therefore went in quest of him, and after having turned and twisted, and searched in every direction, he perceived something like a human form leaning against a tree. This figure was as motionless as a statue, and seemed deeply engaged in looking at a window, although its curtains were closely drawn. As this window happened to be Madame's, Saint-Aignan concluded that the form in question must be that of de Guiche. He advanced cautiously, and found that he was not mistaken. De Guiche had, after his conversation with Madame, carried away such a weight of happiness, that all his strength of mind was hardly sufficient to enable him to support it. On his side, Saint-Aignan knew that de Guiche had had something to do with La Vallière's introduction to Madame's household, for a courtier knows everything and forgets nothing; but he had never heard under what title or conditions de Guiche had conferred his protection upon La Vallière. But, as in asking a great many questions it is singular if a man does not learn something, Saint-Aignan reckoned upon learning much or little, as it might be, if he were to question de Guiche with that extreme tact, and, at the same time, with that persistence in attaining an object, of which he was capable. Saint-Aignan's plan was the following:—if the information obtained was satisfactory, he would inform the King, with effusion, that he had alighted upon a pearl, and claim the privilege of setting the pearl in question in the royal crown. If the information were unsatisfactory, which after all might be possible, he would examine how far the King cared about La Vallière, and make use of his information in such a manner as to get rid of the girl altogether, and thereby obtain all the merit of her banishment with all those ladies of the court who might have any pretensions upon the King's heart, beginning with Madame and finishing with the Queen. In case the King should show himself obstinate in his fancy, then he would not produce the damaging information he had obtained, but would let La Vallière know that this damaging information was carefully preserved in a secret drawer of her confidant's memory; in this manner he would be able to display his generosity before the poor girl's eyes, and so keep her in constant suspense between gratitude and apprehension to such an extent as to make her a friend at court, interested, as an accomplice, in making her accomplice's fortune while she was making her own. As far as concerned the day when the bombshell of the past should burst, if ever there should be any occasion for its bursting, Saint-Aignan promised himself that he would by that time have taken all possible precautions, and would pretend an entire ignorance of the matter to the King; while, with regard to La Vallière, he would still, even on that day, have an opportunity of being considered the personification of generosity. It was with such ideas as these, which the fire of covetousness had caused to dawn into being in half an hour, that Saint-Aignan, the best son in the world, as La Fontaine would have said, determined to get de Guiche into conversation; in other words, to trouble him in his happiness—a happiness of which Saint-Aignan was quite ignorant. It was one o'clock in the morning when Saint-Aignan perceived de Guiche, standing motionless, leaning against the trunk of a tree, with his eyes fastened upon the lighted window. It was precisely at this hour that Saint-Aignan, badly-advised,—selfishness always counsels badly,—came and struck him on the shoulder, at the very moment he was murmuring a word or rather a name.

'Ah!' he cried loudly, 'I was looking for you.'

'For me?' said de Guiche, starting.

'Yes; and I find you seemingly moonstruck. Is it likely, my dear Comte, you have been attacked by a poetical malady, and are making verses.'

The young man forced a smile upon his lips, while a thousand conflicting sensations were muttering against Saint-Aignan in the deep recesses of his heart. 'Perhaps,' he said. 'But by what happy chance——'

'Ah! your remark shows that you did not hear what I said. I began by telling you I was looking for you.'

'You were looking for me?'

'Yes; and I find you now in the very act.'

'Of doing what I should like to know?'

'Of singing the praises of Phillis.'*

'Well, I do not deny it,' said de Guiche, laughing. 'Yes, my dear Comte, I was celebrating Phillis's praises.'

'And you have acquired the right to do so; you, the intrepid protector of every beautiful and clever woman.'

'In the name of goodness what story have you got hold of now?'

'Acknowledged truths, I am well aware. But stay a moment; I am in love.'

'So much the better, my dear Comte; tell me all about it.' And de Guiche, afraid that Saint-Aignan might perhaps presently observe the window where the light was still burning, took the Comte's arm, and endeavoured to lead him away.

'Oh!' said the latter, resisting, 'do not take me toward those dark woods; it is too damp there. Let us stay in the moonlight.' And while he yielded to the pressure of de Guiche's arm he remained in the flower-garden adjoining the château.

'Well,' said de Guiche, resigning himself, 'lead me where you like, and ask me what you please.'

'It is impossible to be more agreeable than you are.' And then, after a moment's silence, Saint-Aignan continued, 'I wish you to tell me something about a certain person in whom you have interested yourself.'

'And with whom you are in love?'

'I will neither admit nor deny it. You understand that a man does not very readily place his heart where there is no hope of return, and that it is most essential he should take measures of security in advance.'

'You are right,' said de Guiche, with a sigh, 'a heart is a precious gift.'

'Mine particularly is very tender, and in that light I present it to you.'

'Oh! you are well known, Comte. Well?'

'It is simply a question of Mademoiselle de Tonnay-Charente.'

'Why, my dear Saint-Aignan, you are losing your senses, I should think. I have never shown or taken any interest in Mademoiselle de Tonnay-Charente.'

'Did you not obtain admission for Mademoiselle de Tonnay-Charente into Madame's household?'

'Mademoiselle de Tonnay-Charente—and you ought to know it better than anyone else, my dear Comte—is of a sufficiently good family to make her presence here desirable, and a greater reason therefore to render her admittance very easy.'

'You are jesting.'

'No; and upon my honour I do not know what you mean.'

'And you had nothing, then, to do with her admission.'

'No; I saw her for the first time the day she was presented to Madame. Therefore, as I have never taken any interest in her, as I do not know her, I am not able to give you the information you require.' And de Guiche made a movement as though he were about to leave his questioner.

'Nay, nay, one moment, my dear Comte,' said Saint-Aignan; 'you shall not escape me in this manner.'

'Why, really, it seems to me that it is now time to return to our apartments.'

'And yet you were not going in when I—did not meet, but found you.'

'Therefore, my dear Comte,' said de Guiche, 'as long as you have anything to say to me, I place myself entirely at your service.'

'And you are quite right in doing so. What matters half an hour more or less? Will you swear that you have no injurious communications to make to me about her, and that any injurious communications you might possibly have to make are not the cause of your silence?'

'Oh! I believe the poor child to be as pure as crystal.'

'You overwhelm me with joy. And yet I do not wish to have towards you the appearance of a man so badly informed as I seem. It is quite certain that you supplied the Princess's household with the ladies of honour. Nay, a song even has been written about it.'

'You know that songs are written about everything.'

'Do you know it?'

'No; sing it to me, and I shall make its acquaintance.'

'I cannot tell you how it begins, I only remember how it ends.'

'Very well, at all events that is something.'

> '"Guiche is the furnisher
> Of the maids of honour."'*

'The idea is weak, and the rhyme poor,' said de Guiche.

'What can you expect, my dear fellow, it is not Racine or Molière, but La Feuillade's;* and a great lord cannot rhyme like a beggarly poet.'

'It is very unfortunate, though, that you only remember how it goes on.'

'Stay, stay; I have just recollected the beginning of the second couplet:—

> ' "He has stock'd the birdcage;
>   Montalais and——" '

'And La Vallière,' exclaimed Guiche impatiently, and completely ignorant besides of Saint-Aignan's object.

'Yes, yes, you have it. You have hit upon the word La Vallière.'

'A grand discovery, indeed.'

'Montalais and La Vallière, these then are the two girls in whom you interested yourself,' said Saint-Aignan, laughing.

'And so Mademoiselle de Tonnay-Charente's name is not to be met with in the song?'

'No; but I find Montalais there,' said Saint-Aignan, still laughing.

'Oh! you will find her everywhere. She is a most active young lady.'

'You know her?'

'Indirectly. She was the protégée of a man named Malicorne, who is a protégé of Manicamp's; Manicamp asked me to get the situation of maid of honour for Montalais in Madame's household, and a situation for Malicorne as an officer in Monsieur's household.* Well, I asked for the appointments, and you know very well that I have a weakness for that droll fellow Manicamp.'

'And you obtained what you sought?'

'For Montalais, yes; for Malicorne, yes and no; for as yet he is only tolerated there; do you wish to know anything else?'

'The last word of the couplet remains La Vallière,' said Saint-Aignan, resuming the smile which had so tormented Guiche.

'Well,' said the latter, 'it is true that I obtained admission for her in Madame's household.'

'Ah, ah!' said Saint-Aignan.

'But,' continued Guiche, assuming a great coldness of manner, 'you will oblige me, Comte, not to jest about that name. Mademoiselle La Baume Le Blanc de la Vallière is a young lady of unimpeachable conduct.'

'Then you have not heard the latest rumour?' exclaimed Saint-Aignan.

'No, and you will do me a service, my dear Comte, in keeping this report to yourself, and to those who circulate it.'

'Ah! bah! you take the matter up very seriously.'

'Yes; Mademoiselle de Vallière is beloved by one of my best friends.' Saint-Aignan started.

'Oh, oh!' he said.

'Yes, Comte,' continued Guiche; 'and consequently, you, the most distinguished man in France for his polished courtesy of manner, will understand that I cannot allow my friend to be placed in a ridiculous position.'

Saint-Aignan began to bite his nails, partially from vexation, and partially from disappointed curiosity. Guiche made him a very profound bow.

'You send me away,' said Saint-Aignan, who was dying to learn the name of the friend.

'I do not send you away, my dear fellow.—I am going to finish my lines to Phillis.'

Saint-Aignan was obliged to accept the notice to quit; he accordingly did so, and disappeared behind the hedge. Their conversation had led Guiche and Saint-Aignan a good distance from the château.

Every mathematician, every poet, and every dreamer has his means of diverting his attention; Saint-Aignan, then, on leaving Guiche, found himself at the extremity of the grove,—at the very spot where the outbuildings for the servants begin, and where, behind thickets of acacias and chestnut-trees interlacing their branches, which were hidden by masses of clematis and young vines, the wall which separated the woods from the courtyard of these outbuildings was erected. Saint-Aignan, alone, took the path which led towards these buildings; Guiche going off in the very opposite direction. The one proceeded towards the flower-garden, while the other bent his steps towards the walls. Saint-Aignan walked on between rows of the mountain ash, lilac, and hawthorn, which formed an almost impenetrable roof above his head; his feet were buried in the soft gravel and in the thick moss. He was deliberating over a means of taking his revenge, which it seemed difficult for him to carry out, and was vexed with himself for not having learnt more about La Vallière, notwithstanding the ingenious measures he had resorted to in order to acquire some information about her, when suddenly the murmur of a human voice attracted his attention. He heard whispers, the complaining tones of a woman's voice mingled with entreaties, smothered laughter, sighs, and half-stifled exclamations of surprise; but above them all, the woman's voice prevailed. Saint-Aignan stopped to look about him; he perceived with the greatest surprise that the voices proceeded, not from the ground, but from the branches of the trees. As he glided along under the covered walk, he raised his head, and observed at the top of the wall a woman perched upon a ladder, in eager conversation with a man seated on a branch of a chestnut-tree, whose head alone could be seen, the rest of his body being concealed in the thick covert of the chestnut. The woman was on the near side of the wall, the man on the other side of it.

XXXI

THE LABYRINTH

SAINT-AIGNAN, who had only been seeking for information, had met with an adventure. This was indeed a piece of good luck. Curious to learn why, and particularly about what, this man and woman were conversing at such an hour and in such a singular position, Saint-Aignan made himself as small as he possibly could, and approached almost under the rounds of the ladder. And taking measures to make himself as comfortable as possible, he leaned his back against a tree and listened, and heard the following conversation. The woman was the first to speak.

'Really, Monsieur Manicamp,' she said, in a voice which, notwithstanding the reproaches she addressed to him, preserved a marked tone of coquetry, 'really your indiscreetness is of a very dangerous character. We cannot talk long in this manner without being observed.'

'That is very probable,' said the man, in the calmest and coolest of tones.

'In that case, then, what would people say? Oh! if any one were to see me, I declare I should die from very shame.'

'Oh! that would be very silly, and I do not believe you capable of it.'

'It might have been different if there had been anything between us; but to do an injury to myself gratuitously, is really very foolish of me; so adieu, Monsieur Manicamp.'

'So far so good; I know the man, and now let me see who the woman is,' said Saint-Aignan, watching the rounds of the ladder, on which were standing two pretty little feet covered with blue satin shoes.

'Nay, nay, for pity's sake, my dear Montalais,' cried Manicamp. 'deuce take it, do not go away; I have a great many things to say to you, of the very greatest importance still.'

'Montalais,' said Saint-Aignan to himself, 'one of the three. Each of the three gossips had her adventure, only I had thought that the hero of this one's adventure was Malicorne and not Manicamp.'

At her companion's appeal, Montalais stopped in the middle of her descent, and Saint-Aignan could observe the unfortunate Manicamp climb from one branch of the chestnut-tree to another, either to improve his situation, or to overcome the fatigue consequent upon his indifferent position.

'Now, listen to me,' said he; 'you quite understand, I hope, that my intentions are perfectly innocent?'

'Of course. But why did you write me a letter stimulating my gratitude towards you? Why did you ask me for an interview at such an hour and in such a place as this?'

'I stimulated your gratitude in reminding you that it was I who had been the means of your becoming attached to Madame's household; because most anxiously desirous of obtaining the interview which you have been kind enough to grant me, I employed the means which appeared to me the most certain to ensure it. And my reason for soliciting it, at such an hour, and in such a locality, was, that the hour seemed to be the most prudent, and the locality the least open to observation. Moreover, I had occasion to speak to you upon certain subjects which require both prudence and solitude.'

'Monsieur Manicamp!'

'But everything in the most perfect honour, I assure you.'

'I think, Monsieur Manicamp, that it will be more becoming in me to take my leave.'

'Nay, listen to me, or I shall jump from my perch here to yours, and be careful how you set me at defiance; for a branch of this chestnut-tree causes me a good deal of annoyance, and may provoke me to extreme measures. Do not follow the example of this branch, then, but listen to me.'

'I am listening, and I will agree to do so; but be as brief as possible, for if you have a branch of the chestnut-tree which annoys you, I wish you to understand that one of the rounds of the ladder is hurting the soles of my feet, and my shoes are being cut through.'

'Do me the kindness to give me your hand.'

'There is my hand; but what are you going to do?'

'To draw you towards me.'

'What for? You surely do not wish me to join you in the tree?'

'No; but I wish you to sit down upon the wall; there, that will do; there is quite room enough, and I would give a great deal to be allowed to sit down beside you.'

'No, no; you are very well where you are; we should be seen.'

'Do you really think so?' said Manicamp, in an insinuating voice.

'I am sure of it.'

'Very well, I remain in my tree, then, although I cannot be worse placed.'

'Monsieur Manicamp, we are wandering away from the subject. You wrote me a letter?'

'I did.'

'Why did you write?'

'Fancy, that at two o'clock to-day, de Guiche left.'

'What then?'

'Seeing him set off, I followed him, as I usually do.'

'Of course, I see that, since you are here now.'

'Don't be in a hurry. You are aware, I suppose, that de Guiche is up to his very neck in disgrace? It was the very height of imprudence on his part, then, to come to Fontainebleau to seek those who had at Paris sent him away into exile, and particularly those from whom he had been separated.'

'Monsieur Manicamp, you reason like Pythagoras* of old.'

'Moreover, de Guiche is as obstinate as a man in love can be, and he refused to listen to any of my remonstrances. I begged, I implored him, but he would not listen to anything. O! the deuce!'

'What's the matter?'

'I beg your pardon, Mademoiselle Montalais, but this confounded branch, about which I have already had the honour of speaking to you, has just made a tear in my clothes.'

'It is quite dark,' replied Montalais, laughing; 'so, pray continue, M. Manicamp.'

'De Guiche set off on horseback as hard as he could, I following him, at a slower pace. You quite understand that to throw oneself into the water, for instance, with a friend with the same headlong speed as he himself would do it, would be the act either of a fool or a madman. I therefore allowed de Guiche to get well ahead, and I proceeded on my way with a commendable slowness of pace, feeling quite sure that my unfortunate friend would not be received, or, if he had been, that he would ride off again at the very first cross, disagreeable answer; and that I should see him returning much faster than he had gone, without having, myself, gone farther than Ris or Melun*—and that even was a good distance you will admit, for it is eleven leagues to get there and as many to return.' Montalais shrugged her shoulders.

'Laugh as much as you like; but if, instead of being comfortably seated on the top of the wall as you are, you were sitting on this branch, as if you were on horseback, you would, like Augustus, aspire to descend.'

'Be patient, my dear M. Manicamp, a few minutes will soon pass away; you were saying, I think, that you had gone beyond Ris and Melun.'

'Yes; I went through Ris and Melun, and I continued to go on, more and more surprised that I did not see him returning; and here I am at Fontainebleau; I look for, and inquire after de Guiche everywhere, but no one has seen him, no one in the town has spoken to him; he arrived riding at full gallop, he entered the château, where he has disappeared. I have been here at Fontainebleau since eight o'clock this evening, inquiring for de Guiche in every direction, but no de Guiche can be found. I am dying from uneasiness. You understand that I have not been running my head into the lion's den, in entering the château, as my imprudent friend has done; I came at once to the servants' offices, and I succeeded in getting a letter conveyed to you; and now, for Heaven's sake, my dear young lady, relieve me from my anxiety.'

'There will be no difficulty in that, my dear M. Manicamp; your friend de Guiche has been admirably received. The King made quite a fuss of him.'

'The King who exiled him!'

'Madame smiled upon him, and Monsieur appears to like him better than ever.'

'Ah! ah!' said Manicamp, 'that explains to me, then, why and how he has remained. And he did not say anything about me?'

'Not a word.'

'That is very unkind. What is he doing now?'

'In all probability he is asleep, or, if not asleep, he is dreaming.'

'And what have they been doing all the evening?'

'Dancing.'

'The famous ballet. How did de Guiche look?'

'Superb.'

'Dear fellow! And now, pray forgive me, Mademoiselle Montalais; but all that I now have to do is to pass from where I now am to your apartment.'

'What do you mean?'

'I cannot suppose that the door of the château will be opened for me at this hour; and as for spending the night upon this branch I possibly might not object to do so, but I declare it is impossible for any other creature than a parrot to do it.'

'But, M. Manicamp, I cannot introduce a man over the wall in that manner.'

'Two, if you please,' said a second voice, but in so timid a tone that it seemed as if its owner felt the utter impropriety of such a request.

'Good gracious!' exclaimed Montalais, 'who is that speaking to me?'

'Malicorne, Mademoiselle Montalais.'

And, as Malicorne spoke, he raised himself from the ground to the lowest branches, and thence to the height of the wall.

'Monsieur Malicorne! why, you are both mad!'

'How do you do, Mademoiselle Montalais?' inquired Malicorne.

'This was all I needed,' said Montalais, in despair.

'Oh! Mademoiselle Montalais,' murmured Malicorne; 'do not be so severe, I beseech you.'

'In fact,' said Manicamp, 'we are your friends, and you cannot possibly wish your friends to lose their lives; and to leave us to pass the night where we are, is, in fact, condemning us both to death.'

'Oh!' said Montalais, 'Monsieur Malicorne is so robust that a night passed in the open air with the beautiful stars above him will not do him any harm, and it will be a just punishment for the trick he has played me.'

'Be it so, then; let Malicorne arrange matters with you in the best way he can; I pass over,' said Manicamp. And bending down the famous branch against which he had directed such bitter complaints, he succeeded, by the assistance of his hands and feet, in seating himself side by side with Montalais, who tried to push him back, while he endeavoured to maintain his position and in which, moreover, he succeeded. Having taken possession of the ladder, he stepped on it, and then gallantly offered his hand to his fair antagonist. While this was going on, Malicorne had installed himself in the chestnut-tree, in the very place Manicamp had just left, determining within himself to succeed him in the one which he now occupied. Manicamp and Montalais descended a few rounds of the ladder, Manicamp insisting and Montalais laughing and objecting.

Suddenly Malicorne's voice was heard in tones of entreaty:—

'I entreat you, Mademoiselle Montalais, not to leave me here. My position is very insecure, and some accident will be sure to befall me, if I attempt unaided to reach the other side of the wall; it does not matter if Manicamp tears his clothes, for he can make use of M. de Guiche's wardrobe; but I shall not be able to use even those belonging to M. Manicamp, for they will be torn.'

'My opinion,' said Manicamp, without taking any notice of Malicorne's lamentations, 'is that the best thing to be done is to go and look for de Guiche without delay, for, by-and-by, perhaps, I may not be able to get to his apartments.'

'That is my own opinion too,' replied Montalais; 'so, go at once, Monsieur Manicamp.'

'A thousand thanks. Adieu, Mademoiselle Montalais,' said Manicamp, jumping to the ground, 'your kindness cannot possibly be exceeded.'

'Farewell, M. Manicamp; I am now going to get rid of M. Malicorne.'

Malicorne sighed. Manicamp went away a few paces, but returning to the foot of the ladder, he said, 'By the bye, which is the way to M. de Guiche's apartments?'

'Nothing is easier. You go along by the hedge until you reach a place where the paths cross.'

'Yes.'

'You will see four paths.'

'Exactly.'

'One of which you will take.'

'Well, let us suppose that I have succeeded in finding that fortunate path.'

'In that case, you are almost there, for you have nothing else to do but to cross the labyrinth.'

'Nothing more than that? The deuce! so there is a labyrinth as well?'

'Yes, and complicated enough too; even in daylight one may sometimes be deceived,—there are turnings and windings without end; in the first place, you must turn three times to the right, then twice to the left, then turn once—stay, is it once or twice though? at all events, when you get clear of the labyrinth, you will see an avenue of sycamores, and this avenue leads straight to the pavilion in which M. de Guiche is lodging.'

'Nothing could be clearer,' said Manicamp; 'and I have not the slightest doubt in the world that if I were to follow your directions, I should lose my way immediately. I have, therefore, a slight service to ask of you.'

'What may that be?'

'That you will offer me your arm and guide me yourself, like another—like another—I used to know mythology, but other important matters have made me forget it; pray come with me, then?'

'And am I to be abandoned, then?' cried Malicorne.

'It is quite impossible, monsieur,' said Montalais to Manicamp; 'if I were to be seen with you at such an hour, what would be said of me?'

'Your own conscience would acquit you,' said Manicamp sententiously.

'Impossible, monsieur, impossible.'

'In that case, let me assist Malicorne to get down; he is a very intelligent fellow, and possesses a very keen scent; he will guide me, and if we lose ourselves, both of us will be lost, and the one will save the other. If we are together, and should be met by any one, we shall look as if we had some matter of business in hand; whilst alone I should have the appearance either of a lover or a robber. Come, Malicorne, here is the ladder.'

Malicorne had already stretched out one of his legs towards the top of the wall, when Manicamp said, in a whisper, 'Hush!'

'What's the matter?' inquired Montalais.

'I hear footsteps.'

In fact the fancied footsteps soon became a reality; the foliage was pushed aside, and Saint-Aignan appeared, with a smile on his lips and his hand stretched out towards them, taking every one by surprise; that is to say, Malicorne upon the tree with his head stretched out, Montalais upon the rounds of the ladder and clinging to it tightly, and Manicamp on the ground with his foot advanced ready to set off. 'Good-evening, Manicamp,' said the Comte, 'I am glad to see you, my dear fellow; we missed you this evening, and a good many inquiries have been made about you. Mademoiselle de Montalais, your most obedient servant.'

Montalais blushed. 'Good heavens!' she exclaimed, hiding her face in both her hands.

'Pray reassure yourself,' said Saint-Aignan, 'I know how perfectly innocent you are, and I shall give a good account of you. Manicamp, follow me: the hedge, the cross-paths, and labyrinth, I am well acquainted with them all; I will be your Ariadne.* There now, your mythological name is found at last.'

'And take M. Malicorne away with you at the same time,' said Montalais.

'No, indeed,' said Malicorne; 'M. Manicamp has conversed with you as long as he liked, and now it is my turn, if you please; I have a multitude of things to tell you about our future prospects.'

'You hear,' said the Comte, laughing; 'stay with him, Mademoiselle Montalais. This is, indeed, a night for secrets.' And taking Manicamp's arm, the Comte led him rapidly away in the direction of the road which Montalais knew so well, and indicated so badly. Montalais followed them with her eyes as long as she could perceive them.

XXXII

HOW MALICORNE HAD BEEN TURNED OUT OF THE HOTEL OF THE BEAU PAON

WHILE Montalais was engaged in looking after the Comte and Manicamp, Malicorne had taken advantage of the young girl's attention being drawn away to render his position somewhat more tolerable, and when she turned round she immediately noticed the change which had taken place; for he had seated himself, like a monkey, upon the wall, with his feet resting upon the top rounds of the ladder. The foliage of the wild vine and honeysuckle curled round his head like a Faun, while the twisted ivy branches represented tolerably enough his cloven feet. Montalais required nothing to make her resemblance to a Dryad* as complete as possible.

'Well,' she said, ascending another round of the ladder, 'are you resolved to render me unhappy? Have you not persecuted me enough, tyrant that you are?'

'I a tyrant?' said Malicorne.

'Yes, you are always compromising me, Monsieur Malicorne; you are a perfect monster of wickedness. Is not Orleans your place of residence?'*

'Do you ask me what I have to do here? I wanted to see you.'

'Ah, great need of that.'

'Not as far as concerns yourself, perhaps, but as far as I am concerned. Mademoiselle Montalais, you know very well that I have left my home, and that, for the future, I have no other place of residence than that which you may happen to have. As you, therefore, are staying at Fontainebleau at the present moment, I have come to Fontainebleau.'

Montalais shrugged her shoulders. 'You wished to see me, did you not?' she said. 'Very well, you have seen me,—you are satisfied; so now go away.'

'Oh, no,' said Malicorne; 'I came to talk with you as well as to see you.'

'Very well, we will talk by-and-by, and in another place than this.'

'By-and-by! Heaven only knows if I shall meet you by-and-by in another place. We shall never find a more favourable one than this.'

'But I cannot this evening nor at the present moment. Mademoiselle de Tonnay-Charente is waiting for me in our room to communicate something of the very greatest importance.'

'How long has she been waiting?'

'For an hour at least.'

'In that case,' said Malicorne tranquilly, 'she will wait a few minutes longer.'

'Monsieur Malicorne,' said Montalais, 'you are forgetting yourself.'

'You should rather say that it is you who are forgetting me, and that I am getting impatient at the part you make me play here, indeed! For the last week I have been prowling about among the company here, and you have not deigned once to notice my presence here.'

'Have you been prowling about here for a week, M. Malicorne?'

'Like a wolf; sometimes I have been burnt by the fireworks, which have singed two of my wigs; at others, I have been completely drenched in the osiers by the evening damps, or the spray from the fountains,—always half-famished, always fatigued to death, with the view of a wall always before me, and the prospect of having to scale it perhaps. Upon my word, this is not the sort of life for any one to lead who is neither a squirrel, nor a salamander, nor an otter; and, since you drive your inhumanity so far as to wish to make me renounce my condition as a man, I declare it openly. A man I am, indeed, and a man I will remain, unless by superior orders.'

'Well, then, tell me, what do you wish,—what do you require, —what do you insist upon?' said Montalais, in a submissive tone.

'Do you mean to tell me that you did not know I was at Fontainebleau?'

'I suspected so.'

'Well, then, could you not have contrived during the last week to have seen me once a day, at least?'

'I have always been prevented, M. Malicorne.'

'Fiddlestick!'

'Ask my companion, if you do not believe me.'

'I shall ask no one to explain matters which I know better than any one.'

'You know that, whether I see you or not, I am thinking of you,' said Montalais, in a coaxing tone of voice.

'Oh, you are thinking of me, are you! well, is there anything new?'

'What about?'

'About my post in Monsieur's household.'

'Ah, my dear Monsieur Malicorne, no one has ventured lately to approach His Royal Highness.'

'Well, but now?'

'Now, it is quite a different thing; since yesterday he has left off being jealous.'

'Bah! how has his jealousy subsided?'

'It has been diverted into another channel.'

'Tell me all about it.'

'A report was spread that the King had fallen in love with some one else, and Monsieur was pacified immediately.'

'And who spread the report?'

Montalais lowered her voice. 'Between ourselves,' she said, 'I think that Madame and the King have come to an understanding about it.'

'Ah, ah!' said Malicorne; 'that was the only way to manage it. But what about poor M. de Guiche?'

'Oh, as for him, he is completely turned away.'

'Have they been writing to each other?'

'No, certainly not; I have not seen a pen in either of their hands for the last week.'

'On what terms are you with Madame?'

'The very best.'

'And with the King?'

'The King always smiles at me whenever I pass him.'

'Good. Now, tell me whom have the two lovers selected to serve for their screen?'

'La Vallière.'

'Oh, oh, poor girl! We must prevent that. If M. Raoul de Bragelonne were to suspect it, he would either kill her or kill himself.'

'Raoul, poor fellow; do you think so?'

'Women always claim to know the state of people's affections,' said Malicorne, 'and they do not even know how to read the thoughts of their own minds and hearts. Well, I can tell you, that M. de Bragelonne loves La Vallière to such a degree that, if she pretended to deceive him, he would, I repeat, either kill himself or kill her.'

'But the King is there to defend her,' said Montalais.

'The King,' exclaimed Malicorne; 'Raoul would kill the King as he would a common thief.'

'Good heavens!' said Montalais; 'you are mad, M. Malicorne.'

'Not in the least. Everything I have told you is, on the contrary, perfectly serious; and, for my own part, I know one thing.'

'What is that?'

'That I shall quietly tell Raoul of the deception.'

'Hush!' said Montalais, ascending another round of the ladder, so as to approach Malicorne more closely, 'do not open your lips to poor Raoul, because, as yet, you know nothing at all.'

'What is the matter then?'

'Why, this evening—but no one is listening, I hope?'

'No.'

'This evening, then, beneath the royal oak, La Vallière said aloud, and innocently enough, "I cannot conceive that when one has once seen the King, one can ever love another man."'

Malicorne almost jumped off the wall. 'Unhappy girl! did she really say that?'

'Word for word.'

'And she thinks so?'

'La Vallière always thinks what she says.'

'That positively cries aloud for vengeance. Why, women are serpents,' said Malicorne.

'Compose yourself, my dear Malicorne, compose yourself.'

'No, no; let us take the evil in time, on the contrary. There is time enough yet to tell Raoul of it.'

'Blunderer, on the contrary, it is too late,' replied Montalais.

'How so?'

'The King knows what La Vallière said of him.'

'The King knows it! The King was told of it I suppose.'

'The King heard it.'

'*Ahimé!* as the Cardinal used to say.'*

'The King was hidden in the thicket close to the royal oak.'

'It follows, then,' said Malicorne, 'that, for the future, the plan which the King and Madame have arranged, will go like clockwork, and will pass over Bragelonne's body.'

'Precisely so.'

'Well,' said Malicorne, after a moment's reflection, 'do not let us interpose our poor selves between a large oak tree and a great King, for we should certainly be ground to pieces.'

'The very thing I was going to say to you.'

'Let us think of ourselves then.'

'My own idea.'

'Open your beautiful eyes, then.'

'And you your large ears.'

'Approach your little mouth for a kiss.'

'Here,' said Montalais, who paid the debt immediately in ringing coin.

'Now, let us consider. First we have M. de Guiche, who is in love with Madame; then La Vallière, who is in love with the King; next, the King, who is in love both with Madame and La Vallière; lastly, Monsieur, who loves no one but himself. Among all these loves, any oaf would make his fortune; a greater reason, therefore, for sensible people like ourselves to do so.'

'There you are with your dreams again.'

'Nay, rather with realities. Let me lead you, darling. I do not think you have been very badly off hitherto?'

'No.'

'Well, the future is guaranteed by the past. Only since all here think of themselves before anything else, let us do so too.'

'Perfectly right.'

'Put out your hand, then, and say, "All for Malicorne."'

'All for Malicorne.'

'And I, "All for Montalais,"' replied Malicorne, stretching out his hand, in his turn.

'And now, what is to be done?'

'Keep your eyes and ears constantly open; collect every means of attack which may be serviceable against others; never let anything lie about which can be used against ourselves.'

'Sworn to. And now the agreement is entered into, good-bye.'

'What do you mean by "good-bye"?'

'Of course you can now return to your inn.'

'To my inn?'

'Have you not a room at the Beau Paon?'*

'I had, but have it no longer.'

'Who has taken it from you, then?'

'I will tell you. Some little time ago I was returning there after I had been running about after you; and having reached my hotel quite out of breath, I perceived a litter, upon which four peasants were carrying a sick monk.'

'A monk?'

'Yes, an old grey-bearded Franciscan. As I was looking at the monk, they entered the hotel; and as they were carrying him up the staircase, I followed; and as I reached the top of the staircase, I observed that they took him into my room.'

'Into your room?'

'Yes, into my own apartment. Supposing it to be a mistake, I summoned the landlord, who says that the room which had been let to me for the past eight days, was let to the Franciscan for the ninth.'

'Oh, oh.'

'That was exactly what I said; nay, I did even more, for I was inclined to get out of temper. I went upstairs again. I spoke to the Franciscan himself, and wished to prove the impropriety of the step; when this monk, dying though he seemed to be, raised himself upon his arm, fixed a pair of blazing eyes upon me, and in a voice which was admirably suited for commanding a charge of cavalry, said, "Turn this fellow out of doors," which was done immediately by the landlord and the four porters, who made me descend somewhat faster than was agreeable. This is how it happens, dearest, that I have no lodging.'

'Who can this Franciscan be?' said Montalais, 'Is he a general?'

'That is exactly the very title that one of the bearers of the litter gave him as he spoke to him in a low tone.'

'So that——' said Montalais.

'So that I have no room, no hotel, no lodging; and that I am as determined as my friend Manicamp was just now, not to pass the night in the open air.'

'What is to be done, then?' said Montalais.

'Nothing easier,' said a third voice; whereupon Montalais and Malicorne uttered a simultaneous cry, and Saint-Aignan appeared. 'Dear Monsieur Malicorne,' said Saint-Aignan, 'a very lucky accident has brought me back to extricate you from your embarrassment. Come, I can offer you a room in my own apartments, which, I can assure you, no Franciscan will deprive you of. As for you, my dear young lady, be easy. I already knew Mademoiselle de la Vallière's secret, and that of Mademoiselle de Tonnay-Charente; your own you have just been kind enough to confide in me; for which I thank you. I can keep three quite as well as one only.' Malicorne and Montalais looked at each other like two children detected in a theft; but as Malicorne saw a great advantage in the proposition which had been made to him, he gave Montalais a sign of resignation, which she returned. Malicorne then descended the ladder, round by round, reflecting at every step upon the means of obtaining piecemeal from M. de Saint-Aignan all he might possibly know about the famous secret. Montalais had already darted away as fleet as a deer, and neither crossroad nor labyrinth was able to deceive her. As for Saint-Aignan, he carried off Malicorne with him to his apartments, showing him a thousand attentions, enchanted to have close at hand, the very two men who, supposing that de Guiche were to remain silent, could give him the best information about the maids of honour.

XXXIII

WHAT REALLY TOOK PLACE AT THE BEAU PAON

In the first place, let us supply our readers with a few details about the inn called the Beau Paon. It owed its name to its sign, which represented a peacock spreading out its tail. But, in imitation of some painters who had bestowed the face of a handsome young man upon the serpent which tempted Eve, the painter of this sign had conferred upon the peacock the features of a woman. This inn, a living epigram against that half of the human race which renders existence delightful, was situated at Fontainebleau, in the first turning on the left-hand side, which divides on the road from Paris, that large artery, which constitutes in itself alone the entire town of Fontainebleau.* The side street in question was then known as the Rue de Lyon, doubtless because, geographically, it advanced in the direction of the second capital of the kingdom. The street itself was composed of two houses occupied by persons of the class of trades-people, the houses being separated by two large gardens, bordered with hedges running round them. Apparently, however, there seemed to be three houses in the street. Let us explain, notwithstanding appearances, how there were only two. The inn of the Beau Paon had its principal front towards the main street; but upon the Rue de Lyon there were two groups of buildings divided by courtyards, which comprised sets of apartments for the reception of all classes of travellers, whether on foot or on horseback, or even with their own carriages; and in which could be supplied, not only board and lodging, but also accommodation for exercise, or opportunities of solitude for even the wealthiest courtiers, whenever, after having received some check at the court, they wished to shut themselves up with their own society, either to devour an affront, or to brood over their revenge. From the windows of this part of the building, the travellers could perceive, in the first place, the street with the grass growing between the stones, which were being gradually loosened by it; next, the beautiful hedges of elder and thorn, which embraced, as though within two green and flowering arms, the houses of which we have spoken; and then, in the spaces between those houses, forming the groundwork of the picture, and appearing like an almost impassable barrier, a line of thick trees, the advanced sentinels of the vast forest which extends itself in front of Fontainebleau. It was therefore easy, provided one secured an apartment at the angle of the building, to obtain, by the main street from Paris, a view of, as well as to hear, the passers-by and the fêtes; and, by the Rue de Lyon, to look upon and to enjoy the calm of the country. And this without reckoning that, in cases of urgent necessity, at the very moment people might be knocking at the principal door in the Rue de Paris, one could make one's escape by the little door in the Rue de Lyon, and, creeping along the gardens of the private houses, attain the outskirts of the forest. Malicorne, who, it will be remembered, was the first to speak about this inn, by way of deploring his being turned out of it, having been absorbed in his own affairs, had not told Montalais all that could be said about this curious inn; and we will try to repair Malicorne's grievous omission. With the exception of the few words he had said about the Franciscan friar, he had not given any particulars about the travellers who were staying in the inn. The manner in which they had arrived, the manner in which they lived, the difficulty which existed for every one but certain privileged travellers, in entering the hotel without a pass-word, and to live there without certain preparatory precautions, must have struck Malicorne; and, we will venture to say, really did so. But Malicorne, as we have already said, had some personal matters of his own to occupy his attention, which prevented him from paying much attention to others. In fact, all the apartments of the hotel were engaged and retained by certain strangers, who never stirred out, who were incommunicative in their address, with countenances full of thoughtful occupation, and not one of whom was known to Malicorne. Every one of these travellers had arrived at the hotel after his own arrival there; each man had entered after having given a kind of pass-word, which had at first attracted Malicorne's attention; but, having inquired, in an indirect manner, about it, he had been informed that the host had given as a reason for this extreme vigilance, that, as the town was so full of wealthy noblemen, it must also be as full of clever and zealous pickpockets. The reputation of an honest inn like that of the

Beau Paon was concerned in not allowing its visitors to be robbed. It occasionally happened that Malicorne asked himself, as he thought matters carefully over in his mind, and reflected upon his own position in the inn, how it was that they had allowed him to become an inmate of the hotel, whilst he had observed, since his residence there, admission refused to so many. He asked himself, too, how it was that Manicamp, who, in his opinion, must be a man to be looked upon with veneration by everybody, having wished to water his horse at the Beau Paon, on arriving there, both horse and rider had been incontinently led away with a *nescio vos** of the most positive character. All this for Malicorne, whose mind being fully occupied by his own love affair and his personal ambition, was a problem he had not applied himself to solve. Had he wished to do so, we should hardly venture, notwithstanding the intelligence we have accorded as his due, to say he would have succeeded. A few words will prove to the reader that nothing less than Œdipus* in person could have solved the enigma in question. During the week, seven travellers had taken up their abode in the inn, all of them having arrived there the day after the fortunate day on which Malicorne had fixed his choice on the Beau Paon. These seven persons, accompanied by a suitable retinue, were the following:*—First of all, a brigadier in the German army, his secretary, physician, three servants, and seven horses. The brigadier's name was the Comte de Wostpur.—A Spanish cardinal, with two nephews, two secretaries, an officer of his household, and twelve horses. The cardinal's name was Monsiegneur Herrebia.— A rich merchant of Bremen, with his manservant and two horses. This merchant's name was Meinheer Bonstett.—A Venetian senator, with his wife and daughter, both extremely beautiful. The senator's name was Signor Marini.—A Scotch laird, with seven Highlanders of his clan, all on foot. The laird's name was MacCumnor.—An Austrian from Vienna, without title or coat of arms, who had arrived in a carriage; a good deal of the priest, and something of the soldier. He was called the Councillor.— And, finally, a Flemish lady, with a manservant, a lady's maid, and a female companion, a large retinue of servants, great display, and immense horses. She was called the Flemish lady.

All these travellers had arrived on the same day, and yet their arrival had occasioned no confusion in the inn, no stoppage in the street; their apartments had been fixed upon beforehand, by their couriers or their secretaries, who had arrived the previous evening or the same morning. Malicorne, who had arrived the previous day, and riding an ill-conditioned horse, with a slender valise, had announced himself at the hotel of the Beau Paon as a friend of a nobleman desirous of witnessing the fêtes, and who would himself arrive almost immediately. The landlord, on hearing these words, had smiled as if he was perfectly well acquainted with either Malicorne or his friend the nobleman, and had said to him, 'Since you are the first arrival, monsieur, choose which apartment you please.' And this was said with that obsequiousness of manners, so full of meaning with landlords, which means, 'Make yourself perfectly easy, monsieur; we know with whom we have to do, and you will be treated accordingly.' These words, and their accompanying gesture, Malicorne had thought very friendly, but rather obscure. However, as he did not wish to be very extravagant in his expenses, and as he thought that if he were to ask for a small apartment he would doubtless have been refused, on account of his want of consequence, he hastened to close at once with the inn-keeper's remark, and deceive him with a cunning equal to his own. So, smiling as a man would do for whom whatever might be done was simply his due, he said, 'My dear host, I shall take the best and the gayest room in the house.'

'With a stable?'

'Yes, with a stable.'

'And when will you take it?'

'Immediately, if it be possible.'

'Quite so.'

'But,' said Malicorne, 'I shall leave the large room unoccupied for the present.'

'Very good!' said the landlord, with a knowing look.

'Certain reasons, which you will understand by-and-by, oblige me to take, at my own cost, this small room only.'

'Yes, yes,' said the host.

'When my friend arrives, he will occupy the large apartment; and, as a matter of course, as this larger apartment will be his own affair, he will settle for it himself.'

'Certainly,' said the landlord, 'certainly; let it be understood in that manner.'

'It is agreed then, that such shall be the terms?'

'Word for word.'

'It is extraordinary,' said Malicorne to himself. 'You quite understand, then?'

'Perfectly.'

'Very well; and now show me to my room.'

The landlord, cap in hand, preceded Malicorne, who installed himself in his room, and became more and more surprised to observe that the landlord, at every ascent or descent, looked and winked at him in a manner which indicated the best possible intelligence between them. 'There is some mistake here,' said Malicorne to himself; 'but until it is cleared up, I shall take advantage of it, which is the best thing I can possibly do.' And he darted out of his room, like a hunting-dog following up a scent, in search of all the news and curiosities of the court, getting himself burnt in one place, and drowned in another, as he had told Mademoiselle de Montalais. The day after he had been installed in his room, he had noticed the seven travellers arrive successively, who speedily filled the whole hotel. When he saw all this number of people, of carriages and retinue, Malicorne rubbed his hands delightedly, thinking that, one day later, he should not have found a bed to lie upon after his return from his exploring expeditions. When all the travellers were lodged, the landlord entered Malicorne's room, and with his accustomed courteousness, said to him, 'You are aware, my dear monsieur, that the large room in the third detached building is still reserved for you?'

'Of course I am aware of it.'

'I am really making you a present of it.'

'Thank you.'

'So that when your friend comes, he will be satisfied with me, I hope; or, if he be not, he will be very difficult to please.'

'Excuse me, but allow me to say a few words about my friend. He intended to come, as you know.'

'And he does so still.'

'He may possibly have changed his opinion.'

'No.'

'You are quite sure, then?'

'Quite sure.'

'But in case you should have some doubt.'

'Well!'

'I can only say that I do not positively assure you that he will come.'

'Yet he told you——'

'He certainly did tell me; but you know that man proposes and God disposes;—*verba volant, scripta manent*.'*

'Which is as much as to say——'

'That what is spoken flies away, and what is written remains; and, as he did not write to me, but contented himself by saying to me, "I will authorise you, yet without specially inviting you," you must feel that it places me in a very embarrassing position.'

'What do you authorise me to do, then?'

'Why, to let your rooms if you find a good tenant for them.'

'Never will I do such a thing, monsieur. If he has not written to you, he has written to me.'

'Ah! ah! what does he say? Let us see if his letter agrees with his words.'

'These are almost his very words. "To the landlord of the Beau Paon Hotel,—You will have been informed of the meeting arranged to take place in your inn between some people of importance; I shall be one of these who will meet the others at Fontainebleau. Keep for me, then, a small room for a friend who will arrive either before or after me——" and you are the friend I suppose,' said the landlord, interrupting his reading of the letter. Malicorne bowed modestly. The landlord continued:—
'"And a large apartment for myself. The large apartment is my own affair, but I wish the price of the smaller room to be moderate, as it is destined for a fellow who is deucedly poor." It is you he is speaking of, is it not?' said the host.

'Oh, certainly,' said Malicorne.

'Then we are agreed; your friend will settle for his apartment, and you for your own.'

'May I be broken alive upon the wheel,' said Malicorne to himself, 'if I understand anything at all about it,' and then he said aloud, 'Well, then, are you satisfied with the name?'

'With what name?'

'With the name at the end of the letter. Does it give you the guarantee you require?'

'I was going to ask you the name.'

'What! was not the letter signed?'

'No,' said the landlord, opening his eyes very wide, full of mystery and curiosity.

'In that case,' replied Malicorne, imitating his gesture and his mysterious look, 'if he has not given you his name, you understand, he must have his reasons for it, and, therefore, that I, his friend, his confidant, must not betray him.'

'You are perfectly right, monsieur,' said the landlord, 'and therefore I do not insist upon it.'

'I appreciate your delicacy. As for myself, as my friend told you, my room is a separate affair, so let us come to terms about it. Short accounts make good friends. How much is it?'

'There is no hurry.'

'Never mind, let us reckon it up all the same. Room, my own board, a place in the stable for my horse, and his feed. How much per day?'

'Four livres, monsieur.'

'Which will make twelve livres for the three days I have been here.'

'Yes, monsieur.'

'Here are your twelve livres, then.'

'But why settle now?'

'Because,' said Malicorne, lowering his voice, and resorting to his former air of mystery, because he saw that the mysterious had succeeded, 'because if I had to set off suddenly, to decamp at any moment, my account would be already settled.'

'You are right, monsieur.'

'I may consider myself at home, then?'

'Perfectly.'

'So far so well. Adieu!' And the landlord withdrew. Malicorne, left alone, reasoned with himself in the following manner:—'No one but de Guiche or Manicamp could have written to this fellow; de Guiche, because he wishes to secure a lodging for himself beyond the precincts of the court, in the event of his success or failure, as the case might be; Manicamp, because de Guiche must have entrusted him with this commission. And de

Guiche or Manicamp will have argued in this manner. The large apartment in which one could receive in a befitting manner a lady very thickly veiled, reserving to the lady in question a double means of exit, either in a street somewhat deserted or closely adjoining the forest. The smaller room, either to shelter Manicamp for a time, who is de Guiche's confidant, and would be the vigilant keeper of the door, or for de Guiche himself, acting for greater safety, the part of master and of confidant at the same time. Yet,' he continued, 'how about this meeting which is to take place, and which indeed has actually taken place, in this hotel? No doubt they are persons who are going to be presented to the King, and the "poor devil" for whom the smaller room is destined, is a trick, in order the better to conceal de Guiche or Manicamp. If this be the case, as very likely it is, there is only half the mischief done, for there is simply the length of one's purse-strings between Manicamp and Malicorne.' After he had thus reasoned the matter out, Malicorne had slept soundly, leaving the seven travellers to occupy, and in every sense of the word to walk up and down, their several lodgings in the hotel. Whenever there was nothing at court to put him out, when he had wearied himself with his excursions and investigations, tired of writing letters which he could never find an opportunity of delivering to whom they were intended, he then returned home to his comfortable little room, and leaning upon the balcony, which was filled with nasturtiums and white pinks, he began to think over these strange travellers, for whom Fontainebleau seemed to possess no attractions in its illuminations, or amusements, or fêtes. Things went on in this manner until the seventh day, a day of which we have given such full details, with its night also, in the preceding chapters. On that night Malicorne was enjoying the fresh air, seated at his window, towards one o'clock in the morning, when Manicamp appeared on horseback, with a thoughtful and listless air.

'Good!' said Malicorne, to himself, recognising him at the first glance; 'there's my friend, who is come to take possession of his apartment, that is to say, of my room.' And he called to Manicamp, who looked up and immediately recognised Malicorne.

'Ah! by Jove!' said the former, his countenance clearing up, 'glad to see you, Malicorne. I have been wandering about

Fontainebleau looking for three things I cannot find: de Guiche, a room, and a stable.'

'Of M. de Guiche I cannot give you either good or bad news, for I have not seen him; but as far as concerns your room and a stable, that's another matter, for they have been retained here for you.'

'Retained—and by whom?'

'By yourself, I suppose.'

'By me?'

'Do you mean to say you have not taken lodgings here?'

'By no means,' said Manicamp.

At this moment the landlord appeared at the threshold of the door.

'I require a room,' said Manicamp.

'Have you engaged one, monsieur?'

'No.'

'Then I have no rooms to let.'

'In that case, I have engaged a room,' said Manicamp.

'By letter?' inquired the landlord. Malicorne nodded affirmatively to Manicamp.

'Of course by letter,' said Manicamp. 'Did you not receive a letter from me.'

'What was the date of the letter?' inquired the host, in whom Manicamp's hesitation had aroused suspicion. Manicamp rubbed his ear, and looked up at Malicorne's window; but Malicorne had left his window and was coming down the stairs to his friend's assistance. At the very same moment, a traveller, wrapped up in a large Spanish cloak, appeared at the porch, near enough to hear the conversation.

'I ask you what was the date of the letter you wrote to me to retain apartments here?' repeated the landlord, again pressing his question.

'Last Wednesday was the date,' said the mysterious stranger, in a soft and polished tone of voice, touching the landlord on the shoulder.

Manicamp drew back, and it was now Malicorne's turn, who appeared on the threshold, to scratch his ear. The landlord saluted the new arrival as a man who recognises his true guest. 'Monsieur,' he said to him, with civility, 'your apartment is ready for you, and the stables too, only——' He looked round him, and inquired, 'Your horses?'

'My horses may or may not arrive. That, however, matters but little to you, provided you are paid for what has been engaged.' The landlord bowed still lower.

'You have,' continued the unknown traveller, 'kept for me, besides, the small room I asked for?'

'Oh!' said Malicorne, endeavouring to hide himself.

'Your friend has occupied it during the last week,' said the landlord, pointing to Malicorne, who was trying to make himself as small as possible. The traveller, drawing his cloak round him so as to cover the lower part of his face, cast a rapid glance at Malicorne, and said, 'This gentleman is no friend of mine.'

The landlord almost started off his feet.

'I am not acquainted with this gentleman,' continued the traveller.

'What!' exclaimed the host, turning to Malicorne, 'are you not this gentleman's friend, then?'

'What does it matter, whether I am or not, provided you are paid?' said Malicorne, parodying the stranger's remark in a very majestic manner.

'It matters so far as this,' said the landlord, who began to perceive that one person had been taken for another, 'that I beg you, monsieur, to leave the rooms, which had been engaged beforehand, and by some one else instead of you.'

'Still,' said Malicorne, 'this gentleman cannot require at the same time a room on the first floor and an apartment on the second. If this gentleman will take the room, I will take the apartment; if he prefers the apartment, I will be satisfied with the room.'

'I am exceedingly distressed, monsieur,' said the traveller in his soft voice, 'but I need both the room and the apartment.'

'At least tell me for whom?' inquired Malicorne.

'The apartment I require for myself.'

'Very well; but the room?'

'Look,' said the traveller, pointing towards a sort of procession which was approaching.

Malicorne looked in the direction indicated, and observed, borne upon a litter, the arrival of the Franciscan* whose installation

in his apartment he had, with a few details of his own, related to
Montalais, and whom he had so uselessly endeavoured to convert to humbler views. The result of the arrival of the stranger,
and of the sick Franciscan, was Malicorne's expulsion, without
any consideration for his feelings, from the inn, by the landlord,
and the peasants who had carried the Franciscan. The details
have already been given of what followed this expulsion; of
Manicamp's conversation with Montalais; how Manicamp, with
greater cleverness than Malicorne had shown, had succeeded
in obtaining news of de Guiche; of the subsequent conversation
of Montalais with Malicorne; and, finally, of the billets with
which the Comte de Saint-Aignan had furnished Manicamp
and Malicorne. It remains for us to inform our readers who
were the traveller with the cloak,—the principal tenant of the
double apartment of which Malicorne had only occupied a
portion,—and the Franciscan, quite as mysterious a personage, whose arrival, together with that of the stranger with the
cloak, had been unfortunate enough to upset the two friends'
plans.

XXXIV

A JESUIT OF THE ELEVENTH YEAR

IN the first place, in order not to weary the reader's patience, we
will hasten to answer the first question. The traveller with the
cloak held over his face was Aramis, who, after he had left
Fouquet, and had taken from a portmanteau, which his servant
had opened, a cavalier's complete costume, had quitted the
château and had gone to the hotel of the Beau Paon, where, by
letters, seven or eight days previously, he had, as the landlord
had stated, directed a room and an apartment to be retained for
him. Immediately Malicorne and Manicamp had been turned
out, Aramis approached the Franciscan, and asked him whether
he would prefer the apartment or the room. The Franciscan
inquired where they were both situated. He was told that the
room was on the first, and the apartment on the second floor.
'The room, then,' he said.

Aramis did not contradict him, but, with great submissiveness, said to the landlord: 'The room.' And, bowing with respect, he withdrew into the apartment, and the Franciscan was accordingly carried at once into the room. Now, is it not extraordinary that this respect should be shown by a prelate of the Church for a simple monk, for one, too, belonging to a mendicant order; to whom was given up, without a request for it even, a room which so many travellers were desirous of obtaining? How, too, explain the unexpected arrival of Aramis at the hotel—he who had entered the château with M. Fouquet, and could have remained at the château with M. Fouquet if he had liked? The Franciscan supported his removal up the staircase without uttering a complaint, although it was evident he suffered very much, and that every time the litter was knocked against the wall or against the railing of the staircase he experienced a terrible shock throughout his frame. And finally, when he had arrived in the room, he said to those who carried him: 'Help me to place myself on that arm-chair.' The bearers of the litter placed it on the ground, and, lifting the sick man up as gently as possible, they carried him to the chair he had indicated, and which was situated at the head of the bed. 'Now,' he added, with a marked benignity of gesture and tone, 'desire the landlord to come.'

They obeyed and five minutes afterwards the landlord appeared at the door.

'Be kind enough,' said the Franciscan to him, 'to send these excellent fellows away; they are vassals of the Vicomte de Melun.* They found me when I had fainted on the road overcome by the heat, and without thinking whether they would be paid for their trouble, they wished to carry me to their own homes. But I know at what cost to themselves is the hospitality which the poor extend to a sick man, and I preferred this hotel, where, moreover, I was expected.'

The landlord looked at the Franciscan in amazement, but the latter, with his thumb, made the sign of the cross in a peculiar manner upon his breast. The host replied by making a similar sign upon his left shoulder. 'Yes, indeed,' he said, 'we did expect you, but we hoped that you would arrive in a better state of health.' And as the peasants were looking at the innkeeper, usually so supercilious, and saw how respectful he had become in the presence of a poor monk, the Franciscan drew from a deep pocket three or four pieces of gold, which he held out.

'My friends,' said he, 'here is something to repay you for the care you have taken of me. So make yourselves perfectly easy, and do not be afraid of leaving me here. The order to which I belong, and for which I am travelling, does not require me to beg; only as the attention you have shown me deserves to be rewarded, take these two louis and depart in peace.'

The peasants did not dare to take them; the landlord took the two louis out of the monk's hand and placed them in that of one of the peasant's, the whole four of them withdrew, opening their eyes wider than ever. The door was then closed; and, while the innkeeper stood respectfully near it, the Franciscan collected himself for a moment. He then passed across his sallow face a hand which seemed dried up by fever, and rubbed his nervous and agitated fingers across his beard. His large eyes, hollowed by sickness and inquietude, seemed to pursue in the vague distance a mournful and fixed idea.

'What physicians have you at Fontainebleau?' he inquired, after a long pause.

'We have three, my father.'

'What are their names?'

'Luiniguet, first; next a brother of the Carmelite order* named brother Hubert; and third, a secular member named Grisart.'

'Ah! Grisart?' murmured the monk. 'Send for M. Grisart immediately.'

The landlord moved in prompt obedience to the direction.

'Tell me what priests there are here.'

'There are Jesuits, Augustines, and Cordeliers;* but the Jesuits are the closest at hand. Shall I send for a confessor belonging to the order of Jesuits?'

'Yes, immediately.'

It will be imagined that at the sign of the cross which they had exchanged, the landlord and the invalid-monk had recognised each other as two affiliated members of the well-known society of Jesus.* Left to himself, the Franciscan drew from his pocket a bundle of papers, some of which he read over with the most careful attention. The violence of his disorder, however, overcame his courage; his eyes rolled in their sockets, a cold sweat poured down his face, and he nearly fainted, and lay with his head thrown backwards and his arms hanging down on both sides of his chair. For more than five minutes he remained without any movement, when the landlord returned, bringing with him the physician, whom he had hardly allowed time to dress himself. The noise they made on entering the room, the current of air which the opening of the door had occasioned, restored the Franciscan to his senses. He hurriedly seized hold of the papers which were lying about, and with his long and bony hand concealed them under the cushions of the chair. The landlord went out of the room, leaving patient and physician together.

'Come here, Monsieur Grisart,' said the Franciscan to the doctor; 'approach closer, for there is no time to lose. Try, by touch and sound, and consider and pronounce your sentence.'

'The landlord,' replied the doctor, 'told me that I had the honour of attending an affiliated brother.'

'Yes,' replied the Franciscan, 'it is so. Tell me the truth, then; I feel very ill, and think I am about to die.'

The physician took the monk's hand and felt his pulse. 'Oh, oh,' he said, 'a dangerous fever.'

'What do you call a dangerous fever?' inquired the Franciscan, with an imperious look.

'To an affiliated member of the first or second year,' replied the physician, looking inquiringly at the monk, 'I should say— a fever that may be cured.'

'But to me?' said the Franciscan. The physician hesitated.

'Look at my grey hair, and my forehead, full of anxious thought,' he continued, 'look at the lines of my face, by which I reckon up the trials I have undergone. I am a Jesuit of the eleventh year, Monsieur Grisart.' The physician started, for, in fact, a Jesuit of the eleventh year was one of those men who had been initiated in all the secrets of the order, one of those for whom the science has no more secrets, the society no further barriers to present—temporal obedience, no more trammels.

'In that case,' said Grisart, saluting him with respect, 'I am in the presence of a Master?'

'Yes; act, therefore, accordingly.'

'And you wish to know?'

'My real state.'

'Well!' said the physician, 'it is a brain fever, which has reached its highest degree of intensity.'

'There is no hope, then?' inquired the Franciscan, in a quick tone of voice.

'I do not say that,' replied the doctor; 'yet, considering the disordered state of the brain, the hurried respiration, the rapidity of the pulse, and the burning nature of the fever which is devouring you——'

'And which has thrice prostrated me since this morning,' said the monk.

'Therefore, I should call it a terrible attack. But why did you not stop on your road?'

'I was expected here, and I was obliged to come.'

'Even at the risk of your life?'

'Yes, at the risk of dying!'

'Very well! considering all the symptoms of your case, I must tell you that your condition is desperate.' The Franciscan smiled in a strange manner.

'What you have just told me is, perhaps, sufficient for what is due to an affiliated member, even of the eleventh year; but for what is due to me, Monsieur Grisart, it is too little, and I have a right to demand more. Come, then, let us be more candid still, and as frank as if you were making your own confession to Heaven. Besides, I have already sent for a confessor.'

'Oh! I hope, however . . .' murmured the doctor.

'Answer me,' said the sick man, displaying with a dignified gesture a golden ring, the stone of which had, until that moment, been turned inside, and which bore engraved thereon the distinguishing mark of the Society of Jesus.

Grisart muttered a loud exclamation. 'The general!'* he cried.

'Silence,' said the Franciscan, 'you now understand that the truth is everything.'

'Monseigneur, monseigneur,' murmured Grisart, 'send for the confessor, for in two hours, at the next seizure, you will be attacked by delirium, and will pass away in the course of it.'

'Very well,' said the patient, for a moment contracting his eyebrows, 'I have still two hours to live, then?'

'Yes; particularly if you take the potion I shall send you presently.'

'And that will give me two hours more? I would take it, were it poison, for those two hours are necessary, not only for myself, but for the glory of the order.'

'What a loss, what a catastrophe for us all!' murmured the physician.

'It is the loss of one man, and nothing more,' replied the Franciscan, 'and Heaven will enable the poor monk, who is about to leave you, to find a worthy successor. Adieu, Monsieur Grisart; already even, through the goodness of Heaven, I have met with you. A physician who had not been one of our holy order, would have left me in ignorance of my condition; and, relying that my existence might have been prolonged a few days further, I should not have taken the necessary precautions. You are a learned man, Monsieur Grisart, and that confers an hon-our upon us all; it would have been repugnant to my feelings to have found one of our order of little standing in his profession. Adieu, Monsieur Grisart; send me the cordial immediately.'

'Give my your blessing at least, monseigneur.'

'In spirit I do, go now;—in spirit I do so, I tell you—*animo*, Maître Grisart, *viribus impossibile*.'* And he again fell back on the arm-chair, in an almost senseless state. M. Grisart hesitated whether he should give him immediate assistance, or should run to prepare the cordial he had promised. He doubtless decided in favour of the cordial, for he darted out of the room and dis-appeared down the staircase.

XXXV

THE STATE SECRET

A FEW moments after the doctor's departure, the confessor arrived. He had hardly crossed the threshold of the door when the Franciscan fixed a penetrating look upon him, and shaking his head, murmured—'A weak mind, I see; may Heaven forgive me for dying without the help of this living piece of human infirmity.' The confessor, on his side, regarded the dying man with astonishment, almost with terror. He had never beheld eyes so burningly bright at the very moment they were about to close, nor looks so terrible at the moment they were about to be quenched in death. The Franciscan made a rapid and imperious movement of his hand. 'Sit down there, my father,' he said, 'and listen to me.' The Jesuit confessor, a good priest, a recent member of the order, who had merely witnessed the initiation into its mysteries, yielded to the superiority assumed by the penitent.

'There are several persons staying in this hotel,' continued the Franciscan.

'But,' inquired the Jesuit, 'I thought I had been summoned to receive a confession. Is your remark, then, a confession?'

'Why do you ask me?'

'In order to know whether I am to keep your words secret.'

'My remarks are part of my confession; I confide them to you in your character of a confessor.'

'Very well,' said the priest, seating himself on the chair which the Franciscan had, with great difficulty, just left to lie down on the bed.

The Franciscan continued—'I repeat, there are several persons staying in this inn.'

'So I have heard.'

'They ought to be eight in number.'

The Jesuit made a sign that he understood him. 'The first to whom I wish to speak,' said the dying man, 'is a German from Vienna, whose name is the Baron de Wostpur. Be kind enough to go to him, and tell him, that the person he expected has arrived.' The confessor, astounded, looked at his penitent; the confession seemed a singular one.

'Obey,' said the Franciscan in a tone of command impossible to resist. The good Jesuit, completely subdued, rose and left the room. As soon as he had gone, the Franciscan again took up the papers which a crisis of the fever had already, once before, obliged him to put aside.

'The Baron de Wostpur? Good!' he said; 'ambitious, a fool, and straitened in his means.'

He folded up the papers, which he thrust under his pillow. Rapid footsteps were heard at the end of the corridor. The confessor returned, followed by the Baron de Wostpur, who walked along with his head raised, as if he were discussing with himself the impropriety of touching the ceiling with the feather of his hat. Therefore, at the appearance of the Franciscan, at his melancholy look, and at the plainness of the room, he stopped, and inquired—'Who summoned me?'

'I,' said the Franciscan, who turned towards the confessor, saying, 'My good father, leave us for a moment together; when this gentleman leaves, you will return here.' The Jesuit left the room, and, doubtless, availed himself of this momentary exile from the presence of the dying man to ask the host for some explanation about this strange penitent, who treated his confessor no better than he would a manservant. The Baron approached the bed, and wished to speak, but the hand of the Franciscan imposed silence upon him.

'Every moment is precious,' said the latter hurriedly. 'You have come here for the competition, have you not?'

'Yes, father.'

'You hope to be elected general of the order?'

'I hope so.'

'You know on what conditions only you can possibly attain this high position, which makes one man the master of monarchs, the equal of Popes?'

'Who are you,' inquired the Baron, 'to subject me to these interrogatories?'

'I am he whom you expected.'

'You are——'

The Franciscan did not give him time to reply; he extended his shrunken hand, on which glittered the ring of the general of the order. The baron drew back in surprise; and then, immediately afterwards, bowing with the profoundest respect, he exclaimed—'Is it possible, that you are here, monseigneur; you, in this wretched room; you, upon this miserable bed; you, in search of and selecting the future general, that is, your own successor!'*

'Do not distress yourself about that, monsieur, but fulfil immediately the principal condition, of furnishing the order with a secret of importance, such as one of the greatest courts of Europe can, by your instrumentality, for ever confer upon the order. Well! do you possess the secret which you promised in your request, addressed to the Grand Council?'

'Monseigneur——'

'Let us proceed, however, in due order,' said the monk. 'You are the Baron de Wostpur?'

'Yes, monseigneur.'

'And this letter is from you?'

'Yes, monseigneur.'

The general of the Jesuits drew a paper from his bundle and presented it to the Baron, who glanced at it, and made a sign in the affirmative, saying, 'Yes, monseigneur, this letter is mine.'

'Can you show me the reply which the secretary of the Grand Council returned to you?'

'This is it,' said the Baron, holding towards the Franciscan a letter, bearing simply the address, 'To His Excellency the Baron de Wostpur,' and containing only this phrase, 'From the 15th to the 22nd May, Fontainebleau, the Hotel of the Beau Paon.— A.M.D.G.'

'Right,' said the Franciscan, 'and now speak.'

'I have a body of troops, composed of 50,000 men; all the officers have been won over to the cause. I am encamped on the Danube. In four days I can overthrow the Emperor,* who is, as you are aware, opposed to the progress of our order, and can replace him by whichever of the princes of his family the order may determine upon.' The Franciscan listened, unmoved.

'Is that all?' he said.

'A revolution* throughout Europe is included in my plan,' said the Baron.

'Very well, Monsieur de Wostpur, you will receive a reply; return to your room, and leave Fontainebleau within a quarter of an hour.' The Baron withdrew backwards, just as obsequiously as if he were taking leave of the Emperor he was ready to betray.

'There is no secret there,' murmured the Franciscan, 'it is a plot. Besides,' he added, after a moment's reflection, 'the future of Europe is no longer in the House of Austria.'*

And with a pencil which he held in his hand, he struck the Baron de Wostpur's name from the list.

'Now for the Cardinal,' he said; 'we ought to get something more serious from the side of Spain.'

Raising his head he perceived the confessor, who was awaiting his orders as submissively as a schoolboy.

'Ah, ah!' he said, noticing his submissive air, 'you have been talking with the landlord.'

'Yes, monseigneur; and to the physician.'

'He is here, then?'

'He is waiting with the potion he promised.'

'Very well; if I require him, I will call; you now understand the great importance of my confession, do you not?'

'Yes, monseigneur.'

'Then go and fetch me the Spanish Cardinal Herrebia. Make haste. Only as you now understand the matter in hand, you will remain near me, for I begin to feel faint.'

'Shall I summon the physician?'

'Not yet, not yet . . . the Spanish Cardinal . . . no one else. Fly.'

Five minutes afterwards, the Cardinal, pale and ill at ease, entered the little room.

'I am informed, monseigneur——' stammered out the Cardinal.

'To the point,' said the Franciscan, in a faint voice, showing the Cardinal a letter which he had written to the Grand Council. 'Is that your handwriting?'

'Yes, but——'

'And your summons here?'

The Cardinal hesitated to answer. His purple clashed with the mean garb of the poor Franciscan, who stretched out his hand and displayed the ring, which produced its effect, greater in proportion as the greatness of the person increased over whom the Franciscan exercised his influence.

'Quick, the secret, the secret!' said the dying man, leaning upon his confessor.

'*Coram isto?*'* inquired the Spanish Cardinal.

'Speak in Spanish,' said the Franciscan, showing the liveliest attention.

'You are aware, monseigneur,' said the Cardinal, continuing the conversation in the Castilian dialect, 'that the condition of the marriage of the Infanta with the King of France is the absolute renunciation of the rights of the said Infanta, as well as King Louis XIV, to all claim to the crown of Spain.'* The Franciscan made a sign in the affirmative.

'The consequence is,' continued the Cardinal, 'that the peace and alliance between the two kingdoms depend upon the observance of that clause of the contract.' A similar sign from the Franciscan. 'Not only France and Spain,' continued the Cardinal, 'but the whole of Europe even would be violently rent asunder should either party refuse to respect it.'* Another movement of the dying man's head.

'It further results', continued the speaker, 'that the man who might be able to foresee events and to render certain that which is no more than a vague idea floating in the mind of man; that is to say, the idea of future good or evil would preserve the world from a great catastrophe; and the event, which has no fixed certainty even in the brain of him who originated it, could be turned to the advantage of our order.'

'*Pronto, pronto!*'* murmured the Franciscan, who suddenly became paler, and leaned upon the priest. The Cardinal approached the ear of the dying man, and said,—'Well, monseigneur, I know that the King of France has determined that, at the first pretext, a death for instance, either that of the King of Spain or that of a brother of the Infanta,* France will, arms in hand, claim the inheritance, and I have in my possession already prepared the plan of policy agreed upon by Louis XIV for this occasion.'

'And this plan,' said the Franciscan.

'Here it is,' returned the Cardinal.

'Have you anything further to say to me?'

'I think I have said a good deal, my lord,' replied the Cardinal.

'Yes, you have rendered the order a great service. But how did you procure the details by the aid of which you have constructed your plan?'

'I have the under-servants of the King of France in my pay, and I obtain from them all the waste papers, which have been saved from being burnt.'

'Very ingenious,' murmured the Franciscan, endeavouring to smile; 'you will leave this hotel, Cardinal, in a quarter of an hour, and a reply will be sent you.' The Cardinal withdrew.

'Call Grisart, and tell the Venetian Marini to come,' said the sick man.

While the confessor obeyed, the Franciscan, instead of striking out the Cardinal's name, as he had done the Baron's, made a cross at the side of it. Then, exhausted by the effort, he fell back on his bed, murmuring the name of Doctor Grisart. When he returned to his senses, he had drunk about half of the potion, of which the remainder was left in the glass, and he found himself supported by the physician, while the Venetian and the confessor were standing close to the door. The Venetian submitted to the same formalities as his two predecessors, hesitated as they had done at the sight of the two strangers, but his confidence restored by the order of the general, he revealed that the Pope, terrified by the power of the order, was weaving a plot for the general expulsion of the Jesuits,* and was tampering with the different courts of Europe, in order to obtain their assistance. He described the Pontiff's auxiliaries, his means of action, and indicated the particular locality in the Archipelago,* where, by a sudden surprise, two cardinals, adepts of the eleventh year, and, consequently, high in authority, were to be transported, together with thirty-two of the principal affiliated members of Rome. The Franciscan thanked the Signor Marini. It was by no means a slight service he had rendered the society by denouncing this pontifical project. The Venetian thereupon received directions to set off in a quarter of an hour, and left as radiant as if he already possessed the ring, the sign of supreme authority of the society. As, however, he was departing, the Franciscan murmured to himself:—'All these men are either spies, or a sort of police, not one of them a general; they have all discovered a plot, but not one of them a secret. It is not by means of ruin, or war, or force, that the Society of Jesus is to be governed, but by that mysterious influence which a moral superiority confers. No, the man is not yet found, and, to complete the misfortune, Heaven strikes me down, and I am dying. Oh! must the society indeed fall with me for want of a column to support it? Must death, which is waiting for me, swallow up with me the future of the order? That future which ten years more of my own life would have rendered eternal; for that future, with the reign of the new king, is opening radiant and full of splendour.' These words, which had been half-reflected, half-pronounced aloud, were listened to by the Jesuit confessor with a terror similar to that with

which one listens to the wanderings of a person attacked by
fever, whilst Grisart, with a mind of a higher order, devoured
them as the revelations of an unknown world, in which his looks
were plunged without ability to attain them. Suddenly the
Franciscan recovered himself.

'Let us finish this,' he said, 'death is approaching. Oh! just
now I was dying resignedly, for I hoped . . . while now I sink in
despair, unless those who remain . . . Grisart, Grisart, make me
live but an hour longer.'

Grisart approached the dying monk, and made him swallow a
few drops, not of the potion which was still left in the glass, but
of the contents of a small bottle he had upon his person.

'Call the Scotchman!' exclaimed the Franciscan; 'call the
Bremen merchant. Call, call quickly. I am dying. I am suffocated.'

The confessor darted forward to seek for assistance, as if
there had been any human strength which could hold back the
hand of death, which was weighing down the sick man; but, at
the threshold of the door, he found Aramis, who, with his finger
on his lips, like a statue of Harpocrates,* the god of silence, with
a look motioned him back to the end of the apartment. The
physician and the confessor after having consulted each other by
their looks, made a movement, however, as if to push Aramis
aside, who, however, with two signs of the cross, each made in
a different manner, transfixed them both in their places.

'A chief!' they both murmured.

Aramis slowly advanced into the room where the dying man
was struggling against the first attack of the agony which had
seized him. As for the Franciscan, whether owing to the effect of
the elixir, or whether the appearance of Aramis had restored his
strength, he made a movement, and his eyes glaring, his mouth
half open, and his hair damp with sweat, sat up upon the bed.
Aramis felt that the air of the room was stifling; the windows
were closed; the fire was burning upon the hearth; a pair of
candles of yellow wax were guttering down in the copper can-
dlesticks, and still further increased, by their thick smoke, the
temperature of the room. Aramis opened the window, and, fixing upon the dying man a look full of intelligence and respect,
said to him: 'Monsiegneur, pray forgive my coming in this manner
before you summoned me, but your state alarms me, and I

thought you might possibly die before you had seen me, for I am only the sixth on your list.'

The dying man started and looked at the list.

'You are, therefore, he who was formerly called Aramis, and since the Chevalier d'Herblay? You are the Bishop of Vannes, then?'

'Yes, my lord.'

'I know you; I have seen you.'

'At the last jubilee,* we were with the Holy Father together.'

'Yes, yes, I remember; and you place yourself on the list of candidates?'

'Monseigneur, I have heard it said that the order required to become possessed of a great State secret, and knowing that from modesty you had in anticipation resigned your functions in favour of the person who should be the depositary of that secret, I wrote to say that I was ready to compete, possessing alone a secret which I believe to be important.'

'Speak,' said the Franciscan, 'I am ready to listen to you, and to judge of the importance of the secret.'

'A secret of the value of that which I have the honour to confide to you, cannot be communicated by word of mouth. Any idea which, when once expressed, has thereby lost its safeguard, and has become vulgarised by any manifestation or communication of it whatever, no longer is the property of him who gave it birth. My words may be overheard by some listener, or perhaps by an enemy; one ought not therefore to speak at random, for, in such a case, the secret would cease to be one.'

'How do you propose, then, to convey your secret?' inquired the dying monk.

With one hand Aramis signed to the physician and the confessor to withdraw, and with the other he handed to the Franciscan a paper enclosed in a double envelope. 'Is not writing more dangerous still than language?'

'No, my lord,' said Aramis, 'for you will find within this envelope characters which you and I can alone understand.' The Franciscan looked at Aramis with an astonishment which momentarily increased.

'It is a cipher,' continued the latter, 'which you used in 1655, and which your secretary, Juan Jujan, who is dead, could alone decipher, if he were to be restored to life.'

'You knew this cipher, then?'

'It was I who taught it him,' said Aramis, bowing with a gracefulness full of respect, and advancing towards the door as if to leave the room; but a gesture of the Franciscan, accompanied by a cry for him to remain, retained him.

'*Ecce homo!*' he exclaimed; then reading the paper a second time, he called out, 'Approach, approach quickly.'

Aramis returned to the side of the Franciscan, with the same calm countenance and the same respectful manner, unchanged. The Franciscan, extending his arm, burnt by the flame of the candle the paper which Aramis had handed him. Then, taking hold of Aramis's hand, he drew him towards him, and inquired:—
'In what manner and by whose means could you possibly become acquainted with such a secret?'

'Through Madame de Chevreuse, the intimate friend and confidante of the Queen, now dead.'*

'Did any others know it?'

'A man and woman only, and they of the lower classes.'

'Who were they?'

'Persons who had brought him up.'

'What has become of them?'

'Dead also. This secret burns like fire.'

'And you have survived?'

'No one is aware that I know it.'

'And for what length of time have you possessed this secret?'

'For the last fifteen years.'*

'And you give it to the order without ambition, without acknowledgement?'

'I give it to the order with ambition and with a hope of return,' said Aramis; 'for if you live, my lord, you will make of me, now you know me, what I can and ought to be.'

'And as I am dying,' exclaimed the Franciscan, 'I constitute you my successor. . . . Thus.' And drawing off the ring, he passed it on Aramis's finger. Then, turning towards the two spectators of this scene, he said: 'Be ye witnesses of this, and testify, if need be, that, sick in body, but sound in mind, I have freely and voluntarily bestowed this ring, the token of supreme authority, upon Monseigneur d'Herblay, Bishop of Vannes, whom I nominate my successor, and before whom I, a humble sinner, about to appear before Heaven, prostrate myself the first, as an example for all to follow.' And the Franciscan bowed lowly and submissively, whilst the physician and the Jesuit fell on their knees. Aramis, even while he became paler than the dying man himself, bent his looks successively upon all the actors of this scene. His gratified ambition flowed with his blood towards his heart.

'We must lose no time,' said the Franciscan; 'what I had to do here is urgent. I shall never succeed in carrying it out.'

'I will do it,' said Aramis.

'That's well,' said the Franciscan, and then turning towards the Jesuit and the doctor, he added, 'Leave us alone,' a direction which they instantly obeyed.

'With this sign,' he said, 'you are the man needed to shake the world from one end to the other; with this sign you will overthrow; with this sign you will build; *in hoc signo vinces!*'*

'Close the door,' continued the Franciscan, after a pause. Aramis shut and bolted the door, and returned to the side of the Franciscan.

'The Pope has conspired against the order,' said the monk, 'the Pope must die.'

'He shall die,'* said Aramis quietly.

'Seven hundred thousand livres are owing to a Bremen merchant of the name of Donstett, who came here to get the guarantee of my signature.'

'He shall be paid,' said Aramis.

'Six knights of Malta, whose names are written here, have discovered, by the indiscreetness of one of the affiliated of the eleventh year, the three mysteries; it must be ascertained what these men have done with the secret, to get it back again and crush it.'

'It shall be done.'

'Three dangerous affiliated members must be sent away into Tibet, to perish there; they are condemned. Here are their names.'

'I will see that the sentence be carried out.'

'Lastly, there is a lady at Anvers, grand-niece of Ravaillac;* she holds certain papers in her hands which compromise the order. There has been payable to the family during the last fifty-one years a pension of fifty-thousand livres. The pension is a heavy one, and the order is not wealthy. Redeem the papers for a sum of money down, or in case of refusal, stop the pension—but without risk.'

'I will think about what is best to be done,' said Aramis.

'A vessel chartered from Lima will have entered the port of Lisbon last week; ostensibly it is laden with chocolate, in reality with gold. Every ingot is concealed by a coating of chocolate. The vessel belongs to the order; it is worth seventeen million livres, you will see that claim is laid to it; here are the bills of lading.'

'To what port shall I direct it to be taken?'

'To Bayonne.'

'Before three weeks are over it shall be there, wind and weather permitting. Is that all?' The Franciscan made a sign in the affirmative, for he could no longer speak; the blood rushed to his throat and his head, and gushed from his mouth, his nostrils, and his eyes. The dying man had barely time to press Aramis's hand, when he fell in convulsions from his bed upon the floor. Aramis placed his hand upon the Franciscan's heart, but it had ceased to beat. As he stooped down, Aramis observed that a fragment of the paper he had given the Franciscan had escaped being burnt. He picked it up, and burnt it to the last atom. Then, summoning the confessor and the physician, he said to the former:—'Your penitent is in heaven; he needs nothing more than prayers and the burial bestowed on the dead. Go and prepare what is necessary for a simple interment such as a poor monk only would require. Go.'

The Jesuit left the room. Then, turning towards the physician, and observing his pale and anxious face, he said, in a low tone of voice:—'Monsieur Grisart, empty and clean this glass; there is too much left in it of what the Grand Council desired you to put in.' Grisart, amazed, overcome, completely astounded, almost fell backwards in his extreme terror. Aramis shrugged his shoulders in sign of pity, took the glass and poured out the contents among the ashes of the hearth. He then left the room carrying the papers of the dead man with him.

XXXVI

A SPECIAL MISSION

THE next day, or rather the same day (for the events we have just described had been concluded only at three o'clock in the morning), before breakfast was served, and as the King was preparing to go to Mass with the two Queens; as Monsieur, with the Chevalier de Lorraine and a few other intimate companions, was mounting his horse to set off for the river, to take one of those celebrated baths about which the ladies of the court were almost mad; as, in fact, no one remained in the château, with the exception of Madame, who, under the pretext of indisposition, would not leave her room; Montalais was seen, or rather was not seen, to glide stealthily out of the room appropriated to the maids of honour, leading La Vallière after her, who tried to conceal herself as much as possible, and both of them, hurrying secretly through the gardens, succeeded, looking round them at every step they took, in reaching the thicket. The weather was cloudy, a hot air bowed the flowers and the shrubs before its blast; the burning dust, swept along in clouds by the wind, was whirled in eddies towards the trees. Montalais, who, during their progress, had discharged the functions of a clever scout, advanced a few steps farther, and, turning round again, to be quite sure that no one was either listening or approaching, said to her companion, 'Thank goodness, we are quite alone! Since yesterday every one spies on us here, and a circle seems to be drawn round us, as if we had the plague.' La Vallière bent down her head and sighed. 'It is positively unheard of,' continued Montalais; 'from M. Malicorne to M. de Saint-Aignan, every one wishes to get hold of our secret. Come, Louise, let us concert a little together, in order that I may know what to do.'

La Vallière lifted up towards her companion her beautiful eyes, pure and deep as the azure of a spring-time sky, 'And I,' she said, 'I will ask you why have we been summoned to Madame's own apartment? Why have we slept close to her apartment, instead of sleeping as usual in our own? Why did you return so late, and whence are these measures of strict supervision which have been adopted since this morning, with respect to us both?'

'My dear Louise, you answer my question by another, or rather, by ten others, which is not answering me at all. I will tell you all you want to know later, and, as they are matters of secondary importance, you can wait. What I ask you—for everything will depend upon that—is, whether there is or is not any secret?'

'I do not know if there is any secret,' said La Vallière; 'but I do know, for my own part at least, that there has been great imprudence committed. Since the foolish remark I made, and my still more silly fainting yesterday, every one here is making remarks about us.'

'Speak for yourself,' said Montalais, laughing, 'speak for yourself and for Tonnay-Charente; for both of you made your declarations of love to the skies, and which unfortunately were intercepted.'

La Vallière hung down her head. 'Really you overwhelm me,' she said.

'Listen to me, Louise. These are no jests, for nothing is more serious; on the contrary, I did not drag you out of the château; I did not miss attending Mass; I did not pretend to have a cold, as Madame did, and which she has as much as I have; and, lastly, I did not display ten times more diplomacy than M. Colbert inherited from M. de Mazarin, and makes use of with respect to M. Fouquet, in order to find means of confiding my perplexities to you, for the sole end and purpose that when, at last, we are alone, and no one can listen to us, you are to deal hypocritically with me. No, no; believe me, that when I ask you any questions, it is not from curiosity alone, but really because the position is a critical one. What you said yesterday is now known,—it is a text on which every one is discoursing. Every one embellishes it to the utmost, and does so according to his own fancy; you had the honour last night, and you have it still to-day, of occupying the whole court, my dear Louise; and the number of tender and witty remarks which have been ascribed to you would make Mademoiselle de Scudery and her brother burst from very spite if they were faithfully reported to them.'

'But, dearest Montalais,' said the poor girl, 'you know better than any one what I did say, since you were present when I said it.'

'Yes, I know. But that is not the question. I have even not forgotten a single syllable you said; but did you think what you were saying?'

Louise became confused. 'What,' she exclaimed, 'more questions still! Oh, heavens! when I would give the whole world to forget what I did say, how does it happen that every one does all he possibly can to remind me of it? Oh, this is indeed terrible!'

'What is?'

'To have a friend who ought to spare me, who might advise me and help me to save myself, and yet who is destroying—is killing me.'

'There, there, that will do,' said Montalais; 'after having said too little, you now say too much. No one thinks of killing you, nor even of robbing you, even of your secret; I wish to have it voluntarily, and in no other way; for the question does not concern your own affairs only, but ours also; and Tonnay-Charente would tell you as I do, if she were here. For, the fact is, that last evening she wished to have some private conversation in our room, and I was going there after the Manicampian and Malicornian colloquies had terminated, when I learnt, on my return, rather late it is true, that Madame had sent away her maids of honour, and that we are to sleep in her apartments, instead of our own room. Moreover, Madame has sent away her maids of honour in order that they should not have the time to concert any measures together, and this morning she was closeted with Tonnay-Charente with the same object. Tell me, then, to what extent Athenaïs and I can rely upon you, as we will tell you in what way you can rely upon us?'

'I do not clearly understand the question you have put,' said Louise, much agitated.

'Hum! and yet, on the contrary, you seem to understand me very well. However, I will put my questions in a more precise manner, in order that you may not be able in the slightest degree to evade them. Listen to me: *Do you love M. de Bragelonne?* That is plain enough, is it not?'

At this question, which fell like the first projectile of a besieging army into a besieged town, Louise started. 'You ask me,' she exclaimed, 'if I love Raoul, the friend of my childhood,*—my brother almost?'

'No, no, no! Again you evade me, or rather, you wish to escape me. I do not ask you if you love Raoul, your childhood's friend,—your brother; but I ask if you love the Vicomte de Bragelonne, your affianced husband?'

'Good heavens! my dear Montalais,' said Louise, 'how severe your tone is!'

'You deserve no indulgence,—I am neither more nor less severe than usual. I put a question to you, so answer it.'

'You certainly do not,' said Louise, in a choking voice, 'speak to me like a friend; but I will answer you as a true friend.'

'Well, do so.'

'Very well; my heart is full of scruples and silly feelings of pride, with respect to everything that a woman ought to keep secret, and in this respect no one has ever read into the bottom of my soul.'

'That I know very well. If I had read it, I should not interrogate you as I have done; I should simply say,—"My good Louise, you have the happiness of an acquaintance with M. de Bragelonne, who is an excellent young man, and an advantageous match for a girl without any fortune. M. de la Fère will leave something like fifteen thousand livres a year to his son. At a future day, then, you, as this son's wife, will have fifteen thousand livres a year; which is not bad. Turn, then, neither to the right hand nor to the left, but go frankly to M. de Bragelonne; that is to say, to the altar to which he will lead you. Afterwards, why—afterwards, according to his disposition, you will be emancipated or enslaved; in other words, you will have a right to commit any act of folly which people commit who have either too much liberty or too little." That is, my dear Louise, what I should have told you at first, if I had been able to read your heart.'

'And I should have thanked you,' stammered out Louise, 'although the advice does not appear to me to be altogether good.'

'Wait, wait. But immediately after having given you that advice, I should add:—"Louise, it is very dangerous to pass whole days with your head reclining on your bosom, your hands unoccupied, your eyes restless and full of thought; it is dangerous to prefer the least frequented paths, and no longer to be amused with such diversions as gladden young girls' hearts; it is dangerous, Louise, to write with the point of your foot, as you do, upon the gravel, certain letters which it is useless for you to efface, but which appear again under your heel, particularly when those letters rather resemble the letter L than the letter B; and, lastly, it is dangerous to allow the mind to dwell on a thousand wild fancies, the fruits of solitude and headaches; these fancies, while they sink into a young girl's mind, make her cheeks sink in also, so that it is not unusual, on these occasions, to find the most delightful persons in the world become the most disagreeable, and the wittiest to become the dullest."'

'I thank you, dearest Aure,' replied La Vallière gently; 'it is like you to speak to me in this manner, and I thank you for it.'

'It was only for the benefit of wild dreamers, such as I described, that I spoke; do not take any of my words, then, to yourself except such as you think you deserve. Stay, I hardly know what story recurs to my memory of some silly or melancholy young girl, who was gradually pining away because she fancied that the Prince, or the King, or the Emperor, whoever it was—and it does not much matter which—had fallen completely in love with her; while, on the contrary, the Prince, or the King, or the Emperor, whichever you please, was plainly in love with some one else, and—a singular circumstance, one, indeed, which she could not perceive, although every one around and about her perceived it clearly enough—made use of her as a screen for his own love affair. You laugh as I do, at this poor silly girl, do you not, Louise?'

'I laugh, of course,' stammered out Louise, pale as death.

'And you are right, too, for the thing is amusing enough. The story, whether true or false, amused me, and so I have remembered it and told it to you. Just imagine, then, my good Louise, the mischief that such a melancholy would create in your brain,—a melancholy, I mean, of that kind. For my own part, I resolved to tell you the story; for, if such a thing were to happen to either of us, it would be most essential to be assured of its truth; to-day it is a snare, to-morrow it will become a jest and mockery, the next day it will be death itself.' La Vallière started again, and became, if possible, still paler.

'Whenever a king takes notice of us,' continued Montalais, 'he lets us see it easily enough, and, if we happen to be the object he covets, he knows very well how to gain his object. You see, then, Louise, that, in such circumstances, between young girls exposed to such a danger as the one in question, the most perfect confidence should exist, in order that those hearts which are not disposed towards melancholy may watch over those who are likely to become so.'

'Silence, silence!' said La Vallière; 'some one approaches.'

'Some one is approaching, in fact,' said Montalais; 'but who can it possibly be? Everybody is away, either at Mass with the King, or bathing with Monsieur.'

At the end of the walk the young girls perceived almost immediately, beneath the arching trees, the graceful carriage and noble height of a young man, who with his sword under his arm and a cloak thrown across his shoulders, and booted and spurred besides, saluted them from the distance with a gentle smile.

'Raoul!' exclaimed Montalais.

'M. de Bragelonne!' murmured Louise.

'A very proper judge to decide upon our difference of opinion,' said Montalais.

'Oh! Montalais, Montalais, for pity's sake,' exclaimed La Vallière, 'after having been so cruel, show me a little mercy.' These words, uttered with all the fervour of a prayer, effaced all trace of irony, if not from Montalais's heart, at least from her face.

'Why you are as handsome as Amadis,* Monsieur de Bragelonne,' she cried to Raoul, 'and armed and booted like him.'

'A thousand compliments, young ladies,' replied Raoul, bowing.

'But why, I ask, are you booted in this manner?' repeated Montalais, whilst La Vallière, although she looked at Raoul with a surprise equal to that of her companion, nevertheless uttered not a word.

'Because I am about to set off,' said Bragelonne, looking at Louise.

The young girl seemed as though smitten by some superstitious feeling of terror, and tottered. 'You are going away, Raoul!' she cried; 'and where are you going?'

'Dearest Louise,' he replied, with that quiet composed manner which was natural to him, 'I am going to England.'

'What are you going to do in England?'

'The King has sent me there.'

'The King!' exclaimed Louise and Aure together, involuntarily exchanging glances, the conversation which had just been interrupted recurring to them both. Raoul intercepted the glance, but he could not understand its meaning, and, naturally enough, attributed it to the interest which both the young girls took in him.

'His Majesty,' he said, 'has been good enough to remember that the Comte de la Fère is high in favour with King Charles II.* This morning, then, as he was on his way to attend Mass, the King, seeing me as he passed, signed to me to approach, which I accordingly did. "Monsieur de Bragelonne," he said to me, "you will call upon M. Fouquet, who has received from me letters for the King of Great Britain; you will be the bearer of them." I bowed. "Ah!" His Majesty added, "before you leave, you will be good enough to take any commissions which Madame may have for the King her brother."'

'Gracious Heaven!' murmured Louise, much agitated, and yet full of thought at the same time.

'So quickly! You are desired to set off in such haste!' said Montalais, almost paralysed by this unforeseen event.

'Properly to obey those whom we respect,' said Raoul, 'it is necessary to obey quickly. Within ten minutes after I had received the order, I was ready. Madame, already informed, is writing the letter which she is good enough to do me the honour of entrusting to me. In the meantime learning from Mademoiselle de Tonnay-Charente that it was likely you would be in this direction, I came here, and am happy to find you both.'

'And both of us very suffering, as you see,' said Montalais, going to Louise's assistance, whose countenance was visibly altered.

'Suffering?' repeated Raoul, pressing Louise's hand with a tender curiosity. 'Your hand is like ice.'

'It is nothing.'

'This coldness does not reach your heart, Louise, does it?' inquired the young man, with a tender smile. Louise raised her head hastily, as if this question had been inspired by some suspicion, and had aroused a feeling of remorse.

'Oh! you know,' she said, with an effort, 'that my heart will never be cold towards a friend like yourself, Monsieur de Bragelonne.'

'Thank you, Louise. I know both your heart and your mind, and it is not by the touch of the hand that one can judge of an affection like yours. You know, Louise, how devotedly I love you, with what perfect and unreserved confidence I have resigned my life to you; will you not forgive me, then, for speaking to you with something like the frankness of a child?'

'Speak, Monsieur Raoul,' said Louise, trembling very much, 'I am listening.'

'I cannot part from you, carrying away with me a thought which torments me; absurd I know it to be, and yet one which rends my very heart.'

'Are you going away, then, for any length of time?' inquired La Vallière, with a thickened utterance, while Montalais turned her head aside.

'No; and probably I shall not be absent more than a fortnight.' La Vallière pressed her hand upon her heart, which felt as though it were breaking.

'It is strange,' pursued Raoul, looking at the young girl with a melancholy expression; 'I have often left you when setting off on adventures fraught with danger. Then I started joyously enough—my heart free, my mind intoxicated by the thought of happiness in store for me, of hopes of which the future was full; and yet, at that time, I was about to face the Spanish cannon, or the halberds of the Walloons.* To-day, without the existence of any danger or uneasiness, and by the easiest manner in the world, I am going in search of a glorious recompense, which this mark of the King's favour seems to indicate, for I am, perhaps, going to win you, Louise; what other favour, more precious than yourself, could the King confer upon me? Yet, Louise, in very truth I know not how or why, but this happiness and this future seem to vanish from my eyes like smoke—like an idle dream; and I feel here, here, at the very bottom of my heart, a deep-seated grief, a dejection which I cannot overcome; something heavy, passionless, death-like,—resembling a corpse. Oh! Louise, too well do I know why; it is because I have never loved you so truly as now. God help me!'

At this last exclamation, which issued as it were from a broken heart, Louise burst into tears, and threw herself into Montalais's arms. The latter, although she was not very easily impressed, felt the tears rush to her eyes. Raoul saw only the tears which Louise shed; his look, however, did not penetrate—nay, sought not to penetrate—beyond those tears. He bent his knee before her, and tenderly kissed her hand; and it was evident that in that kiss he poured out his whole heart before her.

'Rise, rise,' said Montalais to him, herself ready to cry, 'for Athenaïs is coming.'

Raoul rose, brushed his knee with the back of his hand, smiled again upon Louise, whose eyes were fixed on the ground, and, having pressed Montalais's hand gratefully, he turned round to salute Mademoiselle de Tonnay-Charente, the sound of whose silken robe was already heard upon the gravel walk. 'Has Madame finished her letter?' he inquired, when the young girl came within reach of his voice.

'Yes, the letter is finished, sealed, and Her Royal Highness is ready to receive you.'

Raoul, at this remark, hardly gave himself time to salute Athenaïs, cast one last look at Louise, bowed to Montalais, and withdrew in the direction of the château. As he withdrew he again turned round, but at last, at the end of the grand walk, it was useless to do so again, as he could no longer see them. The three young girls, on their side, had, with very different feelings, watched him disappear.

'At last,' said Athenaïs, the first to interrupt the silence, 'at last we are alone, free to talk of yesterday's great affair, and to come to an understanding upon the conduct it is advisable for us to pursue. Besides, if you will listen to me,' she continued, looking round on all sides, 'I will explain to you, as briefly as possible, in the first place, our own duty, such as I imagine it to be, and, if you do not understand a hint, what is Madame's desire on the subject.' And Mademoiselle de Tonnay-Charente pronounced these words in such a tone, as to leave no doubt, in her companions' minds, upon the official character with which she was invested.

'Madame's desire!' exclaimed Montalais and La Vallière together.

'Her ultimatum,' replied Mademoiselle de Tonnay-Charente diplomatically.

'But,' murmured La Vallière, 'does Madame know, then,——'

'Madame knows more about the matter than we said, even,' said Athenaïs, in a formal, precise manner. 'Therefore, let us come to a proper understanding.'

'Yes, indeed,' said Montalais, 'and I am listening in breathless attention.'

'Gracious Heaven!' murmured Louise, trembling, 'shall I ever survive this cruel evening?'

'Oh! do not frighten yourself in that manner,' said Athenaïs; 'we have found a remedy for it.' So, seating herself between her two companions, and taking each of them by the hand, which she held in her own, she began. The first words were hardly spoken, when they heard a horse galloping away over the stones of the public high-road, outside the gates of the château.

XXXVII

AS HAPPY AS A PRINCE

AT the very moment he was about to enter the château, Bragelonne had met de Guiche. But before having been met by Raoul, de Guiche had met Manicamp, who had met Malicorne. How was it that Malicorne had met Manicamp? Nothing more simple, for he had awaited his return from Mass, where he had accompanied M. de Saint-Aignan. When they had met, they congratulated each other upon their good fortune, and Manicamp had availed himself of the circumstance to ask his friend if he had not a few crowns still remaining at the bottom of his pocket.* The latter, without expressing any surprise at the question, and which he expected perhaps, had answered that every pocket, which is always being drawn upon without anything ever being put in it, greatly resembles those wells which can supply water during the winter, but which the gardeners render useless by exhausting them during the summer; that his, Malicorne's pocket, certainly was deep, and that there would be a pleasure in drawing on it in times of plenty, but that, unhappily, abuse had produced barrenness. To this remark Manicamp, deep in thought, had replied, 'Quite true!'

'The question, then, is how to fill it?' Malicorne had added.

'Of course; but in what way?'

'Nothing easier, my dear Monsieur Manicamp.'

'So much the better. How?'

'A post in Monsieur's household, and the pocket is full again.'

'You have the post?'

'That is, I have the promise of being nominated; but the promise of nomination, without the post itself, is the purse without money.'

'Quite true,' Manicamp had replied a second time.

'Let us try for the post, then,' the candidate had persisted.

'My dear fellow,' sighed Manicamp, 'an appointment in His Royal Highness's household is one of the gravest difficulties of our position.'

'Oh! oh!'

'There is no question that, at the present moment, we cannot ask Monsieur for anything. We are not on good terms with him.'

'A great absurdity, too,' said Malicorne promptly.

'Bah! and if we were to show Madame any attention,' said Manicamp, 'frankly speaking, do you think we should please Monsieur?'

'Precisely; if we show Madame any attention, and do so adroitly, Monsieur ought to adore us. Either that, or we are great fools; make haste, therefore, M. Manicamp, you who are so able a politician, to make M. de Guiche and His Royal Highness friendly again.'

'Tell me, what did M. de Saint-Aignan tell you, Malicorne?'

'Nothing; he asked me several questions, and that was all.'

'Well, he was less discreet, then, with me.'

'What did he tell you?'

'That the King is passionately in love with Mademoiselle de la Vallière.'

'We knew that already,' replied Malicorne ironically; 'and everybody talks about it loud enough for every one to know it;

but in the meantime, do what I advise you; speak to M. de Guiche, and endeavour to get him to make an advance towards Monsieur. Deuce take it! he owes His Royal Highness that, at least.'

'But we must see de Guiche, then?'

'There does not seem to be any great difficulty in that: try to see him in the same way I tried to see you. Wait for him; you know that he is naturally very fond of walking.'

'Yes; but whereabouts does he walk?'

'What a question to ask! Do you know not that he is in love with Madame? You will find him walking about on the side of the château where her apartments are.'

'Stay, my dear Malicorne, you were not mistaken, for here he is coming.'

'Why should I be mistaken? Have you ever noticed that I am in the habit of making a mistake? Come, we only need to understand each other. Do you need money?'

'Ah!' exclaimed Manicamp mournfully.

'Well, I want my appointment. Let Malicorne have the appointment, and Manicamp shall have the money. There is no greater difficulty in the way than that.'

'Very well; in that case make yourself easy. I will do my best.'

De Guiche approached, Malicorne stepped aside, and Manicamp caught hold of de Guiche, who was thoughtful and melancholy. 'Tell me, my dear Comte, what rhyme you were trying to find,' said Manicamp. 'I have an excellent one to match yours, particularly if yours ends in *ame*.'*

De Guiche shook his head, and recognising a friend, he took him by the arm. 'My dear Manicamp,' he said, 'I am in search of something very different from a rhyme.'

'What is it you are looking for?'

'You will help me to find what I am in search of,' continued the Comte; 'you who are such an idle fellow, in other words, a man with a mind full of ingenious devices.'

'I am getting my ingenuity ready, then, my dear Comte.'

'This is the state of the case, then: I wish to approach to a particular house, where I have some business.'

'You must get near to the house, then,' said Manicamp.

'Very good; but in this house dwells a husband who happens to be jealous.'

'Is he more jealous than the dog Cerberus?'

'Not more, but quite as much so.'

'Has he three mouths, as that obdurate guardian of the infernal regions had? Do not shrug your shoulders, my dear Comte; I put the question to you with a perfect reason for doing so, since poets pretend that, in order to soften Monsieur Cerberus, the visitor must take something enticing with him—a cake, for instance.* Therefore, I who view the matter in a prosaic light, that is to say, in the light of reality, I say: one cake is very little for three mouths. If your jealous husband has three mouths, Comte, get three cakes.'

'Manicamp, I can get such advice as that from M. de Beautru.'*

'In order to get better advice,' said Manicamp, with a comical seriousness of expression, 'you will be obliged to adopt a more precise formula than you have used towards me.'

'If Raoul were here,' said de Guiche, 'he would be sure to understand me.'

'So I think, particularly if you said to him: "I should very much like to see Madame a little nearer, but I fear Monsieur, because he is jealous."'

'Manicamp!' cried the Comte angrily, and endeavouring to overwhelm his tormentor by a look, who did not, however, appear to be in the slightest degree disturbed by it.

'What is the matter now, my dear Comte?' inquired Manicamp.

'What! is it thus that you blaspheme the most sacred of names!'

'What names?'

'Monsieur! Madame! the highest names in the kingdom.'

'You are very strangely mistaken, my dear Comte, I never mentioned the highest names in the kingdom. I merely answered you in reference to the subject of a jealous husband, whose name you did not tell me, and who, as a matter of course, has a wife. I therefore, I repeat, replied to you. In order to see Madame, you must get a little more intimate with Monsieur.'

'Jester, that you are,' said the Comte, smiling; 'was that what you said?——'

'Nothing else.'

'Very good; what then?'

'Now,' added Manicamp, 'let the question be regarding the Duchess——or the Duke——; very well, I shall say: Let us get into the house in some way or another; for that is a tactic which cannot in any case be unfavourable to your love affair.'

'Ah! Manicamp, if you could find me a pretext, a good pretext.'

'A pretext; I can find you a hundred, nay, a thousand. If Malicorne were here, he would have already hit upon fifty thousand excellent pretexts.'

'Who is Malicorne?'* replied de Guiche, half-shutting his eyes like a person reflecting, 'I seem to know that name.'

'Know him! I should think so; you owe his father thirty thousand crowns.'

'Ah, indeed! so it's that worthy fellow from Orleans.'

'Whom you promised an appointment in Monsieur's household; not the jealous husband, but the other.'

'Well, then, since your friend Malicorne is such an inventive genius, let him find me a means of being adored by Monsieur, and a pretext to make my peace with him.'

'Very good; I'll talk to him about it.'

'But who is that coming? The Vicomte de Bragelonne? Yes, it is he,' said de Guiche, as he hastened forward to meet him. 'You here, Raoul!'

'Yes; I was looking for you to say farewell,' replied Raoul, warmly pressing the Comte's hand. 'How do you do, Monsieur Manicamp?'

'How is this, Vicomte; you are leaving us?'

'Yes; a mission from the King.'

'Where are you going?'

'To London. On leaving you, I am going to Madame; she has a letter to give me for His Majesty Charles II.'

'You will find her alone, for Monsieur has gone out; gone to bathe in fact.'

'In that case, you, who are one of Monsieur's gentlemen-in-waiting, will undertake to make my excuses to him. I should have waited in order to receive any directions he might have to give me, if the desire for my immediate departure had not been intimated to me by M. Fouquet on behalf of His Majesty.'

Manicamp touched de Guiche's elbow, saying, 'there's a pretext for you.'

'You are right, Manicamp: a pretext, whatever it may be, is all

I require. And so a pleasant journey to you, Raoul.' And the two friends thereupon took a warm leave of each other. Five minutes afterwards Raoul entered Madame's apartments, as Mademoiselle de Montalais had begged him to do. Madame was still seated at the table where she had written her letter. Before her was still burning the rose-coloured taper which she had used to seal it. Only in her deep reflection, for Madame seemed to be buried in thought, she had forgotten to extinguish the taper. Bragelonne was expected, and was announced, therefore, as soon as he appeared. Bragelonne was a very model of elegance in every way; it was impossible to see him once without always remembering him; and, not only had Madame seen him once, but it will not be forgotten he was one of the very first who had gone to meet her, and had accompanied her from Le Havre to Paris.* Madame had preserved therefore an excellent recollection of him.

'Ah! M. de Bragelonne,' she said to him, 'you are going to see my brother, who will be delighted to pay to the son a portion of the debt of gratitude he has contracted with the father.'*

'The Comte de la Fère, madame, has been abundantly recompensed for the little service he had the happiness to render the King, by the kindness which the King has shown towards him, and it is I who will have to convey to His Majesty the assurance of the respect, devotion, and gratitude of father and son.'

'Do you know my brother?'

'No, your Highness; I shall have the honour of seeing His Majesty for the first time.'

'You require no recommendation to him. At all events, however, if you have any doubt about your personal merit, take me unhesitatingly for your surety.'

'Your Royal Highness overwhelms me with your kindness.'

'No! M. de Bragelonne, I well remember that we were fellow-travellers once, and that I remarked your extreme prudence in the midst of the extravagant absurdities committed, on both sides, by two of the greatest simpletons in the world, M. de Guiche and the Duke of Buckingham. Let us not speak of them, however; but of yourself. Are you going to England to remain there permanently? Forgive my inquiry, but it is not curiosity, but a desire to be of service to you in anything that I can do.'

'No, Madame; I am going to England to fulfil a mission which His Majesty has been kind enough to confide to me—nothing more.'

'And you propose to return to France?'

'As soon as I shall have accomplished my mission; unless, indeed, His Majesty King Charles II should have other orders for me.'

'He will beg you, at the very least, I am sure, to remain near him as long as possible.'

'In that case, as I shall not know how to refuse, I will now beforehand entreat your Royal Highness to have the goodness to remind the King of France that one of his devoted servants is far away from him.'

'Take care that at the time you are recalled, you do not consider his command as an abuse of power.'

'I do not understand you, Madame.'

'The court of France is not easily matched I am aware; but yet we have some pretty women at the court of England also.' Raoul smiled.

'Oh!' said Madame, 'yours is a smile which portends no good to my countrywomen. It is as though you were telling them, Monsieur de Bragelonne: "I visit you, but I leave my heart on the other side of the Channel." Did not your smile indicate that?'

'Your Highness is gifted with the power of reading the inmost depths of the soul, and you will understand, therefore, why, at present, any prolonged residence at the court of England would be a matter of the deepest regret for me.'

'And I need not inquire if so gallant a knight is recompensed in return?'

'I have been brought up, Madame, with her whom I love, and I believe that our affection is mutual.'

'In that case, do not delay your departure, Monsieur de Bragelonne, and delay not your return, for on your return we shall see two persons happy; for I hope no obstacle exists to your felicity.'

'There is a great obstacle, Madame.'

'Indeed! what is it?'

'The King's wishes on the subject.'

'The King opposes your marriage?'

'He postpones it at least. I solicited His Majesty's consent through the Comte de la Fère, and, without absolutely refusing it, he at least positively said it must be deferred.'

'Is the young lady whom you love unworthy of you, then?'

'She is worthy of a King's affection, Madame.'

'I mean, she is not, perhaps, of birth equal to your own.'

'Her family is excellent.'

'Is she young, beautiful?'

'She is seventeen, and, in my opinion, exceedingly beautiful.'

'Is she in the country, or at Paris?'

'She is here, at Fontainebleau, Madame.'

'Do I know her?'

'She has the honour to form one of your Highness's household.'

'Her name?' inquired the Princess anxiously; 'if, indeed,' she added hastily, 'her name is not a secret.'

'No Madame, my affection is too pure for me to make a secret of it for any one, and with still greater reason for your Royal Highness, whose kindness towards me has been so extreme. It is Mademoiselle Louise de la Vallière.'

Madame could not restrain an exclamation, in which a feeling stronger than surprise might have been detected. 'Ah!' she said, 'La Vallière—she who yesterday——' she paused, and then continued, 'she who was taken ill, I believe.'

'Yes, Madame; it was only this morning that I heard of the accident which had befallen her.'

'Did you see her before you came to me?'

'I had the honour of taking leave of her.'

'And you say,' resumed Madame, making a powerful effort over herself, 'that the King has—deferred your marriage with this young girl.'

'Yes, Madame, deferred it.'

'Did he assign any reason for this postponement?'

'None.'

'How long is it since the Comte de la Fère preferred his request to the King?'

'More than a month, Madame.'

'It is very singular,' said the Princess, as something like a cloud passed across her eyes. 'A month?' she repeated.

'About a month.'

'You are right, Vicomte,' said the Princess, with a smile, in which de Bragelonne might have remarked a kind of restraint, 'my brother must not keep you too long in England; set off at once, and in the first letter I write to England, I will claim you in the King's name.' And Madame rose to place her letter in Bragelonne's hands. Raoul understood that his audience was at an end; he took the letter, bowed lowly to the Princess, and left the room.

'A month!' murmured the Princess; 'could I have been blind, then, to so great an extent, and could he have loved her for the last month?' And as Madame had nothing to do, she sat down to begin a letter to her brother, the postscript of which was a summons for Bragelonne to return.

The Comte de Guiche, as we have seen, had yielded to the pressing persuasions of Manicamp, and allowed himself to be led to the stables, where they desired their horses to be got ready for them; then, by one of the side paths, a description of which has already been given, they advanced to meet Monsieur, who, having just finished bathing, was returning towards the château, wearing a woman's veil to protect his face from getting burnt by the sun, which was already very powerful. Monsieur was in one of those fits of good humour which inspired him sometimes with an admiration of his own good looks. As he was bathing he had been able to compare the whiteness of his body with that of his courtiers, and, thanks to the care which His Royal Highness took of himself, no one, not even the Chevalier de Lorraine, could bear the comparison. Monsieur, moreover, had been tolerably successful in swimming, and his muscles having been exercised by the healthy immersion in the cool water, he was in a light and cheerful state of mind and body. So that, at the sight of Guiche, who advanced to meet him at a hand gallop, mounted upon a magnificent white horse, the Prince could not restrain an exclamation of delight.

'I think matters look well,' said Manicamp, who fancied he could read this friendly disposition upon His Royal Highness's countenance.

'Good-day, de Guiche, good-day,' exclaimed the Prince.

'Long life to your Royal Highness!' replied de Guiche, encouraged by the tone of Philip's voice; 'health, joy, happiness, and prosperity to your Highness.'

'Welcome, de Guiche, come to my right side, but keep your horse in hand, for I wish to return at a walking pace, under the cool shade of these trees.'

'As you please, monseigneur,' said de Guiche, taking his place on the Prince's right, as he had just been invited to do.

'Now, my dear de Guiche,' said the Prince, 'give me a little news of that de Guiche whom I used to know formerly, and who used to pay attentions to my wife.'

Guiche blushed to the very whites of his eyes, while Monsieur burst out laughing, as though he had made the wittiest remark in the world. The few privileged courtiers who surrounded Monsieur thought it their duty to follow his example, although they had not heard the remark, and a noisy burst of laughter immediately followed, beginning with the first courtier, passing on through the whole company, and only terminating with the last. De Guiche, although blushing extremely, put a good countenance on the matter: Manicamp looked at him.

'Ah! monseigneur,' replied de Guiche, 'show a little charity towards such a miserable fellow as I am; do not hold me up to the ridicule of the Chevalier de Lorraine.'

'How do you mean?'

'If he hears you ridicule me, he will go beyond your Highness, and will show no pity.'

'About your passion and the Princess, do you mean?'

'For mercy's sake, monseigneur.'

'Come, come, de Guiche, confess that you did get a little sweet upon Madame.'

'I will never confess such a thing, monseigneur.'

'Out of respect for me, I suppose; but I release you from your respect, de Guiche. Confess, as if it were simply a question about Mademoiselle de Chalais* and Mademoiselle de la Vallière.'

Then breaking off, he said, beginning to laugh again, 'Come, that is very good—a remark like a sword which cuts two ways at once. I hit you and my brother at the same time, Chalais and La Vallière, your affianced bride and his future lady-love.'

'Really, monseigneur,' said the Comte, 'you are in a most brilliant humour to-day.'

'The fact is, I feel well, and then I am pleased to see you again. But you were angry with me, were you not?'

'I, monseigneur? Why should I have been so?'

'Because I interfered with your sarabands and your other Spanish amusements. Nay, do not deny it. On that day you left the Princess's apartments with your eyes full of fury; that brought you ill luck, for you danced in the ballet yesterday in a most miserable manner. Now, don't sulk, de Guiche, for it does you no good, but makes you look as surly as a bear. If the Princess did look at you attentively yesterday, I am quite sure of one thing.'

'What is that, monseigneur? Your Highness alarms me.'

'She has quite forsworn you now,' said the Prince, with a burst of loud laughter.

'Decidedly,' thought Manicamp, 'rank has nothing to do with it, and all men are alike.'

The Prince continued:—'At all events, you are now returned, and it is to be hoped that the Chevalier will become amiable again.'

'How so, monseigneur; and by what miracle can I exercise such an influence over M. de Lorraine?'

'The matter is very simple, he is jealous of you.'

'Bah! it is not possible.'

'It is the case, though.'

'He does me too much honour, then.'

'The fact is, that when you are here he is full of kindness and attention, but when you are gone he makes me suffer martyrdom. I am like a see-saw. Besides, you do not know the idea which has struck me?'

'I do not even suspect it.'

'Well, then; when you were in exile, for you really were exiled, my poor de Guiche——'

'I should think so, indeed; but whose fault was it?' said de Guiche, pretending to speak in an angry tone.

'Not mine, certainly, my dear Comte,' replied His Royal Highness, 'upon my honour, I did not ask the King to exile you.'

'No, not you, monseigneur, I am well aware; but——'

'But Madame; well, as far as that goes, I do not say it is not the case. Why, what the deuce did you do or say to Madame?'

'Really, monseigneur——'

'Women, I know, have their grudges, and my wife is not free from caprices of that nature. But if she were the cause of your being exiled, I bear you no ill will.'

'In that case, monseigneur,' said de Guiche, 'I am not unhappy altogether.'

Manicamp, who was following closely behind de Guiche, and who did not miss a word of what the Prince was saying, bent down to his very shoulders over his horse's neck, in order to conceal the laughter he could not repress.

'Besides, your exile started a project in my head. When the Chevalier—finding you were no longer here, and sure of reigning undisturbed—began to bully me, I, observing that my wife, in the most perfect contrast to him, was most kind and amiable towards me who had neglected her so much, the idea occurred to me of becoming a model husband—a rarity, a curiosity, at the court; and I had an idea of getting very fond of my wife.'

De Guiche looked at the Prince with a stupefied expression of countenance, which was not assumed.

'Oh! monseigneur,' de Guiche stammered out, tremblingly; 'surely, that idea did not seriously occur to you.'

'Indeed, it did. I have some property that my brother gave me on my marriage; she has some money of her own, and not a little, either, for she gets money from her brother and brother-in-law* of England and France at the same time. Well! we should have left the court. I should have retired to my château at Villers-Cotterets,* situated in the middle of a forest, in which we should have led a most sentimental life in the very same spot where my grandfather, Henry IV, did with la belle Gabrielle.* What do you think of that idea, de Guiche?'

'Why, it is enough to make one shudder, monseigneur,' replied de Guiche, who shuddered in reality.

'Ah! I see you would never be able to endure being exiled a second time. I will not carry you off with us, as I had at first intended.'

'What, with you, monseigneur?'

'Yes; if the idea should occur to me again of taking a dislike to the court.'

'Oh! do not let that make any difference, monseigneur; I would follow your Highness to the end of the world.'

'Clumsy fellow that you are!' said Manicamp grumblingly, pushing his horse towards de Guiche, so as almost to unseat him, and then, as he passed close to him, as if he had lost his command over the horse, he whispered, 'For goodness' sake, think what you are saying.'

'Well, it is agreed, then,' said the Prince; 'since you are so devoted to me, I shall take you with me.'

'Anywhere, everywhere, monseigneur,' replied de Guiche in a joyous tone, 'whenever you like, and at once, too. Are you ready?'

And de Guiche, laughingly, gave his horse the rein and galloped forward a few yards.

'One moment,' said the Prince. 'Let us go to the château first.'

'What for?' asked de Guiche.

'Why, since I tell you that it is a project of conjugal affection, it is necessary I shall take my wife with me.'

'In that case, monseigneur,' replied the Comte, 'I am greatly concerned, but no de Guiche for you. Why do you take Madame with you?'

'Because I begin to see that I love her,' said the Prince.

De Guiche turned slightly pale, but endeavoured to preserve his seeming cheerfulness.

'If you love Madame, monseigneur,' he said, 'that ought to be quite enough for you, and you have no further need of your friends.'

'Not bad, not bad,' murmured Manicamp.

'There, your fear of Madame has begun again,' replied the Prince.

'Why, monseigneur, I have experienced that to my cost; a woman who was the cause of my being exiled.'

'What a horrible disposition you have, de Guiche; how terribly you bear malice.'

'I should like the case to be your own, monseigneur.'

'Decidedly, then, that was the reason why you danced so badly yesterday; you wished to revenge yourself, I suppose, by trying to make Madame make a mistake in her dancing; ah! that is very paltry, de Guiche, and I will tell Madame of it.'

'You can tell her whatever you please, monseigneur, for her Highness cannot hate me more than she does.'

'Nonsense, you are exaggerating; and this because, merely, of the fortnight's sojourn in the country she imposed on you.'

'Monseigneur, a fortnight is a fortnight; and when the time was passed in getting sick and tired of everything, a fortnight is an eternity.'

'So that you will not forgive her? Come, come, de Guiche, be a better disposed fellow than that, I wish to make your peace with her; you will find, in conversing with her, that she has no malice or unkindness in her nature, and that she is very talented.'

'Monseigneur——'

'You will see that she can receive her friends like a princess, and laugh like a citizen's wife; you will see that, when she pleases, she can make the hours pass away like minutes. Come, de Guiche, you must really make up your differences with my wife.'

'Upon my word,' said Manicamp, to himself, 'the Prince is a husband whose wife's name will bring him ill-luck, and King Candaules* of old was a complete tiger beside His Royal Highness.'

'At all events,' added the Prince, 'I am sure you will make it up with my wife; I guarantee you will do so. Only, I must show you the way now. There is nothing commonplace about her, and it is not every one who takes her fancy.'

'Monseigneur——'

'No resistance, de Guiche, or I shall get out of temper,' replied the Prince.

'Well, since he will have it so,' murmured Manicamp in Guiche's ear, 'do as he wants you to do.'

'Well, monseigneur,' said the Comte, 'I obey.'

'And to begin,' resumed the Prince, 'there will be cards, this evening, in Madame's apartment. You will dine with me and I will take you there with me.'

'Oh! as for that, monseigneur,' objected de Guiche, 'you will allow me to object.'

'What, again! this is positive rebellion.'

'Madame received me too indifferently, yesterday, before the whole court.'

'Really!' said the Prince, laughing.

'Nay, so much so, indeed, that she did not even answer me when I addressed her; it may be a good thing to have no self-respect at all, but to have too little is not enough, as the saying is.'

'Comte! after dinner, you will go to your own apartments, and dress yourself, and then you will come to fetch me. I shall wait for you.'

'Since your Highness absolutely commands it.'

'He'll not let go his hold,' said Manicamp; 'these are the sort of things which husbands cling most obstinately to.—Ah! what a pity M. Molière* could not have heard this man; he would have turned him into verse if he had.'

The Prince and his court, chatting in this manner, returned to the coolest apartments of the château.

'By the bye,' said de Guiche, as they were standing by the door, 'I had a commission for your Royal Highness.'

'Execute it, then.'

'M. de Bragelonne has, by the King's order, set off for London, and he charged me with his respect for you, monseigneur.'

'A pleasant journey to the Vicomte, whom I like very much. Go and dress yourself, de Guiche, and come back for me. If you don't come back——'

'What will happen then, monseigneur?'

'I will get you sent to the Bastille.'

'Well,' said de Guiche laughing, 'His Royal Highness, monseigneur, is decidedly the counterpart of Her Royal Highness Madame. Madame gets me sent into exile because she does not care for me sufficiently; and Monseigneur gets me imprisoned because he cares for me too much. I thank Monseigneur, and I thank Madame.'

'Come, come,' said the Prince, 'you are a delightful companion, and you know that I cannot do without you. Return as soon as you can.'

'Very well; but I am in the humour to prove myself difficult to be pleased in my turn, monseigneur.'

'Bah!'

'So I will not return to your Royal Highness except upon one condition.'

'Name it.'

'I want to oblige the friend of one of my friends.'

'What's his name?'

'Malicorne. Well, I owe M. Malicorne a place in your household, monseigneur.'

'What kind of place?'

'Any kind of place; a supervision of some sort or another, for instance.'

'That happens very fortunately, for yesterday I dismissed my chief usher of the apartments.'

'That will do admirably. What are his duties?'

'Nothing, except to look about and make his report.'

'A sort of interior police? Ah, how excellently that will suit Malicorne,' Manicamp ventured to say.

'You know the person we are speaking of, M. Manicamp?' inquired the Prince.

'Intimately, monseigneur. I am the friend in question.'

'And your opinion is?'

'That your Highness could never get such an usher of the apartments as he will make.'

'How much does the appointment bring in?' inquired the Comte of the Prince.

'I don't know at all, only I have always been told that he could make as much as he pleased when he was thoroughly employed.'

'What do you call being thoroughly occupied, Prince?'

'It means, of course, when the functionary in question is a man with his wits about him.'

'In that case I think your Highness will be content, for Malicorne is as sharp as the devil himself.'

'Good! the appointment will be an expensive one for me, in that case,' replied the Prince, laughing. 'You are making me a positive present, Comte.'

'I believe so, monseigneur.'

'Well, go and announce to your M. Mélicorne——'

'Malicorne, monseigneur.'

'I shall never get hold of that name.'

'You say Manicamp very well, monseigneur.'

'Oh, I ought to say Malicorne very well, too. Custom will help me.'

'Say what you like, monseigneur, I can promise you that your inspector of apartments will not be annoyed; he is the very happiest disposition that can be met with.'

'Well, then, my dear de Guiche, inform him of his nomination. But stay——'

'What is it, monseigneur?'

'I wish to see him beforehand; if he be as ugly as his name I retract what I have said.'

'Your Highness knows him, for you have already seen him at the Palais-Royal; nay, indeed, it was I who presented him to you.'

'Ah, I remember now—not a bad-looking fellow.'

'I knew you must have noticed him, monseigneur.'

'Yes, yes, yes. You see, de Guiche, I do not wish that either my wife or myself should have ugly faces before our eyes. My wife will have all her maids of honour pretty; I, all the gentlemen about me good-looking.'

Manicamp went off to inform Malicorne of the good news he had just learnt. De Guiche seemed very unwilling to take his departure for the purpose of dressing himself. Monsieur, singing, laughing, and admiring himself, passed away the time until the dinner-hour, in a frame of mind which would have justified the proverb which makes a man as 'Happy as a prince.'

XXXVIII

THE STORY OF A DRYAD AND OF A NAIAD*

EVERY one had partaken of the banquet at the château, and had afterwards assumed their full court dresses. The usual hour for the repast was five o'clock. If we say then, that the repast occupied an hour and the toilet two hours, everybody was ready about eight o'clock in the evening. Towards eight o'clock, therefore, the guests began to arrive at Madame's, for we have already intimated it was Madame who 'received' that evening. And at Madame's soirées no one failed to be present; for the evenings passed in her apartments had always that perfect charm about them which the Queen, that pious and excellent princess, had not been able to confer upon her receptions. For, unfortunately, one of the advantages of goodness of disposition is, that it is far less amusing than wit of an ill-natured character. And yet, let us hasten to add, that such a style of wit could not be applied to Madame, for her disposition of mind, naturally of the very highest order, comprised too much true generosity, too many noble impulses and high-souled thoughts, to warrant her with being termed ill-natured. But Madame was endowed with a spirit of resistance—a gift very frequently fatal to its possessor, for it breaks where another would have bent; the result was that blows did not become deadened upon her as upon what might be termed the wadded feelings of Maria-Theresa. Her heart rebounded at each attack, and therefore, whenever she was attacked, even in a manner almost to stun her, she returned blow for blow to any one who might be imprudent enough to venture to tilt against her. Was this really maliciousness of disposition or simply waywardness of character?* We regard those rich and powerful natures as like the tree of knowledge, producing good and evil at the same time; a double branch, always blooming and fruitful, of which those who wish to eat know how to detect the good fruit, and from which the worthless and frivolous die who have eaten of it—a circumstance which is by no means to be regarded as a great misfortune. Madame, therefore, who had a well-digested plan in her mind of constituting herself the second, if not even the principal, queen of the court, rendered her receptions delightful to all, from the conversation, the opportunities of meeting, and the perfect liberty which she allowed to every one of making any remark he pleased, on the condition, however, that the remark was amusing or sensible. And it will hardly be believed, that, by that means, there was less talking among the society Madame assembled together than elsewhere. Madame hated people who talked much, and took a very cruel revenge upon them, for she allowed them to talk. She disliked pretension, too, and never overlooked that defect, even in the King himself. It was more than a weakness of Monsieur, and the Princess had undertaken the amazing task of curing him of it. As for the rest, poets, wits, beautiful women, all were received by her with the air of a mistress superior to her slaves. Sufficiently meditative in her liveliest humours to make even poets meditate; sufficiently pretty to dazzle by her attractions, even among the

prettiest; sufficiently witty for the most distinguished persons
who were present to listen to her with pleasure—it will easily be
believed that the receptions which were held in Madame's
apartments must naturally have proved very attractive. All who
were young flocked there, and when the King himself happens
to be young, everybody at the court is so too. And so the older
ladies of the court, the strong-minded women of the regency, or
of the last reign,* pouted and sulked at their ease; but others
only laughed at the fits of sulkiness in which these venerable
individuals indulged, who had carried the love of authority so
far as even to have taken the command of bodies of soldiers in
the war of the Fronde, in order, as Madame asserted, not to lose
their influence over men altogether. As eight o'clock struck, Her
Royal Highness entered the great drawing room, accompanied
by her ladies in attendance, and found several gentlemen belonging to the court already there, having been waiting for some
minutes. Among those who had arrived before the hour fixed for
the reception she looked around for the one who, she thought,
ought to have been the first in attendance, but he was not there.
However, almost at the very moment she had completed her
investigation, Monsieur was announced. Monsieur looked
splendid. All the precious stones and jewels of Cardinal Mazarin,
those of course which that minister could not do otherwise than
leave; all the Queen Mother's jewels, as well as a few others
belonging to his wife—Monsieur wore them all, and he was as
dazzling as the sun. Behind him followed de Guiche, with hesitating steps and with an air of contrition admirably assumed; de
Guiche wore a costume of French-grey velvet, embroidered
with silver and trimmed with blue ribbons; he wore also Mechlin
lace, as rare and beautiful of its sort as were the jewels of Monsieur of theirs. The plume in his hat was red. Madame, too,
wore several colours, and preferred red for hangings, grey for
dresses, and blue for flowers. M. de Guiche, dressed as we have
described, looked so handsome that he excited every one's notice. An interesting pallor of complexion, a languid expression of
the eyes, his white hands seen through the masses of lace which
covered them, the melancholy expression of his mouth—it was
only necessary, indeed, to see M. de Guiche to admit that few
men at the court of France could equal him. The consequence

was that Monsieur, who was pretentious enough to fancy he could eclipse a star even, if a star had adorned itself in a similar manner to himself, was, on the contrary, completely eclipsed in all imaginations, which are very silent judges certainly, but very positive and high in their judgement. Madame had looked at de Guiche briefly, but brief as her look had been, it had brought a delightful colour to his face. In fact, Madame had found de Guiche so handsome and so admirably dressed, that she almost ceased regretting the royal conquest which she felt was on the point of escaping her. Her heart, therefore, sent the blood to her face. Monsieur approached her. He had not noticed the Princess blush, or if he had seen it he was far from attributing it to its true cause.

'Madame,' he said, kissing his wife's hand, 'there is some one present here who has fallen into disgrace, an unhappy exile whom I would venture to recommend to your kindness. Do not forget, I beg, that he is one of my best friends, and that your kind reception of him will please me greatly.'

'What exile? what disgraced person are you speaking of?' inquired Madame, looking all round and not permitting her glance to rest more on the count than on the others.

This was the moment to present de Guiche, and the Prince drew aside and let de Guiche pass him, who, with a tolerably well-assumed awkwardness of manner, approached Madame and made his reverence to her.

'What!' exclaimed Madame, as if she were greatly surprised, 'is M. de Guiche the disgraced individual you speak of, the exile in question?'

'Yes, certainly!' returned the Duke.

'Indeed,' said Madame, 'he is almost the only person we see here.'

'You are unjust, Madame,' said the Prince. 'Come, forgive the poor fellow.'

'Forgive him what? What have I to forgive M. de Guiche?'

'Come, explain yourself, de Guiche? What do you wish to be forgiven?' inquired the Prince.

'Alas! Her Royal Highness knows very well what it is,' replied the latter in a hypocritical tone.

'Come, come, give him your hand, Madame,' said Philip.

'If it will give you any pleasure, Monsieur;' and, with a movement of her eyes and shoulders, which it would be impossible to
describe, Madame extended towards the young man her beautiful and perfumed hand, upon which he pressed his lips. It was
evident that he did so for some little time, and that Madame did
not withdraw her hand too quickly, for the Duke added,—

'De Guiche is not wickedly disposed, Madame; so do not be
afraid, he will not bite you.'

A pretext was given in the gallery by the Duke's remark,
which was not perhaps very laughable, for every one to laugh
excessively. The situation was odd enough, and some kindly-
disposed persons had observed it. Monsieur was still enjoying
the effect of his remark, when the King was announced. The
appearance of the room at this moment was as follows:—In the
centre, before the fireplace, which was filled with flowers, Madame was standing up, with her maids of honour formed in two
wings, on either side of her, and around whom the butterflies of
the court were fluttering. Several other groups were formed in
the recesses of the windows, like soldiers stationed in their different towers who belong to the same garrison. From their re-
spective places they could pick up the remarks which fell from
the principal group. From one of these groups, the nearest to
the fireplace, Malicorne, who had been at once raised to the
dignity, through Manicamp and de Guiche, of the post of master of the apartments, and whose official costume had been
ready for the last two months, was brilliant with gold lace, and
shone upon Montalais, standing on Madame's extreme left, with
all the fire of his eyes and all the splendour of his velvet.
Madame was conversing with Mademoiselle de Chatillon and
Mademoiselle de Créquy,* who were next to her, and addressed
a few words to Monsieur, who drew aside as soon as the King
was announced. Mademoiselle de la Vallière, like Montalais,
was on Madame's left hand, and the last but one on the line,
Mademoiselle de Tonnay-Charente being on her right. She was
stationed as certain bodies of troops are, whose weakenss is
suspected, and who are placed between two experienced regiments. Guarded in this manner by her two companions who had
shared her adventure, La Vallière, whether from regret at Raoul's
departure, or still suffering from the emotion caused by recent

events, which had begun to render her name familiar on the lips of the courtiers, La Vallière, we repeat, hid her eyes, red with weeping, behind her fan, and seemed to give the greatest attention to the remarks which Montalais and Athenaïs, alternately, whispered to her from time to time. As soon as the King's name was announced, a general movement took place in the apartment. Madame, in her character as hostess, rose to receive the royal visitor; but as she rose, notwithstanding her pre-occupation of mind, she glanced hastily towards her right; her glance, which the presumptuous de Guiche regarded as intended for himself, rested, as it swept over the whole circle, upon La Vallière, whose warm blush and restless emotion it immediately perceived.

The King advanced to the middle of the group, which had now become a general one, by a movement which took place from the circumference to the centre. Every head bowed low before His Majesty, the ladies bending like frail and magnificent lilies before King Aquilo.* There was nothing very severe, we will even say, nothing very royal that evening about the King, except, however, his youth and good looks. He wore an air of animated joyousness and good humour, which set all imaginations at work, and, thereupon, all present promised themselves a delightful evening, for no other reason than from having remarked the desire which His Majesty had to amuse himself in Madame's apartments. If there was any one in particular whose high spirits and good humour could equal the King's, it was M. de Saint-Aignan, who was dressed in a rose-coloured costume, with face and ribbons of the same colour, and, in addition, particularly rose-coloured in his ideas, for that evening M. de Saint-Aignan was prolific in ideas. The circumstance which had given a new expansion to the numerous ideas germinating in his fertile brain was, that he had just perceived that Mademoiselle de Tonnay-Charente was, like himself, dressed in rose-colour. We would not wish to say, however, that the wily courtier had not known beforehand that the beautiful Athenaïs was to wear that particular colour; for he very well knew the art of unlocking the lips of a dressmaker or ladies'-maid as to her mistress's intentions. He cast as many assassinating glances at Mademoiselle Athenaïs as he had bows of ribbon on his stockings and his doublet; in other words, he discharged an immense number.

The King having paid Madame the customary compliments, and Madame having requested him to be seated, the circle was immediately formed. Louis inquired of Monsieur the particulars of the day's bathing; and stated, looking at the ladies present while he spoke, that certain poets were engaged turning into verse the enchanting diversion of the baths of Vulaines, and that one of them particularly, M. Loret,* seemed to have been entrusted with the confidence of some water-nymph, as he had in his verses recounted many circumstances that were actually true—at which remark more than one lady present felt herself bound to blush. The King at this moment took the opportunity of looking round him more leisurely; Montalais was the only one who did not blush sufficiently to prevent her looking at the King, and she saw him fix his eyes most devouringly upon Mademoiselle de la Vallière. This undaunted maid of honour, Mademoiselle de Montalais, be it understood, forced the King to lower his gaze, and so saved Louise de la Vallière from a sympathetic warmth of feeling which this gaze might possibly have conveyed. Louis was appropriated by Madame, who overwhelmed him with inquiries, and no one in the world knew how to ask questions better than she did. He tried, however, to render the conversation general, and, with the view of effecting this, he redoubled his attention and devotion to her. Madame coveted complimentary remarks, and, determined to procure them at any cost, she addressed herself to the King, saying,—

'Sire, your Majesty, who is aware of everything which occurs in your kingdom, ought to know beforehand the verses confided to M. Loret by this nymph; will your Majesty kindly communicate them to us?'

'Madame,' replied the King, with perfect grace of manner, 'I dare not—you, personally, might be in no little degree confused at having to listen to certain details—but Saint-Aignan tells a story well, and has a perfect recollection of the verses; if he does not remember them, he will invent. I can certify him to be almost a poet himself.' Saint-Aignan, thus brought prominently forward, was compelled to introduce himself as advantageously as possible. Unfortunately, however, for Madame, he thought of his own personal affairs only; in other words, instead of paying Madame the compliments she so much desired and relished, his mind was fixed upon making as much display as possible of his own good fortune. Again glancing, therefore, for the hundredth time, at the beautiful Athenaïs, who thoroughly carried into practice her previous evening's theory of not even deigning to look at her adorer, he said,—

'Your Majesty will perhaps pardon me for having too indifferently remembered the verses which the nymph dictated to Loret; but, if the King has not retained any recollection of them, what could I possibly remember?'

Madame did not receive this shortcoming of the courtier very favourably.

'Ah! madame,' added Saint-Aignan, 'at present it is no longer a question what the water-nymphs have to say; and one would almost be tempted to believe that nothing of any interest now occurs in those liquid realms. It is upon the earth, madame, where important events happen. Ah! madame, upon the earth how many tales are there full of——'

'Well,' said Madame, 'and what is taking place upon the earth?'

'That question must be asked of the Dryads,' replied the Comte; 'the Dryads inhabit the forests, as your Royal Highness is aware.'

'I am aware also, that they are naturally very talkative, Monsieur de Saint-Aignan.'

'Such is the case, madame; but when they say such delightful things, it would be ungracious to accuse them of being too talkative.'

'Do they talk so delightfully, then?' inquired the Princess indifferently. 'Really, Monsieur de Saint-Aignan, you excite my curiosity; and, if I were the King, I would require you immediately to tell us what the delightful things are which these Dryads have been saying, since you alone seem to understand their language.'

'I am perfectly at His Majesty's orders, madame, in that respect,' replied the Comte quickly.

'What a fortunate fellow this Saint-Aignan is, to understand the language of the Dryads,' said Monsieur.

'I understand it perfectly, monseigneur, as I do my own language.'

'Tell us all about them, then,' said Madame.

The King felt embarrassed; for his confidant was, in all probability, about to embark in a difficult matter. He felt that it would be so, from the general attention excited by Saint-Aignan's preamble, and aroused too by Madame's peculiar manner. The most reserved of those who were present seemed ready to devour every syllable the Comte was about to pronounce. They coughed, drew closer together, looked curiously at some of the maids of honour, who, in order to support with greater propriety, or with more steadiness, the fixity of the inquisitorial looks bent upon them, adjusted their fans accordingly, and assumed the bearing of a duellist who is about to be exposed to his adversary's fire. At this epoch, the fashion of ingeniously constructed conversations,* and hazardously-dangerous recitals, so prevailed, that, where, in modern times, a whole company assembled in a drawing-room would begin to suspect some scandal, or disclosure, or tragic event, and would hurry away in dismay, Madame's guests quietly settled themselves in their places, in order not to miss a word or gesture of the comedy composed by Monsieur de Saint-Aignan for their benefit, and the termination of which, whatever the style and the plot might be, must as a matter of course be marked by the most perfect propriety. The Comte was known as a man of extreme refinement, and an admirable narrator. He began courageously, then said, amidst a profound silence, which would have been formidable for any one but himself:—'Madame, by the King's permission, I address myself, in the first place, to your Royal Highness, since you admit yourself to be the person present possessing the greatest curiosity. I have the honour, therefore, to inform your Royal Highness that the Dryad more particularly inhabits the hollows of oaks; and, as Dryads are mythological creatures of great beauty, they inhabit the most beautiful trees, in other words, the largest to be found.'

At this exordium, which recalled, under a transparent veil, the celebrated story of the royal oak, which had played so important a part in the last evening, so many hearts began to beat, both from joy and uneasiness, that, if Saint-Aignan had not had a good and sonorous voice, their throbbings might have been heard above the sound of his voice.

'There must surely be Dryads at Fontainebleau, then,' said

Madame, in a perfectly calm voice; 'for I have never, in all my life, seen finer oaks than in the royal park.' And as she spoke, she directed towards de Guiche a look of which he had no reason to complain, as he had of the one that preceded it; and which, as we have already mentioned, had reserved a certain amount of indefiniteness most painful for so loving a heart as his.

'Precisely, madame, it is of Fontainebleau that I was about to speak to your Royal Highness,' said Saint-Aignan; 'for the Dryad whose story is engaging our attention, lives in the park belonging to the château of His Majesty.' The affair was fairly embarked on; the action was begun, and it was no longer possible for auditory or narrator to draw back.

'It will be worth listening to,' said Madame; 'for the story not only appears to me to have all the interest of a national incident, but still more, seems to be a circumstance of very recent occurrence.'

'I ought to begin at the beginning,' said the Comte. 'In the first place, then, there lived at Fontainebleau, in a cottage of modest and unassuming appearance, two shepherds. The one was the shepherd Tyrcis,* the owner of extensive domains transmitted to him from his parents, by right of inheritance. Tyrcis was young and handsome, and, from his many qualifications, he might be pronounced to be the first and foremost among the shepherds in the whole country; one might even boldly say he was the king of them.' A subdued murmur of approbation encouraged the narrator, who continued:—'His strength equals his courage; no one displays greater address in hunting wild beasts, nor greater wisdom in matters where judgement is required. Whenever he mounts and exercises his horse in the beautiful plains of his inheritance, or whenever he joins with the shepherds who owe him allegiance, in different games of skill and strength, one might say that it is the god Mars darting his lance in the plains of Thrace, or, even better, that it was Apollo himself, the god of day, radiant upon earth, bearing his flaming darts in his hand.' Every one understood that this allegorical portrait of the King was not the worst exordium that the narrator could have chosen; and it, consequently, did not fail to produce its effect, either upon those who, from duty or inclination, applauded it to the very echo, or upon the King himself, to whom flattery was very agreeable when delicately conveyed, and whom, indeed, it did not always displease, even when it was a little too broad. Saint-Aignan then continued:—'It is not in games of glory only, ladies, that the shepherd Tyrcis had acquired that reputation by which he was regarded as the king of shepherds.'

'Of the shepherds of Fontainebleau,' said the King smilingly to Madame.

'Oh!' exclaimed Madame, 'Fontainebleau is selected arbitrarily by the poet; but I should say, of the shepherds of the whole world.' The King forgot his part of a passive auditor, and bowed.

'It was,' pursued Saint-Aignan, amidst a flattering murmur of applause, 'it was with ladies fair especially that the qualities of this king of the shepherds were most prominently displayed. He was a shepherd with a mind as refined as his heart was pure; he can pay a compliment with a charm of manner whose fascination it is impossible to resist; and in his attachments he is so discreet, that his beautiful and happy conquests may regard their lot as more than enviable. Never a syllable of disclosure, never a moment's forgetfulness. Whoever has seen and heard Tyrcis must love him; whoever loves and is beloved by him has indeed found happiness.' Saint-Aignan here paused; he was enjoying the pleasure of his own compliments; and the portrait he had drawn, however grotesquely inflated it might be, had found favour in certain ears, for whom the perfections of the shepherd did not seem to have been exaggerated. Madame begged the orator to continue. 'Tyrcis,' said the Comte, 'had a faithful companion, or rather a devoted servant, whose name was—Amyntas.'

'Ah!' said Madame archly, 'now for the portrait of Amyntas; you are such an excellent painter, Monsieur de Saint-Aignan.'

'Madame——'

'Oh! Comte, do not, I entreat you, sacrifice poor Amyntas; I should never forgive you.'

'Madame, Amyntas is of too humble a position, particularly beside Tyrcis, for his person to be honoured by a parallel. There are certain friends who resemble those followers of ancient times, who caused themselves to be buried alive at their masters' feet. Amyntas's place, too, is at the feet of Tyrcis; he cares for no other; and if, sometimes, the illustrious hero——'

'Illustrious shepherd do you mean?' said Madame, pretending to correct M. de Saint-Aignan.

'Your Royal Highness is right; I was mistaken,' returned the courtier; 'if, I say, the shepherd Tyrcis deigns occasionally to call Amyntas his friend, and to open his heart to him, it is an unparalleled favour, which the latter regards as the most unbounded felicity.'

'All that you say,' interrupted Madame, 'establishes the extreme devotion of Amyntas to Tyrcis, but does not furnish us with the portrait of Amyntas. Comte, do not flatter him, if you like; but describe him to us. I will have Amyntas's portrait.' Saint-Aignan obeyed, after having bowed profoundly towards His Majesty's sister-in-law.

'Amyntas,' he said, 'is somewhat older than Tyrcis; he is not an ill-favoured shepherd; it is even said that the muses condescended to smile upon him at his birth, even as Hebe* smiled upon youth. He is not ambitious of display, but he is ambitious of being loved; and he might not, perhaps, be found unworthy of it, if he were only sufficiently well known.'

This latter paragraph, strengthened by a very killing glance, was directed straight to Mademoiselle de Tonnay-Charente, who received them both unmoved. But the modesty and tact of the allusion had produced a good effect; Amyntas reaped the benefit of it in the applause bestowed on him. Tyrcis's head had even given the signal for it by a consenting bow, full of good feeling.

'One evening,' continued Saint-Aignan, 'Tyrcis and Amyntas were walking together in the forest, talking of their love disappointments. Do not forget, ladies, that the story of the Dryad is now beginning, otherwise it would be easy to tell you what Tyrcis and Amyntas, the two most discreet shepherds of the whole earth, were talking about. They reached the thickest part of the forest, for the purpose of being quite alone, and of confiding their troubles more freely to each other, when suddenly the sound of voices struck upon their ears.'

'Ah, ah!' said those who surrounded the narrator. 'Nothing can be more interesting than this.'

At this point, Madame, like a vigilant general inspecting his army, glanced at Montalais and Tonnay-Charente, who could not help wincing at it as they drew themselves up.

'These harmonious voices,' resumed Saint-Aignan, 'were those of certain shepherdesses, who had been likewise desirous of enjoying the coolness of the shade, and who, knowing the isolated and almost unapproachable situation of the place, had betaken themselves there to interchange their ideas upon——'

A loud burst of laughter occasioned by this remark of Saint-Aignan, and an imperceptible smile of the King, as he looked at Tonnay-Charente, followed this sally.

'The Dryad affirms positively,' continued Saint-Aignan, 'that the shepherdesses were three in number, and that all three were young and beautiful.'

'What were their names?' said Madame quietly.

'Their names!' said Saint-Aignan, who hesitated from the fear of committing an indiscretion.

'Of course; you called your shepherds Tyrcis and Amyntas, give your shepherdesses names in a similar manner.'

'Oh! Madame, I am not an inventor; I relate simply what took place as the Dryad related it to me.'

'What did your Dryad, then, call these shepherdesses? You have a very treacherous memory, I fear. This Dryad must have fallen out with the goddess Mnemosyne.'*

'These shepherdesses, Madame. Pray remember that it is a crime to betray a woman's name.'

'From which a woman absolves you, Comte, on condition that you will reveal the names of the shepherdesses.'

'There names were Phillis, Amaryllis, and Galatea.'

'Very well: they have not lost by the delay,' said Madame, 'and now we have three charming names. But now for their portraits.'

Saint-Aignan again made a slight movement.

'Nay, Comte, let us proceed in due order,' returned Madame. 'Ought we not, sire, to have the portraits of the shepherdesses?'

The King, who expected this determined perseverance, and who began to feel some uneasiness, did not think it safe to provoke so dangerous an interrogator. He thought, too, that Saint-Aignan, in drawing the portraits, would find a means of insinuating some flattering allusions which would be agreeable to the ears of one whom His Majesty was interested in pleasing. It was with this hope and with this fear that Louis authorised

Saint-Aignan to sketch the portraits of the shepherdesses, Phillis, Amaryllis, and Galatea.

'Very well, then, so be it,' said Saint-Aignan, like a man who has made up his mind, and he began.

XXXIX

CONCLUSION OF THE STORY OF A NAIAD AND OF A DRYAD

'PHILLIS,'* said Saint-Aignan, with a glance of defiance at Montalais, just as a fencing-master would give who invites an antagonist worthy of him to place himself on his guard, 'Phillis is neither fair nor dark, neither tall nor short, neither too grave nor too gay; though but a shepherdess, she is as witty as a princess, and as coquettish as the most finished coquette that ever lived. Nothing can equal her excellent vision. Her heart yearns for everything her gaze embraces. She is like a bird, which, always warbling, at one moment skims along the ground, at the next rises fluttering in pursuit of a butterfly, then rests itself upon the topmost branch of a tree, where it defies the bird-catchers either to come and seize it or to entrap it in their nets.' The portrait bore such a strong resemblance to Montalais, that all eyes were directed towards her; she, however, with her head raised, and with a steady unmoved look, listened to Saint-Aignan, as if he were speaking of some one who was a complete stranger to her.

'Is that all, Monsieur de Saint-Aignan?' inquired the Princess.

'Oh! your Royal Highness, the portrait is a mere sketch, and many more additions could be made, but I fear wearying your Royal Highness's patience, or offending the modesty of the shepherdess, and I shall therefore pass on to her companion, Amaryllis.'

'Very well,' said Madame, 'pass on to Amaryllis, Monsieur de Saint-Aignan, we are all attention.'

'Amaryllis is the eldest of the three, and yet,' Saint-Aignan hastened to add, 'this advanced age does not reach twenty years.'

Mademoiselle de Tonnay-Charente, who had slightly knitted her brows at the commencement of the description, unbent them with a smile.

'She is tall, with an immense quantity of hair, which she fastens in the manner of the Grecian statues; her walk is full of majesty, her attitude haughty; she has the air, therefore, rather of a goddess than of a mere mortal, and, among the goddesses, she most resembles Diana the huntress; with this sole difference, however, that the cruel shepherdess, having stolen the quiver of young love, while poor Cupid was sleeping in a thicket of roses, instead of directing her arrows against the inhabitants of the forest, discharges them most pitilessly against all the poor shepherds who pass within reach of her bow and of her eyes.'

'Oh! what a wicked shepherdess!' said Madame. 'She may some day wound herself with one of those arrows she discharges, as you say, so mercilessly on all sides.'

'It is the hope of all the shepherds in general,' said Saint-Aignan.

'And that of the shepherd Amyntas in particular, I suppose?' said Madame.

'The shepherd Amyntas is so timid,' said Saint-Aignan, with the most modest air he could assume, 'that if he cherishes such a hope as that, no one has ever known anything about it, for he conceals it in the very depths of his heart.' A flattering murmur of applause greeted the narrator's profession of faith on the part of the shepherd.

'And Galatea?' inquired Madame. 'I am impatient to see a hand so skilful as yours continue the portrait where Virgil left it,* and finish it before our eyes.'

'Madame,' said Saint-Aignan, 'I am indeed but a very poor poet beside the great Virgil. Still, encouraged by your desire, I will do my best.'

Saint-Aignan extended his foot and his hand, and thus began:—'White as milk, she casts upon the breeze the perfume of her fair hair tinged with golden hues, as are the ears of corn. One is tempted to inquire if she is not the beautiful Europa,* who inspired Jupiter with a tender passion as she played with her companions in the flower-bespangled meadows. From her beautiful eyes, blue as the azure heavens in the brightest summer day, emanates a tender light, which reverie nurtures and which love dispenses. When she frowns, or bends her looks towards the ground, the sun is veiled in token of mourning.

When she smiles, on the contrary, nature resumes her joyousness, and the birds, which had for a moment been silenced, recommence their songs amid the leafy covert of the trees. Galatea,' said Saint-Aignan, in conclusion, 'is worthy of the admiration of the whole world; and if she should ever bestow her heart upon another, happy will that man be to whom she consecrates her first affections.'

Madame, who had attentively listened to the portrait Saint-Aignan had drawn, as, indeed, had all the others too, contented herself by marking her approbation of the most poetic passages by occasional inclinations of her head; but it was impossible to say if these marks of assent had been accorded to the ability of the narrator or to the resemblance of the portrait. The consequence therefore was, that as Madame did not openly exhibit any approbation, no one felt authorised to applaud, not even Monsieur, who secretly thought that Saint-Aignan dwelt too much upon the portraits of the shepherdesses, and had passed rather quickly over the portraits of the shepherds. The whole assembly seemed suddenly chilled. Saint-Aignan, who had exhausted his rhetorical skill and his artist's brush in sketching the portrait of Galatea, and who, after the favour with which his other descriptions had been received, already imagined he could hear the loud applause for this last one, was himself more disappointed than the King and the rest of the company. A moment's silence followed, which was at last broken by Madame.

'Well, sire,' she inquired, 'what is your Majesty's opinion of these three portraits?'

The King, who wished to relieve Saint-Aignan's embarrassment without compromising himself, replied, 'Why, Amaryllis, in my opinion, is beautiful.'

'For my part,' said Monsieur, 'I prefer Phillis; she is a capital girl, or rather a good-sort-of-fellow of a nymph.'

A general laugh followed, and this time the looks were so direct, that Montalais felt herself blushing almost scarlet.

'Well,' resumed Madame, 'what were those shepherdesses saying to each other?'

Saint-Aignan, however, whose vanity had been wounded, did not feel himself in a position to sustain an attack of new and refreshed troops, and merely said, 'Madame, the shepherdesses were confiding to one another their little preferences.'

'Nay, nay! Monsieur de Saint-Aignan, you are a perfect stream of pastoral poesy,' said Madame, with an amiable smile, which somewhat comforted the narrator.

'They confessed that love is a great peril, but that the absence of love is the heart's sentence of death.'

'What was the conclusion they came to?' inquired Madame.

'They came to the conclusion that love was necessary.'

'Very good! Did they lay down any conditions?'

'That of choice, simply,' said Saint-Aignan. 'I ought even to add, remember it is the Dryad who is speaking, that one of the shepherdesses, Amaryllis, I believe, was completely opposed to the necessity of loving, and yet she did not positively deny that she had allowed the image of a certain shepherd to take refuge in her heart.'

'Was it Amyntas or Tyrcis?'

'Amyntas, Madame,' said Saint-Aignan modestly. 'But Galatea, the gentle and soft-eyed Galatea, immediately replied that neither Amyntas, nor Alphesibœus, nor Tityrus, nor indeed any of the handsomest shepherds of the country, were to be compared to Tyrcis; that Tyrcis was as superior to all other men as the oak to all other trees, as the lily in its majesty to all other flowers. She drew even such a portrait of Tyrcis, that Tyrcis himself, who was listening, must have felt truly flattered at it, notwithstanding his rank and position. Thus Tyrcis and Amyntas had been distinguished by Phillis and Galatea; and thus had the secrets of two hearts been revealed beneath the shades of evening, and amid the recesses of the woods. Such, Madame, is what the Dryad related to me; she who knows all that takes place in the hollows of oaks and in grassy dells; she who knows the loves of the birds, and all they wish to convey by their songs; she who understands, in fact, the language of the wind among the branches, the humming of the insects with their golden and emerald wings in the corolla of the wild flowers; it was she who related the particulars to me, and I have repeated them.'

'And now you have finished, Monsieur de Saint-Aignan, have you not?' said Madame, with a smile which made the King tremble.

'Quite finished,' replied Saint-Aignan, 'and only but too happy if I have been able to amuse your Royal Highness for a few moments.'

'Moments which have been too brief,' replied the Princess, 'for you have related most admirably all you know; but, my dear Monsieur de Saint-Aignan, you have been unfortunate enough to obtain your information from one Dryad only, I believe?'

'Yes, Madame, only from one, I confess.'

'The fact was, that you passed by a little Naiad, who pretended to know nothing at all, and yet knew a great deal more than your Dryad, my dear Comte.'

'A Naiad!' repeated several voices, who began to suspect that the story had a continuation.

'Of course; close beside the oak you are speaking of, which, if I am not mistaken, is called the royal oak—is it not so, Monsieur de Saint-Aignan?' Saint-Aignan and the King exchanged glances.

'Yes, Madame,' the former replied.

'Well, close beside the oak there is a pretty little spring which runs murmuringly on over the pebbles, amidst the forget-me-nots and daisies.'

'I believe you are correct,' said the King, with some uneasiness, and listening with some anxiety to his sister-in-law's narrative.

'Oh! there is one, I can assure you,' said Madame; 'and the proof of it is, that the Naiad who resides in that little stream, stopped me as I was about to cross.'

'Bah!' said Saint-Aignan.

'Yes, indeed,' continued the Princess, 'and she did so in order to communicate to me many particulars which Monsieur de Saint-Aignan omitted in his recital.'

'Pray relate them yourself,' said Monsieur, 'you can relate stories in such a charming manner.' The Princess bowed at the conjugal compliment paid her.

'I do not possess the poetical powers of the Comte, nor his ability to bring out all the details.'

'You will not be listened to with less interest on that account,' said the King, who already perceived that something hostile was intended in his sister-in-law's story.

'I speak too,' continued Madame, 'in the name of that poor little Naiad, who is indeed the most charming creature I ever met. Moreover, she laughed so heartily while she was telling me her story, that, in pursuance of that medical axiom that laughter is contagious, I ask permission to laugh a little myself when I recollect her words.'

The King and Saint-Aignan, who noticed spreading over many of the faces present a commencement of the laughter which Madame announced, finished by looking at each other, as if asking themselves whether there was not some little conspiracy concealed beneath her words. But Madame was determined to turn the knife in the wound over and over again; she therefore resumed with an air of the most perfect innocence, in other words, with the most dangerous of all her airs:—'Well, then, I passed that way,' she said, 'and as I found beneath my steps many fresh flowers newly born, no doubt Phillis, Amaryllis, Galatea, and all your shepherdesses had passed the same way before me.'

The King bit his lips, for the recital was becoming more and more threatening. 'My little Naiad,' continued Madame, 'was murmuring her little song in the bed of her rivulet; as I perceived that she accosted me by touching the bottom of my dress, I did not think of receiving her advances ungraciously, and more particularly so, since, after all, a divinity, even though she be of a second grade, is always of greater importance than a mortal, though a princess. I, thereupon, accosted the Naiad. Bursting into laughter, this is what she said to me:—

'"Fancy, Princess——" You understand, sire, it is the Naiad who is speaking.'

The King bowed assentingly, and Madame continued:—

'"Fancy, Princess, the banks of my little stream have just witnessed a most amusing scene. Two shepherds, full of curiosity, even indiscreetly so, have allowed themselves to be mystified in a most amusing manner by three nymphs, or three shepherdesses." I beg your pardon, but I do not now remember if it were a nymph or a shepherdess, she said; but it does not much matter, so we will continue.'

The King, at this opening, coloured visibly, and Saint-Aignan, completely losing countenance, began to open his eyes in the greatest possible anxiety.

'"The two shepherds," pursued my nymph, still laughing,

"followed in the wake of the three young ladies—no, I mean of the three nymphs; forgive me, I ought to say, of the three shepherdesses." It is not always wise to do that, for it may be awkward for those who are followed. I appeal to all the ladies present, and not one of them, I am sure, will contradict me.'

The King, who was much disturbed by what he suspected was about to follow, signified his assent by a gesture.

'"But," continued the Naiad, "the shepherdesses had noticed Tyrcis and Amyntas gliding into the wood, and, by the light of the moon, they had recognised them through the grove of trees." Ah, you laugh!' interrupted Madame; 'wait, wait, you are not yet at the end.'

The King turned pale; Saint-Aignan wiped his forehead, which was bedewed with perspiration. Among the groups of ladies present could be heard smothered laughter and stealthy whispers.

'"The shepherdesses, I was saying, noticing how indiscreet the two shepherds were, proceeded to sit down at the foot of the royal oak; and, when they perceived that their indiscreet listeners were sufficiently near, so that not a syllable of what they might say could be lost, they addressed towards them very innocently, in the most innocent manner in the world indeed, a passionate declaration, which from the vanity natural to all men, and even to the most sentimental of shepherds, seemed to the two listeners as sweet as honey."'

The King, at these words, which the assembly was unable to hear without laughing, could not restrain a flash of anger darting from his eyes. As for Saint-Aignan, he let his head fall upon his breast, and concealed, under a bitter laugh, the extreme annoyance he felt.

'Oh,' said the King, drawing himself up to his full height, 'upon my word, that is a most amusing jest certainly; but, really and truly, are you sure you quite understood the language of the Naiads?'

'The Comte, sire, pretends to have perfectly understood that of the Dryads,' retorted Madame eagerly.

'No doubt,' said the King; 'but you know the Comte has the weakness to aspire to become a member of the Academy,* so that, with this object in view, he has learnt all sorts of things of which very happily you are ignorant; and it might possibly happen that the language of the Nymph of the Waters might be among the number of things which you have not studied.'

'Of course, sire,' replied Madame, 'for facts of that nature one does not altogether rely upon oneself alone; a woman's ear is not infallible, so says Saint Augustine; and I, therefore, wished to satisfy myself by other opinions besides my own, and as my Naiad, who, in her character of a goddess, is polyglot,—is not that the expression, M. de Saint-Aignan?'

'Yes,' said the latter, quite out of countenance.

'Well,' continued the Princess, 'as my Naiad, who, in her character of a goddess, had, at first, spoken to me in English, I feared, as you suggest, that I might have misunderstood her, and I requested Mademoiselle de Montalais, de Tonnay-Charente, and de la Vallière, to come to me, begging my Naiad to repeat to me in the French language the recital she had already communicated to me in English.'

'And did she do so?' inquired the King.

'Oh, she is the most polite divinity that exists! Yes, sire, she did so; so that no doubt whatever remains on the subject. Is it not so, young ladies?' said the Princess, turning towards the left of her army; 'did not the Naiad say precisely what I have related, and have I, in any one particular, exceeded the truth, Phillis? I beg your pardon, I mean Mademoiselle Aure de Montalais.'

'Precisely as you have stated, Madame,' articulated Mademoiselle de Montalais, very distinctly.

'Is it true, Mademoiselle de Tonnay-Charente?'

'The perfect truth,' replied Athenaïs, in a voice quite as firm, but yet not so distinct.

'And you, La Vallière?' asked Madame.

The poor girl felt the King's ardent look fixed upon her,— she dared not deny it, she dared not tell a falsehood, and bowed her head simply in token of assent. Her head, however, was not raised again, half-chilled as she was by a coldness more bitter than that of death. This triple testimony overwhelmed the King. As for Saint-Aignan, he did not even attempt to dissemble his despair, and, hardly knowing what he said, he stammered out, 'An excellent jest! admirably played!'

'A just punishment for curiosity,' said the King, in a hoarse voice. 'Oh! who would think, after the chastisement that Tyrcis and Amyntas had suffered, of endeavouring to surprise what is passing in the heart of shepherdesses? Assuredly I shall not for one; and you, gentlemen?'

'Nor I! nor I!' repeated, in a chorus, the group of courtiers.

Madame was filled with triumph at the King's annoyance; and was full of delight, thinking that her story had been, or was to be, the termination of the whole matter. As for Monsieur, who had laughed at the two stories without comprehending anything about them, he turned towards de Guiche, and said to him, 'Well, Comte, you say nothing; can you not find something to say? Do you pity M. Tyrcis and M. Amyntas, for instance?'

'I pity them with all my soul,' replied de Guiche; 'for in very truth, love is so sweet a fancy, that to lose it, fancy though it may be, is to lose more than life itself. If, therefore, these two shepherds thought themselves beloved,—if they were happy in that idea, and if, instead of that happiness, they meet with not only that empty void which resembles death, but jeers and jests at that love, which is worse than a thousand deaths,—in that case, I say that Tyrcis and Amyntas are the two most unhappy men I know.'

'And you are right, too, Monsieur de Guiche,' said the King; 'for, in fact, the death we speak of is a very hard return for a little curiosity.'

'That is as much as to say, then, that the story of my Naiad has displeased the King?' asked Madame innocently.

'Nay, Madame, undeceive yourself,' said Louis, taking the Princess by the hand; 'your Naiad, on the contrary, has pleased me, and the more so, because she has been more truthful, and because her tale, I ought to add, is confirmed by the testimony of unimpeachable witnesses.'

These words fell upon La Vallière accompanied by a look that no one, from Socrates to Montaigne,* could have exactly defined. The look and the King's remark succeeded in over-powering the unhappy girl, who, with her head upon Montalais's shoulder, seemed to have fainted away. The King rose, without remarking this circumstance, of which no one, moreover, took any notice, and, contrary to his usual custom, for generally he remained late in Madame's apartments, he took his leave and retired to his own side of the palace. Saint-Aignan followed him leaving the rooms in as great a state of despair as he had entered them in a state of delight. Mademoiselle de Tonnay-Charente, less sensitive than La Vallière, was not much frightened, and did not faint. However, the last look of Saint-Aignan had hardly been so majestic as the last look of the King.

XL

ROYAL PSYCHOLOGY

THE King returned to his apartments with hurried steps. The reason he walked as fast as he did was probably to avoid tottering in his gait. He seemed to leave behind him as he went along a trace of a mysterious sorrow. This gaiety of manner, which every one had remarked in him on his arrival, and which they had been delighted to perceive, had not perhaps been understood in its true sense; but this stormy departure, his disordered countenance, all knew, or at least thought they could tell the reason of. Madame's levity of manner, her somewhat bitter jests —bitter for persons of a sensitive disposition, and particularly for one of the King's character: the great resemblance which naturally existed between the King and an ordinary mortal, were among the reasons assigned for the precipitate and unexpected departure of His Majesty. Madame, keen-sighted enough in other respects, did not, however, at first see anything extraordinary in it. It was quite sufficient for her to have inflicted some slight wound upon the vanity or self-esteem of one who, so soon forgetting the engagements he had contracted, seemed to have undertaken to disdain, without cause, the noblest and highest prizes. It was not an unimportant matter for Madame, in the present position of affairs, to let the King perceive the difference which existed between the bestowal of his affections on one in a high station and the running after some passing fancy, like a youth fresh from the provinces. With regard to those higher placed affections, recognising their dignity and their unlimited influence, acknowledging in some respects a certain etiquette and display—a monarch not only did not act in a manner derogatory to his high position, but found even a repose, security, mystery, and general respect therein. On the contrary, in the debasement of a common or humble attachment, he would encounter, even among his meanest subjects, carping and sarcastic remarks; he would forfeit his character of infallibility and inviolability. Having descended to the region of petty human miseries, he would be subjected to its paltry contentions. In one word, to convert the royal divinity into a mere mortal by striking at his heart, or rather even at his face, like the meanest of his subjects, was to inflict a terrible blow upon the pride of that generous nature; Louis was more easily captivated by vanity than by affection. Madame had wisely calculated her vengeance, and it has been seen also in what manner she carried it out. Let it not be supposed, however, that Madame possessed such terrible passions* as the heroines of the Middle Ages possessed, or that she regarded things in a sombre point of view; on the contrary, Madame, young, amiable, of cultivated intellect, coquettish, loving in her nature, but rather from fancy, or imagination, or ambition, than from her heart—Madame, we say, on the contrary, inaugurated that epoch of light and fleeting amusements which distinguished the hundred and twenty years which intervened between the half of the seventeenth century and the three-fourths of the eighteenth.* Madame saw, therefore, or rather fancied she saw, things under their true aspect; she knew that the King, her august brother-in-law, had been the first to ridicule the humble La Vallière, and that, in accordance with his usual custom, it was hardly probable he would ever love the person who had excited his laughter, even had it been only for a moment. Moreover, was not her vanity present, that evil influence which plays so important a part in that comedy of dramatic incidents called the life of a woman; did not her vanity tell her, aloud, in a subdued voice, in a whisper, in every variety of tone, that she could not, in reality, she a Princess, young, beautiful, and rich, be compared to the poor La Vallière, as youthful as herself it is true, but far less pretty certainly, and utterly poor? And surprise need not be excited with respect to Madame; for it is known that the greatest characters are those who flatter themselves the most in the comparison they draw between themselves and others, between others and themselves. It may perhaps be asked what was Madame's motive for an attack which had been so skilfully

combined? Why was there such a display of forces, if it were not
seriously the intention to dislodge the King from a heart that
had never been occupied before, in which he seemed disposed to
take refuge? Was there any necessity, then, for Madame to attach so great an importance to La Vallière if she did not fear her.
Yet, Madame did not fear La Vallière, in that point of view in
which an historian, who knows everything, sees into the future,
or rather the past; Madame was neither a prophetess nor a
sibyl;* nor could she, any more than another, read what was
written in that terrible and fatal book of the future, which records
in its most secret pages the most serious events. No, Madame
desired simply to punish the King for having availed himself of
secret means utterly feminine in their nature; she wished to
prove to him, that if he made use of offensive weapons of that
nature, she, a woman of ready wit and high descent, would
assuredly discover in the arsenal of her imagination defensive
weapons proof even against the thrusts of a monarch. Moreover,
she wished him to learn, that, in a warfare of that description,
kings are held of no account, or, at all events, that kings who
fight on their own behalf, like ordinary individuals, may witness
the fall of their crown in the first encounter; and that, in fact, if
he had expected to be adored by all the ladies of the court from
the very first, from a confident reliance on his mere appearance,
it was a pretension which was most preposterous and insulting
even for certain persons who filled a higher position than others,
and that a lesson being taught in season to this royal personage,
who assumed too high and haughty a carriage, would be rendering him a great service. Such, indeed, were Madame's reflections with respect to the King. The event itself was not thought
of. And in this manner, it will have been seen that she had
exercised her influence over the minds of her maids of honour,
and, with all its accompanying details, had arranged the comedy
which had just been acted. The King was completely bewildered
by it; for the first time since he had escaped from the trammels
of M. de Mazarin he found himself treated as a man.* A similar
severity from any of his subjects would have been at once resisted by him. But to attack women, to be attacked by them, to
have been imposed upon by mere girls from the country, who
had come from Blois expressly for that purpose; it was the depth

of dishonour for a young sovereign full of that pride which his personal advantages and his royal power inspired him with. There was nothing he could do, neither reproaches, nor exile, nor even could he show the annoyance he felt. To show any vexation would have been to admit that he had been touched, like Hamlet, by a sword from which the button had been removed*—the sword of ridicule. To show vexation towards women, what humiliation! especially when these women in question have laughter on their side as a means of vengeance. Oh! if, instead of leaving all the responsibility of the affair to these women, one of the courtiers had had anything to do with the intrigue, how delightedly would Louis have seized the opportunity of turning the Bastille to a profitable account. But there, again, the King's anger paused, checked by reason. To be the master of armies, of prisons, of an almost divine authority, and to exert that almost almighty power in the service of a petty grudge, would be unworthy not only of a monarch, but even of a man. It was necessary, therefore, simply to swallow the affront in silence, and to wear his usual gentleness and graciousness of expression. It was essential to treat Madame as a friend. As a friend! . . . Well, and why not? Either Madame had been the instigator of the affair, or the affair itself had found her passive. If she had been the instigator of it, it certainly was a bold measure on her part, but at all events, it was but natural in her.

If, on the contrary, she had remained passive in the whole affair, what grounds had the King to be angry with her on that account? Was it for her to restrain, or rather could she restrain, the chattering of a few country girls? and was it for her, by an excess of zeal which might have been misinterpreted, to check, at the risk of increasing it, the impertinence of their conduct? All these various reasonings were like so many stings to the King's pride; but when he had carefully, in his own mind, gone over all the various causes of complaint, Louis was surprised, upon due reflection—in other words, after the wound had been dressed—to find that there were other causes of suffering, secret, unendurable, and unrevealed. There was one circumstance which he dared not confess, even to himself; namely, that the acute pain from which he was suffering had its seat in his heart. The fact is, he had permitted his heart to be gratified by La

Vallière's innocent confession. He had dreamed of a pure affection—of an affection for Louis the man, and not the sovereign—of an affection free from all self-interest; and his heart, more youthful and more simple than he had imagined it to be, had bounded forward to meet that other heart which had just revealed itself to him by its aspirations. The commonest thing in the complicated history of love, is the double inoculation of love to which any two hearts are subjected; the one loves nearly always before the other, in the same way that the latter finishes nearly always by loving after the other. In this way, the electric current is established, in proportion to the intensity of the passion which is first kindled. The more Mademoiselle de la Vallière had shown her affection, the more the King's affection had increased. And it was precisely that which had surprised His Majesty. For it had been fairly demonstrated to him, that no sympathetic current had been the means of hurrying his heart away in its course, because there had been no confession of love in the case—because the confession was, in fact, an insult towards the man and towards the sovereign; and finally, because—and the word, too, burnt like a hot iron—because, in fact, it was nothing but a mystification after all. This girl, therefore, who, in strictness, could not lay claim to beauty, or birth, or great intelligence—who had been selected by Madame herself, on account of her unpretending position, had not only aroused the King's regard, but had, moreover, treated him with disdain—he, the King, a man who, like an eastern potentate, had but to bestow a glance, to indicate with his finger, to throw his handkerchief. And, since the previous evening, his mind had been so absorbed with this girl that he could think and dream of nothing but her. Since the previous evening his imagination had been occupied by clothing her image with all those charms to which she could not lay claim. In very truth, he whom such vast interests summoned, and whom so many women smiled upon invitingly, had, since the previous evening, consecrated every moment of his time, every throb of his heart, to this sole dream. It was, indeed, either too much, or not sufficient. The indignation of the King, making him forget everything, and, among others, that Saint-Aignan was present, was poured out in the most violent imprecations. True it is, that Saint-Aignan had taken refuge in a corner of the room; and from his corner regarded the tempest passing over. His own personal disappointment seemed contemptible, in comparison with the anger of the King. He compared with his own petty vanity the prodigious pride of offended majesty; and, being well read in the hearts of kings in general, and in those of powerful kings in particular, he began to ask himself if this weight of anger, as yet held in suspense, would not soon terminate by falling upon his own head, for the very reason that others were guilty, and he innocent. In point of fact, the King, all at once, did arrest his hurried pace; and, fixing a look full of anger upon Saint-Aignan, suddenly cried out, 'And you, Saint-Aignan?'

Saint-Aignan made a sign, which was intended to signify, 'Well, sire?'

'Yes; you have been as silly as myself, I think.'

'Sire,' stammered out Saint-Aignan.

'You permitted yourself to be deceived by this shameful trick.'

'Sire,' said Saint-Aignan, whose agitation was such as to make him tremble in every limb, 'let me entreat your Majesty not to exasperate yourself. Women, you know, are creatures full of imperfections, created for the misfortune of others; to expect anything good from them is to require them to do impossibilities.'

The King, who had the greatest consideration for himself, and who had begun to acquire over his emotions that command which he preserved over them all his life, perceived that he was doing an outrage to his own dignity in displaying so much animation about so trifling an object. 'No,' he said hastily; 'you are mistaken, Saint-Aignan; I am not angry; I can only wonder that we should have been turned into ridicule so cleverly and with such boldness, by these two young girls. I am particularly surprised that, although we might have informed ourselves accurately on the subject, we were silly enough to leave the matter for our own hearts to decide upon.'

'The heart, sire, is an organ which requires positively to be reduced to its physical functions, but which must be deprived of all its moral functions. For my own part, I confess, that when I saw that your Majesty's heart was so taken up by this little——'

'My heart taken up! I!—my mind might perhaps have been

so; but as for my heart, it was——' Louis again perceived that, in order to conceal one blank, he was about to disclose another. 'Besides,' he added, 'I have no fault to find with the girl. I was quite aware that she was in love with some one else.'

'The Vicomte de Bragelonne. I informed your Majesty of the circumstance.'

'You did so; but you were not the first who told me. The Comte de la Fère had solicited from me Mademoiselle de la Vallière's hand for his son. And, on his return from England, the marriage shall be celebrated, since they love each other.'

'I recognise your Majesty's generosity of disposition in that act.'

'So, Saint-Aignan, we will cease to occupy ourselves with these matters any longer,' said Louis.

'Yes, we will digest the affront, sire,' replied the courtier, with resignation.

'Besides, it will be a very easy matter to do so,' said the King, checking a sigh.

'And, by way of a beginning, I will set about the composition of an epigram upon all three of them. I will call it "The Naiad and Dryad," which will please Madame.'

'Do so, Saint-Aignan, do so,' said the King indifferently. 'You shall read me your verses; they will amuse me. Ah! it does not signify, Saint-Aignan,' added the King, like a man breathing with difficulty, 'the blow requires more than human strength to support in a dignified manner.' As the King thus spoke, assuming an air of the most angelic patience, one of the servants in attendance knocked gently at the door. Saint-Aignan drew aside, out of respect.

'Come in,' said the King. The servant partially opened the door. 'What is it?' inquired Louis.

The servant held out a letter of a triangular shape. 'For your Majesty,' he said.

'From whom?'

'I do not know. One of the officers on duty gave it me.'

The valet, in obedience to a gesture of the King, handed him the letter. The King advanced towards the candles, opened the note, read the signature, and uttered a loud cry. Saint-Aignan was sufficiently respectful not to look on; but, without looking on, he saw and heard all, and ran towards the King, who, with a gesture, dismissed the servant. 'Oh, heavens!' said the King, as he read the note.

'Is your Majesty unwell?' inquired Saint-Aignan, stretching forward his arms.

'No, no, Saint-Aignan—read!' and he handed him the note.

Saint-Aignan's eyes fell upon the signature. 'La Vallière!' he exclaimed. 'Oh, sire!'

'Read, read!'

And Saint-Aignan read,—'Forgive my importunity, sire, and forgive, also, the absence of the formalities which may be wanting in this letter. A note seems to me more speedy and more urgent than a despatch. I venture, therefore, to address this note to your Majesty. I have returned to my own room, overcome with grief and fatigue, sire; and I implore your Majesty to grant me the favour of an audience which will enable me to confess the truth to my sovereign.

'LOUISE DE LA VALLIÈRE.'

'Well?' asked the King, taking the letter from Saint-Aignan's hands, who was completely bewildered by what he had just read.

'What do you think of it?'

'I hardly know.'

'Still, what is your opinion?'

'Sire, the young lady must have heard the muttering of the thunder, and has got frightened.'

'Frightened at what?' asked Louis, with dignity.

'Why, your Majesty has a thousand reasons to be angry with the author or authors of so hazardous a joke; and, if your Majesty's memory were to be awakened in a disagreeable sense, it would be a perpetual menace hanging over the head of this imprudent girl.'

'Saint-Aignan, I do not think as you do.'

'Your Majesty doubtless sees more clearly than myself.'

'Well! I see affliction and restraint in these lines, and more particularly since I recollect some of the details of the scene which took place this evening in Madame's apartments——'
The King suddenly stopped, leaving his meaning unexpressed.

'In fact,' resumed Saint-Aignan, 'your Majesty will grant an audience; nothing is clearer than that in the whole affair.'

'I will do better still, Saint-Aignan. Put on your cloak.'

'But, sire——'

'You know the room where Madame's maids of honour are lodged?'

'Certainly.'

'You know some means of obtaining an entrance there.'

'As far as that is concerned, I do not.'

'At all events, you must be acquainted with some one there.'

'Really, your Majesty is the source of every good idea.'

'You do know some one, then. Who is it?'

'I know a certain gentleman, who is on very good terms with a certain young lady there.'

'With Mademoiselle de Tonnay-Charente, I suppose?' said the King, laughing.

'Unfortunately, no, sire; with Montalais.'

'What is his name?'

'Malicorne.'

'And you can depend on him?'

'I believe so, sire. He ought to have a key of some sort in his possession; and if he should happen to have one, as I have done him a service, why, he will return it.'

'Nothing could be better. Let us set off, then.' The King threw his own cloak over Saint-Aignan's shoulders, asked him for his, and then both went out into the vestibule.

XLI

SHOWING WHAT NEITHER THE NAIAD NOR DRYAD HAD ANTICIPATED

SAINT-AIGNAN stopped at the foot of the staircase which led to the entresol, where the maids of honour were lodged, and to the first door, where Madame's apartments were situated. Then, by means of one of the servants who was passing, he sent to apprise Malicorne, who was still with Monsieur. After having waited ten minutes, Malicorne arrived, looking full of suspicion and importance. The King drew back towards the darkest part of the vestibule. Saint-Aignan, on the contrary, advanced to meet him, but at the first words, indicating his wish, Malicorne drew back abruptly.

'Oh! oh!' he said, 'you want me to introduce you into the rooms of the maids of honour. You know very well that I cannot do anything of the kind, without being made acquainted with your object.'

'Unfortunately, my dear Monsieur Malicorne, it is quite impossible for me to give you any explanation; you must therefore confide in me as in a friend who got you out of a great difficulty yesterday, and who now begs you to draw him out of one to-day.'

'Yet I told you, monsieur, what my object was; that my object was, not to sleep out in the open air, and any man might express the same wish, whilst you, however, admit nothing.'

'Believe me, my dear Monsieur Malicorne,' Saint-Aignan persisted, 'that if I were permitted to explain myself, I would do so.'

'In that case, my dear monsieur, it is impossible for me to allow you to enter Mademoiselle de Montalais's apartment.'

'Why so?'

'You know why, better than any one else, since you caught me on the wall paying my addresses to Mademoiselle de Montalais; it would, therefore, be an excess of kindness on my part, you will admit, since I am paying my attentions to her, to open the door of her room to you.'

'But who told you it was on her account I asked you for the key?'

'For whom, then?'

'She does not lodge there alone, I suppose?'

'No, certainly; for Mademoiselle de la Vallière shares her rooms with her; but really, you have nothing more to do with Mademoiselle de la Vallière than with Mademoiselle de Montalais, and there are only two men to whom I would give this key; to M. de Bragelonne, if he begged me to give it him, and to the King, if he ordered me to do so.'

'In that case, give me the key, monsieur, I order you to do so,' said the King, advancing from the obscurity, and partially opening his cloak. 'Mademoiselle de Montalais will step down to talk with you, while we go upstairs to Mademoiselle de la Vallière, for, in fact, it is she only whom we require.'

'The King!' exclaimed Malicorne, bowing down to the very ground.

'Yes, the King,' said Louis smiling; 'the King, who is as pleased with your resistance as with your capitulation. Rise, monsieur, and render us the service we request of you.'

'I obey your Majesty,' said Malicorne, leading the way up the staircase.

'Get Mademoiselle de Montalais to come down,' said the King, 'and do not breathe a word to her of my visit.'

Malicorne bowed in sign of obedience, and proceeded up the staircase. But the King, after a hasty reflection, followed him, and that, too, with such rapidity, that, although Malicorne was already more than half-way up the staircase, the King reached the room at the same moment he did. He then observed, by the door which remained half opened behind Malicorne, La Vallière, sitting in an arm-chair with her head thrown back, and in the opposite corner Montalais, who, in her dressing-gown, was standing before a looking-glass, engaged in arranging her hair, and parleying all the while with Malicorne. The King hurriedly opened the door and entered the room. Montalais called out at the noise made by the opening of the door, and, recognising the King, made her escape. La Vallière rose from her seat, like a dead person who had been galvanised, and then fell back again in her arm-chair. The King advanced slowly towards her.

'You wished for an audience, I believe,' he said coldly; 'I am ready to hear you. Speak.'

Saint-Aignan, faithful to his character of being deaf, blind, and dumb, had stationed himself in a corner of the door, upon a stool which he fortuitously found there. Concealed by the tapestry which covered the doorway, and leaning his back against the wall, he could in this way listen without being seen; resigning himself to the post of a good watch-dog, who patiently waits and watches without ever getting in his master's way.

La Vallière, terror-stricken at the King's irritated aspect, again rose a second time, and assuming a posture full of humility and entreaty, murmured, 'Forgive me, sire.'

'What need is there for my forgiveness?' asked Louis.

'Sire, I have been guilty of a great fault; nay, more than a great fault, a great crime. Sire, I have offended your Majesty.'

'Not the slightest degree in the world,' replied Louis XIV.

'I implore you, sire, not to maintain towards me that terrible seriousness of manner which reveals your Majesty's just anger. I feel I have offended you, sire; but I wish to explain to you how it was that I have not offended you of my own accord.'

'In the first place,' said the King, 'in what way can you possibly have offended me? I cannot perceive how. Surely not on account of a young girl's harmless and very innocent jest? You turned the credulity of a young man into ridicule—it was very natural to do so; any other woman in your place would have done the same.'

'Oh! your Majesty overwhelms me by your remark. If I had been the author of the jest, it would not have been innocent.'

'Well! is that all you had to say to me in soliciting an audience?' said the King, as though about to turn away.

Thereupon, La Vallière, in an abrupt and broken voice, her eyes dried up by the fire of her tears, made a step towards the King, and said, 'Did your Majesty hear everything?'

'Everything, what?'

'Everything I said beneath the royal oak.'

'I did not miss a syllable.'

'And when your Majesty heard me, you were able to think I had abused your credulity?'

'Credulity; yes, indeed, you have selected the very word.'

'And your Majesty did not suppose that a poor girl like myself might possibly be compelled to submit to the will of others?'

'Forgive me,' returned the King; 'but I shall never be able to understand that she, who of her own free-will could express herself so unreservedly beneath the royal oak, would allow herself to be influenced to such an extent by the direction of others.'

'But the threat held out against me, sire.'

'Threat! who threatened you—who dared to threaten you?'

'They who have the right to do so, sire.'

'I do not recognise any one as possessing the right to threaten in my kingdom.'

'Forgive me, sire, but near your Majesty, even, there are persons sufficiently high in position to have, or to believe that they possess, the right of injuring a young girl, without fortune, and possessing only her reputation.'

'In that way injure her?'

'In depriving her of her reputation, by disgracefully expelling her from the court.'

'Oh! Mademoiselle de la Vallière,' said the King bitterly; 'I prefer those persons who exculpate themselves without incriminating others.'

'Sire!'

'Yes; and I confess that I greatly regret to perceive, that an easy justification, as your own might be, should have been complicated in my presence by a tissue of reproaches and imputations against others.'

'And which you do not believe?' exclaimed La Vallière. The King remained silent.

'Nay, but tell me!' repeated La Vallière vehemently.

'I regret to confess it,' repeated the King, bowing coldly.

The young girl uttered a deep groan, striking her hands together in despair. 'You do not believe me, then,' she said to the King, who still remained silent, while poor La Vallière's features became visibly changed at his continued silence. 'Therefore, you believe,' she said, 'that I settled this ridiculous, this infamous plot, in so shameless a manner, with your Majesty?'

'Nay,' said the King, 'it is neither ridiculous nor infamous, it is not even a plot; it is merely a jest, more or less amusing, and nothing more.'

'Oh!' murmured the young girl, 'the King does not, and will not, believe me, then?'

'No, indeed, I will not believe you,' said the King. 'Besides, in point of fact, what can be more natural? The King, you argue, follows me, listens to me, watches me; the King wishes perhaps to amuse himself at my expense. I will amuse myself at his, and as the King is very tender-hearted I will take his heart by storm.'

La Vallière hid her face in her hands, as she stifled her sobs. The King continued most pitilessly, he revenged himself upon the poor victim before him for all that he had himself suffered.

'Let us invent, then, this story of my loving him and preferring him to others. The King is so simple and so conceited that he will believe me; and then we can go and tell others how credulous the King is, and can enjoy a laugh at his expense.'

'Oh!' exclaimed La Vallière, 'to think that, to believe that! it is frightful.'

'And,' pursued the King, 'that is not all; if this self-conceited prince should take our jest seriously, if he should be imprudent enough to exhibit before others anything like delight at it, well, in that case, the King will be humiliated before the whole court; and what a delightful story it will be, too, for him to whom I am really attached, a part of my dowry for my husband, to have the adventure to relate of the King who was so amusingly deceived by a young girl.'

'Sire!' exclaimed La Vallière, her mind bewildered, almost wandering indeed, 'not another word, I implore you; do you not see that you are killing me?'

'A jest, nothing but a jest,' murmured the King, who, however, began to be somewhat affected.

La Vallière fell upon her knees, and that so violently that their sound could be heard upon the hard floor. 'Sire,' she said, 'I prefer shame to disloyalty.'

'What do you mean?' inquired the King, without moving a step to raise the young girl from her knees.

'Sire, when I shall have sacrificed my honour and my reason both to you, you will perhaps believe in my loyalty. The tale which was related to you in Madame's apartments, and by Madame herself, is utterly false; and that which I said beneath the great oak——'

'Well!'

'That only is the truth.'

'What!' exclaimed the King.

'Sire,' exclaimed La Vallière, hurried away by the violence of her emotions, 'were I to die of shame on the very spot where my knees are fixed, I would repeat it until my latest breath; I said that I loved you, and it is true; I do love you.'

'You!'

'I have loved you, sire, from the very day I first saw you; from the moment when at Blois, where I was pining away my exist-ence, your royal looks, full of light and life, were first bent upon me.* I love you still, sire; It is a crime of high treason, I know, that a poor girl like myself should love her sovereign and should presume to tell him so. Punish me for my audacity, despise me

for my shameless immodesty; but do not ever say, do not ever
think, that I have jested with or deceived you. I belong to a
family whose loyalty has been proved, sire; and I, too, love my
King.'

Suddenly her strength, voice, and respiration ceased, and she
fell forward, like the flower Virgil alludes to,* which the scythe
of the reaper touched as it passed over. The King, at these
words, at this vehement entreaty, no longer retained either ill
will or doubt in his mind; his whole heart seemed to expand at
the glowing breath of an affection which proclaimed itself in
such a noble and courageous language. When, therefore, he
heard the passionate confession of that young girl's affection, his
strength seemed to fail him, and he hid his face in his hands.
But when he felt La Vallière's hands clinging to his own, when
their warm pressure fired his blood, he bent forward, and passing
his arm round La Vallière's waist, he raised her from the ground
and pressed her against his heart. But she, her drooping head
fallen forward on her bosom, seemed to have ceased to live. The
King, terrified, called out for Saint-Aignan. Saint-Aignan, who
had carried his discretion so far as to remain without stirring in
his corner, pretending to wipe away a tear, ran forward at the
King's summons. He then assisted Louis to seat the young girl
upon a couch, slapped her hands, sprinkled some Hungary water*
over her face, calling out all the while 'Come, come, it is all over;
the King believes you, and forgives you. There, there now! take
care, or you will agitate His Majesty too much; His Majesty is so
sensitive, so tender-hearted. Now, really, Mademoiselle de la
Vallière, you must pay attention for the King is very pale.'

The fact was, the King was visibly losing colour. But La
Vallière did not move.

'Do pray recover,' continued Saint-Aignan, 'I beg, I implore
you; it is really time you should; think only of one thing, that if
the King should become unwell, I should be obliged to summon
his physician. What a state of things that would be! So do pray
rouse yourself; make an effort, pray do, and do it at once, too.'

It was difficult to display more persuasive eloquence than
Saint-Aignan did, but something still more powerful and of a
more energetic nature than this eloquence, aroused La Vallière.
The King, who was kneeling before her, covered the palms of

her hands with those burning kisses which are to the hands what a kiss upon the lips is to the face. La Vallière's senses returned to her; she languidly opened her eyes, and, with a dying look, murmured, 'Oh! sire, has your Majesty pardoned me, then?'

The King did not reply, for he was still too much overcome. Saint-Aignan thought it his duty again to retire, for he observed the passionate devotion which was displayed in the King's gaze. La Vallière rose.

'And now, sire, that I have justified myself, at least I trust so, in your Majesty's eyes, grant me leave to retire into a convent. I shall bless your Majesty all my life, and I shall die there thanking and loving Heaven for having granted me one day of perfect happiness.'

'No, no,' replied the King, 'on the contrary you will live here blessing Heaven, but loving Louis, who will make your existence one of perfect felicity—Louis who loves you—Louis who swears it.'

'Oh! sire, sire!'

And upon this doubt of La Vallière the King's kisses became so warm that Saint-Aignan thought it his duty to retire behind the tapestry. These kisses, however, which she had not had the strength at first to resist, began to intimidate the young girl.

'Oh! sire,' she exclaimed, 'do not make me repent my loyalty for it would show me that your Majesty despises me still.'

'Mademoiselle de la Vallière,' said the King suddenly, drawing back with an air full of respect, 'there is nothing in the world I love and honour more than yourself, and nothing in my court, I call Heaven to witness, shall be so highly regarded as you shall be henceforward. I entreat your forgiveness for my transport; it arose from an excess of affection, but I can prove to you that I shall love still more than ever by respecting you as much as you can possibly desire.' Then bending before her, and taking her by the hand, he said to her, 'Will you honour me by accepting the kiss I press upon your hand?' And the King's lips were pressed respectfully and lightly upon the young girl's trembling hand. 'Henceforth,' added Louis, rising and bending his glance upon La Vallière, 'henceforth you are under my safeguard. Do not speak to any one of the injury I have done you, forgive others that which they may have been able to do you. For the future, you shall be so far above all those, that, far from inspiring you with fear, they shall be even beneath your pity.' Then calling to Saint-Aignan, who approached with great humility, he said, 'I hope, Comte, that Mademoiselle de la Vallière will kindly confer a little of her friendship upon you, in return for that which I have vowed to her eternally.'

Saint-Aignan bent his knee before La Vallière, saying, 'How happy, indeed, would such an honour make me!'

'I shall send your companion back to you,' said the King. 'Farewell! or, rather, adieu till we meet again; do not forget me in your prayers, I entreat.'

'Oh! sire,' said La Vallière, 'be assured that you and Heaven are in my heart together.'

These words of Louise elated the King, who, full of happiness, hurried Saint-Aignan down the stairs. Madame had not anticipated this termination, and neither the Naiad nor the Dryad had said a word about it.

XLII

THE NEW GENERAL OF THE JESUITS

WHILE La Vallière and the King were mingling together, in their first confession of love, all the bitterness of the past, all the happiness of the present, and all the hopes of the future, Fouquet had retired to the apartments which had been assigned to him in the château, and was conversing with Aramis precisely upon the very subjects which the King at that moment was forgetting.

'Now tell me,' began Fouquet, after having installed his guest in an arm-chair and seated himself by his side, 'tell me, Monsieur d'Herblay, what is our position with regard to the Belle-Isle affair,* and whether you have received any news about it.'

'Everything is going on in that direction as we wish,' replied Aramis; 'the expenses have been paid, and nothing has transpired of our designs.'

'But what about the soldiers whom the King wished to send there?'

'I have received news this morning that they had arrived there two weeks ago.'*

'And how have they been treated?'

'In the best manner possible.'

'What has become of the former garrison?'

'The soldiers were landed at Sarzeau, and were sent off at once towards Quimper.'*

'And the new garrison?'

'Belong to us from this very moment.'

'Are you sure of what you say, my dear Monsieur de Vannes?'

'Quite sure, and, moreover, you will see by-and-by how matters have turned out.'

'Still you are very well aware that, of all the garrison towns, Belle-Isle is the least agreeable.'

'I know it, and have acted accordingly; no space to move about, no communications, no cheerful society, no gambling permitted; well, it is a great pity,' added Aramis, with one of those smiles so peculiar to him, 'to see how much young people at the present day seek amusement, and how much, consequently, they incline towards the man who procures and pays for such amusements for them.'

'But if they amuse themselves at Belle-Isle?'

'If they amuse themselves through the King's means they will attach themselves to the King; but if they get bored to death through the King's means, and amuse themselves through M. Fouquet, they will attach themselves to M. Fouquet.'

'And you informed my intendant, of course, so that immediately on their arrival——'

'By no means; they were left alone a whole week, to weary themselves at their ease; but, at the end of the week, they cried out, saying that the last officers amused themselves more than they did. Whereupon they were told that the old officers had been able to make a friend of M. Fouquet, and that M. Fouquet, knowing them to be friends of his, had from that moment done all he possibly could to prevent their getting wearied or bored upon his estates. Upon this they began to reflect. Immediately afterwards, however, the intendant added, that without anticipating M. Fouquet's orders, he knew his master sufficiently well to be aware that he took an interest in every gentleman in the

King's service, and that, although he did not know the new-comers, he would do as much for them as he had done for the others.'

'Excellent! and I trust that the promises were followed up; I desire, as you know, that no promise should ever be made in my name without being kept.'

'Without a moment's loss of time, our two privateers, and your own horses, were placed at the disposal of the officers; the keys of the principal mansion were handed over to them, so that they make up hunting-parties and walking-excursions with such ladies as are to be found in Belle-Isle; and such others as they are able to enlist from the neighbourhood who have no fear of sea-sickness.'

'And there is a fair sprinkling to be met with at Sarzeau and Vannes, I believe, your Eminence?'

'Yes; all along the coast,' said Aramis quietly.

'And now for the soldiers?'

'Everything is precisely the same, in a relative degree, you understand; the soldiers have plenty of wine, excellent provisions, and good pay. So that this garrison can be depended upon, and it is a better one than the last.'

'Good.'

'The result is, if Fortune favours us so that the garrisons are changed in this manner, only every two months, that at the end of every three years the whole army will in its turn have been there; and, therefore, instead of having one regiment in our favour, we shall have fifty thousand men.'

'Yes, yes; I knew perfectly well,' said Fouquet, 'that no friend could be more incomparable and invaluable than yourself, my dear Monsieur d'Herblay; but,' he added, laughing, 'all this time we are forgetting our friend, Du Vallon; what has become of him?* During the three days I have spent at Saint-Mandé, I confess I have forgotten him completely.'

'I do not forget him, however,' returned Aramis. 'Porthos is at Saint-Mandé; all his joints are kept well greased, the greatest care is being taken of him, with regard to the food he eats and to the wines he drinks; I advise him to take daily airings in the small park, which you have kept for your own use, and he makes use of it accordingly. He begins to walk again, he exercises his muscular powers by bending down young elm trees, or making the old oaks fly into splinters, as Milo of Crotona* used to do; and, as there are no lions in the park, it is not unlikely we shall find him alive. Porthos is a brave fellow.'

'Yes, but in the meantime he will get wearied to death. He will be asking questions?'

'He sees no one.'

'At all events, he is looking or hoping for something or another?'

'I have inspired him a hope which we will realise some fine morning, and he subsists on that.'

'What is it?'

'That of being presented to the King, as the engineer of Belle-Isle.'*

'Shall we not be obliged, then, to send him back to Belle-Isle?'

'Most certainly; I am even thinking of sending him back as soon as possible. Porthos is very fond of display; he is a man whose weaknesses d'Artagnan, Athos, and myself are alone acquainted with; he never commits himself in any way; he is dignity itself; to the officers there, he would seem like a Paladin* of the time of the Crusades. He would make the whole staff drunk, without getting so himself, and every one will regard him as an object of admiration and sympathy; if, therefore, it should happen, that we should have any orders requiring to be carried out, Porthos is an incarnation of the order itself, and whatever he chose to do, others would find themselves obliged to submit to.'

'Send him back, then.'

'That is what I intend to do; but in a few days only, for I must not omit to tell you one thing. I begin to suspect d'Artagnan. He is not at Fontainebleau, as you may have noticed, and d'Artagnan is never absent, or apparently idle, without some object in view. And now that my own affairs are settled, I am going to try and ascertain what the affairs are which d'Artagnan is engaged in.'

'Your own affairs are settled, you say. You are very fortunate in that case, then, and I should like to be able to say the same.'

'I hope you do not make yourself uneasy. Nothing could be better than the King's reception of you.'

'True.'

'And Colbert lets you alone.'

'Almost so.'

'In that case,' said Aramis, with that connection of ideas which marked him, 'in that case, then, we can bestow a thought upon the young girl I was speaking to you about yesterday.'

'Whom do you mean?'

'What! have you forgotten already? I mean La Vallière.'

'Ah! of course, of course.'

'Do you object, then, to try and make a conquest of her?'

'In one respect only, my heart is engaged in another direction; and I positively do not care about the girl in the least.'

'Oh! oh!' said Aramis, 'your heart is engaged you say. The deuce! we must take care of that! It is terrible to have the heart occupied, when others, beside yourself, have so much need of the head.'

'You're right. So you see, at your first summons, I left everything. But to return to this girl. What good do you see in my troubling myself about her?'

'This.—The King, it is said, has taken a fancy to her; at least, so it is supposed.'

'But you, who know everything, know very differently.'

'I know that the King has changed with great rapidity; that the day before yesterday, he was mad about Madame; that a few days ago, Monsieur complained of it even to the Queen-Mother; and that some conjugal misunderstandings and maternal scoldings were the consequence.'

'How do you know all that?'

'I do know it; at all events, since these misunderstandings and scoldings, the King has not addressed a word, has not paid the slightest attention, to Her Royal Highness.'

'Well, what next?'

'Since, then, he has been taken up with Mademoiselle de la Vallière. Now, Mademoiselle de la Vallière is one of Madame's maids of honour. You happen to know, I suppose, what is called a chaperone in matters of love. Well, then, Mademoiselle de la Vallière is Madame's chaperone. It is for you, therefore, to take advantage of this state of things. You have no occasion for me to tell you that. But, at all events, wounded vanity will render the conquest an easier one; the girl will get hold of the King, and

Madame's secret, and you can hardly tell what a man of intelligence can do with a secret.'

'But how to get at her?'

'Nay, you, of all men, to ask me such a question?' said Aramis.

'Very true. I shall not have any time to take any notice of her.'

'She is poor and unassuming, you will create a position for her, and, whether she becomes the King's master, as his mistress; or whether she only becomes his confidante, you will only have made a new proficient.'

'Very good,' said Fouquet. 'What is to be done, then, with regard to this girl?'

'Whenever you have taken a fancy to any lady, Monsieur Fouquet, what steps have you taken?'

'I have written to her, protesting my devotion to her. I have added, how happy I should be to render her any service in my power, and have signed 'Fouquet,' at the end of the letter.'

'And has any one offered any resistance?'

'One person only,' replied Fouquet. 'But four days ago, she yielded, as the others had done.'

'Will you take the trouble to write?' said Aramis, holding a pen towards him, which Fouquet took, saying,—

'I will write at your dictation. My head is so taken up in another direction, that I should not be able to write a couple of lines.'

'Very well,' said Aramis, 'write.'

And he dictated, as follows:—'I have seen, and you will not be surprised to learn, how beautiful I have found you. But, for want of the position you merit at the court, your presence there is a waste of time. The devotion of a man of honour, should ambition of any kind inspire you, might possibly serve as a means of display for your talents and beauty. I place my devotion at your feet; but, as an affection, however reserved and unpresuming it may be, might, possibly, compromise the object of its worship, it would ill become a person of your merit running the risk of being compromised, without her future being ensured. If you would deign to accept, and reply to my affection, my affection shall prove its gratitude to you in making you free and independent for ever.' Having finished writing, Fouquet looked at Aramis.

'Sign it,' said the latter.

'Is it absolutely necessary?'

'Your sign re at the foot of that letter is worth a million; you forget that.' Fouquet signed.

'Now, by whom do you intend to send the letter?' asked Aramis.

'By an excellent servant of mine.'

'Can you rely on him?'

'He is a man who has been with me all my life.'

'Very well. Besides, in this case, we are not playing for very heavy stakes.'

'How so? For if what you say be true of the accommodating disposition of this girl for the King and Madame, the King will give her all the money she can ask for.'

'The King has money, then?' asked Aramis.

'I suppose so, for he has not asked me for any more.'

'Be easy, he will ask for some, soon.'

'Nay, more than that, I had thought he would have spoken to me about the fête at Vaux,* but he never said a word about it.'

'He will be sure to do so, though.'

'You must think the King's disposition a very cruel one, Monsieur d'Herblay.'

'It is not he who is so.'

'He is young, and therefore his disposition is a kind one.'

'He is young, and either he is weak, or his passions are strong; and Monsieur Colbert holds his weaknesses and his passions in his villainous grasp.'

'In that case I am lost.'

'Why so?'

'My only influence with the King has been through the money I commanded, and now I am a ruined man.'

'Not so.'

'What do you mean by "not so"? Do you know my affairs better than myself?'

'That is not unlikely.'

'If he were to request this fête to be given?'

'You will give it, of course.'

'But where is the money to come from?'

'Have you ever been in want of any?'

'Oh! if you only knew at what a cost I procured the last supply?'

'The next shall cost you nothing.'

'But who will give it me?'

'I will.'

'What, give me six millions?'

'Ten, if necessary.'

'Upon my word, d'Herblay,' said Fouquet, 'your confidence alarms me more than the King's displeasure. Who can you possibly be after all?'

'You know me well enough, I should think.'

'Of course; but what is it you are aiming at?'

'I wish to see upon the throne of France a king devoted to Monsieur Fouquet, and I wish Monsieur Fouquet to be devoted to me.'*

'Oh!' exclaimed Fouquet, pressing his hand, 'as for belonging to you, I am yours entirely; but believe me, my dear d'Herblay, you are deceiving yourself.'

'In what respect?'

'The King will never become devoted to me.'

'I do not remember to have said that the King would be devoted to you.'

'Why, on the contrary, you have this moment said so.'

'I did not say the King; I said a king.'

'Is it not all the same?'

'No, on the contrary, it is quite different.'

'I do not understand you.'

'You will do so, shortly, then; suppose, for instance, the King in question were to be a very different person to Louis XIV.'

'Another person.'

'Yes, who is indebted for everything to you.'

'Impossible.'

'His very throne, even.'

'You are mad, d'Herblay. There is no man living besides Louis XIV who can sit on the throne of France. I see none, not one.'

'But I see one.'

'Unless it be Monsieur,' said Fouquet, looking at Aramis uneasily; 'yet Monsieur——'

'It is not Monsieur.'

'But how can it be, that a prince not of the royal line, that a prince without any right——'

'My King, or rather your King, will be everything that is necessary, be assured of that.'

'Be careful, Monsieur d'Herblay, you make my blood run cold, and my head swim.'

Aramis smiled. 'There is but little occasion for that,' he replied.

'Again, I repeat, you terrify me,' said Fouquet. Aramis smiled.

'You laugh,' said Fouquet.

'The day will come when you will laugh too; only at the present moment I must laugh alone.'

'But explain yourself.'

'When the proper day shall have arrived, I will explain all, fear nothing. Have faith in me, and doubt nothing.'

'The fact is, I cannot but doubt, because I do not see clearly, or at all even.'

'That is because of your blindness; but a day will come when you will be enlightened.'

'Oh!' said Fouquet, 'now willingly would I believe.'

'You, without belief! you, who, through my means, have ten times crossed the abyss yawning at your feet, and in which had you been alone, you would have been irretrievably swallowed up. You without belief! you, who from procureur-general attained the rank of intendant, from the rank of intendant that of first minister of the crown, and who from the rank of first minister will pass to that of mayor of the palace.* But no,' he said, with the same unaltered smile, 'no, no, you cannot see, and consequently cannot believe that.' And Aramis rose to withdraw.

'One word more,' said Fouquet, 'you have never yet spoken to me in this manner, you have never yet shown yourself so confident, I should rather say so daring.'

'Because it is necessary in order to speak confidently to have the lips unfettered.'

'And that is now your case?'

'Yes; since yesterday.'

'Oh! Monsieur d'Herblay, take care, your confidence is becoming audacity.'

'One can well be audacious when one is powerful.'

'And you are powerful?'

'I have already offered you ten millions, I offer them again to you.'

Fouquet rose much agitated and disturbed.

'Come,' he said, 'come; you spoke of overthrowing kings and replacing them by others. If, indeed, I am not really out of my senses, is or is not that what you said just now?'

'You are by no means out of your senses, for it is perfectly true I did say all that just now.'

'And why did you say so?'

'Because it is easy to speak in this manner of thrones being cast down, and kings being raised up, when one is oneself far above all kings and thrones, of this world at least.'

'Your power is infinite, then?' cried Fouquet.

'I have told you so already, and I repeat it,' replied Aramis, with glistening eyes and trembling lips.

Fouquet threw himself back in his chair, and buried his face in his hands. Aramis looked at him for a moment, as the angel of human destinies might have looked upon a simple mortal being.

'Adieu,' he said to him, 'sleep undisturbed, and send your letter to La Vallière. To-morrow we shall see each other again.'

'Yes, to-morrow,' said Fouquet, shaking his hand like a man returning to his senses. 'At the King's promenade.'

XLIII

THE STORM

THE dawn of the following day was dark and gloomy, and as every one knew that the promenade was set down in the royal programme, every one's gaze, as his eyes were opened, was directed towards the sky. Just above the tops of the trees a thick, suffocating vapour seemed to remain suspended with hardly sufficient power to rise thirty feet above the ground under the influence of the sun's rays, which could barely be seen through the veil of a heavy and thick mist. No dew had fallen in the

morning; the turf was dried up for want of moisture, the flowers
were withered. The birds sang less inspiritingly than usual amid
the boughs, which remained as motionless as death. The strange
confused and animated murmurs, which seemed born of, and to
exist by the sun, that respiration of nature which is unceasingly
heard amidst all other sounds, could not be heard now, and
never had the silence been so profound. The King had noticed
the cheerless aspect of the heavens as he approached the window
immediately after rising. But as all the necessary directions had
been given respecting the promenade, and every preparation
had been made accordingly, and as, which was far more imperious than everything else, Louis relied upon this promenade to
satisfy the cravings of his imagination, and we will even already
say, the clamorous desires of his heart—the King unhesitatingly
decided that the appearance of the heavens had nothing whatever to do with the matter; that the promenade was arranged,
and that, whatever the state of the weather might be, the promenade should take place. Besides there are certain terrestrial
sovereigns who seem to have accorded them privileged exist-
ences, and there are certain times when it might almost be
supposed that the expressed wish of an earthly monarch has its
influence over the Divine will. It was Virgil who observed of
Augustus:—*Nocte pluit tota redeunt spectacula mane.** Louis attended mass as usual, but it was evident that his attention was
somewhat distracted from the presence of the Creator by the
remembrance of the creature. His mind was occupied during the
service in reckoning more than once the number of minutes,
then of seconds, which separated him from the blissful moment
when the promenade would begin, that is to say, the moment
when Madame would set out with her maids of honour. Besides,
as a matter of course, everybody at the château was ignorant of
the interview which had taken place between La Vallière and the
King. Montalais, perhaps, with her usual chattering propensity,
might have been disposed to talk about it; but Montalais on this
occasion was held in check by Malicorne, who had placed upon
her lips the padlock of mutual interest. As for Louis XIV, his
happiness was so extreme that he had forgiven Madame, or
nearly so, her little piece of ill-nature of the previous evening. In
fact, he had occasion to congratulate himself about it rather than

to complain of it. Had it not been for her ill-natured action, he would not have received the letter from La Vallière; had it not been for the letter, he would have had no interview; and had it not been for the interview, he would have remained undecided. His heart was filled with too much happiness for any ill feeling to remain in it, at that moment at least. Instead, therefore, of knitting his brows into a frown when he perceived his sister-in-law, Louis resolved to receive her in a more friendly and gracious manner than usual. But on one condition only, that she would be ready to set out early. Such was the nature of Louis's thoughts during Mass, and which made him, during the ceremony, forget matters, which, in his character of Most Christian King and of the eldest son of the Church, ought to have occupied his attention. He returned to the château, and as the promenade was fixed for midday only, and it was at present just ten o'clock, he set to work most desperately with Colbert and Lyonne.* But even while he worked Louis went from the table to the window, inasmuch as the window looked out upon Madame's pavilion; he could see M. Fouquet in the courtyard, to whom the courtiers, since the favour shown towards him on the previous evening, paid greater attention than ever. The King instinctively, on noticing Fouquet, turned towards Colbert, who was smiling, and seemed full of benevolence and delight, a state of feeling which had arisen from the very moment one of his secretaries had entered and handed him a pocket-book, which he had put unopened into his pocket. But, as there was always something sinister at the bottom of any delight expressed by Colbert, Louis preferred, of the smiles of the two men, that of Fouquet. He beckoned to the superintendent to come up, and then turning towards Lyonne and Colbert, he said:—'Finish this matter, place it on my desk, and I will read it at my leisure.' And he left the room. At the sign the King had made to him, Fouquet had hastened up the staircase, while Aramis, who was with the superintendent, quietly retired among the group of courtiers and disappeared without having been even observed by the King. The King and Fouquet met at the top of the staircase.

'Sire,' said Fouquet, remarking the gracious manner in which Louis was about to receive him, 'your Majesty has overwhelmed me with kindness during the last few days. It is not a youthful monarch, but a being of a higher order, who reigns over France, one whom pleasure, happiness, and love acknowledge as their master.' The King coloured. The compliment, although flattering, was not the less somewhat direct. Louis conducted Fouquet to a small room which separated his study from his sleeping apartment.

'Do you know why I summoned you?' said the King, as he seated himself upon the edge of the window, so as not to lose anything that might be passing in the gardens which fronted the opposite entrance to Madame's pavilion.

'No sire,' replied Fouquet, 'but I am sure for something agreeable, if I am to judge from your Majesty's gracious smile.'

'You are mistaken, then, for I summoned you, on the contrary, to pick a quarrel with you.'

'With me, sire?'

'Yes; and that a serious one.'

'Your Majesty alarms me—and yet I wait most confident in your justice and goodness.'

'Do you know I am told, Monsieur Fouquet, that you are preparing a grand fête at Vaux?'*

Fouquet smiled, as a sick man would do at the first shiver of a fever which has left him but returns again.

'And that you have not invited me!' continued the King.

'Sire,' replied Fouquet, 'I have not even thought of the fête you speak of, and it was only yesterday evening that one of my *friends*,' Fouquet laid stress upon the word, 'was kind enough to make me think of it.'

'Yet I saw you yesterday evening, Monsieur Fouquet, and you said nothing to me about it.'

'How dared I hope that your Majesty would so greatly descend from your own exalted station as to honour my dwelling with your royal presence?'

'Excuse me, Monsieur Fouquet, you did not speak to me about your fête.'

'I did not allude to the fête to your Majesty, I repeat, in the first place, because nothing had been decided with regard to it, and, secondly, because I feared a refusal.'

'And something made you fear a refusal, Monsieur Fouquet? You see I am determined to push you hard.'

'The profound wish I had that your Majesty should accept my invitation——'

'Well, Monsieur Fouquet, nothing is easier, I perceive, than our coming to an understanding. Your wish is to invite me to your fête, my own is to be present at it; invite me, and I will go.'

'Is it possible that your Majesty will deign to accept?' murmured the surintendent.

'Why really, monsieur,' said the King, laughing; 'I think I do more than accept; I think I invite myself.'

'Your Majesty overwhelms me with honour and delight,' exclaimed Fouquet, 'but I shall be obliged to repeat what M. de Vieuville said to your ancestor Henry IV, *Domine non sum dignus*.'*

'To which I reply, Monsieur Fouquet, that if you give a fête I will go whether I am invited or not.'

'I thank your Majesty deeply,' said Fouquet, as he raised his head beneath this favour, which he was convinced would be his ruin.

'But how could your Majesty have been informed of it?'

'By public rumour, Monsieur Fouquet, which says such wonderful things of yourself and of the marvels of your house. Would you become proud, Monsieur Fouquet, if the King were to be jealous of you?'

'I should be the happiest man in the world, sire, since the very day on which your Majesty were to be jealous of Vaux I should possess something worthy of being offered to you.'

'Very well, Monsieur Fouquet, prepare your fête, and open the doors of your house as wide as possible.'

'It is for your Majesty to fix the day.'

'This day month, then.'

'Has your Majesty any further commands?'

'Nothing, Monsieur Fouquet, except from the present moment until then to have you near me as much as possible.'

'I have the honour to form one of your Majesty's party for the promenade.'

'Very good; I am now going out indeed, for there are the ladies, I see, who are going to start.'

With this remark the King, with all the eagerness, not only of a young man, but of a young man in love, withdrew from the window, in order to take his gloves and cane, which his valet held ready for him. The neighing of the horses and the rumbling of the wheels on the gravel of the courtyard could be distinctly heard. The King descended the stairs, and at the moment he made his appearance upon the flight of steps every one stopped. The King walked straight up to the young Queen. The Queen-Mother, who was still suffering more than ever from the illness* with which she was afflicted, did not wish to go out. Maria Theresa accompanied Madame in her carriage, and asked the King in what direction he wished the promenade to take place. The King, who had just seen La Vallière, still pale from the events of the previous evening, get into a carriage with three of her companions, told the Queen that he had no preference, and wherever she would wish to go there would he be with her. The Queen then desired that the outriders should proceed in the direction of Apremont.* The outriders set off accordingly before the others. The King rode on horseback and for a few minutes accompanied the carriage of the Queen and Madame, with his hand resting on the door. The weather had cleared up a little; but a kind of veil of dust like a thick gauze was still spread over the surface of the heavens, and the sun made every glittering atom of dust glisten again within the circuit of its rays. The heat was stifling; but, as the King did not seem to pay any attention to the appearance of the heavens, no one made himself uneasy about it, and the promenade, in obedience to the orders which had been given by the Queen, took its course in the direction of Apremont. The courtiers who followed were merry and full of spirits; it was very evident that everyone tried to forget, and to make others forget, the bitter discussions of the previous evening. Madame, particularly, was delightful. In fact, seeing the King at the door of her carriage, as she did not suppose he would be there for the Queen's sake, she hoped that her prince had returned to her. Hardly, however, had they proceeded a quarter of a mile on the road when the King, with a gracious smile, saluted them and drew up his horse, leaving the Queen's carriage to pass on, then that of the principal ladies of honour, and then all the others in succession, who, seeing the King stop, wished in their turn to stop too; but the King made a sign to them to continue their progress.* When La Vallière's carriage passed the King approached it, saluted the ladies who were inside, and was preparing to accompany the carriage containing the maids of honour, in the same way he had followed that in which Madame was, when suddenly the whole file of carriages stopped. It was probably that Madame, uneasy at the King having left her, had just given directions for the performance of this manœuvre, the direction in which the promenade was to take place having been left to her. The King having sent to inquire what her object was in stopping the carriages, was informed in reply that she wished to walk. She very likely hoped that the King, who was following the carriages of the maids of honour on horseback, would not venture to follow the maids of honour themselves on foot. They had arrived in the middle of the forest. The promenade, in fact, was not ill-timed, especially for those who were dreamers or lovers. From the little open space where the halt had taken place three beautiful long walks, shady and undulating, stretched out before them. All alighted from their carriages as soon as they observed that the Queen was doing so. Maria Theresa took the arm of one of her ladies of honour, and, with a side-glance towards the King, who did not perceive that he was in the slightest degree the object of the Queen's attention, entered the forest by the first path before her. Two of the outriders preceded Her Majesty with long poles, which they used for the purpose of putting the branches of the trees aside, or removing the bushes which might impede her progress. As soon as Madame alighted she found the Comte de Guiche at her side, who bowed and placed himself at her disposal. Monsieur, delighted with his bath of the two previous days, had announced his preference for the river, and, having given de Guiche leave of absence, remained at the château with the Chevalier de Lorraine and Manicamp. He was not in the slightest degree jealous. He had been looked for to no purpose among those present; but as Monsieur was a man who thought a great deal of himself, and usually added very little to the general pleasure, his absence had rather been a subject of satisfaction than of regret. Every one had followed the example which the Queen and Madame had set, doing just as they pleased, according as chance or fancy influenced them. The King, we have already observed, remained near La Vallière, and, throwing himself off his horse at the moment the door of her carriage was opened, he offered her his hand to alight. Montalais and Tonnay-Charente immediately drew back and kept at a distance; the former from calculated, the latter from prudent motives. There was this difference, however, between the two, that the one had withdrawn from a wish to please the King, the other for a very opposite reason. During the last half-hour the weather also had undergone a change; the veil which had been spread over the sky, as if driven by a blast of heated air, had become massed together in the western part of the heavens; and afterwards, as if driven back by a current of air from the opposite direction, was now advancing slowly and heavily towards them. The approach of the storm could be felt, but as the King did not perceive it no one thought it was right to do so. The promenade was therefore continued; some of the company, with minds ill at ease on the subject, raised their eyes from time to time towards the sky; others, even more timid still, walked about without wandering too far from the carriages, where they relied upon taking shelter in case the storm burst. The greater number of these, however, observing that the King fearlessly entered the wood with La Vallière, followed His Majesty. The King noticing this, took La Vallière's hand, and led her away by a side-path, where no one this time ventured to follow him.

XLIV

THE SHOWER OF RAIN

AT this moment, and in the same direction, too, that the King and La Vallière were proceeding, except that they were walking in the wood itself instead of following the path—two men were walking together, utterly indifferent to the appearance of the heavens. Their heads were bent down in the manner of people occupied with matters of great moment. They had not observed either de Guiche or Madame, or the King or La Vallière. Suddenly something passed through the air like a stream of fire followed by a loud but distant rumbling noise.

'Ah!' said one of them, raising his head, 'here is the storm. Let us reach our carriages, my dear d'Herblay.'

Aramis looked inquiringly at the heavens. 'There is no occasion to hurry yet,' he said; and then resuming the conversation where it had doubtlessly been interrupted he said, 'You were observing that the letter we wrote last evening must by this time have reached its destination?'

'I was saying that she certainly has it.'

'Whom did you send it by?'

'By my own servant, as I have already told you.'

'Did he bring back an answer?'

'I have not seen him since; the young girl was probably in attendance on Madame, or was in her own room dressing, and he may have had to wait. Our time for leaving arrived, and we set off of course: I cannot, therefore, know what is going on yonder.'

'Did you see the King before leaving? How did he seem?'

'Nothing could be better or worse; according as he be sincere or hypocritical.'

'And the fête?'

'Will take place in a month.'*

'He invited himself, you say?'

'With a pertinacity in which I detected Colbert's influence. But has not last night removed your illusions?'

'What illusions?'

'With respect to the assistance you may be able to give me in this circumstance.'

'No; I have passed the night writing, and all my orders are given.'

'Do not conceal it from yourself, d'Herblay, but the fête will cost some millions.'

'I will give six; do you on your side get two or three.'

'You are a wonderful man, my dear d'Herblay. But,' inquired Fouquet, with some remaining uneasiness, 'how is it that while now you are squandering millions in this manner, a few days ago you did not pay the fifty thousand francs to Baisemeaux out of your own pocket?'

'Because a few days ago I was as poor as Job.'

'And to-day?'

'To-day I am wealthier than the King himself.'

'Very well,' said Fouquet; 'I understand men pretty well; I

know you are incapable of going back on your word; I do not wish to wrest your secret from you, and so let us talk no more about it.'

At this moment a dull, heavy rumbling was heard, which suddenly burst forth in a violent clap of thunder.

'Oh, oh!' said Fouquet, 'I was quite right in what I said.'

'Come,' said Aramis, 'let us rejoin the carriages.'

'We shall not have time,' said Fouquet, 'for here comes the rain.'

In fact, as he spoke, and as if the heavens were opened, a shower of large drops of rain was suddenly heard falling on the trees about them.

'We shall have time,' said Aramis, 'to reach the carriages before the foliage becomes saturated.'

'It will be better,' said Fouquet, 'to take shelter somewhere—in a grotto, for instance.'

'Yes, but where are we to find a grotto?' inquired Aramis.

'I know one,' said Fouquet smiling, 'not ten paces from here.' Then looking round about him he added: 'Yes, we are quite right.'

'You are very fortunate to have so good a memory,' said Aramis, smiling in his turn; 'but are you not afraid that your coachman, finding we do not return, will suppose we have taken another road back, and that he will not follow the carriages belonging to the court?'

'Oh, there is no fear of that,' said Fouquet; 'whenever I place my coachman and my carriage in any particular spot, nothing but an express order from the King could stir them; and more than that, too, it seems that we are not the only ones who have come so far, for I hear footsteps and the sound of voices.'

As he spoke, Fouquet turned round, opened with his cane a mass of foliage which hid the path from his view. Aramis's glance as well as his own plunged at the same moment through the opening he had made.

'A woman,' said Aramis.

'And a man,' said Fouquet.

'It is La Vallière and the King,' they both exclaimed together.

'Oh, oh!' said Aramis, 'is His Majesty aware of your cavern as well? I should not be astonished if he were, for he seems to be on very good terms with the nymphs of Fontainebleau.'

'It matters little,' said Fouquet; 'let us get there; if he is not aware of it we shall see what he will do; if he should know it, as it has two entrances, whilst he enters by one, we can leave by the other.'

'Is it far?' asked Aramis, 'for the rain is beginning to penetrate.'

'We are there now,' said Fouquet, as he put aside a few branches, and an excavation of the rock could be observed, which had been entirely concealed by broom, ivy, and a thick covert of small shrubs.

Fouquet led the way, followed by Aramis; but as the latter entered the grotto, he turned round, saying: 'Yes, they are now entering the wood; and, see, they are bending their steps this way.'

'Very well; let us make room for them,' said Fouquet, smiling and pulling Aramis by his cloak; 'but I do not think the King knows of my grotto.'

'Yes,' said Aramis, 'they are looking about them, but it is only for a thicker tree.'

Aramis was not mistaken, the King's looks were directed upwards and not around him. He held La Vallière's arm within his own, and held her hand in his. La Vallière's feet began to slip on the damp grass. Louis again looked round him with greater attention than before, and perceiving an enormous oak with wide-spreading branches, he hurriedly drew La Vallière beneath its protecting shelter. The poor girl looked round her on all sides, and seemed half afraid, half desirous, of being followed. The King made her lean her back against the trunk of the tree, whose vast circumference, protected by the thickness of the foliage, was as dry as if at that moment the rain had not been falling in torrents. He himself remained standing before her with his head uncovered. After a few minutes, however, some drops of rain penetrated through the branches of the tree and fell on the King's forehead, who did not pay any attention to it.

'Oh, sire!' murmured La Vallière, pushing the King's hat towards him. But the King simply bowed, and determinedly refused to cover his head.

'Now or never is the time to offer your place,' said Fouquet in Aramis's ear.

'Now or never is the time to listen, and not lose a syllable of what they may have to say to each other,' replied Aramis in Fouquet's ear.

In fact they both remained perfectly silent, and the King's voice reached them where they were.

'Believe me,' said the King, 'I perceive, or rather I can imagine your uneasiness; believe how sincerely I regret to have isolated you from the rest of the company, and to have brought you, also, to a spot where you will be inconvenienced by the rain. You are wet already, and perhaps are cold too?'

'No, sire.'

'And yet you tremble?'

'I am afraid, sire, that my absence may be misinterpreted; at a moment, too, when all the others are reunited.'

'I would not hesitate to propose returning to the carriages, Mademoiselle de la Vallière, but pray look and listen, and tell me if it be possible to attempt to make the slightest progress at the present?'

In fact the thunder was still rolling, and the rain continued to fall in torrents.

'Besides,' continued the King, 'no possible interpretation can be made which would be to your discredit. Are you not with the King of France; in other words with the first gentleman of the kingdom?'

'Certainly, sire,' replied La Vallière, 'and it is a very distinguished honour for me; it is not, therefore, for myself that I fear the interpretations that may be made.'

'For me?' said the King, smiling, 'I do not understand you.'

'Has your Majesty already forgotten what took place yesterday evening in Her Royal Highness's apartments?'

'Oh! forget that, I beg, or allow me to remember it for no other purpose than to thank you once more for your letter, and——'

'Sire,' interrupted La Vallière, 'the rain is falling, and your Majesty's head is uncovered.'

'I entreat you not to think of anything but yourself.'

'Oh! I,' said La Vallière smiling, 'I am a country girl, accustomed to roaming through the meadows of the Loire and the gardens of Blois, whatever the weather may be. And, as for my clothes,' she added, looking at her simple muslin dress, 'your Majesty sees they do not run much risk.'

'Indeed, I have already noticed more than once that you owed nearly everything to yourself and nothing to your toilet. Your freedom from coquetry is one of your greatest charms in my eyes.'

'Sire, do not make me out better than I am, and say merely, "You cannot be a coquette."'

'Why so?'

'Because,' said La Vallière, smiling, 'I am not rich.'

'You admit then,' said the King quickly, 'that you have a love for beautiful things?'

'Sire, I only regard those things as beautiful which are within my reach. Everything which is too highly placed for me——'

'You are indifferent to?'

'Is foreign to me, as being prohibited.'

'And I,' said the King, 'do not find that you are at my court on the footing you should be. The services of your family have not been sufficiently brought under my notice. The advancement of your family has been cruelly neglected by my uncle.'

'On the contrary, sire. His Royal Highness, the Duke of Orleans, had always been exceedingly kind towards M. de Saint-Remy, my step-father. The services rendered were humble, and, properly speaking, our services have been adequately recognised. It is not every one who is happy enough to find opportunities of serving his sovereign with distinction. I have no doubt at all, that, if ever opportunities had been met with, my family's actions would; but that happiness has never been ours.'

'In that case, Mademoiselle de la Vallière, it belongs to kings to repair the want of opportunity, and most delightedly do I undertake to repair, in your instance, and with the least possible delay, the wrongs of fortune towards you.'

'Nay, sire,' cried La Vallière eagerly; 'leave things, I beg, as they now are.'

'Is it possible! you refuse what I ought and what I wish to do for you?'

'All I desired has been granted me, when the honour was conferred upon me of forming one of Madame's household.'

'But if you refuse for yourself, at least accept for your family.'

'Your generous intention, sire, bewilders and makes me apprehensive, for, in doing for my family what your kindness urges you to do, your Majesty will raise up enemies for us and enemies for yourself too. Leave me in my mediocrity, sire; of all the feelings and sentiments I experience, leave me to enjoy that pleasing delicacy of disinterestedness.'

'The sentiments you express,' said the King, 'are indeed admirable.'

'Quite true,' murmured Aramis in Fouquet's ear, 'and he cannot be accustomed to them.'

'But,' replied Fouquet, 'suppose she were to make a similar reply to my letter.'

'True!' said Aramis, 'let us not anticipate, but wait the conclusion.'

'And then, dear Monsieur d'Herblay,' added the super-intendant, hardly able to appreciate the sentiments which La Vallière had just expressed, 'it is very often a good policy to seem disinterested with monarchs.'

'Exactly what I was thinking this very minute,' said Aramis. 'Let us listen.'

The King approached nearer to La Vallière, and as the rain dripped more and more through the foliage of the oak, he held his hat over the head of the young girl, who raised her beautiful blue eyes towards the royal hat which sheltered her, and shook her head, sighing deeply as she did so.

'What melancholy thought,' said the King, 'can possibly reach your heart when I place mine as a rampart before it?'

'I will tell you, sire. I had already once before broached this question, which is so difficult for a young girl of my age to discuss, but your Majesty imposed silence on me. Your Majesty belongs not to yourself alone, you are married; and every sentiment which would separate your Majesty from the Queen, in leading your Majesty to take notice of me, will be a source of the profoundest sorrow for the Queen.' The King endeavoured to interrupt the young girl, but she continued with a suppliant gesture. 'The Queen Maria, with an attachment which can be so well understood, follows with her eyes every step of your Majesty which separates you from her. Happy enough in having had her fate united to your own, she weepingly implores Heaven to preserve you to her, and is jealous of the faintest throb of your heart bestowed elsewhere.' The King again seemed anxious to speak, but again did La Vallière venture to prevent him. 'Would it not, therefore, be a most blamable action,' she continued, 'if your Majesty, a witness of this anxious and disinterested affection, gave the Queen any cause for her jealousy? Forgive me, sire, for the expression I have used. I well know it is impossible, or rather that it would be impossible, that the greatest queen of the whole world could be jealous of a poor girl like myself. But, though a queen, she is still a woman, and her heart, like that of any of her sex, cannot close itself against the suspicions which such as are evilly disposed insinuate. For Heaven's sake, sire, think no more of me, I am unworthy of your regard.'

'Do you not know that in speaking as you have done, you change my esteem for you into admiration?'

'Sire, you assume my words to be contrary to the truth; you suppose me to be better than I really am, and attach a greater merit to me than God ever intended should be the case. Spare me, sire; for, did I not know that your Majesty was the most generous man in your kingdom, I should believe you were jesting.'

'You do not, I know, fear such a thing; I am quite sure of that,' exclaimed Louis.

'I shall be obliged to believe it, if your Majesty continues to hold such language towards me.'

'I am most unhappy, then,' said the King, in a tone of regret which was not assumed; 'I am the unhappiest prince in the whole Christian world, since I am powerless to induce belief in my words in one whom I love the best in the wide world, and who almost breaks my heart by refusing to credit my regard for her.'

'Oh, sire!' said La Vallière, gently putting the King aside, who had approached nearer to her, 'I think the storm has passed away now, and the rain has ceased.' At the very moment, however, as the poor girl, fleeing, as it were, from her own heart, which doubtless throbbed too much in unison with the King's, uttered these words, the storm undertook to contradict her. A bluish flash of lightning illumined the forest with a wild, weird-like glare, and a peal of thunder like a discharge of artillery, burst over their very heads, as if the height of the oak which sheltered them had attracted the storm. The young girl could not repress a cry of terror. The King with one hand drew her towards his heart, and stretched the other above her head, as though to shield her from the lightning. A moment's silence ensued, as the group, delightful as everything young and loving is delightful, remained motionless, while Fouquet and Aramis contemplated it in attitudes as motionless as La Vallière and the King. 'Oh, sire, sire!' murmured La Vallière, 'do you hear?' and her head fell upon his shoulder.

'Yes,' said the King. 'You see, the storm has not passed away.'

'It is a warning, sire.' The King smiled. 'Sire, it is the voice of Heaven in anger.'

'Be it so,' said the King. 'I agree to accept that peal of thunder as a warning, and even as a threat, if, in five minutes from the present moment, it is renewed with equal violence; but if not, permit me to think that the storm is a storm simply, and nothing more.' And the King, at the same moment, raised his head, as if to interrogate the heavens. But, as if the remark had been heard and accepted, during the five minutes which elapsed after the burst of thunder which had alarmed them, no renewed peal was heard; and, when the thunder was again heard, it was passing away in so audible a manner, as if, during those same five minutes, the storm, put to flight, had traversed the heavens with the speed of the wings of the wind. 'Well, Louise,' said the King, in a low tone of voice, 'will you still threaten me with the anger of heaven? and, since you wished to regard the storm as a presentiment, will you still believe that presentiment to be one of misfortune?'

The young girl looked up, and saw that while they had been talking, the rain had penetrated the foliage above them, and was trickling down the King's face. 'Oh, sire, sire!' she exclaimed, in accents of eager apprehension, which greatly agitated the King. 'Is it for me,' she murmured, 'that the King remains thus uncovered, and exposed to the rain? What am I, then?'

'You are, you perceive,' said the King, 'the divinity who dissipates the storm and brings back fine weather.' In fact, a ray of sunlight streamed through the forest, and caused the raindrops which rested upon the leaves, or fell vertically among the openings in the branches of the trees, to glisten like diamonds.

'Sire,' said La Vallière, almost overcome, but making a powerful effort over herself, 'think of the anxieties your Majesty will
have to submit to on my account. At this very moment they
are seeking you in every direction. The Queen must be full of
uneasiness; and Madame—oh, Madame!' the young girl exclaimed, with an expression which almost resembled terror.

This name had a certain effect upon the King. He started,
and disengaged himself from La Vallière, whom he had, till that
moment, held pressed against his heart. He then advanced towards
the path, in order to look round, and returned, somewhat thoughtfully, to La Vallière. 'Madame, did you say?' he remarked.

'Yes, Madame; she too is jealous,' said La Vallière, with a
marked tone of voice; and her eyes, so timorous in their expression, and so modestly fugitive in their glance, for a moment
ventured to look inquiringly in the King's eyes.

'Still,' returned Louis, making an effort over himself, 'it seems
to me that Madame has no reason, no right to be jealous of me.'

'Alas!' murmured La Vallière.

'Are you too,' said the King, almost in a tone of reproach, 'are
you among those who think the sister has a right to be jealous of
the brother?'

'It is not for me, sire, to penetrate your Majesty's secrets.'

'You do believe it then?' exclaimed the King.

'I do believe Madame is jealous, sire,' La Vallière replied firmly.

'Is it possible,' said the King, with some anxiety, 'that you
have perceived it, then, from her conduct towards you? Have
her manners in any way been such towards you that you can
attribute them to the jealousy you speak of?'

'Not at all, sire; I am of so little importance.'

'Oh! if it were really the case——' exclaimed Louis violently.

'Sire,' interrupted the young girl, 'it has ceased raining; some
one is coming, I think.' And, forgetful of all etiquette, she had
seized the King by the arm.

'Well,' replied the King, 'let them come. Who is there who
would venture to think I had done wrong in remaining alone
with Mademoiselle de la Vallière?'

'For pity's sake, sire! they will think it strange to see you wet
through in this manner, and that you should have run such risk
for me.'

'I have simply done my duty as a gentleman,' said Louis; 'and woe to him who may fail in his in criticising his sovereign's conduct.' In fact, at this moment, a few eager and curious faces were seen in the walk, as if engaged in a search, and who, observing the King and La Vallière, seemed to have found what they were seeking. They were some of the courtiers who had been sent by the Queen and Madame, and who immediately uncovered themselves, in token of having perceived His Majesty. But, Louis, notwithstanding La Vallière's confusion, did not quit his respectful and tender attitude. Then, when all the courtiers were assembled in the walk—when every one had been able to perceive the mark of deference with which he had treated the young girl, by remaining standing and bare-headed during the storm—he offered her his arm, led her towards the group who were waiting, recognised by an inclination of the head the respectful salutations which were paid him on all sides; and still holding his hat in his hand, he conducted her to her carriage. And, as the rain still continued to fall—a last adieu of the disappearing storm—the other ladies, whom respect had prevented getting into their carriages before the King, remained, and altogether unprotected by hood and cloak, exposed to the rain from which the King with his hat over her, was protecting, as much as he was able, the humblest among them. The Queen and Madame must, like the others, have witnessed this exaggerated courtesy of the King. Madame was so disconcerted at it, that she touched the Queen with her elbow, saying at the same time, 'Look there, look there.'

The Queen closed her eyes as if she had been suddenly seized with a fainting attack. She lifted her hand to her face and entered her carriage, Madame following her. The King again mounted his horse, and without showing a preference for any particular carriage door, he returned to Fontainebleau, the reins hanging over his horse's neck, absorbed in thought. As soon as the crowd had disappeared, and the sound of the horses and carriages grew fainter in the distance, and when they were certain, in fact, that no one could see them, Aramis and Fouquet came out of their grotto, and both of them in silence passed slowly on toward the walk. Aramis looked most narrowly not only at the whole extent of the open space stretching out before and behind him, but even into the very depth of the wood.

'Monsieur Fouquet,' he said, when he had quite satisfied himself that they were alone, 'we must get back, at any cost, the letter you wrote to La Vallière.'

'That will be easy enough,' said Fouquet, 'if my servant has not given it to her.'

'In any case it must be done, do you understand?'

'Yes; the King is in love with this girl, you mean?'

'Exceedingly so, and what is worse is, that on her side, the girl is passionately attached to the King.'

'As much as to say that we must change our tactics I suppose?'

'Not a doubt of it; you have no time to lose. You must see La Vallière, and, without thinking any more of becoming her lover, which is out of the question, must declare yourself her dearest friend and her most humble servant.'

'I will do so,' replied Fouquet, 'and without the slightest feeling of disinclination, for she seems a good-hearted girl.'

'Or a clever one,' said Aramis; 'but in that case the greater reason.' Then he added, after a moment's pause, 'If I am not mistaken, that girl will become the strongest passion of the King. Let us return to our carriage, and, as fast as possible, to the château.'

XLV

TOBY

TWO hours after the superintendant's carriage had set off by Aramis's directions, conveying them both towards Fontainebleau with the fleetness of the clouds which the last breath of the tempest was hurrying across the face of the heavens, La Vallière was closeted in her own apartment, with a simple muslin wrapper round her, having just finished a light repast, which was placed upon a small marble table. Suddenly the door was opened and a servant entered to announce M. Fouquet, who had called to request permission to pay his respects to her. She made him repeat the message twice over, for the poor girl only knew M. Fouquet by name, and could not conceive what she could possibly have to do with a superintendant of finances. However, as he might possibly come from the King—and, after the conversation we have recorded it was very likely—she glanced at her mirror, drew out still more the long ringlets of her hair, and desired him to be admitted. La Vallière could not, however, refrain from a certain feeling of uneasiness. A visit from the superintendant was not an ordinary event in the life of any woman attached to the court. Fouquet, so notorious for his generosity, his gallantry, and his sensitive delicacy of feeling with regard to women generally, had received more invitations than he had requested audiences. In many houses, the presence of the superintendant had been significant of fortune; in many hearts of love. Fouquet entered the apartment with a manner full of respect, presenting himself with that ease and gracefulness of manner which was the distinctive characteristic of the men of eminence of that period, and which at the present day seems no longer to be understood,* even in the portraits of the period in which the painter has endeavoured to recall them into being. La Vallière acknowledged the ceremonious salutation which Fouquet addressed to her by a gentle inclination of the head, and motioned him to a seat. But Fouquet, with a bow, said, 'I will not sit down until you have pardoned me.'

'I?' asked La Vallière, 'pardoned what?'

Fouquet fixed a most piercing look upon the young girl, and fancied he could perceive in her face nothing but the most unaffected surprise. 'I observe,' he said, 'that you have as much generosity as intelligence, and I read in your eyes the forgiveness I solicit. A pardon pronounced by your lips is insufficient for me, and I need the forgiveness of your heart and mind.'

'Upon my honour, monsieur,' said La Vallière, 'I assure you most positively I do not understand your meaning.'

'Again, that is a delicacy on your part which charms me,' replied Fouquet, 'and I see you do not wish me to blush before you.'

'Blush! blush before me! Why should you blush?'

'Can I have deceived myself,' said Fouquet; 'and can I have been happy enough not to have offended you by my conduct towards you?'

'Really, monsieur,' said La Vallière, shrugging her shoulders, 'you speak in enigmas, and I suppose I am too ignorant to understand you.'

'Be it so,' said Fouquet; 'I will not insist. Tell me, only, I entreat you, that I may rely upon your full and complete forgiveness.'

'I have but one reply to make to you, monsieur,' said La Vallière, somewhat impatiently, 'and I hope that will satisfy you. If I knew the wrong you have done me, I would forgive you, and I would do so with still greater reason since I am ignorant of the wrong you allude to.'

Fouquet bit his lips, as Aramis would have done. 'In that case,' he said, 'I may hope that, notwithstanding what has happened, our good understanding will remain undisturbed, and that you will kindly confer the favour upon me of believing in my respectful friendship.'

La Vallière fancied that she now began to understand, and said to herself, 'I should not have believed M. Fouquet so eager to seek the source of a favour so very recent,' and then added aloud, 'Your friendship, monsieur! you offer me your friendship. The honour, on the contrary, is mine, and I feel overpowered by it.'

'I am aware,' replied Fouquet, 'that the friendship of the master may appear more brilliant and desirable than that of the servant, but I assure you the latter will be quite as devoted, quite as faithful, and altogether disinterested.'

La Vallière bowed, for, in fact, the voice of the superintendant seemed to convey both conviction and real devotion in its tone, and she held out her hand to him, saying, 'I believe you.'

Fouquet eagerly took hold of the young girl's hand. 'You see no difficulty, therefore,' he added, 'in restoring me that unhappy letter.'

'What letter?' inquired La Vallière.

Fouquet interrogated her with his most searching gaze, as he had already done before, but the same innocent expression, the same candid look met his. 'I am obliged to confess,' he said, after this denial, 'that your system is the most delicate in the world, and I should not feel I was a man of honour and uprightness if I were to suspect anything from a woman so generous as yourself.'

'Really, Monsieur Fouquet,' replied La Vallière, 'it is with profound regret I am obliged to repeat that I absolutely understand nothing of what you refer to.'

'In fact, then, upon your honour, mademoiselle, you have not received any letter from me?'

'Upon my honour, none,' replied La Vallière firmly.

'Very well, that is quite sufficient; permit me, then, to renew the assurance of my utmost esteem and respect,' said Fouquet. Then, bowing, he left the room to seek Aramis, who was waiting for him in his own apartment and leaving La Vallière to ask herself whether the superintendant had not lost his senses.

'Well!' inquired Aramis, who was impatiently waiting Fouquet's return, 'are you satisfied with the favourite?'

'Enchanted,' replied Fouquet; 'she is a woman full of intelligence and fine feeling.'

'She did not get angry, then?'

'Far from that, she did not even seem to understand.'

'To understand what?'

'To understand that I had written to her.'

'She must, however, have understood you sufficiently to give the letter back to you, for I presume she returned it.'

'Not at all.'

'At least, you satisfied yourself that she had burned it.'

'My dear Monsieur d'Herblay, I have been playing at cross purposes for more than an hour, and, however amusing it may be, I begin to have had enough of this game. So understand me thoroughly: the girl pretended not to understand what I was saying to her; she denied having received any letter; therefore, having positively denied its receipt, she was unable either to return or burn it.'

'Oh! oh!' said Aramis, with uneasiness, 'what is that you say?'

'I say that she swore most positively she had not received any letter.'

'That is too much. And you did not insist?'

'On the contrary, I did insist, almost impertinently so, even.'

'And she persisted in her denial?'

'Unhesitatingly.'

'And she did not contradict herself once?'

'Not once.'

'But, in that case, then, you have left our letter in her hands?'

'How could I do otherwise.'

'Oh! it was a great mistake.'

'What the deuce would you have done in my place?'

'One could not force her, certainly, but it is very embarrassing; such a letter ought not to remain in existence against us.'

'Oh! the young girl's disposition is generosity itself; I looked at her eyes, and I can read eyes well.'

'You think she can be relied upon?'

'From my heart I do.'

'Well, I think we are mistaken.'

'In what way?'

'I think that, in point of fact, as she herself told you, she did not receive the letter.'

'What! do you suppose——'

'I suppose that, from some motive, of which we know nothing, your man did not deliver the letter to her.'

Fouquet rang the bell. A servant appeared. 'Send Toby here,' he said. A moment afterwards a man made his appearance, with an anxious, restless look, shrewd expression of the mouth, with short arms, and his back somewhat bent. Aramis fixed a penetrating look upon him.

'Will you allow me to interrogate him myself?' inquired Aramis.

'Do so,' said Fouquet.

Aramis was about to say something to the lackey, when he paused. 'No,' he said; 'he would see that we attach too much importance to his answer, question him yourself; I will pretend to write.' Aramis accordingly placed himself at a table, his back turned towards the old attendant, whose every gesture and look he watched in a looking-glass opposite to him.

'Come here, Toby,' said Fouquet to the valet, who approached with a tolerably firm step. 'How did you execute my commission?' inquired Fouquet.

'In the usual way, monseigneur,' replied the man.

'But how, tell me?'

'I succeeded in penetrating as far as Mademoiselle de la Vallière's apartment; but she was at Mass, and so I placed the note on her toilet-table. Is not that what you told me to do?'

'Precisely; and is that all?'

'Absolutely all, monseigneur.'

'No one was there?'

'No one.'

'Did you conceal yourself as I told you?'

'Yes.'

'And she returned?'

'Ten minutes afterwards.'

'And no one could have taken the letter?'

'No one; for no one had entered the room.'

'From the outside, but from the interior?'

'From the place where I was secreted I could see to the very end of the room.'

'Now listen to me,' said Fouquet, looking fixedly at the lackey; 'if this letter did not reach its proper destination, confess it; for, if a mistake has been made, your head shall be the forfeit.'

Toby started, but immediately recovered himself. 'Monseigneur,' he said, 'I placed the letter on the very place I told you; and I ask only half an hour to prove to you that the letter is in Mademoiselle de la Vallière's hands or to bring you back the letter itself.'

Aramis looked at the valet scrutinisingly. Fouquet was ready in placing confidence in people, and for twenty years this man had served him faithfully. 'Go,' he said; 'but bring me the proof you speak of.' The lackey quitted the room.

'Well, what do you think of it?' inquired Fouquet of Aramis.

'I think that you must, by some means or another, assure yourself of the truth, either that the letter has or has not reached La Vallière; that, in the first case, La Vallière must return it to you, or satisfy you by burning it in your presence; that, in the second, you must have the letter back again, even were it to cost you a million. Come, is not that your opinion?'

'Yes; but still, my dear Bishop, I believe you are exaggerating the position of the affair.'

'Blind, how blind you are!' murmured Aramis.

'La Vallière,' returned Fouquet, 'whom we assume to be a politician of the greatest ability, is simply nothing more than a coquette, who hopes that I shall pay my court to her, because I have already done so, and who, now that she has received a confirmation of the King's regard, hopes to keep me in leading strings with the letter. It is natural enough.' Aramis shook his head.

'Is not that your opinion?' said Fouquet.

'She is not a coquette,' he replied.

'Allow me to tell you——'

'Oh! I am well enough acquainted with women who are coquettes,'* said Aramis.

'My dear friend!'

'It is a long time ago since I finished my studies, you mean. But women do not change.'

'True; but men change, and you at the present day are far more suspicious than you formerly were.' And then, beginning to laugh, he added, 'Come, if La Vallière is willing to love me only to the extent of a third, and the King two-thirds, do you think the condition acceptable?'

Aramis rose impatiently. 'La Vallière,' he said, 'has never loved, and will never love any one but the King.'

'At all events,' said Fouquet, 'what would you do?'

'Ask me rather what I would have done?'

'Well! what would you have done?'

'In the first place, I should not have allowed that man to go.'

'Toby!'

'Yes; Toby is a traitor. Nay, I am sure of it, and I would not have let him go until he had told me the truth.'

'There is still time. I will recall him, and do you question him in your turn.'

'Agreed.'

'But I assure you it is quite useless. He has been with me for the last twenty years, and has never made the slightest mistake, and yet,' added Fouquet, laughing, 'it has been easy enough.'

'Still, call him back. This morning I fancy I saw that face in earnest conversation with one of M. Colbert's men.'

'Where was that?'

'Opposite the stables.'

'Bah! all my people are at daggers drawn with that fellow.'

'I saw him, I tell you, and his face, which I ought not to have recognised when he entered just now, struck me in a disagreeable manner.'

'Why did you not say something, then, while he was here?'

'Because it is only at this very minute that my memory is clear upon the subject.'

'Really,' said Fouquet, 'you alarm me.' And he again rang the bell.

'Provided that it is not already too late,' said Aramis.

Fouquet once more rang impatiently. The valet usually in attendance appeared. 'Toby!' said Fouquet, 'send Toby.' The valet again shut the door.

'You leave me at perfect liberty, I suppose?'

'Entirely so.'

'I may employ all means, then, to ascertain the truth.'

'All.'

'Intimidation, even?'

'I constitute you public prosecutor in my place.'

They waited ten minutes longer, but uselessly, and Fouquet, thoroughly out of patience, again rang loudly. 'Toby?' he exclaimed.

'Monseigneur,' said the valet, 'they are looking for him.'

'He cannot be far distant, I have not given him any commission to execute.'

'I will go and see, monseigneur,' replied the valet, as he closed the door. Aramis, during this interval, walked impatiently, but silently, up and down the cabinet. Again they waited another ten minutes. Fouquet rang in a manner to awaken the very dead. The valet again presented himself, trembling in a way to induce a belief that he was the bearer of bad news.

'Monseigneur is mistaken,' he said, before even Fouquet could interrogate him, 'you must have given Toby some commission, for he has been to the stables and taken your lordship's swiftest horse, and saddled it himself.'

'Well?'

'And he has gone off.'

'Gone!' exclaimed Fouquet. 'Let him be pursued, let him be captured.'

'Nay, nay,' said Aramis, taking him by the hand, 'be calm, the evil is done now.'

'The evil is done, you say?'

'No doubt; I was sure of it. And now, let us give no cause for suspicion; we must calculate the result of the blow and ward it off, if possible.'

'After all,' said Fouquet, 'the evil is not great.'

'You think so?' said Aramis.

'Of course. Surely a man is allowed to write a love-letter to a woman.'

'A man, certainly; a subject, no: especially, too, when the woman in question is one with whom the King is in love.'

'But the King was not in love with La Vallière a week ago! he was not in love with her yesterday, and the letter is dated yesterday; I could not guess the King was in love when the King's affection was not even yet in existence.'

'As you please,' replied Aramis; 'but unfortunately the letter is not dated, and it is that circumstance particularly which annoys me. If it had only been dated yesterday, I should not have the slightest shadow of uneasiness on your account.' Fouquet shrugged his shoulders.

'Am I not my own master,' he said, 'and is the King, then, King of my brain and of my flesh?'

'You are right,' replied Aramis, 'do not let us give more importance to matters than is necessary; and besides . . . Well! if we are threatened, we have means of defence.'

'Oh! threatened!' said Fouquet, 'you do not place this gnat bite, as it were, among the number of threats which may compromise my fortune and my life, do you?'

'Do not forget, Monsieur Fouquet, that the bite of an insect can kill a giant, if the insect be venomous.'

'But has this sovereign power you were speaking of already vanished?'

'I am all-powerful, it is true, but I am not immortal.'

'Come, then, the most pressing matter is to find Toby again, I suppose. Is not that your opinion?'

'Oh! as for that, you will not find him again,' said Aramis, 'and if he were of any great value to you, you must give him up for lost.'

'At all events he is somewhere or another in the world,' said Fouquet.

'You're right, let me act,' replied Aramis.

XLVI

ANNE OF AUSTRIA had begged the young Queen to pay her a visit. For some time past suffering most acutely, and losing both her youth and beauty with that rapidity which signalises the decline of women for whom life has been a long contest, Anne of Austria had, in addition to her physical sufferings, to experience the bitterness of being no longer held in any esteem, except as a living remembrance of the past, amidst the youthful beauties, wits, and influences of her court. Her physician's opinions, her mirror also, grieved her far less than the inexorable warnings which the society of the courtiers afforded, who, like the rats in a ship, abandon the hold in which the water is on the point of penetrating, owing to the ravages of decay. Anne of Austria did not feel satisfied with the time her eldest son devoted to her. The King, a good son, more from affectation than from affection, had at first been in the habit of passing an hour in the morning and one in the evening with his mother; but since he had himself undertaken the conduct of State affairs, the duration of the morning and evening's visit had been reduced to half; and then, by degrees, the morning visit had been suppressed altogether. They met at mass; the evening visit was replaced by a meeting, either at the King's assembly or at Madame's, which the Queen attended obligingly enough out of regard to her two sons. The result was, that Madame had acquired an immense influence over the court, which made her apartments the true royal place of meeting. This, Anne of Austria had perceived; feeling herself to be suffering, and condemned by her sufferings to frequent retirement, she was distressed at the idea that the greater part of her future days and evenings would pass away solitary, useless, and in despondency. She recalled with terror the isolation in which Cardinal Richelieu had formerly left her, those dreaded and insupportable evenings, during which, however, she had her youth and beauty, which are always accompanied by hope, to console her. She next formed the project of transporting the court to her own apartments, and of attracting

Madame, with her brilliant escort, to her gloomy and already sorrowful abode, where the widow of a king of France, and the mother of a king of France, was reduced to console, in her anticipated widowhood, the always weeping wife of a king of France.

Anne began to reflect. She had intrigued a good deal in her life.* In the good times past, when her youthful mind nursed projects which were invariably successful, she then had by her side, to stimulate her ambition and her love, a friend of her own sex, more eager, more ambitious than herself,—a friend who had loved her, a rare circumstance at court, and whom some petty considerations had removed from her for ever. But for many years past—except Madame de Motteville, and except La Molena, her Spanish nurse, a confidante in her character of countrywoman and woman too—who could boast of having given good advice to the Queen?* Who, too, among all the youthful heads there, could recall the past for her,—that past in which alone she lived? Anne of Austria remembered Madame de Chevreuse,* in the first place exiled rather by her wish than the King's, and then dying in exile, the wife of a gentleman of obscure birth and position. She asked herself what Madame de Chevreuse would formerly have advised her in a similar circumstance, in their mutual difficulties arising from their intrigues; and after serious reflection, it seemed as if the clever subtle mind of her friend, full of experience and sound judgement, answered her in her ironical tone of voice: 'All these insignificant young people are poor and greedy of gain. They require gold and incomes to keep alive their means of amusements; it is by interest you must gain them over.'* And Anne of Austria adopted this plan. Her purse was well filled, and she had at her disposal a considerable sum of money, which had been amassed by Mazarin for her and lodged in a place of safety. She possessed the most magnificent jewels in France, and especially pearls of a size so large that they made the King sigh every time he saw them, because the pearls of his crown were like millet-seed compared to them. Anne of Austria had neither beauty nor charms any longer at her disposal. She gave out, therefore, that her wealth was great, and as an inducement for others to visit her apartments she let it be known that there were good gold crowns to be won at play, or that handsome presents were likely to be made on days when all went well with her; or windfalls, in the shape of annuities which she had wrung from the King by entreaty, and which she determined to do to maintain her credit. And, in the first place, she tried these means upon Madame, because, to gain her consent was of more importance than anything else. Madame, notwithstanding the bold confidence with which her wit and beauty inspired her, blindly ran head foremost into the net which had been stretched out to catch her. Enriched by degrees by these presents and transfers of property, she took a fancy to these inheritances by anticipation. Anne of Austria adopted the same means towards Monsieur, and even towards the King himself. She instituted lotteries in her apartments. The day on which the present chapter opens, invitations had been issued for a late supper in the Queen-Mother's apartments, as she intended that two beautiful diamond bracelets of exquisite workmanship should be put into lottery. The medallions were antique cameos of the greatest value; the diamonds, in point of intrinsic value, did not represent a very considerable amount, but the originality and rarity of the workmanship were such, that every one at court not only wished to possess the bracelets, but even to see the Queen herself wear them, for, on the days she wore them, it was considered as a favour to be admitted to admire them in kissing her hands. The courtiers had, even with regard to this subject, adopted various expressions of gallantry to establish the aphorism that the bracelets would have been priceless in value if they had not been unfortunate enough to be placed in contact with arms as beautiful as the Queen's. This compliment had been honoured by a translation into all the languages of Europe, and numerous were the verses in Latin and French which had been circulated on the subject. The day that Anne of Austria had selected for the lottery was a decisive moment; the King had not been near his mother for a couple of days; Madame, after the great scene of the Dryads and Naiads, was sulking by herself. The King's fit of sulkiness was over, but his mind was absorbingly occupied by a circumstance which raised him above the stormy disputes and the giddy pleasures of the court.

Anne of Austria effected a diversion by the announcement of the famous lottery to take place in her apartments on the following evening. With this object in view she saw the young Queen, whom, as we have already seen, she had invited to pay her a visit in the morning. 'I have good news to tell you,' she said to her; 'the King has been saying the most tender things about you. He is young, you know, and easily drawn away; but so long as you keep near me, he will not venture to keep away from you, to whom, besides, he is most warmly and affectionately attached. I intend to have a lottery this evening, and shall expect to see you.'

'I have heard,' said the young Queen, with a sort of timid reproach, 'that your Majesty intends to put in lottery those beautiful bracelets whose rarity is so great that we ought not to allow them to pass out of the custody of the Crown, even were there no other reason than that they had once belonged to you.'

'My daughter,' said Anne of Austria, who read the young Queen's thoughts, and wished to console her for not having received the bracelets as a present, 'it is positively necessary that I should induce Madame to pass her time always in my apartments.'

'Madame!' said the young Queen blushing.

'Of course; would you not prefer to have a rival near you whom you could watch and rule over, than to know that the King is with her, always as ready to flirt with as to be flirted with by her. The lottery I have proposed is my means of attraction for that purpose; do you blame me?'

'Oh, no!' returned Maria Theresa, clapping her hands with a childlike expression of delight.

'And you no longer regret, then, that I did not give you these bracelets, as I had at first intended to do?'

'Oh, no, no!'

'Very well; make yourself look as beautiful as possible, that our supper may be very brilliant; the gayer you seem the more charming you appear, and you will eclipse all the ladies present as much by your brilliancy as by your rank.'

Maria Theresa left full of delight. An hour afterwards Anne of Austria received a visit from Madame, whom she covered with caresses, saying, 'Excellent news! the King is charmed with my lottery.'

'But I,' replied Madame, 'am not quite charmed; to see such beautiful bracelets on any one's arms but yours or mine is what I cannot reconcile myself to.'

'Well, well,' said Anne of Austria, concealing by a smile a violent pang which she had just experienced; 'do not alarm yourself, young lady, and do not look at things in the worst light immediately.'

'Ah, madame, fortune is blind, and I am told there are two hundred tickets.'

'Quite as many as that; but you cannot surely forget that there can only be one winner.'

'No doubt. But who will that be? Can you tell?' said Madame, in despair.

'You remind me that I had a dream last night; my dreams are always good,—I sleep so little.'

'What was your dream?—But are you suffering?'

'No,' said the Queen, stifling with wonderful command the torture of a renewed attack of shooting pains in her bosom;* 'I dreamt that the King won the bracelets.'

'The King?'

'You are going to ask me, I think, what the King could possibly do with the bracelets?'

'Yes.'

'And you will not add, perhaps, that it would be very fortunate if the King were really to win, for he would be obliged to give the bracelets to some one else.'

'To restore them to you, for instance.'

'In which case I should immediately give them away; for you do not think, I suppose,' said the Queen, laughing, 'that I have put these bracelets up to a lottery from necessity. My object was to give them without arousing any one's jealousy; but if fortune will not get me out of my difficulty—well, I will teach fortune a lesson—and I know very well to whom I intend to offer the bracelets.' These words were accompanied by so expressive a smile that Madame could not resist paying her by a grateful kiss.

'But,' added Anne of Austria, 'do you not know, as well as I do, that if the King were to win the bracelets he would not restore them to me?'

'You mean, he would give them to the Queen?'

'No; and for the very same reason, that he would not give them back again to me; since, if I had wished to make the Queen a present of them, I had no need of him for that purpose.'

Madame cast a side-glance upon the bracelets, which, in their casket, were dazzlingly exposed to view upon a table close beside her.

'How beautiful they are,' she said, sighing. 'But stay,' Madame continued, 'we are quite forgetting that your Majesty's dream is nothing but a dream.'

'I should be very much surprised,' returned Anne of Austria, 'if my dream were to deceive me; that has happened to me very seldom.'

'We may look upon you as a prophetess, then.'

'I have already said that I dream but very rarely; but the coincidence of my dream about this matter, with my own ideas, is extraordinary! it agrees so wonderfully with my own views and arrangements.'

'What arrangements do you allude to?'

'That you will win the bracelets, for instance.'

'In that case, it will not be the King.'

'Oh!' said Anne of Austria, 'there is not such a very great distance between His Majesty's heart and your own; for are not you his sister, for whom he has a great regard? There is not, I repeat, so very wide a distance, that my dream can be pronounced false on that account. Come, let us reckon up the chances in its favour.'

'I will count them.'

'In the first place, we will begin with the dream. If the King wins, he is sure to give you the bracelets.'

'I admit that is one.'

'If you win them, they are yours.'

'Naturally; that may be admitted also.'

'Lastly;—if Monsieur were to win them!'

'Oh!' said Madame, laughing heartily, 'he would give them to the Chevalier de Lorraine.'

Anne of Austria laughed as heartily as her daughter-in-law; so much so, indeed, that her sufferings again returned and made her turn suddenly pale in the very midst of her enjoyment.

'What is the matter?' inquired Madame almost terrified.

'Nothing, nothing; a pain in my side. I have been laughing too much. We were at the fourth chance, I think.'

'I cannot see a fourth.'

'I beg your pardon; I am not excluded from the chance of winning, and if I be winner, you are sure of me.'

'Oh! thank you, thank you!' exclaimed Madame.

'I hope you look upon yourself as one whose chances are good, and that my dream now begins to assume the solid form of reality.'

'Yes, indeed; you give me both hope and confidence,' said Madame, 'and the bracelets, won in this manner, will be a hundred times more precious to me.'

'Well! then, good-bye, until this evening.' And the two princesses separated. Anne of Austria, after her daughter-in-law had left her, said to herself, as she examined the bracelets, 'They are, indeed, precious; since, by their means, this evening, I shall have won over a heart to my side, and, at the same time, shall have guessed a secret.'

Then, turning towards the deserted recess in her room, she said, addressing vacancy—'Is it not thus that you would have acted, my poor Chevreuse? Yes, yes; I know it is.'

And, like a perfume of days gone by, her youth, her imagination, and her happiness, seemed to return to her with the echo of this invocation.

XLVII
THE LOTTERY

AT eight o'clock in the evening every one had assembled in the Queen-Mother's apartments. Anne of Austria, in full dress, beautiful still, from former loveliness, and from all the resources which coquetry can command at the hands of clever assistants, concealed, or rather pretended to conceal, from the crowd of young courtiers who surrounded her, and who still admired her, thanks to the combination of circumstances which we have indicated in the preceding chapter, the ravages, which were already visible, of the acute suffering to which she finally yielded a few years later. Madame, almost as great a coquette as Anne of Austria, and the Queen, simple and natural as usual, were seated beside her, each contending for her good graces. The ladies of honour, united in a body in order to resist with greater effect, and consequently with more success, the witty and lively conversations which the young men held about them, were enabled, like a battalion formed in square, to offer each other the means of attack and defence which were thus at their command. Montalais, learned in that species of warfare which consists of a skirmishing character, protected the whole line by the sort of rolling fire which she directed against the enemy. Saint-Aignan, in utter despair at the rigour, which became insulting almost, from the very fact of her persisting in it, which Mademoiselle de Tonnay-Charente displayed, tried to turn his back upon her; but, overcome by the irresistible brilliancy of her large eyes, he, every moment, returned to consecrate his defeat by new submissions, to which Mademoiselle de Tonnay-Charente did not fail to reply by fresh acts of impertinence. Saint-Aignan did not know which way to turn. La Vallière had about her, not exactly a court, but sprinklings of courtiers. Saint-Aignan, hoping by this manœuvre to attract Athenaïs's attention towards him, had approached the young girl, and saluted her with a respect which induced some to believe that he wished to balance Athenaïs by Louise. But these were persons who had neither been witnesses of the scene during the shower nor had heard it spoken of. But, as the majority was already informed, and well informed too, on the matter, the acknowledged favour with which she was regarded had attracted to her side some of the most astute, as well as the least sensible, members of the court. The former, because they said with Montaigne, 'What do I know?' and the latter, who said with Rabelais, 'Perhaps.'* The greatest number had followed in the wake of the latter, just as in hunting five or six of the best hounds alone follow the scent of the animal hunted, whilst the remainder of the pack follow only the scent of the hounds. The two Queens and Madame examined with particular attention the toilets of their ladies and maids of honour; and they condescended to forget they were Queens in recollecting that they were women. In other words, they pitilessly tore in pieces every person there who wore a petticoat. The looks of both princesses simultaneously fell upon La Vallière, who, as we have just said, was completely surrounded at that moment. Madame knew not what pity was, and said to the Queen-Mother, as she turned towards her, 'If fortune were just she would favour that poor La Vallière.'

'That is not possible,' said the Queen-Mother, smiling.

'Why not?'

'There are only two hundred tickets, so that it was not possible to inscribe every one's name on the list.'

'And hers is not there, then?'

'No!'

'What a pity! she might have won them, and then sold them.'

'Sold them!' exclaimed the Queen.

'Yes; it would have been a dowry for her, and she would not have been obliged to marry without her trousseau, as will probably be the case.'

'Really,' answered the Queen-Mother, 'poor little thing, has she no dresses, then?'

And she pronounced these words like a woman who has never been able to understand the inconveniences of a slenderly-filled purse.

'Stay, look at her. Heaven forgive me, if she is not wearing the very same skirts this evening that she had on this morning during the promenade, and which she managed to keep clean, thanks to the care the King took of her in sheltering her from the rain.'

At the very moment Madame uttered these words the King entered the room. The two Queens would not perhaps have observed his arrival, so completely were they occupied in their ill-natured remarks, had not Madame noticed that, all at once, La Vallière, who was standing up facing the gallery, exhibited certain signs of confusion, and then said a few words to the courtiers who surrounded her, who immediately dispersed. This movement induced Madame to look towards the door, and at that moment, the captain of the guards announced the King. At this moment, La Vallière, who had hitherto kept her eyes fixed upon the gallery, suddenly cast them down as the King entered. His Majesty was dressed magnificently and in the most perfect taste; he was conversing with Monsieur and the Duc de

Roquelaure,* Monsieur on his right and the Duc de Roquelaure on his left. The King advanced, in the first place, towards the Queens, to whom he bowed with an air full of graceful respect. He took his mother's hand and kissed it, addressed a few compliments to Madame upon the beauty of her toilet, and then began to make the round of the assembly. La Vallière was saluted in the same manner as the others, but with neither more nor less attention. His Majesty then returned to his mother and his wife. When the courtiers noticed that the King had only addressed some ordinary remark to the young girl who had been so particularly noticed in the morning, they immediately drew their own conclusion to account for this coldness of manner; this conclusion being, that although the King may have taken a sudden fancy to her, that fancy had already disappeared. One thing, however, must be remarked, that close beside La Vallière, among the number of the courtiers, M. Fouquet was to be seen; and his respectfully attentive manner served to sustain the young girl in the midst of the varied emotions which visibly agitated her.

M. Fouquet was just on the point, moreover, of speaking in a more friendly manner with Mademoiselle de la Vallière, when M. de Colbert approached, and after having bowed to Fouquet with a formality which the rules of the most respectful politeness could require, he seemed to take up a post beside La Vallière for the purpose of entering into conversation with her. Fouquet immediately quitted his place. These proceedings were eagerly devoured by the eyes of Montalais and Malicorne, who mutually exchanged their several observations on the subject. De Guiche, standing within the embrasure of one of the windows, saw no one but Madame. But as Madame, on her side, frequently glanced at La Vallière, de Guiche's eyes, following Madame's, were from time to time cast upon the young girl. La Vallière instinctively felt herself sinking beneath the weight of all the different looks, inspired, some by interest, others by envy. She had nothing to compensate her for her sufferings, not a kind word from her companions, nor a look of affection from the King. No one could possibly express the misery the poor girl was suffering. The Queen-Mother next directed the small table to be brought forward, on which the lottery-tickets were placed, two hundred in number, and begged Madame de Motteville to read the list of the names. It was a matter of course that this list had been drawn out in strict accordance with the laws of etiquette; the King's name was first on the list, next the Queen-Mother, then the Queen, Monsieur, Madame, and so on. All hearts throbbed anxiously as the list was read out; more than three hundred persons had been invited, and each of them was anxious to learn whether his or her name was likely to be found among the number of privileged names. The King listened with as much attention as the others, and when the last name had been pronounced he noticed that La Vallière had been omitted from the list. Every one, of course, could remark this omission. The King flushed as if he had been much annoyed; but La Vallière, gentle and resigned, as usual, exhibited nothing of the sort. While the list was being read, the King had not taken his eyes off the young girl, who seemed to expand, as it were, beneath the happy influence she felt was shed around her, and who was delighted and too pure in spirit for any other thought than that of love to find an entrance either in her mind or her heart. Acknowledging this touching self-denial by the fixedness of his attention, the King showed La Vallière how much he appreciated its delicacy. When the list was finished, the different faces of those who had been omitted or forgotten fully expressed their disappointment. Malicorne also was forgotten among the number of men; and the grimace he made plainly said to Montalais, who was also forgotten, 'Cannot we contrive to arrange matters with Fortune in such a manner that she shall not forget us?' to which a smile full of intelligence from Mademoiselle Aure, replied: 'Certainly we can.'

The tickets were distributed to each person according to the number held. The King received his first, next the Queen-Mother, then Monsieur, then the Queen and Madame, and so on. After this, Anne of Austria opened a small Spanish leather bag, containing two hundred numbers engraved upon small balls of mother-of-pearl and presented the open sack to the youngest of her maids of honour, for the purpose of taking one of the balls out of it. The eager expectation, amidst all these tediously slow preparations, was rather that of avidity than of curiosity. Saint-Aignan bent towards Mademoiselle de Tonnay-Charente to whisper to her, 'Since we have each a number, let us unite our two chances. The bracelets shall be yours if I win, and if you are successful deign to give me but one look of your beautiful eyes.'

'No,' said Athenaïs, 'if you win the bracelets keep them; every one for himself.'

'You are without any pity,' said Saint-Aignan, 'and I will punish you by a quatrain:—

> 'Beautiful Iris, to my vows
> You are too opposed——'

'Silence,' said Athenaïs, 'you will prevent me hearing the winning number.'

'Number one,' said the young girl who had drawn the mother-of-pearl from the Spanish leather bag.

'The King!' exclaimed the Queen-Mother.

'The King has won,' repeated the Queen delightedly.

'Oh! the King! your dream!' said Madame joyously, in the ear of Anne of Austria.

The King was the only one who did not exhibit any satisfaction. He merely thanked Fortune for what she had done for him, in addressing a slight salutation to the young girl who had been chosen as her proxy. Then, receiving from the hands of Anne of Austria, amid the eager desire of the whole assembly, the casket enclosing the bracelets, he said, 'Are these bracelets really beautiful, then?'

'Look at them,' said Anne of Austria, 'and judge for yourself.'

The King looked at them, and said, 'Yes, indeed, an admirable medallion. What perfect finish!'

'What perfect finish!' repeated Madame.

Queen Maria Theresa easily saw, and that, too, at the very first glance, that the King would not offer the bracelets to her; but, as he did not seem either the least degree in the world disposed to offer them to Madame, she felt almost satisfied, or nearly so. The King sat down. The most intimate among the courtiers approached, one by one, for the purpose of admiring more closely the beautiful piece of workmanship, which soon, with the King's permission, was handed about from person to person. Immediately, every one, connoisseurs or not, uttered various exclamations of surprise, and overwhelmed the King with congratulations. There was, in fact, something for everybody to admire—the brilliants for some and the cutting for others. The ladies present visibly displayed their impatience to see such a treasure monopolised by the gentlemen.

'Gentlemen, gentlemen,' said the King, whom nothing escaped, 'one would almost think that you wore bracelets as the Sabines* used to do; hand them for a little while for the inspection of the ladies, who seem to me to have, and with far greater right, some excuse for understanding such matters better than you.'

These words appeared to Madame the commencement of a decision she expected. She gathered, besides, this happy belief from the glances of the Queen-Mother. The courtier who held them at the moment the King made this remark, amidst the general agitation, hastened to place the bracelets in the hands of the Queen, Maria Theresa, who, knowing too well, poor woman, that they were not destined for her, hardly looked at them, and almost immediately passed them on to Madame. The latter, and—even more minutely than herself—Monsieur, gave the bracelets a long look of anxious and almost covetous desire. She then handed the jewels to those ladies who were near her, pronouncing this single word, but with an accent which was worth a long phrase, 'Magnificent!'

The ladies who had received the bracelets from Madame's hands looked at them as long as they chose to examine them, and then made them circulate by passing them on towards the right. During this time the King was tranquilly conversing with de Guiche and Fouquet, rather letting them talk than himself listening. Accustomed to the set form of ordinary phrases, his ear, like that of all men who exercise an incontestable superiority over others, merely selected from the conversations held in various directions the indispensable word which requires reply. His attention, however, was now elsewhere, for it wandered as his eyes did.

Mademoiselle de Tonnay-Charente was the last of the ladies inscribed for tickets; and, as if she had ranked according to her name upon the list, she only had Montalais and La Vallière after her. When the bracelets reached these two latter, no one appeared to take any further notice of them. The humble hands which for a moment touched these jewels deprived them of all their importance—a circumstance which did not, however, prevent Montalais from starting with joy and envy, covetous desire, at the sight of the beautiful stones still more than at their magnificent workmanship. It is evident that if she were compelled to decide between the pecuniary value and the artistic beauty, Montalais would unhesitatingly have preferred diamonds to cameos, and her disinclination, therefore, to pass them to her companion, La Vallière, was very great. La Vallière fixed a look almost of indifference upon the jewels.

'Oh, how beautiful, how magnificent these bracelets are!' exclaimed Montalais; 'and yet you do not go into ecstasies about them, Louise! You are no true woman, I am sure.'

'Yes, I am indeed,' replied the young girl, with an accent of the most charming melancholy; 'but why desire that which cannot be ours?'

The King, his head bent forward, listened to what the young girl was saying. Hardly had the vibration of her voice reached his ear than he rose radiant with delight, and passing across the whole assembly, from the place where he stood, to La Vallière, 'You are mistaken, mademoiselle,' he said; 'you are a woman, and every woman has a right to wear jewels, which are a woman's property.'

'Oh, sire!' said La Vallière, 'your Majesty will not absolutely believe my modesty?'

'I believe you possess every virtue, mademoiselle; frankness as well as every other; I entreat you, therefore, to say frankly what you think of these bracelets?'

'That they are beautiful, sire, and cannot be offered to any other than a queen.'

'I am delighted that such is your opinion, mademoiselle; the bracelets are yours, and the King begs your acceptance of them.'

And as with a movement almost resembling terror, La Vallière eagerly held out the casket to the King, the King gently pushed back La Vallière's trembling hand. A silence of astonishment, more profound than that of death, reigned in the assembly. And yet, from the side where the Queens were, no one had heard what he had said, nor understood what he had done. A charitable friend, however, took upon herself to spread the news; it was Tonnay-Charente, to whom Madame had made a sign to approach.

'Good heavens!' exclaimed Tonnay-Charente, 'how happy that La Vallière is! the King has just given her the bracelets.'

Madame bit her lips to such a degree that the blood appeared upon the surface of the skin. The young Queen looked first at La Vallière and then at Madame, and began to laugh. Anne of Austria rested her chin upon her beautiful white hand, and remained for a long time absorbed by a suspicion which disturbed her mind and by a terrible pang which stung her heart. De Guiche, observing Madame turn pale, and guessing the cause of her change of colour, abruptly quitted the assembly and disappeared. Malicorne was then able to approach Montalais very quietly, and under cover of the general din of conversation, said to her:—

'Aure, you have our fortune and our future close beside you.'

'Yes,' was her reply, as she tenderly embraced La Vallière, whom, inwardly, she was tempted to strangle.

XLVIII

MALAGA

DURING the continuance of the long and violent debates between the opposite ambitions of the court and those of the heart, one of our characters, the least deserving of neglect, perhaps, was, however, very much neglected, very much forgotten, and exceedingly unhappy. In fact, d'Artagnan, we say, for we must call him by his name, to remind our readers of his existence— d'Artagnan, we repeat, had absolutely nothing whatever to do, amid this brilliant, light-hearted world of fashion. After having followed the King during two whole days at Fontainebleau, and having critically observed all the pastoral fancies and heroico-comic transformations of his sovereign, the musketeer felt that he needed something more than this to satisfy the cravings of his existence. At every moment assailed by people asking him, 'How do you think this costume suits me, Monsieur d'Artagnan?' he would reply to them in quiet sarcastic tones, 'Why, I think, you are quite as well dressed as the best dressed monkey to be found in the fair of Saint-Laurent.'* It was just such a compliment as d'Artagnan would choose to pay, where he did not feel disposed to pay any other; and, whether agreeable or not, the inquirer was obliged to be satisfied with it. Whenever any one asked him, 'How do you intend to dress yourself this evening?' he replied, 'I shall undress myself'; at which all the ladies laughed. But after a couple of days passed in this manner, the musketeer, perceiving that nothing serious was likely to arise which would concern him, and that the King had completely or, at least, appeared to have completely, forgotten Paris, Saint-Mandé, and Belle-Isle—that M. Colbert's mind was occupied with illuminations and fireworks—that for the next month, at least, the ladies had plenty of glances to bestow, and also to receive in exchange; d'Artagnan asked the King for leave of absence for a matter of private business. At the moment d'Artagnan made his request His Majesty was on the point of going to bed, quite exhausted from dancing.

'You wish to leave me, Monsieur d'Artagnan?' inquired the King, with an air of astonishment; for Louis XIV could never understand that any one who had the distinguished honour of being near him could wish to leave him.

'Sire,' said d'Artagnan, 'I leave you simply because I am not of the slightest service to you in anything. Ah! if I could only hold the balancing-pole while you were dancing, it would be a very different affair.'

'But, my dear Monsieur d'Artagnan,' said the King gravely, 'people dance without a balancing-pole.'

'Ah! indeed,' said the musketeer, continuing his imperceptible tone of irony, 'I had no idea.'

'You have not seen me dance, then?' inquired the King.

'Yes; but I always thought it would make you firmer. I was mistaken; a greater reason, therefore, that I should leave for a time. Sire, I repeat, you have no present occasion for my services; besides, if your Majesty should have any need of me, you would know where to find me.'

'Very well,' said the King, and he granted him his leave of absence.

We shall not look for d'Artagnan, therefore, at Fontainebleau, for this would be quite useless; but, with the permission of our readers, we shall follow him to the Rue des Lombards, where he was located at the sign of the Golden Pestle, in the house of our old friend Planchet.* It was about eight o'clock in the evening, and the weather was exceedingly warm; there was only one window open, and that one belonging to a room on the entresol. A perfume of spices, mingled with another perfume less exotic, but more penetrating, namely, that which arose from the street, ascended to salute the nostrils of the musketeer. D'Artagnan, reclining upon an immense straight-backed chair, with his legs not stretched out, but simply placed up on a stool, formed an angle of the most obtuse form that could possibly be seen. Both his arms were crossed over his head, his head reclining upon his left shoulder, like Alexander the Great. His eyes, usually so quick and intelligent in their expression, were now half-closed, and seemed fastened, as it were, upon a small corner of blue sky which was visible behind the opening of the chimneys; there was just enough blue, and no more, to put a piece into one of sacks of lentils, or haricots, which formed the principal furniture of the shop on the ground-floor. Thus extended at his ease, and thus sheltered in his place of observation behind the window, d'Artagnan seemed as if he had ceased to be a soldier, as if he were no longer an officer belonging to the palace, but was, on the contrary, a quiet, easy-going citizen in a state of stagnation between his dinner and supper, or between his supper and his bed; one of those strong, ossified brains, which have no more room for a single idea, so fiercely does animal matter keep watch at the doors of intelligence, narrowly inspecting the contraband trade which might result from the introduction into the brain of a symptom of thought. We have already said night was closing in, the shops were being lighted, while the windows of the upper apartments were being closed, and the irregular steps of a patrol of soldiers forming the night-watch could be heard in the distance. D'Artagnan continued, however, to think of nothing, and to look at nothing, except the blue corner of the sky. A few paces from him, completely in the shade, lying on his stomach upon a sack of Indian corn, was Planchet, with both his arms under his chin and his eyes fixed on d'Artagnan, who was either thinking, dreaming, or sleeping, with his eyes open. Planchet had been watching him for a tolerably long time, and, by way of interruption, he began by exclaiming, 'Hum! hum!' But d'Artagnan did not stir. Planchet then saw that it was necessary to have recourse to a more effectual means still: after a prolonged reflection on the subject, the most ingenious means which suggested itself to him under present circumstances was to let himself roll off the sack on to the floor, murmuring, at the same time, against himself, the word 'stupid'. But, notwithstanding the noise produced by Planchet's fall, d'Artagnan, who had in the course of his existence heard many other, and very different noises, did not appear to pay the least attention to the present one. Besides, an enormous cart, laden with stones, passing from la Rue Saint-Médéric,* absorbed, in the noise of its wheels, the noise of Planchet's fall. And yet Planchet fancied that, in token of tacit approval, he saw him imperceptibly smile at the word 'stupid'. This emboldened him to say, 'Are you asleep, Monsieur d'Artagnan?'

'No, Planchet, I am not *even* asleep,' replied the musketeer.

'I am in despair,' said Planchet, 'to hear such a word as *even*.'

'Well, and why not; is it not a good French word, Monsieur Planchet?'

'Of course, Monsieur d'Artagnan.'

'Well!'

'Well, then, the word distresses me beyond measure.'

'Tell me why you are distressed, Planchet,' said d'Artagnan.

'If you say that you are not *even* asleep, it is as much as to say that you have not even the consolation of being able to sleep; or, better still, it is precisely the same as telling me that you are bored to death.'

'Planchet, you know I am never bored.'

'Except to-day, and the day before yesterday.'

'Bah!'

'Monsieur d'Artagnan, it is a week* since you returned here from Fontainebleau; in other words, you have no longer your orders to issue, or your men to review and manœuvre. You need the sound of guns, drums, and all that din and confusion; I who have myself carried a musket can easily believe that.'

'Planchet,' replied d'Artagnan, 'I assure you I am not the least bored.'

'In that case, what are you doing, lying there, as if you were dead?'

'My dear Planchet, there was, once upon a time, at the siege of La Rochelle,* when I was there, when you were there, when we both were there, a certain Arab, who was celebrated for the manner in which he aimed culverins.* He was a clever fellow, although very singular with regard to his complexion, which was the same colour as your olives. Well, this Arab, whenever he had done eating or working, used to sit down to rest himself, as I am resting myself now, and smoked I cannot tell you what sort of magical leaves,* in a large amber-mouthed tube; and if any officer, happening to pass, reproached him for being always asleep, he used quietly to reply: "Better to sit down than to stand up, to lie down than to sit down, to be dead than to lie down." He was a very melancholy Arab, and I remember him perfectly well, from his colour and his style of conversation. He used to cut off the heads of the Protestants with extreme satisfaction.'

'Precisely; and then used to embalm them, when they were worth the trouble.'

'Yes; and when he was engaged in his embalming occupations, with his herbs and other plants about him, he looked like a basket-maker making baskets.'

'You are quite right, Planchet, he did so.'

'Oh! I can remember things very well, at times!'

'I have no doubt of it; but what do you think of his mode of reasoning?'

'I think it very good in one sense, but very stupid in another.'

'Propound your meaning, M. Planchet.'

'Well, monsieur, in point of fact, then, "better to sit down than to stand up," is plain enough, especially when one may be fatigued under certain circumstances,' and Planchet smiled in a roguish way; 'as for "better to be lying down than sitting down," let that pass; but as for the last proposition, that it is "better to be dead than alive," it is, in my opinion, very absurd, my own undoubted preference being for my bed; and if you are not of my opinion, it is simply, as I have already had the honour of telling you, because you are boring yourself to death.'

'Planchet, do you know M. la Fontaine?'

'The chemist at the corner of the Rue Saint-Médéric?'

'No, the writer of fables.'

'Oh! *Maître Corbeau*!'

'Exactly so; well, then, I am like his hare.'*

'He has got a hare also, then?'

'He has all sorts of animals.'

'Well, what does his hare do, then?'

'His hare thinks.'

'Ah, ah!'

'Planchet, I am like M. la Fontaine's hare—I am thinking.'

'You're thinking, you say?' said Planchet uneasily.

'Yes; your house is dull enough to drive people to think; you will admit that, I hope.'

'And yet, monsieur, you have a look out upon the street.'

'Yes; and wonderfully interesting that is, of course.'

'But it is no less true, monsieur, that, if you were living at the back of the house, you would bore yourself—I mean, you would think—more than ever.'

'Upon my word, Planchet, I hardly know that.'

'Still,' said the grocer, 'if your reflections were at all like those which led you to restore King Charles II——'* and Planchet finished by a little laugh which was not without its meaning.

'Ah! Planchet, my friend,' returned d'Artagnan—'you are getting ambitious.'

'Is there no other king to be restored, M. d'Artagnan—no other Monk to be put into a box?'*

'No, my dear Planchet; all the kings are seated on their various thrones—less comfortably so, perhaps, than I am upon this chair; but at all events, there they are.' And d'Artagnan sighed very deeply.

'Monsieur d'Artagnan,' said Planchet, 'you are making me very uneasy.'

'You're very good, Planchet.'

'I begin to suspect something.'

'What is it?'

'Monsieur d'Artagnan, you are getting thin.'

'Oh!' said d'Artagnan, striking his chest, which sounded like an empty cuirass; 'that is impossible, Planchet.'

'Ah!' said Planchet, slightly overcome; 'if you were to get thin in my house——'

'Well?'

'I should do something rash.'

'What would you do? tell me.'

'I should look out for the man who was the cause of all your anxieties.'

'Ah! according to your account I am anxious now.'

'Yes, you are anxious; and you are getting thin, visibly getting thin. *Malaga!* if you go on getting thin in this way, I will take my sword in my hand, and go straight to M. d'Herblay, and have it out with him.'

'What!' said d'Artagnan, starting in his chair; 'what's that you say? And what has M. d'Herblay's name to do with your groceries?'

'Just as you please. Get angry if you like, or call me names— if you prefer it; but, the deuce is in it, I know what I know.'

D'Artagnan had, during this second outburst of Planchet, so placed himself as not to miss a single look of his face; that is, he sat with both his hands resting on both his knees, and his head stretched out towards the grocer. 'Come, explain yourself,' he said, 'and tell me how you could possibly utter such a blasphemy. M. d'Herblay, your old master, my friend, an ecclesiastic, a musketeer turned bishop—do you mean to say you would raise your sword against him, Planchet?'

'I could raise my sword against my own father, when I see you in such a state as you are now.'

'M. d'Herblay, a gentleman!'

'It's all the same to me whether he's a gentleman or not. He gives you the blue devils, that is all I know. And the blue devils make people get thin. *Malaga!* I have no notion of M. d'Artagnan leaving my house thinner than he entered it.'

'How does he give me the blue devils as you call it? Come, explain, explain.'

'You have had a nightmare during the last three nights.'

'I?'

'Yes, you; and in your nightmare you called out several times, "Aramis, sly Aramis!"'

'Ah! I said that, did I?' said d'Artagnan uneasily.

'Yes, those very words, upon my honour.'

'Well, what else? You know the saying, Planchet, "dreams go by contraries."'

'Not so; for, every time during the last three days when you went out, you have not once failed to ask me on your return, "Have you seen M. d'Herblay?" or else, "Have you received any letters for me from M. d'Herblay?" '

'Well, it is very natural I should take an interest in my old friend,' said d'Artagnan.

'Of course; but not to such an extent as to get thin from it.'

'Planchet, I'll get fatter; I give you my word of honour I will.'

'Very well, monsieur, I accept it; for I know that when you give your word of honour, it is sacred.'

'I will not dream of Aramis any longer; and I will never ask you again if there are any letters from M. d'Herblay; but on condition that you explain one thing to me.'

'Tell me what it is, monsieur?'

'I am a great observer, and just now you made use of a very singular oath, which is unusual for you.'

'You mean *Malaga!* I suppose?'

'Precisely.'

'It is the oath I have used ever since I have been a grocer.'

'Very proper, too; it is the name of a dried grape, or raisin,* I believe?'

'It is my most ferocious oath; when I have once said *Malaga!* I am a man no longer.'

'Still, I never knew you use that oath before.'

'Very likely not, monsieur. I had a present made me of it,' said Planchet; and as he pronounced these words, he winked his eye with a cunning expression, which thoroughly awakened d'Artagnan's attention.

'Come, come, M. Planchet.'

'Why, I am not like you, monsieur,' said Planchet. 'I don't pass my life in thinking.'

'You are wrong then.'

'I mean in boring myself to death. We have but a very short time to live—why not make the best of it?'

'You are an Epicurean philosopher,* I begin to think, Planchet.'

'Why not? My hand is still as steady as ever; I can write, and can weigh out my sugars and spices; my foot is firm; I can dance and walk about; my stomach has its teeth still, for I eat and digest well; my heart is not quite hardened. Well, monsieur?'

'Well, what, Planchet?'

'Why, you see——' said the grocer, rubbing his hands together.

D'Artagnan crossed one leg over the other, and said, 'Planchet, my dear friend, I am astounded by surprise; for you are revealing yourself to me under a perfectly new light.'

Planchet, flattered in the highest degree by this remark, continued to rub his hands very hard together. 'Ah, ah!' he said, 'because I happen to be only stupid, you think me, perhaps, a positive fool.'

'Very good, Planchet; very well reasoned.'

'Follow my idea, monsieur, if you please. I said to myself,' continued Planchet, 'that, without enjoyment, there is no happiness on this earth.'

'Quite true, what you say, Planchet,' interrupted d'Artagnan.

'At all events, if we cannot obtain pleasure—for pleasure is not so common a thing after all—let us, at least, get consolations of some kind or other.'

'And so you console yourself?'

'Exactly so.'

'Tell me how you console yourself.'

'I put on a buckler for the purpose of confronting ennui. I place my time at the direction of patience; and on the very eve of feeling I am going to get bored, I amuse myself.'

'And you don't find any difficulty in that?'

'None.'

'And you found it out quite by yourself?'

'Quite so.'

'It is miraculous.'

'What do you say?'

'I say that your philosophy is not to be matched in the whole world.'

'You think so?—follow my example then.'

'It is a very tempting one.'

'Do as I do.'

'I could not wish for anything better; but all minds are not of the same stamp; and it might possibly happen that if I were required to amuse myself in the manner you do, I should bore myself horribly.'

'Bah! at least try it first.'

'Well, tell me what you do.'

'Have you observed that I leave home occasionally?'

'Yes.'

'In any particular way?'

'Periodically.'

'That's the very thing. You have noticed it then?'

'My dear Planchet, you must understand that when people see each other every day, and one of the two absents himself, the other misses him. Do not you feel the want of my society when I am in the country?'

'Prodigiously; that is to say I feel like a body without a soul.'

'That being understood, then, let us go on.'

'What are the periods when I absent myself?'

'On the fifteenth and thirtieth of every month.'

'And I remain away?'

'Sometimes two, sometimes three, and sometimes four days at a time.'

'Have you ever given it a thought what I have been absent for?'

'To look after your debts, I suppose.'

'And when I returned, how did you think I looked, as far as my face was concerned?'

'Exceedingly satisfied.'

'You admit, you say, that I always look very satisfied. And what have you attributed my satisfaction to?'

'That your business was going on very well; that your purchases of rice, prunes, raw sugar, dried apples and pears, and treacle, were advantageous. You were always very picturesque in your notions and ideas, Planchet; and I was not in the slightest degree surprised to find you had selected grocery as an occupation, which is of all trades the most varied, and the very pleasantest, as far as character is concerned; inasmuch as one handles so many natural and perfumed productions.'

'Perfectly true, monsieur; but you are very greatly mistaken.'

'In what way?'

'In thinking that I leave here every fortnight to collect my money, or to make purchases. Oh, oh! how could you have

possibly thought such a thing? Oh, oh, oh!' And Planchet began
to laugh in a manner that inspired d'Artagnan with very serious
misgivings as to his sanity.

'I confess,' said the musketeer, 'that I do not precisely catch
your meaning.'

'Very true, monsieur.'

'What do you mean by "very true"?'

'It must be true, since you say it; but pray, be assured that it
in no way lessens my opinion of you.'

'Ah! that is very fortunate.'

'No; you are a man of genius; and whenever the question
happens to be of war, tactics, surprises, or good honest blows to
be dealt, why, kings are all nonsense compared to you. But for the
consolations of the mind, the proper care of the body, the agreeable things of life, if one may say so—ah! monsieur, don't talk to
me about men of genius; they are nothing short of executioners.'

'Good,' said d'Artagnan, quite fidgety with curiosity, 'upon
my word you interest me in the highest degree.'

'You feel already less bored than you did just now, do you
not?'

'I was not bored; yet since you have been talking to me I feel
more amused.'

'Very good, then; that is not a bad beginning. I will cure you,
rely upon that.'

'There is nothing I should like better.'

'Will you let me try, then?'

'Immediately, if you like.'

'Very well. Have you any horses here?'

'Yes; ten, twenty, thirty.'

'Oh, there is no occasion for so many as that; two will be quite
sufficient.'

'They are quite at your disposal, Planchet.'

'Very good; then I shall carry you off with me.'

'When?'

'To-morrow.'

'Where?'

'Ah, you are asking me too much.'

'You will admit, however, that it is important I should know
where I am going.'

'Do you like the country?'

'Only moderately, Planchet.'

'In that case you like town better?'

'That is as it may be.'

'Very well; I am going to take you to a place, half town and half country.'

'Good.'

'To a place where I am sure you will amuse yourself.'

'Is it possible?'

'Yes; and more wonderful still, to a place from which you have just returned, for the purpose only, it would seem, of getting bored here.'

'It is to Fontainebleau you are going, then?'

'Exactly; to Fontainebleau.'

'And, in Heaven's name, what are you going to do at Fontainebleau?'

Planchet answered d'Artagnan with a wink full of sly humour.

'You have some property there, you sly rascal.'

'Oh, a very paltry affair; a little bit of a house—nothing more.'

'I understand you.'

'But it is tolerable enough, after all.'

'I am going to Planchet's country seat!' exclaimed d'Artagnan.

'Whenever you like.'

'Did we not fix to-morrow?'

'Let us say to-morrow, if you like; and then, besides, to-morrow is the fourteenth,* that is to say, the day before the one when I am afraid of getting bored; so we will look upon it as an understood thing.'

'Agreed, by all means.'

'You will lend me one of your horses?'

'The best I have.'

'No; I prefer the gentlest of all; I never was a very good rider, as you know, and in my grocery business I have got more awkward than ever; besides——'

'Besides what?'

'Why,' added Planchet, 'I do not wish to fatigue myself.'

'Why so?' d'Artagnan ventured to ask.

'Because I should lose half the pleasure I expect to enjoy,' replied Planchet. And thereupon he rose from his sack of Indian corn, stretching himself, and making all his bones crack, one after the other, with a sort of harmony.

'Planchet, Planchet,' exclaimed d'Artagnan, 'I do declare that there is no sybarite upon the whole face of the globe who can for a moment be compared to you. Oh, Planchet, it is very clear that we have never yet eaten a ton of salt together.'

'Why so, monsieur?'

'Because even now I can scarcely say I know you,' said d'Artagnan, 'and because, in point of fact, I return to the opinion which, for a moment, I had formed of you on that day at Boulogne,* when you strangled, or did so as nearly as possible, M. de Wardes's valet, Lubin; in plain language, Planchet, that you are a man of great resources.'

Planchet began to laugh with a laugh full of self-conceit; bade the musketeer good-night, and went downstairs to his back shop, which he used as a bedroom. D'Artagnan resumed his original position upon his chair, and his brow, which had been unruffled for a moment, became more pensive than ever. He had already forgotten the whims and dreams of Planchet. 'Yes,' said he, taking up again the thread of his thoughts, which had been broken by the agreeable conversation in which we have just permitted our readers to participate. 'Yes, yes, those three points include everything; First, to ascertain what Baisemeaux wanted with Aramis; secondly, to learn why Aramis does not let me hear from him; and thirdly, to ascertain where Porthos is. The whole mystery lies in these three points. Since, therefore,' continued d'Artagnan, 'our friends tell us nothing, we must have recourse to our own poor intelligence. I must do what I can, *mordioux*,* or rather *Malaga*, as Planchet would say.'

XLIX

A LETTER FROM M. DE BAISEMEAUX

D'ARTAGNAN, faithful to his plan, went the very next morning to pay a visit to M. de Baisemeaux. It was the cleaning-up or tidying day at the Bastille; the cannons were furbished up, the staircases scraped and cleaned; and the jailers seemed to be carefully engaged in polishing even the keys themselves. As for the soldiers belonging to the garrison, they were walking about in the different courtyards, under the pretence that they were clean enough. The governor, Baisemeaux, received d'Artagnan with more than ordinary politeness, but he behaved towards him with so marked a reserve of manner, that all d'Artagnan's tact and cleverness could not get a syllable out of him. The more he kept himself within bounds, the more d'Artagnan's suspicion increased. The latter even fancied he remarked that the governor was acting under the influence of a recent recommendation. Baisemeaux had not been at the Palais Royal* with d'Artagnan the same cold and impenetrable man which the latter now found in the Baisemeaux of the Bastille. When d'Artagnan wished to make him talk about the urgent money matters which had brought Baisemeaux in search of d'Artagnan, and had rendered him expansive; notwithstanding what had passed on that evening, Baisemeaux pretended that he had some orders to give in the prison, and left d'Artagnan so long alone, waiting for him, that our musketeer, feeling sure that he should not get another syllable out of him, left the Bastille without waiting until Baisemeaux returned from his inspection. But d'Artagnan's suspicions were aroused, and when once that was the case, d'Artagnan could not sleep or remain quiet for a moment. He was among men what the cat is among quadrupeds, the emblem of restlessness and impatience, at the same moment. A restless cat no more remains in the same place than a silk thread does which is wafted idly to and fro with every breath of air. A cat on the watch is as motionless as death stationed at its place of observation, and neither hunger nor thirst can possibly draw it away from its meditation. D'Artagnan, who was burning with impatience, suddenly threw aside the feeling, like a cloak which he felt too heavy on his shoulders, and said to himself that what they were concealing from him was the very thing it was important he should know; and, consequently, he reasoned that Baisemeaux would not fail to put Aramis on his guard, if Aramis had given him any particular recommendation, and which was, in fact, the very thing that did happen.

Baisemeaux had hardly had time to return from the donjon,

than d'Artagnan placed himself in ambuscade close to the Rue
du Petit-Musc, so as to see every one who might leave the gates
of the Bastille. After he had spent an hour on the look-out from
the Golden Portcullis,* under the penthouse of which he could
keep himself a little in the shade, d'Artagnan observed a soldier
leave the Bastille. This was, indeed, the surest indication he
could possibly have wished for, as every jailer or warder has
certain days, and even certain hours, for leaving the Bastille,
since all are alike prohibited from having either wives or lodgings in the castle, and can accordingly leave without exciting any
curiosity; but a soldier once in barracks is kept there for four-
and-twenty hours when on duty,—and no one knew this better
than d'Artagnan. The soldier in question, therefore, was not
likely to leave in his regimentals except on an express and urgent
order. The soldier, we were saying, left the Bastille at a slow and
lounging pace, like a happy mortal, in fact, who, instead of
keeping sentry before a wearisome guard-house, or upon a bas-
tion no less wearisome, has the good luck to get a little liberty,
in addition to a walk—the two pleasures being reckoned as part
of his time on duty. He bent his steps towards the Faubourg
Saint-Antoine,* enjoying the fresh air and the warmth of the
sun, and looking at all the pretty faces he passed. D'Artagnan
followed him at a distance; he had not yet arranged his ideas as
to what was to be done. 'I must first of all,' he thought, 'see the
fellow's face. A man seen is a man judged of.' D'Artagnan
increased his pace, and, which was not very difficult, by the bye
soon got in advance of the soldier. Not only did he observe that
his face showed a tolerable amount of intelligence and resolution,
but he noticed also that his nose was a little red. 'He has a
weakness for brandy,* I see,' said d'Artagnan to himself. At the
same moment that he remarked his red nose, he saw that the
soldier had a white paper in his belt. 'Good, he has a letter,'
added d'Artagnan. The only difficulty was to get hold of the
letter. But a soldier would, of course, be too delighted at having
been selected by M. de Baisemeaux for a special messenger, and
would not be likely to sell his message. As d'Artagnan was biting
his nails, the soldier continued to advance more and more into
the Faubourg Saint-Antoine. 'He is certainly going to Saint-
Mandé,' he said to himself, 'and I shall not be able to learn what

the letter contains.' It was enough to drive him wild. 'If I were in uniform,' said d'Artagnan to himself, 'I would have this fellow seized, and his letter with him. I could easily get assistance at the very first guard-house; but the devil take me if I mention my name in an affair of this kind. If I were to treat him to something to drink, his suspicions would be roused; and besides, he would make me drunk. *Mordioux!* my wits seem to have left me,' said d'Artagnan; 'it is all over with me. Yet, supposing I were to attack this poor devil, make him draw his sword, and kill him for the sake of his letter. No harm in that, if it were a question of a letter from a queen to a nobleman, or a letter from a cardinal to a queen; but what miserable intrigues are those of Messieurs Aramis and Fouquet with M. Colbert. A man's life for that! No, no, indeed; not even ten crowns.' As he philosophised in this manner, biting first his nails and then his moustaches, he perceived a group of archers and an inspector of the police* engaged in forcibly carrying away a man of very gentlemanly exterior, who was struggling with all his might against them. The archers had torn his clothes, and were dragging him roughly away. He begged they would lead him along more respectfully, asserting that he was a gentleman and a soldier. And observing our soldier walking in the street, he called out, 'Help, comrade.'

The soldier walked on with the same step towards the man who had called out to him, followed by the crowd. An idea suddenly occurred to d'Artagnan; it was his first one, and we shall find it was not a bad one either. During the time the gentleman was relating to the soldier that he had just been seized in a house as a thief, when the truth was he had only been there as a lover; and while the soldier was pitying him, and offering him consolation and advice, with that gravity which a French soldier has always ready whenever his vanity or his *esprit de corps* is concerned, d'Artagnan glided behind the soldier, who was closely hemmed in by the crowd, and with a rapid gesture drew the paper out of his belt. As at this moment the gentleman with the torn clothes was pulling about the soldier to show how the inspector of police had pulled him about, d'Artagnan effected his capture of the letter without the slightest inconvenience. He stationed himself about ten paces distant, behind the pillar of an adjoining house, and read on the address, 'To Monsieur du Vallon at Monsieur Fouquet's, Saint-Mandé.'

'Good!' he said, and then he unsealed without tearing the letter, drew out the paper, which was folded in four, from the inside, and which contained only these words:—

'DEAR MONSIEUR DE VALLON,—Will you be good enough to tell Monsieur d'Herblay that *he* has been to the Bastille, and has been making inquiries.

'Your devoted DE BAISEMEAUX.'

'Very good! all right!' exclaimed d'Artagnan; 'it is clear enough now. Porthos is involved in this business.' Being now satisfied of what he wished to know; '*Mordioux!*' thought the musketeer, 'what is to be done with that poor devil of a soldier? That hot-headed, cunning fellow de Baisemeaux, will make him pay dearly for my trick,—if he returns without the letter, what will they do to him? Besides, I don't want the letter; when the egg has been sucked, what is the good of the shell?' D'Artagnan perceived that the inspector and the archers of the watch had succeeded in convincing the soldier, and went on their way with the prisoner, the latter being still surrounded by the crowd, and continuing his complaints. D'Artagnan advanced into the very middle of the crowd, let the letter fall, without any one having observed him, and then retreated rapidly. The soldier resumed his route towards Saint-Mandé, his mind occupied with the gentleman who had implored his protection. Suddenly he thought of his letter, and, looking at his belt, saw that it was no longer there. D'Artagnan derived no little satisfaction from his sudden terri-fied cry. The poor soldier in the greatest anguish of mind looked round him on every side, and at last, about twenty paces behind him, he perceived the blessed envelope. He pounced on it like a falcon on its prey. The envelope was certainly a little dusty, and rather crumpled, but at all events the letter itself was found again. D'Artagnan observed that the broken seal attracted the soldier's attention a good deal, but he finished apparently by consoling himself, and returned the letter to his belt. 'Go on,' said d'Artagnan, 'I have plenty of time before me, so you may precede me. It appears that Aramis is not at Paris, since Baisemeaux writes to Porthos. Dear Porthos, how delighted I shall be to see him again, and to have some conversation with him!' said the Gascon. And, regulating his pace according to that of the soldier, he promised himself to arrive a quarter of an hour after him at M. Fouquet's.

L

IN WHICH THE READER WILL BE DELIGHTED TO FIND THAT PORTHOS HAS LOST NOTHING OF HIS STRENGTH

D'ARTAGNAN had, according to his usual style, calculated that every hour is worth sixty minutes, and every minute worth sixty seconds. Thanks to this perfectly exact calculation of minutes and seconds, he reached the superintendant's door at the very moment the soldier was leaving it with his belt empty. D'Artagnan presented himself at the door, which a porter with a profusely embroidered livery held half-opened for him. D'Artagnan would very much have liked to enter without giving his name, but this was impossible, and so he gave it. Notwithstanding this concession, which ought to have removed every difficulty in the way, at least d'Artagnan thought so, the concierge hesitated; however, at the second repetition of the title, captain of the King's Guards, the concierge, without quite leaving the passage clear for him, ceased to bar it completely. D'Artagnan understood that orders of the most positive character had been given. He decided, therefore, to tell a falsehood,*—a circumstance, moreover, which did not very seriously affect his peace of mind, when he saw that beyond the falsehood the safety of the State itself, or even purely and simply his own individual personal interest, might be at stake. He moreover added to the declarations which he had already made that the soldier sent to M. du Vallon was his own messenger, and that the only object that letter had in view was to announce his intended arrival. From that moment no one opposed M. d'Artagnan's entrance any further, and he entered accordingly. A valet wished to accompany him, but he answered that it was useless to take that trouble on his account, inasmuch as he knew perfectly well where M. du Vallon was. There was nothing, of course, to say to a man so thoroughly and completely informed on all points, and d'Artagnan was permitted therefore to do as he liked. The terraces, the magnificent apartments, the gardens, were all reviewed and narrowly inspected by the musketeer. He walked for a quarter of an hour in this more than royal residence, which included as many wonders as articles of furniture, and as many servants as there were columns and doors. 'Decidedly,' he said to himself, 'this mansion has no other limits than the limits of the earth. Is it probable Porthos has taken it into his head to go back to Pierrefonds* without even leaving M. Fouquet's house?' He finally reached a remote part of the château enclosed by a stone wall, which was covered with a profusion of thick plants, luxuriant in blossoms as large and solid as fruit. At equal distances on the top of this wall were placed various statues in modest or mysterious attitudes. These were vestals hidden beneath the long Greek peplum, with its thick, heavy folds; agile watchers, covered with their marble veils, and guarding the palace with their furtive glances. A statue of Hermes, with his fingers on his lips, one of Iris, with extended wings;* another of Night sprinkled all over with poppies, dominated in the gardens and the out-buildings, which could be seen through the trees. All these statues threw in white relief their profiles upon the dark ground of the tall cypresses, which darted their black summits toward the sky. Around these cypresses were entwined climbing roses, whose flowering rings were fastened to every fork of every branch, and spread over the lower branches and upon the various statues showers of flowers of the richest fragrance. These enchantments seemed to the musketeer the result of the greatest efforts of the human mind. He felt in a dreamy, almost poetical frame of mind. The idea that Porthos was living in so perfect an Eden gave him a higher idea of Porthos, showing how true it is, that even the very highest orders of minds are not quite exempt from the influence of surrounding circumstances. D'Artagnan found the door, and at the door a kind of spring which he detected; having touched it, the door flew open. D'Artagnan entered, closed the door behind him, and advanced into a pavilion built in a circular form, in which no other sound could be heard but cascades and the songs of birds. At the door of the pavilion he met a lackey.

'It is here, I believe,' said d'Artagnan without hesitation, 'that M. le Baron du Vallon is staying?'

'Yes, monsieur,' answered the lackey.

'Have the goodness to tell him that M. le Chevalier d'Artagnan, captain of the King's musketeers, is waiting to see him.'

D'Artagnan was introduced into the salon, and had not long to remain in expectation; a well-remembered step shook the floor of the adjoining room, a door opened, or rather flew open, and Porthos appeared, and threw himself into his friend's arms with a sort of embarrassment which did not ill become him. 'You here?' he exclaimed.

'And you?' replied d'Artagnan. 'Ah, you shy fellow!'

'Yes,' said Porthos with a somewhat embarrassed smile; 'yes, you see I am staying in M. Fouquet's house, at which you are not a little surprised, I suppose?'

'Not at all; why should you not be one of M. Fouquet's friends? M. Fouquet has a very large number, particularly among clever men.'

Porthos had the modesty not to take the compliment to himself.

'Besides,' he added, 'you saw me at Belle-Isle.'*

'A greater reason for believing you to be one of M. Fouquet's friends.'

'The fact is I am acquainted with him,' said Porthos with a certain embarrassment of manner.

'Ah, friend Porthos,' said d'Artagnan, 'how treacherously you have behaved towards me.'

'In what way?' exclaimed Porthos.

'What! you complete so admirable a work as the fortifications of Belle-Isle, and you did not tell me of it!' Porthos coloured. 'Nay, more than that,' continued d'Artagnan, 'you saw me out yonder, you know I am in the King's service, and yet you could not guess that the King, jealously desirous of learning the name of the man whose abilities have wrought a work of which he has heard the most wonderful accounts,—you could not guess, I say, that the King sent me to learn who this man was?'

'What! the King sent you to learn——'

'Of course, but don't let us speak of that any more.'

'Not speak of it!' said Porthos; 'on the contrary, we will speak of it; and so the King knew that we were fortifying Belle-Isle?'

'Of course; does not the King know everything?'

'But he did not know who was fortifying it?'

'No, he only suspected from what he had been told of the nature of the works, that it was some celebrated soldier or another.'

'The devil!' said Porthos; 'if I had only known that!'

'You would not have run away from Vannes* as you did, perhaps?'

'No; what did you say when you couldn't find me?'

'My dear fellow, I reflected.'

'Ah, indeed; you reflect, do you? Well, and what has that reflection led to?'

'It led me to guess the whole truth.'

'Come, then, tell me, what did you guess after all?' said Porthos, settling himself into an arm-chair, and assuming the airs of a sphinx.

'I guessed, in the first place, that you were fortifying Belle-Isle.'

'There was no great difficulty in that, for you saw me at work.'

'Wait a minute; I also guessed something else—that you were fortifying Belle-Isle by M. Fouquet's orders.'

'That's true.'

'But not all. Whenever I feel myself in train for guessing, I do not stop on my road; and so I guessed that M. Fouquet wished to preserve the most absolute secrecy respecting these fortifications.'

'I believe that was his intention, in fact,' said Porthos.

'Yes; but do you know why he wished to keep it secret?'

'Because it should not be known, perhaps,' said Porthos.

'That was his principal reason. But his wish was subservient to an affair of generosity——'

'In fact,' said Porthos, 'I have heard it said that M. Fouquet was a very generous man.'

'To an affair of generosity which he wished to exhibit towards the King.'

'Oh, oh!'

'You seem surprised at it?'

'Yes.'

'And you did not know that?'

'No.'

'Well, I know it, then.'

'You're a wizard.'

'Not in the slightest degree.'

'How do you know it, then?'

'By a very simple means. I heard M. Fouquet himself say so to the King.'

'Say what to the King?'

'That he had fortified Belle-Isle on His Majesty's account, and that he made him a present of Belle-Isle.'*

'And you heard M. Fouquet say that to the King?'

'In those very words. He even added, "Belle-Isle has been fortified by an engineer, one of my friends, a man of a great deal of merit, whom I shall ask your Majesty's permission to present to you."

'"What is his name?" said the King.

'"The Baron du Vallon," M. Fouquet replied.

'"Very well," returned His Majesty, "you will present him to me."

'The King said that?'

'Upon the word of a d'Artagnan!'

'Oh, oh!' said Porthos. 'Why have I not been presented, then?'

'Have they not spoken to you about this presentation?'

'Yes, certainly; but I am always kept waiting for it.'

'Be easy, it will be sure to come.'

'Humph! humph!' grumbled Porthos, which d'Artagnan pretended not to hear; and, changing the conversation, he said, 'You seem to be living in a very solitary place here, my dear fellow?'

'I always preferred retirement. I am of a melancholy disposition,' replied Porthos with a sigh.

'Really, that is odd,' said d'Artagnan; 'I never remarked that before.'

'It is only since I have taken to reading,' said Porthos with a thoughtful air.

'But the labours of the mind have not affected the health of the body, I trust.'

'Not in the slightest degree.'

'Your strength is as great as ever?'

'Too great, my friend, too great.'

'Ah! I had heard that, for a short time after your arrival——'

'That I could hardly move a limb, I suppose.'

'How was it?' said d'Artagnan, smiling; 'and why was it you could not move?'

Porthos, perceiving that he had made a mistake, wished to correct it. 'Yes, I came from Belle-Isle here upon very hard horses,' he said, 'and that fatigued me.'

'I am no longer astonished then, since I, who followed you, found seven or eight lying dead on the road.'

'I am very heavy, you know,' said Porthos.

'So that you were bruised all over.'

'My fat melted, and that made me very ill.'

'Poor Porthos! But how did Aramis act towards you under those circumstances?'

'Very well indeed. He had me attended to by M. Fouquet's own doctor. But just imagine, at the end of a week I could not breathe any longer.'

'What do you mean?'

'The room was too small, I absorbed too much air.'

'Indeed?'

'I was told so, at least; and so I was removed into another apartment.'

'Where you were able to breathe that time, I hope.'

'Yes, more freely; but no exercise—nothing to do. The doctor pretended that I was not to stir; I, on the contrary, felt that I was stronger than ever; that was the cause of a very serious accident.'

'What accident?'

'Fancy, my dear fellow, that I revolted against the directions of that ass of a doctor, and I resolved to go out, whether it suited him or not; and, consequently, I told the valet who waited on me to bring me my clothes.'

'You were quite naked, then?'

'Oh, no, on the contrary, I had a magnificent dressing-gown to wear; the lackey obeyed; I dressed myself in my own clothes, which had become too large for me; but a strange circumstance had happened, my feet had become too large.'

'Yes, I quite understand.'

'And my boots had become too small.'

'You mean your feet were still swollen.'

'Exactly; you have hit it.'

'*Pardieu!* And is that the accident you were going to tell me about?'

'Oh, yes! I did not make the same reflection you have done. I said to myself, "Since my feet have entered my boots ten times, there is no reason why they should not go in an eleventh."'

'Allow me to tell you, my dear Porthos, that on this occasion you failed in your logic.'

'In short, then, they placed me opposite to a part of the room which was partitioned; I tried to get my boot on; I pulled it with my hands, I pushed with all the strength of the muscles of my leg, making the most unheard-of efforts, when suddenly, the two tags of my boots remained in my hands, and my foot struck out like a catapult.'

'Catapult! how learned you are in fortification, dear Porthos.'

'My foot darted out like a catapult, and came against the partition, which it broke in; I really thought that, like Samson, I had demolished the temple.* And the number of pictures, the quantity of china, vases of flowers, carpets, and window-poles which fell down were really wonderful.'

'Indeed!'

'Without reckoning that, on the other side of the partition was a small table laden with porcelain——'

'Which you knocked over?'

'Which I dashed to the other side of the room,' said Porthos, laughing.

'Upon my word it is, as you say, astonishing,' replied d'Artagnan, beginning to laugh also; whereupon Porthos laughed louder than ever.

'I broke,' said Porthos, in a voice half-choked from his increasing mirth, 'more than three thousand francs' worth of china—oh! oh! oh!'

'Good,' said d'Artagnan.

'I smashed more than four thousand francs' worth of glass—oh! oh! oh!'

'Excellent.'

'Without counting a chandelier, which fell on my head and was broken into a thousand pieces—oh! oh! oh!'

'Upon your head?' said d'Artagnan holding his sides.

'On the top.'

'But your head was broken, I suppose?'

'No, since I tell you, on the contrary, my dear fellow, that it was the chandelier which broke like glass, as it was, indeed.'

'Ah! the chandelier was glass, you say.'

'Venetian glass! a perfect curiosity, quite matchless, indeed, and weighed two hundred pounds.'

'And it fell upon your head!'

'Upon my head. Just imagine, a globe of crystal, gilded all over, the lower part beautifully encrusted, perfumes burning at the top, and jets from which flame issued when they were lighted.'

'I quite understand, but they were not lighted at the time, I suppose?'

'Happily not, or I should have been set on fire.'

'And you were only knocked down flat, instead?'

'Not at all.'

'How, not at all?'

'Why the chandelier fell on my skull. It appears that we have upon the top of our heads an exceedingly thick crust.'

'Who told you that, Porthos?'

'The doctor. A sort of dome which would bear Notre-Dame at Paris.'

'Bah!'

'Yes, it seems that our skulls are made in that manner.'

'Speak for yourself, my dear fellow, it is your own skull that is made in that manner, and not the skulls of other people.'

'Well, that may be so,' said Porthos conceitedly, 'so much, however, was that the case, in my instance, that no sooner did the chandelier fall upon the dome which we have on the top of our head, than there was a report like a cannon, the crystal was broken to pieces, and I fell, covered from head to foot.'

'With blood, poor Porthos!'

'Not at all; with perfumes, which smelt like rich cream; it was delicious, but the odour was too strong, and I felt quite giddy from it; perhaps you have experienced it sometimes yourself, d'Artagnan?'

'Yes, in inhaling the scent of the lily of the valley; so that, my poor friend, you were knocked over by the shock and over-powered by the odour?'

'Yes; but what is very remarkable, for the doctor told me he had never seen anything like it——'

'You had a bump on your head, I suppose?' interrupted d'Artagnan.

'I had five.'

'Why five?'

'I will tell you; the chandelier had at its lower extremity, five gilt ornaments, excessively sharp.'

'Oh!'

'Well, these five ornaments penetrated my hair, which, as you see, I wear very thick.'

'Fortunately so.'

'And they made a mark on my skin. But just notice the singularity of it, these things really seem only to happen to me! Instead of making indentations, they made bumps. The doctor could never succeed in explaining that to me satisfactorily.'

'Well, then, I will explain it to you.'

'You will do me a great service if you will,' said Porthos, winking his eyes, which, with him, was a sign of the profoundest attention.

'Since you have been employing your brain in studies of an exalted character, in important calculations, and so on, the head has gained a certain advantage, so that your head is now too full of science.'

'Do you think so?'

'I am sure of it. The result is, that, instead of allowing any foreign matter to penetrate the interior of the head, your bony box or skull, which is already too full, avails itself of the open-ings which are made in it in allowing this excess to escape.'

'Ah!' said Porthos, to whom this explanation appeared clearer than that of the doctor.

'The five protuberances, caused by the five ornaments of the lustre, must certainly have been scientific masses, brought to the surface by the force of circumstances.'

'In fact,' said Porthos, 'the real truth is, that I felt far worse outside my head than inside. I will even confess that when I put

my hat upon my head, clapping it on my head with that graceful energy which we gentlemen of the sword possess, if my fist
was not very gently applied, I experienced the most painful
sensations.'

'I quite believe you, Porthos.'

'Therefore, my friend,' said the giant, 'M. Fouquet decided,
seeing how slightly built the house was, to give me another
lodging, and so they brought me here.'

'It is the private park, I think, is it not?'

'Yes.'

'Where the rendezvous are made; that park, indeed, which is
so celebrated in some of those mysterious stories about the
superintendant.'

'I don't know; I have had no rendezvous or heard mysterious
stories myself, but they have authorised me to exercise my
muscles, and I take advantage of the permission by rooting up
some of the trees.'

'What for?'

'To keep my hand in, and also to take some birds' nests; I find
that more convenient than climbing up the trees.'

'You are as pastoral as Tyrcis, my dear Porthos.'

'Yes, I like the small eggs; I like them very much better than
larger ones. You have no idea how delicate an omelette is, if made
of four or five hundred eggs of linnets, chaffinches, starlings,
blackbirds, and thrushes.'

'But five hundred eggs is perfectly monstrous!'

'A salad bowl will hold them easily enough,' said Porthos.

D'Artagnan looked at Porthos admiringly for fully five minutes,
as if he had seen him for the first time, while Porthos spread
himself out joyously and proudly. They remained in this state
several minutes, Porthos smiling and d'Artagnan looking at him.
D'Artagnan was evidently trying to give the conversation a new
turn. 'Do you amuse yourself much here, Porthos?' he asked at
last, very likely after he had found out what he was searching
for.

'Not always.'

'I can imagine that; but when you get thoroughly bored, by-
and-by, what do you intend to do?'

'Oh! I shall not be here for any length of time. Aramis is

waiting until the last bump on my head disappears, in order to present me to the King, who I am told cannot endure the sight of a bump.'

'Aramis is still in Paris, then?'

'No.'

'Whereabouts is he, then?'

'At Fontainebleau.'

'Alone?'

'With M. Fouquet.'

'Very good. But do you happen to know one thing?'

'No, tell it me, and then I shall know.'

'Well, then, I think that Aramis is forgetting you.'

'Do you really think so?'

'Yes; for at Fontainebleau yonder, you must know, they are laughing, dancing, banqueting, and drawing the corks of M. de Mazarin's wine in fine style. Are you aware that they have a ballet every evening there?'

'The deuce they have!'

'I assure you that your dear Aramis is forgetting you.'

'Well, that is not at all unlikely, and I have myself thought so sometimes.'

'Unless he is playing you a trick, the sly fellow.'

'Oh!'

'You know that Aramis is as sly as a fox.'

'Yes, but to play me a trick——'

'Listen; in the first place he puts you under a sort of sequestration.'

'He sequestrates me! Do you mean to say I am sequestrated?'

'I think so.'

'I wish you would have the goodness to prove that to me.'

'Nothing easier. Do you ever go out?'

'Never.'

'Do you ever ride on horseback?'

'Never.'

'Are your friends allowed to come and see you?'

'Never.'

'Very well, then, never to go out, never to ride on horseback, never to be allowed to see your friends, that is called being sequestrated.'

'But why should Aramis sequestrate me?' inquired Porthos.

'Come,' said d'Artagnan, 'be frank, Porthos.'

'As gold.'

'It was Aramis who drew the plan of the fortifications at Belle-Isle, was it not?'

Porthos coloured as he said, 'Yes, but that was all that he did.'

'Exactly, and my own opinion is that it was no very great affair after all.'

'That is mine, too.'

'Very good, I am delighted we are of the same opinion.'

'He never even came to Belle-Isle,' said Porthos.

'There now, you see.'

'It was I who went to Vannes, as you may have seen.'*

'Say rather, as I did see. Well, that is precisely the state of the case, my dear Porthos. Aramis, who only drew the plans, wishes to pass himself off as the engineer, whilst you, who, stone by stone, built the wall, the citadel, and the bastions, he wishes to reduce to the rank of a mere builder.'

'By builder you mean mason, perhaps?'

'Mason; the very word.'

'Plasterer, in fact?'

'Precisely.'

'A labourer?'

'Exactly.'

'Oh! oh! my dear Aramis, you seem to think you are only five-and-twenty years of age still.'

'Yes, and that is not all, for he believes you are fifty.'

'I should have liked to have seen him at work.'

'Yes, indeed.'

'A fellow who has the gout?'

'Yes.'

'Who has lost three of his teeth?'

'Four.'

'While I, look at mine.' And Porthos, opening his large mouth very wide, displayed two rows of teeth rather less white than snow, but as even, hard, and sound as ivory.

'You can hardly believe, Porthos,' said d'Artagnan, 'what a fancy the King has for good teeth. Yours decide me; I will present you to the King myself.'

'You?'

'Why not? Do you think I have less credit at court than Aramis?'

'Oh, no!'

'Do you think that I have the slightest pretension upon the fortifications at Belle-Isle?'

'Certainly not.'

'It is your own interest alone, which would induce me to do it.'

'I don't doubt it in the least.'

'Well! I am the intimate friend of the King; and a proof of that is, that whenever there is anything disagreeable to tell him, it is I who have to do it.'

'But dear d'Artagnan, if you present me——'

'Well!'

'Aramis will be angry.'

'With me?'

'No, with me.'

'Bah! whether he or I present you, since you are to be presented, what does it matter?'

'They were going to get me some clothes made.'

'Your own are splendid.'

'Oh! those I had ordered were far more beautiful.'

'Take care; the King likes simplicity.'

'In that case, I will be simple. But what will M. Fouquet say, when he learns that I have left?'

'Are you a prisoner, then, on parole?'

'No, not quite that. But I promised him I would not leave without letting him know.'

'Wait a minute, we shall return to that presently. Have you anything to do here?'

'I, nothing; nothing of any importance, at least.'

'Unless, indeed, you are Aramis's representative for something of importance?'

'By no means.'

'What I tell you, pray understand that, is out of interest for you. I suppose, for instance, that you are commissioned to send messages and letters to him?'

'Ah! letters, yes. I send certain letters to him.'

'Where?'

'To Fontainebleau.'

'Have you any letters, then?'

'But——'

'Nay, let me speak. Have you any letters, I say?'

'I have just received one for him.'

'Interesting?'

'I suppose so.'

'You do not read them then?'

'I am not at all curious,' said Porthos as he drew out of his pocket the soldier's letter, which Porthos had not read but which d'Artagnan had.

'Do you know what to do with it?' said d'Artagnan.

'Of course, do as I always do, send it to him.'

'Not so.'

'Why not. Keep it then?'

'Did they not tell you that this letter was important?'

'Very important.'

'Well, you must take it yourself to Fontainebleau.'

'To Aramis?'

'Yes.'

'Very good.'

'And since the King is there——'

'You will make the most of it . . . ?'

'I shall take the opportunity to present you to the King.'

'Ah! d'Artagnan, there is no one like you to find expedients.'

'Therefore, instead of forwarding to our friend any messages, which may or may not be faithfully delivered, we will ourselves be the bearers of the letter.'

'I had never even thought of that, and yet it is simple enough.'

'And therefore, because it is urgent, Porthos, we ought to set off at once.'

'In fact,' said Porthos, 'the sooner we set off the less chance there is of Aramis's letter meeting with any delay.'

'Porthos, your reasoning is always very accurate, and, in your case, logic seems to serve as an auxiliary to the imagination.'

'Do you think so?' said Porthos.

'It is the result of your hard reading,' replied d'Artagnan. 'So come along, let us be off.'

'But,' said Porthos, 'my promise to M. Fouquet?'

'Which?'

'Not to leave St Mandé without telling him of it.'

'Ah! Porthos,' said d'Artagnan, 'how very young you are.'

'In what way?'

'You are going to Fontainebleau, are you not, where you will find M. Fouquet?'

'Yes.'

'Probably in the King's palace?'

'Yes,' repeated Porthos, with an air full of majesty.

'Well, you will accost him with these words, "M. Fouquet, I have the honour to inform you that I have just left St Mandé."'

'And,' said Porthos with the same majestic mien, 'seeing me at Fontainebleau at the King's, M. Fouquet will not be able to tell me I am not speaking the truth.'

'My dear Porthos, I was just on the point of opening my lips to make the same remark, but you anticipate me in everything. Oh! Porthos, how fortunately you are gifted; age has not made any impression on you.'

'Not over-much, certainly.'

'Then there is nothing more to say?'

'I think not.'

'All your scruples are removed?'

'Quite so.'

'In that case I shall carry you off with me.'

'Exactly; and I shall go and get my horses saddled.'

'You have horses here, then?'

'I have five.'

'You had them sent from Pierrefonds, I suppose?'

'No, M. Fouquet gave them to me.'

'My dear Porthos, we shall not want five horses for two persons; besides, I have already three in Paris, which will make eight, and that will be too many.'

'It would not be too many if I had some of my servants here; but, alas! I have not got them.'

'Do you regret them, then?'

'I regret Mousqueton; I need Mousqueton.'*

'What a good-hearted fellow you are, Porthos,' said d'Artagnan; 'but the best thing you can do is to leave your horses here, as you have left Mousqueton out yonder.'

'Why so?'

'Because, by-and-by, it might turn out a very good thing if M. Fouquet had never given you anything at all.'

'I don't understand you,' said Porthos.

'It is not necessary you should understand.'

'But yet——'

'I will explain it to you later, Porthos.'

'I'll wager it is some piece of politics or other.'

'And of the most subtle character,' returned d'Artagnan.

Porthos bent his head at this word politics; then after a moment's reflection, he added, 'I confess, d'Artagnan, that I am no politician.'

'I know that well.'

'Oh! no one knows what you told me yourself, you the bravest of the brave.'

'What did I tell you, Porthos?'

'That every man has his day. You told me so, and I have experienced it myself. There are certain days when one feels less pleasure than others in exposing oneself to a bullet or a sword-thrust.'

'Exactly my own idea.'

'And mine too, although I can hardly believe in blows or thrusts which kill outright.'

'The deuce! and yet you have killed a few in your time.'

'Yes; but I have never been killed.'

'Your reason is a very good one.'

'Therefore, I do not believe I shall ever die from a thrust of a sword, or a gun-shot.'

'In that case, then you are afraid of nothing. Ah! water perhaps?'

'Oh! I swim like an otter.'

'Of a quartan fever,* then?'

'I never had one yet, and I don't believe I ever shall; but there is one thing I will admit,' and Porthos dropped his voice.

'What is that?' asked d'Artagnan, adopting the same tone of voice as Porthos.

'I must confess,' repeated Porthos, 'that I am horribly afraid of political matters.'

'Ah! bah!' exclaimed d'Artagnan.

'Upon my word, it's true,' said Porthos in a stentorian voice. 'I have seen His Eminence Monsieur le Cardinal de Richelieu, and His Eminence Monsieur le Cardinal de Mazarin; the one was a red politician, the other a black politician;* I have never felt very much more satisfied with the one than with the other; the first struck off the heads of M. de Marillac, M. de Thou, M. de Cinq-Mars, M. Chalais, M. de Bouteville, and M. de Montmorency;* the second got a whole crowd of Frondeurs cut in pieces; and we belonged to them.'

'On the contrary, we did not belong to them,' said d'Artagnan.

'Oh! indeed, yes; for, if I unsheathed my sword for the Cardinal, I struck for the King.'*

'Dear Porthos!'

'Well, I have done. My dread of politics is such, that if there is any question of politics in the matter, I should far sooner prefer to return to Pierrefonds.'

'You would be quite right, if that were the case. But with me, dear Porthos, no politics at all, that is quite clear. You have laboured hard in fortifying Belle-Isle; the King wished to know the name of the clever engineer under whose directions the works were carried on; you are modest, as all men of true genius are; perhaps Aramis wishes to put you under a bushel. But I happen to seize hold of you; I make it known who you are; I produce you; the King rewards you; and that is the only policy I have to do with.'

'And the only one I will have to do with either,' said Porthos, holding out his hand to d'Artagnan.

But d'Artagnan knew Porthos's grasp; he knew that once imprisoned within the Baron's five fingers, no hand ever left it without being half-crushed. He therefore held out, not his hand, but his fist, and Porthos did not even perceive the difference. The servants talked a little with each other in an undertone, and whispered a few words, which d'Artagnan understood, but which he took very good care not to let Porthos understand. 'Our friend,' he said to himself, 'was really and truly Aramis's prisoner. Let us now see what the result will be of the liberation of the captive.'

LI

THE RAT AND THE CHEESE

D'ARTAGNAN and Porthos returned on foot, as D'Artagnan had arrived. When d'Artagnan, as he entered the shop of the Golden Pestle, had announced to Planchet that M. du Vallon would be one of the privileged travellers, and when the plume in Porthos's hat had made the wooden candles suspended over the front jingle together, something almost like a melancholy presentiment troubled the delight which Planchet had promised himself for the next day. But the grocer's heart was of sterling metal, a precious relic of the good old time, which always remains what it has always been. For those who are getting old it is the time of their youth, and for those who are young it is the old age of their ancestors. Planchet, notwithstanding the sort of internal shiver, which he checked immediately he experienced it, received Porthos, therefore, with a respect mingled with the most tender cordiality. Porthos, who was a little cold and stiff in his manners at first, on account of the social difference which existed at that period between a baron and a grocer, soon began to get a little softened when he perceived so much good-feeling and so many kind attentions in Planchet. He was particularly touched by the liberty which was permitted him to plunge his large hands into the boxes of dried fruits and preserves, into the sacks of nuts and almonds, and into the drawers full of sweet-meats. So that, notwithstanding Planchet's pressing invitations to go upstairs to the entresol, he chose as his favourite seat, during the evening which he had to spend at Planchet's house, the shop itself, where his fingers could always find whatever his nose had first detected for him. The delicious figs from Provence, filberts from the forest, Tours plums, were subjects of his interrupted attention for five consecutive hours. His teeth, like millstones, cracked heaps of nuts, the shells of which were scattered all over the floor, where they were trampled by every one who went in and out of the shop; Porthos pulled from the stalk with his lips, at one mouthful, bunches of the rich Muscatel raisins with their beautiful bloom, and a half-pound of which passed at one gulp from his mouth to his stomach. In one of the corners of the shop, Planchet's assistants, crouching down in a fright, looked at each other without venturing to open their lips. They did not know who Porthos was, for they had never seen him before. The race of those Titans who had worn the cuirasses of Hugues Capet, Philip Augustus and Francis I had already begun to disappear. They could not help thinking he might possibly be the ogre of the fairy tale, who was going to turn the whole contents of Planchet's shop into his insatiable stomach, and that, too, without in the slightest degree displacing the barrels and chests that were in it. Cracking, munching, chewing, nibbling, sucking, and swallowing, Porthos occasionally said to the grocer,—

'You do a very good business here, friend Planchet.'

'He will very soon have none at all to do, if this continues,' grumbled the foreman, who had Planchet's word that he should be his successor. And, in his despair, he approached Porthos, who blocked up the whole of the passage leading from the back shop to the shop itself. He hoped that Porthos would rise, and that this movement would distract his devouring ideas.

'What do you want, my man?' asked Porthos very affably.

'I should like to pass you, monsieur, if it is not troubling you too much.'

'Very well,' said Porthos, 'it does not trouble me in the least.'

At the same moment he took hold of the young fellow by the waistband, lifted him off the ground, and placed him very gently on the other side, smiling all the while with the same affable expression. As soon as Porthos had placed him on the ground, the lad's legs so shook under him, that he fell back upon some sacks of corks. But noticing the giant's gentleness of manner, he ventured again, and said,—

'Ah, monsieur! pray be careful.'

'What about?' inquired Porthos.

'You are positively putting fire into your body.'

'How is that, my good fellow?' said Porthos.

'All those things are very heating to the system.'

'Which?'

'Raisins, nuts, and almonds.'

'Yes, but if raisins, nuts, and almonds are heating——'

'There is no doubt at all of it, monsieur.'

'Honey is very cooling,' said Porthos, stretching out his hand towards a small barrel of honey which was opened, and he plunged the scoop with which the wants of the customers were supplied into it, and swallowed a good half-pound at one gulp.

'I must trouble you for some water now, my man,' said Porthos.

'In a pail, monsieur?' asked the lad simply.

'No, in a water-bottle; that will be quite enough;' and raising the bottle to his mouth, as a trumpeter does his trumpet, he emptied the bottle at a single draught.

Planchet was moved in all the sentiments which correspond to the fibres of propriety and self-love. However, a worthy representative of the hospitality which prevailed in early days, he feigned to be talking very earnestly with d'Artagnan, and incessantly repeated—'Ah! monsieur, what a happiness! what an honour!'

'What time shall we have supper, Planchet?' inquired Porthos; 'I feel hungry.'

The foreman clasped his hands together. The two others got under the counters, fearing that Porthos might have a taste for human flesh.

'We shall only take a short snack here,' said d'Artagnan, 'and when we get to Planchet's country-seat we shall have supper.'

'Ah! ah! so we are going to your country-house, Planchet,' said Porthos; 'so much the better.'

'You overwhelm me, Monsieur le Baron'.

The 'Monsieur le Baron' had a great effect upon the men, who detected a personage of the highest quality in an appetite of that kind. This title too, reassured them. They had never heard that an ogre was ever called 'Monsieur le Baron'.

'I will take a few biscuits to eat on the road,' said Porthos carelessly; and he emptied a whole jar of aniseed biscuits into the huge pocket of his doublet.

'My shop is saved!' exclaimed Planchet.

'Yes, as the cheese was,' said the foreman.

'What cheese?'

'That Dutch cheese, inside which a rat had made his way, and we only found the rind left.'*

Planchet looked all round his shop, and observing the different articles which had escaped Porthos's teeth, he found the comparison somewhat exaggerated. The foreman, who remarked what was passing in his master's mind, said, 'Take care; he is not gone yet.'

'Have you any fruit here?' said Porthos as he went upstairs to the entresol, where it had just been announced that some refreshment was prepared.

'Alas!' thought the grocer, addressing a look at d'Artagnan full of entreaty, which the latter half understood.

As soon as they had finished eating they set off. It was late in the evening when the three riders, who had left Paris about six in the evening, arrived at Fontainebleau. The journey had passed very agreeably. Porthos took a fancy to Planchet's society, because the latter was very respectful in his manners and seemed delighted to talk to him about his meadows, his woods, and his rabbit warrens. Porthos had all the taste and pride of a landed proprietor. When d'Artagnan saw his two companions in earnest conversation, he took the opposite side of the road, and letting his bridle drop upon his horse's neck, separated himself from the whole world, as he had done from Porthos and from Planchet. The moon shone softly through the foliage of the forest. The odours of the open country rose deliciously perfumed to the horses' nostrils, and they snorted and pranced about delightedly. Porthos and Planchet began to talk about hay-crops. Planchet admitted to Porthos that in the more advanced years of his life, he had certainly neglected agricultural pursuits for commerce, but that his childhood had been passed in Picardy in the beautiful meadows where the grass grew as high as the knees, and where he had played under the green apple-trees covered with red-cheeked fruit; he went on to say, that he had solemnly promised himself that as soon as he made his fortune, he would return to nature, and end his days, as he had begun them, as near as he possibly could to the earth itself, where all men must go at last.

'Eh! eh!' said Porthos; 'in that case, my dear Monsieur Planchet, your retreat is not far distant.'

'How so?'

'Why, you seem to be in the way of making your fortune very soon.'

'Well, we are getting on pretty well, I must admit,' replied Planchet.

'Come, tell me, what is the extent of your ambition, and what is the amount you intend to retire upon?'

'There is one circumstance, monsieur,' said Planchet without answering the question, 'which occasions me a good deal of anxiety.'

'What is it?' inquired Porthos, looking all round him as if in search of the circumstance that annoyed Planchet, and desirous of freeing him from it.

'Why, formerly,' said the grocer, 'you used to call me Planchet quite short, and you would have spoken to me then in a much more familiar manner than you do now.'

'Certainly, certainly, I should have said so formerly,' replied the good-natured Porthos with an embarrassment full of delicacy; 'but formerly——'

'Formerly I was M. d'Artagnan's lackey; is not that what you mean?'

'Yes.'

'Well, if I am not quite his lackey, I am as much as ever I was his devoted servant; and more than that, since that time——'

'Well, Planchet?'

'Since that time, I have had the honour of being in partnership with him.'*

'Oh! oh!' said Porthos. 'What, has d'Artagnan gone into the grocery business?'

'No, no,' said d'Artagnan, whom these words had drawn out of his reverie, and who entered into the conversation with that readiness and rapidity which distinguished every operation of his mind and body. 'It was not d'Artagnan who entered into the grocery business, but Planchet who entered into a political affair with me.'

'Yes,' said Planchet with mingled pride and satisfaction, 'we transacted a little matter of business which brought me in a hundred thousand francs, and M. d'Artagnan two hundred thousand.'

'Oh, oh!' said Porthos with admiration.

'So that, Monsieur le Baron,' continued the grocer, 'I again beg you to be kind enough to call me Planchet, as you used to do; and to speak to me as familiarly as in old times. You cannot possibly imagine the pleasure that it would give me.'

'If that be the case, my dear Planchet, I will do so certainly,' replied Porthos. And as he was quite close to Planchet, he raised his hand as if to strike him on the shoulder, in token of friendly cordiality; but a fortunate movement of the horse made him miss his aim, so that his hand fell on the crupper of Planchet's horse instead, which made the animal's legs almost give way.

D'Artagnan burst out laughing as he said, 'Take care, Planchet; for if Porthos begins to like you too much, he will caress you; and if he caresses you, he will knock you as flat as a pancake. Porthos is still as strong as ever, you know.'

'Oh,' said Planchet, 'Mousqueton is not dead, and yet Monsieur le Baron is very fond of him.'

'Certainly,' said Porthos with a sign that made all the three horses rear, 'and I was only saying, this very morning, to d'Artagnan, how much I regretted him. But tell me, Planchet?'

'Thank you, Monsieur le Baron, thank you.'

'Good lad, good lad! How many acres of park have you got?'

'Of park?'

'Yes; we will reckon up the meadows presently, and the woods afterwards.'

'Whereabouts, monsieur?'

'At your château.'

'Oh, Monsieur le Baron, I have neither château, nor park, nor meadows, nor woods.'

'What have you got, then?' inquired Porthos, 'and why do you call it a country-seat?'

'I did not call it a country-seat, Monsieur le Baron,' replied Planchet, somewhat humiliated, 'but a country-box.'

'Ah! ah! I understand. You are modest.'

'No, Monsieur le Baron; I speak the plain truth. I have rooms for a couple of friends, that is all.'

'But, in that case, whereabouts do your friends walk?'

'In the first place they can walk about the King's forest, which is very beautiful.'

'Yes, I know the forest is very fine,' said Porthos; 'nearly as beautiful as my forest at Berry.'*

Planchet opened his eyes very wide. 'Have you a forest of the

same kind as the forest at Fontainebleau, Monsieur le Baron?'
he stammered out.

'Yes; I have two, indeed, but the one at Berry is my favourite.'

'Why so?' asked Planchet.

'Because I don't know where it ends; and, also, because it is
full of poachers.'

'How can the poachers make the forest so agreeable to you?'

'Because they hunt my game, and I hunt them—which in
these peaceful times is for me a picture of war on a small scale.'

They had reached this turn of the conversation, when Planchet,
looking up, perceived the houses at the commencement of
Fontainebleau, the outline of which stood out strongly upon the
dark face of the heavens; whilst, rising above the compact and
irregularly-formed mass of buildings, the pointed roofs of the
château were clearly visible, the slates of which glistened beneath the light of the moon, like the scales of an immense fish.
'Gentlemen,' said Planchet, 'I have the honour to inform you
that we have arrived at Fontainebleau.'

LII

PLANCHET'S COUNTRY-HOUSE

THE cavaliers looked up, and saw that what Planchet had announced to them was true. Ten minutes afterwards, they were
in the street called the Rue de Lyon, on the opposite side of the
inn of the sign of Beau Paon. A high hedge of bushy elders,
hawthorn, and wild hops, formed an impenetrable fence, behind
which rose a white house, with a large tiled roof. Two of the
windows, which were quite dark, looked upon the street. Between the two, a small door, with a porch supported by a couple
of pillars, formed the entrance to the house. The door was
gained by a step raised a little from the ground. Planchet got off
his horse, as if he intended to knock at the door; but, on second
thoughts, he took hold of his horse by the bridle, and led it
about thirty paces farther on, his two companions following
him. He then advanced about another thirty paces, until he
arrived at the door of a cart-house, lighted by an iron grating;

and, lifting up a wooden latch, pushed open one of the folding-doors. He entered first, leading his horse after him by the bridle, into a small courtyard, where an odour met them which revealed their close vicinity to a stable. 'That smells all right,' said Porthos loudly, getting off his horse, 'and I almost begin to think I am near my own cows at Pierrefonds.'

'I have only one cow,' Planchet hastened to say, modestly.

'And I have thirty,' said Porthos; 'or, rather, I don't exactly know how many I have.'

When the two cavaliers had entered, Planchet fastened the door behind them. In the meantime, d'Artagnan, who had dismounted with his usual agility, inhaled the fresh perfumed air with the delight a Parisian feels at the sight of green fields and fresh foliage, plucked a piece of honeysuckle with one hand, and of sweet-brier with the other. Porthos had laid hold of some peas which were twined round poles stuck into the ground, and ate, or rather browsed upon them, shells and all; and Planchet was busily engaged trying to wake up an old and infirm peasant, who was fast asleep in a shed, lying on a bed of moss, and dressed in an old stable suit of clothes. The peasant, recognising Planchet, called him 'the master,' to the grocer's great satisfaction. 'Stable the horses well, old fellow, and you shall have something good for yourself,' said Planchet.

'Yes, yes; fine animals they are too,' said the peasant. 'Oh! they shall have as much as they like.'

'Gently, gently, my man,' said d'Artagnan, 'we are getting on a little too fast. A few oats, and a good bed—nothing more.'

'Some bran and water for my horse,' said Porthos, 'for it is very warm, I think.'

'Don't be afraid, gentlemen,' replied Planchet; 'Old Celestin is a former soldier, who fought at Ivry.* He knows all about stables; so, come into the house.' And he led the way along a well-sheltered walk, which crossed a kitchen-garden, then a small paddock, and came out into a little garden behind the house, the principal front of which, as we have already noticed, was facing the street. As they approached, they could see, through two open windows on the ground floor, which led into a sitting-room, the interior of Planchet's residence. This room, softly lighted by a lamp placed on the table, seemed, from the end of

the garden, like a smiling image of repose, comfort, and happiness. In every direction where the rays of light fell, whether
upon a piece of old china, or upon an article of furniture shining
from excessive neatness, or upon the weapons hanging against
the wall, the soft light was so softly reflected; and its rays seemed
to linger everywhere, upon something or another agreeable to
the eye. The lamp which lighted the room, whilst the foliage of
jasmine and climbing roses hung in masses from the window-
frames, splendidly illuminated a damask table-cloth as white as
snow. The table was laid for two persons. An amber-coloured
wine sparkled in the long cut-glass bottle; and a large jug of
blue china, with a silver lid, was filled with foaming cider. Near
the table in a high-backed arm-chair, reclined, fast asleep, a
woman of about thirty years of age, her face the very picture
of health and freshness. Upon her knees lay a large cat, with
her paws folded under her, and her eyes half-closed, purring in
that significant manner which, according to feline habits, indicates perfect contentment. The two friends paused before the
window, in complete amazement, while Planchet, perceiving
their astonishment, was, in no little degree, secretly delighted at
it.

'Ah! Planchet, you rascal,' said d'Artagnan, 'I now understand your absences.'

'Oh, oh! there is some white linen,' said Porthos, in his turn,
in a voice of thunder. At the sound of this voice, the cat took
flight, the housekeeper woke up suddenly, and Planchet, assuming a gracious air, introduced his two companions into the room,
where the table was already laid.

'Permit me, my dear,' he said, 'to present you to Monsieur le
Chevalier d'Artagnan, my patron.' D'Artagnan took the lady's
hand in his in the most courteous manner, and with precisely
the same chivalrous air as he would have taken Madame's.

'Monsieur le Baron du Vallon de Bracieux de Pierrefonds,'
added Planchet. Porthos bowed with a reverence which Anne of
Austria would have approved of.

It was then Planchet's turn, and he, unhesitatingly, embraced
the lady in question, not, however, until he had made a sign as
if requesting d'Artagnan's and Porthos's permission, a permission
which was of course frankly conceded. D'Artagnan complimented

Planchet, and said, 'You are indeed a man who knows how to make life agreeable.'

'Life, monsieur,' said Planchet laughing, 'is a capital which a man ought to invest as sensibly as he possibly can.'

'And you get very good interest for yours,' said Porthos, with a burst of laughter like a peal of thunder.

Planchet turned to his housekeeper. 'You have before you,' he said to her, 'the two men who have influenced no small portion of my life. I have spoken to you about them both very frequently.'

'And two others as well,' said the lady, with a very decided Flemish accent.

'Madame is Dutch?' inquired d'Artagnan. Porthos curled his moustache, a circumstance which was not lost upon d'Artagnan, who remarked everything.

'I am from Antwerp,' said the lady.

'And her name is Madame Gechter,' said Planchet.

'You should not call her madame,' said d'Artagnan.

'Why not?' asked Planchet.

'Because it would make her seem older every time you call her so.'

'Well, I call her Trüchen.'

'And a very pretty name too,' said Porthos.

'Trüchen,' said Planchet, 'came to me from Flanders with her virtue and two thousand florins. She ran away from a brute of a husband who was in the habit of beating her. Being myself a Picard born, I was always very fond of the Artesian women, and it is only a step from Artois to Flanders; she came crying bitterly to her godfather, my predecessor in the Rue des Lombards; she placed her two thousand florins in my establishment, which I have turned to very good account, and which bring her in ten thousand.'

'Bravo, Planchet.'

'She is free and well off; she has a cow, a maid-servant, and old Celestin at her orders; she mends my linen, knits my winter stockings; she only sees me every fortnight, and seems anxious to make herself happy.'

'And I am very happy indeed,' said Trüchen, with perfect ingenuousness.

Porthos began to curl the other side of his moustache. 'The deuce,' thought d'Artagnan, 'can Porthos have any intentions in that quarter?'

In the meantime Trüchen had set her cook to work, had laid the table for two more, and covered it with every possible delicacy, which converts a light supper into a substantial meal, and a meal into a regular feast. Fresh butter, salt beef, anchovies, tunny, a shopful of Planchet's commodities, fowls, vegetables, salad, fish from the pond and the river, game from the forest—all the produce in fact of the province. Moreover, Planchet returned from the cellar, laden with ten bottles of wine, the glass of which could hardly be seen for the thick coating of dust which covered them. Porthos's heart seemed to expand as he said, 'I am hungry,' and he sat himself beside Madame Trüchen, whom he looked at in the most killing manner. D'Artagnan seated himself on the other side of her, while Planchet, discreetly and full of delight, took his seat opposite.

'Do not trouble yourselves,' he said, 'if Trüchen should leave the table now and then during supper; for she will have to look after your bedrooms.'

In fact, the housekeeper made her escape very frequently, and they could hear, on the first floor above them, the creaking of the wooden bedsteads and the rolling of the castors on the floor. While this was going on, the three men, Porthos especially, ate and drank gloriously,—it was wonderful to see them. The ten full bottles were ten empty ones by the time Trüchen returned with the cheese. D'Artagnan still preserved his dignity and self-possession, but Porthos had lost a portion of his; the mirth soon began to be somewhat uproarious. D'Artagnan recommended a new descent into the cellar, and, as Planchet did not walk with the steadiness of a well-trained foot-soldier, the captain of the musketeers proposed to accompany him. They set off, humming songs wild enough to frighten anybody who might be listening. Trüchen remained behind at table with Porthos. While the two wine-bibbers were looking behind the firewood for what they wanted, a sharp sonorous sound was heard, like the impression of a pair of lips on a cheek.

'Porthos fancies himself at La Rochelle,' thought d'Artagnan as they returned freighted with bottles. Planchet was singing so loudly that he was incapable of noticing anything. D'Artagnan, whom nothing ever escaped, remarked how much redder Trüchen's left cheek was than her right. Porthos was sitting on Trüchen's left, and was curling with both his hands both sides of his moustache at once, and Trüchen was looking at him with a most bewitching smile. The sparkling wine of Anjou very soon produced a remarkable effect upon the three companions. D'Artagnan had hardly strength enough left to take a candlestick to light Planchet up his own staircase. Planchet was pulling Porthos along, who was following Trüchen, who was herself jovial enough. It was d'Artagnan who found out the rooms and the beds. Porthos threw himself into the one destined for him, after his friend had undressed him. D'Artagnan got into his own bed, saying to himself, '*Mordioux!* I had made up my mind never to touch that light-coloured wine which brings my early camp days back again. Fie! fie! if my musketeers were only to see their captain in such a state.' And drawing the curtains of his bed, he added, 'Fortunately enough, though, they will not see me.'

'The country is very amusing,' said Porthos, stretching out his legs, which passed through the wooden footboard, and made a tremendous noise, of which, however, no one in the house was capable of taking the slightest notice. By two o'clock in the morning every one was fast asleep.

LIII

SHOWING WHAT COULD BE SEEN FROM PLANCHET'S HOUSE

THE next morning found the three heroes sleeping soundly. Trüchen had closed the outside blinds to keep the first rays of the sun from the heavy eyes of her guests, like a kind good woman. It was still perfectly dark, then, beneath Porthos's curtains and under Planchet's canopy, when d'Artagnan, awakened by an indiscreet ray of light which made its way through the windows, jumped hastily out of bed, as if he wished to be the first at the assault. He took by assault Porthos's room, which was next to his own. The worthy Porthos was sleeping with a noise like distant thunder; and in the dim obscurity of the room his gigantic frame was prominently displayed, and his swollen fist hung down outside the bed upon the carpet. D'Artagnan awoke Porthos, who rubbed his eyes in a tolerably good humour. In the meantime Planchet was dressing himself, and met at the bedroom doors his two guests, who were still somewhat unsteady from their previous evening's entertainment. Although it was yet very early, the whole household was already up. The cook was mercilessly slaughtering poultry in the poultry-yard, and Celestin was gathering cherries in the garden. Porthos, brisk and lively as ever, held out his hand to Planchet, and d'Artagnan requested permission to embrace Madame Trüchen. The latter, to show that she bore no ill will, approached Porthos, upon whom she conferred the same favour. Porthos embraced Madame Trüchen, heaving an enormous sigh. Planchet took both his friends by the hand.

'I am going to show you over the house,' he said; 'when we arrived last evening it was as dark as pitch, and we were unable to see anything; but in broad daylight, everything looks different, and you will be satisfied, I hope.'

'If we begin by the view you have,' said d'Artagnan, 'that charms me beyond everything; I have always lived in royal mansions, you know, and royal personages have some very good ideas upon the selection of points of view.'

'I am a great stickler for a good view myself,' said Porthos. 'At my Château de Pierrefonds, I have had four avenues laid out, and at the end of each is a landscape of a different character altogether to the others.'

'You shall see my prospect,' said Planchet; and he led his two guests to a window.

'Ah!' said d'Artagnan, 'this is the Rue de Lyon.'

'Yes, I have two windows on this side, a paltry insignificant view, for there is always that bustling and noisy inn, which is a very disagreeable neighbour. I had four windows here, but I have only kept two.'

'Let us go on,' said d'Artagnan.

They entered a corridor leading to the bedrooms, and Planchet pushed open the outside blinds.

'Hallo! what is that out yonder?' said Porthos.

'The forest,' said Planchet. 'It is the horizon—a thick line of green, which is yellow in the spring, green in the summer, red in the autumn, and white in the winter.'

'All very well, but it is like a curtain, which prevents one seeing a greater distance.'

'Yes,' said Planchet; 'still one can see, at all events, everything between.'

'Ah, the open country,' said Porthos. 'But what is that I see out there, crosses and stones?'

'Ah, that is the cemetery,' exclaimed d'Artagnan.

'Precisely,' said Planchet; 'I assure you it is very curious. Hardly a day passes that some one is not buried there; for Fontainebleau is by no means an inconsiderable place. Sometimes we see young girls clothed in white carrying banners; at others, some of the town council, or rich citizens, with choristers and all the parish authorities; and then, too, we see some of the officers of the King's household.'

'I should not like that,' said Porthos.

'There is not much amusement in it at all events,' said d'Artagnan.

'I assure you it encourages religious thoughts,' replied Planchet.

'Oh, I don't deny that.'

'But,' continued Planchet, 'we must all die one day or another, and I once met with a maxim somewhere which I have remembered, that the thought of death is a thought that will do us all good.'

'I am far from saying the contrary,' said Porthos.

'But,' objected d'Artagnan, 'the thought of green fields, flowers, rivers, blue horizons, extensive and boundless plains is no less likely to do us good.'

'If I had any, I should be far from rejecting them,' said Planchet; 'but possessing only this little cemetery, full of flowers so moss-grown, shady, and quiet, I am contented with it, and I think of those who live in town, in the Rue des Lombards, for instance, and who have to listen to the rumbling of a couple of thousand vehicles every day, and to the trampling of a hundred and fifty thousand pedestrians.'

'But living,' said Porthos; 'living, remember that.'

'That is exactly the reason,' said Planchet timidly, 'why I feel it does me good to see a few dead.'

'Upon my word,' said d'Artagnan, 'that fellow Planchet was born to be a poet as well as a grocer.'

'Monsieur,' said Planchet, 'I am one of those good-humoured sort of men whom Heaven created for the purpose of living a certain space of time, and of considering all things good which they meet with during their stay on earth.'

D'Artagnan sat down close to the window, and as there seemed to be something substantial in Planchet's philosophy, he mused over it.

'Ah, ah!' exclaimed Porthos, 'if I am not mistaken, we are going to have a show now, for I think I heard something like chanting.'

'Yes,' said d'Artagnan, 'I hear singing too.'

'Oh, it is only a burial of a very poor description,' said Planchet disdainfully; 'the officiating priest, the beadle, and only one chorister boy, nothing more. You observe, messieurs, that the defunct lady or gentleman could not have been of very high rank.'

'No; no one seems to be following the coffin.'

'Yes,' said Porthos; 'I see a man.'

'You are right; a man wrapped up in a cloak,' said d'Artagnan.

'It is not worth looking at,' said Planchet.

'I find it interesting,' said d'Artagnan, leaning on the window.

'Come, come, you are beginning to take a fancy to the place already,' said Planchet delightedly; 'it is exactly my own case. I was so melancholy at first that I could do nothing but make the sign of the cross all day, and the chants were like nails being driven into my head; but now, the chants lull me to sleep, and no bird I have ever seen or heard can sing better than those which are to be met with in this cemetery.'

'Well,' said Porthos, 'this is beginning to get a little dull for me, and I prefer going downstairs.'

Planchet with one bound was beside his guest, to whom he offered his hand to lead him into the garden.

'What!' said Porthos to d'Artagnan, as he turned round, 'are you going to remain here?'

'Yes, I shall join you presently.'

'Well, M. d'Artagnan is right after all,' said Planchet; 'are they beginning to bury yet?'

'Not yet.'

'Ah! yes; the grave-digger is waiting until the cords are fastened round the bier. But, see, a woman has just entered the cemetery at the other end.'

'Yes, yes, my dear Planchet,' said d'Artagnan quickly, 'leave me, leave me; I feel I am beginning already to be much comforted by my meditations, so do not interrupt me.'

Planchet left, and d'Artagnan remained, devouring with his eager gaze from behind the half-closed blinds what was taking place just before him. The two bearers of the corpse had unfastened the straps by which they carried the litter, and were letting their burden glide gently into the open grave. At a few paces distant, the man with the cloak wrapped round him, the only spectator of this melancholy scene, was leaning with his back against a large cypress tree, and kept his face and person entirely concealed from the grave-diggers and the priests; the corpse being buried in five minutes. The grave having been filled up, the priests turned away, and the grave-digger having addressed a few words to them, followed them as they moved away. The man in the mantle bowed as they passed him and put a piece of money into the grave-digger's hand.

'*Mordioux!*' murmured d'Artagnan; 'why that man is Aramis himself.'

Aramis, in fact, remained alone, on that side at least; for hardly did he turn his head than a woman's footstep, and the rustling of her dress, were heard in the path close to him. He immediately turned round, and took off his hat with the most ceremonious respect; he led the lady under the shelter of some walnut and lime trees, which overshadowed a magnificent tomb.

'Ah! who would have thought it,' said d'Artagnan; 'the Bishop of Vannes at a rendezvous! He is still the same Abbé Aramis as he was at Noisy-le-Sec.* Yes,' he added after a pause; 'but as it is in a cemetery, the rendezvous is sacred.' And he began to laugh.

The conversation lasted for fully half an hour. D'Artagnan could not see the lady's face, for she kept her back turned towards him; but he saw perfectly well, by the erect attitude of both the speakers, by their gestures, by the measured and careful manner with which they glanced at each other, either by way of attack or defence, that they must be conversing about any other subject than that of love. At the end of the conversation, the lady rose, and bowed most profoundly to Aramis.

'Oh, oh!' said d'Artagnan; 'this rendezvous finishes like one of a very tender nature though. The cavalier kneels at the beginning, the young lady by-and-by gets tamed down, and then it is she who has to supplicate.—Who is this girl? I would give anything to ascertain.'

This seemed impossible, however, for Aramis was the first to leave; the lady carefully concealed her head and face, and then immediately separated. D'Artagnan could hold out no longer; he ran to the window which looked out on the Rue de Lyon, and saw Aramis just entering the inn. The lady was proceeding in quite an opposite direction, and seemed, in fact, to be about to rejoin an equipage, consisting of two led horses and a carriage, which he could see standing close to the borders of the forest. She was walking slowly, her head bent down, absorbed in the deepest meditation.

'*Mordioux! mordioux!* I must and will learn who that woman is,' said the musketeer again; and then, without further deliberation, he set off in pursuit of her. As he was going along, he tried to think how he could contrive to make her raise her veil. 'She is not young,' he said, 'and is a woman of high rank in society. I ought to know that figure and peculiar style of walk.' As he ran, the sound of his spurs and of his boots upon the hard ground of the street made a strange jingling noise; a fortunate circumstance in itself, which he was far from reckoning upon. For the noise disturbed the lady; she seemed to fancy she was being either followed or pursued, which was indeed the case, and turned round. D'Artagnan started as if he had received a charge of small shot in his legs, and then turning suddenly round as if he were going back the same way he had come, he murmured, 'Madame de Chevreuse!'* D'Artagnan would not go home until he had learnt everything. He asked Celestin to inquire of the grave-digger whose body it was they had buried that morning.

'A poor Franciscan mendicant friar,' replied the latter, 'who had not even a dog to love him in this world, and to accompany him to his last resting-place.'

'If that were really the case,' thought d'Artagnan, 'we should not have found Aramis present at his funeral. The Bishop of Vannes is not precisely a dog as far as devotion goes; his scent, however, is quite as keen, I admit.'

LIV

HOW PORTHOS, TRÜCHEN, AND PLANCHET PARTED WITH EACH OTHER ON FRIENDLY TERMS, THANKS TO D'ARTAGNAN

THERE was good living in Planchet's house. Porthos broke a ladder and two cherry trees, stripped the raspberry bushes, and was only unable to succeed in reaching the strawberry-beds on account, as he said, of his belt. Trüchen, who had been quite sociable with the giant, said that it was not the belt so much as his corporation; and Porthos, in a state of the highest delight, embraced Trüchen, who gathered him a handful of strawberries, and made him eat them out of her hand. D'Artagnan, who arrived in the midst of these little innocent flirtations, scolded Porthos for his indolence, and silently pitied Planchet. Porthos breakfasted with a very good appetite, and when he had finished, he said, looking at Trüchen, 'I could make myself very happy here.' Trüchen smiled at his remark, and so did Planchet, but the latter not without some embarrassment.

D'Artagnan then addressed Porthos,—'You must not let the delights of Capua* make you forget the real object of our journey to Fontainebleau.'

'My presentation to the King!'

Certainly. I am going to take a turn in the town to get everything ready for that. Do not think of leaving the house, I beg.'

'Oh, no!' exclaimed Porthos.

Planchet looked at d'Artagnan nervously. 'Will you be away long?' he inquired.

'No, my friend; and this very evening I will release you from two troublesome guests.'

'Oh! Monsieur d'Artagnan! can you say——'

'No, no; you are an excellent-hearted fellow, but your house is very small. Such a house, with only a couple of acres of land, would be fit for a King, and make him very happy, too. But you were not born a great lord.'

'No more was M. Porthos,' murmured Planchet.

'But he has become so, my good fellow; his income has been a hundred thousand francs a year for the last twenty years, and for the last fifty years* has been the owner of a couple of fists and a backbone, which are not to be matched throughout the whole realm of France. Porthos is a man of the very greatest consequence compared to you, and . . . well, I need say no more, for I know you are an intelligent fellow.'

'No, no, monsieur, explain what you mean.'

'Look at your orchard, how stripped it is, how empty your larder, your bedstead broken, your cellar almost exhausted, look too . . . at Madame Trüchen——'

'Oh! my good gracious!' said Planchet.

'Madame Trüchen is an excellent person,' continued d'Artagnan, 'but keep her for yourself, do you understand?' and he slapped him on the shoulder.

Planchet at this moment perceived Porthos and Trüchen sitting close together in an arbour; Trüchen, with a grace of manner peculiarly Flemish, was making a pair of earrings for Porthos out of a double cherry, while Porthos was laughing as amorously as Samson did with Delilah.* Planchet pressed d'Artagnan's hand, and ran towards the arbour. We must do Porthos the justice to say that he did not move as they approached, and very likely he did not think he was doing any harm. Nor indeed did Trüchen move either, which rather put Planchet out; but he, too, had been so accustomed to see fashionable people in his shop, that he found no difficulty in putting a good countenance on what was disagreeable to him. Planchet seized Porthos by the arm, and proposed to go and look at the horses, but Porthos pretended he was tired. Planchet then suggested that the Baron du Vallon should taste some hazel-nut liqueur of his own manufacture, which was not to be equalled anywhere; an offer which the Baron immediately accepted; and, in this way, Planchet managed to engage his enemy's attention during the whole of the day, by dint of sacrificing his cellar in preference to his *amour propre*. Two hours afterwards d'Artagnan returned.

'Everything is arranged,' he said; 'I saw His Majesty at the very moment he was setting off for the chase; the King expects us this evening.'

'The King expects me!' cried Porthos, drawing himself up. It is a sad thing to have to confess, but a man's heart is like a restless billow; for, from that very moment, Porthos ceased to look at Madame Trüchen in that touching manner which had so softened her heart. Planchet encouraged these ambitious leanings in the best way he could. He talked over, or rather gave exaggerated accounts of all the splendours of the last reign, its battles, sieges, and grand court ceremonies. He spoke of the luxurious display which the English had made; the prizes which the three brave companions had won, and how d'Artagnan, who, at the beginning, had been the humblest of the three, had finished by becoming the head. He fired Porthos with a generous feeling of enthusiasm, by reminding him of his early youth, now passed away; he boasted as much as he could of the moral life this great lord had led, and how religiously he respected the ties of friendship. He was eloquent, and skilful in his choice of subjects. He delighted Porthos, frightened Trüchen, and made d'Artagnan think. At six o'clock, the musketeer ordered the horses to be brought round, and told Porthos to get ready. He thanked Planchet for his kind hospitality, whispered a few words about a post he might succeed in obtaining for him at court, which immediately raised Planchet in Trüchen's estimation, where the poor grocer—so good, so generous, so devoted—had become much lowered ever since the appearance and comparison with him of the two great gentlemen. Such, however, is woman's nature; they are anxious to possess what they have not got, and disdain it as soon as it is acquired. After having rendered this service to his friend Planchet, d'Artagnan said in a low tone of voice to Porthos; 'That is a very beautiful ring you have on your finger.'

'It's worth three hundred pistoles,' said Porthos.

'Madame Trüchen will remember you better if you leave her that ring,' replied d'Artagnan, a suggestion which Porthos seemed to hesitate to adopt.

'You think it is not beautiful enough perhaps,' said the musketeer; 'I understand your feelings; a great lord as you are would not think of accepting the hospitality of an old servant without paying him most handsomely for it; but I am sure that Planchet is too good-hearted a fellow to remember that you have an income of a hundred thousand francs a year.'

'I have more than half a mind,' said Porthos, flattered by the remark, 'to make Madame Trüchen a present of my little farm at Bracieux; it has twelve acres.'

'It is too much, my good Porthos, too much just at present. . . . Keep it for a future occasion.' He then took the ring off Porthos's finger—and approaching Trüchen, said to her,—'Madame, Monsieur le Baron hardly knows how to entreat you out of your regard for him, to accept this little ring. M. du Vallon is one of the most generous and discreet men of my acquaintance. He wished to offer you a farm that he has at Bracieux, but I dissuaded him from it.'

'Oh!' said Trüchen, looking eagerly at the diamond.

'Monsieur le Baron!' exclaimed Planchet quite overcome.

'My good friend,' stammered out Porthos, delighted at having been so well represented by d'Artagnan. These several exclamations, uttered at the same moment, made quite a pathetic winding up of a day which might have finished in a very ridiculous manner. But d'Artagnan was there, and on every occasion, wherever d'Artagnan had exercised any control, matters had ended only just in the way he wished and desired. There were general embracings. Trüchen, whom the Baron's munificence had restored to her proper position, very timidly, and blushing all the while, presented her forehead to the great lord with whom she had been on such very excellent terms the evening before. Planchet himself was overcome by a feeling of the deepest humility. Still, in the same generosity of disposition, Porthos would have emptied his pockets into the hands of the cook and of Celestin; but d'Artagnan stopped him.

'No,' he said, 'it is now my turn,' And he gave one pistole to the woman and two to the man; and the benedictions which were showered down upon them would have rejoiced the heart of Harpagon* himself, and have rendered even him prodigal of his money.

D'Artagnan made Planchet lead them to the château, and introduce Porthos into his own apartment, where he arrived

safely without having been perceived by those he was afraid of
meeting.

LV

THE PRESENTATION OF PORTHOS AT COURT

AT seven o'clock the same evening, the King gave an audience
to an ambassador from the United Provinces* in the grand
reception-room. The audience lasted a quarter of an hour. His
Majesty afterwards received those who had been recently presented, together with a few ladies, who paid their respects first.
In one corner of the salon, concealed behind a column, Porthos
and d'Artagnan were conversing together, waiting until their
turn arrived.

'Have you heard the news?' inquired the musketeer of his
friend.

'No.'

'Well, look then.' Porthos raised himself on tiptoe, and saw
M. Fouquet in full court dress, leading Aramis towards the King.

'Aramis,' said Porthos.

'Presented to the King by M. Fouquet.'

'Ah!' ejaculated Porthos.

'For having fortified Belle-Isle,' continued d'Artagnan.

'And I?'

'You—oh, you! as I have already had the honour of telling
you, are the good-natured, kind-hearted Porthos, and so they
begged you to look after Saint-Mandé a little.'

'Ah!' repeated Porthos.

'But very happily, I was there,' said d'Artagnan, 'and presently it will be my turn.'

At this moment, Fouquet addressed the King. 'Sire,' he said,
'I have a favour to solicit of your Majesty. M. d'Herblay is not
ambitious, but he knows he can be of some service. Your Majesty
needs a representative at Rome, who should be able to exercise
a powerful influence there; may I request a cardinal's hat for M.
d'Herblay?' The King started. 'I do not often solicit anything of
your Majesty,' said Fouquet.

'That is a reason, certainly,' replied the King, who always expressed any hesitation he might have in that manner, and to which remark there was nothing to say in reply.

Fouquet and Aramis looked at each other. The King resumed,—'M. d'Herblay can serve us equally well in France; an archbishopric for instance.'

'Sire,' objected Fouquet, with a grace of manner peculiarly his own, 'your Majesty overwhelms M. d'Herblay; the archbishopric may, in your Majesty's extreme kindness, be conferred in addition to the hat; the one does not exclude the other.'

The King admired the readiness which he displayed, and smiled, saying, 'D'Artagnan himself could not have answered better.' He had no sooner pronounced the name than d'Artagnan appeared.

'Did your Majesty call me?' he said.

Aramis and Fouquet drew back a step, as if they were about to retire.

'Will your Majesty allow me,' said d'Artagnan quickly, as he led forward Porthos, 'to present to your Majesty M. le Baron du Vallon, one of the bravest gentlemen of France?'

As soon as Aramis saw Porthos, he turned as pale as death, while Fouquet clenched his hands under his ruffles. D'Artagnan smiled at both of them, while Porthos bowed, visibly overcome before the royal presence.

'Porthos here?' murmured Fouquet in Aramis's ear.

'Hush! there is some treachery at work,' said the latter.

'Sire,' said d'Artagnan, 'it is more than six years ago that I ought to have presented M. du Vallon to your Majesty; but certain men resemble stars, they move not unless their friends accompany them. The Pleiades* are never disunited, and that is the reason I have selected, for the purpose of presenting him to you, the very moment when you would see M. d'Herblay by his side.'

Aramis almost lost countenance. He looked at d'Artagnan with a proud haughty air, as though willing to accept the defiance which the latter seemed to throw down.

'Ah! these gentlemen are good friends then?' said the King.

'Excellent friends, sire, the one can answer for the other. Ask M. de Vannes now in what manner Belle-Isle was fortified.' Fouquet moved back a step.

'Belle-Isle,' said Aramis coldly, 'has been fortified by that gentleman,' and he indicated Porthos with his hand, who bowed a second time. Louis could not withhold his admiration, though at the same time his suspicions were aroused.

'Yes,' said d'Artagnan, 'but ask Monsieur le Baron whose assistance he had in carrying the works out?'

'Aramis's,' said Porthos frankly; and he pointed to the Bishop.

'What the deuce does all this mean,' thought the Bishop, 'and what sort of a termination are we to expect to this comedy?'

'What!' exclaimed the King, 'is the Cardinal's—I mean the Bishop's name, Aramis?'

'A *nom de guerre*,'* said d'Artagnan.

'A name of friendship,' said Aramis.

'A truce to modesty,' exclaimed d'Artagnan; 'beneath the priest's robe, sire, is concealed the most brilliant officer, a gentleman of the most unparalleled intrepidity, and the wisest theologian in your kingdom.'

Louis raised his head. 'And an engineer, also, it appears,' he said, admiring Aramis's calm imperturbable self-possession.

'An engineer for a particular purpose, sire,' said the latter.

'My companion in the musketeers, sire,' said d'Artagnan with great warmth of manner, 'the man who has more than a hundred times aided your father's ministers by his advice—M. d'Herblay, in a word, who, with M. du Vallon, myself, and M. le Comte de la Fère, who is known to your Majesty, formed that quadrille which was a good deal talked about during the late King's reign, and during your Majesty's minority.'

'And who has fortified Belle-Isle?' the King repeated in a significant tone.

Aramis advanced and said: 'In order to serve the son as I have served the father.'

D'Artagnan looked at Aramis most narrowly while he uttered these words, which displayed so much true respect, so much warm devotion, such entire frankness and sincerity, that even he, d'Artagnan, the eternal doubter, he, the almost infallible in his judgement, was deceived by it. 'A man who lies cannot speak in such a tone as that,' he said.

Louis was overcome by it. 'In that case,' he said to Fouquet, who anxiously awaited the result of this proof, 'the cardinal's hat is promised. Monsieur d'Herblay, I pledge you my honour that the first promotion shall be yours. Thank M. Fouquet for it.' Colbert overheard these words; they stung him to the quick, and he left the salon abruptly. 'And you, Monsieur du Vallon,' said the King, 'what have you to ask? I am pleased to have it in my power to acknowledge the services of those who were faithful to my father.'

'Sire——' began Porthos; but he was unable to proceed with what he was going to say.

'Sire,' exclaimed d'Artagnan, 'this worthy gentleman is overpowered by your Majesty's presence, he who has so valiantly sustained the looks and the fire of a thousand foes. But, knowing what his thoughts are, I—who am more accustomed to gaze upon the sun—can translate his thoughts; he needs nothing, his sole desire is to have the happiness of gazing upon your Majesty for a quarter of an hour.'

'You shall sup with me this evening,' said the King, saluting Porthos with a gracious smile.

Porthos became crimson with delight and from pride. The King dismissed him, and d'Artagnan pushed him into the adjoining apartment, after he had embraced him warmly.

'Sit next to me at table,' said Porthos in his ear.

'Yes, my friend.'

'Aramis is annoyed with me, I think.'

'Aramis has never liked you so much as he does now. Fancy, it was I who was the means of his getting the cardinal's hat.'

'Of course,' said Porthos. 'By the bye, does the King like his guests to eat much at his table?'

'It is a compliment to himself if you do,' said d'Artagnan, 'for he possesses a royal appetite.'*

LVI

EXPLANATIONS

ARAMIS had cleverly managed to effect a diversion for the purpose of finding d'Artagnan and Porthos. He came up to the latter, behind one of the columns, and, as he pressed his hand, said, 'So you have escaped from my prison?'

'Do not scold him,' said d'Artagnan; 'it was I, dear Aramis, who set him free.'

'Ah! my friend,' replied Aramis, looking at Porthos, 'could you not have waited with a little more patience?'

D'Artagnan came to the assistance of Porthos, who already began to breathe hard in perplexity.

'You see, you members of the Church are great politicians; we, mere soldiers, go at once to the point. The facts are these; I went to pay Baisemeaux a visit——'

Aramis pricked up his ears at this announcement.

'Stay!' said Porthos; 'you make me remember that I have a letter from Baisemeaux for you, Aramis.' And Porthos held out to the Bishop the letter we have already seen. Aramis begged to be allowed to read it, and read it without d'Artagnan feeling in the slightest degree embarrassed by the circumstance that he was so well acquainted with the contents of it. Besides, Aramis's face was so impenetrable, that d'Artagnan could not but admire him more than ever; after he had read it, he put the letter into his pocket, with the calmest possible air.

'You were saying, captain?' he observed.

'I was saying,' continued the musketeer, 'that I had gone to pay Baisemeaux a visit on His Majesty's service.'

'On His Majesty's service?' said Aramis.

'Yes,' said d'Artagnan, 'and, naturally enough, we talked about you and your friends. I must say that Baisemeaux received me coldly; so I soon took my leave of him. As I was returning, a soldier accosted me, and said (no doubt he recognised me, notwithstanding I was in private clothes), 'Captain, will you be good enough to read me the name written on this envelope?' and I read, 'To Monsieur du Vallon, at M. Fouquet's Saint-Mandé.' The deuce, said I to myself, Porthos has not returned, then, as I fancied, to Belle-Isle, or to Pierrefonds, but is at M. Fouquet's house, at Saint-Mandé; and as M. Fouquet is not at Saint-Mandé, Porthos must be quite alone, or, at all events, with Aramis; I will go and see Porthos, and I accordingly went to see Porthos.'

'Very good,' said Aramis thoughtfully.

'You never told me that,' said Porthos.

'I did not have the time, my friend.'

'And you brought back Porthos with you to Fontainebleau?'

'Yes, to Planchet's house.'

'Does Planchet live at Fontainebleau?' inquired Aramis.

'Yes, near the cemetery,' said Porthos thoughtlessly.

'What do you mean by "near the cemetery"?' said Aramis suspiciously.

'Come,' thought the musketeer, 'since there is to be a squabble, let us take advantage of it.'

'Yes, the cemetery,' said Porthos. 'Planchet is a very excellent fellow, who makes very excellent preserves; but his house has windows which look out upon the cemetery. And a very melancholy prospect it is! So this morning——'

'This morning?' said Aramis, more and more excited.

D'Artagnan turned his back to them, and walked to the window, where he began to tap a march upon one of the panes of glass with his fingers.

'Yes, this morning, we saw a man buried there.'

'Ah! ah!'

'Very depressing, was it not? I should never be able to live in a house where burials can always be seen from it. D'Artagnan, on the contrary, seems to like it very much.'

'So d'Artagnan saw it as well?'

'Not simply saw it, he literally never took his eyes off the whole time.'

Aramis started, and turned to look at the musketeer, but the latter was engaged in earnest conversation with Saint-Aignan. Aramis continued to question Porthos, and when he had squeezed all the juice out of this enormous lemon, he threw the peel aside. He turned towards his friend d'Artagnan, and clapping him on the shoulder, when Saint-Aignan had left him, the King's supper having been announced, said, 'D'Artagnan.'

'Yes, my dear fellow,' he replied.

'We do not sup with His Majesty, I believe.'

'Yes, indeed, I do.'

'Can you give me ten minutes' conversation?'

'Twenty, if you like. His Majesty will take quite that time to get properly seated at table.'

'Where shall we talk then?'

'Here, upon these seats, if you like; the King has left; we can sit down, and the apartment is empty.'

'Let us sit down, then.'

They sat down, and Aramis took one of d'Artagnan's hands in his.

'Tell me, candidly, my dear friend, whether you have not counselled Porthos to distrust me a little?'

'I admit I have, but not as you understand it. I saw that Porthos was bored to death, and I wished, by presenting him to the King, to do for him and for you, what you would never do for yourselves.'

'What is that?'

'Speak in your own praise.'

'And you have done it most nobly, I thank you.'

'And I brought the cardinal's hat a little nearer, just as it seemed to be retreating from you.'

'Ah! I admit that,' said Aramis, with a singular smile, 'you are, indeed, not to be matched for making your friends' fortunes for them.'

'You see, then, that I only acted with the view of making Porthos's fortune for him.'

'I meant to have done that myself; but your arm reaches farther than ours.'

It was now d'Artagnan's turn to smile.

'Come,' said Aramis, 'we ought to deal truthfully with each other; do you still love me, d'Artagnan?'

'The same as I used to do,' replied d'Artagnan, without compromising himself too much by this reply.

'In that case, thanks; and now, for the most perfect frankness,' said Aramis; 'you went to Belle-Isle for the King?'

'Pardieu!'

'You wished to deprive us of the pleasure of offering Belle-Isle completely fortified to the King?'

'But before I could deprive you of that pleasure, I ought to have been made acquainted with your intention of doing so?'

'You came to Belle-Isle without knowing anything?'

'Of you? yes. How the devil could I imagine that Aramis had become so clever an engineer, as to be able to fortify like Polybius, or Archimedes?'*

'True. And yet you guessed my plans when we met?'*

'Oh, yes!'

'And Porthos, too?'

'I did not guess that Aramis was an engineer. I was only able to guess that Porthos might have become one. There is a saying,* one becomes an orator, one is born a poet; but it has never been said, one is born Porthos, and one becomes an engineer.'

'Your wit is always amusing,' said Aramis coldly. 'Well, then, I will go on.'

'Do so.'

'When you found out our secret, you made all the haste you could to communicate it to the King.'

'I certainly made as much haste as I could, since I saw that you were making still more. When a man weighing 258 pounds,* as Porthos does, rides post; when a gouty prelate—I beg your pardon, but you told me you were so—when a prelate does not let the dust settle on the road; I naturally suppose that my two friends, who did not wish to be communicative with me, had certain matters of the highest importance to conceal from me, and so I made as much haste as my leanness and the absence of gout would allow.'

'Did it not occur to you, my dear friend, that you might be rendering Porthos and myself a very sad service?'

'Yes, I thought it not unlikely; but you and Porthos made me play a very ridiculous part at Belle-Isle.'*

'I beg your pardon,' said Aramis.

'Excuse me,' said d'Artagnan.

'So that,' pursued Aramis, 'you now know everything?'

'No, indeed.'

'You know I was obliged to inform M. Fouquet of what had happened, in order that he might anticipate what you might have to tell the King?'

'That is rather obscure.'

'Not at all; M. Fouquet has his enemies—you will admit that, I suppose.'

'Certainly.'

'And one in particular.'

'A dangerous one?'

'A mortal enemy. Well! in order to counteract that man's influence, it was necessary that M. Fouquet should give the King a proof of a great devotion to him and of his readiness to make the greatest sacrifices. He surprised His Majesty by offering him Belle-Isle. If you had been the first to reach Paris, the surprise would have been destroyed, it would have looked as if we had yielded to fear.'

'I understand.'

'That is the whole mystery,' said Aramis, satisfied that he had quite convinced the musketeer.

'Only,' said the latter, 'it would have been more simple to have taken me aside, and said to me, "My dear d'Artagnan, we are fortifying Belle-Isle, and intend to offer it to the King. Tell us frankly, for whom you are acting. Are you a friend of M. Colbert, or of M. Fouquet?" Perhaps I should not have answered you, but you would have added—"Are you my friend?" I should have said yes.' Aramis hung down his head. 'In this way,' continued d'Artagnan, 'you would have paralysed my movements, and I should have gone to the King, and said, "Sire, M. Fouquet is fortifying Belle-Isle, and exceedingly well, too; but here is a note, which the governor of Belle-Isle gave me for your Majesty"; or, "M. Fouquet is about to wait upon your Majesty to explain his intentions with regard to it." I should not have been placed in an absurd position; you would have enjoyed the surprise you wished for, and we should not have had any occasion to look askance at each other when we met.'

'While, on the contrary,' replied Aramis, 'you have acted altogether as one friendly to M. Colbert. And you really are a friend of his, I suppose?'

'Certainly not, indeed!' exclaimed the captain. 'M. Colbert is a mean fellow, and I hate him as I used to hate Mazarin, but without fearing him.'

'Well, then,' said Aramis, 'I love M. Fouquet, and his interests are mine. You know my position———. I have no property or means whatever. M. Fouquet gave me several livings, a bishopric as well; M. Fouquet has served and obliged me like the generous-hearted man he is, and I know the world sufficiently well to appreciate a kindness when I meet with it. M. Fouquet has won my regard, and I have devoted myself to his service.'

'You couldn't do better. You will find him a very good master.'

Aramis bit his lips; and then said, 'The best a man could possibly have.' He then paused for a minute, d'Artagnan taking good care not to interrupt him.

'I suppose you know how Porthos got mixed up in all this?'

'No,' said d'Artagnan; 'I am curious of course, but I never question a friend when he wishes to keep a real secret from me.'

'Well, then, I will tell you.'

'It is hardly worth the trouble, if the confidence is to bind me in any way.'

'Oh! do not be afraid; there is no man whom I love better than Porthos; because he is so simple-minded and good. Porthos is so straightforward in everything. Since I have become a bishop, I have looked for those simple natures, which make me love truth and hate intrigue.'

D'Artagnan simply stroked his moustache but said nothing.

'I saw Porthos, and again cultivated his acquaintance; his own time hanging idly on his hands, his presence recalled my earlier and better days without engaging me in any present evil. I sent for Porthos to come to Vannes. M. Fouquet, whose regard for me is very great, having learned that Porthos and I were attached to each other by old ties of friendship, promised him increase of rank at the earliest promotion, and that is the whole secret.'

'I shall not abuse your confidence,' said d'Artagnan.

'I am sure of that, my dear friend; no one has a finer sense of honour than yourself.'

'I flatter myself you are right, Aramis.'

'And now——' and here the prelate looked searchingly and scrutinisingly at his friend—'now, let us talk of ourselves and for ourselves; will you become one of M. Fouquet's friends? Do not interrupt me until you know what that means.'

'Well, I am listening.'

'Will you become a marshal of France, peer, duke, and the possessor of a duchy, with a revenue of a million francs?'

'But, my friend,' replied d'Artagnan, 'what must one do to get all that?'

'Belong to M. Fouquet.'

'But I already belong to the King.'

'Not exclusively, I suppose.'

'Oh! d'Artagnan cannot be divided.'

'You have, I presume, ambitions, as noble hearts like yours have?'

'Yes; certainly I have.'

'Well?'

'Well! I wish to be a marshal; the King will make me marshal, duke, peer,—the King will make me all that.'*

Aramis fixed a searching look upon d'Artagnan.

'Is not the King master?' said d'Artagnan.

'No one disputes it; but Louis XIII was master also.'

'Oh! my dear friend, between Richelieu and Louis XIII there was no d'Artagnan,' said the musketeer very quietly.

'There are many stumbling-blocks round the King,' said Aramis.

'Not for the King.'

'Very likely not, still——'

'One moment, Aramis; I observe that every one thinks of himself, and never of this poor young Prince; I will myself maintain him.'

'And if you meet with ingratitude?'

'The weak alone are afraid of that.'

'Are you quite certain of yourself?'

'I think so.'

'Still the King may have no further need of you?'

'On the contrary, I think his need of me will be greater than ever; and hearken, my dear fellow, if it became necessary to arrest a new Condé,* who would do it? This, this alone in all France,' and d'Artagnan struck his sword.

'You are right,' said Aramis, turning very pale; and then he rose and pressed d'Artagnan's hand.

'That is the last summons for supper,' said the captain of the musketeers; 'you will excuse me.'

Aramis threw his arm round the musketeer's neck, and said, 'A friend like you is the brightest jewel in the royal crown.' And they immediately separated.

'I was right,' thought d'Artagnan; 'there is something on foot.'

'We must make haste with the explosion,' said Aramis, 'for d'Artagnan has discovered the plot.'

LVII

MADAME AND GUICHE

IT will not be forgotten that the Comte de Guiche had left the Queen-Mother's apartment on the day when Louis XIV presented La Vallière with the beautiful bracelets he had won at the lottery.* The Comte walked to and fro for some time outside the palace, in the greatest distress, from a thousand suspicions and anxieties with which his mind was beset. Presently he stopped and waited on the terrace opposite the grove of trees, watching for Madame's departure. More than half an hour passed; and as he was at that moment quite alone, the Comte could hardly have had any very diverting ideas at his command. He drew his tablets from his pocket, and, after hesitating over and over again, determined to write these words,—'Madame, I implore you to grant me one moment's conversation. Do not be alarmed at this request which contains nothing in any way opposed to the profound respect with which I subscribe myself, etc., etc.' He then signed and folded this singular supplication, when he suddenly observed several ladies leaving the château, and afterwards several men also, in fact almost every person who had formed the Queen's circle. He saw La Vallière herself, then Montalais talking with Malicorne; he saw the departure of the very last of the numerous guests who had a short time before thronged the Queen-Mother's apartment.

Madame herself had not passed; she would be obliged, however, to cross the courtyard in order to enter her own quarters; and, from the terrace where he was standing, de Guiche could see all that was passing in the courtyard. At last, he saw Madame leave, attended by a couple of pages, who were carrying torches before her. She was walking very quickly; as soon as she reached the door, she said,—

'Let some one go and see after de Guiche. He has to render me an account of a mission he had to discharge for me; if he should be disengaged, request him to be good enough to come to my apartment.'

De Guiche remained silent and concealed in the shade; but, as soon as Madame had withdrawn, he darted from the terrace down the steps, and assumed a most indifferent air, so that the pages who were hurrying towards his rooms might meet him.

'Ah! it is Madame then who is seeking me!' he said to himself, quite overcome; and he crushed in his hand the letter which had now become useless.

'M. le Comte,' said one of the pages approaching him, 'we are indeed most fortunate in meeting you.'

'Why so, messieurs?'

'A command from Madame.'

'From Madame!' said de Guiche, looking surprised.

'Yes, M. le Comte, Her Royal Highness has been asking for you; she expects to hear, she told us, the result of a commission you had to execute for her. Are you at liberty?'

'I am quite at Her Royal Highness's orders.'

'Will you have the goodness to follow us, then?'

When de Guiche ascended to the Princess's apartments, he found her pale and agitated. Montalais was standing at the door, apparently in some degree uneasy about what was passing in her mistress's mind. De Guiche appeared.

'Ah! is that you, Monsieur de Guiche?' said Madame; 'come in, I beg. Mademoiselle de Montalais, I do not require your attendance any longer.'

Montalais, more puzzled than ever, curtseyed and withdrew, and de Guiche and the Princess were left alone. The Comte had every advantage in his favour; it was Madame who had summoned him to a rendezvous. But how was it possible for the Comte to make use of this advantage? Madame was so whimsical and her disposition was so changeable. She soon allowed this to be perceived, for, suddenly opening the conversation, she said, 'Well, have you nothing to say to me?'

He imagined she must have guessed his thoughts; he fancied (for those who are in love are so constituted, they are as credulous and blind as poets or prophets), he fancied she knew how ardent was his desire to see her, and also the subject of it.

'Yes, Madame,' he said, 'and I think it very singular.'

'The affair of the bracelets,' she exclaimed eagerly, 'you mean that, I suppose?'

'Yes, Madame.'

'And you think the King is in love; do you not?'

Guiche looked at her for some time; her eyes sunk under his gaze, which seemed to read her very heart.

'I think,' he said, 'that the King may possibly have had an idea of annoying some one here; were it not for that, the King would not show himself so earnest in his attentions as he is; he would not run the risk of compromising from mere thoughtlessness of disposition, a young girl against whom no one has been hitherto able to say a word.'

'Indeed! the bold shameless girl,' said the Princess haughtily.

'I can positively assure your Royal Highness,' said de Guiche, with a firmness marked by great respect, 'that Mademoiselle de la Vallière is beloved by a man who merits every respect, for he is a brave and honourable gentleman.'

'Bragelonne, perhaps?'

'My friend; yes, Madame.'

'Well, and although he is your friend, what does that matter to the King?'

'The King knows that Bragelonne is affianced to Mademoiselle de la Vallière; and as Raoul has served the King most valiantly, the King will not inflict an irreparable injury upon him.'

Madame began to laugh in a manner that produced a mournful impression upon de Guiche.

'I repeat, Madame, I do not believe the King is in love with Mademoiselle de la Vallière; and the proof that I do not believe it is, that I was about to ask you whose *amour propre* it is likely the King is, in this circumstance, desirous of wounding? You, who are well acquainted with the whole court, can perhaps assist me in ascertaining that; and assuredly, with greater reason too, since it is everywhere said that your Royal Highness is on very intimate terms with the King.'

Madame bit her lips, and, unable to assign any good and sufficient reasons, changed the conversation. 'Prove to me,' she said, fixing on him one of those looks in which the whole soul seems to pass into the eyes, 'prove to me, I say, that you intended to interrogate me at the very moment I sent for you.'

De Guiche gravely drew from his tablets what he had written, and showed it to her.

'Sympathy,' she said.

'Yes,' said the Comte with an indescribable tenderness of tone, 'sympathy. I have explained to you how and why I sought you; you, however, have yet to tell me, Madame, why you sent for me.'

'True,' replied the Princess. She hesitated, and then suddenly exclaimed, 'Those bracelets will drive me mad.'

'You expected the King would offer them to you,' replied de Guiche.

'Why not?'

'But before you, Madame, before you, his sister-in-law, was there not the Queen herself to whom the King should have offered them?'

'Before La Vallière,' cried the Princess, wounded to the quick, 'could he not have presented them to me? Was there not the whole court, indeed, to choose from?'

'I assure you, Madame,' said the Comte respectfully, 'that if any one heard you speak in this manner, if any one were to see how red your eyes are, and, Heaven forgive me, to see, too, that tear trembling on your eyelids, it would be said that your Royal Highness was jealous.'

'Jealous!' cried the Princess haughtily, 'jealous of La Vallière!'

She expected to see de Guiche yield beneath her haughty gesture and her proud tone; but he simply and boldly replied, 'Jealous of La Vallière; yes, Madame.'

'Am I to suppose, monsieur,' she stammered out, 'that your object is to insult me?'

'It is not possible, Madame,' replied the Comte slightly agitated, but resolved to master that fiery nature.

'Leave the room,' said the Princess, thoroughly exasperated; de Guiche's coolness and silent respect having made her completely lose her temper.

De Guiche fell back a step, bowed slowly, but with great respect, drew himself up, looking as white as his lace cuffs, and, in a voice slightly trembling, said, 'It was hardly worth while to have hurried here to be subjected to this unmerited disgrace.' And he turned away with hasty steps.

He had scarcely gone half a dozen paces when Madame darted like a tigress after him, seized him by the cuff, and, making him turn round again, said, trembling with passion, as she did so, 'The respect that you pretend to have is more insulting than insult itself. Insult me, if you please, but at least speak.'

'And do you, Madame,' said the Comte gently, as he drew his sword, 'thrust this sword into my heart, rather than kill me by slow degrees.'

At the look he fixed upon her—a look full of love, resolution, and despair even—she knew how readily the Comte, so outwardly calm in appearance, would pass his sword through his own breast if she added another word. She tore the blade from his hands, and, pressing his arm with a feverish impatience, which might pass for tenderness, said, 'Do not be too hard with me, Comte. You see how I am suffering, and you have no pity for me.'

Tears, which were the last crisis of the attack, stifled her voice. As soon as de Guiche saw her weep, he took her in his arms and carried her to an arm-chair; in another moment she would have been suffocated from suppressed passion.

'Oh, why,' he murmured, as he knelt by her side, 'why do you conceal your troubles from me? Do you love any one—tell me? It would kill me, I know, but not until after I should have comforted, consoled, and served you even.'

'And do you love me to that extent?' she replied, completely conquered.

'I do indeed love you to that extent, Madame.'

She placed both her hands in his. 'My heart is indeed another's,' she murmured in so low a tone that her voice could hardly be heard; but he heard it, and said, 'Is it the King you love?'

She gently shook her head, and her smile was like a clear bright streak in the clouds, through which, after the tempest has passed away, one almost fancies Paradise is opening. 'But,' she added, 'there are other passions stirring in a high-born heart. Love is poetry; but the life of the heart is pride. Comte, I was born upon a throne, I am proud and jealous of my rank. Why does the King gather such unworthy objects round him?'

'Once more, I repeat,' said the Comte, 'you are acting unjustly towards that poor girl, who will one day be my friend's wife.'

'Are you simple enough to believe that, Comte?'

'If I did not believe it,' he said, turning very pale, 'Bragelonne should be informed of it to-morrow; indeed he should, if I thought that poor La Vallière had forgotten the vows she had exchanged with Raoul. But no, it would be cowardly to betray any woman's secret; it would be criminal to disturb a friend's peace of mind.'

'You think, then,' said the Princess, with a wild burst of laughter, 'that ignorance is happiness?'

'I believe it,' he replied.

'Prove it to me, then,' she said hurriedly.

'It is easily done, Madame. It is reported through the whole court that the King loves you, and that you return his affection.'

'Well?' she said, breathing with difficulty.

'Well; admit for a moment that Raoul, my friend, had come and said to me, "Yes, the King loves Madame, and has made an impression upon her heart," I possibly should have slain Raoul.'

'It would have been necessary,' said the Princess, with the obstinacy of a woman who feels herself not easily overcome, 'for M. de Bragelonne to have had proofs, before he could venture to speak to you in that manner.'

'Such, however, is the case,' replied de Guiche, with a deep sigh, 'that not having been warned, I have never examined the matter seriously; and I now find that my ignorance has saved my life.'

'So, then, you would drive your selfishness and coldness to that extent,' said Madame, 'that you would let this unhappy young man continue to love La Vallière?'

'I would, until La Vallière's guilt were revealed.'

'But the bracelets?'

'Well, Madame, since you yourself expected to receive them from the King, what could I possibly have said?'

The argument was a telling one, and the Princess was overwhelmed by it, and from that moment her defeat was assured. But as her heart and mind were instinct with noble and generous feelings, she understood de Guiche's extreme delicacy. She saw that in his heart he really suspected that the King was in love with La Vallière, and that he did not wish to resort to the common expedient of ruining a rival in the mind of a woman, by giving the latter the assurance and certainty that this rival's affections were transferred to another woman. She guessed that his suspicions of La Vallière were aroused, and that, in order to leave himself time for his conviction to undergo a change, so as not to ruin her utterly, he was determined to pursue a certain straightforward line of conduct. She could read so much real greatness of character, and such true generosity of disposition in her lover, that her heart seemed to warm with affection towards him, whose passion for her was so pure and delicate in its nature. Despite his fear of incurring her displeasure, de Guiche, by retaining his position as a man of proud independence of feeling and of deep devotion, became almost a hero in her estimation, and reduced her to the state of a jealous and little-minded woman. She loved him for it so tenderly, that she could not refuse to give him a proof of her affection.

'See, how many words we have wasted,' she said, taking his hand; 'suspicions, anxieties, mistrust, sufferings—I think we have mentioned all those words.'

'Alas! Madame, yes.'

'Efface them from your heart as I drive them from mine. Whether La Vallière does or does not love the King, and whether the King does or does not love La Vallière—from this moment you and I will draw a distinction in the two characters I have to perform. You open your eyes so wide that I am sure you do not understand me.'

'You are so impetuous, Madame, that I always tremble at the fear of displeasing you.'

'And see how he trembles now, poor fellow,' she said with the most charming playfulness of manner. 'Yes, monsieur, I have two characters to perform. I am the sister of the King, the sister-in-law of the King's wife. In this character ought I not to take an interest in these domestic intrigues? Come, tell me what you think?'

'As little as possible, Madame.'

'Agreed, monsieur; but it is a question of dignity; and then, you know, I am the wife of the King's brother.' Guiche sighed. 'A circumstance,' she added, with an expression of great tenderness, 'which will remind you that I am always to be treated with the profoundest respect.' Guiche fell at her feet, which he kissed, with the religious fervour of a worshipper. 'And I begin to think that, really and truly, I have another character to perform. I was almost forgetting it.'

'Name it, oh! name it,' said Guiche.

'I am a woman,' she said in a voice lower than ever, 'and I love another.' He rose; she opened her arms, and their lips were pressed together. A footstep was heard behind the tapestry, and Mademoiselle de Montalais appeared.

'What do you want?'

'M. de Guiche is wanted,' replied Montalais, who was just in time to see the agitation of the actors of these four characters; for Guiche had constantly carried out his part with the greatest heroism.

LVIII

MONTALAIS AND MALICORNE

MONTALAIS was right. M. de Guiche, summoned in every direction, was very much exposed, even from the multiplication of matters, to the risk of not answering in any one direction. It so happened that, considering the awkwardness of the interruption, Madame, notwithstanding her wounded pride, and her secret anger, could not, for the moment at least, reproach Montalais for having violated, in so bold a manner, the semi-royal order with which she had been dismissed on Guiche's entrance. Guiche, also, lost his presence of mind, or, it would be better to say, that he had already lost it before Montalais's arrival; for, scarcely had he heard the young girl's voice, than without taking leave of Madame, as the most ordinary politeness required, even between persons equal in rank and station, he fled from her presence, his heart tumultuously throbbing, and his brain on fire, leaving the Princess with one hand raised, as though about to bid him adieu. Montalais was at no loss, therefore, to perceive the agitation of the two lovers—the one who fled was agitated and the one who remained was equally so.

'So, so,' murmured the young girl as she glanced inquisitively round her, 'this time, at least, I think I know as much as the most curious woman could possibly wish to know.' Madame felt so embarrassed by this inquisitorial look, that, as if she had heard Montalais's muttered side-remark, she did not speak a word to her maid of honour, but, casting down her eyes, retired at once to her bedroom. Montalais, observing this, stood listening for a moment, and then heard Madame lock and bolt her door. By this she knew that the rest of the evening was at her disposal; and making, behind the door which had just been closed, a gesture which indicated but little real respect for the Princess, she went down the staircase in search of Malicorne, who was very busily engaged at that moment in watching a courier, who, covered with dust, had just left the Comte de Guiche's apartments. Montalais knew that Malicorne was engaged in a matter of some importance; she therefore allowed him to look and stretch out his neck as much as he pleased; and it was only when Malicorne had resumed his natural position that she touched him on the shoulder. 'Well,' said Montalais, 'what is the latest intelligence you have?'

'M. de Guiche is in love with Madame.'

'Fine news, truly! I know something more recent than that.'

'Well, what do you know?'

'That Madame is in love with M. de Guiche.'

'The one is the consequence of the other.'

'Not always, my good monsieur.'

'Is that remark intended for me?'

'Present company are always excepted.'

'Thank you,' said Malicorne. 'Well, and in the other direction what is there fresh?'

'The King wished, this evening, after the lottery, to see Mademoiselle de la Vallière.'

'Well, and he has seen her?'

'No, indeed.'

'What do you mean by that?'

'The door was shut and locked.'

'So that——'

'So that the King was obliged to go back again, looking very sheepish, like a thief who has forgotten his implements.'

'Good.'

'And in the third direction?' inquired Montalais.

'The courier who has just arrived for de Guiche came from M. de Bragelonne.'

'Excellent,' said Montalais, clapping her hands together.

'Why so?'

'Because we have work to do. If we get weary now, something unfortunate will be sure to happen.'

'We must divide the work, then,' said Malicorne, 'in order to avoid confusion.'

'Nothing easier,' replied Montalais. 'Three intrigues, carefully nursed and carefully encouraged, will produce, one with another, and taking a low average, three love-letters a day.'*

'Oh!' exclaimed Malicorne shrugging his shoulders, 'you cannot mean what you say, darling; three letters a day, that may be for sentimental common people. A musketeer on duty, a young girl in a convent, may exchange letters with their lovers once a day, perhaps, from the top of a ladder, or through a hole in the wall. A letter contains all the poetry their poor little hearts have to boast of. But the cases we have in hand require to be dealt with very differently.'

'Well, finish,' said Montalais out of patience with him. 'Some one may come.'

'Finish! Why I am only at the beginning. I have still three points as yet untouched.'

'Upon my word, he will be the death of me, with his Flemish indifference,' exclaimed Montalais.

'And you will drive me mad with your Italian vivacity.* I was going to say that our lovers here will be writing volumes to each other. But what are you driving at?'

'At this: Not one of our lady correspondents will be able to keep the letters they may receive.'

'Very likely not.'

'M. de Guiche will not be able to keep his either.'

'That is probable.'

'Very well, then; I will take care of all that.'

'That is the very thing which is impossible,' said Malicorne.

'Why so?'

'Because you are not your own mistress; your room is as much La Vallière's as yours; and there are certain persons who will think nothing of visiting and searching a maid of honour's room; so that I am terribly afraid of the Queen, who is as jealous as a Spaniard; of the Queen-Mother, who is as jealous as a couple of Spaniards; and, last of all, of Madame herself, who has jealousy enough for ten Spaniards.'

'You've left someone out.'

'Who?'

'Monsieur.'

'I was only speaking of the women. Let us add them up, then: we will call Monsieur No. 1.'

'Guiche?'

'No. 2.'

'The Vicomte de Bragelonne?'

'No. 3.'

'And the King, the King?'

'No. 4. Of course the King, who not only will be more jealous, but still more powerful than all the rest put together. Ah, my dear!'

'Well?'

'Into what a wasp's nest you have thrust yourself!'

'As yet not quite far enough, if you will follow me into it.'

'Most certainly I will follow you where you like. Yet——'

'Well, yet——'

'While we have time enough left, I think it will be more prudent to turn back.'

'But I, on the contrary, think the most prudent course to take is to put ourselves at once at the head of all these intrigues.'

'You will never be able to do it.'

'With you I could carry on ten of them. I am in my element, you must know. I was born to live at court, as the salamander is made to live in fire.'

'Your comparison does not reassure me in the slightest degree in the world, my dear Montalais. I have heard it said, and by men very learned too, that, in the first place, there are no salamanders at all, and that, if there had been any, they would have been perfectly baked or roasted on leaving the fire.'

'Your learned men may be very wise as far as salamanders are concerned, but your learned men will never tell you what I can tell you; namely, that Aure de Montalais is destined, before a month is over, to become the greatest diplomatic genius in the court of France.'

'Be it so, but on condition that I shall be the second.'

'Agreed; an offensive and defensive alliance of course.'

'Only be very careful of any letters.'

'I will hand them to you as I receive them.'

'What shall we tell the King about Madame?'

'That Madame is still in love with His Majesty.'

'What shall we tell Madame about the King?'

'That she would be exceedingly wrong not to humour him.'

'What shall we tell La Vallière about Madame?'

'Whatever we choose, for La Vallière is in our power.'

'How so?'

'In two ways.'

'What do you mean?'

'In the first place, through the Vicomte de Bragelonne.'

'Explain yourself?'

'You do not forget, I hope, that Monsieur de Bragelonne has written many letters to Mademoiselle de la Vallière?'

'I forget nothing.'

'Well, then, it was I who received, and I who kept, those letters.'

'And consequently, it is you who have them still?'

'Yes.'

'Where—here?'

'Oh, no; I have them safe at Blois, in the little room you know well enough.'

'That dear little room—that darling little room, the ante-chamber of the palace I intend you to live in one of these days. But I beg your pardon, you said that all those letters are in that little room?'

'Yes.'

'Did you not put them in a box?'

'Of course; in the same box where I put all the letters I received from you, and where I put mine also when your business or your amusements prevented you from coming to our rendezvous.'

'Ah, very good,' said Malicorne.

'Why are you so satisfied?'

'Because I see there is a possibility of not having to run to Blois after the letters, for I have them here.'

'You have brought the box away?'

'It was very dear to me, because it belonged to you.'

'Be sure and take care of it, for it contains original documents which will be of very great value by-and-by.'

'I am perfectly well aware of that indeed, and that is the very reason why I laugh as I do, and with all my heart too.'

'And now, one last word.'

'Why the last?'

'Do we need any one to assist us?'

'No one at all.'

'Valets, or maid-servants.'

'Bad—detestable. You will give the letters—you will receive them. Oh! we must have no pride in this affair, otherwise M. Malicorne and Mademoiselle Aure, not transacting their own affairs themselves, will have to make up their minds to see them done by others.'

'You are quite right; but what is going on yonder in M. de Guiche's room?'

'Nothing; he is only opening his window.'

'Let us be gone.' And they both immediately disappeared, all the terms of the compact having been agreed upon.

The window which had just been opened was, in fact, that of the Comte de Guiche. But it was not alone with the hope of catching a glimpse of Madame through her curtains that he seated himself by the open window, for his pre-occupation of mind had at that time a different origin. He had just received, as we have already stated, the courier who had been despatched to him by Bragelonne, the latter having written to de Guiche a letter which had made the deepest impression upon him, and which he had read over and over again. 'Strange, strange!' he murmured. 'How powerful are the means by which destiny hurries men on towards their fate!' Leaving the window in order to approach nearer to the light, he again read over the letter he had just received,—

                                                        'CALAIS.'

'MY DEAR COUNT,—I found M. de Wardes at Calais; he has been seriously wounded in an affair with the Duke of Buckingham. De Wardes is, as you know, unquestionably brave, but full of malevolent and wicked feelings. He conversed with me about yourself, for whom, he says, he has a warm regard; and also about Madame, whom he considers a beautiful and amiable woman. He has guessed your affection for a certain person. He also talked to me about the person for whom I have so ardent a regard, and showed the greatest interest on my behalf in expressing a deep pity for me, accompanied, however, by dark hints which alarmed me at first, but which I at last looked upon as the result of his usual love of mystery. These are the facts: He had received news of the court; you will understand, however, that it was only through M. de Lorraine. The report is, so says the news, that a change has taken place in the King's affections. You know whom that concerns. Afterwards, the news continues, people are talking about one of the maids of honour, respecting whom various slanderous reports are being circulated. These vague phrases have not allowed me to sleep. I have been deploring, ever since yesterday, that my diffidence and vacillation of purpose should, notwithstanding a certain obstinacy of character I may possess, have left me unable to reply to these insinuations. In a word, therefore, M. de Wardes was setting off for Paris, and I did not delay his departure with explanations; for it seemed rather hard, I confess, to cross-examine a man whose wounds are hardly yet closed. In short, he travelled by short stages, as he was anxious to leave, he said, in order to be present at a curious spectacle which the court cannot fail to offer within a very short time. He added a few congratulatory words, accompanied by certain sympathising expressions—I could not understand the one any more than the other. I was bewildered by my own thoughts, and then tormented by a mistrust of this man—a mistrust which, you know better than any one else, I have never been able to overcome. As soon as he left, my perception seemed to become clearer. It is hardly possible that a man of de Wardes's character should not have communicated something of his own malicious nature to the statements he made to me. It is not unlikely, therefore, that in the mysterious hints which de Wardes threw out in my presence, there may not be a mysterious signification, which I might have some difficulty in applying either to myself or to some one with whom you are acquainted. Being compelled to leave as soon as possible, in obedience to the King's commands, the idea did not occur to me of running after de

Wardes in order to ask him to explain his reserve, but I have despatched a courier to you with this letter, which will explain in detail all my various doubts. I regard you as myself; it is you who have thought—and it will be for you to act. M. de Wardes will arrive very shortly; endeavour to learn what he meant, if you do not already know it. M. de Wardes, moreover, pretended that the Duke of Buckingham left Paris on the very best of terms with Madame. This was an affair which would have unhesitatingly made me draw my sword, had I not felt that I was under the necessity of despatching the King's mission before undertaking any quarrel. Burn this letter, which Olivain will hand you. Whatever Olivain says you may confidently rely upon. Will you have the goodness, my dear Comte, to recall me to the remembrance of Mademoiselle de la Vallière, whose hands I kiss with the greatest respect.

'Your devoted,   'DE BRAGELONNE.'

'P.S.—If anything serious should happen—we should be prepared for everything—despatch a courier to me with this one single word, "Come," and I shall be in Paris within six-and-thirty hours after I shall have received your letter.'

De Guiche sighed, folded the letter up a third time, and, instead of burning it as Raoul had recommended him to do, placed it in his pocket. He felt that he needed to read it over and over again.

'How much distress of mind, and yet how great a confidence, he shows!' murmured the Comte; 'he has poured out his whole soul in that letter. He says nothing of the Comte de la Fère, and speaks of his respect for Louise. He cautions me on my account, and entreats me on his own. Ah!' continued de Guiche, with a threatening gesture, 'you interfere in my affairs, Monsieur de Wardes, do you? Very well, then; I shall now occupy myself with yours. And for you, poor Raoul,—you who entrust your heart to my keeping, be assured I will watch over it.'

With this promise, de Guiche begged Malicorne to come immediately to his apartments, if it were possible. Malicorne acknowledged the invitation with an activity which was the first result of his conversation with Montalais. And while de Guiche, who thought that his motive was undiscovered, cross-examined Malicorne, the latter, who appeared to be working in the dark, soon guessed his questioner's motives. The consequence was, that, after a quarter of an hour's conversation, during which de Guiche thought he had ascertained the whole truth with regard to La Vallière and the King, he had learned absolutely nothing more than his own eyes had already acquainted him with, while Malicorne learned or guessed that Raoul, who was absent, was fast becoming suspicious, and that de Guiche intended to watch over the treasure of the Hesperides.* Malicorne accepted the office of dragon. De Guiche fancied he had done everything for his friend, and soon began to think of nothing but his own personal affairs. The next evening, de Wardes's return and his first appearance at the King's reception were announced. When that visit had been paid, the convalescent waited on Monsieur; de Guiche taking care, however, to be at Monsieur's apartments before the visit took place.

LIX

HOW DE WARDES WAS RECEIVED AT COURT

MONSIEUR had received de Wardes with that marked favour which all light and frivolous minds bestow on every novelty that may come in their way. De Wardes, who had been absent for a month,* was like fresh fruit to him. To treat him with marked kindness was an infidelity to his old friends, and there was always something fascinating in that; moreover, it was a sort of reparation to de Wardes himself. Nothing, consequently, could exceed the favourable notice Monsieur took of him. The Chevalier de Lorraine, who feared this rival not a little, but who respected a character and disposition which were precisely parallel to his own in every particular, with the addition of a courage he did not himself possess, received de Wardes with a greater display of regard and affection than even Monsieur had done. De Guiche, as we have said, was there also, but kept a little in the background, waiting very patiently until all these embraces were over. De Wardes, while talking to the others, and even to Monsieur himself, had not for a moment lost sight of de Guiche, who, he instinctively felt, was there on his account. As soon as he had finished with the others he went up to de Guiche. They both exchanged the most courteous compliments, after which de Wardes returned to Monsieur and to the other gentlemen. In the midst of these congratulations Madame was announced. She had been informed of de Wardes's arrival, and knowing all the details of his voyage and of his duel, she was not sorry to be present at the remarks she knew would be made, without delay, by one who, she felt assured, was her personal enemy. Two or three of her ladies accompanied her. De Wardes saluted Madame in the most graceful and respectful manner, and, as a commencement of hostilities, announced, in the first place, that he could furnish the Duke of Buckingham's friends with the latest news about him. This was a direct answer to the coldness with which Madame had received him. The attack was a vigorous one, and Madame felt the blow, but without appearing to have even noticed it. He rapidly cast a glance at Monsieur and at de Guiche—the former had coloured, and the latter had turned very pale, Madame alone preserved an unmoved countenance; but, as she knew how many unpleasant thoughts and feelings her enemy could awaken in the two persons who were listening to him, she smilingly bent forward towards the traveller, as if to listen to the news he had brought, but he was speaking of other matters. Madame was brave, even to imprudence; if she were to retreat, it would be inviting an attack; so, after the first disagreeable impression had passed away, she returned to the charge.

'Have you suffered much from your wounds, Monsieur de Wardes?' she inquired, 'for we have been told that you had the misfortune to get wounded.'

It was now de Wardes's turn to wince; he bit his lips, and replied, 'No, Madame, hardly at all.'

'Indeed, and yet in this terrible hot weather——'

'The sea-breezes are fresh and cool, Madame, and then I had one consolation.'

'Indeed. What was it?'

'The knowledge that my adversary's sufferings were still greater than my own.'

'Ah! you mean he was more seriously wounded than you were; I was not aware of that,' said the Princess with utter indifference.

'Oh! Madame, you are mistaken, or rather you pretend to misunderstand my remark. I did not say that he was suffering more in body than myself; but his heart was seriously affected.'

De Guiche comprehended in what direction the struggle was approaching; he ventured to make a sign to Madame, as if entreating her to retire from the contest. But she, without acknowledging de Guiche's gesture, without pretending to have noticed it even, and still smiling, continued,—

'Is it possible,' she said, 'that the Duke of Buckingham's heart was touched? I had no idea, until now, that a heart-wound could be cured.'

'Alas! Madame,' replied de Wardes politely, 'every woman believes that; and it is such a belief which gives them over us that superiority which confidence imposes.'

'You misunderstand altogether, dearest,' said the Prince impatiently; 'M. de Wardes means that the Duke of Buckingham's heart had been touched, not by a sword, but by something else.'

'Ah! very good, very good!' exclaimed Madame. 'It is a jest of M. de Wardes; very good; but I should like to know if the Duke of Buckingham would appreciate the jest. It is, indeed, a very great pity he is not here, M. de Wardes.'

The young man's eyes seemed to flash fire. 'Oh!' he said, as he clenched his teeth, 'there is nothing I should like better.'

De Guiche did not move. Madame seemed to expect that he would come to her assistance. Monsieur hesitated. The Chevalier de Lorraine advanced and continued the conversation.

'Madame,' he said, 'de Wardes knows perfectly well that for a Buckingham's heart to be touched is nothing new, and what he has said has already taken place.'

'Instead of an ally, I have two enemies,' murmured Madame; 'two determined enemies, and in league with each other.' And she changed the conversation. To change the conversation is, as every one knows, a right possessed by princes which etiquette requires all to respect. The remainder of the conversation was moderate enough in its tone; the principal actors had finished their parts. Madame withdrew early, and Monsieur, who wished to question her on several matters, offered her his hand on leaving. The Chevalier was seriously afraid that a good understanding might be established between the husband and wife if he were to leave them quietly together. He therefore made his way to Monsieur's apartments, in order to surprise him on his return, and to destroy with a few words all the good impressions that Madame might have been able to sow in his heart. De Guiche advanced towards de Wardes, who was surrounded by a large number of persons, and thereby indicated his wish to converse with him; de Wardes, at the same time, showing both by his looks and by a movement of his head that he perfectly understood him. There was nothing in these signs to enable strangers to suppose they were otherwise than upon the most friendly footing. De Guiche could therefore turn away from him, and wait until he was at liberty. He had not long to wait; for de Wardes, freed from his questioners, approached de Guiche, and both of them, after salutation, began to walk side by side together.

'You have made a good impression since your return, my dear de Wardes,' said the Comte.

'Excellent, as you see.'

'And your spirits are just as lively as ever?'

'More than ever.'

'And a very great happiness too.'

'Why not? Everything is so ridiculous in this world, everything so absurd around us.'

'You are right.'

'You are of my opinion, then?'

'I should think so. And what news do you bring us from yonder?'

'I? none at all. I have come to look for news here.'

'But tell me, you surely must have seen some people at Boulogne, one of our friends, for instance; it is no great time ago?'

'Some people—one of our friends——'

'Your memory is short.'

'Ah! true; Bragelonne, you mean?'

'Exactly so.'

'Who was on his way to fulfil a mission, with which he was intrusted, to King Charles II.'

'Precisely. Well, then, did he not tell you, or did not you tell him——'

'I do not precisely know what I told him, I must confess, but I do know what I did not tell him.' De Wardes was *finesse* itself. He perfectly well knew from de Guiche's tone and manner, which was cold and dignified, that the conversation was about to assume a disagreeable turn. He resolved to let it take what course it pleased, and to keep strictly on his guard.

'May I ask what it was you did not tell him?' inquired de Guiche.

'About La Vallière.'

'La Vallière . . . What is it? and what was the strange circumstance you seem to have known out yonder, which Bragelonne, who was here on the spot, was not acquainted with?'

'Do you really ask me that in a serious manner?'

'Nothing can be more so.'

'What! you, a member of the court, living in Madame's household, a friend of Monsieur's, a guest at their table, the favourite of our lovely Princess?'

Guiche coloured violently from anger. 'What Princess are you alluding to?' he said.

'I am only acquainted with one, my dear fellow. I am speaking of Madame herself. Are you devoted to another Princess, then? Come, tell me.'

Guiche was on the point of launching out, but he saw the drift of the remark. A quarrel was imminent between the two young men. De Wardes wished the quarrel to be only in Madame's name, while de Guiche would not accept it except on La Vallière's account. From this moment, it became a series of feigned attacks, which would have continued until one of the two had been touched home. De Guiche therefore resumed all the self-possession he could command.

'There is not the slightest question in the world of Madame in this matter, my dear de Wardes,' said Guiche, 'but simply of what you were talking about just now.'

'What was I saying?'

'That you had concealed certain things from Bragelonne.'

'Certain things which you know as well as I do,' replied de Wardes.

'No, upon my honour.'

'Nonsense.'

'If you tell me what it is, I shall know, but not otherwise, I swear.'

'What! I, who have just arrived from a distance of sixty leagues, and you who have not stirred from this place, who have witnessed with your own eyes that which rumour informed me of at Calais! Do you now tell me seriously that you do not know what it is about? Oh! Comte, this is hardly charitable of you.'

'As you like, de Wardes; but I again repeat, I know nothing.'

'You are very discreet—well!—perhaps it is prudent of you.'

'And so you will not tell me anything, will not tell me any more than you told Bragelonne?'

'You are pretending to be deaf, I see. I am convinced that Madame could not possibly have more command over herself than you have over yourself.'

'Double hypocrite,' murmured Guiche to himself, 'you are again returning to the old subject.'

'Very well, then,' continued de Wardes, 'since we find it so difficult to understand each other about La Vallière and Bragelonne, let us speak about your own affairs.'

'Nay,' said Guiche, 'I have no affairs of my own to talk about. You have not said anything about me, I suppose, to Bragelonne, which you cannot repeat to myself?'

'No, but understand me, Guiche, that however much I may be ignorant of certain matters, I am quite as conversant with others. If, for instance, we were conversing about certain intimacies of the Duke of Buckingham at Paris, as I did during my journey with the Duke, I could tell you a great many interesting circumstances. Would you like me to mention them?'

Guiche passed his hand across his forehead, which was covered with perspiration. 'No, no,' he said, 'a hundred times no! I have no curiosity for matters which do not concern me. The Duke of Buckingham is for me nothing more than a simple acquaintance, whilst Raoul is an intimate friend. I have not the slightest curiosity to learn what happened to the Duke, while I have, on the contrary, the greatest interest in learning what happened to Raoul.'

'At Paris?'

'Yes, at Paris, or at Boulogne. You understand, I am on the spot; if anything should happen, I am here to meet it; whilst

Raoul is absent, and has only myself to represent him; so, Raoul's affairs before my own.'

'But Raoul will return.'

'Not, however, until his mission is completed. In the meantime, you understand, evil reports cannot be permitted to circulate about him without my looking into them.'

'And for a greater reason still, that he will remain some time in London,' said de Wardes chuckling.

'You think so,' said Guiche simply.

'Think so, indeed! do you suppose that he was sent to London for no other purpose than to go there and return again immediately. No, no; he was sent to London to remain there.'

'Ah! de Wardes,' said Guiche seizing de Wardes's hand violently, 'that is a very serious suspicion concerning Bragelonne, which completely confirms what he wrote to me from Boulogne.'

De Wardes resumed his former coldness of manner, his love of raillery had led him too far, and by his own imprudence, he had laid himself open to attack.

'Well, tell me, what did he write to you about?' he inquired.

'He told me that you had artfully insinuated some injurious remarks against La Vallière, and that you had seemed to laugh at his great confidence in that young girl.'

'Well, it is perfectly true I did so,' said de Wardes, 'and I was quite ready, at the time, to hear from the Vicomte de Bragelonne what every man expects from another, whenever anything may have been said to displease him. In the same way, for instance, if I were seeking a quarrel with you, I should tell you that Madame, after having shown the greatest preference for the Duke of Buckingham, is at this moment supposed to have sent the handsome Duke away for your benefit.'

'Oh! that would not wound me in the slightest degree, my dear de Wardes,' said de Guiche smiling, notwithstanding the shiver which ran through his whole frame. 'Why, such a favour as that would be too great a happiness.'

'I admit that, but if I absolutely wished to quarrel with you, I should try and invent a falsehood perhaps and should speak to you about a certain arbour, where you and that illustrious Princess were together—I should speak also of certain genuflections, of certain kissings of the hand; and you, who are so secret on all occasions, so hasty, and punctilious——'

'Well,' said Guiche, interrupting him, with a smile upon his lips, although he almost felt as if he were going to die; 'I swear I should not care for that, nor should I in any way contradict you; for you must know, my dear Marquis, that for all matters which concern myself, I am a block of ice; but it is a very different thing when an absent friend is concerned, a friend who, on leaving, confided his interests to my safe keeping; for such a friend, de Wardes, believe me, I am like fire itself.'

'I understand you, Monsieur de Guiche; in spite of what you say, there cannot be any question between us just now, either of Bragelonne or of this young insignificant girl, whose name is La Vallière.'

At this moment some of the younger courtiers were crossing the apartment, and having already heard the few words which had just been pronounced, were able also to hear those which were about to follow. De Wardes observed this, and continued aloud,—'Oh! if La Vallière were a coquette like Madame, whose very innocent flirtations, I am sure, were first of all, the cause of the Duke of Buckingham being sent back to England, and afterwards were the reason of your being sent into exile; for you will not deny, I suppose, that Madame's seductive manners did have a certain influence over you?'

The courtiers drew nearer to the two speakers, Saint-Aignan at their head, and then Manicamp.

'But my dear fellow, whose fault was that?' said Guiche laughing. 'I am a vain conceited fellow, I know, and everybody else knows it, too. I took seriously that which was only intended as a jest, and I got myself exiled for my pains. But I saw my error. I overcame my vanity, and I obtained my recall, by making amends, and promising myself to overcome this defect; and the consequence is, that I am so thoroughly cured, that I now laugh at the very thing which, three or four days ago, would have almost broken my heart. But Raoul is in love, and is loved in return; he cannot laugh at the reports which disturb his happiness—reports which you seem to have undertaken to interpret, which you know, Marquis, as I do, as those gentlemen do, as every one does in fact, that these reports are pure slander.'

'Slander!' exclaimed de Wardes, furious at seeing himself caught in the snare by de Guiche's coolness of temper.

'Yes, slander. Look at this letter from him, in which he tells me you have spoken ill of Mademoiselle de la Vallière; and where he asked me, if what you reported about this young girl be true or not. Do you wish me to appeal to these gentlemen, de Wardes, to decide?' And with admirable coolness, Guiche read aloud the paragraph of the letter which referred to La Vallière. 'And now,' continued de Guiche, 'there is no doubt in the world, as far as I am concerned, that you wished to disturb Bragelonne's peace of mind, and that your remarks were maliciously intended.'

De Wardes looked round him, to see if he could find support from any one; but, at the idea, that de Wardes had insulted, either directly or indirectly, the idol of the day, every one shook his head; and de Wardes saw that there was no one present who would have refused to say he was in the wrong.

'Messieurs,' said de Guiche intuitively sensing the general feeling, 'my discussion with Monsieur de Wardes refers to a subject so delicate in its nature, that it is most important no one should hear more than you have already heard. Close the doors, then, I beg you, and let us finish our conversation in the manner which becomes two gentlemen, one of whom has given the other the lie.'

'Messieurs, messieurs!' exclaimed those who were present.

'Is it your opinion, then, that I was wrong in defending Mademoiselle de la Vallière?' said de Guiche. 'In that case I pass judgment upon myself, and am ready to withdraw the offensive words I may have used to Monsieur de Wardes.'

'The deuce! certainly not!' said Saint-Aignan, 'Mademoiselle de la Vallière is an angel.'

'Virtue and purity itself,' said Manicamp.

'You see, Monsieur de Wardes,' said Guiche, 'I am not the only one who undertakes the defence of that poor girl. I entreat you, therefore, messieurs, a second time, to leave us. You see, it is impossible we could be more calm and composed than we are.'

It was the very thing the courtiers wished; some went out at one door, and the rest at the other, and the two young men were left alone.

'Well played,' said de Wardes to the Comte.

'Was it not?' replied the latter.

'How can it be wondered at, my dear fellow; I have got quite rusty in the country, while the command you have acquired over yourself, Comte, confounds me; a man always gains something in women's society; so, pray accept my congratulations.'

'I do accept them.'

'And I will make Madame a present of them.'

'And now, my dear Monsieur de Wardes, let us speak as loud as you please.'

'Do not push me too far.'

'I shall push you hard, for you are known to be an evil-minded man; if you do that, you will be looked upon as a coward, too; and Monsieur would have you hanged, this evening, at his window-casement. Speak, my dear de Wardes, speak.'

'I have fought already.'

'But not quite enough yet.'

'I see, you would not be sorry to fight with me while my wounds are still open.'

'No; better still.'

'The deuce! you are unfortunate in the moment you have chosen; a duel, after the one I have just fought, would hardly suit me; I have lost too much blood at Boulogne; at the slightest effort my wounds would open again, and you would really have too good a bargain with me.'

'True,' said Guiche; 'and yet, on your arrival here your looks and your arms showed there was nothing the matter with you.'

'Yes, my arms are all right, but my legs are weak; and then, I have not had a foil in my hand since that devil of a duel; and you, I am sure, have been fencing every day, in order to carry your little conspiracy against me to a successful issue.'

'Upon my honour, monsieur,' replied de Guiche, 'it is six months since I last practised.'

'No, Comte, after due reflection, I will not fight, at least, with you. I shall await Bragelonne's return, since you say that it is Bragelonne who has fault to find with me.'

'Oh, no, indeed!—You shall not wait until Bragelonne's return,' exclaimed the Comte, losing all command over himself, 'for you have said that Bragelonne might, possibly, be some time before he returns; and, in the meanwhile, your wicked insinuations would have had their effect.'

'Yet, I shall have my excuse. So take care.'

'I will give you a week to finish your recovery.'

'That is better. So let us wait a week.'

'Yes, yes, I understand; a week will give time to my adversary to make his escape. No, no; I will not give you one day even.'

'You are mad, monsieur,' said de Wardes retreating a step.

'And you are a coward, if you do not fight willingly. Nay, what is more, I will denounce you to the King, as having refused to fight, after having insulted La Vallière.'

'Ah!' said de Wardes, 'you are dangerously treacherous, though you pass for a man of honour.'

'There is nothing more dangerous than the treachery, as you term it, of the man whose conduct is always loyal and upright.'

'Restore me the use of my legs, then, or get yourself bled, till you are as white as I am, so as to equalise our chances.'

'No, no; I have something better than that to propose.'

'What is it?'

'We will fight on horseback, and will exchange three pistol-shots each. You are a first-rate marksman. I have seen you bring down swallows with single balls, and at full gallop. Do not deny it, for I have seen you myself.'

'I believe you are right,' said de Wardes; 'and as that is the case, it is not unlikely I might kill you.'

'You would be rendering me a very great service, if you did.'

'I will do my best.'

'Is it agreed? Give me your hand upon it.'

'There it is; but, on one condition, however.'

'Name it.'

'That not a word shall be said about it to the King.'

'Not a word, I swear.'

'I shall go and get my horse, then.'

'And I mine.'

'Where shall we meet?'

'In the open plain; I know an admirable place.'

'Shall we go together?'

'Why not.'

And both of them on their way to the stables passed beneath

Madame's windows, which were faintly lighted; a shadow could be seen behind the lace curtains. 'There is a woman,' said de Wardes smiling, 'who does not suspect that we are going to fight*—to die, perhaps, on her account.'

LX

THE COMBAT

DE WARDES and de Guiche selected their horses, and then saddled them with their own hands, with holster saddles. De Guiche, having two pairs of pistols, went to his apartments to get them; and after having loaded them gave the choice to de Wardes, who selected the pair he had made use of twenty times before, the same, indeed, with which de Guiche had seen him kill swallows flying. 'You will not be surprised,' he said, 'if I take every precaution. You know the weapons well, and, consequently, I am only making the chances equal.'

'Your remark was quite useless,' replied de Guiche, 'and you have done no more than you are entitled to do.'

'Now,' said de Wardes, 'I beg you to have the goodness to help me to mount; for I still experience a little difficulty in doing so.'

'In that case, we had better settle the matter on foot.'

'No; once in the saddle, I shall be all right.'

'Very good, then; so we will not speak of it again,' said de Guiche, as he assisted de Wardes to mount his horse.

'And now,' continued the young man, 'in our eagerness to kill each other, we have neglected one circumstance.'

'What is that?'

'That it is quite dark, and we shall almost be obliged to grope about, in order to kill each other.'

'Oh!' said de Guiche, 'you are as anxious as I am that everything should be done in proper order.'

'Yes; but I do not wish people to say that you have assassinated me, any more than, supposing I were to kill you, I should myself like to be accused of such a crime.'

'Did any one make a similar remark about your duel with the

Duke of Buckingham?' said de Guiche, 'it took place precisely under the same conditions as ours.'

'Very true; but there was still light enough to see by; and we were up to our middles almost in the water; besides, there were a good number of spectators on shore, looking at us.'

De Guiche reflected for a moment, and the thought which had already presented itself to him became more confirmed— that de Wardes wished to have witnesses present, in order to bring back the conversation about Madame, and to give a new turn to the combat. He avoided saying a word in reply, therefore; and, as de Wardes once more looked at him interrogatively, he replied by a movement of the head, that it would be best to let things remain as they were. The two adversaries consequently set off, and left the château by the same gate, close to which we may remember to have seen Montalais and Malicorne together. The night, as if to counteract the extreme heat of the day, had gathered the clouds together in masses which were moving slowly along from the west to the east. The vault above, without a clear spot anywhere visible, or without the faintest indication of thunder, seemed to hang heavily over the earth, and soon began, by the force of the wind, to be split up into fragments, like a huge sheet torn into shreds. Large and warm drops of rain began to fall heavily, and gathered the dust into globules, which rolled along the ground. At the same time, the hedges, which seemed conscious of the approaching storm, the thirsty plants, the drooping branches of the trees, exhaled a thousand aromatic odours, which revived in the mind tender recollections, thoughts of youth, endless life, happiness, and love. 'How fresh the earth smells,' said de Wardes; 'it is a piece of coquetry to draw us to her.'

'By the bye,' replied de Guiche, 'several ideas have just occurred to me; and I wish to have your opinion upon them.'

'Relative to?'

'Relative to our engagement.'

'It is quite time, in fact, that we should begin to arrange matters.'

'Is it to be an ordinary combat, and conducted according to established custom?'

'Let me first know what your established custom is.'

'That we dismount in any particular plain that may suit us, then fasten our horses to the nearest object, meet each without our pistols in our hands, afterwards retire for a hundred and fifty paces, in order to advance on each other.'

'Very good; that is precisely the way in which I killed poor Follivent, three weeks ago, at Saint-Denis.'*

'I beg your pardon, but you forget one circumstance.'

'What is that?'

'That in your duel with Follivent you advanced towards each other on foot, your swords between your teeth, and your pistols in your hands.'

'True.'

'While now, on the contrary, as you cannot walk, you yourself admit that we shall have to mount our horses again, and charge; and the first who wishes to fire will do so.'

'That is the best course, no doubt; but it is quite dark; we must make allowance for more missed shots than would be the case in the daytime.'

'Very well; each will fire three times; the pair of pistols already loaded and one reload.'

'Excellent! Where shall our engagement take place?'

'Have you any preference?'

'No.'

'You see that small wood which lies before us.'

'The wood which is called Rochin?'*

'Exactly.'

'You know it, then?'

'Perfectly.'

'You know that there is an open glade in the centre?'

'Yes.'

'Well, this glade is admirably adapted for such a purpose, with a variety of roads, by-places, paths, ditches, windings, and avenues. We could not find a better spot.'

'I am perfectly satisfied if you are so. We have arrived, if I am not mistaken.'

'Yes. Look at the beautiful open space in the centre. The faint light which the stars afford seems concentrated in this spot; the woods which surround it seem, with their barriers, to form its natural limits.'

'Very good. Do, then, as you say.'

'Let us first settle the conditions.'

'These are mine; if you have any objection to make you will state it.'

'I am listening.'

'If the horse be killed, its rider will be obliged to fight on foot.'

'That is a matter of course, since we have no change of horses here.'

'But that does not oblige his adversary to dismount.'

'His adversary will, in fact, be free to act as he likes.'

'The adversaries, having once met in close contact, cannot quit each other under any circumstances, and may, consequently, fire muzzle to muzzle.'

'Agreed.'

'Three shots, and no more will do, I suppose?'

'Quite sufficient, I think. Here are powder and balls for your pistols; measure out three charges, take three balls; I will do the same; then we will throw the rest of the powder and the balls away.'

'And we will solemnly swear,' added de Wardes, 'that we have neither balls nor powder about us?'

'Agreed; and I swear it,' said de Guiche holding his hand towards heaven, a gesture which de Wardes imitated.

'And now, my dear Comte,' said de Wardes, 'allow me to tell you that I am in no way your dupe. You already are, or you soon will be, the accepted lover of Madame. I have detected your secret, and you are afraid I shall tell others of it. You wish to kill me to insure my silence; that is very clear; and in your place, I should do the same.' De Guiche hung down his head. 'Only,' continued de Wardes triumphantly, 'was it really worth while, tell me, to throwh this affair of Bragelonne's upon my shoulders? But take care, my dear fellow; in bringing the wild boar to bay, you enrage him; in running down the fox, you give him the ferocity of the jaguar. The consequence is, that, brought to bay by you, I shall defend myself to the very last.'

'You will be quite right in doing so.'

'Yes, but take care; I shall work more harm than you think. In the first place, as a beginning, you will readily suppose that I have not been absurd enough to lock up my secret, or your secret rather, in my own breast. There is a friend of mine, who resembles me in every way, a man whom you know very well, who shares my secret with me; so, pray, understand, that if you kill me, my death will not have been of much service to you; whilst on the contrary, if I kill you—and everything is possible, you know——you understand?' De Guiche shuddered. 'If I kill you,' continued de Wardes, 'you will have secured two mortal enemies to Madame, who will do their very utmost to ruin her.'

'Oh! monsieur,' exclaimed de Guiche furiously, 'do not reckon upon my death so easily. Of the two enemies you speak of, I trust most heartily to dispose of one immediately, and the other at the earliest opportunity.'

The only reply de Wardes made was a burst of laughter so diabolical in its sound, that a superstitious man would have been terrified by it. But de Guiche was not so impressionable as that. 'I think,' he said, 'that everything is now settled, Monsieur de Wardes; so have the goodness to take your place first, unless you would prefer me to do so.'

'By no means,' said de Wardes. 'I shall be delighted to save you the slightest trouble.' And putting his horse into a gallop, he crossed the wide open space, and took his stand at that point of the circumference of the crossroads which was immediately opposite to where de Guiche was stationed. De Guiche remained motionless. At the distance of a hundred paces the two adversaries were absolutely invisible to each other, being completely concealed by the thick shade of elms and chestnuts. A minute elapsed amidst the profoundest silence. At the end of the minute, each of them, in the deep shade in which he was concealed, heard the double click of the trigger, as they put the pistols on full cock. De Guiche adopting the usual tactics, set his horse into a gallop, persuaded that he should render his safety doubly sure, both by the movement, as well as by the speed of the animal. He directed his course in a straight line towards the point where, in his opinion, de Wardes would be stationed; and he expected to meet de Wardes about half way; but in this he was mistaken. He continued his course, presuming that his adversary was impatiently awaiting his approach. When, however, he had gone about two thirds of the distance, he saw the place suddenly illuminated and a ball flew by, cutting the plume of his hat in two. Nearly at the same moment, and as if the flash of the first shot had served to indicate the direction of the other, a second report was heard, and a second ball passed through the head of de Guiche's horse, a little below the ear. The animal fell. These two reports proceeding from the very opposite direction to that in which he expected to find de Wardes surprised him a great deal; but as he was a man of amazing self-possession, he prepared himself for his horse falling, but not so completely, however, that the toe of his boot escaped being caught under the animal as it fell. Very fortunately the horse in its dying agonies moved so as to enable him to release the leg which was less entangled than the other. De Guiche rose, felt himself all over, and found that he was not wounded. At the very moment he had felt the horse tottering under him, he placed his pistols in the holsters, afraid that the force of the fall might explode one at least, if not both of them, by which he would have been disarmed, and left utterly without defence. Once on his feet, he took the pistols out of the holsters, and advanced towards the spot, where, by the light of the flash, he had seen de Wardes appear. De Guiche had, at the first shot, accounted for the manœuvre, than which nothing could have been simpler. Instead of advancing to meet de Guiche, or remaining in his place to await his approach, de Wardes had, for about fifteen paces, followed the circle of the shadow which hid him from his adversary's observation, and at the very moment when the latter presented his flank in his career, he had fired from the place where he stood, carefully taking his aim, and assisted instead of being inconvenienced by the horse's gallop. It has been seen that, notwithstanding the darkness, the first ball had passed hardly more than an inch above de Guiche's head. De Wardes had so confidently relied upon his aim, that he thought he had seen de Guiche fall; his astonishment was extreme when he saw that he still remained erect in his saddle. He hastened to fire his second shot, but his hand trembled, and he killed the horse instead. It would be a most fortunate chance for him if de Guiche were to remain held fast under the animal. Before he could have freed himself de Wardes would have loaded his pistol and had de Guiche at his mercy. But de Guiche, on the contrary, was up, and had three shots to fire. De Guiche immediately understood the position of affairs. It would be necessary to exceed de Wardes in rapidity of execution. He advanced, therefore, so as to reach him before he should have had time to reload his pistol. De Wardes saw him approaching like a tempest. The ball was rather tight, and offered some resistance to the ramrod. To load it carelessly would be to expose himself to lose his last chance; to take the proper care in loading it would be to lose his time, or rather it would be throwing away his life. He made his horse bound on one side. De Guiche turned round also, and, at the moment the horse was quiet again, he fired, and the ball carried off de Wardes's hat from his head. De Wardes now knew that he had a moment's time at his own disposal; he availed himself of it in order to finish loading his pistol. De Guiche, noticing that his adversary did not fall, threw the pistol he had just discharged aside, and walked straight towards de Wardes, elevating the second pistol as he did so. He had hardly proceeded more than two or three paces, when de Wardes took aim at him as he was walking, and fired. An exclamation of anger was de Guiche's answer; the Comte's arm contracted and dropped motionless by his side, and the pistol fell from his grasp. De Wardes observed the Comte stoop down, pick up the pistol with his left hand, and again advance towards him. His anxiety was excessive. 'I am lost,' murmured de Wardes, 'he is not mortally wounded.' At the very moment, however, that de Guiche was about to raise his pistol against de Wardes, the head, shoulders, and limbs of the Comte seemed all to give way. He heaved a deep-drawn sigh, tottered, and fell at the feet of de Wardes's horse.

'That is all right,' said de Wardes, and, gathering up the reins, he struck his spurs into his horse's sides. The horse cleared the Comte's motionless body, and bore de Wardes rapidly back to the château. When he arrived there, he remained a quarter of an hour deliberating within himself as to the proper course to be adopted. In his impatience to leave the field of battle he had omitted to ascertain whether de Guiche were dead or not. A double hypothesis presented itself to de Wardes's agitated mind; either de Guiche was killed, or de Guiche was wounded only. If he were killed, why should he leave his body in that manner to the tender mercies of the wolves?* It was a perfectly useless piece of cruelty, for if de Guiche were dead, he certainly would not breathe a syllable of what had passed; if he were not killed, why should he, de Wardes, in leaving him there uncared for, allow himself to be regarded as a savage, incapable of one generous feeling? This last consideration determined his line of conduct.

De Wardes immediately instituted inquiries after Manicamp. He was told that Manicamp had been looking after de Guiche, and, not knowing where to find him, had retired to bed. De Wardes went and woke the sleeper without any delay, and related the whole affair to him, which Manicamp listened to in perfect silence, but with an expression of momentarily increasing energy, of which his face could hardly have been supposed capable. It was only when de Wardes had finished that Manicamp uttered the words, 'Let us go.'

As they proceeded, Manicamp became more and more excited, and in proportion as de Wardes related the details of the affair to him, his countenance assumed every moment a darkening expression. 'And so,' he said, when de Wardes had finished, 'you think he is dead?'

'Alas, I do.'

'And you fought in that manner, without witnesses?'

'He insisted upon it.'

'It is very singular.'

'What do you mean by saying it is singular?'

'That it is so very unlike Monsieur de Guiche's disposition.'

'You do not doubt my word, I suppose?'

'Hum! hum!'

'You do doubt it, then?'

'A little. But I shall doubt it more than ever, I warn you, if I find the poor fellow is really dead.'

'Monsieur Manicamp!'

'Monsieur de Wardes!'

'It seems you intend to insult me.'

'Just as you please. The fact is, I never could like those people who come and say, "I have killed such and such a gentleman in a corner; it is a great pity, but I killed him in a perfectly honourable manner." It has a very ugly appearance, M. de Wardes.'

'Silence! we have arrived.'

In fact the open glade could now be seen, and in the open space lay the motionless body of the dead horse. To the right of the horse, upon the dark grass, with his face against the ground, the poor Comte lay, bathed in his blood. He had remained in the same spot, and did not even seem to have made the slightest movement. Manicamp threw himself on his knees, lifted the Comte in his arms, and found him quite cold, and steeped in blood. He let him gently fall again. Then, stretching out his hand, and feeling all over the ground close to where the Comte lay, he sought until he found de Guiche's pistol.

'By Heaven!' he said, rising to his feet, pale as death, and with the pistol in his hand, 'you are not mistaken, he is quite dead.'

'Dead!' repeated de Wardes.

'Yes; and his pistol is still loaded,' added Manicamp, looking into the pan.

'But I told you that I took aim as he was walking towards me, and fired at him at the very moment he was going to fire at me.'

'Are you quite sure that you have fought with him, Monsieur de Wardes? I confess that I am very much afraid that it has been a foul assassination. Nay, nay, no exclamations! You have had your three shots, and his pistol is still loaded. You have killed his horse, and he, de Guiche, one of the best marksmen in France, has not even wounded either your horse or yourself. Well, Monsieur de Wardes, you have been very unlucky in bringing me here; all the blood in my body seems to have mounted to my head, and I believe that since so good an opportunity presents itself, I shall blow out your brains on the spot. So, Monsieur de Wardes, recommend your soul to Heaven.'

'Monsieur Manicamp, you cannot think of such a thing!'

'On the contrary, I am thinking of it very strongly.'

'Would you assassinate me?'

'Without the slightest remorse, at least for the present.'

'Are you a gentleman?'

'I have given a great many proofs of it.'

'Let me defend my life, then, at least.'

'Very likely; in order, I suppose, that you may do to me what you have done to poor de Guiche.'

And Manicamp slowly raised his pistol to the height of de Wardes's breast, and, with his arm stretched out, and a fixed, determined look on his face, took a careful aim. De Wardes did not attempt a flight; he was completely terrified. In the midst, however, of this horrible silence, which lasted about a second, but which seemed an age to de Wardes, a faint sigh was heard.

'Oh,' exclaimed de Wardes, 'he still lives! Help, de Guiche, I am about to be assassinated!'

Manicamp fell back a step or two, and the two young men saw the Comte raise himself slowly and painfully upon one hand. Manicamp threw the pistol away a dozen paces, and ran to his friend, uttering a cry of delight. De Wardes wiped his forehead, which was covered with a cold perspiration.

'It was just in time,' he murmured.

'Where are you hurt?' inquired Manicamp of de Guiche, 'and whereabouts are you wounded?'

De Guiche showed him his mutilated hand and his chest covered with blood.

'Comte,' exclaimed de Wardes, 'I am accused of having assassinated you; speak, I implore you, and say that I fought loyally.'

'Perfectly so,' said the wounded man; 'Monsieur de Wardes fought quite loyally, and whoever may say the contrary will make me his enemy.'

'Then, sir,' said Manicamp, 'assist me, in the first place, to carry this poor fellow back, and I will afterwards give you every satisfaction you please; or, if you are in a hurry, we can do better still; let us stanch the blood from the Comte's wounds here, with your pocket-handkerchief and mine, and then, as there are two shots left, we can have them between us.'

'Thank you,' said de Wardes. 'Twice already, in one hour, I have seen death too close at hand to be agreeable; I don't like his look at all, and I prefer your apologies.'

Manicamp burst out laughing, and Guiche, too, in spite of his sufferings. The two young men wished to carry him, but he declared he felt himself quite strong enough to walk alone. The ball had broken his ring-finger and his little finger, and then had glanced along his side, but without penetrating deeply into his chest. It was the pain rather than the seriousness of the wound, therefore, which had overcome de Guiche. Manicamp passed his arm under one of the Comte's shoulders, and de Wardes did the same with the other, and in this way they brought him back to Fontainebleau, to the house of the same doctor who had been present at the death of the Franciscan, Aramis's predecessor.

LXI

THE KING'S SUPPER

THE King, while these matters were being arranged, had sat down to the supper-table, and the not very large number of guests invited for that day had taken their seats, after the usual gesture intimating the royal permission to be seated. At this period of Louis XIV's reign, although etiquette was not governed by the strict regulations which subsequently were adopted, the French court had entirely thrown aside the traditions of good fellowship and patriarchal affability which existed in the time of Henry IV; and which the suspicious mind of Louis XIII had gradually replaced by the pompous state, forms, and ceremonies which he despaired of being able fully to realise.*

The King, therefore, was seated alone, at a small separate table, which, like the desk of a presiding chairman, overlooked the adjoining tables. Although we say a small table, we must not omit to add that this small table was the largest one there. Moreover, it was the one on which were placed the greatest number and quantity of dishes; consisting of fish, game, meat, fruit, vegetables, and preserves. The King was young and full of vigour and energy, very fond of hunting, addicted to all violent exercises of the body, possessing besides, like all members of the Bourbon family,* a rapid digestion and an appetite speedily renewed. Louis XIV was a formidable table-companion; he delighted to criticise his cooks; but when he honoured them by praise and commendation, the honour was overwhelming. The King began by eating several kinds of soup, either mixed together or taken separately. He intermixed, or rather he separated, each of the soups by a glass of old wine. He ate quickly, and some-what greedily. Porthos, who from the beginning had, out of respect, been waiting for a jog of d'Artagnan's arm, seeing that the King made such rapid progress, turned to the musketeer and said in a low tone,—

'It seems as if one might go on now; His Majesty is very encouraging from the example he sets. Look.'

'The King eats,' said d'Artagnan, 'but he talks at the same time; try and manage matters in such a manner that, if he should happen to address a remark to you, he should not find you with your mouth full, which would be very disrespectful.'

'The best way in that case,' said Porthos, 'is to eat no supper at all; and yet I am very hungry, I admit, and everything looks and smells most invitingly, as if appealing to all my senses at once.'

'Don't think of not eating for a moment,' said d'Artagnan; 'that would put his Majesty out terribly. The King has a saying "that he who works well, eats well," and does not like people to eat indifferently at his table.'

'How can I avoid having my mouth full if I eat?' said Porthos.

'All you have to do,' replied the captain of the musketeers, 'is simply to swallow what you have in it, whenever the King does you the honour to address a remark to you.'

'Very good,' said Porthos; and from that moment he began to eat with a well-bred enthusiasm of manner.

The King occasionally looked at the different persons who were at table with him, and *en connoisseur*, could appreciate the different dispositions of his guests.

'Monsieur du Vallon!' he said.

Porthos was enjoying a jugged hare, and swallowed half of the back. His name pronounced in such a manner had made him start, and by a vigorous effort of his gullet he absorbed the whole mouthful.

'Sire,' replied Porthos, in a stifled voice, but sufficiently intelligible nevertheless.

'Let those *filets d'agneau* be handed to Monsieur du Vallon,' said the King; 'do you like brown meats, M. du Vallon?'

'Sire, I like everything,' replied Porthos.

D'Artagnan whispered: 'Everything your Majesty sends me.'

Porthos repeated, 'Everything your Majesty sends me,' an observation which the King apparently received with great satisfaction.

'People eat well who work well,' replied the King, delighted to have *en tête-à-tête* a guest who could eat as Porthos did.

Porthos received the dish of lamb, and put a portion of it on his own plate.

'Well!' said the King.

'Exquisite,' said Porthos calmly.

'Have you as good mutton in your part of the country, Monsieur du Vallon?' continued the King.

'Sire, I believe that from my own province, as everywhere else, the best of everything is sent to Paris for your Majesty's use; but, on the other hand, I do not eat lamb in the same way your Majesty does.'

'Ah, ah! and how do you eat it?'

'Generally I have a lamb dressed quite whole.'

'Quite whole?'

'Yes, sire.'

'In what manner, then?'

'In this, sire; my cook, who is a German, first stuffs the lamb in question with small sausages which he procures from Strasburg, force-meat balls which he procures from Troyes, and larks which he procures from Pithiviers; by some means or other, which I am not acquainted with, he bones the lamb as he would do a fowl, leaving the skin on, however, which forms a brown crust all over the animal; when it is cut into slices, like an enormous sausage, a rose-coloured gravy pours forth, which is as agreeable to the eye as it is exquisite to the palate.'* And Porthos finished by smacking his lips.

The King opened his eyes with delight, and, while cutting some of the stewed pheasant which was being handed to him, he said,—

'That is a dish I should very much like to taste, Monsieur du Vallon. Is it possible! a whole lamb!'

'Completely so, sire.'

'Pass those pheasants to M. du Vallon; I perceive he is a gourmet.'

The order was immediately obeyed. Then, continuing the conversation, he said, 'And you do not find the lamb too fat?'

'No, sire, the fat is rendered down at the same time as the gravy forms, and remains on the surface; then the servant who carves removes the fat with a spoon, which I have had expressly made for that purpose.'

'Where do you reside?' inquired the King.

'At Pierrefonds, sire.'

'At Pierrefonds; where is that, M. du Vallon—near Belle-Isle?'

'Oh, no, sire! Pierrefonds is in the Soissonnais.'

'I thought you alluded to the lamb on account of the salt marshes.'*

'No, sire, I have marshes which are not salt, it is true, but which are not the less valuable on that account.'

The King had now arrived at the *entremets*,* but without losing sight of Porthos, who continued to play his part in the best manner.

'You have an excellent appetite, M. du Vallon,' said the King, 'and you make an admirable guest at table.'

'Ah! sire, if your Majesty were ever to pay a visit to Pierrefonds, we would both of us eat our lamb together; for your appetite is not an indifferent one by any means.'

D'Artagnan gave Porthos a severe kick under the table, which made Porthos colour up.

'At your Majesty's present happy age,' said Porthos, in order to repair the mistake he had made, 'I was in the musketeers, and nothing could ever satisfy me then. Your Majesty has an excellent appetite, as I have already had the honour of mentioning, but you select what you eat with too much refinement to be called a great eater.'

The King seemed charmed at his guest's politeness.

'Will you try some of these creams?' he said to Porthos.

'Sire, your Majesty treats me with far too much kindness to prevent me speaking the whole truth.'

'Pray do so, M. du Vallon.'

'Well, sire, with regard to sweet dishes, I only recognise pastry, and even that should be rather solid; all these frothy substances swell the stomach, and occupy a place which seems to me to be too precious to be so badly tenanted.'

'Ah! gentlemen,' said the King, indicating Porthos by a gesture, 'here is indeed a perfect model of gastronomy. It was in such a manner that our fathers, who so well knew what good living was, used to eat, while we,' added His Majesty, 'can do nothing but trifle with our food.' And as he spoke he took the breast of a chicken with ham, while Porthos attacked a dish of partridges and land-rails. The cup-bearer filled His Majesty's glass. 'Give M. du Vallon some of my wine,' said the King. This was one of the greatest honours of the royal table. D'Artagnan pressed his friend's knees.

'If you could only manage to swallow the half of that boar's head I see yonder,' said he to Porthos, 'I shall believe you will be a duke and peer* within the next twelvemonth.'

'Presently,' said Porthos phlegmatically; 'I shall come to it by-and-by.'

In fact it was not long before it came to the boar's turn, for the King seemed to take a pleasure in urging on his guest; he did not pass any of the dishes to Porthos until he had tasted them himself, and he accordingly took some of the boar's head. Porthos showed that he could keep pace with his sovereign; and, instead of eating the half, as d'Artagnan had told him, he ate three-fourths of it. 'It is impossible,' said the King in an undertone, 'that a gentleman who eats so good a supper every day, and who has such beautiful teeth, can be otherwise than the most straightforward, upright man in my kingdom.'

'Do you hear?' said d'Artagnan in his friend's ear.

'Yes; I think I am rather in favour,' said Porthos, balancing himself on his chair.

'Oh! you are in luck's way.'

The King and Porthos continued to eat in the same manner, to the great satisfaction of the other guests, some of whom, from emulation, had attempted to follow them, but had been obliged to give up on the way. The King soon began to get flushed, and the reaction of the blood to his face announced that the moment of repletion had arrived. It was then that Louis XIV, instead of becoming gay and cheerful, as most good livers generally do, became dull, melancholy, and taciturn. Porthos, on the contrary, was lively and communicative. D'Artagnan's foot had more than once to remind him of this peculiarity of the King. The dessert now made its appearance. The King had ceased to think anything further of Porthos; he turned his eyes anxiously towards the entrance-door and was heard occasionally to inquire how it happened that Monsieur de Saint-Aignan was so long in arriving. At last, at the moment when his Majesty was finishing a pot of preserved plums with a deep sigh, Saint-Aignan appeared. The King's eyes, which had become somewhat dull, immediately began to sparkle. The Comte advanced towards the King's table, and Louis arose at his approach. Everybody arose at the same time, including Porthos, who was just finishing an almond-cake, capable of making the jaws of a crocodile stick together. The supper was over.

LXII

AFTER SUPPER

THE King took Saint-Aignan by the arm, and passed into the adjoining apartment. 'What has detained you, Comte?' said the King.

'I was bringing the answer, sire,' replied the Comte.

'She has taken a long time to reply to what I wrote her.'

'Sire, your Majesty had deigned to write in verse, and Mademoiselle de la Vallière wished to repay your Majesty in the same coin; that is to say, in gold.'

'Verses! Saint-Aignan,' exclaimed the King in ecstasy. 'Give them to me at once.' And Louis broke the seal of a little letter, enclosing the verses* which history has preserved entire for us, and which are more meritorious in intention than in execution. Such as they were, however, the King was enchanted with them, and exhibited his satisfaction by unequivocal transports of delight; but the universal silence which reigned in the rooms warned Louis, so sensitively particular with regard to good breeding, that his delight might give rise to various interpretations. He turned aside and put the note in his pocket, and then advancing a few steps, which brought him again to the threshold of the door, close to his guests, he said, 'M. du Vallon, I have seen you to-day with the greatest pleasure, and my pleasure will be equally great to see you again.' Porthos bowed as the Colossus of Rhodes* would have done, and retired from the room with his face towards the King. 'M. d'Artagnan,' continued the King, 'you will await my orders in the gallery; I am obliged to you for having made me acquainted with M. du Vallon. Gentlemen,' addressing himself to the other guests, 'I return to Paris to-morrow, on account of the departure of the Spanish and Dutch ambassadors. Until to-morrow, then.'

The apartment was immediately cleared of the guests. The King took Saint-Aignan by the arm, made him read La Vallière's verses over again, and said, 'What do you think of them?'

'Charming, sire.'

'They charm me, in fact, and if it were known——'

'Oh! the professional poets would be jealous of them; but it is not at all likely they will know anything about them.'

'Did you give her mine?'

'Oh! sire, she positively devoured them.'

'They were very weak, I am afraid.'

'That is not what Mademoiselle de la Vallière said of them.'

'Do you think she was pleased with them?'

'I am sure of it, sire.'

'I must answer them, then.'

'Oh! sire, immediately after supper? Your Majesty will fatigue yourself.'

'You're right; study after eating is very injurious.'

'The labour of a poet especially so, and, besides, there is great excitement prevailing at Mademoiselle de la Vallière's.'

'What do you mean?'

'With her as with all the ladies of the court.'

'Why?'

'On account of poor de Guiche's accident.'

'Has anything serious happened to de Guiche, then?'

'Yes, sire, he has one hand nearly destroyed, a hole in his breast; in fact he is dying.'

'Good heavens! who told you that?'

'Manicamp brought him back just now to the house of a doctor here in Fontainebleau, and the rumour soon reached us all here.'

'Brought back! Poor de Guiche; and how did it happen?'

'Ah! that is the very question, how did it happen?'

'You say that in a very singular manner, Saint-Aignan. Give me the details. What does he say himself?'

'He says nothing, sire, but others do.'

'What others?'

'Those who brought him back, sire.'

'Who are they?'

'I do not know, sire; but M. de Manicamp knows. M. de Manicamp is one of his friends.'

'As everybody is, indeed,' said the King.

'Oh! no!' returned Saint-Aignan, 'you are mistaken, sire; every one is not precisely friends with M. de Guiche.'

'How do you know that?'

'Does your Majesty require me to explain myself?'

'Certainly I do.'

'Well, sire, I believe I have heard something said about a quarrel between two gentlemen.'

'When?'

'This very evening, before your Majesty's supper was served.'

'That can hardly be. I have issued such stringent and severe ordinances with respect to duelling* that no one, I presume, would dare to disobey them.'

'In that case, Heaven preserve me from excusing any one!' exclaimed Saint-Aignan. 'Your Majesty commanded me to speak, and I spoke accordingly.'

'Tell me, then, in what way the Comte de Guiche has been wounded?'

'Sire, it is said to have been at a boar-hunt.'

'This evening?'

'Yes, sire.'

'One of his hands shattered, and a hole in his breast? Who was at the hunt with M. de Guiche?'

'I do not know, sire; but M. de Manicamp knows, or ought to know.'

'You are concealing something from me, Saint-Aignan.'

'Nothing, sire, I assure you.'

'Then explain to me how the accident happened; was it a musket that burst?'

'Very likely, sire. But yet, on reflection, it could hardly have been that, for Guiche's pistol was found close by him still loaded.'

'His pistol? But a man does not go to a boar-hunt with a pistol.'

'Sire, it is also said, that Guiche's horse was killed, and that the horse is still to be found in the wide open glade of the forest.'

'His horse?—Guiche go on horseback to a boar-hunt—Saint-

Aignan, I do not understand a syllable of what you have been telling me. Where did the affair happen?'

'At the Rond-point, in that part of the forest called the Bois-Rochin.'

'That will do. Call M. d'Artagnan.' Saint-Aignan obeyed, and the musketeer entered.

'Monsieur d'Artagnan,' said the King, 'you will leave this place by the little door of the private staircase.'

'Yes, sire.'

'You will mount your horse.'

'Yes, sire.'

'And you will proceed to the Rond-point du Bois-Rochin. Do you know the spot?'

'Yes, sire. I have fought there twice.'

'What!' exclaimed the King, amazed at the reply.

'Under the edicts,* sire, of Cardinal Richelieu,' returned d'Artagnan, with his usual impassibility.

'That is very different, monsieur. You will, therefore, go there, and will examine the locality very carefully. A man has been wounded there, and you will find a horse lying dead. You will tell me what your opinion is upon the whole affair.'

'Very good, sire.'

'It is a matter of course that it is your own opinion I require, and not that of any one else.'

'You shall have it in an hour's time, sire.'

'I prohibit you speaking with any one, whoever it may be.'

'Except with the person who must give me a lantern,' said d'Artagnan.

'Oh! that is a matter of course,' said the King laughing at the liberty, which he tolerated in no one but his captain of musketeers. D'Artagnan left by the little staircase.

'Now, let my physician* be sent for,' said Louis. Ten minutes afterwards the King's physician arrived, quite out of breath.

'You will go, monsieur,' said the King to him, 'and accompany M. de Saint-Aignan wherever he may take you; you will render me an account of the state of the person you may see in the house you will be taken to.' The physician obeyed without a remark, as at that time people began to obey Louis XIV, and left the room preceding Saint-Aignan.

'Saint-Aignan, send Manicamp to me, before the physician can possibly have spoken to him.' And Saint-Aignan left in his turn.

LXIII

SHOWING IN WHAT WAY D'ARTAGNAN DISCHARGED THE MISSION WITH WHICH THE KING HAD ENTRUSTED HIM

WHILE the King was engaged in making these last-mentioned arrangements in order to ascertain the truth, d'Artagnan, without wasting a second, ran to the stable, took down the lantern, saddled his horse himself, and proceeded towards the place which His Majesty had indicated. According to the promise he had made, he had neither seen nor met any one; and, as we have observed, he had carried his scruples so far as to do without the assistance of the helpers in the stables altogether. D'Artagnan was one of those who in moments of difficulty pride themselves on increasing their own value. By dint of hard galloping, he in less than five minutes reached the wood, fastened his horse to the first tree he came to, and penetrated to the broad open space on foot. He then began to inspect most carefully, on foot and with his lantern in his hand, the whole surface of the Rond-point, went forward, turned back again, measured, examined, and after half an hour's minute inspection, he returned silently to where he had left his horse, and pursued his way in deep reflection and at a foot-pace to Fontainebleau. Louis was waiting in his cabinet; he was alone, and with a pencil was scribbling on paper certain lines which d'Artagnan at the first glance recognised as being very unequal and very much scratched about. The conclusion he arrived at was, that they must be verses. The King raised his head and perceived d'Artagnan. 'Well, monsieur,' he said, 'do you bring me any news?'

'Yes, sire.'

'What have you seen?'

'As far as probability goes, sire——' d'Artagnan began to reply.

'It was certainty I requested of you.'

'I will approach it as near as I possibly can. The weather was very well adapted for investigations of the character I have just made; it has been raining this evening, and the roads were wet and muddy——'

'Well, the result, M. d'Artagnan?'

'Sire, your Majesty told me that there was a horse lying dead in the crossroad of the Bois-Rochin, and I began therefore by studying the roads. I say the roads, because the centre of the crossroad is reached by four separate roads. The one that I myself took was the only one that presented any fresh traces. The two horses had followed it side by side; their eight feet were marked very distinctly in the clay. One of the riders was more impatient than the other, for the footprints of the one were invariably in advance of the other about half a horse's length.'

'Are you quite sure they came together?' said the King.

'Yes, sire, the horses are two rather large animals of equal pace,—horses well used to manœuvres of all kinds, for they wheeled round the barrier of the Rond-point together.'

'Well—and after?'

'The two cavaliers paused there for a minute, no doubt to arrange the conditions of the engagement; the horses grew restless and impatient. One of the riders spoke, while the other listened and seemed to have contented himself by simply answering. His horse pawed the ground, which proves that his attention was so taken up by listening that he let the bridle fall from his hand.'

'A hostile meeting did take place, then?'

'Undoubtedly.'

'Continue; you are a most accurate observer.'

'One of the two cavaliers remained where he was standing, the one, in fact, who had been listening; the other crossed the open space, and at first placed himself directly opposite to his adversary. The one who had remained stationary traversed the Rond-point at a gallop about two thirds of its length, thinking that by this means he would gain upon his opponent; but the latter had followed the circumference of the wood.'

'You are ignorant of their names, I suppose?'

'Completely so, sire. Only he who followed the circumference of the wood was mounted on a black horse.'

'How do you know that?'

'I found a few hairs of his tail among the brambles which bordered the sides of the ditch.'

'Go on.'

'As for the other horse, there can be no trouble in describing him, since he was left dead on the field of battle.'

'What was the cause of his death?'

'A ball which had passed through his temple.'

'Was the ball that of a pistol or a gun?'

'It was a pistol-bullet, sire. Besides, the manner in which the horse was wounded explained to me the tactics of the man who had killed it. He had followed the circumference of the wood in order to take his adversary in flank. Moreover, I followed his foot-tracks on the grass.'

'The tracks of the black horse, do you mean?'

'Yes, sire.'

'Go on, Monsieur d'Artagnan.'

'As your Majesty now perceives the position of the two adversaries, I will, for a moment, leave the cavalier who had remained stationary for the one who started off at a gallop.'

'Do so.'

'The horse of the cavalier who rode at full speed was killed on the spot.'

'How do you know that?'

'The cavalier had not time even to throw himself off his horse, and so fell with it. I observed the impression of his leg, which, with a great effort, he was enabled to extricate from under the horse. The spur, pressed down by the weight of the animal, had ploughed up the ground.'

'Very good, and what did he do as soon as he rose up again?'

'He walked straight up to his adversary.'

'Who still remained upon the verge of the forest?'

'Yes, sire. Then, having reached a favourable distance, he stopped firmly—for the impression of both his heels are left in the ground quite close to each other—fired, and missed his adversary.'

'How do you know he did not hit him?'

'I found a hat with a ball through it.'

'Ah, a proof, then!' exclaimed the King.

'Insufficient, sire,' replied d'Artagnan coldly; 'it is a hat without any letters indicating its ownership, without arms; a red feather, as all hats have; the lace, even, had nothing particular in it.'

'Did the man with the hat through which the bullet had passed fire a second time?'

'Oh, sire, he had already fired twice.'

'How did you ascertain that?'

'I found the waddings of the pistol.'

'And what became of the bullet which did not kill the horse?'

'It cut in two the feather of the hat belonging to him against whom it was directed, and broke a small birch at the other end of the open glade.'

'In that case, then, the man on the black horse was disarmed, whilst his adversary had still one more shot to fire?'

'Sire, while the dismounted rider was extricating himself from his horse, the other was reloading his pistol. Only, he was much agitated while he was loading it, and his hand trembled greatly.'

'How do you know that?'

'Half the charge fell to the ground, and he threw the ramrod aside, not having time to replace it in the pistol.'

'Monsieur d'Artagnan, it is marvellous what you tell me.'

'It is only close observation,* sire, and the commonest highwayman would do as much.'

'The whole scene is before me from the manner in which you relate it.'

'I have, in fact, reconstructed it in my own mind, with merely a few alterations.'

'And now,' said the King, 'let us return to the dismounted cavalier. You were saying that he had walked towards his adversary while the latter was loading his pistol.'

'Yes; but at the very moment he himself was taking aim, the other fired.'

'Oh!' said the King; 'and the shot?'

'The shot told terribly, sire; the dismounted cavalier fell upon his face, after having staggered forward three or four paces.'

'Where was he hit?'

'In two places; in the first place, in his right hand, and then, by the same bullet, in his chest.'

'But how could you ascertain that?' inquired the King, full of admiration.

'By a very simple means; the butt-end of the pistol was covered with blood, and the trace of the bullet could be observed with fragments of a broken ring. The wounded man, in all probability, had the ring-finger and the little finger carried off.'

'As far as the hand goes, I have nothing to say; but the chest?'

'Sire, there were two small pools of blood, at a distance of about two feet and a half from each other. At one of these pools of blood the grass was torn up by the clenched hand; at the other, the grass was simply pressed down by the weight of the body.'

'Poor de Guiche!' exclaimed the King.

'Ah! it was M. de Guiche, then?' said the musketeer very quietly. 'I suspected it, but did not venture to mention it to your Majesty.'

'And what made you suspect it?'

'I recognised the de Gramont* arms upon the holsters of the dead horse.'

'And you think he is seriously wounded?'

'Very seriously, since he fell immediately, and remained a long time in the same place; however, he was able to walk, as he left the spot supported by two friends.'

'You met him returning, then?'

'No, but I observed the footprints of three men; the one on the right and the one on the left walked freely and easily, but the one in the middle dragged his feet as he walked, besides, he left traces of blood at every step he took.'

'Now, monsieur, since you saw the combat so distinctly that not a single detail seems to have escaped you, tell me something about de Guiche's adversary.'

'Oh, sire, I do not know him.'

'And yet you see everything very clearly?'

'Yes, sire, I see everything; but I do not tell all I see; and, since the poor devil has escaped, your Majesty will permit me to say that I do not intend to denounce him.'

'And yet he is guilty, since he has fought a duel, monsieur.'

'Not guilty in my eyes, sire,' said d'Artagnan coldly.

'Monsieur!' exclaimed the King, 'are you aware of what you are saying?'

'Perfectly, sire; but, according to my notion, a man who fights a duel is a brave man; such, at least, is my own opinion; but your Majesty may have another; that is very natural—you are the master here.'

'Monsieur d'Artagnan, I ordered you, however——'

D'Artagnan interrupted the King by a respectful gesture. 'You ordered me, sire, to gather what particulars I could respecting a hostile meeting that had taken place; those particulars you have. If you order me to arrest M. de Guiche's adversary I will do so; but do not order me to denounce him to you, for in that case I will not obey.'

'Very well, arrest him, then.'

'Give me his name, sire.'

The King stamped his foot angrily, but after a moment's reflection, he said, 'You are right—ten times, twenty times, a hundred times right.'

'That is my opinion, sire; I am happy that, this time, it accords with your Majesty's.'

'One word more. Who assisted Guiche?'

'I do not know, sire.'

'But you speak of two men. There was a person present, then, as second?'

'There was no second, sire. Nay, more than that, when M. de Guiche fell, his adversary fled without giving him any assistance.'

'The miserable coward!' exclaimed the King.

'The consequence of your ordinances, sire. If a man has fought well, and fairly, and has already escaped one chance of death he naturally wishes to escape a second. M. de Bouteville cannot be forgotten very easily.'

'And so men turn cowards?'

'No, they become prudent.'

'And he has fled, then, you say?'

'Yes; and as fast as his horse could possibly carry him.'

'In what direction?'

'In the direction of the château.'

'Well, and after——'

'Afterwards, as I have had the honour of telling your Majesty, two men on foot arrived, who carried M. de Guiche back with them.'

'What proof have you that these men arrived after the combat?'

'A very evident proof, sire; at the moment the encounter took place, the rain had just ceased, the ground had not had time to imbibe the moisture, and had, consequently, become damp; the footsteps sank in the ground, but, while M. de Guiche was lying there in a fainting condition, the ground became firm again, and the footsteps made a less sensible impression.'

Louis clapped his hands together in sign of admiration. 'Monsieur d'Artagnan,' he said, 'you are positively the cleverest man in my kingdom.'

'The very thing that M. de Richelieu thought, and M. de Mazarin said, sire.'

'And, now, it remains for us to see if your sagacity is in fault.'

'Oh! sire, a man may be mistaken; *errare humanum est*,'* said the musketeer philosophically.

'In that case, you are not human, Monsieur d'Artagnan, for I believe you never are mistaken.'

'Your Majesty said that we were going to see whether such was the case or not.'

'Yes.'

'In what way, may I venture to ask?'

'I have sent for M. de Manicamp, and M. de Manicamp is coming.'

'And M. de Manicamp knows the secret.'

'Guiche has no secrets for M. de Manicamp.'

D'Artagnan shook his head. 'No one was present at the combat, I repeat; and, unless M. de Manicamp was one of the two men who brought him back——'

'Hush!' said the King, 'he is coming; remain there, and listen attentively.'

'Very good, sire.'

And, at the same moment, Manicamp and Saint-Aignan appeared at the threshold of the door.

LXIV

THE ENCOUNTER

THE King with his hand made, first to the musketeer, and then to Saint-Aignan, an imperious and significant gesture, as much as to say, 'On your lives, not a word.' D'Artagnan withdrew, like a soldier, into a corner of the room; Saint-Aignan, in his character of favourite, leaned over the back of the King's chair. Manicamp, with his right foot properly advanced, a smile upon his lips, and his white and well-formed hands gracefully disposed, advanced to make his reverence to the King, who returned the salutation by a bow. 'Good evening, M. de Manicamp,' he said.

'Your Majesty did me the honour to send for me,' said Manicamp.

'Yes, in order to learn from you all the details of the unfortunate accident which has befallen the Comte de Guiche.'

'Oh, sire, it is very grievous indeed.'

'You were there?'

'Not precisely so, sire.'

'But you arrived on the scene where the accident occurred a few minutes after it took place?'

'I did so, sire, about half an hour afterwards.'

'And where did the accident happen?'

'I believe, sire, the place is called the Rond-point du Bois-Rochin.'

'Oh! the rendezvous of the hunt.'

'The very spot, sire.'

'Very good; tell me what details you are acquainted with respecting this unhappy affair, Monsieur de Manicamp.'

'Perhaps your Majesty has already been informed of them, and I fear to fatigue you by useless repetitions.'

'No, do not be afraid of that.'

Manicamp looked all round him; he only saw d'Artagnan leaning with his back against the wainscot—d'Artagnan, calm, kind, and good-natured as usual—and Saint-Aignan whom he had accompanied, and who still leaned over the King's armchair with an expression of countenance equally full of good feeling. He determined, therefore, to speak out. 'Your Majesty is perfectly aware,' he said, 'that accidents are very frequent in hunting.'

'In hunting, do you say?'

'I mean, sire, when an animal is brought to bay.'

'Ah, ah!' said the King, 'it was when the animal was brought to bay, then, that the accident happened.'

'Alas! sire, unhappily it was so.'

The King paused for a moment before he said, 'What animal was being hunted?'

'A wild boar, sire.'

'And what could possibly have possessed de Guiche to go to a wild-boar hunt by himself; that is but a clownish idea of sport, and only fit for that class of people who, unlike the Marshal de Gramont, have no dogs and huntsmen to hunt as gentlemen should do.'

Manicamp shrugged his shoulders. 'Youth is very rash,' he said sententiously.

'Well, go on,' said the King.

'At all events,' continued Manicamp, not venturing to be too precipitate and hasty, and letting his words fall very slowly one by one, 'at all events, sire, poor de Guiche went hunting—quite alone.'

'Quite alone, indeed! What a sportsman. And is not M. de Guiche aware that the wild boar always stands at bay?'

'That is the very thing that really happened, sire.'

'He had some idea, then, of the beast being there?'

'Yes, sire, some peasants had seen it among their potatoes.'*

'And what kind of animal was it?'

'A short, stocky beast.'

'You may as well tell me, monsieur, that Guiche had some idea of committing suicide; for I have seen him hunt, and he is an active and vigorous hunter. Whenever he fires at an animal brought to bay and held in check by the dogs, he takes every possible precaution, and yet he fires with a carbine,* and on this occasion he seems to have faced the boar with pistols only.'

Manicamp started.

'A costly pair of pistols, excellent weapons to fight a duel with a man and not with a wild boar. What absurdity!'

'There are some things, sire, which are difficult of explanation.'

'You are quite right, and the event which we are now discussing is one of those things. Go on.'

During the recital, Saint-Aignan, who had probably made a sign to Manicamp to be careful what he was about, found that the King's glance was constantly fixed upon himself, so that it was utterly impossible to communicate with Manicamp in any way. As for d'Artagnan, the statue of Silence* at Athens was far more noisy and far more expressive than he. Manicamp, therefore, was obliged to continue in the same way he had begun, and so contrived to get more and more entangled in his explanation. 'Sire,' he said, 'this is probably how the affair happened. Guiche was waiting to receive the boar as it rushed towards him.'

'On foot or on horseback?' inquired the King.

'On horseback. He fired upon the brute and missed his aim, and then it dashed upon him.'

'And the horse was killed.'

'Ah! your Majesty knows that, then?'

'I have been told that a horse has been found lying dead in the cross-roads of the Bois-Rochin, and I presumed it was de Guiche's horse.'

'Perfectly true, sire, it was his.'

'Well, so much for the horse, and now for Guiche?'

'Guiche, once down, was attacked and worried by the wild boar, and wounded in the hand and in the chest.'

'It is a horrible accident, but it must be admitted it was de Guiche's own fault. How could he possibly have gone to hunt such an animal merely armed with pistols; he must have forgotten the fable of Adonis?'*

Manicamp rubbed his ear in seeming perplexity. 'Very true,' he said, 'it was very imprudent.'

'Can you explain it, Monsieur Manicamp?'

'Sire, what is written is written!'

'Ah! you are a fatalist.'

Manicamp looked very uncomfortable and ill at ease. 'I am angry with you, Monsieur Manicamp,' continued the King.

'With me, sire?'

'Yes. How was it that you, who are de Guiche's intimate

friend, and who know that he is subject to such acts of folly, did not stop him in time?'

Manicamp hardly knew what to do; the tone in which the King spoke was not exactly that of a credulous man. On the other hand, the tone did not indicate any particular severity, nor did he seem to care much about the cross-examination. There was more of raillery in it than of menace. 'And you say, then,' continued the King, 'that it was positively de Guiche's horse that was found dead?'

'Quite positive, sire.'

'Did that astonish you?'

'No, sire; for your Majesty will remember that, at the last hunt, M. de Saint-Maure* had a horse killed under him, and in the same way.'

'Yes, but that one was ripped open.'

'Of course, sire.'

'Had Guiche's horse been ripped open like M. de Saint-Maure's horse, that would not have astonished me, indeed,'

Manicamp opened his eyes very wide. 'Am I mistaken,' resumed the King, 'was it not in the temple that de Guiche's horse was struck? You must admit, Monsieur de Manicamp, that that is a very singular wound.'

'You are aware, sire, that the horse is a very intelligent animal, and he endeavoured to defend himself.'

'But a horse defends himself with his hind feet, and not with his head.'

'In that case the terrified horse may have slipped or fallen down,' said Manicamp, 'and the boar, you understand, sire, the boar——'

'Oh! I understand that perfectly, as far as the horse is concerned; but how about his rider?'

'Well! that, too, is simple enough; the boar left the horse and attacked the rider; and, as I have already had the honour of informing your Majesty, shattered de Guiche's hand at the very moment he was about to discharge his second pistol at him, and then, with a blow of his tusk, made that terrible hole in his chest.'

'Nothing can possibly be more likely; really, Monsieur de Manicamp, you are wrong in placing so little confidence in your own eloquence, and you can tell a story most admirably.'

'Your Majesty is exceedingly kind,' said Manicamp, saluting him in the most embarrassed manner.

'From this day, henceforth, I will prohibit any gentleman attached to my court going to a similar encounter. Really, one might just as well permit duelling.'

Manicamp started, and moved as if he were about to withdraw. 'Is your Majesty satisfied?' he inquired.

'Delighted; but do not withdraw yet, Monsieur de Manicamp,' said Louis, 'I have something to say to you.'

'Well, well!' thought d'Artagnan, 'there is another who is not up to our mark;' and he uttered a sigh which might signify, 'Oh! the men of our stamp, where are they now?'*

At this moment an usher lifted up the curtain before the door, and announced the King's physician.

'Ah,' exclaimed Louis, 'here comes Monsieur Valot, who has just been to see M. de Guiche. We shall now hear news of the wounded man.'

Manicamp felt more uncomfortable than ever. 'In this way, at least,' added the King, 'our conscience will be quite clear.' And he looked at d'Artagnan, who did not seem in the slightest degree discomposed.

LXV

THE PHYSICIAN

M. VALOT entered. The position of the different persons was precisely the same; the King was seated, Saint-Aignan still leaning over the back of his arm-chair, d'Artagnan with his back against the wall, and Manicamp still standing.

'Well, M. Valot,' said the King, 'have you obeyed my directions?'

'With the greatest alacrity, sire.'

'You went to the doctor's house in Fontainebleau?'

'Yes, sire.'

'And you found M. de Guiche there?'

'I did, sire.'

'What state was he in?—speak unreservedly.'

'In a very sad state, indeed, sire.'

'The wild boar did not quite devour him, however?'

'Devour whom?'

'Guiche.'

'What wild boar?'

'The boar that wounded him.'

'M. de Guiche wounded by a boar?'

'So it is said, at least.'

'By a poacher, rather, or by a jealous husband, or an ill-used lover, who, in order to be revenged, fired upon him.'

'What is that you say, Monsieur Valot; are not M. de Guiche's wounds produced by defending himself against a wild boar?'

'M. de Guiche's wounds are produced by a pistol-bullet which broke his ring-finger and the little finger of the right hand, and afterwards buried itself in the intercostal muscles of the chest.'

'A bullet! Are you sure, Monsieur de Guiche has been wounded by a bullet?' exclaimed the King, pretending to look much surprised.

'Indeed I am, sire; so sure, in fact, that here it is.' And he presented to the King a half-flattened bullet, which the King looked at, but did not touch.

'Did he have that in his chest, poor fellow?' he asked.

'Not precisely. The ball did not penetrate, but was flattened, as you see, either upon the trigger of the pistol or upon the right side of the breast-bone.'

'Good heavens!' said the King seriously, 'You said nothing to me about this, Monsieur de Manicamp.'

'Sire——'

'What does all this mean, then, this invention about hunting a wild boar at nightfall? Come, speak, monsieur.'

'Sire——'

'It seems, then, that you are right,' said the King, turning round towards the captain of musketeers, 'and that a duel actually took place.'

The King possessed, to a greater extent than any one else, the faculty enjoyed by the great in power or position of compromising and divining those beneath them. Manicamp darted a look full of reproaches at the musketeer. D'Artagnan understood the look at once, and not wishing to remain beneath the weight of such an accusation, advanced a step forward, and said,—'Sire, your Majesty commanded me to go and explore the place where the cross-roads meet in the Bois-Rochin, and to report to you, according to my own ideas, what had taken place there. I submitted my observations to you, but without denouncing any one. It was your Majesty yourself who was the first to name the Comte de Guiche.'

'Well, monsieur, well,' said the King haughtily; 'you have done your duty, and I am satisfied with you. But you, Monsieur de Manicamp, have failed in yours, for you have told me a falsehood.'

'A falsehood, sire? The expression is a hard one.'

'Find another instead, then.'

'Sire, I will not attempt to do so. I have already been unfortunate enough to displease your Majesty, and it will, in every respect, be far better for me to accept most humbly any reproaches you may think proper to address to me.'

'You are right, monsieur; whoever conceals the truth from me, risks my displeasure.'

'Sometimes, sire, one is ignorant of the truth.'

'No further falsehood, monsieur, or double the punishment.'

Manicamp bowed and turned pale. D'Artagnan again made another step forward, determined to interfere if the still increasing anger of the King attained certain limits.

'You see, monsieur,' continued the King, 'that it is useless to deny the thing any longer. M. de Guiche has fought a duel.'

'I do not deny it, sire, and it would have been generous in your Majesty not to have forced me to tell a falsehood.'

'Forced? Who forced you?'

'Sire, M. de Guiche is my friend. Your Majesty has forbidden duels under pain of death. A falsehood might save my friend's life, and I told it.'

'Good!' murmured d'Artagnan, 'an excellent fellow, upon my word.'

'Instead of telling a falsehood, monsieur, you should have prevented him from fighting,' said the King.

'Oh! sire, your Majesty, who is the most accomplished gentleman in France, knows quite as well as any of us other gentlemen that we have never considered M. de Bouteville dishonoured for having suffered death on the Place de Grève.* That which does in truth dishonour a man is to avoid meeting his enemy, and not to avoid meeting his executioner?'

'Well, monsieur, that may be so,' said Louis XIV; 'I am very desirious of suggesting a means of your repairing all.'

'If it be a means of which a gentleman may avail himself, I shall most eagerly do so.'

'The name of M. de Guiche's adversary?'

'Oh! oh!' murmured d'Artagnan, 'we are going to take Louis XIII as a model.'*

'Sire!' said Manicamp with an accent of reproach.

'You will not name him, it appears, then?' said the King.

'Sire, I do not know him.'

'Bravo!' murmured d'Artagnan.

'Monsieur de Manicamp, hand your sword to the captain.'

Manicamp bowed very gracefully, unbuckled his sword, smiling as he did so, and handed it for the musketeer to take. But Saint-Aignan advanced hurriedly between him and d'Artagnan. 'Sire,' he said, 'will your Majesty permit me to say a word?'

'Do so,' said the King, delighted perhaps at the bottom of his heart for some one to step between him and the wrath which he felt had carried him too far.

'Manicamp, you are a brave man, and the King will appreciate your conduct; but to wish to serve your friends too well is to destroy them. Manicamp, you know the name the King asks your for?'

'It is perfectly true—I do know it.'

'You will give it up, then?'

'If I felt I ought to have mentioned it I should have already done so.'

'Then I will tell it, for I am not so extremely sensitive on such points of honour as you are.'

'You are at liberty to do so, but it seems to me, however——'

'Oh! a truce to magnanimity; I will not permit you to go to the Bastille in that way. Do you speak, or I will.'

Manicamp was keen-witted enough, and perfectly understood that he had done quite sufficient to procure a good opinion of his conduct; it was now only a question of persevering in such a manner as to regain the good graces of the King. 'Speak, monsieur,' he said to Saint-Aignan; 'I have on my own behalf done all that my conscience told me to do, and it must have been very importunate,' he added, turning towards the King, 'since its mandates led me to disobey your Majesty's command; but your Majesty will forgive me, I hope, when you learn that I was anxious to preserve the honour of a lady.'

'Of a lady?' said the King with some uneasiness.

'Yes, sire.'

'A lady was the cause of this duel?'

Manicamp bowed.

'If the position of the lady in question warrants it,' he said, 'I shall not complain of your having acted with so much circumspection; on the contrary, indeed.'

'Sire, everything which concerns your Majesty's household, or the household of your Majesty's brother is of importance in my eyes.'

'In my brother's household,' repeated Louis XIV, with a slight hesitation, 'The cause of the duel was a lady belonging to my brother's household, do you say?'

'Or to Madame's.'

'Ah! to Madame's?'

'Yes, sire.'

'Well, and this lady?'

'Is one of the maids of honour of Her Royal Highness Madame la Duchesse d'Orléans.'

'For whom M. de Guiche fought—do you say?'

'Yes, sire, and this time I tell no falsehood.'

Louis seemed restless and anxious. 'Gentlemen,' he said, turning towards the spectators of this scene, 'will you have the goodness to retire for a moment; I wish to be alone with M. de Manicamp. I know he has some very important communications to make for his own justification, and which he will not venture to do before witnesses. . . . Put up your sword, Monsieur de Manicamp.'

Manicamp returned his sword to his belt.

'The fellow decidedly has his wits about him,' murmured the musketeer, taking Saint-Aignan by the arm, and withdrawing with him.

'He will get out of it,' said the latter in d'Artagnan's ear.

'And with honour, too, Comte.'

Manicamp cast a glance of recognition at Saint-Aignan and the captain which passed unnoticed by the King.

'Come, come,' said d'Artagnan, as he left the room, 'I had an indifferent opinion of the new generation. Well, I was mistaken after all, and there is some good in them, I perceive.'

Valot preceded the favourite and the captain, leaving the King and Manicamp alone in the cabinet.

LXVI

WHEREIN D'ARTAGNAN PERCEIVES THAT IT WAS HE WHO WAS MISTAKEN AND MANICAMP WHO WAS RIGHT

THE King determined to be satisfied that no one was listening went himself to the door, and then returned precipitately and placed himself opposite to Manicamp. 'And now we are alone, Monsieur de Manicamp, explain yourself.'

'With the greatest frankness, sire,' replied the young man.

'And, in the first place, pray understand,' added the King, 'that there is nothing to which I personally attach a greater importance than the honour of any lady.'

'That is the very reason, sire, why I endeavoured to study your delicacy of sentiment and feeling.'

'Yes, I understand it all, now. You say it was one of the maids of honour of my sister-in-law who was the subject of the dispute, and that the person in question, Guiche's adversary, the man, in point of fact, whom you will not name——'

'But whom M. de Saint-Aignan will name, Monsieur.'

'Yes; you say, however, that this man has insulted some one belonging to the household of Madame.'

'Yes, sire, Mademoiselle de la Vallière.'

'Ah!' said the King, as if he had expected the name, and yet as if its announcement had caused him a sudden pang; 'ah! it was Mademoiselle de la Vallière who was insulted?'

'I do not say precisely that she was insulted, sire.'

'But at all events——'

'I merely say that she was spoken of in terms far from respectful.'

'A man dares to speak in disrespectful terms of Mademoiselle de la Vallière, and yet you refused to tell me the name of the insulter?'

'Sire, I thought it was quite understood that your Majesty had abandoned the idea of making me denounce him.'

'Perfectly true, monsieur,' returned the King, controlling his anger; 'besides I shall always know in sufficient time the name of the man whom I shall feel it my duty to punish.'

Manicamp perceived that they had returned to the question again. As for the King, he saw he had allowed himself to be hurried away a little too far, and he therefore continued,—'And I will punish him—not because there is any question of Mademoiselle de la Vallière, although I esteem her very highly—but because a lady was the object of the quarrel. And I intend that ladies shall be respected at my court, and that quarrels shall be put a stop to altogether.'

Manicamp bowed.

'And now, Monsieur de Manicamp,' continued the King, 'what was said about Mademoiselle de la Vallière?'

'Cannot your Majesty guess?'

'I?'

'Your Majesty can imagine the character of the jests in which young men permit themselves to indulge.'

'They very probably said that she was in love with some one?' the King ventured to remark.

'Probably so.'

'But Mademoiselle de la Vallière has a perfect right to love any one she pleases,' said the King.

'That is the very point de Guiche maintained.'

'And on account of which he fought, do you mean?'

'Yes, sire, the very sole cause.'

The King coloured. 'And you do not know anything more, then?'

'In what respect, sire?'

'In the very interesting respect which you are now referring to.'

'What does your Majesty wish me to know?'

'Why, the name of the man with whom La Vallière is in love, and whom de Guiche's adversary disputed her right to love.'

'Sire, I know nothing—I have heard nothing—and have learnt nothing, even accidentally; but de Guiche is a noble hearted fellow, and if, momentarily, he substituted himself in the place or stead of La Vallière's protector, it was because that protector was himself of too exalted a position to undertake her defence.'

These words were more than transparent; they made the King blush, but this time with pleasure. He struck Manicamp gently on the shoulder. 'Well, well, Monsieur de Manicamp, you are not only a ready, witty fellow, but a brave gentleman besides, and your friend de Guiche is a Paladin* after my own heart; you will express that to him from me?'

'Your Majesty forgives me, then?'

'Completely.'

'And I am free?'

The King smiled and held out his hand to Manicamp, which he took and kissed respectfully. 'And then,' added the King, 'you relate stories so charmingly.'

'I, sire?'

'You told me in the most admirable manner the particulars of the accident which happened to Guiche. I can see the wild boar rushing out of the wood—I can see the horse fall down, and the boar rush from the horse to the rider. You do not simply relate a story well, but you paint its incidents in the most vivid colours.'

'Sire, I think your Majesty deigns to laugh at my expense,' said Manicamp.

'On the contrary,' said Louis seriously, 'I have so little intention of laughing, Monsieur de Manicamp, that I wish you to relate this adventure to every one.'

'The adventure of the hunt?'

'Yes; in the same manner you told it to me, without changing a single word—you understand.'

'Perfectly, sire.'

'And you will relate it, then?'

'Without wasting a minute.'

'Very well! and now summon M. d'Artagnan; I hope you are no longer afraid of him.'

'Oh! sire, from the very moment I am sure of your Majesty's kind dispositions, I no longer fear anything.'

'Call him, then,' said the King.

Manicamp opened the door, and said, 'Gentlemen, the King wishes you to return.'

D'Artagnan, Saint-Aignan, and Valot entered.

'Gentlemen,' said the King, 'I summoned you for the purpose of saying that Monsieur de Manicamp's explanation has entirely satisfied me.'

D'Artagnan glanced at Valot and Saint-Aignan, as much as to say, 'Well! did I not tell you so?'

The King led Manicamp to the door, and then in a low tone of voice said,—'See that M. de Guiche takes care of himself, and, particularly, that he recovers as soon as possible; I am very desirous of thanking him in the name of every lady, but let him take special care that he does not do it again.'

'Were he to die a hundred times, sire, he would begin again if your Majesty's honour were in any way called in question.'

This remark was direct enough. But we have already said that the incense of flattery was very pleasing to the King, and, provided he received it, he was not very particular as to its quality.

'Very well, very well,' he said, as he dismissed Manicamp. 'I will see de Guiche myself, and make him listen to reason.' And as Manicamp left the apartment, the King turned round towards the three spectators of this scene, and said, 'Tell me, Monsieur d'Artagnan, how does it happen that your sight is so imperfect?— you whose eyes are generally so very good.'

'My sight bad, sire?'

'Certainly.'

'It must be the case, since your Majesty says so; but in what respect may I ask?'

'Why, with regard to what occurred in the Bois-Rochin.'

'Ah! ah!'

'Certainly. You pretend to have seen the tracks of two horses, to have detected the foot-prints of two men; and have described the particulars of an engagement, which you assert took place. Nothing of the sort occurred, pure illusion on your part.'

'Ah! ah!' said d'Artagnan.

'Exactly the same thing with the galloping to and fro of the horses, and the other indications of a struggle. It was the struggle of de Guiche against the wild boar, and absolutely nothing else; only the struggle was a long and a terrible one, it seems.'

'Ah! ah!' continued d'Artagnan.

'And when I think that I almost believed it for a moment; but, then, you speak with such confidence.'

'I admit, sire, that I must have been very shortsighted,' said d'Artagnan, with a readiness of humour which delighted the King.

'You do admit, then?'

'Admit it, sire, most assuredly I do.'

'So that now you see the thing——'

'In quite a different light to what I saw it half an hour ago.'

'And to what, then, do you attribute this difference in your opinion?'

'Oh! a very simple thing, sire; half an hour ago I returned from the Bois-Rochin, where I had nothing to light me but a stupid stable lantern——'

'While now?'

'While now, I have all the wax-lights of your apartments, and more than that, your Majesty's own eyes, which illuminate everything like the blazing sun at noonday.'

The King began to laugh, and Saint-Aignan broke out into convulsions of merriment.

'It is precisely like M. Valot,' said d'Artagnan, resuming the conversation where the King had left off; 'he has been imagining all along, that, not only was M. de Guiche wounded by a bullet, but still more that he extracted it, even, from his chest.'

'Upon my word,' said Valot, 'I assure you——'

'Now, did you not believe that?' continued d'Artagnan.

'Yes,' said Valot; 'not only did I believe it, but, at this very moment I would swear it.'

'Well, my dear doctor, you have dreamt it.'

'I have dreamt it?'

'M. de Guiche's wound—a mere dream; the bullet, a dream. So, take my advice, and say no more about it.'

'Well said,' returned the King; 'M. d'Artagnan's advice is very good. Do not speak of your dream to any one, Monsieur Valot, and upon the word of a gentleman, you will have no occasion to repent it. Good-evening, gentlemen; a very sad affair, indeed, is a wild-boar hunt!'

'A very serious thing, indeed,' repeated d'Artagnan, in a loud voice, 'is a wild-boar hunt!' and he repeated it in every room through which he passed; and left the château, taking Valot with him.

'And now we are alone,' said the King to Saint-Aignan, 'what is the name of de Guiche's adversary?'

Saint-Aignan looked at the King.

'Oh! do not hesitate,' said the King; 'you know that I must forgive.'

'De Wardes,' said Saint-Aignan.

'Very good,' said Louis XIV; and then, hastily retiring to his own room, added to himself, 'to forgive is not to forget.'

LXVII

SHOWING THE ADVANTAGE OF HAVING TWO STRINGS TO ONE'S BOW

MANICAMP quitted the King's apartment, delighted at having succeeded so well, when, just as he reached the bottom of the staircase, and was about passing before a doorway, he felt that some one suddenly pulled him by the sleeve. He turned round and recognised Montalais, who was waiting for him in the passage, and who, in a very mysterious manner, with her body bent forward, and, in a low tone of voice, said to him, 'Follow me, monsieur, and without any delay, if you please.'

'Where to, mademoiselle?' inquired Manicamp.

'In the first place, a true knight would not have asked such a question, but would have followed me without requiring any explanation.'

'Well, mademoiselle, I am quite ready to conduct myself as a true knight.'

'No; it is too late, and you cannot take the credit of it. We are going to Madame's apartments, so come at once.'

'Ah! ah!' said Manicamp. 'Lead on, then.'

And he followed Montalais, who ran before him as light as Galatea.*

'This time,' said Manicamp, as he followed his guide, 'I do not think that the stories about hunting expeditions would be acceptable. We will try, however, and if need be—why, if there should be any occasion for it, we must try something else.'

Montalais still ran on.

'How fatiguing it is,' thought Manicamp, 'to have need of one's head and legs at the same time.'

At last, however, they arrived. Madame had just finished undressing, and was in a most elegant *déshabille*, but it must be understood that she had changed her dress before she had any idea of being subjected to the emotions which agitated her. She was waiting with the most restless impatience, and Montalais and Manicamp found her standing near the door. At the sound of their approaching footsteps, Madame came forward to meet them.

'Ah!' she said, 'at last!'

'Here is M. Manicamp,' replied Montalais.

Manicamp bowed with the greatest respect; Madame signed to Montalais to withdraw, and she immediately obeyed. Madame followed her with her eyes, in silence, until the door closed behind her, and then, turning towards Manicamp, said, 'What is the matter?—and is it true, as I am told, Monsieur de Manicamp, that some one is lying wounded in the château?'

'Yes, Madame, unfortunately so—Monsieur de Guiche.'

'Yes! Monsieur de Guiche,' repeated the Princess. 'I had, in fact, heard it rumoured, but not confirmed. And so, in perfect truth, it is Monsieur de Guiche who has been so unfortunate?'

'M. de Guiche himself, Madame.'

'Are you aware, M. de Manicamp,' said the Princess hastily, 'that the King has the strongest antipathy to duels?'

'Perfectly so, Madame, but a duel with a wild beast is not amenable to His Majesty.'

'Oh, you will not insult me by supposing that I should credit the absurd fable which has been reported, with what object I cannot tell, respecting M. de Guiche having been wounded by a wild boar. No, no, monsieur, the real truth is known, and in addition to the inconvenience of his wound, M. de Guiche runs the risk of losing his liberty.'

'Alas! Madame, I am well aware of that, but what is to be done?'

'You have seen the King?'

'Yes, Madame.'

'What did you say to him?'

'I told him how M. de Guiche had been to the chase, and how a wild boar had rushed forth out of the Bois-Rochin; how M. de Guiche fired at it, and how, in fact, the furious brute dashed at de Guiche, killed his horse, and grievously wounded himself.'

'And the King believed that?'

'Perfectly.'

'Oh, you surprise me, Monsieur de Manicamp; you surprise me very much.' And Madame walked up and down the room, casting a searching look from time to time at Manicamp, who remained motionless and impassible in the same place. At last she stopped. 'And yet,' she said, 'every one here seems united in giving another cause for this wound.'

'What cause, Madame,' said Manicamp; 'may I be permitted, without indiscretion, to ask your Highness?'

'You ask such a question! You, M. de Guiche's intimate friend, his confidant, indeed!'

'Oh, Madame! the intimate friend—yes; the confidant—no; de Guiche is a man who can keep his own secrets, who has some of his own certainly, but who never breathes a syllable about them. De Guiche is discretion itself, Madame.'

'Very well, then; those secrets which M. de Guiche keeps so scrupulously, I shall have the pleasure of informing you of,' said the Princess almost spitefully; 'for the King may possibly question you a second time, and if, on the second occasion, you were to repeat the same story to him he possibly might not be very well satisfied with it.'

'But, Madame, I think your Highness is mistaken with regard to the King. His Majesty has been perfectly satisfied with me, I assure you.'

'In that case, permit me to assure you, Monsieur de Manicamp, that only proves one thing, which is, that His Majesty is very easily satisfied.'

'I think your Highness is mistaken in arriving at such an opinion; His Majesty is well known not to be contented except with very good reasons.'

'And do you suppose that he will thank you for your officious falsehood, when he will learn to-morrow that M. de Guiche had, on behalf of his friend M. de Bragelonne, a quarrel which ended in a hostile meeting?'

'A quarrel on M. de Bragelonne's account,' said Manicamp, with the most innocent expression in the world; 'what does your Royal Highness do me the honour to tell me!'

'What is there astonishing in that? M. de Guiche is susceptible, irritable, and easily loses his temper.'

'On the contrary, Madame, I know M. de Guiche to be very patient, and never susceptible or irritable except upon very good grounds.'

'But is not friendship a just ground?' said the Princess.

'Oh, certainly, Madame; and particularly for a heart like his.'

'Very good; you will not deny, I suppose, that M. de Bragelonne is M. de Guiche's friend?'

'A very great friend.'

'Well, then, M. de Guiche has taken M. de Bragelonne's part; and as M. de Bragelonne was absent, and could not fight, he fought for him.'

Manicamp began to smile, and moved his head and shoulders very slightly, as much as to say, 'Oh, if you will positively have it so——'

'But speak at all events,' said the Princess, out of patience, 'speak!'

'I?'

'Of course; it is quite clear you are not of my opinion, and that you have something to say.'

'I have only one thing to say, Madame.'

'Name it!'

'That I do not understand a single word of what you have just been telling me.'

'What!—you do not understand a single word about M. de Guiche's quarrel with M. de Wardes!' exclaimed the Princess, almost out of temper.

Manicamp remained silent.

'A quarrel,' she continued, 'which arose out of a conversation scandalous in its tone and purport, and more or less well-founded, respecting the virtue of a certain lady.'

'Ah! of a certain lady,—that is quite another thing,' said Manicamp.

'You begin to understand, do you not?'

'Your Highness will excuse me, but I dare not——'

'You dare not,' said Madame, exasperated; 'very well, then, wait one moment, and I will dare.'

'Madame, Madame!' exclaimed Manicamp, as if in great dismay, 'be careful of what you are going to say.'

'It would seem, monsieur, that if I happened to be a man, you would challenge me, notwithstanding his Majesty's edicts, as Monsieur de Guiche challenged M. de Wardes; and that, too, on account of the virtue of Mademoiselle de la Vallière.'

'Of Mademoiselle de la Vallière?' exclaimed Manicamp, starting backwards, as if hers was the very last name he expected to hear pronounced.

'What makes you start in that manner, Monsieur de Manicamp?' said Madame ironically; 'do you mean to say you would be impertinent enough to suspect that young lady's honour?'

'Madame, in the whole course of this affair, there has not been the slightest question of Mademoiselle de la Vallière's honour.'

'What! when two men have almost blown each other's brains out on a woman's behalf, do you mean to say she has had nothing to do with the affair, and that her name has not been called in question at all? I did not think you so good a courtier, Monsieur de Manicamp.'

'Pray forgive me, Madame,' said the young man, 'but we are very far from understanding each other. You do me the honour to speak one kind of language, while I am speaking altogether another.'

'I beg your pardon, but I do not understand your meaning.'

'Forgive me, then; but I fancied I understood your Highness to remark that de Guiche and de Wardes had fought on Mademoiselle de la Vallière's account.'

'Certainly.'

'On account of Mademoiselle de la Vallière, I think you said?' repeated Manicamp.

'I do not say that M. de Guiche personally took an interest in Mademoiselle de la Vallière, but I say that he did so as representing or acting on behalf of another.'

'On behalf of another?'

'Come, do not always assume such a bewildered look. Does not every one here know that M. de Bragelonne is affianced to Mademoiselle de la Vallière, and that before he went on the mission with which the King entrusted him, he charged his friend M. de Guiche to watch over that interesting young lady.'

'There is nothing more for me to say, then. Your Highness is well informed.'

'Of everything; so I beg you to understand that clearly.'

Manicamp began to laugh, which almost exasperated the Princess, who was not, as we know, of a very patient and enduring disposition.

'Madame,' resumed the discreet Manicamp, saluting the Princess, 'let us bury this affair altogether in forgetfulness, for it will never be quite cleared up.'

'Oh, as far as that goes, there is nothing more to do, and the information is complete. The King will learn that M. de Guiche has taken up the cause of this little adventuress, who gives herself all the airs of a grand lady; he will learn that Monsieur de Bragelonne, having nominated his friend M. de Guiche his guardian-in-ordinary of the garden of the Hesperides,* the latter immediately fastened, as he was required to do, upon the Marquis de Wardes, who ventured to touch the golden apple. Moreover, you cannot pretend to deny, Monsieur Manicamp— you who know everything so well—that the King, on his side, casts a longing eye upon this famous treasure, and that he will bear no light grudge against M. de Guiche for constituting himself the defender of it. Are you sufficiently well-informed now, or do you require anything further—if so, speak, monsieur.'

'No, Madame, there is nothing more I wish to know.'

'Learn, however—for you ought to know it, Monsieur de Manicamp—learn that His Majesty's indignation will be followed by terrible consequences. In princes of a similar temperament to that of His Majesty, the passion which jealousy causes sweeps down like a whirlwind.'

'Which you will temper, Madame.'

'I!' exclaimed the Princess with a gesture of indescribable irony; 'I! and by what title may I ask?'

'Because you detest injustice, Madame.'

'And according to your account, then, it would be an injustice to prevent the King arranging his love affairs as he pleases.'

'You will intercede, however, in M. de Guiche's favour?'

'You are mad, monsieur,' said the Princess in a haughty tone of voice.

'On the contrary, I am in the most perfect possession of my senses; and, I repeat, you will defend M. de Guiche before the King.'

'Why should I?'

'Because the cause of M. de Guiche is your own, Madame,' said Manicamp with all the ardour with which his eyes were kindled.

'What do you mean by that?'

'I mean, Madame, that, with respect to the defence which Monsieur de Guiche undertook in M. de Bragelonne's absence, I am surprised that your Highness has not detected a pretext in La Vallière's name having been brought forward.'

'A pretext? But a pretext for what?' repeated the Princess hesitantly, for Manicamp's steady look had just revealed something of the truth to her.

'I trust, Madame,' said the young man, 'I have said sufficient to induce your Highness not to overwhelm before His Majesty my poor friend de Guiche, against whom all the malevolence of a party bitterly opposed to your own will now be directed.'

'You mean, on the contrary, I suppose, that all those who have no great affection for Mademoiselle de la Vallière, and even, perhaps, a few of those who have some regard for her, will be angry with the Comte?'

'Oh, Madame! why will you push your obstinacy to such an extent, and refuse to open your ears and listen to the counsel of one whose devotion to you is unbounded? Must I expose myself to the risk of your displeasure—am I really to be called upon to name, contrary to my own wish, the person who was the real cause of this quarrel?'

'The person?' said Madame, blushing.

'Must I,' continued Manicamp, 'tell you how poor de Guiche

became irritated, furious, exasperated beyond all control, at the different rumours which are circulating about this person? Must I, if you persist in this wilful blindness, and if respect should continue to prevent me naming her—must I, I repeat, recall to your recollection that the various scenes which Monsieur had with the Duke of Buckingham, and the insinuations which were reported respecting the Duke's exile? Must I remind you of the anxious care the Comte always took in his efforts to please, to watch, to protect that person for whom alone he lives,—for whom alone he breathes? Well! I will do so; and when I shall have made you recall all the particulars I refer to, you will perhaps understand how it happened that the Comte, having lost all control over himself, and having been for some time past almost harassed to death by de Wardes, became, at the first disrespectful expression which the latter pronounced respecting the person in question, inflamed with passion, and panted only for an opportunity of revenging the affront.'

The Princess concealed her face in her hands. 'Monsieur, monsieur!' she exclaimed; 'do you know what you are saying, and to whom you are speaking?'

'Therefore, Madame,' pursued Manicamp as if he had not heard the exclamations of the Princess, 'nothing will astonish you any longer—neither the Comte's ardour in seeking the quarrel, nor his wonderful address in transferring it to a quarter foreign to your own personal interests. That latter circumstance was, indeed, a marvellous instance of tact and perfect coolness, and if the person in whose behalf the Comte so fought and shed his blood does, in reality, owe some gratitude to the poor wounded sufferer, it is not on account of the blood he has shed, or for the agony he has suffered, but for the steps he has taken to preserve from comment or reflection an honour which is more precious to him than his own.'

'Oh!' cried Madame, as if she had been alone, 'is it possible the quarrel was on my account!'

Manicamp felt he could now breathe for a moment—and gallantly had he won the right to do so. Madame, on her side, remained for some time plunged in a painful reverie. Her agitation could be seen by her quick respiration, by her languishing looks, by the frequency with which she pressed her hand upon her heart. But, in her, coquetry was not so much a passive quality as, on the contrary, a fire which sought for fuel to maintain itself, and which found what it required.

'If it be as you assert,' she said, 'the Comte will have obliged two persons at the same time; for Monsieur de Bragelonne also owes a deep debt of gratitude to M. de Guiche—and with far greater reason indeed, because everywhere, and on every occasion, Mademoiselle de la Vallière will be regarded as having been defended by this generous champion.'

Manicamp perceived that there still remained some lingering doubt in the Princess's heart. 'A truly admirable service indeed,' he said, 'is the one he has rendered to Mademoiselle de la Vallière! A truly admirable service to M. de Bragelonne! The duel has created a sensation which, in some respects, casts a dishonourable suspicion on that young girl; a sensation, indeed, which will embroil her with the Vicomte. The consequence is, that de Wardes's pistol-bullet has had three results instead of one; it destroys at the same time the honour of a woman, the happiness of a man, and, perhaps, it has wounded to death one of the best gentlemen in France. Oh, Madame! your logic is cold and calculating; it always condemns—it never absolves.'

Manicamp's concluding words scattered to the winds the last doubt which lingered, not in Madame's heart, but in her head. She was no longer a Princess full of scruples, nor a woman with ever-returning suspicions, but one whose heart had just felt the mortal chill of a wound. 'Wounded to death!' she murmured in a faltering voice, 'oh, Monsieur de Manicamp, did you not say wounded to death?'

Manicamp returned no other answer than a deep sigh.

'And so you said that the Comte is dangerously wounded?' continued the Princess.

'Yes, Madame; one of his hands is shattered, and he has a bullet lodged in his breast.'

'Gracious heavens!' resumed the Princess with a feverish excitement, 'this is horrible, Monsieur de Manicamp! a hand shattered, do you say, and a bullet in his breast? And that coward! that wretch! that assassin de Wardes, who did it!'

Manicamp seemed overcome by a violent emotion. He had, in fact, displayed no little energy in the latter part of his speech. As for Madame, she entirely threw aside all regard for the formal observances of propriety which society imposes; for when, with her, passion spoke in accents either of anger or sympathy, nothing could any longer restrain her impulses. Madame approached Manicamp, who had sunk down upon a seat, as if his grief were a sufficiently powerful excuse for his infraction of one of the laws of etiquette. 'Monsieur,' she said, seizing him by the hand, 'be frank with me.'

Manicamp looked up.

'Is M. de Guiche in danger of death?'

'Doubly so, Madame,' he replied; 'in the first place on account of the hæmorrhage which has taken place, an artery having been injured in the hand; and next, in consequence of the wound in his breast, which may, the doctor is afraid of it at least, have injured some vital part.'

'He may die, then?'

'Die, yes, Madame; and without even having had the consolation of knowing that you had been told of his devotion.'

'You will tell him.'

'I?'

'Yes; are you not his friend?'

'I? oh, no, Madame; I will only tell M. de Guiche—if, indeed, he is still in a condition to hear me—I will only tell him what I have seen; that is, your cruelty for him.'

'Oh, monsieur, you will not be guilty of such barbarity!'

'Indeed, Madame, I shall speak the truth, for nature is very energetic in a man of his age. The physicians are clever men, and if, by chance, the poor Comte should survive his wound, I should not wish him to die of a wound of the heart, after having escaped that of the body.' And Manicamp rose, and with an expression of profound respect, seemed to be desirous of taking leave.

'At least, monsieur,' said Madame, stopping him with almost a suppliant air, 'you will be kind enough to tell me in what state your wounded friend is, and who is the physician who attends him?'

'As regards the state he is in, Madame, he is seriously ill; his physician is M. Valot, His Majesty's private medical attendant. M. Valot is moreover assisted by a professional friend, to whose house M. de Guiche has been carried.'

'What! he is not in the château?' said Madame.

'Alas, Madame! the poor fellow was so ill that he could not even be conveyed hither.'

'Give me the address, monsieur,' said the Princess hurriedly; 'I will send to inquire after him.'

'Rue du Feurre;* a brick-built house with white outside blinds. The doctor's name is on the door.'

'You are returning to your wounded friend, Monsieur de Manicamp?'

'Yes, Madame.'

'You will be able, then, to do me a service.'

'I am at your Highness's orders.'

'Do what you intended to do; return to M. de Guiche, send away all those whom you may find there, and have the kindness yourself to go away too.'

'Madame——'

'Let us waste no time in useless explanations. Accept the fact as I present it to you; see nothing in it beyond what is really there, and ask nothing further than what I tell you. I am going to send one of my ladies, perhaps two, because it is now getting late; I do not wish them to see you, or rather, I do not wish you to see them. These are scruples which you can understand—you particularly, Monsieur de Manicamp, who seem to be capable of divining everything.'

'Oh, Madame, perfectly; I can even do better still—I will precede, or rather walk, in advance of your attendants; it will, at the same time, be a means of showing them the way more accurately, and of protecting them, if it happened any occasion might occur, though there is no probability of their needing protection.'

'And by this means, then, they would be sure of entering without any difficulty, would they not?'

'Certainly, Madame, for as I should be the first to pass, I should remove any difficulties which might chance to be in the way.'

'Very well, go, go, Monsieur de Manicamp, and wait at the bottom of the staircase.'

'I go at once, Madame.'

'Stay.' Manicamp paused. 'When you hear the footsteps of

two women descending the stairs, go out, and, without once turning round, take the road which leads to where the poor Comte is lying.'

'But if, by any mischance, two other persons were to descend, and I were to be mistaken?'

'You will hear one of the two clap her hands together very softly. So go.'

Manicamp turned round, bowed once more, and left the room, his heart overflowing with joy. In fact, he knew very well that the presence of Madame herself would be the best balm to apply to his friend's wounds. A quarter of an hour had hardly elapsed when he heard the sound of a door being opened softly, and closed with the same precaution. He listened to the light footfalls gliding down the staircase, and then heard the signal agreed upon. He immediately went out, and, faithful to his promise, bent his way, without once turning round his head, through the streets of Fontainebleau, towards the doctor's dwelling.

LXVIII

M. MALICORNE THE KEEPER OF THE RECORDS OF THE REALM OF FRANCE

Two women, whose figures were completely concealed by their mantles, and whose masks effectually hid the upper portion of their faces, timidly followed Manicamp's steps. On the first floor, behind curtains of red damask, the soft light of a lamp placed upon a low table faintly illuminated the room, at the other extremity of which, on a large bedstead supported by spiral columns, around which curtains of the same colour as those which deadened the rays of the lamp had been closely drawn, lay de Guiche, his head supported by pillows, his eyes looking as if the mists of death seemed gathering there; his long black hair, scattered over the pillow, set off the young man's hollowed and pale temples to great advantage. It could be easily perceived that fever was the principal occupant of that chamber. Guiche was dreaming. His wandering mind was pursuing, through gloom and mystery, one of those wild creations which delirium engenders. Two or three drops of blood, still liquid, stained the floor. Manicamp hurriedly ran up the stairs, but paused at the threshold of the door, looked into the room, and seeing that everything was perfectly quiet, he advanced towards the foot of the large leathern arm-chair, a specimen of furniture of the reign of Henry IV, and seeing that the nurse, as a matter of course, had dropped off to sleep, he awoke her, and begged her to pass into the adjoining room. Then, standing by the side of the bed, he remained for a moment deliberating whether it would be better to awaken Guiche, in order to acquaint him with the good news. But, as he began to hear behind the door the rustle of the silk dresses and the hurried breathing of his two companions, and as he already saw that the curtain which hung before the doorway seemed on the point of being impatiently drawn aside, he passed round the bed and followed the nurse into the next room. As soon as he had disappeared the curtain was raised, and his two female companions entered the room he had just left. The one who entered the first made a gesture to her companion, which riveted her to the spot where she stood, close to the door, and then resolutely advanced towards the bed, drew back the curtains along the iron rod, and threw them in thick folds behind the head of the bed. She gazed upon the Comte's pallid face, remarked his right hand enveloped in linen whose dazzling whiteness was increased by the counterpane decorated with dark leaves which was thrown across a portion of the sick couch. She shuddered as she saw a spot of blood becoming larger and larger upon the linen bandages. The young man's white chest was quite uncovered, as if the cool night air would assist his respiration. A small bandage fastened the dressings of the wound, around which a bluish circle of escaping blood was gradually increasing in size. A deep sigh broke from her lips. She leaned against one of the columns of the bed, and gazed through the holes in her mask, upon the harrowing spectacle before her. A hoarse harsh sigh passed like a death rattle through the Comte's clenched teeth. The masked lady seized his left hand, which felt as scorching as burning coals. But at the very moment she placed her icy hand upon it the action of the cold was such that Guiche opened his eyes, and by a look in which revived intelligence was dawning, seemed as if struggling back again into existence. The first thing upon which he fixed his gaze was this phantom standing erect by his bedside. At that sight his eyes became dilated, but without any appearance of consciousness in them. The lady thereupon made a sign to her companion, who had remained at the door; and in all probability the latter had already received her lesson, for in a clear tone of voice and without any hesitation whatever, she pronounced these words:—'Monsieur le Comte, Her Royal Highness Madame is desirous of knowing how you are able to bear your wound, and to express to you, by my lips, her great regret at seeing you suffer.'

As she pronounced the word Madame, Guiche started. He had not as yet remarked the person to whom the voice belonged, and he naturally turned towards the direction whence it proceeded. But, as he felt the cold hand still resting on his own, he again turned towards the motionless figure beside him. 'Was it you who spoke, Madame?' he asked, in a weak voice, 'or is there another person beside you in the room?'

'Yes,' replied the figure in an almost unintelligible voice, as she bent down her head.

'Well!' said the wounded man with a great effort, 'I thank you. Tell Madame that I no longer regret dying, since she has remembered me.'

At this word 'dying,' pronounced by one whose life seemed to hang on a thread, the masked lady could not restrain her tears, which flowed under her mask, and which appeared upon her cheeks just where the mask left her face bare. If Guiche had been in fuller possession of his senses, he would have seen her tears roll like glistening pearls, and fall upon his bed. The lady, forgetting that she wore her mask, raised her hand as though to wipe her eyes, and meeting the rough velvet, she tore away her mask in anger and threw it on the floor. At the unexpected apparition before him, which seemed to issue from a cloud, Guiche uttered a cry and stretched out his arms towards her; but every word perished on his lips, and his strength seemed utterly abandoning him. His right hand, which had followed his first impulse, without calculating the amount of strength he had left, fell back again upon the bed, and immediately afterwards the white linen was stained with a larger spot than before. In the meantime, the young man's eyes became dim, and closed as if he were already struggling with the angel of death; and then, after a few involuntary movements, his head fell back motionless on his pillow; from pale he had become livid. The lady was frightened; but on this occasion, contrary to what is usually the case, fear became attractive. She leaned over the young man, gazed earnestly, fixedly at his pale cold face, which she almost touched, then imprinted a rapid kiss upon de Guiche's left hand, who, trembling as if an electric shock had passed through him, awoke a second time, opened his large eyes incapable of recognition, and again fell into a state of complete insensibility. 'Come,' she said to her companion, 'we must not remain here any longer; I shall be committing some folly or other.'

'Madame, Madame, your Highness is forgetting your mask!' said her vigilant companion.

'Pick it up,' replied her mistress, as she tottered almost senseless towards the staircase, and as the street door had been left only half closed, the two women, light as birds, passed through it, and with hurried steps returned to the palace. One of them ascended towards Madame's apartments where she disappeared; the other entered the room belonging to the maids of honour, namely, on the entresol, and having reached her own room, she sat down before a table, and without giving herself time even to breathe, wrote the following letter:—

'This evening Madame has been to see M. de Guiche. Everything is going on well on this side. See that yours is the same, and do not forget to burn this paper.'

She then folded the letter in a long thin form, and leaving her room with every possible precaution, crossed a corridor which led to the apartments appropriated to the gentlemen attached to Monsieur's service. She stopped before a door, under which, having previously knocked twice in a short quick manner, she thrust the paper, and fled. Then, returning to her own room, she removed every trace of her having gone out, and also of having written the letter. Amid the investigations she was so diligently pursuing she perceived on the table the mask which belonged to Madame, and which, according to her mistress's directions, she had brought back, but had forgotten to restore to her. 'Oh! oh!' she said, 'I must not forget to do to-morrow what I have forgotten to do to-day.'

And as she took hold of the velvet mask by that part of it which covered the cheeks, and feeling that her thumb was wet, she looked at it. It was not only wet, but reddened. The mask had fallen upon one of the pools of blood which, we have already said, stained the floor, and from the black velvet outside which had accidentally come into contact with it, the blood had passed through to the inside and stained the white cambric lining. 'Oh! oh!' said Montalais, for doubtless our readers have already recognised her by these various manœuvres, 'I shall not give her back her mask, it is far too precious now.'

And rising from her seat, she ran towards a box made of maple wood, which enclosed different articles of toilet and perfumery. 'No, not here,' she said, 'such a treasure must not be abandoned to the slightest chance of detection.'

Then, after a moment's silence, and with a smile which was peculiarly her own, she added,—'Beautiful mask, stained with the blood of that brave knight, you shall go and join that collection of wonders, La Vallière's and Raoul's letters, that loving collection, indeed, which will some day or other form part of the history of France and of royalty. You shall be taken under M. Malicorne's care,' said the laughing girl, as she began to undress herself, 'under the protection of that worthy M. Malicorne,' she said, blowing out the taper, 'who thinks he was born only to become the chief usher of Monsieur's apartments, and whom I will make keeper of the records and historiographer* of the house of Bourbon and of the first houses in the kingdom. Let him grumble now, that discontented Malicorne,' she added as she drew the curtains and fell fast asleep.

LXIX

THE JOURNEY

THE next day, being agreed upon for the departure, the King, at eleven o'clock precisely, descended the grand staircase with the two Queens and Madame, in order to enter his carriage drawn by six horses which were pawing the ground in impatience at the foot of the staircase. The whole court awaited the royal appearance in the *Fer-à-cheval* crescent,* in their travelling costumes; the large number of saddled horses and carriages of ladies and gentlemen of the court, surrounded by their attendants, servants, and pages, formed a spectacle whose brilliancy could scarcely be equalled. The King entered his carriage with the two Queens; Madame was in the same with Monsieur. The maids of honour followed the example, and took their seats, two by two, in the carriages destined for them. The weather was exceedingly warm, a light breeze, which early in the morning all had thought would have been just sufficient to cool the air, soon became fiercely heated by the rays of the sun, although it was hidden behind the clouds, and filtered through the heated vapour which rose from the ground like a scorching wind, bearing particles of fine dust against the faces of the hasty travellers. Madame was the first to complain of the heat. Monsieur's only reply was to throw himself back in the carriage, as if he were about to faint, and to inundate himself with scents and perfumes, uttering the deepest sighs all the while; whereupon Madame said to him, with her most amiable expression, 'Really, Monsieur, I fancied that you would have been polite enough on account of the terrible heat, to have left me my carriage to myself, and to have performed the journey yourself on horseback.'

'Ride on horseback!' cried the Prince, 'you cannot suppose such a thing, Madame; my skin would peel off if I were to expose myself to such a burning air as this.'

'You can take my parasol,' she said.

'But the trouble of holding it!' replied Monsieur with the greatest coolness; 'besides, I have no horse.'

'How, no horse?' replied the Princess, who, if she did not obtain the solitude she required at least obtained the amusement of teasing. 'No horse! You are mistaken Monsieur; for I see your favourite bay out yonder.'

'My bay horse!' exclaimed the Prince, attempting to lean forward to look out of the door; but the movement he was obliged to make cost him so much trouble that he soon hastened to resume his immobility.

'Yes,' said Madame; 'your horse, led by M. de Malicorne.'

'Poor beast,' replied the Prince; 'how warm it will soon be!'

And with these words he closed his eyes, like a man on the point of death. Madame, on her side, reclined indolently in the other corner of the carriage, and closed her eyes also, not however to sleep, but to think more at her ease. In the meantime the King, seated in the front seat of the carriage, the back of which he had yielded up to the two Queens, was a prey to that restless feverish contrariety experienced by anxious lovers, who, without being able to quench their ardent thirst, are ceaselessly desirous of seeing the loved object, and then go away partially satisfied, without perceiving that they have acquired a more burning thirst than ever. The King, whose carriage headed the procession, could not from the place he occupied perceive the carriages of the ladies and maids of honour, which followed in a line behind it. Besides, he was obliged to answer the eternal questions of the young Queen, who, happy to have with her '*her dear husband*,' as she called him in utter forgetfulness of royal etiquette, invested him with all her affection, stifled him with her attentions, afraid that some one might come to take him from her, or that he himself might suddenly take a fancy to leave her society. Anne of Austria, whom nothing at that moment occupied except the occasional sharp throbbings in her bosom, looked pleased and delighted, and although she perfectly conceived the King's impatience, tantalisingly prolonged his sufferings by unexpectedly resuming the conversation at the very moment the King, absorbed in his own reflections, began to muse over his secret attachment. Everything seemed to combine——not alone the little teasing attentions of the Queen, but also the Queen-Mother's tantalising interruptions——to make the King's position almost unbearable; for he knew not how to control the restless longings of his heart. At first, he complained of the heat, a complaint which was merely preliminary to other complaints, but with sufficient tact to prevent Maria Theresa guessing his real object. Understanding the King's remark literally, she began to fan him with her ostrich plumes. But the heat passed away, and the King then complained of cramps and stiffness in his legs, and as the carriages at that moment stopped to change horses, the Queen said,—'Shall I get out with you? I too feel tired of sitting. We can walk on a little distance; the carriage will overtake us, and we can resume our places again presently.'

The King frowned; it is a hard trial a jealous woman makes her husband submit to whose fidelity she suspects, when, although herself a prey to jealousy, she watches herself so narrowly that she avoids giving any pretext for an angry feeling. The King, therefore, in the present case, could not refuse; he accepted the offer; alighted from the carriage, gave his arm to the Queen, and walked up and down with her while the horses were being changed. As he walked along, he cast an envious glance upon the courtiers, who were fortunate enough to be performing the journey on horseback. The Queen soon found out that the promenade she had suggested afforded the King as little pleasure as he had experienced from riding in the carriage. She accordingly expressed a wish to return to her carriage, and the King conducted her to the door, but did not get in with her. He stepped back a few paces, and looked among the file of carriages for the purpose of recognising the one in which he took so strong an interest. At the door of the sixth carriage he saw La Vallière's fair countenance. As the King thus stood motionless, wrapt in thought, without perceiving that everything was ready, and that he alone was causing the delay, he heard a voice close beside him, addressing him in the most respectful manner. It was M. Malicorne, in a complete costume of an equerry, holding over his left arm the bridles of a couple of horses.

'Your Majesty asked for a horse, I believe?' he said.

'A horse? Have you one of my horses here?' inquired the King, who endeavoured to remember the person who addressed him, and whose face was not as yet very familiar to him.

'Sire,' replied Malicorne, 'at all events I have a horse which is at your Majesty's service.'

And Malicorne pointed at Monsieur's bay horse, which Madame had observed. It was a beautiful creature and most royally caparisoned.

'This is not one of my horses, monsieur,' said the King.

'Sire, it is a horse out of His Royal Highness's stables but His Royal Highness does not ride when the weather is as hot as it is now.'

The King did not reply, but hastily approached the horse, which stood pawing the ground with his foot. Malicorne hastened to hold the stirrup for him, but the King was already in the saddle. Restored to good humour by this lucky accident, the King hastened towards the Queens' carriages, where he was anxiously expected; and notwithstanding Maria Theresa's thoughtful and preoccupied air, he said, 'I have been fortunate enough to find this horse, and I intend to avail myself of it. I felt stifled in the carriage. Adieu, ladies.'

Then bending most gracefully over the arched neck of his beautiful steed, he disappeared in a second. Anne of Austria leaned forward, in order to look after him as he rode away; he did not go very far, for when he reached the sixth carriage he reined in his horse suddenly, and took off his hat. He saluted La Vallière, who uttered a cry of surprise as she saw him, blushing at the same time with pleasure. Montalais, who occupied the other seat in the carriage, made the King a most respectful bow. And then, with all the tact of a woman, she pretended to be exceedingly interested in the landscape, and withdrew herself into the left-hand corner. The conversation between the King and La Vallière began, as all lovers' conversations generally do, namely, by eloquent looks and a few words utterly void of common sense. The King explained how warm he had felt in his carriage, so much so indeed that he could almost regard the horse he then rode as a blessing thrown in his way. 'And,' he added, 'my benefactor is an exceedingly intelligent man, for he seemed to guess my thoughts intuitively. I have now only one wish, that of learning the name of the gentleman who so cleverly assisted his King out of his dilemma, and extricated him from his cruel position.'

Montalais, during this colloquy, the first words of which had awakened her attention, had slightly altered her position, and had contrived so as to meet the King's look as he finished his remark. It followed very naturally that the King looked inquiringly as much at her as at La Vallière; she had every reason to suppose that it was she who was appealed to, and consequently might be permitted to answer. She therefore said, 'Sire, the horse which your Majesty is riding belongs to Monsieur, and was being led by one of His Royal Highness's gentlemen.'

'And what is that gentleman's name, may I ask, mademoiselle?'

'M. de Malicorne, sire.'

The name produced its usual effect, for the King repeated it smilingly.

'Yes, sire,' replied Aure. 'Stay, it is that gentleman who is galloping on my left hand;' and she pointed out Malicorne, who, with a very sanctified expression, was galloping on the left side of the carriage, knowing perfectly well that they were talking of him at that very moment, but sitting in his saddle as if he were deaf and dumb.

'Yes,' said the King, 'that is the gentleman; I remember his face, and will not forget his name;' and the King looked tenderly at La Vallière.

Aure had now nothing further to do; she had let Malicorne's name fall; the soil was good; all that was now left to be done was to let the name take root, and the event would bear its fruit in due time. She, consequently, threw herself back in her corner, feeling perfectly justified in making as many agreeable signs of recognition as she liked to Malicorne, since the latter had had the happiness of pleasing the King. As it will very readily be believed, Montalais was not mistaken; and, Malicorne, with his quick ear and his sly look, seemed to interpret her remark as 'All goes on well,' the whole being accompanied by a pantomimic action which he fancied conveyed something resembling a kiss.

'Alas! mademoiselle,' said the King after a moment's pause, 'the liberty and freedom we enjoy in the country is soon about to cease; your attendance upon Madame will be more strictly enforced, and we shall see each other no more.'

'Your Majesty is too much attached to Madame,' replied Louise, 'not to come and see her very frequently; and whenever your Majesty may pass across the apartments——'

'Ah!' said the King in a tender voice, which was gradually lowered in its tone, 'to perceive is not to see, and yet it seems that it would be quite sufficient for you.'

Louise did not answer a syllable; a sigh filled her heart almost to bursting, but she stifled it.

'You exercise a great control over yourself,' said the King to Louise, who smiled upon him with a melancholy expression.

'Exert the strength you have in loving fondly,' he continued, 'and I will bless Heaven for having bestowed it on you.'

La Vallière still remained silent, but raised her eyes, brimful of affection, towards the King. Louis, as if he had been overcome by this burning glance, passed his hand across his forehead, and pressing the sides of his horse with his knees, made him bound several paces forward. La Vallière, leaning back in her carriage, with her eyes half-closed, gazed fixedly upon the King, whose plumes were floating in the air; she could not but admire his graceful carriage, his delicate and nervous limbs, which pressed his horse's side, and the regular outline of his features, which his beautiful curling hair set off to great advantage, revealing occasionally his small and well-formed ear. In fact the poor girl was in love, and she revelled in her innocent affection. In a few moments the King was again by her side.

'Do you not perceive,' he said, 'how terribly your silence affects me? Oh! mademoiselle, how pitilessly immovable you would become if you were ever to resolve to break off all acquaintance with any one; and then, too, I think you changeable; in fact, I dread this deep affection which fills my whole being.'

'Oh! sire, you are mistaken,' said La Vallière; 'if ever I love, it will be for my whole life.'

'If you love, you say,' exclaimed the King; 'you do not love now, then.' She hid her face in her hands.

'You see,' said the King, 'that I am right in accusing you; you must admit that you are changeable, capricious, a coquette, perhaps.'

'Oh, no! sire, be perfectly satisfied on that. No, I say again; no, no!'

'Promise me, then, that for me you will always be the same.'

'Oh! always, sire.'

'That you will never show any of that severity which would break my heart, none of that fickleness of manner which would be worse than death to me.'

'Oh! no, no.'

'Very well, then! but listen. I like promises, I like to place under the guarantee of an oath, under the protection of heaven in fact, everything which interests my heart and my affections. Promise me, or rather swear to me, that if in the life we are about to commence, a life which will be full of sacrifice, mystery, anxiety, disappointment, and misunderstanding, swear to me that if we should be deceiving, or should misunderstand each other, or should be judging each other unjustly, for that indeed would be criminal in love such as ours; swear to me, Louise——'

She trembled with agitation to the very depths of her heart; it was the first time she had heard her name pronounced in that manner by her royal lover. As for the King, taking off his glove, and placing his ungloved hand within the carriage, he continued,—'Swear, that never in all our quarrels will we allow one night even to pass by, if any misunderstanding should arise between us, without a visit, or at least a message, from either, in order to convey consolation and repose to the other.'

La Vallière took her lover's burning hand between her own icy palms, and pressed it softly, until a movement of the horse, frightened by the proximity of the wheels, obliged her to abandon her happiness. She had sworn as he wished her.

'Return, sire,' she said, 'return to the Queen; I foresee a storm rising yonder which threatens my peace of mind.'

Louis obeyed, saluted Mademoiselle de Montalais, and set off at a gallop to rejoin the Queen's carriage. As he passed Monsieur's carriage he observed that he was fast asleep, although Madame, on her part, was wide awake. As the King passed her she said, 'What a beautiful horse, sire! is it not Monsieur's bay horse?' The young Queen merely remarked, 'Are you better now, sire?'

LXX

TRIUMFEMINATE*

ON the King's arrival in Paris, he sat at the council which had been summoned, and worked for a certain portion of the day. The Queen remained with the Queen-Mother, and burst into tears as soon as she had taken leave of the King. 'Ah, Madame!' she said, 'the King no longer loves me! What will become of me?'

'A husband always loves his wife when she is like you,' replied Anne of Austria.

'A time may come when he will love another woman instead
of me.'

'What do you call loving?'

'Always thinking of a person—always seeking her society.'

'Do you happen to have remarked,' said Anne of Austria,
'that the King has ever done anything of the sort?'

'No, Madame,' said the young Queen hesitantly.

'What is there to complain of, then, Marie?'*

'You will admit that the King leaves me?'

'The King, my daughter, belongs to his people.'

'And that is the very reason why he no longer belongs to me;*
and that is the reason too, why I shall find myself, as so many
Queens have been before me, forsaken and forgotten, whilst
glory and honours will be reserved for others. Oh, mother! the
King is so handsome! how often will others tell him that they
love him, and how much, indeed, they must do so!'

'It is very seldom that women love the man in loving the
King. But should that happen, which I doubt, you should rather
wish, Marie, that such women should really love your husband.
In the first place, the devoted love of a mistress is a rapid
element of the dissolution of a lover's affection; and then, by
dint of loving, the mistress loses all influence over her lover,
whose power or wealth she does not covet, caring only for his
affection. Wish, therefore, that the King should love but lightly,
and that his mistress should love with all her heart.'*

'Oh, my mother, what power may not a deep affection exercise
over him!'

'And yet you say you are abandoned?'

'Quite true, quite true; I speak absurdly. There is a feeling of
anguish, however, which I can never control.'

'And that is?'

'The King may make a happy choice—may find a home, with
all the tender influences of home, not far from that we can offer
him—a home with children around him, the children of another
woman than myself. Oh, Madame, I should die if I were but to
see those children.'

'Marie, Marie,' replied the Queen-Mother with a smile, and she took the young Queen's hand in her own, 'remember what I am going to say, and let it always be a consolation to you, the King cannot have a Dauphin without you.'*

With this remark the Queen-Mother quitted her daughter-in-law in order to meet Madame, whose arrival in the grand cabinet had just been announced by one of the pages. Madame had scarcely taken time to change her dress. Her face revealed her agitation, which betrayed a plan the execution of which occupied, while the result disturbed, her mind.

'I came to ascertain,' she said, 'if your Majesties are suffering any fatigue from our journey.'

'None at all,' said the Queen-Mother.

'But a slight one,' replied Maria Theresa.

'I have suffered from annoyance more than from anything else,' said Madame.

'What annoyance?' inquired Anne of Austria.

'The fatigue the King undergoes in riding about on horseback.'

'That does the King good.'

'And it was I who advised him to do it,' said Maria Theresa turning pale.

Madame said not a word in reply; but one of those smiles which were peculiarly her own flitted for a moment across her lips without passing over the rest of her face; then, immediately changing the conversation, she continued, 'We shall find Paris precisely like the Paris we left; the same intrigues, plots, and flirtations going on.'

'Intrigues! What intrigues do you allude to?' inquired the Queen-Mother.

'People are talking a good deal about M. Fouquet and Madame Plessis-Bellière.'

'Who makes up the number to about ten thousand,' replied the Queen-Mother. 'But what are the plots you speak of?'

'We have, it seems, certain misunderstandings with Holland to settle.'

'What about?'

'Monsieur has been telling me the story of the medals.'

'Oh!' exclaimed the young Queen, 'you mean those medals which were struck in Holland, on which a cloud is seen passing across the sun, which is the King's device. You are wrong in calling that a plot—it is an insult.'*

'But so contemptible that the King can well despise it,' replied the Queen-Mother. 'Well, what are the flirtations alluded to? Do you mean that of Madame d'Olonne?'*

'No, no; nearer ourselves than that.'

'*Casa de usted*,'* murmured the Queen-Mother, and without moving her lips, in her daughter-in-law's ear, and also without being overheard by Madame, who thus continued,—'You know the terrible news?'

'Oh, yes; M. de Guiche's wound?'

'And you attribute it, I suppose, as every one else does, to an accident which happened to him while hunting?'

'Yes, of course,' said both the Queens together, their interest awakened.

Madame drew closer to them, as she said, in a low tone of voice, 'It was a duel.'

'Ah!' said Anne of Austria in a severe tone; for in her ears the word 'duel,' which had been forbidden in France during the time she reigned over it, had a strange sound.

'A most deplorable duel, which has nearly cost Monsieur two of his best friends, and the King two of his best servants.'

'What was the cause of the duel?' inquired the young Queen, animated by a secret instinct.

'Flirtations,' repeated Madame triumphantly. 'The gentlemen in question were conversing about the virtue of a particular lady belonging to the court. One of them thought that Pallas was a very second-rate person compared to her; the other pretended that the lady in question was an imitation of Venus alluring Mars; and thereupon the two gentlemen fought as fiercely as Hector and Achilles.'*

'Venus alluring Mars?' said the young Queen in a low tone of voice, without venturing to examine into the allegory very deeply.

'Who is the lady?' inquired Anne of Austria abruptly. 'You say, I believe, she was one of the ladies of honour?'

'Did I say so?' replied Madame.

'Yes; at least I thought I heard you mention it.'

'Are you not aware that such a woman is of ill-omen to a royal house?'

'Is it not Mademoiselle de la Vallière?' said the Queen-Mother.

'Yes, indeed, that plain-looking creature.'

'I thought she was affianced to a gentleman who certainly is not, at least I suppose so, either M. de Guiche or M. de Wardes?'

'Very possibly, Madame.'

The young Queen took up a piece of tapestry, and began to unpick with an affectation of tranquillity which her trembling fingers contradicted.

'What were you saying about Venus and Mars?' pursued the Queen-Mother; 'is there a Mars also?'

'She boasts of that being the case.'

'Do you say she boasts of it?'

'That was the cause of the duel.'

'And M. de Guiche upheld the cause of Mars?'

'Yes, certainly; like the devoted servant he is.'

'The devoted servant of whom?' exclaimed the young Queen, forgetting her reserve in allowing her jealous feeling to escape her.

'Mars, not being able to be defended except at the expense of this Venus,' replied Madame, 'M. de Guiche maintained the perfect innocence of Mars, and no doubt affirmed that it was a mere boast of Venus.'

'And M. de Wardes,' said Anne of Austria quietly, 'spread the report that Venus was right, I suppose?'

'Oh, de Wardes,' thought Madame, 'you shall pay most dearly for the wound you have given that noblest—that best of men!' And she began to attack de Wardes with the greatest bitterness; thus discharging her own and de Guiche's debt with the assurance that she was working the future ruin of her enemy. She said so much, in fact, that had Manicamp been there he would have regretted that he had shown such strong regard for his friend, inasmuch as it resulted in the ruin of his unfortunate foe.

'I see nothing in the whole affair but one cause of mischief, and that is La Vallière herself,' said the Queen-Mother.

The young Queen resumed her work with a perfect indifference of manner, while Madame listened eagerly.

'I do not yet quite understand what you said just now about the danger of coquetry,' resumed Anne of Austria.

'It is quite true,' Madame hastened to say, 'that if the girl had not been a coquette Mars would not have thought at all about her.'

The repetition of this word Mars brought a passing colour on the Queen's face; but she still continued her work.

'I will not permit that in my court gentlemen should be set against each other in this manner,' said Anne of Austria calmly. 'Such manners were useful enough, perhaps, in a time when the divided nobility had no other rallying-point than mere gallantry. At that time women, whose sway was absolute and undivided, were privileged to encourage men's valour by frequent trials of their courage. But now, thank Heaven! there is but one master in France,* and to him every thought of the mind, and every pulse of the body are due. I will not allow my son to be deprived of any one of his servants.' And she turned towards the young Queen saying, 'What is to be done with this La Vallière?'

'La Vallière?' said the Queen apparently surprised, 'I do not even know the name;' and she accompanied this remark by one of those cold fixed smiles which are only observed on royal lips.

Madame was herself a Princess great in every respect, great in intelligence, great by birth and pride; the Queen's reply, however, completely astonished her, and she was obliged to pause for a moment in order to recover herself. 'She is one of my maids of honour,' she replied with a bow.

'In that case,' retorted Maria Theresa, in the same tone, 'it is your affair, sister, and not ours.'

'I beg your pardon,' resumed Anne of Austria, 'it is my affair. And I perfectly well understand,' she pursued, addressing a look full of intelligence at Madame, 'Madame's motive for saying what she has just said.'

'Everything which emanates from you, Madame,' said the English Princess, 'proceeds from the lips of Wisdom.'

'If you send this girl back again to her own family,' said Maria Theresa gently, 'we must bestow a pension upon her.'

'Which I will provide for out of my income,' exclaimed Madame.

'No, no,' interrupted Anne of Austria, 'no fuss, I beg. The King dislikes that the slightest disrespectful remark should be made of any lady. Let everything be done quite quietly. Will you have the kindness, Madame, to send for this girl here; and you, my daughter, will have the goodness to retire to your own room.'

The old Queen's entreaties were commands, and as Maria Theresa rose to return to her own apartments, Madame rose in order to send a page to summon La Vallière.

LXXI

THE FIRST QUARREL

LA VALLIÈRE entered the Queen-Mother's apartments without in the least suspecting that a serious plot was being concerted against her. She thought it was for something connected with her duties, and never had the Queen-Mother been unkind to her when such was the case. Besides, not being immediately under the control or direction of Anne of Austria, she could only have an official connection with her, to which her own gentleness of disposition and the rank of the august Princess, made her yield on every occasion with the best possible grace. She therefore advanced towards the Queen-Mother with that soft and gentle smile which constituted her principal charm, and as she did not approach sufficiently close, Anne of Austria signed to her to come nearer. Madame then entered the room, and with a perfectly calm air took her seat beside her mother-in-law and continued the work which Maria Theresa had begun. When La Vallière, instead of the directions which she had expected to receive immediately on entering the room, perceived these preparations, she looked with curiosity, if not with uneasiness, at the two Princesses. Anne seemed full of thought, while Madame maintained an affectation of indifference which would have alarmed a less timid person even than Louise.

'Mademoiselle,' said the Queen-Mother suddenly, without attempting to moderate or disguise her Spanish accent, which she never failed to do except when she was angry, 'come closer; we were talking of you, as every one else seems to be doing.'

'Of me!' exclaimed La Vallière turning pale.

'Do you pretend to be ignorant of it; are you not aware of the duel between M. de Guiche and M. de Wardes?'

'Oh, Madame! I heard of it yesterday,' said La Vallière clasping her hands together.

'And did you not foresee this quarrel?'

'Why should I, Madame?'

'Because two men never fight without a motive, and because you must be aware of the motive which awakened the animosity of the two in question.'

'I am perfectly ignorant of it, Madame.'

'A persevering denial is a very commonplace mode of defence, and you, who have great pretensions to be witty and clever, ought to avoid commonplaces. What else have you to say?'

'Oh! Madame, your Majesty terrifies me with your cold severity of manner; but I do not understand how I can have incurred your displeasure, or in what respect people can occupy themselves about me.'

'Then I will tell you. M. de Guiche has been obliged to undertake your defence.'

'My defence?'

'Yes. He is a gallant knight, and beautiful adventuresses like to see brave knights couch their lances in their honour. But, for my part, I hate fields of battle, and more than all, do I hate adventuresses, and—take my remark as you please.'

La Vallière sank at the Queen's feet, who turned her back upon her. She stretched out her hands towards Madame, who laughed in her face. A feeling of pride made her rise to her feet.

'I have begged your Majesty to tell me what is the crime I am accused of—I can claim this at your Majesty's hands; and I observe that I am condemned before I am even permitted to justify myself.'

'Eh! indeed,' cried Anne of Austria, 'listen to her beautiful phrases, Madame, and to her fine sentiments; she is an inexhaustible well of tenderness and of heroic expressions. One can easily see, young lady, that we have cultivated our mind in the society of crowned heads.'

La Vallière felt struck to the heart; she became, not paler, but as white as a lily, and all her strength forsook her.

'I wished to inform you,' interrupted the Queen disdainfully, 'that if you continue to nourish such feeling, you will humiliate us other women to such a degree that we shall be ashamed of

appearing before you. Become simple in your manners. By the
bye, I am informed that you are affianced; is that the case?'

La Vallière pressed her hand over her heart, which was wrung
with a fresh pang.

'Answer when you are spoken to.'

'Yes, Madame.'

'To a gentleman?'

'Yes, Madame.'

'His name?'

'The Vicomte de Bragelonne.'

'Are you aware that it is an exceedingly fortunate circumstance
for you, mademoiselle, that such is the case; and without fortune
or position as you are, or without any very great personal advantages, you ought to bless Heaven for having procured you
such a future as seems to be in store for you.'

La Vallière did not reply. 'Where is this Vicomte de
Bragelonne?' pursued the Queen.

'In England,' said Madame, 'where the report of this young
lady's success will not fail to reach him.'

'Oh, Heaven!' murmured La Vallière in despair.

'Very well, mademoiselle,' said Anne of Austria, 'we will get
this young gentleman to return, and send you away somewhere
with him. If you are of a different opinion—for girls have strange
views and fancies at times, trust to me, I will put you in a proper
path again. I have done as much for girls who are not so good as
you are, perhaps.'

La Vallière ceased to hear the Queen, who pitilessly added: 'I
will send you somewhere by yourself, where you will be able to
procure a little serious reflection. Reflection calms the ardour of
the blood, and swallows up all the illusions of youth. I suppose
you have understood what I have been saying?'

'Madame, madame!'

'Not a word!'

'I am innocent of everything your Majesty can suppose. Oh,
madame! you are a witness of my despair. I love, I respect your
Majesty so much.'

'It would be far better not to respect me at all,' said the
Queen, with a chilling irony of manner. 'It would be far better
if you were not innocent. Do you presume to suppose that I

should be satisfied simply to leave you unpunished if you had committed the fault?'

'Oh, madame! you are killing me.'

'No acting, if you please, or I will undertake the *dénouement* of the comedy; leave the room; return to your own apartment, and I trust my lesson may be of service to you.'

'Madame!' said La Vallière to the Duchesse d'Orléans, whose hands she seized in her own, 'do you, who are so good, intercede for me.'

'I!' replied the latter, with an insulting joy, 'I—good!—Ah, mademoiselle, you think nothing of the kind;' and with a rude, hasty gesture, she repulsed the young girl's hand.

La Vallière, instead of giving way, as from her extreme pallor, and from her tears the two princesses might possibly have expected, suddenly resumed her calm and dignified air; she bowed profoundly, and left the room.

'Well!' said Anne of Austria to Madame, 'do you think she will begin again?'

'I always suspect those gentle and patient characters,' replied Madame. 'Nothing is more full of courage than a patient heart, nothing is more self-reliant than a gentle spirit.'

'I feel I may almost venture to assure you she will think twice before she looks at the god Mars again.'

'So long as she does not obtain the protection of his buckler, I do not care,' retorted Madame.

A proud, defiant look of the Queen-Mother was the reply to this objection, which was by no means deficient in finesse; and both of them, almost sure of their victory, went to look for Maria Theresa, who had been engaged, while awaiting their arrival, in endeavouring to disguise her impatience.

It was about half-past six in the evening, and the King had just partaken of some refreshment. He lost no time; but no sooner was the repast finished, and business matters settled, than he took Saint-Aignan by the arm, and desired him to lead him to La Vallière's apartments. The courtier uttered a loud exclamation.

'Well, what is that for? It is a habit you will have to adopt, and in order to adopt a habit, you must begin by something or another at first.'

'Oh, sire!' said Saint-Aignan, 'it is hardly possible, for every one can be seen entering or leaving those apartments. If, however, some pretext was made use of—if your Majesty, for instance, would wait until Madame were in her own apartments——'

'No pretexts; no delays. I have had enough of these impediments and these mysteries; I cannot conceive in what respect the King of France dishonours himself in conversing with an amiable and clever girl. Evil be to him who evil thinks.'

'Will your Majesty forgive an excess of zeal on my part?'

'Speak freely.'

'And the Queen?'

'True, true; I always wish the most entire respect to be shown to Her Majesty. Well, then, this evening only will I pay Mademoiselle de la Vallière a visit, and after to-day I will make use of any pretext you like. To-morrow we will devise all sorts of means; to-night I have not the time.'

Saint-Aignan did not reply; he descended the steps, preceding the King, and crossed the different courtyards with a feeling of shame, which the distinguished honour of accompanying the King did not remove. The reason was, that Saint-Aignan wished to stand well with Madame, as well as the two Queens; and, also that he did not, on the other hand, wish to displease Mademoiselle de la Vallière; and in order to carry out so many promising affairs, it was difficult to avoid jostling against some obstacle or other. Besides, the windows of the young Queen's rooms, those of the Queen-Mother's, and of Madame herself, looked out upon the courtyard of the maids of honour. To be seen, therefore, accompanying the King, would be effectually to quarrel with three great and influential princesses—with three women whose authority was unbounded—for the purpose of supporting the ephemeral credit of a mistress. The unhappy Saint-Aignan, who had not displayed a very great amount of courage in taking La Vallière's part in the park of Fontainebleau, did not feel himself any braver in the broad daylight, and found a thousand defects in the poor girl which he was most eager to communicate to the King. But his trial soon finished,—the courtyards were crossed; not a curtain was drawn aside, nor a window opened. The King walked hastily because of his impatience, and then also because of the long legs of Saint-Aignan, who preceded him. At the door, however, Saint-Aignan wished to retire, but the King desired him to remain; this was a delicate consideration on the King's part which the courtier could very well have dispensed with. He had to follow Louis into La Vallière's apartment. As soon as the King arrived the young girl dried her tears, but did it so precipitately that the King perceived it. He questioned her most anxiously and tenderly, and pressed her to tell him the cause of her emotion.

'I have nothing the matter with me, sire,' she said.

'And yet you were weeping.'

'Oh, no, indeed, sire.'

'Look, Saint-Aignan, and tell me if I am mistaken.'

Saint-Aignan ought to have answered, but he was greatly embarrassed.

'At all events your eyes are red, mademoiselle,' said the King.

'The dust of the road, merely, sire.'

'No, no; you no longer possess that air of supreme contentment which renders you so beautiful and so attractive. You do not look at me. Why avoid my gaze?' he said, as she turned aside her head. 'In Heaven's name, what is the matter?' he inquired, beginning to lose all command over himself.

'Nothing at all, sire; and I am perfectly ready to assure your Majesty that my mind is as free from anxiety as you could possibly wish.'

'Your mind at ease, when I see you are embarrassed at the slightest thing. Has any one wounded or annoyed you?'

'No, no, sire.'

'I insist upon knowing if such really be the case,' said the young prince, his eyes sparkling.

'No one sire, no one has in any way offended me.'

'In that case, do resume your gentle air of gaiety, or that sweet melancholy look which I loved so in you this morning; for pity's sake do so.'

'Yes, sire, yes.'

The King struck the ground impatiently with his foot, saying, 'Such a change is positively inexplicable.' And he looked at Saint-Aignan, who had also remarked La Vallière's heavy languor of manner as well as the King's impatience.

It was utterly useless for the King to entreat, and as useless for him to try his utmost to overcome her positiveness, which was but too apparent, and did not in reality exist; the poor girl was completely overwhelmed,—the aspect of death itself could not have awakened her from her torpor. The King saw in her repeated negative replies a mystery full of unkindness; he began to look all round the apartment with a suspicious air. There happened to be in La Vallière's room a miniature of Athos. The King remarked this portrait, which bore a considerable resemblance to Bragelonne, for it had been taken when the Comte was quite a young man. He looked at it with a threatening air. La Vallière, in her depressed state of mind, and very far indeed from thinking of this portrait, could not conjecture the King's preoccupation. And yet the King's mind was occupied with a terrible remembrance, which had more than once taken possession of his mind, but which he had always driven away. He recalled* the intimacy which had existed between the two young people from their birth; the engagement which had followed; and that Athos had himself come to solicit La Vallière's hand for Raoul. He, therefore, could not but suppose that, on her return to Paris, La Vallière had found news from London awaiting her, and that this news had counterbalanced the influence which he had been enabled to exert over her. He immediately felt himself stung, as it were, by feelings of the wildest jealousy; and he again questioned her, with increased bitterness. La Vallière could not reply, unless she were to acknowledge everything, which would be to accuse the Queen, and Madame also; and the consequence would be that she would have to enter upon an open warfare with these two great and powerful princesses. She thought within herself that as she made no attempt to conceal from the King what was passing in her own mind, the King ought to be able to read in her heart, in spite of her silence; and that, if he really loved her, he would have understood, and guessed everything. What was sympathy then, if it were not that divine flame which possesses the property of enlightening the heart, and of saving lovers the necessity of an expression of their thoughts and feelings. She maintained her silence, therefore, satisfying herself with sighing, weeping, and concealing her face in her hands. These sighs and tears, which had at first distressed, and then terrified, Louis XIV, now irritated him. He could not bear any opposition—not the opposition which tears and sighs exhibited, any more than opposition of any other kind. His remarks, therefore, became bitter, urgent, and openly aggressive in their nature. This was a fresh cause of distress for the poor girl. From that very circumstance, therefore, which she regarded as an injustice on her lover's part, she drew sufficient courage to bear, not only her other troubles, but even this one also.

The King next began to accuse her in direct terms. La Vallière did not even attempt to defend herself; she endured all his accusations without according any other reply than that of shaking her head; without making any other remark than that which escapes every heart in deep distress, by a prayerful appeal to Heaven for help. But this ejaculation, instead of calming the King's displeasure, rather increased it. He, moreover, saw himself seconded by Saint-Aignan, for Saint-Aignan, as we have observed, having seen the storm increasing, and not knowing the extent of the regard of which Louis XIV was capable, felt, by anticipation, all the collected wrath of the three princesses, and the near approach of poor La Vallière's downfall; and he was not true knight enough to resist the fear that he himself might possibly be dragged down in the impending ruin. Saint-Aignan did not reply to the King's questions except by short, dry remarks, pronounced half-aloud; and by abrupt gestures, whose object was to make things worse, and bring about a misunderstanding, the result of which would be to free him from the annoyance of having to cross the courtyards in broad open day, in order to follow his illustrious companion to La Vallière's apartments. In the meantime the King's anger momentarily increased; he made two or three steps towards the door, as if to leave the room, but then returned; the young girl did not, however, raise her head, although the sound of his footsteps might have warned her that her lover was leaving her; he drew himself up, for a moment, before her, with his arms crossed.

'For the last time, mademoiselle,' he said, 'will you speak? Will you assign a reason for this change, for this fickleness, for this caprice?'

'What can I say?' murmured La Vallière. 'Do you not see, sire, that I am completely overwhelmed at this moment; that I have no power of will, or thought, or speech?'

'Is it so difficult, then, to speak the truth? You would have told me the truth in fewer words than those in which you have just now expressed yourself.'

'But the truth about what, sire?'

'About everything.'

La Vallière was just on the point of revealing the whole truth to the King; her arms made a sudden movement as if they were about to open, but her lips remained silent, and her arms again fell listlessly by her side. The poor girl had not yet endured sufficient unhappiness to risk the necessary revelation. 'I know nothing,' she stammered out.

'Oh!' exclaimed the King, 'this is no longer mere coquetry or caprice, it is treason.'

And this time nothing could restrain him, the impulses of his heart were not sufficient to induce him to turn back, and he darted out of the room with a gesture full of despair. Saint-Aignan followed him, wishing for nothing better than to leave the place.

Louis XIV did not pause until he reached the staircase, and grasping the balustrade, said: 'You see how shamefully I have been duped.'

'How, sire?' inquired the favourite.

'Guiche fought on the Vicomte de Bragelonne's account, and this Bragelonne . . . oh! Saint-Aignan, she still loves him. I vow to you, Saint-Aignan, that, if in three days hence, there were to remain but an atom of affection for her in my heart, I should die from very shame.' And the King resumed his way to his own apartments.

'I assured your Majesty how it would be,' murmured Saint-Aignan, continuing to follow the King, and timidly glancing up at the different windows. Unfortunately, their return was different to what their departure had been. A curtain was stealthily drawn aside; Madame was behind it. She had seen the King leave the apartments of the maids of honour, and as soon as she observed that His Majesty had passed, she left her own apartments with hurried steps, and ran up the staircase, which led to the room the King had just left.

LXXII

DESPAIR

As soon as the King had left her, La Vallière raised herself from the ground, and extended her arms, as if to follow and detain him; but when, having violently closed the door, the sound of his retreating footsteps could be heard in the distance, she had hardly sufficient strength left to totter towards and fall at the foot of her crucifix. There she remained, broken-hearted, absorbed, and overwhelmed by her grief, forgetful of and indifferent to everything but her profound grief itself—a grief which she could not comprehend otherwise than by instinct and acute sensation. In the midst of the wild tumult of her thoughts, La Vallière heard her door open again; she started, and turned round, thinking that it was the King who had returned. She was deceived, however, for it was Madame who appeared at the door. What did she now care for Madame! Again she sank down, her head supported by her *prie-Dieu* chair. It was Madame, agitated, irritated, and threatening. But what was that to her? 'Mademoiselle,' said the Princess, standing before La Vallière, 'this is very fine, I admit, to kneel and pray, and make a pretence of being religious; but however submissive you may be in your addresses to Heaven, it is desirable that you should pay some little attention to the wishes of those who reign and rule here below.'

La Vallière raised her head painfully in token of respect.

'Not long since,' continued Madame, 'a certain recommendation was addressed to you, I believe.'

La Vallière's fixed and wild gaze showed how entire her forgetfulness or her ignorance was.

'The Queen recommended you,' continued Madame, 'to conduct yourself in such a manner that no one could be justified in spreading any reports about you.'

La Vallière darted an inquiring look towards her.

'I will not,' continued Madame, 'allow my household, which is that of the first Princess of the blood, to set an evil example to the court; you would be the cause of such an example. I beg you to understand, therefore, in the absence of any witness of your shame, for I do not wish to humiliate you, that you are from this moment at perfect liberty to leave, and that you can return to your mother at Blois.'

La Vallière could not sink lower, nor could she suffer more than she had already suffered. Her countenance did not even change, but she remained with her hands crossed over her knees like the figure of the Magdalen.

'Did you hear me?' said Madame.

A shiver, which passed through her whole frame, was La Vallière's only reply. And as the victim gave no other sign of life, Madame left the room. And then, her very respiration suspended, and her blood almost congealed, as it were, in her veins, La Vallière by degrees felt that the pulsations of her wrists, her neck, and temples, began to throb more and more heavily. These pulsations, as they gradually increased, soon changed into a species of brain fever, and in her temporary delirium she saw the figures of her friends contending with her enemies floating before her vision. She heard, too, mingled together in her deafened ears, words of menace and words of fond affection; she seemed raised out of her first existence as though it were upon the wings of a mighty tempest, and in the dim horizon of the path along which her delirium hurried her, she saw the stone which covered her tomb upraised, and the dark and appalling interior of eternal night revealed to her distracted gaze. But the horror of the dream which had possessed her senses soon faded away, and she was again restored to the habitual resignation of her character. A ray of hope penetrated her heart, as a ray of sunlight streams into the dungeon of some unhappy captive. Her mind reverted to the journey from Fontainebleau, she saw the King riding beside her carriage, telling her that he loved her, asking for her love in return, requiring her to swear, and himself swearing too, that never should an evening pass by, if ever a misunderstanding were to arise between them, without a visit, a letter, a sign of some kind, being sent, to replace the troubled anxiety of the evening by the calm repose of the night. It was the King who had suggested that, who had imposed a promise upon her, who had himself sworn it also. It was impossible, therefore, she reasoned, that the King should fail in keeping the promise which he had himself exacted from her, unless, indeed, the King were a despot who enforced love as he enforced obedience; unless, too, the King were truly indifferent, that the first obstacle in his way were sufficient to arrest his further progress. The King, that kind protector, who, by a word, by a single word, could relieve her distress of mind, the King even joined her persecutors. Oh! his anger could not possibly last. Now that he was alone, he would be suffering all that she herself was a prey to. But he was not tied hand and foot as she was; he could act, could move about, could come to her, while she could do nothing but wait. And the poor girl waited, and waited with breathless anxiety, for she could not believe it possible that the King would not come.

It was now about half-past ten. He would either come to her, or write to her, or send some kind word by M. de Saint-Aignan. If he were to come, oh! how she would fly to meet him; how she would thrust aside that excess of delicacy which she now discovered was misunderstood; how eagerly she would explain: 'It is not I who do not love you, it is the fault of others who will not allow me to love you.' And then it must be confessed that as she reflected upon it, and also the more she reflected, Louis appeared to her to be less guilty. In fact, he was ignorant of everything. What must he have thought of the obstinacy with which she remained silent. Impatient and irritable as the King was known to be, it was extraordinary that he had been able to preserve his temper so long. And yet, had it been her own case, she undoubtedly would not have acted in such a manner; she would have understood everything, have guessed everything. Yes, but she was nothing but a poor simple-minded girl, and not a great and powerful monarch. Oh! if he did but come, if he would but come!—how eagerly she would forgive him for all he had just made her suffer! how much more tenderly she would love him because she had so suffered! And so as she sat, with her head bent forward in eager expectation towards the door, her lips slightly parted, as if—and Heaven forgive her for the thought, she mentally exclaimed—they were awaiting the kiss which the King's lips had in the morning so sweetly indicated when he pronounced the word *love!* If the King did not come at least he would write; it was a second chance; a chance less delightful certainly than the other, but which would show an affection just as strong, but only more timorous in its nature. Oh! how she would devour his letter, how eager she would be to answer it; and when the messenger who had brought it had left her, how she would kiss, read over and over again, press upon her heart, the happy paper which would have brought her ease of mind, tranquillity, and perfect happiness. At all events, if the King did not come, if, however, the King did not write, he could not do otherwise than send Saint-Aignan, or Saint-Aignan could not do otherwise than come of his own accord. Even if it were a third person, how openly she would speak to him; the royal presence would not be there to freeze her words upon her tongue, and then no suspicious feeling would remain a moment longer in the King's heart.

Everything with La Vallière, heart and look, body and mind, was concentrated in eager expectation. She said to herself that there was still an hour left in which to indulge hope; that until midnight had struck, the King might come, or write, or send; that at midnight only would every expectation be useless, every hope lost. Whenever there was any noise in the palace the poor girl fancied she was the cause of it; whenever she heard any one pass in the courtyard below she imagined they were messengers of the King coming to her. Eleven o'clock struck; then a quarter past eleven; then half-past. The minutes dragged slowly on in this anxiety, and yet they seemed to pass far too quickly. And now it struck a quarter to twelve. Midnight, midnight was near, the last, the final hope which remained came in its turn. With the last stroke of the clock the last ray of light seemed to fade away; and with the last ray, so faded her final hope. And so the King himself had deceived her; it was he who had been the first to fail in keeping the oath which he had sworn that very day; twelve hours only between his oath and his perjured vow; it was not long, certainly, to have preserved the illusion. And so, not only did the King not love her, but, still more, he despised her whom every one overwhelmed; he despised her to the extent even of abandoning her to the shame of an expulsion which was equivalent to having an ignominious sentence passed upon her; and yet it was he, the King himself, who was the first cause of this ignominy. A bitter smile, the only symptom of anger which during this long conflict had passed across the victim's angelic face, appeared upon her lips. What, in fact, now remained on earth for her, after the King was lost to her? Nothing. But Heaven still remained, and her thoughts flew thither. She prayed that the proper course for her to follow might be suggested. 'It is from Heaven,' she thought, 'that I do expect everything; it is from Heaven I ought to expect everything.' And she looked at her crucifix with a devotion full of tender love. 'There,' she said, 'hangs before me a Master who never forgets and never abandons those who do not abandon and who do not forget Him; it is to Him alone that we must sacrifice ourselves.' And, thereupon, could any one have gazed into the recesses of that chamber, they would have seen the poor despairing girl adopt a final resolution, and determine upon one last plan in her mind. Thereupon, and as her knees were no longer able to support her, she gradually sank down upon the *prie-Dieu*, and with her head pressed against the wooden cross, her eyes fixed, and her respiration short and quick, she watched for the earliest rays of approaching daylight. At two o'clock in the morning she was still in the same bewilderment of mind, or rather in the same ecstasy of feeling. Her thoughts had almost ceased to hold any communion with the things of this world. And when she saw the violet tints of early dawn visible upon the roofs of the palace, and vaguely revealing the outlines of the ivory cross which she held embraced, she rose from the ground with a new-born strength, kissed the feet of the divine martyr, descended the staircase leading from the room, and wrapped herself from head to foot in a mantle as she went along. She reached the wicket at the very moment the guard of musketeers opened the gate to admit the first relief-guard belonging to one of the Swiss regiments.* And then, gliding behind the soldiers, she reached the street before the officer in command of the patrol had even thought of asking who the young girl was who was making her escape from the palace at so early an hour.*

LXXIII

THE FLIGHT

LA VALLIÈRE followed the patrol as it left the courtyard. The patrol bent its steps towards the right by the Rue St. Honoré, and mechanically La Vallière went to the left. Her resolution was taken—her determination fixed; she wished to betake herself to the convent of the Carmelites at Chaillot,* the superior of which enjoyed a reputation for severity which made the worldly-minded people of the court tremble. La Vallière had never seen Paris,—she had never gone out on foot, and so, would have been unable to find her way even had she been in a calmer frame of mind than was then the case, and this may explain why she ascended instead of descending* the Rue St. Honoré. Her only thought was to get away from the Palais Royal, and this she was doing; she had heard it said that Chaillot looked out upon the Seine, and she accordingly directed her steps towards the Seine. She took the Rue du Coq, and not being able to cross the Louvre, bore towards the church of St. Germain l'Auxerrois, proceeding along the site of the colonnade which was subsequently built there by Perrault. In a very short time she reached the quays. Her steps were rapid and agitated; she scarcely felt the weakness which reminded her of having sprained her foot when very young, and which obliged her to limp slightly. At any other hour of the day her countenance would have awakened the suspicions of the least clear-sighted persons, or have attracted the attention of the most indifferent passers-by. But at half-past two in the morning, the streets of Paris are almost, if not quite, deserted, and scarcely any one is to be seen but the hard-working artisan on his way to earn his daily bread, or the dangerous idlers of the streets, who are returning to their homes after a night of riot and debauchery; for the former the day was beginning, for the latter it was just closing. La Vallière was afraid of those faces, in which her ignorance of Parisian types did not permit her to distinguish the type of probity from that of dishonesty. The appearance of misery alarmed her, and all whom she met seemed wretched and miserable. Her toilet, which

was the same she had worn during the previous evening, was
elegant even in its careless disorder; for it was the one in which
she had presented herself to the Queen-Mother; and, moreover,
when she drew aside the mantle which covered her face, in order
to enable her to see the way she was going, her pallor and her
beautiful eyes spoke an unknown language to the men she met,
and, ignorantly, the poor fugitive seemed to invite the brutal
remarks of the one class or to appeal to the compassion of the
other. La Vallière still walked on in the same way, breathless
and hurried, until she reached the top of the Place de Grève.*
She stopped from time to time, placed her hand upon her heart,
leant against a wall until she could breathe freely again, and then
continued her course more rapidly than before. On reaching the
Place de Grève La Vallière suddenly came upon a group of three
drunken men, reeling and staggering along, who were just leaving a boat, which they had made fast to a quay; the boat was
freighted with wines, and it was apparent that they had done
complete justice to the merchandise. They were singing their
convivial exploits in three different keys, when suddenly, as they
reached the end of the railing leaning down to the quay, they
found an obstacle in their path in the shape of this young girl.
La Vallière stopped; while they, on their side, at the appearance
of the young girl dressed in court costume, also halted, and
seizing each other by the hand, they surrounded La Vallière,
singing,—

> 'O! you who sadly are wandering alone,
> Come, come, and laugh with us.'

La Vallière at once understood that the men were addressing
her, and wished to prevent her passing; she tried to do so several
times, but all her efforts were useless. Her limbs failed her; she
felt she was on the point of falling and uttered a cry of terror. At
the same moment the circle which surrounded her was suddenly
broken through in a most violent manner. One of her insulters
was knocked to the left, another fell rolling over and over to the
right, close to the water's edge, while the third could hardly
keep his feet. An officer of the musketeers stood face to face
with the young girl with threatening brow and his hand raised to

carry out his threat. The drunken fellows at the sight of the
uniform made their escape with all despatch, and the greater for
the proof of strength which the wearer of the uniform had just
afforded them.

'Is it possible,' exclaimed the musketeer, 'that it can be Mademoiselle de la Vallière?'

La Vallière, bewildered by what had just happened and confounded by hearing her name pronounced, looked up and recognised d'Artagnan. 'Oh, M. d'Artagnan! it is indeed I;' and at the
same moment she seized hold of his arm. 'You will protect me,
will you not?' she added, in a tone of entreaty.

'Most certainly I will protect you; but, in Heaven's name,
where are you going at this hour?'

'I am going to Chaillot.'

'You're going to Chaillot by the way of La Rapée!* why,
mademoiselle, you are turning your back to it.'

'In that case, monsieur, be kind enough to put me in the right
way, and to go with me a short distance.'

'Most willingly.'

'But how does it happen that I have found you here? By what
merciful direction were you so near at hand to come to my assistance? I almost seem to be dreaming, or to be losing my senses.'

'I happened to be here, mademoiselle, because I have a house*
in the Place de Grève, at the sign of Notre-Dame, the rent of
which I went to receive yesterday, and where I, in fact, passed
the night. And I also wished to be at the palace early, for the
purpose of inspecting my posts.'

'Thank you,' said La Vallière.

'That was what I was doing,' said d'Artagnan to himself; 'but
what was she doing, and why was she going to Chaillot at such
an hour?' And he offered her his arm, which she took, and began
to walk with increased precipitation, which concealed, however,
a great weakness. D'Artagnan perceived it, and proposed to La
Vallière that she should take a little rest, which she refused.

'You are ignorant, perhaps, where Chaillot is?' inquired
d'Artagnan.

'Quite so.'

'It is a great distance.'

'That matters very little.'

'It is at least a league.'

'I can walk it.'

D'Artagnan did not reply; he could tell, merely by the tone of a voice, when a resolution was real or not. He rather bore along than accompanied La Vallière, until they perceived the elevated ground of Chaillot.

'What house are you going to, mademoiselle?' inquired d'Artagnan.

'To the Carmelites, monsieur.'

'To the Carmelites?' repeated d'Artagnan, in amazement.

'Yes; and since Heaven has directed you towards me to give me your support on my road, accept both my thanks and my adieux.'

'To the Carmelites! Your adieux! Are you going to become a nun?' exclaimed d'Artagnan.

'Yes, monsieur.'

'What, you! ! !' There was in this 'you,' which we have marked by three notes of exclamation in order to render it as expressive as possible,—there was, we repeat, in this 'you,' a complete poem; it recalled to La Vallière her old recollections of Blois, and her new recollections of Fontainebleau; it said to her, '*You*, who might be happy with Raoul; *you*, who might be powerful with Louis; *you*, about to become a nun!'

'Yes, monsieur,' she said, 'I am going to devote myself to the service of Heaven; and to renounce the world altogether.'

'But are you not mistaken with regard to your vocation,—are you not mistaken in supposing it to be the will of Heaven?'

'No; since Heaven has been pleased to throw you in my way. Had it not been for you, I should certainly have sunk from fatigue on the road; and since Heaven, I repeat, has thrown you in my way, it is because it has willed that I should carry out my intention.'

'Oh!' said d'Artagnan doubtingly, 'that is a rather subtle distinction, I think.'

'Whatever it may be,' returned the young girl, 'I have acquainted you with the steps I have taken, and with my fixed resolution. And, now, I have one last favour to ask of you, even while I return you thanks. The King is entirely ignorant of my flight from the Palais Royal, and is ignorant also of what I am about to do.'

'The King ignorant, you say!' exclaimed d'Artagnan. 'Take care, mademoiselle; you are not aware of what you are doing. No one ought to do anything with which the King is unacquainted, especially those who belong to the court.'

'I no longer belong to the court, monsieur.'

D'Artagnan looked at the girl with increasing astonishment.

'Do not be uneasy, monsieur,' she continued; 'I have well calculated everything; and were it not so, it would now be too late to reconsider my resolution,—it is decided.'

'Well, mademoiselle, what do you wish me to do?'

'In the name of that sympathy which misfortune inspires, by your generous feelings, and by your honour as a gentleman, I entreat you to swear to me one thing.'

'Name it.'

'Swear to me, Monsieur d'Artagnan, that you will not tell the King that you have seen me and that I am at the Carmelites.'

'I will not swear that,' said d'Artagnan, shaking his head.

'Why?'

'Because I know the King, I know you, I know myself even, nay, the whole human race, too well; no, no, I will not swear that!'

'In that case,' cried Vallière, with an energy of which one would hardly have thought her capable, 'instead of the blessing which I should have implored for you until my dying day, I will invoke a curse, for you are rendering me the most miserable creature that ever lived.'

We have already observed that d'Artagnan could easily recognise the accents of truth and sincerity, and he could not resist this last appeal. He saw by her face how bitterly she suffered from a feeling of degradation, he remarked her trembling limbs, how her whole slight and delicate frame was violently agitated by some internal struggle, and clearly perceived that resistance might be fatal. 'I will do as you wish, then,' he said. 'Be satisfied, mademoiselle, I will say nothing to the King.'

'Oh! thanks, thanks,' exclaimed La Vallière, 'you are the most generous man breathing.'

And in her extreme delight she seized hold of d'Artagnan's hands, and pressed them between her own. D'Artagnan, who felt himself quite overcome, said: 'This is touching, upon my word; she begins where others leave off.'

And La Vallière, who, in the extremity of her distress had sunk down upon the ground, rose and walked towards the convent of the Carmelites, which could now, in the dawning light, be perceived just before them. D'Artagnan followed her at a distance. The entrance-door was half-open, she glided in like a shadow, and thanking d'Artagnan by a parting gesture, disappeared from his sight. When d'Artagnan found himself quite alone, he reflected profoundly upon what had just taken place. 'Upon my word,' he said, 'this looks very much like what is called a false position. To keep such a secret as that is to keep a burning coal in one's breeches-pocket, and trust that it may not burn the stuff. And yet, not to keep it when I have sworn to do so is dishonourable. It generally happens that some bright idea or other occurs to me as I am going along; but I am very much mistaken if I shall not, now, have to go a long way in order to find the solution of this affair. Yes, but which way to go? Oh! towards Paris, of course; that is the best way, after all. Only one must make haste, and in order to make haste, four legs are better than two, and I, unhappily, have only two. 'A horse, a horse,' as I heard them say in the theatre in London,* 'my kingdom for a horse.' And, now I think of it, it need not cost me so much as that, for at the Barrière de la Conférence* there is a guard of musketeers, and instead of the one horse I need I shall find ten there.'

So, in pursuance of this resolution, which he had adopted with his usual rapidity, d'Artagnan immediately turned his back upon the heights of Chaillot, reached the guardhouse, took the fastest horse he could find there, and was at the Palace in less than ten minutes. It was striking five as he reached the Palais Royal. The King, he was told, went to bed at his usual hour, after having been engaged with M. Colbert, and in all probability was still fast asleep. 'Come,' said d'Artagnan, 'she spoke the truth, and the King is ignorant of everything; if he only knew one half of what has happened, the Palais Royal by this time would be turned upside down.'

LXXIV

WHEN the King left the apartment of the maids of honour, he found Colbert awaiting him to receive his directions with regard to the next day's ceremony, as the King was then to receive the Dutch and Spanish ambassadors. Louis XIV had serious causes of dissatisfaction with the Dutch; the States had already been guilty of many mean shifts and evasions with France,* and without perceiving or without caring about the chances of a rupture, they again abandoned the alliance with His Most Christian Majesty, for the purpose of entering into all kinds of plots with Spain. Louis XIV at his accession, that is to say, at the death of Cardinal Mazarin, had found this political question roughly sketched out; the solution was difficult for a young man, but at that time, the King represented the whole nation; anything that the head resolved upon, the body would be found ready to carry out. Any sudden impulse of anger, the reaction of young and hot blood to the brain, would be quite sufficient to change an old form of policy and to create another and new system altogether. The part that diplomatists had to play in those days was that of arranging among themselves the different *coups-d'état* which their sovereign masters might wish to effect. Louis was not in that calm state of mind which could make him capable of determining upon a wise course of policy. Still much agitated from the quarrel he had just had with La Vallière, he walked hastily into his cabinet, exceedingly desirous of finding an opportunity of producing an explosion after he had controlled himself for so long a time. Colbert, as he saw the King enter, knew the position of affairs at a glance, understood the King's intentions, and resolved therefore to manœuvre a little. When Louis requested to be informed what it would be necessary to say on the morrow, Colbert began by expressing his surprise that His Majesty had not been properly informed by M. Fouquet. 'M. Fouquet,' he said, 'is perfectly acquainted with the whole of the Dutch affair; he receives the despatches himself direct.'

The King, who was accustomed to hear M. Colbert speak in not over-scrupulous terms of M. Fouquet, allowed this remark to pass by unanswered, and merely listened. Colbert noticed the effect it had produced, and hastened to back out, saying, that M. Fouquet was not on all occasions as blameable as at the first glance might seem to be the case, inasmuch as at that moment he was greatly occupied. The King looked up. 'What do you allude to?' he said.

'Sire, men are but men, and M. Fouquet has his defects as well as his great qualities.'

'Ah! defects, who is without them, M. Colbert?'

'Your Majesty is not,' said Colbert boldly; for he knew how to convey a good deal of flattery in a light amount of blame, like the arrow which cleaves the air, not withstanding its weight, thanks to the feathers which bear it up.

The King smiled. 'What defect has M. Fouquet, then?' he said.

'Still the same, sire; it is said he is in love.'

'In love! with whom?'

'I am not quite sure, sire; I have very little to do with matters of gallantry.'

'At all events you know, since you speak of it.'

'I have heard a name mentioned.'

'Whose?'

'I cannot now remember whose, but I think it is one of Madame's maids of honour.'

The King started. 'You know more than you like to say, M. Colbert,' he murmured.

'I assure you no, sire.'

'At all events, Madame's maids of honour are all known, and in mentioning their names to you, you will perhaps recollect the one you allude to.'

'No, sire.'

'At least, try.'

'It would be useless, sire. Whenever the name of any lady who runs the risk of being compromised is concerned, my memory is like a coffer of brass, the key of which I have lost.'

A dark cloud seemed to pass over the mind as well as across the face of the King; then, wishing to appear as if he were perfect master of himself and of his feelings, he said, 'And now for the affair concerning Holland.'

'In the first place, sire, at what hour will your Majesty receive the ambassadors?'

'Early in the morning.'

'Eleven o'clock?'

'That is too late—say, nine o'clock.'

'That will be too early, sire.'

'For friends that would be a matter of no importance, one does what one likes with one's friends; but for one's enemies, in that case nothing could be better than if they were to feel hurt. I should not be sorry, I confess, to have to finish altogether with these marsh-birds, who annoy me with their cries.'

'It shall be precisely as your Majesty desires. At nine o'clock, therefore—I will give the necessary orders. Is it to be a formal audience?'

'No. I wish to have an explanation with them, and not to embitter matters, as is always the case when many persons are present; but, at the same time, I wish to clear everything with them, in order not to have to begin over again.'

'Your Majesty will inform me of the persons whom you wish to be present at the reception.'

'I will draw out a list of them. Let us speak of the ambassadors; what do they want?'

'Allies with Spain, they gain nothing; allies with France they lose much.'

'How is that?'

'Allied with Spain, they see themselves bounded and protected by the possessions of their allies; they cannot touch them, however anxious they may be to do so. From Antwerp to Rotterdam is but a step, and that by way of the Scheldt and the Meuse. If they wish to make a bite at the Spanish cake, you, sire, the son-in-law of the King of Spain, could with your cavalry go from your dominions to Brussels in a couple of days. Their design is, therefore, only to quarrel so far with you, and only to make you suspect Spain so far as will be sufficient to induce you not to interfere with their own affairs.'

'It would be far more simple, I should think,' replied the

King, 'to form a solid alliance with me, by means of which I should gain something, while they would gain everything.'

'Not so; for if, by chance, they were to have you, or France rather, as a boundary, your Majesty is not an agreeable neighbour; young, ardent, warlike, the King of France might inflict some serious mischief on Holland, especially if he were to get near her.'

'I perfectly understand, M. Colbert, and you have explained it very clearly; but be good enough to tell me the conclusion you have arrived at.'

'Your Majesty's decisions are never deficient in wisdom.'

'What will these ambassadors say to me?'

'They will tell your Majesty that they are ardently desirous of forming an alliance with you, which will be a falsehood; they will tell Spain that the three powers ought to unite so as to check the prosperity of England, and that will equally be a falsehood; for, at present, the natural ally of your Majesty is England, who has ships when you have none; England, who can counteract Dutch influence in India;* England, in fact, a monarchical country to which your Majesty is attached by ties of blood.'*

'Good; but how would you answer?'

'I should answer, sire, with the greatest possible moderation of tone, that the disposition of Holland does not seem friendly towards the King of France; that the symptoms of public feeling among the Dutch are alarming as regards your Majesty; that certain medals have been struck with insulting devices.'

'Towards me!' exclaimed the young King excitedly.

'Oh! no, sire, no, insulting is not the word; I was mistaken, I ought to have said immeasurably flattering for the Dutch.'

'Oh! if that be so, the pride of the Dutch is a matter of indifference to me,' said the King sighing.

'Your Majesty is right, a thousand times right. However, it is never a mistake in politics, your Majesty knows better than myself, to be unjust in order to obtain a concession in your own favour. If your Majesty were to complain as if your susceptibility were offended, you will stand in a far higher position with them.'

'What are those medals you speak of?' inquired Louis; 'for if I allude to them, I ought to know what to say.'

'Upon my word, sire, I cannot very well tell you—some overweeningly conceited device—that is the sense of it, the words have nothing to do with the thing itself.'

'Very well, I will mention the word medal, and they can understand it if they like.'

'Oh! they will understand without any difficulty. Your Majesty can also slip in a few words about certain pamphlets which are being circulated.'

'Never! Pamphlets befoul those who write them much more than those against whom they are written, M. Colbert. I thank you, you can leave me now. Do not forget the hour I have fixed, and be there yourself.'

'Sire, I await your Majesty's list.'

'True,' returned the King; and he began to meditate; he did not think of the list in the slightest degree. The clock struck half-past eleven. The King's face revealed a violent conflict between pride and love. The political conversation had dispelled a good deal of the irritation which Louis had felt, and La Vallière's pale, worn features, in his imagination, spoke a very different language to that of the Dutch medals or the Batavian pamphlets.* He sat for ten minutes debating within himself whether he should or should not return to La Vallière; but Colbert having with some urgency respectfully requested that the list might be furnished him, the King blushed at thinking of mere matters of affection when matters of business required his attention. He, therefore, dictated: the Queen-Mother, the Queen, Madame, Madame de Motteville, Madame de Châtillon, Madame de Navailles; and, for the men, M. le Prince,* M. de Gramont, M. de Manicamp. M. de Saint-Aignan, and the officers on duty.

'The ministers,' said Colbert.

'As a matter of course, and the secretaries also.'

'Sire, I will leave at once, in order to get everything prepared; the orders will be at the different residences to-morrow.'

'Say rather to-day,' replied Louis mournfully, as the clock struck twelve. It was the very hour when poor La Vallière was almost dying from anguish and bitter suffering. The King's attendants entered, it being the hour for his retiring to rest; the Queen, indeed, had been waiting for more than an hour. Louis accordingly retired to his bedroom with a sigh; but as he sighed, he congratulated himself on his courage, and applauded himself for having been as firm in love as in affairs of State.

LXXV

THE AMBASSADORS

D'ARTAGNAN had, with a very few exceptions, learnt almost all the particulars of what we have just been relating; for among his friends he reckoned all the useful, serviceable people in the royal household,—officious attendants who were proud of being recognised by the captain of the musketeers, for the captain's influence was very great; and then, in addition to any ambitious views they may have imagined he could promote, they were proud of being regarded as worth being spoken to by a man as brave as d'Artagnan. In this manner d'Artagnan learnt every morning what he had not been able either to see or to ascertain the night before, from the simple fact of his not being ubiquitous; so that, with the information he had been able by his own means to pick up during the day, and with what he had gathered from others, he succeeded in making up a bundle of weapons, which he untied as occasion might require. In this way, d'Artagnan's two eyes rendered him the same service as the hundred eyes of Argus.* Political secrets, bedside revelations, hints or scraps of conversation dropped by the courtiers on the threshold of the royal antechamber, in this way d'Artagnan managed to ascertain, and to put away everything in the vast and impenetrable tomb of his memory, by the side of those royal secrets so dearly bought and so faithfully preserved. He, therefore, knew of the King's interview with Colbert, and of the appointment made for the ambassadors in the morning, and consequently he knew that the question of the medals would be brought under debate; and, while he was arranging and constructing the conversation upon a few chance words which had reached his ears, he returned to his post in the royal apartments, so as to be there at the very moment the King would awake. It happened that the King woke very early,—proving thereby that he, too, on his side had slept but indifferently. Towards seven o'clock, he half-opened his door very gently. D'Artagnan was at his post. His Majesty was pale, and seemed wearied; he had not, moreover, quite finished dressing.

'Send for M. de Saint-Aignan,' he said.

Saint-Aignan very probably awaited a summons, for the messenger, when he reached his apartment, found him already dressed. Saint-Aignan hastened to the King in obedience to the summons. A moment afterwards the King and Saint-Aignan passed by together, but the King walking first. D'Artagnan went to the window which looked out upon the courtyards; he had no need to put himself to the trouble of watching in what direction the King went, for he had no difficulty in guessing beforehand where His Majesty was going. The King, in fact, bent his steps towards the apartments of the maids of honour,—a circumstance which in no way astonished d'Artagnan, for he more than suspected, although La Vallière had not breathed a syllable on the subject, that the King had some kind of reparation to make. Saint-Aignan followed him as he had done the previous evening, rather less uneasy in his mind, though still slightly agitated, for he fervently trusted that at seven o'clock in the morning there might be only himself and the King awake among the august guests at the palace. D'Artagnan stood at the window, careless and perfectly calm in his manner. One could almost have sworn that he noticed nothing and was utterly ignorant who were these two hunters after adventures who were passing across the courtyards wrapped up in their cloaks. And yet, all the while that d'Artagnan appeared not to be looking at them at all, he did not for one moment lose sight of them, and while he whistled that old march of the musketeers, which he rarely recalled except under great emergencies, he conjectured and prophesied how terrible would be the storm which would be raised on the King's return. In fact, when the King entered La Vallière's apartment,* and found the room empty and the bed untouched, he began to be alarmed, and called out to Montalais, who immediately answered the summons; but her astonishment was equal to the King's. All that she could tell His Majesty was, that she had fancied she had heard La Vallière weep during a portion of the night, but, knowing that His Majesty had returned, she had not dared to inquire what was the matter.

'But,' inquired the King, 'where do you suppose she is gone to?'

'Sire,' replied Montalais, 'Louise is of a very sentimental disposition, and as I have often seen her rise at daybreak in order to go out into the garden, she may perhaps be there now.'

This appeared probable, and the King immediately ran down the staircase in search of the fugitive. D'Artagnan saw him appear very pale, and talking in an excited manner with his companion, as he went towards the gardens, Saint-Aignan following him, out of breath. D'Artagnan did not stir from the window, but went on whistling, looking as if he saw nothing, and yet seeing everything. 'Come, come,' he murmured, when the King disappeared, 'His Majesty's passion is stronger than I thought; he is now doing, I think, what he never did for Mademoiselle de Mancini.'*

In a quarter of an hour the King again appeared; he had looked everywhere, was completely out of breath, and, as a matter of course, had not discovered anything. Saint-Aignan, who still followed him, was fanning himself with his hat, and, in a gasping voice, asking for information about La Vallière from such of the servants as were about, in fact from every one he met. Among others he came across Manicamp, who had arrived from Fontainebleau by easy stages; for whilst others had performed the journey in six hours, he had taken four-and-twenty.

'Have you seen Mademoiselle de la Vallière?' Saint-Aignan asked him.

Whereupon Manicamp, dreamy and absent as usual, answered, thinking that some one was asking him about de Guiche, 'Thank you, the Comte is a little better.'

And he continued on his way until he reached the antechamber where d'Artagnan was, and whom he asked to explain how it was the King looked, as he thought, so bewildered; to which d'Artagnan replied that he was quite mistaken; that the King, on the contrary, was as lively and as merry as he could possibly be.

In the midst of all this eight o'clock struck. It was usual for the King to take his breakfast at this hour, for the code of etiquette prescribed that the King should always be hungry at eight o'clock. His breakfast was laid upon a small table in his bedroom, and he ate very fast. Saint-Aignan, of whom he would not lose sight, held his napkin in his hand. He then disposed of several military audiences, during which he despatched Saint-Aignan to see what he could find out. Then, still occupied, still full of anxiety, still watching Saint-Aignan's return, who had sent out his servants in every direction to make inquiries, and who had also gone himself, the hour of nine struck, and the King forthwith passed into his large cabinet.

As the clock was striking nine the ambassadors entered, and as it finished the two Queens and Madame made their appearance. There were three ambassadors from Holland and two from Spain. The King glanced at them and then bowed; and, at the same moment, Saint-Aignan entered,—an entrance which the King regarded as far more important, in a different sense, however, than that of the ambassadors, however numerous they were, and from whatever country they came; and so, setting everything else aside, the King made a sign of interrogation to Saint-Aignan which the latter answered by a most decisive negative. The King almost entirely lost his courage; but as the Queens, the members of the nobility who were present, and the ambassadors, had their eyes fixed upon him, he overcame this emotion by a violent effort, and invited the latter to speak. Whereupon one of the Spanish deputies made a long oration, in which he boasted the advantages which the Spanish alliance would offer.

The King interrupted him, saying, 'Monsieur, I trust that whatever is advantageous for France must be exceedingly advantageous for Spain.'

This remark, and particularly the peremptory tone in which it was pronounced, made the ambassadors pale, and brought the colour into the cheeks of the two Queens, who, being Spanish, felt wounded by this reply in their pride of relationship and nationality.

The Dutch ambassador then began to address himself to the King, and complained of the injurious suspicions which the King exhibited against the Government of his country.

The King interrupted him, saying, 'It is very singular, monsieur, that you should come here with any complaint, when it is

I rather who have reason to be dissatisfied; and yet, you see, I do not complain.'

'Complain, sire; and in what respect?'

The King smiled bitterly. 'Will you blame me, monsieur,' he said, 'if I should happen to entertain suspicions against a Government which authorises and protects public insulters?'

'Sire!'

'I tell you,' resumed the King, exciting himself by a recollection of his own personal annoyance rather than from political grounds, 'that Holland is a land of refuge for all who hate me, and especially for all who malign me.'

'Oh, sire!'

'You wish for proofs, perhaps? Very good; they can be had easily enough. Whence proceed all those insulting pamphlets which represent me as a monarch without glory and without authority. Your printing presses groan under their number. If my secretaries were here I would mention the titles of the works as well as the names of the printers.'

'Sire,' replied the ambassador, 'a pamphlet can hardly be regarded as the work of a whole nation. Is it just, is it reasonable, that a great and powerful monarch like your Majesty should render a whole nation responsible for the crime of a few madmen, who are starving or dying of hunger?'

'That may be the case, I admit. But when the Mint at Amsterdam strikes off medals which reflect disgrace upon me, is that also the crime of a few madmen?'

'Medals!' stammered out the ambassador.

'Medals,' repeated the King, looking at Colbert.

'Your Majesty,' the ambassador ventured, 'should be quite sure——'

The King still looked at Colbert; but Colbert appeared not to understand him, and maintained an unbroken silence, notwithstanding the King's repeated hints. D'Artagnan then approached the King, and taking a metal disc out of his pocket, he placed it in the King's hands, saying: 'That is the medal your Majesty refers to.'

The King looked at it, and with a glance which, ever since he had become his own master, had been always soaring in its gaze, observed an insulting device representing Holland arresting the progress of the sun, with this inscription: '*In conspectu meo stetit sol.*'*

'In my presence the sun stands still,' exclaimed the King furiously. 'Ah! you will hardly deny it now, I suppose.'

'And the sun,' said d'Artagnan, 'is this,' as he pointed to the panels of the cabinet, where the sun was brilliantly represented in every direction with this motto, '*Nec pluribus impar.*'*

Louis's anger, increased by the bitterness of his own personal sufferings, hardly required this additional circumstance to foment it. Every one saw, from the kindling passion in the King's eyes, that an explosion was most imminent. A look from Colbert kept back the storm from bursting forth. The ambassador ventured to frame excuses by saying that the vanity of nations was a matter of little consequence; that Holland was proud that, with such limited resources, she had maintained her rank as a great nation, even against the powerful monarchs, and that if a little smoke had intoxicated his countrymen, the King would be kindly disposed, and would excuse this intoxication. The King seemed as if he would be glad of some one's advice; he looked at Colbert, who remained impassible; then at d'Artagnan, who simply shrugged his shoulders, a movement which was like the opening of the floodgates whereby the King's anger, which he had restrained for so long a period, now burst forth. As no one knew what direction his anger might take, all preserved a dead silence. The second ambassador took advantage of it to begin his excuses also. While he was speaking, and while the King, who had again gradually returned to his own personal reflections, listened to the voice, full of nervous anxiety, with the air of an absent man listening to the murmuring of a cascade, d'Artagnan, on whose left hand Saint-Aignan was standing, approached the latter, and, in a voice which was loud enough to reach the King's ears, said: 'Have you heard the news?'

'What news?' said Saint-Aignan.

'About La Vallière?'

The King started, and involuntarily advanced a step nearer to them.

'What has happened to La Vallière?' inquired Saint-Aignan, in a tone which can very easily be imagined.

'Ah! poor girl! she is going to take the veil.'

'The veil!' exclaimed Saint-Aignan.

'The veil!' cried the King, in the midst of the ambassador's discourse; but then, mindful of the rules of etiquette, he mastered himself, still listening, however, with rapt attention.

'Which Order?' inquired Saint-Aignan.

'The Carmelites of Chaillot.'

'Who the deuce told you that?'

'She did herself.'

'You have seen her, then?'

'Nay, I even went with her to the Carmelites.'

The King did not miss a syllable of this conversation; and again he could hardly control his feelings.

'But what was the cause of her flight?' inquired Saint-Aignan.

'Because the poor girl was driven away from the court yesterday,' replied d'Artagnan.

He had no sooner said this than the King, with an authoritative gesture, said to the ambassador, 'Enough, monsieur, enough.' Then, advancing towards the captain he exclaimed: 'Who says that La Vallière is going to take religious vows?'

'M. d'Artagnan,' answered the favourite.

'Is it true what you say?' said the King, turning towards the musketeer.

'As true as truth itself.'

The King clenched his hands and turned pale. 'You have something further to add, M. d'Artagnan?' he said.

'I know nothing more, sire.'

'You added that Mademoiselle de la Vallière had been driven away from the court?'

'Yes, sire.'

'Is that true also?'

'Ascertain it for yourself, sire.'

'And from whom?'

'Oh!' said d'Artagnan, like a man declining to say anything further.

The King almost bounded from his seat, regardless of ambassadors, ministers, courtiers, and politics. The Queen-Mother rose; she had heard everything, or, if she had not heard everything, she had guessed it. Madame, almost fainting from anger and fear, endeavoured to rise as the Queen-Mother had done;

but she sank down again upon her chair, which by an instinctive movement she made to roll back a few paces.

'Gentlemen,' said the King, 'the audience is over; I will communicate my answer, or rather my will, to Spain and to Holland;' and with a proud, imperious gesture he dismissed the ambassadors.

'Take care, my son,' said the Queen-Mother indignantly, 'take care, you are hardly master of yourself, I think.'

'Ah! madame,' returned the young lion, with a terrible gesture, 'if I am not master of myself, I will be, I promise you, of those who do me outrage; come with me, d'Artagnan, come.' And he quitted the room in the midst of the general stupefaction and dismay. The King hastily descended the staircase, and was about to cross the courtyard.

'Sire,' said d'Artagnan, 'your Majesty mistakes the way.'

'No; I am going to the stables.'

'That is useless, sire, for I have horses ready for your Majesty.'

The King's only answer was a look, but this look promised more than the ambition of three d'Artagnans could have dared to hope.

LXXVI

CHAILLOT

ALTHOUGH they had not been summoned, Manicamp and Malicorne had followed the King and d'Artagnan. They were both exceedingly intelligent men, except that Malicorne was generally too precipitate, owing to his ambition; while Manicamp was frequently too tardy, owing to his idleness. On this occasion, however, they arrived at precisely the proper moment. Five horses were waiting in readiness. Two were seized upon by the King and d'Artagnan, two others by Manicamp and Malicorne, while a groom belonging to the stables mounted the fifth.* The whole cavalcade set off at a gallop. D'Artagnan had been very careful in his selection of the horses; they were the very animals for distressed lovers—horses which did not simply run but flew. Within ten minutes after their departure, the cavalcade, amidst a cloud of dust, arrived at Chaillot. The King literally threw himself off his horse; but, notwithstanding the rapidity with which he accomplished this manœuvre, he found d'Artagnan already holding his stirrup. With a sign of acknowledgement to the musketeer, he threw the bridle to the groom, then darted into the vestibule, violently pushed open the door, and entered the reception-room. Manicamp, Malicorne and the groom remained outside, d'Artagnan alone following him. When he entered the reception-room, the first object which met his gaze was Louise herself, not simply on her knees, but lying at the foot of the large stone crucifix. The young girl was stretched upon the damp flagstones, scarcely visible in the gloom of the apartment, which was lighted only by means of a narrow window protected by bars, and completely shaded by creeping plants. She was alone, inanimate, cold as the stone to which she was clinging. When the King saw her in this state he thought she was dead, and uttered a loud cry, which made d'Artagnan hurry into the room. The King had already passed one of his arms round her body, and d'Artagnan assisted him in raising the poor girl, whom the torpor of death seemed already to have taken possession of. D'Artagnan seized hold of the alarm-bell, and rang with all his might. The Carmelite Sisters immediately hastened at the summons, and uttered loud exclamations of alarm and indignation at the sight of the two men holding a woman in their arms. The superior also hurried to the scene of action; but far more a creature of the world than any of the female members of the court, notwithstanding her austerity of manners, she recognised the King at the first glance, by the respect which those present exhibited for him, as well as by the imperious and authoritative way in which he had thrown the whole establishment into confusion. As soon as she saw the King, she retired to her own apartments, in order to avoid compromising her dignity. But by one of the nuns she sent various cordials, Hungary water, etc., etc., and ordered that all the doors should be immediately closed, a command which was just in time, for the King's distress was fast becoming of a most clamorous and despairing character. He had almost decided to send for his own physician, when La Vallière exhibited signs of returning animation. The first object which met her gaze as she opened her eyes, was the

King at her feet; in all probability she did not recognise him, for she uttered a deep sigh full of anguish and distress. Louis fixed his eyes devouringly upon her face; and, when, in the course of a few moments, she recognised the King, she endeavoured to tear herself from his embrace.

'Oh, heavens!' she murmured, 'is not the sacrifice yet made?'

'No, no,' exclaimed the King, 'and it shall not be made, I swear.'

Notwithstanding her weakness and utter despair, she rose from the ground, saying, 'It must be made, however; it must be; so do not stay me in my purpose.'

'I leave you to sacrifice yourself! I, never, never!' exclaimed the King.

'Well,' murmured d'Artagnan, 'I may as well go now. As soon as they begin to speak we may as well save their having any listeners.' And he quitted the room, leaving the two lovers alone.

'Sire,' continued La Vallière, 'not another word, I implore you. Do not destroy the only future I can hope for—my salvation; do not destroy the glory and brightness of your own future for a mere caprice.'

'A caprice!' cried the King.

'Oh, sire! it is now, only, that I can see clearly into your heart.'

'You, Louise, what mean you?'

'An inexplicable impulse, foolish and unreasonable in its nature, may momentarily appear to offer a sufficient excuse for your conduct; but there are duties imposed upon you which are incompatible with your regard for a poor girl such as I am. So forget me.'

'Forget you!'

'You have already done so.'

'Rather would I die.'

'You cannot love one whose peace of mind you hold so lightly, and whom you so cruelly abandoned, last night, to the bitterness of death.'

'What can you mean? Explain yourself, Louise.'

'What did you ask me yesterday morning? To love you. What did you promise me in return? Never to let midnight pass without offering me an opportunity of reconciliation, whenever your anger might be aroused against me.'

'Oh! forgive me, Louise, forgive me! I was almost mad from jealousy.'

'Jealousy is an unworthy thought, sire. You may become jealous again, and will end by killing me. Be merciful then, and leave me now to die.'

'Another word, mademoiselle, in that strain, and you will see me expire at your feet.'

'No, no, sire, I am better acquainted with my own failings; and believe me, that to sacrifice yourself for one whom all despise would be needless.'

'Give me the names of those you have cause to complain of.'

'I have no complaints, sire, to prefer against any one; no one but myself to accuse. Farewell, sire; you are compromising yourself in speaking to me in such a manner.'

'Oh! be careful, Louise, in what you say; for you are reducing me to the very depths of despair.'

'Oh! sire, sire, leave me to the protection of Heaven, I implore you.'

'No, no; Heaven itself shall not tear you from me.'

'Save me, then,' cried the poor girl, 'from those determined and pitiless enemies who are thirsting to destroy my very life and honour too. If you have courage enough to love me, show at least that you have power enough to defend me. But no; she whom you say you love, others insult and mock and drive shamelessly away.' And the gentle-hearted girl, forced, by her own bitter distress to accuse others, wrung her hands in an uncontrollable agony of tears.

'You have been driven away!' exclaimed the King. 'This is the second time I have heard that said.'

'I have been driven away with shame and ignominy, sire. You see, then, that I have no other protector but Heaven, no consolation but prayer, and this cloister is my only refuge.'

'My palace, my whole court, shall be yours. Oh! fear nothing further now, Louise; those, be they men or women, who yesterday drove you away, shall to-morrow tremble before you—to-morrow, do I say? nay, this very day have I already shown my displeasure—have already threatened. It is in my power, even now, to hurl the thunderbolt which I have hitherto withheld. Louise, Louise, you shall be cruelly revenged; tears of blood shall repay you for the tears you have shed. Give me only the names of your enemies.'

'Never, never.'

'How can I show my anger, then?'

'Sire, those upon whom your anger would have to fall would force you to draw back your hand upraised to punish.'

'Oh! you do not know me,' cried the King, exasperated. 'Rather than draw back I would sacrifice my kingdom and would curse my family. Yes, I would strike until this arm had utterly annihilated all those who had ventured to make themselves the enemies of the gentlest and best of creatures.' And, as he said these words, Louis struck his fist violently against the oaken wainscoting with a force which alarmed La Vallière; for his anger, owing to his unbounded power, had something imposing and threatening in it, and, like the tempest, might be mortal in its effects. She, who thought that her own sufferings could not be surpassed, was overwhelmed by a suffering which revealed itself by menace and by violence.

'Sire,' she said, 'for the last time, I implore you to leave me; already do I feel strengthened by the calm seclusion of this asylum; and the protection of Heaven has reassured me; for all the petty human meannesses of this world are forgotten beneath Divine protection. Once more then, sire, and for the last time, I again implore you to leave me.'

'Confess, rather,' cried Louis, 'that you have never loved me; admit that my humility and my repentance are flattering to your pride; but that my distress affects you not; that the King of this wide realm is no longer regarded as a lover whose tenderness of devotion is capable of working out your happiness; but that he is a despot whose caprice has utterly destroyed in your heart the very last fibre of human feeling.'

Louise's heart was wrung within her as she listened to his passionate utterance, which made the fever of passion course through every vein in her body. 'But did you not hear me say, that I have been driven away, scorned, despised?'

'I will make you the most respected, the most adored, and the most envied of my whole court.'

'Prove to me that you have not ceased to love me.'

'In what way?'

'By leaving me.'

'I will prove it to you by never leaving you again.'

'But do you imagine, sire, that I shall allow that; do you imagine that I will let you come to an open rupture with every member of your family; do you imagine that for my sake, you could abandon mother, wife, and sister?'

'Ah! you have named them then at last; it is they, then, who have wrought this grievous injury? By the heaven above us, then, upon them shall my anger fall.'

'That is the reason why the future terrifies me, why I refuse everything, why I do not wish you to revenge me. Tears enough have already been shed, sufficient sorrow and affliction have already been occasioned. I, at least, will never be the cause of sorrow, or affliction, or distress, to whomsoever it may be, for I have mourned and suffered and wept too much myself.'

'And do you count my sufferings, my distress, and my tears, as nothing?'

'In Heaven's name, sire, do not speak to me in that manner. I need all my courage to enable me to accomplish the sacrifice.'

'Louise, Louise, I implore you! whatever you desire, whatever you command, whether vengeance or forgiveness, your slightest wish shall be obeyed, but do not abandon me.'

'Alas! sire, we must part.'

'You do not love me, then!'

'Heaven knows I do!'

'It is false, Louise, it is false.'

'Oh! sire, if I did not love you, I should let you do what you please; I should let you avenge me, in return for the insult which has been inflicted on me; I should accept the sweet triumph to my pride which you propose; and yet, you cannot deny, that I reject even the sweet compensation which your affection affords, that affection which for me is life itself, for I wished to die when I thought that you loved me no longer.'

'Yes, yes; I now know, I now perceive it; you are the holiest, the best, the purest of women. There is no one so worthy as yourself, not alone of my own respect and devotion, but also of the respect and devotion of all who surround me; and therefore shall no one be loved like yourself; no one shall ever possess the influence over me that you wield. You wish me to be calm, to forgive; be it so, you shall find me perfectly unmoved. You wish to reign by gentleness and clemency, I will be clement and gentle. Dictate for me the conduct you wish me to adopt, and I will obey blindly.'

'In Heaven's name, no, sire; what am I, a poor girl, to dictate to so great a monarch as yourself?'

'You are my life, the very spirit and principle of my being. Is it not the spirit that rules the body?'

'You love me, then, sire?'

'On my knees, yes; with my hands upraised to you, yes; with all the strength and power of my being, yes; I love you so deeply, that I would happily lay down my life for you at your merest wish.'

'Oh! sire, now that I know you love me, I have nothing to wish for in the whole world. Give me your hand, sire; and then, farewell! I have enjoyed in this life all the happiness which I was destined to meet with.'

'Oh! no, no! your happiness is not a happiness of yesterday, it is of to-day, of to-morrow, ever-enduring. The future is yours, everything which is mine is yours too. Away with these ideas of separation, away with these gloomy, despairing thoughts. You will live for me, as I will live for you, Louise.' And he threw himself at her feet, embracing her knees with the wildest transports of joy and gratitude.

'Oh! sire, sire! all that is but a wild dream.'

'Why a wild dream?'

'Because I cannot return to the court. Exiled, how can I see you again? Would it not be far better to bury myself in a cloister for the rest of my life, with the rich consolation that your affection gives me, with the latest pulses of your heart beating for me, and your latest confession of attachment still ringing in my ears?'

'Exiled, you!' exclaimed Louis XIV, 'and who dares to exile, let me ask, when I recall?'

'Oh! sire, something which is greater than and superior to kings even—the world and public opinion. Reflect for a moment; you cannot love a woman who has been ignominiously driven away—love one whom your mother has stained with suspicion; one whom your sister has threatened with disgrace; such a woman, indeed, would be unworthy of you.'

'Unworthy! one who belongs to me?'

'Yes, sire! precisely on that account; from the very moment she belongs to you, the character of your mistress renders her unworthy.'

'You are right, Louise, every shade of delicacy of feeling is yours. Very well, you shall not be exiled.'

'Ah! from the tone in which you speak you have not heard Madame, that is very clear.'

'I will appeal from her to my mother.'

'Again, sire, you have not seen your mother.'

'She also! poor Louise! every one's hand then is against you.'

'Yes, yes, poor Louise, who was already bending beneath the fury of the storm when you arrived and crushed her beneath the weight of your displeasure.'

'Oh! forgive me.'

'You will not, I know, be able to make either of them yield; believe me, the evil cannot be repaired, for I will not allow you to use violence, or to exercise your authority.'

'Very well, Louise, to prove to you how fondly I love you I will do one thing, I will see Madame; I will make her revoke her sentence, I will compel her to do so.'

'Compel? Oh! no, no!'

'True, you are right. I will bend her.'

Louise shook her head.

'I will entreat her, if it be necessary,' said Louis. 'Will you believe in my affection after that?'

Louise drew herself up. 'Oh! never, never, shall you humiliate yourself on my account; sooner, a thousand times, would I die.'

Louis reflected, his features assumed a dark expression. 'I will love as much as you have loved; I will suffer as keenly as you have suffered; this shall be my expiation in your eyes. Come, mademoiselle, put aside these paltry considerations; let us show ourselves as great as our sufferings, as strong as our affection for each other.' And as he said this, he took her in his arms, and encircled her waist with both his hands, saying, 'My own love! my own dearest and best-beloved, follow me.'

She made a final effort, in which she concentrated—no longer all her firmness of will, for that had long since been overcome,

but all her physical strength. 'No!' she replied weakly, 'no! no!
I should die of shame.'

'No! you shall return like a queen. No one knows of your
having left—except indeed, d'Artagnan.'

'He has betrayed me, then?'

'In what way?'

'He promised me faithfully——'

'I promised not to say anything to the King,' said d'Artagnan,
putting his head in through the half-opened door, 'and I kept
my word; I was speaking to M. de Saint-Aignan, and it was not
my fault if the King overheard me; was it, sire?'

'It is quite true,' said the King, 'forgive him.'

La Vallière smiled, and held out her small white hand to the
musketeer.

'Monsieur d'Artagnan,' said the King, 'be good enough to see
if you can find a carriage for Mademoiselle de la Vallière.'

'Sire,' replied the captain, 'the carriage is waiting at the gate.'

'You are the most perfect model of thoughtfulness,' exclaimed
the King.

'You have taken a long time to find it out,' muttered d'Artagnan, notwithstanding he was flattered by the praise bestowed
upon him.

La Vallière was overcome: after a little further hesitation she
allowed herself to be led away half-fainting by her royal lover.
But, as she was on the point of leaving the room, she tore herself
from the King's grasp, and returned to the stone crucifix, which
she kissed, saying, 'Oh! Heaven! it was Thou who drewest me
hither! Thou who hast rejected me; but Thy grace is infinite.
Whenever I shall again return, forget that I have ever separated
myself from Thee, for, when I return, it will be—never to leave
Thee again!'*

The King could not restrain his emotion, and d'Artagnan
even was overcome. Louis bore the young girl away, lifted her
into the carriage, and directed d'Artagnan to seat himself beside
her, while he mounting his horse, spurred violently towards the
Palais Royal, where immediately on his arrival he sent to request
an audience of Madame.

LXXVII

MADAME

FROM the manner in which the King had dismissed the ambassadors, even the least clear-sighted persons belonging to the court had imagined war would ensue. The ambassadors themselves, but slightly acquainted with the King's domestic disturbances, had interpreted as directed against themselves the celebrated sentence, 'If I be not master of myself, I, at least, will be of those who insult me.' Happily for the destinies of France and Holland, Colbert had followed them out of the King's presence, for the purpose of explaining matters to them; but the two Queens and Madame, who were perfectly aware of every particular circumstance that had taken place in their several households, having heard the remark so full of dark meaning, retired to their own apartments in no little fear and chagrin. Madame, especially, felt that the royal anger might fall upon her; and, as she was brave and exceedingly proud, instead of seeking support and encouragement from the Queen-Mother, she had returned to her own apartments, if not without some uneasiness, at least without any intention of avoiding the encounter. Anne of Austria, from time to time at frequent intervals, sent messages to learn if the King had returned. The silence which the whole palace preserved upon the matter, and upon Louise's disappearance, was indicative of a long train of misfortunes to all those who knew the haughty and irritable humour of the King. But Madame remained perfectly unmoved in spite of all the flying rumours, shut herself up in her apartments, sent for Montalais, and, with a voice as calm as she could possibly command, desired her to relate all she knew about the event itself. At the moment when the eloquent Montalais was concluding, with all kinds of oratorical precautions, and was recommending, if not in actual language, at least in spirit, that she should show a forbearance towards La Vallière, M. Malicorne made his appearance to beg an audience of Madame on behalf of His Majesty. Montalais's worthy friend bore upon his countenance all the signs of the very liveliest emotion. It was impossible to be mistaken: the interview which the King requested would be one of the most interesting chapters in the history of the hearts of kings and of men. Madame was disturbed by her brother-in-law's arrival. She did not expect it so soon, nor had she, indeed, expected any direct step on Louis's part. Besides, all women who wage war successfully by indirect means are invariably neither very skilful nor very strong when it becomes a question of accepting a pitched battle. Madame, however, was not one who ever drew back; she had the very opposite defect or qualification, in whichever light it may be considered; she took an exaggerated view of what constituted real courage; and therefore the King's message, of which Malicorne had been the bearer, was regarded by her as the trumpet proclaiming the commencement of hostilities. She, therefore, boldly accepted the gage of battle. Five minutes afterwards the King ascended the staircase.* His colour was heightened from having ridden hard. His dusty and disordered clothes formed a singular contrast with the fresh and perfectly arranged toilet of Madame, who, notwithstanding her rouge, turned pale as the King entered the room. Louis lost no time in approaching the object of his visit; he sat down, and Montalais disappeared.

'My dear sister,' said the King, 'you are aware that Mademoiselle de la Vallière fled from her own room this morning, and that she has retired to a cloister, overwhelmed by grief and despair.' As he pronounced these words, the King's voice was singularly moved.

'Your Majesty is the first to inform me of it,' replied Madame.

'I should have thought that you might have learnt it this morning, during the reception of the ambassadors,' said the King.

'From your emotion, sire, I imagined that something extraordinary had happened, but without knowing what.'

The King with his usual frankness went straight to the point. 'Why have you sent Mademoiselle de la Vallière away?'

'Because I had reason to be dissatisfied with her conduct,' she replied dryly.

The King became crimson, and his eyes kindled with a fire which it required all Madame's courage to support. He mastered his anger, however, and continued, 'A stronger reason than that is surely requisite, for one so good and kind as you are, to turn away and dishonour, not only the young girl herself, but every member of her family as well. You know that the whole city has its eyes fixed upon the conduct of the female portion of the court. To dismiss a maid of honour is to attribute a crime to her—at the very least a fault. What crime, what fault has Mademoiselle de la Vallière been guilty of?'

'Since you constitute yourself the protector of Mademoiselle de la Vallière,' replied Madame coldly, 'I will give you those explanations which I should have a perfect right to withhold from every one.'

'Even from the King!' exclaimed Louis, as, with a sudden gesture, he covered his head with his hat.

'You have called me your sister,' said Madame, 'and I am in my own apartments.'

'It matters not,' said the youthful monarch, ashamed at having been hurried away by his anger; 'neither you, nor any one else in this kingdom can assert a right to withhold an explanation in my presence.'

'Since that is the way you regard it,' said Madame, in a hoarse, angry tone of voice, 'all that remains for me to do is to bow submissively to your Majesty and to be silent.'

'No; let there be no equivocation between us.'

'The protection with which you surround Mademoiselle de la Vallière does not impose any respect.'

'No equivocation, I repeat; you are perfectly aware that, as head of the nobility of France, I am accountable to all for the honour of every family. You dismiss Mademoiselle de la Vallière, or whoever else it may be——' Madame shrugged her shoulders.

'Or whoever else it may be, I repeat,' continued the King; 'and as, in acting in that manner, you cast a dishonourable reflection upon that person, I ask you for an explanation, in order that I may confirm or annul the sentence.'

'Annul my sentence!' exclaimed Madame haughtily. 'What! when I have discharged one of my attendants, do you order me to take her back again?' The King remained silent.

'This would cease to be an excess of power merely, sire; it would be indecorous and unseemly.'

'Madame!'

'As a woman I should revolt against an abuse so insulting to me; I should no longer be able to regard myself as a princess of your blood, a daughter of a monarch; I should be the meanest of creatures, more humble and disgraced than the servant I had sent away.'

The King rose from his seat with anger. 'It cannot be a heart,' he cried, 'you have beating in your bosom; if you act in such a way with me, I may have reason to act with similar severity.'

It sometimes happens that in a battle a chance ball may reach its mark. The observation which the King had made, without any particular intention, struck Madame home, and staggered her for a moment; some day or other she might indeed have reason to dread reprisals. 'At all events, sire,' she said, 'explain what you require.'

'I ask, madame, what has Mademoiselle de la Vallière done to warrant your conduct towards her?'

'She is the most cunning fomenter of intrigues I know; she was the occasion of two personal friends engaging in mortal combat; and has made people talk of her in such shameless terms that the whole court is indignant at the mere sound of her name.'

'She! she!' cried the King.

'Under her soft and hypocritical manner,' continued Madame, 'she hides a disposition full of foul and dark deceit.'

'She!'

'You may possibly be deceived, sire, but I know her well; she is capable of creating dispute and misunderstanding between the most affectionate relatives and the most intimate friends. You see that she has already sown discord between us two.'

'I do assure you——' said the King.

'Sire, look well into the case as it stood; we were living on the most friendly understanding, and by the artfulness of her tales and complaints, she has set your Majesty against me.'

'I swear to you,' said the King, 'that on no occasion has a bitter word ever passed her lips; I swear that, even in my wild bursts of passion, she would never allow me to threaten any one; and I swear, too, that you do not possess a more devoted and respectful friend than she is.'

'Friend!' said Madame, with an expression of supreme disdain.

'Take care, madame!' said the King; 'you forget that you now understand me, and that from this moment everything is equalised. Mademoiselle de la Vallière will be whatever I may choose her to become; and, to-morrow, if I were to determine to do so, I could seat her on a throne.'

'She will not have been born to a throne, at least, and whatever you may do can affect the future alone, but cannot affect the past.'

'Madame, towards you I have shown every kind consideration, and every eager desire to please you; do not remind me that I am master here.'

'That is the second time, sire, that you have made that remark, and I have already informed you that I am ready to submit.'

'In that case, then, will you confer upon me the favour of receiving Mademoiselle de la Vallière back again.'

'For what purpose, sire, since you have a throne to bestow upon her. I am too insignificant to protect so exalted a personage.'

'Nay, a truce to this bitter and disdainful spirit. Grant me her forgiveness.'

'Never!'

'You drive me, then, to open warfare with my own family.'

'I, too, have my own family, where I can find refuge.'

'Do you mean that as a threat, and could you forget yourself so far? Do you believe that, if you push the affront to that extent, your family would encourage you?'

'I hope, sire, that you will not force me to take any step which would be unworthy of my rank.'

'I hoped that you would remember our friendship, and that you would treat me as a brother.'

Madame paused for a moment. 'I do not disown you as a brother,' she said, 'in refusing your Majesty an injustice.'

'An injustice!'

'Oh, sire, if I informed others of La Vallière's conduct; if the Queen knew——'

'Come, come, Henriette, let your heart speak; remember that you have loved me; remember, too, that human hearts should be as merciful as the heart of our sovereign master. Do not be inflexible with others; forgive La Vallière.'

'I cannot; she has offended me.'

'But for my sake.'

'Sire, for your sake I would do anything in the world except that.'

'You will drive me to despair—you compel me to turn to the last resource of weak people, and seek counsel of my angry and wrathful disposition.'

'I advise you to be reasonable.'

'Reasonable!—I can be so no longer.'

'Nay, sire! I pray you——'

'For pity's sake, Henriette; it is the first time I have entreated any one, and I have no hope in any one but in you.'

'Oh, sire! you are weeping.'

'From rage, from humiliation. That I, the King, should have been obliged to descend to entreaty. I shall hate this moment during my whole life. You have made me suffer in one moment more distress and more degradation of feeling than I could have anticipated in the greatest extremity in life.' And the King rose and gave free vent to his tears, which, in fact, were tears of anger and of shame.

Madame was not touched exactly—for the best women, when their pride is hurt, are without pity; but she was afraid that the tears the King was shedding might possibly carry away every soft and tender feeling in his heart. 'Give what commands you please, sire,' she said; 'and since you prefer my humiliation to your own—although mine is public and yours has been witnessed but by myself alone—speak, I will obey your Majesty.'

'No, no, Henriette!' exclaimed Louis, transported with gratitude, 'you will have yielded to a brother's wishes.'

'I no longer have any brother since I obey.'

'Will you accept my kingdom in grateful acknowledgement?'

'How passionately you love, sire, when you do love!'

He did not answer. He had seized upon Madame's hand and covered it with kisses. 'And so you will receive this poor girl back again, and will forgive her; you will find how gentle and pure-hearted she is.'

'I will maintain her in my household.'

'No, you will give her your friendship, my sister.'

'I have never liked her.'

'Well, for my sake, you will treat her kindly, will you not, Henriette?'

'I will treat her as your mistress.'

The King rose suddenly to his feet. By this word, which had so unfortunately escaped her lips, Madame had destroyed the whole merit of her sacrifice. The King felt freed from all obligation. Exasperated beyond measure, and bitterly offended, he replied:—

'I thank you, madame; I shall never forget the service you have rendered me.' And, saluting her with an affectation of ceremony, he took his leave of her. As he passed before a mirror he saw that his eyes were red, and angrily stamped his foot on the ground. But it was too late, for Malicorne and d'Artagnan, who were standing at the door, had seen his eyes.

'The King has been crying,' thought Malicorne. D'Artagnan approached the King with a respectful air, and said in a low tone of voice:—

'Sire, it would be better to return to your apartments by the small staircase.'

'Why?'

'Because the dust of the road has left its traces on your face,' said d'Artagnan. 'By Heaven!' he thought, 'when the King has been giving way like a child, let those look to it who may make her weep for whom the King has shed tears.'

LXXVIII

MADEMOISELLE DE LA VALLIÈRE'S POCKET-HANDKERCHIEF

MADAME was not bad-hearted, she was only hasty and impetuous. The King was not imprudent, he was only in love. Hardly had they both entered into this sort of compact, which terminated in La Vallière's recall, when they both sought to make as much as they could by their bargain. The King wished to see La Vallière every moment in the day; while Madame, who was sensible of the King's annoyance ever since he had so entreated her, would not abandon La Vallière without a contest. She planted every conceivable difficulty in the King's path; he was, in fact, obliged, in order to get a glimpse of La Vallière, to be exceedingly devoted in his attentions to his sister-in-law, and this, indeed, was Madame's plan of policy. As she had chosen some one to second her efforts, and as this person was our old friend Montalais, the King found himself completely hemmed in every time he paid Madame a visit; he was surrounded, and was never left a moment alone. Madame displayed in her conversations a charm of manner and brilliancy of wit which eclipsed everything. Montalais followed her, and soon rendered herself perfectly insupportable to the King, which was, in fact, the very thing she expected would happen. She then set Malicorne at the King, who found the means of informing His Majesty that there was a young person belonging to the court who was exceedingly miserable; and on the King inquiring who this person was, Malicorne replied that it was Mademoiselle de Montalais. To this the King answered that it was perfectly just that a person should be unhappy when she rendered others so. Whereupon Malicorne explained how matters stood; for he had received his directions from Montalais. The King began to open his eyes; he remarked that, as soon as he made his appearance, Madame made hers too; that she remained in the corridors until after he had left; that she accompanied him back to his own apartments, fearing that he might speak in the antechambers to one of her maids of honour. One evening she went further still. The King was seated, surrounded by the ladies who were present, and holding in his hand, concealed by his lace ruffle, a small note which he wished to slip into La Vallière's hand. Madame guessed both his intention and the letter too. It was very difficult to prevent the King going wherever he pleased, and yet it was necessary to prevent his going near La Vallière, to speak to her, as by so doing he could let the note fall into her lap behind her fan, and into her pocket-handkerchief. The King, who was also on the watch, suspected that a snare was being laid for him. He rose and pushed his chair, without affectation, near Mademoiselle de Châtillon, with whom he began to talk in a light tone. They were amusing themselves in making rhymes; from Mademoiselle de Châtillon he went to Montalais, and then to Mademoiselle de Tonnay-Charente. And thus, by this skilful manœuvre, he found himself seated opposite to La Vallière, whom he completely concealed. Madame pretended to be greatly occupied; she was altering a group of flowers that she was working in tapestry. The King showed the corner of the letter to La Vallière, and the latter held out her handkerchief with a look which signified, 'Put the letter inside.' Then, as the King had placed his own handkerchief upon his chair, he was adroit enough to let it fall on the ground, so that La Vallière slipped her handkerchief on the chair. The King took it up quietly, without any one observing what he did, placed the letter within it, and returned the handkerchief to the place he had taken it from. There was only just time for La Vallière to stretch out her hand to take hold of the handkerchief with its valuable contents.

But Madame, who had observed everything that had passed, said to Mademoiselle de Châtillon, 'Châtillon, be good enough to pick up the King's handkerchief, if you please; it has fallen on the carpet.'

The young girl obeyed with the utmost precipitation, the King having moved from his seat, and La Vallière being in no little degree nervous and confused.

'Ah! I beg your Majesty's pardon,' said Mademoiselle de Châtillon, 'you have two handkerchiefs I perceive.'

And the King was accordingly obliged to put into his pocket La Vallière's handkerchief as well as his own. He certainly gained that souvenir of Louise, who lost, however, a copy of verses which had cost the King ten hours' hard labour, and which, as far as he was concerned, was perhaps as good as a long poem.* It would be impossible to describe the King's anger and La Vallière's despair; but shortly afterwards a circumstance occurred which was more than remarkable. When the King left, in order to retire to his own apartments, Malicorne, informed of what had passed, one can hardly tell how, was waiting in the antechamber. The antechambers of the Palais Royal are naturally very dark, and in the evening they were but indifferently lighted. Nothing pleased the King more than this dim light. As a general rule, love, whose mind and heart are constantly in a blaze, dislikes light anywhere else than in the mind and heart. And so the antechamber was dark; a page carried a torch before the King, who walked on slowly, greatly annoyed at what had recently occurred. Malicorne passed close to the King, almost stumbled against him, in fact, and begged his forgiveness with the profoundest humility; but the King, who was in an exceedingly ill temper, was very sharp in his reproof to Malicorne, who disappeared as soon and as quietly as he possibly could. Louis retired to rest, having had a misunderstanding with the Queen; and the next day, as soon as he entered the cabinet, he wished to have La Vallière's handkerchief in order to press his lips to it. He called his valet.

'Fetch me,' he said, 'the coat I wore yesterday evening, but be very sure you do not touch anything it may contain.'

The order being obeyed, the King himself searched the pocket of the coat; he found only one handkerchief, and that his own; La Vallière's had disappeared. Whilst busied with all kinds of conjectures and suspicions, a letter was brought to him from La Vallière; it ran in these terms:—

'How kind and good of you to have sent me those beautiful verses; how full of ingenuity and perseverance your affection is; how is it possible to help loving you so dearly!'

'What does this mean?' thought the King; 'there must be some mistake. Look well about,' he said to the valet, 'for a pocket-handkerchief must be in one of my pockets; and if you do not find it or if you have touched it——' He reflected for a moment. To make a State matter of the loss of a handkerchief would be to act too absurdly, and he therefore added, 'There was a letter of some importance inside the handkerchief which had somehow got among the folds of it.'

'Sire,' replied the valet, 'your Majesty had only one handkerchief, and that is it.'

'True, true,' replied the King, setting his teeth together hard. 'Oh, poverty, how I envy you! Happy is the man who can empty his own pockets of letters and handkerchiefs!'

He read La Vallière's letter over again, endeavouring to imagine in what conceivable way his verses could have reached their destination. There was a postscript to the letter:—

'I send you back by your messenger this reply, so unworthy of what you sent me.'

'So far so good; I shall find out something now,' he said delightedly. 'Who is waiting, and who brought me this letter?'

'M. Malicorne,' replied the *valet de chambre* timidly.

'Desire him to come in.'

Malicorne entered.

'You come from Mademoiselle de la Vallière?' said the King with a sigh.

'Yes, sire.'

'And you took Mademoiselle de la Vallière something from me?'

'I, sire?'

'Yes, you.'

'Oh no, sire.'

'Mademoiselle de la Vallière says so distinctly.'

'Oh, sire, Mademoiselle de la Vallière is mistaken.'

The King frowned. 'What jest is this?' he said; 'explain yourself; why does Mademoiselle de la Vallière call you my messenger? What did you take to that lady? Speak, monsieur, and quickly.'

'Sire, I merely took Mademoiselle de la Vallière a pocket-handkerchief, that was all.'

'A handkerchief,—what handkerchief?'

'Sire, at the very moment when I had the misfortune to stumble against your Majesty yesterday, a misfortune which I shall deplore to the last day of my life, especially after the dissatisfaction which you exhibited, I remained, sire, motionless with despair, your Majesty being at too great a distance to hear my excuses, when I saw something white lying on the ground.'

'Ah!' said the King.

'I stooped down—it was a pocket-handkerchief. For a moment I had an idea that when I stumbled against your Majesty I must have been the cause of the handkerchief falling from your pocket; but as I felt it all over very respectfully, I perceived an emblem at one of the corners, and, on looking at it closely, I found it was Mademoiselle de la Vallière's emblem. I presumed that on her way to Madame's apartments in the earlier part of the evening she had let her handkerchief fall, and I accordingly hastened to restore it to her as she was leaving; and that is all I gave Mademoiselle de la Vallière, I entreat your Majesty to believe.' Malicorne's manner was so simple, so full of contrition, and marked with such extreme humility, that the King was greatly amused in listening to him. He was as pleased with him at what he had done as if he had rendered him the greatest service.

'This is the second fortunate meeting I have had with you, monsieur,' he said; 'you may count upon my friendly feeling.'

The plain and sober truth was, that Malicorne had picked the King's pocket of the handkerchief as dexterously as any of the pickpockets of the good city of Paris could have done. Madame never knew of this little incident, but Montalais gave La Vallière some idea of the manner in which it had really happened, and La Vallière afterwards told the King, who laughed exceedingly at it and pronounced Malicorne to be a first-rate politician. Louis XIV was right, and it is well known that he was tolerably acquainted with human nature.

LXXIX

WHICH TREATS OF GARDENERS, OF LADDERS, AND MAIDS OF HONOUR

MIRACLES, unfortunately, could not always last for ever, whilst Madame's ill humour still continued to last. In a week's time, matters had reached such a point, that the King could no longer look at La Vallière without a look full of suspicion crossing his own. Whenever a promenade was proposed, Madame, in order to avoid the recurrence of similar scenes to that of the thunder-storm, or the royal oak, had a variety of indispositions ready prepared; and, thanks to them, she was unable to go out, and her maids of honour were obliged to remain indoors also. There was not the slightest chance or means of paying a nocturnal visit; for, in this respect, the King had, on the very first occasion, experi-enced a severe check, which happened in the following manner. As at Fontainebleau, he had taken Saint-Aignan with him one evening, when he wished to pay La Vallière a visit; but he had found no one but Mademoiselle de Tonnay-Charente, who had begun to call out fire and thieves in such a manner that a perfect legion of chambermaids, attendants, and pages ran to her assist-ance; so that Saint-Aignan, who had remained in order to save the honour of his royal master, who had fled precipitately, was obliged to submit to a severe scolding from the Queen-Mother as well as from Madame herself. In addition, he had the next morning received two challenges from the de Mortemart family,* and the King had been obliged to intervene. This mistake had been owing to the circumstance of Madame having suddenly ordered a change in the apartments of her maids of honour, and directed La Vallière and Montalais to sleep in her own quarters. Nothing, therefore, was now possible, not even any communication by letter; to write under the eyes of so ferocious an Argus as Madame, whose kindness of disposition was so uncertain, was to run the risk of exposure to the greatest dangers; and it can well be conceived into what a state of continuous irritation, and of ever increasing anger, all these petty annoyances threw the young lion. The King almost tormented himself to death in endeavouring to discover a means of communication; and, as he did not think proper to call in the aid of Malicorne or d'Artagnan, the means were not discovered at all. Malicorne had, indeed, some occasional brilliant flashes of imagination, with which he tried to inspire the King with confidence; but whether from shame or suspicion, the King, who had at first begun to nibble at the bait soon abandoned the hook. In this way, for instance, one evening, while the King was crossing the garden, and looking up at Madame's windows, Malicorne stumbled over a ladder lying beside a border of box, and said to Manicamp, who was walking with him behind the King, and who had not either stumbled over or seen anything, 'Did you not see that I just now stumbled against a ladder, and was nearly thrown down?'

'No,' said Manicamp, as usual very absent, 'but it appears you did not fall.'

'That doesn't matter; but it is not, on that account, the less dangerous to leave ladders lying about in that manner.'

'True, one might hurt oneself, especially when troubled with fits of absence of mind.'

'I don't mean that; what I did mean was, that it is dangerous to allow ladders to lie about so near the windows of the maids of honour.' Louis started imperceptibly.

'Why so?' inquired Manicamp.

'Speak louder,' whispered Malicorne, as he touched him with his arm.

'Why so?' said Manicamp, louder. The King listened.

'Because, for instance,' said Malicorne, 'a ladder nineteen feet high is just the height of the cornice of those windows.' Manicamp, instead of answering, was dreaming of something else.

'Ask me, can't you, what windows I mean,' whispered Malicorne.

'But what windows are you referring to?' said Manicamp, aloud.

'The windows of Madame's apartments.'

'Eh!'

'Oh! I don't say that any one would ever venture to go up a ladder into Madame's room; but in Madame's apartments, merely separated by a partition, sleep two exceedingly pretty girls, Mesdemoiselles de la Vallière and de Montalais.'

'By a partition,' said Manicamp.

'Look; you see how brilliantly lighted Madame's apartments are—well, do you see those two windows?'

'Yes.'

'And that window close to the others, but more dimly lighted?'

'Yes.'

'Well, that is the room of the maids of honour. Look, look, there is Mademoiselle de la Vallière opening the window. Ah! how many soft things could an enterprising lover say to her, if he only suspected that there was lying here a ladder nineteen feet long which would just reach the cornice.'

'But she is not alone; you said Mademoiselle de Montalais is with her.'

'Mademoiselle de Montalais counts for nothing; she is her oldest friend, and exceedingly devoted to her—a positive well, into which can be thrown all sorts of secrets one might wish to get rid of.'

The King did not miss a single syllable of this conversation. Malicorne had even remarked that His Majesty had slackened his pace, in order to give him time to finish. So, when he arrived at the door, he dismissed every one with the exception of Malicorne, a circumstance which excited no surprise, for it was known that the King was in love; and they suspected he was going to compose some verses by moonlight; and, although there was no moon that evening, the King might, nevertheless, have some verses to compose. Every one, therefore, took his leave, and immediately afterwards the King turned towards Malicorne, who respectfully waited until His Majesty should address him. 'What were you saying just now about a ladder, Monsieur Malicorne?' he asked.

'Did I say anything about ladders, sire?' said Malicorne, looking up as if in search of his words which had flown away.

'Yes, of a ladder nineteen feet long.'

'Oh, yes, sire, I remember; but I spoke to Monsieur Manicamp, and I should not have said a word had I known your Majesty could have heard us.'

'And why would you not have said a word?'

'Because I should not have liked to have got the gardener scolded who had left it there—poor fellow.'

'Don't make yourself uneasy on that account. What is this ladder like?'

'If your Majesty wishes to see it, nothing is easier, for there it is.'

'In that box hedge?'

'Exactly.'

'Show it to me.'

Malicorne turned back, and led the King up to the ladder, saying, 'This is it, sire.'

'Pull it this way a little.'

When Malicorne had brought the ladder on to the gravel walk, the King began to step its whole length, 'Hum!' he said; 'you say it is nineteen feet long?'

'Yes, sire.'

'Nineteen feet—that is rather long; I can hardly believe it can be so long as that.'

'You cannot judge very accurately with the ladder in that position, sire. If it were upright against a tree or a wall, for instance, you would be better able to judge, because the comparison would assist you a good deal.'

'Oh! it does not matter, M. Malicorne; but I can hardly believe that the ladder is nineteen feet high.'

'I know how accurate your Majesty's glance is, and yet I would wager.'

The King shook his head. 'There is one unanswerable means of verifying it,' said Malicorne.

'What is that?'

'Every one knows, sire, that the ground-floor of the palace is eighteen feet high.'

'True, that is very well known.'

'Well, sire, if I place the ladder against the wall, we shall be able to ascertain.'

'True.'

Malicorne took up the ladder like a feather, and placed it upright against the wall. And, in order to try the experiment, he chose, or chance, perhaps, directed him to choose, the very window of the cabinet where La Vallière was. The ladder just reached the edge of the cornice, that is to say, the sill of the window; so that, by standing upon the last rung but one of the ladder a man of about the middle height,* as the King was, for instance, could easily hold a communication with those who might be in the room. Hardly had the ladder been properly placed than the King, dropping the assumed part he had been playing in the comedy, began to ascend the rungs of the ladder, which Malicorne held at the bottom. But hardly had he completed half the distance when a patrol of Swiss guards appeared in the garden and advanced straight towards them. The King descended with the utmost precipitation, and concealed himself among the trees. Malicorne at once perceived that he must offer himself as a sacrifice; for, if he, too, were to conceal himself, the guard would search everywhere until they had found either himself or the King, perhaps both. It would be far better, therefore, that he alone should be discovered. And, consequently, Malicorne hid himself so clumsily that he was the only one arrested. As soon as he was arrested Malicorne was taken to the guard-house; when there, he declared who he was, and was immediately recognised. In the meantime, by concealing himself first behind one clump of trees and then behind another, the King reached the side-door of his apartments, very much humiliated, and still more disappointed. More than that, the noise made in arresting Malicorne had drawn La Vallière and Montalais to their window; and even Madame herself had appeared at her own, with a pair of wax candles, asking what was the matter.

In the meantime, Malicorne sent for d'Artagnan, who did not waste a moment in hurrying to him. But it was in vain he attempted to make him understand his reasons, and in vain also that d'Artagnan did understand them; and, further, it was equally in vain that both their sharp and inventive minds endeavoured to give another turn to the adventure; there was no other resource left to Malicorne but to let it be supposed that he had wished to enter Mademoiselle de Montalais's apartment, as Saint-Aignan had passed for having wished to force Mademoiselle de Tonnay-Charente's door. Madame was inflexible; in the first place, because if Malicorne had, in fact, wished to enter her apartment at night through the window, and by means of the ladder, in order to see Montalais, it was a punishable offence on Malicorne's part, and he must be punished accordingly; and, in the second place, if Malicorne, instead of acting in his own name, had acted as an intermediary between La Vallière and a person whose name need not be mentioned, his crime was in that case even greater, since love, which is an excuse for everything, did not exist in the present case as an excuse for him. Madame therefore made the greatest possible disturbance about the matter, and obtained his dismissal from Monsieur's household, without reflecting, poor blind creature, that both Malicorne and Montalais held her fast in their clutches in consequence of her visit to de Guiche, and in a variety of other ways equally delicate. Montalais, who was furious, wished to revenge herself immediately, but Malicorne pointed out to her that the King's countenance would repay them for all the disgraces in the world, and that it was a great thing to have to suffer on His Majesty's account.

Malicorne was perfectly right, and, therefore, although Montalais had the spirit of ten women in her, he succeeded in bringing her round to his own opinion. And we must not omit to state that the King helped them to console themselves, for, in the first place, he presented Malicorne with fifty thousand francs as a compensation for the post he had lost, and, in the next place, he gave him an appointment in his own household, delighted to have an opportunity of revenging himself in such a manner upon Madame for all she had made him and La Vallière suffer. But as he no longer had Malicorne to steal his pocket-handkerchiefs and to measure ladders for him, the poor lover was in a terrible state. There seemed to be no hope, therefore, of ever getting near La Vallière again, so long as she should remain at the Palais Royal. All the dignities and all the money in the world could not remedy that. Fortunately, however, Malicorne was on the look-out, and this he did so successfully that he met Montalais, who, to do her justice, did her best to meet Malicorne. 'What do you do during the night in Madame's apartment,' he asked the young girl.

'Why, I go to sleep, of course,' she replied.

'But it is very wrong to sleep; it can hardly be possible that with the pain you are suffering you can manage to do so.'

'And what am I suffering from, may I ask.'

'Are you not in despair at my absence?'

'Of course not, since you have received fifty thousand francs and an appointment in the King's household.'

'That is a matter of no moment; you are exceedingly afflicted at not seeing me as you used to see me formerly, and more than all, you are in despair at my having lost Madame's confidence; come now, is not that true?'

'Perfectly true.'

'Very good; your distress of mind prevents you sleeping at night, and so you sob, and sigh, and blow your nose ten times every minute as loud as possible.'

'But, my dear Malicorne, Madame cannot endure the slightest noise near her.'

'I know that perfectly well; of course she can't endure anything; and so, I tell you, she will not waste a minute, when she sees your deep distress, in turning you out of her room without a moment's delay.'

'I understand——'

'Very fortunate you do.'

'Well, and what will happen next?'

'The next thing that will happen will be, that La Vallière finding herself alone without you, will groan and utter such loud lamentations that she will exhibit despair enough for two persons.'

'In that case she will be put into another room.'

'Precisely so.'

'Yes, but which?'

'Which?'

'Yes, that will puzzle you to say, Mr Inventor-General.'

'Not at all; wherever and whatever the room may be it will always be preferable to Madame's own room.'

'That is true.'

'Very good; so begin your lamentations a little to-night.'

'I certainly will not fail to do so.'

'And give La Vallière a hint also.'

'Oh! don't fear her, she cries quite enough already to herself.'

'Very well! all she has to do is to cry out loud.'

And they separated.

LXXX

WHICH TREATS OF CARPENTRY OPERATIONS, AND FURNISHES DETAILS UPON THE MODE OF CONSTRUCTING STAIRCASES

THE advice which had been given to Montalais was communicated by her to La Vallière, who could not but acknowledge that it was by no means deficient in judgment, and who, after a certain amount of resistance, arising rather from her timidity than from the indifference to the project, resolved to put it into execution. This story of the two girls weeping, and filling Madame's bedroom with the noisiest lamentations, was Malicorne's *chef-d'œuvre*. As nothing is so probable as improbability, so natural as romance, this kind of Arabian Nights story succeeded perfectly with Madame. The first thing she did was to send Montalais away, then, three days, or rather, three nights, afterwards, she had La Vallière removed. She gave to the latter one of the small rooms on the top storey, situated immediately over the apartments allotted to the gentlemen of Monsieur's suite. One storey only, that is to say, a mere flooring, separated the maids of honour from the officers and gentlemen of her husband's household. A private staircase, which was placed under Madame de Navailles's surveillance, was the only means of communication. For greater safety, Madame de Navailles, who had heard of His Majesty's previous attempts, had the windows of the rooms, and the openings of the chimneys carefully barred. There was, therefore, every possible security provided for Mademoiselle de la Vallière, whose room bore more resemblance to a cage than to anything else. When Mademoiselle de la Vallière was in her own room, and she was there very frequently, for Madame scarcely ever had any occasion for her services, since she once knew she was safe under Madame de Navailles's inspection. Mademoiselle de la Vallière had no other means of amusing herself than that of looking through the bars of her windows. It happened, therefore, that one morning, as she was looking out as usual, she perceived Malicorne at one of the windows exactly opposite to her own. He held a carpenter's rule in his hand, was surveying the buildings, and seemed to be adding up some figures on paper. La Vallière recognised Malicorne and bowed to him; Malicorne in his turn replied by a profound bow, and disappeared from the window. She was surprised at this marked coolness, so unusual with his unfailing good humour, but she remembered that he had lost his appointment on her account, and that he could hardly be very amiably disposed towards her, since, in all probability, she would never be in a position to recompense him for what he had lost. She knew how to forgive offences, and with still greater reason could she sympathise with misfortune. La Vallière would have asked Montalais her opinion, if she had been there; but she was absent, it being the hour she usually devoted to her own correspondence. Suddenly, La Vallière observed something thrown from the window where Malicorne had been standing, pass across the open space which separated the two windows from each other, enter her room through the iron bars, and roll upon the floor. She advanced with no little curiosity towards this object, and picked it up; it was a winder for silk, only, in this instance, instead of silk, a small piece of paper was rolled round it. La Vallière unrolled it, and read the following:—

'MADEMOISELLE.—I am exceedingly anxious to learn two things: the first is, to know if the flooring of your apartment is wood or brick; the second, to know at what distance your bed is placed from the window. Forgive my importunity, and will you be good enough to send me an answer by the same way you receive this letter—that is to say by means of the silk winder;

only, instead of throwing it into my room, as I have thrown it into yours, which will be too difficult for you to attempt, have the goodness merely to let it fall. Believe me, mademoiselle, your most humble and most respectful servant, MALICORNE.'

'Write the reply, if you please, upon the letter itself.'

'Ah! poor fellow,' exclaimed La Vallière, 'he must have gone out of his mind;' and she directed towards her correspondent— of whom she caught but a faint glimpse, in consequence of the darkness of his room, a look full of compassionate consideration. Malicorne understood her, and shook his head, as if he meant to say, 'No, no, I am not out of my mind; be quite satisfied.' She smiled as if still in doubt.

'No, no,' he signified by a gesture, 'my head is perfectly right,' and pointed to his head; then, after moving his hand like a man who writes very rapidly, he put his hands together as if entreating her to write.

La Vallière, even if he were mad, saw no impropriety in doing what Malicorne requested her; she took a pencil and wrote 'wood'; and then counted ten paces from her window to her bed, and wrote, 'ten feet'; and having done this, she looked out again at Malicorne, who bowed to her, signifying that he was about to descend. La Vallière understood that it was to pick up the silk winder. She approached the window, and, in accordance with Malicorne's instructions, let it fall. The winder was still rolling along the flagstones as Malicorne started after it, overtook and picked it up, began to peel it as a monkey would do with a nut, and ran straight towards M. de Saint-Aignan's apartments. Saint-Aignan had selected, or rather solicited, that this room might be as near the King as possible, as certain plants seek the sun's rays in order to develop themselves more luxuriantly. His apartment consisted of two rooms in that portion of the palace occupied by Louis XIV himself. M. de Saint-Aignan was very proud of this proximity, which afforded easy access to His Majesty, and, more than that, the favour of unexpected occasional meetings. At the moment we are now referring to he was engaged in having both his rooms magnificently carpeted, with the expectation of re- ceiving the honour of frequent visits from the King; for His

Majesty, since his passion for La Vallière, had chosen Saint-Aignan as his confidant, and could not, in fact, do without him, either night or day. Malicorne introduced himself to the Comte and met with no difficulties, because he had been favourably noticed by the King; and, also, because the credit which one man may happen to enjoy is always a bait for others. Saint-Aignan asked his visitor if he brought any news for him.

'Yes; great news,' replied the latter.

'Ah! ah!' said Saint-Aignan, 'what is it?'

'Mademoiselle de la Vallière has changed her quarters.'

'What do you mean?' said Saint-Aignan, opening his eyes very wide. 'She was living in the same apartments as Madame.'

'Precisely so; but Madame got tired of her proximity, and has installed her in a room which is situated exactly above your future apartment.'

'What! up there,' exclaimed Saint-Aignan, with surprise, and pointing at the floor above him with his finger.

'No' said Malicorne, 'yonder,' and indicated the building opposite.

'What do you mean then, by saying, that her room is above my apartment?'

'Because I am sure that your apartment ought most naturally to be under Mademoiselle de la Vallière's room.'

Saint-Aignan, at this remark, gave poor Malicorne a look similar to one of those La Vallière had already given him a quarter of an hour before, that is to say, he thought he had lost his senses.

'Monsieur,' said Malicorne to him, 'I wish to answer what you are thinking about.'

'What do you mean by "what I am thinking about"?'

'My reason is that you have not clearly understood what I want to convey.'

'I admit it.'

'Well, then, you are aware that underneath the apartments set apart for Madame's maids of honour the gentlemen in attendance on the King and on Monsieur are lodged.'

'Yes, I know that, since Manicamp, de Wardes, and others are living there.'

'Precisely. Well, monsieur, admire the singularity of the

circumstances; the two rooms destined for M. de Guiche are exactly the very two rooms situated underneath those which Mademoiselle de Montalais and Mademoiselle de la Vallière occupy.'

'Well; what then?'

'"What then," do you say? Why, these two rooms are empty, since M. de Guiche is now lying wounded at Fontainebleau.'

'I assure you, my dear monsieur, I cannot guess your meaning.'

'Well! if I had the happiness to call myself Saint-Aignan I should guess immediately.'

'And what would you do then?'

'I should at once change the rooms I am occupying here for those which M. de Guiche is not using yonder.'

'Can you suppose such a thing?' said Saint-Aignan disdainfully; 'What! abandon the chief post of honour, the proximity to the King, a privilege conceded only to princes of the blood, to dukes, and peers! Permit me to tell you, my dear Monsieur de Malicorne, that you must be out of your senses.'

'Monsieur,' replied the young man seriously, 'you commit two mistakes. My name is Malicorne simply; and I am in perfect possession of all my senses.' Then, drawing a paper from his pocket, he said, 'Listen to what I am going to say; and, afterwards, I will show you this paper.'

'I am listening,' said Saint-Aignan.

'You know that Madame looks after La Vallière as carefully as did Argus after the nymph Io.'

'I do.'

'You know that the King has sought for an opportunity, but uselessly, of speaking to the prisoner, and that neither you nor myself have yet succeeded in procuring him this piece of good fortune.'

'You certainly ought to know something on that subject, my poor Malicorne.'

'Very good; what do you suppose would happen to the man whose imagination devised some means of bringing the two lovers together?'

'Oh! the King would have no bounds to his gratitude.'

'Let me ask you, then, M. de Saint-Aignan, whether you would not be curious to taste a little of this royal gratitude?'

'Certainly,' replied Saint-Aignan, 'any favour of my master, as a recognition of the proper discharge of my duty, would assuredly be most precious to me.'

'In that case, look at this paper, Monsieur le Comte.'

'What is it—a plan?'

'Yes; a plan of M. de Guiche's two rooms, which, in all probability, will soon be your two rooms.'

'Oh! no, whatever may happen.'

'Why so?'

'Because my own rooms are the envy of too many gentlemen, to whom I shall not certainly give them up; M. de Roquelaure, for instance, M. de la Ferté, and M. de Dangeau, would all be anxious to get them.'

'In that case I shall leave you, Monsieur le Comte, and I shall go and offer to one of those gentlemen the plan I have just shown you, together with the advantages annexed to it.'

'But why do you not keep them for yourself?' inquired Saint-Aignan suspiciously.

'Because the King would never do me the honour of paying me a visit openly, whilst he would readily go and see any one of those gentlemen.'

'What! the King would go and see any one of those gentlemen?'

'Go! most certainly would he, ten times instead of once. Is it possible you can ask me if the King would go to an apartment which would bring him nearer to Mademoiselle de la Vallière?'

'Yes, indeed, admirably near her, with a whole floor between them.'

Malicorne unfolded the piece of paper which had been wrapped round the bobbin. 'Monsieur le Comte,' he said, 'have the goodness to observe that the flooring of Mademoiselle de la Vallière's room is merely a wooden flooring.'

'Well?'

'Well! all you would have to do would be to get hold of a journeyman carpenter, lock him up in your apartments, without letting him know where you have taken him to; and let him make a hole in your ceiling, and consequently in the flooring of Mademoiselle de la Vallière's room.'

'Good Heavens!' exclaimed Saint-Aignan as if dazzled.

'What is the matter?' said Malicorne.

'Nothing, except that you have hit upon a singularly bold idea, monsieur.'

'It will seem a very trifling one to the King, I assure you.'

'Lovers never think of the risk they run.'

'What danger do you apprehend, Monsieur le Comte?'

'Why effecting such an opening as that will make a terrible noise; it will be heard over the whole palace.'

'Oh! Monsieur le Comte, I am quite sure that the carpenter I shall select shall not make the slightest noise in the world. He will saw an opening six feet square, with a saw covered with oakum, and no one, not even those immediately adjoining, will know that he is at work.'

'My dear Monsieur Malicorne, you astound, you positively bewilder me.'

'To continue,' replied Malicorne quietly, 'in the room, the ceiling of which you have cut through, you will put up a staircase, which will either allow Mademoiselle de la Vallière to descend into your room or the King to ascend into Mademoiselle de la Vallière's room.'

'But the staircase will be seen.'

'No; for in your room it will be hidden by a partition over which you will hang a tapestry similar to that which covers the rest of the apartment; and in Mademoiselle de la Vallière's room it will not be seen, for the trap-door which will be a part of the flooring itself will be made to open under the bed.'

'Of course,' said Saint-Aignan, whose eyes began to sparkle with delight.

'And now, Monsieur le Comte, there is no occasion to make you admit that the King will frequently come to the room where such a staircase is constructed. I think that M. Dangeau, particularly, will be struck by my idea, and I shall now go and explain it to him.'

'But, my dear Monsieur Malicorne, you forget that you spoke to me about it first, and that I have consequently the right of priority.'

'Do you wish for the preference?'

'Do I wish it? Of course I do.'

'The fact is, Monsieur de Saint-Aignan, I am presenting you with that which is as good as the promise of an additional step in the peerage, and perhaps even a good estate to accompany your dukedom.'

'At least,' replied Saint-Aignan, 'it will give me an opportunity of showing the King that he is not mistaken in occasionally calling me his friend; an opportunity, dear M. Malicorne, for which I am indebted to you.'

'And which you will not forget to remember?' inquired Malicorne smiling.

'Nothing will delight me more, monsieur.'

'But I am not the King's friend, I am simply his attendant.'

'Yes; and if you imagine that that staircase is as good as a dukedom for myself, I think there will certainly be letters of nobility for you.' Malicorne bowed.

'All I have to do now,' said Saint-Aignan, 'is to move as soon as possible.'

'I do not think the King will object to it; ask his permission, however.'

'I will go and see him this very moment.'

'And I will run and get the carpenter I was speaking of.'

'When will he be here?'

'This very evening.'

'Do not forget your precautions.'

'He shall be brought with his eyes bandaged.'

'And I will send you one of my carriages.'

'Without your coat of arms.'

'With one of my servants without livery. But, stay, what will La Vallière say if she sees what is going on?'

'Oh! I can assure you she will be very much interested in the operation, and equally sure that if the King has not courage enough to ascend to her room she will have sufficient curiosity to come down to him.'

'We will live in hope,' said Saint-Aignan; 'and now I am off to His Majesty; at what time will the carpenter be here?'

'At eight o'clock.'

'How long do you suppose he will take to make this opening?'

'About a couple of hours; only afterwards he must have sufficient time to effect what might be called the junction between the two rooms. One night and a portion of the following day will do; we must not reckon upon less than two days, including putting up the staircase.'

'Two days; that is very long.'

'Nay; when one undertakes to open a door into paradise itself, we must at least take care it is properly done.'

'Quite right; so farewell for a short time, dear M. Malicorne. I shall begin to remove the day after to-morrow, in the evening.'

LXXXI

THE PROMENADE BY TORCHLIGHT

SAINT-AIGNAN, delighted with what he had just heard, and rejoiced at what the future foreshadowed for him, bent his steps towards de Guiche's two rooms. He who, a quarter of an hour previously, would not have yielded up his own rooms for a million francs, was now ready to expend a million, if it were necessary, upon the acquisition of the two happy rooms he coveted so eagerly. But he did not meet with so many obstacles. M. de Guiche did not yet know whereabouts he was to lodge, and besides, he was still far too suffering to trouble himself about his lodgings; and so Saint-Aignan obtained de Guiche's two rooms without difficulty. As for M. Dangeau, he was so immeasurably delighted that he did not even give himself the trouble to think whether Saint-Aignan had any particular reason for removing. Within an hour after Saint-Aignan's new resolution, he was in possession of the two rooms; and ten minutes after Malicorne entered, followed by the decorators and movers. During this time, the King asked for Saint-Aignan; the valet ran to his late apartments and found M. Dangeau there; Dangeau sent him on to M. de Guiche's, and Saint-Aignan was found there; but a little delay had, of course, taken place, and the King had already exhibited once or twice evident signs of impatience, when Saint-Aignan entered his royal master's presence, quite out of breath. 'You, too, abandon me, then,' said Louis XIV in a similar tone of lamentation to that which Cæsar, eighteen hundred years previously, had used the *tu quoque*.*

'Sire, I am very far from abandoning you, for, on the contrary, I am busily occupied in changing my lodgings.'

'What do you mean? I thought you had finished moving three days ago.'

'Yes, sire. But I don't find myself comfortable where I am, and so I am going to change to the opposite side of the building.'

'Was I not right when I said you were abandoning me!' exclaimed the King. 'Oh! this exceeds all endurance. But so it is: there was only one woman for whom my heart cared at all, and all my family is leagued together to tear her from me; and my friend, to whom I confided my distress, and who helped me to bear up under it, has become wearied of my complaints and is going to leave me without even asking my permission.'

Saint-Aignan began to laugh. The King at once guessed there must be some mystery in this want of respect.

'What is it?' cried the King, full of hope.

'This, sire, that the friend whom the King slanders is going to try if he cannot restore to his sovereign the happiness he has lost.'

'Are you going to let me see La Vallière?' said Louis XIV.

'I cannot say so, positively, but I hope so.'

'How—how? tell me that, Saint-Aignan. I wish to know what your plan is, and to help you with all my power.'

'Sire,' replied Saint-Aignan, 'I cannot, even myself, tell very well how I must set about attaining success; but I have every reason to believe that from to-morrow——'

'To-morrow, do you say! What happiness! But why are you changing your rooms?'

'In order to serve your Majesty to greater advantage.'

'How can your moving serve me?'

'Do you happen to know where the two rooms destined for de Guiche are situated?'

'Yes.'

'Well, your Majesty now knows where I am going.'

'Very likely; but that does not help me.'

'What! is it possible you do not understand, sire, that above de Guiche's lodgings are two rooms, one of which is Mademoiselle de Montalais's and the other——'

'La Vallière's, is it not so, Saint-Aignan? Oh, yes, yes. It is a brilliant idea, Saint-Aignan, a true friend's idea, a poet's idea; in bringing me nearer her from whom the whole world seems to unite to separate me; you are far more than Pylades was for Orestes, or Patroclus for Achilles.'*

'Sire,' said Aignan, with a smile, 'I question whether, if your Majesty were to know my projects in their full extent, you would continue to confer such grandiose qualifications upon me. Ah! sire, I know how very different are the epithets which certain puritans of the court will not fail to apply to me when they learn what I intend to do for your Majesty.'

'Saint-Aignan, I am dying from impatience; I am in a perfect fever; I shall never be able to wait until to-morrow—— To-morrow! why, to-morrow is an eternity!'

'And yet, sire, I shall require you, if you please, to go out presently and divert your impatience by a good walk.'

'With you—agreed; we will talk about your projects, we will talk of her.'

'Nay, sire, I remain here.'

'Whom shall I go out with, then?'

'With the Queens and all the ladies of the court.'

'Nothing shall induce me to do that, Saint-Aignan.'

'And yet, sire, you must do it.'

'No, no—a thousand times no! I will never again expose myself to the horrible torture of being close to her, of seeing her, of touching her dress as I pass by her, and yet not to be able to say a word to her. No, I renounce a torture which you suppose to be happiness, but which consumes and eats away my very life; to see her in the presence of strangers and not to tell her that I love her, when my whole being reveals my affection and betrays me to every one; no! I have sworn never to do it again, and I will keep my oath.'

'Yet, sire, pray listen to me for a moment.'

'I will listen to nothing, Saint-Aignan.'

'In that case, I will continue; it is most urgent, sire—pray understand me, it is of the greatest importance—that Madame and her maids of honour should be absent for two hours from the palace.'

'I cannot understand your meaning at all, Saint-Aignan.'

'It is hard for me to give my sovereign directions what to do;

but in this circumstance I do give you directions, sire; and either
a hunting or promenade party must be got up.'

'But if I were to do what you wish it would be a caprice, a
mere whim. In displaying such an impatient humour I show my
whole court that I have no control over my own feelings. Do not
people already say that I am dreaming of the conquest of the
world, but that I ought previously to begin by achieving a conquest over myself.'

'Those who say so, sire, are insolent and factious persons; but
whoever they may be, if your Majesty prefers to listen to them,
I have nothing further to say. In such a case, that which we have
fixed to take place to-morrow must be postponed indefinitely.'

'Nay, Saint-Aignan, I will go out this evening—I will go by
torchlight to sleep at Saint-Germain; I will breakfast there to-
morrow, and will return to Paris by three o'clock. Will that do?'

'Admirably.'

'In that case I will set out this evening at eight o'clock.'

'Your Majesty had fixed upon the exact minute.'

'And you will positively tell me nothing more?'

'It is because I have nothing more to tell you. Industry goes
for something in this world, sire; but yet chance plays so important a part in it that I have been accustomed to leave her the
narrowest part, confident that she will manage so as to always
take the widest.'

'Well, I abandon myself entirely to you.'

'And you are quite right.'

Comforted in this manner, the King went immediately to
Madame, to whom he announced the intended expedition.
Madame fancied at the first moment that she saw in this unexpectedly arranged party a plot of the King's to converse with
La Vallière, either on the road, under cover of the darkness, or
in some other way, but she took especial care to show nothing
of her fancies to her brother-in-law, and accepted the invitation
with a smile upon her lips. She gave directions aloud that her
maids of honour should accompany her, secretly intending in
the evening to take the most effectual steps to interfere with His
Majesty's attachment. Then when she was alone, and at the very
moment the poor lover, who had issued his orders for the departure, was revelling in the idea that Mademoiselle de la Vallière

would form one of the party—at the very moment, perhaps, when he was luxuriating in the sad happiness which persecuted lovers enjoy, of realising by the sense of sight alone all the delights of an interdicted possession—at that very moment, we say, Madame, who was surrounded by her maids of honour, said:—'Two ladies will be enough for me this evening. Mademoiselle de Tonnay-Charente and Mademoiselle de Montalais.'

La Vallière had anticipated the omission of herself and was prepared for it; but persecution had rendered her courageous, and she did not give Madame the pleasure of seeing on her face the impression of the shock her heart had received. On the contrary, smiling with that ineffable gentleness which gave an angelic expression to her features—'In that case, Madame, I shall be at liberty this evening, I suppose?' she said.

'Of course.'

'I shall be able to employ it, then, in progressing with that piece of tapestry which your Highness has been good enough to notice, and which I have already had the honour of offering to you.'

And having made a respectful obeisance, she withdrew to her own apartment; Mesdemoiselles de Tonnay-Charente and de Montalais did the same. The rumour of the intended promenade was soon spread all over the palace; ten minutes afterwards Malicorne learned Madame's resolution, and slipped under Montalais's door a note in the following terms:—

'La Vallière must positively pass the night with Madame.'

Montalais, in pursuance of the compact she had entered into, began by burning the paper, and then sat down to reflect. Montalais was a girl full of expedients, and so had very soon arranged her plan. Towards five o'clock, which was the hour for her to repair to Madame's apartment, she was running across the courtyard, and had reached within a dozen paces of a group of officers, when she uttered a cry, fell gracefully on one knee, rose again, and walked on limpingly. The gentlemen ran forward to her assistance; Montalais had sprained her foot. Faithful to the discharge of her duty, she insisted, however, notwithstanding her accident, upon going to Madame's apartment.

'What is the matter, and why do you limp so?' she inquired: 'I mistook you for La Vallière.'

Montalais related how it had happened, that in hurrying on, in order to arrive as quickly as possible, she had sprained her foot. Madame seemed to pity her, and wished to have a surgeon sent for immediately, but she, assuring her that there was nothing really serious in the accident, said: 'My only regret, Madame, is, that it will preclude my attendance on you, and I should have begged Mademoiselle de la Vallière to take my place with your royal Highness, but——' seeing that Madame frowned, she added,—'I have not done so.'

'Why did not you do so?' inquired Madame.

'Because poor La Vallière seemed so happy to have her liberty for a whole evening and night too that I did not feel courageous enough to ask her to take my place.'

'What, is she so delighted as that?' inquired Madame, struck by these words.

'She is wild with delight; she, who is always so melancholy, was singing like a bird. Besides, your Highness knows how much she detests going out, and also that her character has a spice of wildness in it.'

'Oh, oh,' thought Madame, 'this extreme delight hardly seems natural to me.'

'She has already made all her arrangements for dining in her own room *tête-à-tête* with one of her favourite books. And then, as your Highness has six other young ladies who would be delighted to accompany you, I did not make my proposal to La Vallière.' Madame did not say a word in reply.

'Have I acted properly?' continued Montalais, with a slight fluttering of the heart, seeing the little success that attended the *ruse de guerre* which she had relied upon with so much confidence that she had not thought it even necessary to try and find another. 'Does Madame approve of what I have done?' she continued.

Madame was reflecting that the King could very easily leave Saint-Germain* during the night, and that, as it was only four leagues and a half from Paris to Saint-Germain, he might very easily be in Paris in an hour's time. 'Tell me,' she said, 'whether La Vallière, when she heard of your accident, offered at least to bear you company?'

'O! she does not yet know of my accident; but even did she

know of it, I shall not most certainly ask her to do anything which might interfere with her own plans. I think she wishes this evening to realise quietly by herself that amusement of the late King, when he said to M. de Cinq-Mars, "Let us amuse ourselves by doing nothing and making ourselves miserable."'

Madame felt convinced that some mysterious love adventure was hidden beneath this strong desire for solitude. This mystery might possibly be Louis's return during the night; it could not be doubted any longer La Vallière had been informed of his intending return, and that was the reason of her delight at having to remain behind at the Palais Royal. It was a plan settled and arranged beforehand.

'I will not be their dupe, though,' said Madame, and she took a decisive step. 'Mademoiselle de Montalais,' she said, 'will you have the goodness to inform your friend, Mademoiselle de la Vallière, that I am exceedingly sorry to disarrange her projects of solitude, but that instead of being bored by remaining behind alone as she wished, she will be good enough to accompany us to Saint-Germain and be bored there.'

'Ah! poor La Vallière,' said Montalais compassionately, but with her heart throbbing with delight, 'oh, Madame! could there not be some means——'

'Enough,' said Madame, 'I desire it! I prefer Mademoiselle La Baume Le Blanc's society to that of any one else. Go, and send her to me, and take care of your foot.'

Montalais did not wait for the order to be repeated; she returned to her room, wrote an answer to Malicorne, and slipped it under the carpet. The answer simply said: 'She is going.' A Spartan could not have written more laconically.

'By this means,' thought Madame, 'I will look narrowly after all on the road; she shall sleep near me during the night, and His Majesty must be very clever if he can exchange a single word with Mademoiselle de la Vallière.'

La Vallière received the order to set off with the same indifferent gentleness with which she had received the order to remain. But, inwardly, her delight was extreme, and she looked upon this change in the Princess's resolution as a consolation which Providence had sent her. With less penetration than Madame possessed, she attributed all to chance. While every one, with the exception of those in disgrace, of those who were ill, and those who were suffering from sprains, were proceeding towards Saint-Germain, Malicorne smuggled his workman into the palace in one of M. de Saint-Aignan's carriages, and led him into the room corresponding to La Vallière's room. The man set to work, tempted by the splendid reward which had been promised him. As the very best tools and implements had been selected from the reserve stock belonging to the engineers attached to the King's household—and among others, a saw with teeth so sharp and well tempered that it could, under water even, cut through oaken joists as hard as iron—the work in question advanced very rapidly, and a square portion of the ceiling, taken from between two of the joists, fell into the arms of Saint-Aignan, Malicorne, the workman, and a confidential valet, the latter being one brought into the world to see and hear everything but to repeat nothing. In accordance with a new plan indicated by Malicorne, the opening was effected in an angle of the room, and for this reason. As there was no dressing-closet adjoining La Vallière's room, she had solicited, and had that very morning obtained, a large screen intended to serve as a partition. The screen which had been conceded was perfectly sufficient to conceal the opening, which would, besides, be hidden by all the artifices which cabinet-makers have at their command. The opening having been made, the workman glided between the joists, and found himself in La Vallière's room. When there, he cut a square opening in the flooring, and out of the boards he manufactured a trap so accurately fitting into the opening that the most practised eye could hardly detect the necessary interstices made by joining the flooring. Malicorne had provided for everything; a ring and a couple of hinges which had been bought for the purpose were affixed to the trap-door; and a small circular staircase had been bought ready-made by the industrious Malicorne, who had paid two thousand francs for it. It was higher than was required, but the carpenter reduced the number of steps, and it was found to suit exactly. This staircase, destined to receive so illustrious a weight, was merely fastened to the wall by a couple of iron clamps, and its base was fixed into the floor of the Comte's room by two iron pegs screwed down tightly, so that the King and all his cabinet councillors too, might pass up and down the staircase without any fear. Every blow of the hammer fell upon a thick pad or cushion, and the saw was not used until the handle had been wrapped in wool, and the blade steeped in oil. The noisiest part of the work, moreover, had taken place during the night and early in the morning, that is to say, when La Vallière and Madame were both absent. When, about two o'clock in the afternoon, the court returned to the Palais Royal, La Vallière went up into her own room. Everything was in its place, and not the smallest particle of sawdust, not the smallest chip, was left to bear witness to the violation of her domicile. Saint-Aignan, however, who had wished to do his utmost in getting the work done, had torn his fingers and his shirt too, and had expended no ordinary quantity of perspiration in the King's service. The palms of his hands especially were covered with blisters, occasioned by his having held the ladder for Malicorne. He had, moreover, brought, one by one, the five pieces of the staircase, each consisting of two steps. In fact, we can safely assert, that if the King had seen him so ardently at work, His Majesty would have sworn an eternal gratitude towards his faithful attendant. As Malicorne had anticipated, the workman had completely finished the job in twenty-four hours; he received twenty-four louis, and left overwhelmed with delight, for he had gained in one day as much as six months' hard work would have procured him. No one had the slightest suspicion of what had taken place in the room under Mademoiselle de la Vallière's apartment. But in the evening of the second day, at the very moment La Vallière had just left Madame's circle and had returned to her own room, she heard a slight creaking sound at the end of it. Astonished, she looked to see whence it proceeded, and the noise began again. 'Who is there?' she said in a tone of alarm.

'I,' replied the well-known voice of the King.

'You! you!' cried the young girl, who for a moment fancied herself under the influence of a dream. 'But, where? You, sire?'

'Here,' replied the King, opening one of the folds of the screen, and appearing like a ghost at the end of the room.

La Vallière uttered a loud cry, and fell trembling into an armchair as the King advanced respectfully towards her.*

LXXXII

THE APPARITION

LA VALLIÈRE very soon recovered from her surprise, for, owing to his respectful bearing, the King inspired her with more confidence by his presence than his sudden appearance had deprived her of. But, as he noticed that that which made La Vallière most uneasy was the means by which he had effected an entrance into her room, he explained to her the system of the staircase concealed by the screen, and strongly disavowed the notion of his being a supernatural appearance.

'Oh! sire!' said La Vallière, shaking her fair head with a most engaging smile, 'present or absent, you do not appear to my mind more at one time than at another.'

'Which means, Louise——'

'Oh, what you know so well, sire; that there is not one moment in which the poor girl whose secret you surprised at Fontainebleau, and whom you came to snatch from the foot of the cross itself, does not think of you.'

'Louise, you overwhelm me with joy and happiness.'

La Vallière smiled mournfully and continued: 'But, sire, have you reflected that your ingenious invention could not be of the slightest service to us.'

'Why so? Tell me—I am waiting most anxiously.'

'Because this room may be subject to being searched at any moment of the day. Madame herself may, at any time, come here accidentally; my companions run in at any moment they please. To fasten the door on the inside is to denounce myself as plainly as if I had written above, "No admittance,—the King is here." Even now, sire, at this very moment, there is nothing to prevent the door opening and your Majesty being seen here.'

'In that case,' said the King laughingly, 'I should indeed be taken for a phantom, for no one can tell in what way I came here. Besides it is only phantoms who can pass through brick walls, or floors and ceilings.'

'Oh! sire, reflect for a moment how terrible the scandal would be! Nothing equal to it could ever have been previously said about the maids of honour, poor creatures! whom evil report, however, hardly ever spares.'

'And your conclusion from all this, my dear Louise,—come, explain yourself.'

'Alas! it is a hard thing to say—but your Majesty must suppress staircase plots, surprises and all; for the evil consequences which would result from your being found here would be far greater than the happiness of seeing each other.'

'Well, Louise,' replied the King tenderly, 'instead of removing this staircase, by which I have ascended, there is a far more simple means, of which you have not thought.'

'A means—another means!'

'Yes, another. Oh, you do not love me as I love you, Louise, since my invention is quicker than yours.'

She looked at the King, who held out his hand to her, which she took and gently pressed between her own.

'You were saying,' continued the King, 'that I shall be detected coming here, where any one who pleases can enter.'

'Stay, sire; at this very moment, even while you are speaking about it, I tremble with dread of your being discovered.'

'But you would not be found out, Louise, if you were to descend the staircase which leads to the rooms underneath.'

'Oh, sire! what do you say?' cried Louise in alarm.

'You do not quite understand me, Louise, since you get offended at my very first word; first of all, do you know to whom the apartments underneath belong?'

'To M. de Guiche, sire, I know.'

'Not at all; they are M. de Saint-Aignan's.'

'Are you sure?' cried La Vallière; and this exclamation which escaped from the young girl's joyous heart made the King's heart throb with delight.

'Yes, to Saint-Aignan, our friend,' he said.

'But, sire,' returned La Vallière, 'I cannot visit M. de Saint-Aignan's rooms any more than I could M. de Guiche's. It is impossible—impossible.'

'And yet, Louise, I should have thought that, under the safeguard of the King, you could venture anything.'

'Under the safeguard of the King,' she said, with a look full of tenderness.

'You have faith in my word, I hope, Louise?'

'Yes, sire, when you are not present; but when you are present—when you speak to me,—when I look upon you, I have faith in nothing.'

'What can possibly be done to reassure you?'

'It is scarcely respectful, I know, to doubt the King, but you are not the King for me.'

'Thank Heaven!—I, at least, hope so most fervently; you see how anxiously I am trying to find or invent a means of removing all difficulties. Stay; would the presence of a third person reassure you?'

'The presence of M. de Saint-Aignan would certainly.'

'Really, Louise, you wound me by your suspicions.'

Louise did not answer, she merely looked steadfastly at him with that clear, piercing gaze which penetrates the very heart, and said softly to herself, 'Alas! alas! it is not you of whom I am afraid—it is not you upon whom my doubts would fall.'

'Well,' said the King sighing, 'I agree; and M. de Saint-Aignan, who enjoys the inestimable privilege of reassuring you, shall always be present at our conversations, I promise you.'

'You promise that, sire?'

'Upon my honour as a gentleman; and you, on your side——'

'Oh, wait, sire, that is not all yet; for such conversations, ought, at least, to have a reasonable motive of some kind for M. de Saint-Aignan.'

'Dear Louise, every shade of delicacy of feeling is yours, and my only wish is to equal you on that point. It shall be just as you wish; therefore, our conversations shall have a reasonable motive, and I have already hit upon one; so that from to-morrow, if you like——'

'To-morrow?'

'Do you mean that that is not soon enough?' exclaimed the King, caressing La Vallière's hand between his own.

At this moment the sound of steps was heard in the corridor.

'Sire, sire!' cried La Vallière, 'some one is coming; do you hear? Oh, fly! fly! I implore you.'

The King made but one bound from the chair where he was

sitting to his hiding place behind the screen. He had barely time, for as he drew one of the folds before him, the handle of the door was turned, and Montalais appeared at the threshold. As a matter of course she entered quite naturally, and without any ceremony, for she knew perfectly well that to knock at the door beforehand would be showing a suspicion towards La Vallière which would be displeasing to her. She accordingly entered, and after a rapid glance round the room, whereby she observed two chairs very close to each other, she was so long in shutting the door, which seemed difficult to close, one can hardly tell how or why, that the King had ample time to raise the trap door, and to descend again to Saint-Aignan's room.

'Louise,' she said to her, 'I want to talk to you, and seriously, too.'

'Good heavens! my dear Aure, what is the matter now?'

'The matter is, that Madame suspects everything.'

'Explain yourself.'

'Is there any occasion for us to enter into explanations, and do you not understand what I mean? Come, you must have noticed the fluctuations in Madame's humour during several days past; you must have noticed how she first kept you close beside her, then dismissed you, and then sent for you again.'

'Yes, I have noticed it, of course.'

'Well, it seems that Madame has now succeeded in obtaining sufficient information, for she has now gone straight to the point, as there is nothing further left in France to withstand the torrent which sweeps away all obstacles before it—you know what I mean by the torrent?'

La Vallière hid her face in her hands.

'I mean,' continued Montalais pitilessly, 'that torrent which has burst through the gates of the Carmelites of Chaillot, and overthrown all the prejudices of the court, both at Fontainebleau and at Paris.'

'Alas! alas!' murmured La Vallière, her face still covered by her hands, and her tears streaming through her fingers.

'Oh, don't distress yourself in that manner, for you have only heard half of your troubles.'

'In Heaven's name,' exclaimed the young girl in great anxiety, 'what is the matter?'

'Well, then, this is how the matter stands; Madame, who can no longer rely upon any further assistance in France; for she has, one after the other, made use of the two Queens, of Monsieur, and the whole court too, now bethinks herself of a certain person who has certain pretended rights over you.'

La Vallière became as white as a marble statue.

'This person,' continued Montalais, 'is not in Paris at this moment; but, if I am not mistaken, is in England.'

'Yes, yes,' breathed La Vallière, almost overwhelmed with terror.

'And is to be found, I think, at the court of Charles II; am I right?'

'Yes.'

'Well, this evening a letter has been despatched by Madame to Saint James's, with directions for the courier to go straight on to Hampton Court,* which I believe is one of the royal residences, situated about a dozen miles from London.'

'Yes; well?'

'Well; as Madame writes regularly to London once a fortnight, and as the ordinary courier left for London not more than three days ago, I have been thinking that some serious circumstance could alone have induced her to write again so soon, for you know she is a very indolent correspondent.'

'Yes.'

'This letter has been written, therefore, something tells me so at least, on your account.'

'On my account?' repeated the unhappy girl, mechanically.

'And I, who saw the letter lying on Madame's desk before she sealed it, fancied I could read——'

'What did you fancy you could read?'

'I might possibly have been mistaken, though——'

'Tell me,—what was it?'

'The name of Bragelonne.'

La Vallière rose hurriedly from her chair, a prey to the most painful agitation. 'Montalais,' she said, her voice broken by sobs, 'all the smiling dreams of youth and innocence have fled already. I have nothing now to conceal, either from you or from any one else. My life is exposed to every one's inspection, and can be opened like a book, in which all the world can read, from the

King himself to the first passer-by. Aure, dearest Aure, what can I do—what will become of me?'

Montalais approached close to her, and said, 'Consult your own heart, of course.'

'Well; I do not love M. de Bragelonne; when I say I do not love him, understand that I love him as the most affectionate sister could love the best of brothers, but that is not what he requires, nor what I have promised him.'

'In fact, you love the King,' said Montalais, 'and that is a sufficiently good excuse.'

'Yes, I do love the King,' hoarsely murmured the young girl, 'and I have paid dearly enough to pronounce those words. And now, Montalais, tell me—what can you do, either for me or against me, in my present position?'

'You must speak more clearly still.'

'What am I to say, then?'

'And so you have nothing very particular to tell me?'

'No!' said Louise in astonishment.

'Very good; and so all you have to ask me is my advice respecting M. Raoul?'

'Nothing else.'

'It is a very delicate subject,' replied Montalais.

'No, it is nothing of the kind. Ought I to marry him in order to keep the promise I made, or ought I to continue to listen to the King?'

'You have really placed me in a very difficult position,' said Montalais, smiling; 'you ask me if you ought to marry Raoul, whose friend I am, and whom I shall mortally offend in giving my opinion against him; and then, you ask me if you should cease to listen to the King, whose subject I am, and whom I should also offend if I were to advise you in a particular way. Ah, Louise, you seem to hold a difficult position at a very cheap rate.'

'You have not understood me, Aure,' said La Vallière, wounded by the slightly mocking tone of her companion; 'if I were to marry M. de Bragelonne, I should be far from bestowing on him the happiness he deserves; but, for the same reason, if I listen to the King he would become the possessor of one indifferently good in very many respects I admit, but one on whom his affection confers an appearance of value. What, I ask you, then, is to tell me some means of disengaging myself honourably either from the one or from the other; or, rather, I ask you, from which side you think I can free myself most honourably.'

'My dear Louise,' replied Montalais, after a pause, 'I am not one of those seven wise men of Greece,* and I have no perfectly invariable rules of conduct to govern me; but, on the other hand, I have a little experience and I can assure you that no woman ever asks for advice of the nature of which you have just asked me, without being in a terrible state of embarrassment. Besides, you have made a solemn promise, which every principle of honour would require you to fulfil;—if, therefore, you are embarrassed in consequence of having undertaken such an engagement, it is not a stranger's advice (every one is a stranger to a heart full of love), it is not my advice, I repeat, which will extricate you from your embarrassment. I shall not give it you, therefore; and for a greater reason still—because, were I in your place, I should feel much more embarrassed after the advice than before it. All I can do is to repeat what I have already told you; shall I assist you?'

'Yes, yes.'

'Very well; that is all. Tell me in what way you wish me to help you; tell me for and against whom,—in this way we shall not make any blunders.'

'But first of all,' said La Vallière, pressing her companion's hand, 'for whom or against whom do you decide?'

'For you, if you are really and truly my friend.'

'Are you not Madame's confidante?'

'A greater reason for being of service to you; if I were not to know what is going on in that direction I should not be able to be of any service at all, and consequently you would not obtain any advantage from my acquaintance. Friendships live and thrive upon a system of reciprocal benefit.'

'The result is, then, that you will remain at the same time Madame's friend also?'

'Evidently. Do you complain of that?'

'No,' said La Vallière thoughtfully, for that cynical frankness appeared to her an offence addressed both to the woman as well as to the friend.

'All well and good then,' said Montalais, 'for, in that case, you would be very foolish.'

'You will serve me, then?'

'Devotedly so, if you will serve me in return?'

'One would almost say that you do not know my heart,' said La Vallière, looking at Montalais with her eyes wide open.

'Why, the fact is, that since we have belonged to the court, my dear Louise, we are very much changed.'

'In what way?'

'It is very simple. Were you the second Queen of France yonder at Blois?'

La Vallière hung down her head and began to weep. Montalais looked at her in an indefinable manner, and murmured, 'Poor girl!' and then, adding, 'Poor King,' she kissed Louise on the forehead, and returned to her apartment, where Malicorne was waiting for her.

LXXXIII

THE PORTRAIT

In that malady which is termed love the paroxysms succeed each other at intervals, always more rapid from the moment the disease declares itself. By and by, the paroxysms are less frequent, in proportion as the cure approaches. This being laid down as a general axiom, and as the heading of a particular chapter, we will now proceed with our recital. The next day, the day fixed by the King for the first conversation in Saint-Aignan's room, La Vallière, on opening one of the folds of the screen, found upon the floor a letter in the King's handwriting. The letter had been passed through the slit in the floor, from the lower apartment to her own. No indiscreet hand or curious gaze could have brought or did bring this simple paper. This was one of Malicorne's ideas. Having seen how very serviceable Saint-Aignan would become to the King on account of his apartment, he did not wish that the courtier should become still more indispensable as a messenger, and so he had, on his own private account, reserved this last post for himself. La Vallière most eagerly read the letter, which fixed two o'clock that same afternoon for the rendezvous, and which indicated the way of raising the trap-door which was constructed out of the flooring. 'Make yourself look as beautiful as possible,' added the postscript of the letter, words which astonished the young girl, but at the same time reassured her. The hours passed away very slowly, but the time fixed, however, arrived at last. As punctual as the priestess Hero,* Louise lifted up the trap-door at the last stroke of the hour of two, and found the King upon the top steps waiting for her with the greatest respect, in order to give her his hand to descend. The delicacy and deference shown in this attention affected her very powerfully. At the foot of the staircase the two lovers found the Comte, who, with a smile and a low reverence distinguished by the best taste, expressed his thanks to La Vallière for the honour she conferred upon him. Then turning towards the King, he said:—

'Sire, our man is here.' La Vallière looked at the King with some uneasiness.

'Mademoiselle,' said the King, 'if I have begged you to do me the honour of coming down here, it was from an interested motive. I have procured a most admirable portrait-painter, who is celebrated for the fidelity of his likenesses, and I wish you to be kind enough to authorise him to paint yours.* Besides, if you positively wish it, the portrait shall remain in your own possession.' La Vallière blushed.

'You see,' said the King to her, 'we shall not be three, as you wished, but four instead. And, so long as we are not alone, there can be as many present as you please.' La Vallière gently pressed her royal lover's hand.

'Shall we pass into the next room, sire?' said Saint-Aignan, opening the door to let his guests precede him. The King walked behind La Vallière, and fixed his eyes lingeringly and passionately upon her neck as white as snow, upon which her long fair ringlets fell in heavy masses. La Vallière was dressed in a thick silk robe of pearl-grey colour, with a tinge of rose, with jet ornaments, which displayed to greater effect the dazzling purity of her skin, holding in her slender and transparent hands a bouquet of heartsease, Bengal roses, and clematis, surrounded with leaves of the tenderest green, above which rose, like a tiny goblet shedding perfumes, a tulip of grey and violet tints, of a pure and beautiful species, which had cost the gardener five years' toil, and the King five thousand francs. Louis had placed this bouquet in La Vallière's hand as he saluted her. In the room, the door of which Saint-Aignan had just opened, a young man was standing, dressed in a loose velvet coat, with beautiful black eyes and long brown hair. It was the painter; his canvas was ready, and his palette prepared for use. He bowed to La Vallière with that grave curiosity of an artist who is studying his model, saluted the King discreetly, as if he did not recognise him, and as he would, consequently, have saluted any other gentleman. Then, leading Mademoiselle de la Vallière to the seat which he had arranged for her, he begged her to sit down. The young girl assumed an attitude graceful and unrestrained, her hands occupied and her limbs reclining on cushions; and in order that her gaze might not assume a vague or affected expression, the painter begged her to choose some kind of occupation, so as to engage her attention; whereupon Louis XIV, smiling, sat down on the cushions at La Vallière's feet; so that she, in the reclining posture she had assumed, leaning back in the arm-chair, holding her flowers in her hand, and he, with his eyes raised towards her and fixed devouringly on her face—they, both together, formed so charming a group, that the artist contemplated it with professional delight; while, on his side, Saint-Aignan regarded them with feelings of envy. The painter sketched rapidly; and very soon, beneath the earliest touches of the brush, there started into life, out of the grey background, the gentle poetry-breathing face, with its soft calm eyes, and delicately tinted cheeks, framed in the masses of hair which fell about her neck. The lovers, however, spoke but little, and looked at each other a good deal; sometimes their eyes became so languishing in their gaze, that the painter was obliged to interrupt his work in order to avoid representing an Erycina* instead of a La Vallière. It was on such occasions that Saint-Aignan came to the rescue, and recited verses, or repeated one of those little tales as Patru related them, and which Tallemant des Réaux* wrote so cleverly. Or, it might be, that La Vallière was fatigued, and the sitting was, therefore, suspended for a while; and, immediately a tray of precious porcelain, laden with the most beautiful fruits which could be obtained, and rich wines distilling their bright colours in silver goblets, beautifully chased, served as accessories to the picture of which the painter could but retrace the most ephemeral resemblance. Louis was intoxicated with love, La Vallière with happiness, Saint-Aignan with ambition, and the painter was storing up recollections for his old age. Two hours passed away in this manner, and four o'clock having struck, La Vallière rose and made a sign to the King. Louis also rose, approached the picture, and addressed a few flattering remarks to the painter. Saint-Aignan also praised the picture, which, as he pretended, was already beginning to assume an accurate resemblance. La Vallière in her turn blushingly thanked the painter, and passed into the next room, where the King followed her after having previously summoned Saint-Aignan.

'Will you not come to-morrow?' he said to La Vallière.

'Oh! sire, pray think that some one will be sure to come to my room, and will not find me there.'

'Well?'

'What will become of me in that case?'

'You are very apprehensive, Louise.'

'But, at all events, suppose Madame were to send for me.'

'Oh!' replied the King, 'will the day never come when you yourself will tell me to brave everything, so that I may not have to leave you again.'

'On that day, then, sire, I shall be quite out of my mind, and you ought not to believe me.'

'To-morrow, Louise?'

La Vallière sighed, but, without the courage to oppose her royal lover's wish, she repeated, 'To-morrow, then, since you desire it, sire,' and, with these words, she ran up the stairs lightly, and disappeared from her lover's gaze.

'Well, sire?' inquired Saint-Aignan, when she had left.

'Well, Saint-Aignan; yesterday I thought myself the happiest of men.'

'And does your Majesty, then regard yourself to-day,' said the Comte, smiling, 'as the unhappiest of men?'

'No; but my love for her is an unquenchable thirst; in vain do I drink, in vain do I swallow the drops of water which your industry procures for me; the more I drink, the more unquench-able is my thirst.'

'Sire, that is in some degree your own fault, and your Majesty alone has made the position such as it is.'

'You are right.'

'In that case, therefore, the means to be happy is to fancy yourself satisfied and to wait.'

'Wait! you know that word, then?'

'There, there, sire—do not despair; I have already been at work on your behalf—I have still other resources in store.' The King shook his head in a despairing manner.

'What, sire, have you not been satisfied hitherto?'

'Oh! yes, indeed, yes, my dear Saint-Aignan; but find, for Heaven's sake, find some further means yet.'

'Sire, I undertake to do my best, and that is all I can do.'

The King wished to see the portrait again, as he was unable to see the original. He pointed out several alterations to the painter, and left the room, and then Saint-Aignan dismissed the artist. The easel, paints, and painter himself, had scarcely gone, when Malicorne showed his head at the doorway. He was received by Saint-Aignan with open arms, but still with a little sadness, for the cloud which had passed across the royal sun, veiled, in its turn, the faithful satellite, and Malicorne at a glance perceived the melancholy look which was visible upon Saint-Aignan's face.

'Oh! Monsieur le Comte,' he said, 'how sad you seem.'

'And good reason too, my dear Monsieur Malicorne. Will you believe that the King is not satisfied?'

'Not satisfied with his staircase, do you mean?'

'Oh, no; on the contrary, he is delighted with the staircase.'

'The decorations of the apartments, I suppose, don't please him.'

'Oh! he has not even thought of that. No, indeed, it seems that what has dissatisfied the King——'

'I will tell you, Monsieur le Comte—he is dissatisfied at find-ing himself the fourth person at a rendezvous of this kind. How is it possible you could not have guessed that?'

'Why, how is it likely I could have done so, dear M. Malicorne, when I followed the King's instructions to the very letter.'

'Did His Majesty really insist upon your being present?'

'Positively so.'

'And also required that the painter whom I met downstairs just now should be here, too?'

'He insisted upon it.'

'In that case, I can easily understand why His Majesty is dissatisfied.'

'What! dissatisfied that I have so punctually and literally obeyed his orders. I don't understand you.'

Malicorne began to scratch his ear, as he asked, 'What time did the King fix for the rendezvous in your apartment?'

'Two o'clock.'

'And you were waiting for the King?'

'Ever since half-past one; for it would have been a fine thing indeed, to have been unpunctual with His Majesty.'

Malicorne, nowithstanding his respect for Saint-Aignan, could not resist shrugging his shoulders. 'And the painter,' he said, 'did the King wish him to be here at two o'clock also?'

'No; but I had him waiting here from midday. Far better, you know, for a painter to be kept waiting a couple of hours, than the King a single minute.'

Malicorne began to laugh to himself. 'Come, dear Monsieur Malicorne,' said Saint-Aignan, 'laugh less at me, and speak a little more freely, I beg.'

'Well, then, Monsieur le Comte, if you wish the King to be a little more satisfied the next time he comes——'

'*Ventre saint-gris!* as his grandfather* used to say; of course I wish it.'

'Well, all you have to do is, when the King comes to-morrow, to be obliged to go away on a most pressing matter of business, which cannot possibly be postponed, and stay away for twenty minutes.'

'What! leave the King alone for twenty minutes?' cried Saint-Aignan, in alarm.

'Very well, do as you like; don't pay any attention to what I say,' said Malicorne, moving towards the door.

'Nay, nay, dear Monsieur Malicorne; on the contrary go on— I begin to understand you. But the painter——'

'Oh! the painter must be half an hour late.'

'Half an hour—do you really think so?'

'Yes, I do, decidedly.'

'Very well, then, I will do as you tell me.'

'And my opinion is that you will be doing perfectly right. Will you allow me to come and inquire to-morrow a little?'

'Of course.'

'I have the honour to be your most respectful servant, M. de Saint-Aignan,' said Malicorne, bowing profoundly, and retiring from the room backwards.

'There is no doubt that fellow has more invention than I have,' said Saint-Aignan, as if compelled by his conviction to admit it.

LXXXIV

HAMPTON COURT

THE revelation of which we have been witnesses, that Montalais made to La Vallière, in a preceding chapter, very naturally makes us return to the principal hero of this tale, a poor wandering knight, roving about at the King's caprice. If our reader will be good enough to follow us, we will, in his company, cross that strait more stormy than the Euripus*—that which separates Calais from Dover; we will speed across that green and fertile country, with its numerous little streams; through Maidstone, and many other villages and towns, each prettier than the other; and, finally, arrive at London. From thence, like bloodhounds following a track, after having ascertained that Raoul had made his first stay at Whitehall, his second at St James's, and having learned that he had been warmly received by Monk, and introduced into the best society of Charles II's court, we will follow him to one of Charles II's summer residences, near the town of Kingston, at Hampton Court, situated on the Thames. The river is not, at that spot, the boastful highway which bears upon its broad bosom its thousands of travellers; nor are its waters black and troubled as those of Cocytus,* as it boastfully asserts, 'I, too, am the sea.' No; at Hampton Court it is a soft and murmuring stream, with moss-grown banks, reflecting, in its broad mirror, the willows and beeches which ornament its sides, and on which may occasionally be seen a light bark indolently reclining among the tall reeds, in a little creek formed of alders and forget-me-nots. The surrounding country on all sides seemed smiling in happiness and wealth; the brick cottages, from whose chimneys the blue smoke was slowly ascending in wreaths, peeped forth from the belts of green holly which environed them; children dressed in red frocks appeared and disappeared amidst the high grass, like poppies bowed by the gentle breath of the passing breeze. The sheep, ruminating with closed eyes, lay lazily about under the shadow of the stunted aspens; while, far and near, the kingfisher, clad in emerald and gold, skimmed swiftly along the surface of the water, like a magic ball, heedlessly touching, as he passed, the line of his brother angler, who sat watching in his boat the fish as they rose to the surface of the sparkling stream. High above this Paradise of dark shadows and soft light, arose the palace of Hampton Court, which had been built by Wolsey*—a residence which the haughty cardinal had been obliged, timid courtier that he was, to offer to his master, Henry VIII, who had frowned with envy and feelings of cupidity at the aspect of the new palace. Hampton Court, with its brick walls, its large windows, its handsome iron gates, as well as its curious bell-turrets, its retired covered walks, and interior fountains, like those of the Alhambra,* was a perfect bower of roses, jasmine, and clematis. Every sense, of sight and smell particularly, was gratified, and formed a most charming framework for the picture of love which Charles II unrolled among the voluptuous paintings of Titian, of Pordenone, and of Van Dyck;* the same Charles whose father's portrait—the martyr King—was hanging in his gallery, and who could show upon the wainscots of the various apartments the holes made by the balls of the puritanical followers of Cromwell, on the 24th August, 1648, at the time they had brought Charles I prisoner to Hampton Court.* There it was that the King, intoxicated with pleasure and amusement, held his court—he who, a poet in feeling, thought himself justified in redeeming, by a whole day of voluptuousness, every minute which had been formerly passed in anguish and misery. It was not the soft green sward of Hampton Court—so soft, that it almost resembled the richest velvet, in the thickness of its texture—nor was it the beds of flowers, with their variegated hues, which encircled the foot of every tree, with rose-trees many feet in height, embracing most lovingly their trunks—nor even the enormous lime-trees, whose branches swept the earth like willows, offering a ready concealment for love or reflection beneath the shade of their foliage—it was none of these things for which Charles II loved his palace of Hampton Court. Perhaps it might have been that beautiful sheet of water, which the cool breeze rippled like the wavy undulations of Cleopatra's hair; waters bedecked with cresses and white water-lilies, with hardy bulbs, which, half unfolding themselves beneath the sun's warm rays, reveal the golden-coloured germs which lie concealed in their milk-white covering—murmuring waters, on the bosom of which the black swans majestically floated; and the restless water-fowl, with their tender broods covered with silken down, darted restlessly in every direction, in pursuit of the insects among the flags, or the frogs in their mossy retreats. Perhaps it might have been the enormous hollies, with their dark and tender green foliage; or the bridges which united the banks of the canals in their embrace; or the fawns browsing in the endless avenues of the park; or the numberless birds which hopped about the gardens, or flew from branch to branch, amidst the dense foliage of the trees.

It might well have been any of these charms, for Hampton Court possessed them all; and possessed, too, almost forests of white roses, which climbed and trailed along the lofty trellises, showering down upon the ground their snowy leaves rich with odorous perfumes. But, no, what Charles II most loved in Hampton Court was the charming figures who, when midday was passed, flitted to and fro along the broad terraces of the gardens; like Louis XIV he had had their wealth of beauties painted for his cabinet by one of the great artists of the period—an artist who well knew the secret of transferring to canvas a ray of light which had escaped from their beaming eyes laden with love and love's delights.

The day of our arrival at Hampton Court is almost as clear and bright as a summer's day in France; the atmosphere is laden with the delicious perfume of the geraniums, sweet-peas, seringas, and heliotrope, which are scattered in profusion around. It is past mid-day, and the King, having dined after his return from hunting, paid a visit to Lady Castlemaine,* the lady who was reputed at the time to hold his heart in bondage; and with this proof of his devotion discharged, he was readily permitted to pursue his infidelities until evening arrived. Love and amusement ruled the whole court; it was the period when ladies would seriously interrogate their ruder companions as to their opinion upon a foot more or less captivating, according to whether it wore a pink or green silk stocking—for it was the period when Charles II had declared that there was no hope of safety for a woman who wore green silk stockings, because Miss Lucy Stewart* wore them of that colour. While the King is endeavouring in all directions to inoculate others with his preferences on this point, we will ourselves bend our steps towards an avenue of beech-trees opposite the terrace, and listen to the conversation of a young girl in a dark-coloured dress, who is walking with another of about her own age dressed in lilac and dark blue. They crossed a beautiful lawn in the middle of which arose a fountain, with the figure of a siren executed in bronze, and strolled on, talking as they went, towards the terrace, along which, looking out upon the park, and interspersed at frequent intervals, were erected summer-houses, various in form and ornaments; these summer-houses were nearly all occupied; the two young women passed on, the one blushing deeply, while the other seemed dreamily silent. At last, having reached the end of the terrace which looks on the river, and finding there a cool retreat, they sat down close to each other.

'Where are we going, Stewart?' said the younger to her companion.

'My dear Grafton,* we are going where you yourself led the way.'

'I?'

'Yes, you; to the extremity of the palace, towards that seat yonder where the young Frenchman is seated, wasting his time in sighs and lamentations.'

Miss Mary Grafton hurriedly said, 'No, no; I am not going there.'

'Why not?'

'Let us go back, Stewart.'

'Nay, on the contrary, let us go on, and have an explanation.'

'About what?'

'About how it happens that the Vicomte de Bragelonne always accompanies you in all your walks, as you invariably accompany him in his.'

'And you conclude either that he loves me, or that I love him?'

'Why not?—he is a most agreeable and charming companion—No one can hear me, I hope,' said Lucy Stewart, as she turned round with a smile, which indicated, moreover, that her uneasiness on the subject was not extreme.

'No, no,' said Mary, 'the King is engaged in his summerhouse with the Duke of Buckingham.'

'Oh! à propos of the Duke; Mary, it seems he has shown you great attention since his return from France; how is your own heart in that direction?'

Mary Grafton shrugged her shoulders with seeming indifference.

'Well, well, I will ask Bragelonne about that,' said Stewart, laughing; 'let us go and find him at once.'

'What for?'

'I wish to speak to him.'

'Not yet; one word before you do; come, Stewart, you who know so many of the King's secrets, tell me why M. de Bragelonne is in England?'

'Because he was sent as an envoy from one sovereign to another.'

'That may be; but, seriously, although politics do not much concern us, we know enough to be satisfied that M. de Bragelonne has no mission of any serious import here.'

'Well, then, listen,' said Stewart, with assumed gravity, 'for your sake I am going to betray a State secret. Shall I tell you the nature of the letter which King Louis XIV gave M. de Bragelonne for King Charles II? I will; these are the very words, "My brother, the bearer of this is a gentleman attached to my court, and the son of one* whom you regard most warmly. Treat him kindly, I beg, and try to make him like England."'

'Did it say that?'

'Word for word—or something very like it. I will not answer for the form, but the substance I am sure of.'

'Well, and what conclusion do you, or rather what conclusion does the King, draw from that?'

'That the King of France has his own reasons for removing M. de Bragelonne, and for getting him married—somewhere else than in France.'

'So that, then, in consequence of this letter——'

'King Charles received M. de Bragelonne, as you are aware, in the most distinguished and friendly manner; the handsomest apartments in Whitehall were allotted to him; and as you are the most valuable and precious person in his court, inasmuch as you have rejected his heart—nay, do not blush—he wished you to take a fancy to this Frenchman, and he was desirous to confer upon him so costly a prize. And this is the reason why you, the heiress of three hundred thousand pounds, a future duchess, and one so beautiful and so good, have been thrown in Bragelonne's way, in all the promenades and parties of pleasure to which he was invited. In fact it was a plot—a kind of conspiracy.'

Mary Grafton smiled with that charming expression which was habitual to her, and, pressing her companion's arm, said, 'Thank the King, Lucy.'

'Yes, yes, but the Duke of Buckingham is jealous, so take care.'

Hardly had she pronounced these words, than the Duke appeared from one of the pavilions on the terrace, and, approaching the two girls, with a smile, said, 'You are mistaken, Miss Lucy; I am not jealous; and the proof, Miss Mary, is yonder, in the person of M. de Bragelonne himself, who ought to be the cause of my jealousy, but who is dreaming in pensive solitude. Poor fellow! Allow me to leave you for a few minutes, while I avail myself of those few minutes to converse with Miss Lucy Stewart, to whom I have something to say.' And then, bowing to Lucy, he added, 'Will you do me the honour to accept my hand, in order that I may lead you to the King, who is waiting for us.' With these words, Buckingham, still smiling, took Miss Stewart's hand, and led her away. When by herself, Mary Grafton, her head gently inclined towards her shoulder, with that indolent gracefulness of action which distinguishes young English girls, remained for a moment with her eyes fixed on Raoul, but as if uncertain what to do. At last, after first blushing violently, and then turning deadly pale, thus revealing the internal combat which assailed her heart, she seemed to make up her mind to adopt a decided course, and, with a tolerably firm step, advanced towards the seat on which Raoul was reclining, buried in the profoundest meditation, as we have already said. The sound of Miss Mary's steps, though they could be hardly heard upon the green sward, awakened Raoul from his musing attitude; he turned round, perceived the young girl, and walked forward to meet the companion whom his happy destiny had thrown in his way.

'I have been sent to you, monsieur,' said Mary Grafton; 'will you accept me?'

'To whom is my gratitude due, for so great a happiness?' inquired Raoul.

'To the Duke of Buckingham,' replied Mary, affecting a gaiety she did not really feel.

'To the Duke of Buckingham, do you say?—he who so passionately seeks your charming society! Am I really to believe you are serious, mademoiselle?'

'The fact is, monsieur, you perceive, that everything seems to conspire to make us pass the best, or rather the longest part of our days together. Yesterday it was the King who desired me to beg you to seat yourself next to me at dinner; to-day, it is the Duke of Buckingham who begs me to come and place myself near you on this seat.'

'And he has gone away in order to leave us together?' asked Raoul with some embarrassment.

'Look yonder, at the turning of that path; he is just out of sight, with Miss Stewart. Are these polite attentions usual in France, Monsieur le Comte?'

'I cannot very precisely say what people do in France, mademoiselle, for I can hardly be called a Frenchman. I have resided in many countries, and almost always as a soldier; and then, I have spent a long period of my life in the country. I am almost a savage.'*

'You do not like your residence in England, I fear.'

'I scarcely know,' said Raoul inattentively, and sighing deeply at the same time.

'What! you do not know.'

'Forgive me,' said Raoul shaking his head, and collecting his thoughts, 'I did not hear you.'

'Oh!' said the young girl, sighing in her turn, 'how wrong the Duke was to send me here!'

'Wrong!' said Raoul, 'perhaps so; for I am but a rude, uncouth companion, and my society annoys you. The Duke was, indeed, very wrong to send you.'

'It is, precisely,' replied Mary Grafton, in a clear, calm voice, 'because your society does not annoy me, that the Duke was wrong to send me to you.'

It was now Raoul's turn to blush. 'But,' he resumed, 'how is it that the Duke of Buckingham should send you to me; and why should you have come? the Duke loves you, and you love him.'

'No,' replied Mary seriously, 'the Duke does not love me, because he is in love with the Duchesse d'Orléans; and, as for myself, I have no affection for the Duke.'

Raoul looked at the young girl with astonishment.

'Are you a friend of the Duke of Buckingham?' she inquired.

'The Duke has honoured me by calling me so ever since we met in France.'*

'You are simple acquaintances, then?'

'No; for the Duke is the most intimate friend of one whom I regard as a brother.'

'The Duc de Guiche?'

'Yes.'

'He who is in love with Madame la Duchesse d'Orléans.'

'Oh! what is that you are saying?'

'And who loves him in return,' continued the young girl quietly.

Raoul bent down his head, and Mary Grafton, sighing deeply, continued, 'They are very happy. But, leave me, Monsieur de Bragelonne, for the Duke of Buckingham has given you a very troublesome commission in offering me as a companion in your promenade. Your heart is elsewhere, and it is with the greatest difficulty you can be charitable enough to lend me your attention. Confess truly; it would be unfair on your part, Vicomte, not to confess it.'

'Madame, I do confess it.'

She looked at him steadily. He was so noble and so handsome in his bearing, his eye revealed so much gentleness, candour, and resolution, that the idea could not possibly enter her mind, that he was either rudely discourteous, or a mere simpleton. She only perceived clearly enough, that he loved another woman, and not herself, with the whole strength of his heart. 'Ah! I now understand you,' she said; 'you have left your heart behind you in France.' Raoul bowed. 'The Duke is aware of your affection.'

'No one knows it,' replied Raoul.

'Why, therefore, do you tell me? Nay, answer me.'

'I cannot.'

'It is for me, then, to anticipate an explanation; you do not wish to tell me anything, because you are now convinced that I do not love the Duke; because you see that I possibly might have loved you; because you are a gentleman of noble and delicate sentiments; and because, instead of accepting, even were it for the mere amusement of the passing hour, a hand which is almost pressed upon you; and because, instead of meeting my smiles with a smiling lip, you, who are young, have preferred to tell me, whom men have called beautiful, "My heart is far away in France." For this, I thank you, Monsieur de Bragelonne; you are, indeed, a noble-hearted, noble-minded man, and I regard you yet more for it. As a friend only. And now let us cease speaking of myself, and talk of your own affairs. Forget that I have ever spoken to you of myself; tell me why you are sad, and why you have become more than usually so during these past four days?'*

Raoul was deeply and sensibly moved by her sweet and melancholy tone; and as he could not, at the moment, find a word to say, the young girl again came to his assistance.

'Pity me,' she said. 'My mother was born in France, and I can truly affirm that I, too, am French in blood, as well as in feeling; but the heavy atmosphere and characteristic gloom of England seem to weigh like a burden upon me. Sometimes my dreams are golden-hued and full of wondrous enjoyment, but suddenly a mist arises and overspreads my dreams, and blots them out for ever. Such, indeed, is the case at the present moment. Forgive me; I have now said enough on that subject, give me your hand, and relate your griefs to me as to a friend.'

'You say you are French in heart and soul.'

'Yes, not only, I repeat it, that my mother was French, but, further still, as my father, a friend of King Charles I, was exiled in France, I, during the trial of that Prince, as well as during the Protector's life, was brought up in Paris; at the restoration of King Charles II my poor father returned to England, where he died almost immediately afterwards; and then the King created me a duchess, and has dowered me according to my rank.'

'Have you any relation in France?' Raoul inquired, with the deepest interest.

'I have a sister there, my senior by seven or eight years, who was married in France, and was early left a widow; her name is Madame de Bellières. Do you know her?'* she added, observing Raoul start suddenly.

'I have heard her name mentioned.'

'She, too, loves with her whole heart; and her last letters inform me that she is happy, and her affection is I conclude, returned. I told you, Monsieur de Bragelonne, that although I possess half of her nature, I do not share her happiness. But let us now speak of yourself; whom do you love in France?'

'A young girl, as soft and as pure as a lily.'

'But if she loves you, why are you sad?'

'I have been told that she has ceased to love me.'

'You do not believe it, I trust?'

'He who wrote me so, does not sign his letter.'

'An anonymous denunciation! some treachery, be assured,' said Miss Grafton.

'Stay,' said Raoul, showing the young girl a letter which he had read over a thousand times; she took it from his hands and read as follows:—

'VICOMTE,—You are perfectly right to amuse yourself yonder with the lovely faces of Charles II's court, for, at Louis XIV's court, the castle in which your affections are enshrined is being besieged. Stay in London altogether, poor Vicomte, or return without delay to Paris.'

'There is no signature,' said Miss Mary.

'None.'

'Believe it not, then.'

'Very good; but here is a second letter, from my friend de

Guiche, which says, "I am lying here wounded and ill. Return, Raoul, oh, return!" '

'What do you intend doing?' inquired the young girl with a feeling of oppression at her heart.

'My intention, as soon as I received this letter, was immediately to take my leave of the King.'

'When did you receive it?'

'The day before yesterday.'

'It is dated from Fontainebleau.'

'A singular circumstance, do you not think, for the court is now at Paris? At all events, I would have set off; but when I mentioned my intention to the King, he began to laugh, and said to me, "How comes it, monsieur l'ambassadeur, that you think of leaving? Has your sovereign recalled you?" I coloured, naturally enough, for I was confused by the question, for the fact is, the King himself sent me here, and I have received no order to return.'

Mary frowned in deep thought, and said, 'Do you remain, then?'

'I must, mademoiselle.'

'Do you ever receive any letters from her to whom you are so devoted?'

'Never.'

'Never, do you say? Does she not love you, then?'

'At least she has not written to me since my departure, although she used occasionally to write to me before.* I trust she may have been prevented.'

'Hush! the Duke is here.'

And Buckingham at that moment was seen at the end of the walk, approaching towards them, alone and smiling; he advanced slowly, and held out his hands to them both. 'Have you arrived at an understanding?' he said.

'About what?'

'About whatever might render you happy, dear Mary, and make Raoul less miserable.'

'I do not understand you, my lord,' said Raoul.

'That is my view of the subject, Miss Mary; do you wish me to mention it before M. de Bragelonne?' he added with a smile.

'If you mean,' replied the young girl haughtily, 'that I was not indisposed to love M. de Bragelonne, that is useless, for I have told him so myself.'

Buckingham reflected for a moment, and, without seeming in any way discountenanced, as she expected, he said, 'My reason for leaving you with M. de Bragelonne was, that I thoroughly knew your refined delicacy of feeling, no less than the perfect loyalty of your mind and heart, and I hoped that M. de Bragelonne's cure might be effected by the hands of a physician such as you are.'

'But, my lord, before you spoke of M. de Bragelonne's heart, you spoke to me of your own. Do you mean me to effect the cure of two hearts at the same time?'

'Perfectly true, madam, but you will do me the justice to admit that I have long discontinued a useless pursuit, acknowledging that my own wound is incurable.'

'My lord,' said Mary, collecting herself for a moment before she spoke, 'M. de Bragelonne is happy, for he loves and is beloved. He has no need of such a physician as I can be.'

'M. de Bragelonne,' said Buckingham, 'is on the very eve of experiencing a serious misfortune, and he has greater need than ever of sympathy and affection.'

'Explain yourself, my lord,' inquired Raoul anxiously.

'No; gradually I will explain myself, but, if you desire it, I can tell Miss Grafton what you may not listen to yourself.'

'My lord, you are putting me to the torture; you know something you wish to conceal from me?'

'I know that Miss Mary Grafton is the most charming object that a heart ill at ease could possibly meet with in its way through life.'

'I have already told you that the Vicomte de Bragelonne loves elsewhere,' said the young girl.

'He is wrong, then.'

'Do you assume to know, my lord, that I am wrong?'

'Yes.'

'Whom is it that he loves, then?' exclaimed the young girl.

'He loves a woman who is unworthy of him,' said Buckingham with that calm, collected manner peculiar to an Englishman.

Miss Grafton uttered a cry, which, together with the remark the Buckingham had that moment made, spread over de

Bragelonne's features a deadly paleness, arising from the sudden surprise, and also from a vague fear of impending misfortune. 'My lord,' he exclaimed, 'you have just pronounced words which compel me, without a moment's delay, to seek their explanation in Paris.'

'You will remain here,' said Buckingham, 'because you have no right to leave; and no one has the right to quit the service of the King for that of any woman, even were she as worthy of being loved as Mary Grafton is.'

'You will tell me all, then?'

'I will, on condition that you will remain.'

'I will remain, if you will promise to speak openly and without reserve.'

Thus far had their conversation proceeded, and Buckingham, in all probability, was on the point of revealing, not indeed all that had taken place, but at least all he was aware of, when one of the King's attendants appeared at the end of the terrace, and advanced towards the summer-house where the King was sitting with Lucy Stewart. A courier followed him, covered with dust from head to foot, and who seemed as if he had but a few moments before dismounted from his horse.

'The courier from France! Madame's courier!' exclaimed Raoul, recognising the Princess's livery; and while the attendant and the courier advanced towards the King, Buckingham and Miss Grafton exchanged a look full of intelligence with each other.

LXXXV

THE COURIER FROM MADAME

CHARLES II was busily engaged in proving, or in endeavouring to prove, to Miss Stewart that she was the only person for whom he cared at all, and consequently he was swearing for her an affection similar to that which his ancestor Henry IV had entertained for Gabrielle. Unfortunately for Charles II he had hit upon an unlucky day, upon a day when Miss Stewart had taken it into her head to make him jealous, and therefore, instead of being touched by his offer, as the King had hoped, she laughed heartily. 'Oh! sire, sire,' she cried, laughing all the while; 'if I were to be unfortunate enough to ask you for a proof of the affection you profess, how easy it would be to see that you are telling a falsehood.'

'Nay, listen to me,' said Charles, 'you know my cartoons by Raphael;* you know whether I care for them or not; the whole world envies me their possession, as you well know also; my father got Van Dyck to purchase them. Would you like me to send them to your house this very day?'

'Oh! no,' replied the young girl; 'pray keep them yourself, sire; my house is far too small to accommodate such visitors.'

'In that case you shall have Hampton Court to put the cartoons in.'

'Be less generous, sire, and learn to love a little while longer, that is all I have to ask you.'

'I shall never cease to love you; is not that enough?'

'You are laughing, sire.'

'Do you wish me to weep, then?'

'No; but I should like to see you a little more melancholy.'

'Thank Heaven, I have been so long enough; fourteen years of exile, poverty, and misery,* I think I may well regard it is a debt discharged; besides, melancholy makes people look so plain.'

'Far from that, for look at the young Frenchman.'

'What! the Vicomte de Bragelonne! are you smitten too! By Heaven, they will all become mad about him, one after the other; but he, on the contrary, has a reason for being melancholy.'

'Why so?'

'Oh! indeed! you wish me to betray State secrets, do you?'

'If I wish it, you must do it, since you told me you were quite ready to do everything I wished.'

'Well, then, he is bored in his own country. Does that satisfy you?'

'Bored?'

'Yes, a proof that he is a simpleton; I allow him to fall in love with Miss Mary Grafton, and he feels bored. Can you believe it?'

'Very good; it seems then, that if you were to find Miss Lucy Stewart indifferent to you, you would console yourself by falling in love with Miss Mary Grafton?'

'I don't say that; in the first place, you know that Mary Grafton does not care for me; besides, a man can only console himself for a lost affection by the discovery of a new one. Again, however, I repeat, the question is not of myself, but of that young man. One might almost be tempted to call the girl he has left behind him a Helen*—a Helen before her introduction to Paris, of course.'

'He has left some one, then?'

'That is to say, some one has left him.'

'Poor fellow! so much the worse!'

'What do you mean by "so much the worse"?'

'Why not? why did he leave?'

'Do you think it was of his own wish or will that he left?'

'Was he obliged to leave, then?'

'He left Paris under orders; and—prepare to be surprised—by express orders of the King.'

'Ah! I begin to see now.'

'At least say nothing at all about it.'

'You know very well that I am quite as discreet as any man could be. And so the King sent him away?'

'Yes.'

'And during his absence, he takes his mistress away from him?'

'Yes; and will you believe it? the silly fellow, instead of thanking the King, is making himself miserable.'

'What! thank the King for depriving him of the woman he loves! Really, sire, yours is a most ungallant speech.'

'But, pray understand me. If she whom the King had run off with was either a Miss Grafton or a Miss Stewart, I should be of his opinion; nay, I should even think him not half miserable enough; but she is a little, thin, lame thing. Deuce take such fidelity as that! Surely, one can hardly understand how a man can refuse a girl who is rich for one who is poverty itself—a girl who loves him for one who deceives and betrays him.'

'Do you think that Mary seriously wishes to please the Vicomte, sire?'

'I do, indeed.'

'Very good! the Vicomte will settle down in England, for Mary has a clear head, and when she fixes her mind upon anything, she does so thoroughly.'

'Take care, my dear Miss Stewart, if the Vicomte has any idea of adopting our country, he has not long to do so, for it was only the day before yesterday that he again asked me for permission to leave.'

'Which you refused him, I suppose?'

'I should think so, indeed; my royal brother is far too anxious for his absence; and, for myself, my *amour propre* is enlisted on his side, for I will never have it said that I had held out as a bait to this young man the noblest and gentlest creature in England——'

'You are very gallant, sire,' said Miss Stewart with a pretty pout.

'I do not allude to Miss Stewart, for she is worthy a King's devotion; and since she has captivated me, I trust that no one else will be caught by her; I say, therefore, finally, that the attention I have shown this young man will not have been thrown away; he will stay with us here, will marry here, or I am very much mistaken.'

'And I hope that when he is once married and settled, instead of being angry with your Majesty, he will be grateful to you, for every one tries his utmost to please him; even the Duke of Buckingham, whose brilliancy, which is hardly credible, seems to pale before that of this young Frenchman.'

'And including Miss Stewart even, who calls him the most finished gentleman she ever saw.'

'Stay, sire; you have spoken quite enough, and quite highly enough, of Miss Grafton, to overlook what I may have said about de Bragelonne. But, by the bye, sire, your kindness for some time past astonishes me; you think of those who are absent, you forgive those who have done wrong, in fact, you are, as nearly as possible, perfect. How does it happen——'

'It is because you allow yourself to be loved,' he said, beginning to laugh.

'Oh! there must be some other reason.'

'Well, I am doing all I can to oblige my brother Louis XIV.'

'Nay, I must have another reason.'

'Well, then, the true motive is that Buckingham strongly recommended the young man to me, saying, "Sire, I begin by yielding up all claim to Miss Grafton; I pray you follow my example."'

'The Duke is, indeed, a true gentleman.'

'Oh! of course, of course; it is Buckingham's turn now, I suppose, to turn your head. You seem determined to cross me in everything to-day.'

At this moment someone scratched at the door.

'Who is it who presumes to interrupt us?' exclaimed Charles impatiently.

'Really, sire, you are extremely vain with your "who is it who presumes?" and in order to punish you for it——'

She went to the door and opened it.

'It is a courier from France,' said Miss Stewart.

'A courier from France!' exclaimed Charles; 'from my sister, perhaps.'

'Yes, sire,' said the usher, 'a special messenger.'

'Let him come in at once,' said Charles.

'You have a letter for me,' said the King to the courier as he entered, 'from the Duchess of Orléans?'

'Yes, sire,' replied the courier, 'and so urgent in its nature that I have only been twenty-six hours bringing it to your Majesty, and yet I lost three quarters of an hour at Calais.'

'Your zeal shall not be forgotten,' said the King as he opened the letter. When he had read it, he burst out laughing, and exclaimed, 'Upon my word, I am at a loss to understand anything about it.' He then read the letter a second time, Miss Stewart assuming a manner marked by the greatest reserve, and doing her utmost to restrain her ardent curiosity.

'Francis,' said the King to his valet, 'see that this excellent fellow is well taken care of and sleeps soundly, and that on waking to-morrow morning he finds a purse of fifty sovereigns by his bedside.'

'Sire!' said the courier amazed.

'Begone, begone; my sister was perfectly right in desiring you to use the utmost diligence, the affair was most pressing.' And he again began to laugh louder than ever. The courier, the valet, and Miss Stewart, hardly knew what sort of countenance to assume. 'Ah!' said the King, throwing himself back in his arm-chair; 'when I think that you have worn out—how many horses?'

'Two.'

'Two horses to bring this intelligence to me! That will do, you can leave us now.'

The courier retired with the valet. Charles went to the window, which he opened, and, leaning forward, called out,—'Duke! Buckingham! come here, there's a good fellow.'

The Duke hurried to him, in obedience to the summons; but when he reached the door, and perceived Miss Stewart, he hesitated to enter.

'Come in, and shut the door,' said the King. The Duke obeyed; and, perceiving in what an excellent humour the King was, he advanced, smilingly, towards him. 'Well, my dear Duke, how do you get on with your Frenchman?'

'Sire, I am in the most perfect state of utter despair about him.'

'Why so?'

'Because charming Miss Grafton is willing to marry him, but he is unwilling.'

'Why, he is a perfect Bœotian!'* cried Miss Stewart. 'Let him say either "Yes," or "No," and let the affair end.'

'But,' said Buckingham seriously, 'you know, or you ought to know, madam, that M. de Bragelonne is in love in another direction.'

'In that case,' said the King, coming to Miss Stewart's help, 'nothing is easier; let him say "No," then.'

'Very true; and I have proved to him he was wrong not to say "Yes."'

'You told him candidly, I suppose, that La Vallière was deceiving him?'

'Yes, without the slightest reserve; and, as soon as I had done so, he gave a start, as if he were going to clear the Channel at a bound.'

'At all events,' said Miss Stewart, 'he has done something; and a very good thing, too, upon my word.'

'But,' said Buckingham, 'I stopped him; I have left him and Miss Mary in conversation together, and I sincerely trust that now he will not leave, as he seemed to have had an idea of doing.'

'An idea of leaving England?' cried the King.

'I, at one moment, hardly thought that any human power

could have prevented him; but Miss Mary's eyes are now bent fully on him, and he will remain.'

'Well, that is the very thing which deceives you, Buckingham,' said the King with a peal of laughter; 'the poor fellow is predestined.'

'Predestined to what?'

'If it were to be simply deceived, that is nothing; but, to look at him, it is a great deal.'

'At a distance, and with Miss Grafton's aid, the blow will be warded off.'

'Far from it, far from it; neither distance nor Miss Grafton's help will be of the slightest avail. Bragelonne will set off for Paris within an hour's time.'

Buckingham started, and Miss Stewart opened her eyes very wide in astonishment.

'But, sire,' said the Duke, 'your Majesty knows that is impossible.'

'That is to say, my dear Buckingham, that it is impossible until the contrary happens.'

'Do not forget, sire, that the young man is a lion, and that his wrath is terrible.'

'I don't deny it, my dear Duke.'

'And that if he sees that his misfortune is certain, so much the worse for the author of it.'

'I don't deny it; but what the deuce am I to do?'

'Were it the King himself,' cried Buckingham, 'I would not answer for him.'

'Oh, the King has his musketeers to take care of him,' said Charles quietly; 'I know that perfectly well, for I was kept dancing attendance in his antechamber at Blois.* He has M. d'Artagnan, and what better guardian could the King have than M. d'Artagnan? I should make myself perfectly easy with twenty storms of passion, such as Bragelonne might display, if I had four guardians like d'Artagnan.'

'But I entreat your Majesty, who is so good and kind, to reflect a little.'

'Stay,' said Charles II, presenting the letter to the Duke, 'read and answer yourself what you would do in my place.'

Buckingham slowly took hold of Madame's letter, and,

trembling with emotion, read the following words: 'For your own sake, for mine, for the honour and safety of every one, send M. de Bragelonne back to France immediately. Your devoted sister,

'HENRIETTA.'

'Well, Villiers, what do you say?'

'Really, sire, I have nothing to say,' replied the Duke stupefied.

'Nay, would you, of all persons,' said the King artfully, 'advise me not to listen to my sister when she writes so urgently?'

'Oh, no, no, sire; and yet——'

'You've not read the postscript, Villiers; it is under the fold of the letter, and escaped me at first; read it.' And as the Duke turned down a fold of the letter, he read, 'A thousand kind remembrances to those who love me.'

The Duke's head sank gradually on his breast; the paper trembled in his fingers, as if it had been changed to lead. The King paused for a moment, and seeing that Buckingham did not speak, 'He must follow his destiny, as we ours,' continued the King; 'every man has his share of grief in this world; I have had my own—I have had that of others who belong to me—and have thus had a double weight of woe to endure! But the deuce take all my cares now! Go, and bring our friend here, Villiers.'

The Duke opened the trellised door of the summer-house, and pointing at Raoul and Mary, who were walking together side by side, said, 'What a cruel blow, sire, for poor Miss Grafton!'

'Nonsense; call him,' said Charles II, knitting his black brows together; 'every one seems to be sentimental here. There, look at Miss Stewart, who is wiping her eyes,—now deuce take the French fellow!'

The Duke called Raoul, and taking Miss Grafton by the hand, he led her towards the King.

'Monsieur de Bragelonne,' said Charles II, 'did you not ask me the day before yesterday for permission to return to Paris?'

'Yes, sire,' replied Raoul, greatly puzzled by this address.

'And I refused you, I think?'

'Yes, sire.'

'Were you not angry with me for it?'

'No, sire; your Majesty had no doubt excellent reasons for

withholding it; for you are so wise and so good that everything you do is well done.'

'I alleged, I believe, as a reason that the King of France had not recalled you?'

'Yes, sire, that was the reason you assigned.'

'Well, M. de Bragelonne, I have reflected over the matter since; if the King did not, in fact, fix your return, he begged me to render your sojourn in England as agreeable as possible; since, however, you ask my permission to return, it is because your residence in England is no longer agreeable to you.'

'I do not say that, sire.'

'No, but your request, at least,' said the King, 'signified that another place of residence would be more agreeable to you than this.'

At this moment Raoul turned towards the door, against which Miss Grafton was leaning, pale and sorrow-stricken; her other arm was passed through the arm of the Duke.

'You do not reply,' pursued Charles; 'the proverb is plain enough, that "Silence gives consent."* Very good, Monsieur de Bragelonne; I am now in a position to satisfy you; whenever you please, therefore, you can leave for Paris, for which you have my authority.'

'Sire!' exclaimed Raoul, while Mary stifled an exclamation of grief which rose to her lips, unconsciously pressing Buckingham's arm.

'You can be at Dover this evening,' continued the King; 'the tide serves at two o'clock in the morning.'

Raoul, astounded, stammered out a few broken sentences, which equally answered the purpose both of thanks and of excuse.

'I therefore bid you adieu, Monsieur de Bragelonne, and wish you every sort of prosperity,' said the King rising; 'you will confer a pleasure on me by keeping this diamond in remembrance of me; I had intended it as a marriage-gift.'

Miss Grafton felt her limbs almost giving way; and, as Raoul received the diamond from the King's hand, he, too, felt his strength and courage failing him. He addressed a few respectful words to the King, a passing compliment to Miss Stewart, and looked for Buckingham to bid him adieu. The King profited by this moment to disappear. Raoul found the Duke engaged in endeavouring to encourage Miss Grafton.

'Tell him to remain, I implore you!' said Buckingham to Mary.

'No, I will tell him to go,' replied Miss Grafton, with returning animation; 'I am not one of those women who have more pride than heart; if she whom he loves is in France, let him return there and bless me for having advised him to go and seek his happiness there. If, on the contrary, she shall have ceased to love him, let him come back here again, I shall still love him, and his unhappiness will not have lessened him in my regard. In the arms of my house you will find that which Heaven has engraven on my heart,—*Habenti parum, egenti cuncta.** "To the rich is accorded little, to the poor everything."'

'I do not believe, Bragelonne, that you will find yonder the equivalent of what you leave behind you here.'

'I think, or at least I hope,' said Raoul with a gloomy air, 'that she whom I love is worthy of my affection; but if it be true she is unworthy of me, as you have endeavoured to make me believe, I will tear her image from my heart, Duke, even were my heart broken in the attempt.'

Mary Grafton gazed on him with an expression of the most indefinable pity, and Raoul returned her look with a sad, sorrowful smile, saying, 'Mademoiselle, the diamond which the King has given me was destined for you,—give me leave to offer it for your acceptance; if I marry in France, you will send it me back; if I do not marry, keep it.' And he bowed and left her.

'What does he mean?' thought Buckingham, while Raoul pressed Mary's icy hand with marks of the most reverential respect.

Mary understood the look that Buckingham fixed upon her. 'If it were a wedding-ring, I would not accept it,' she said.

'And yet you were willing to ask him to return to you.'

'Oh! Duke,' cried the young girl in heart-broken accents, 'a woman such as I am is never accepted as a consolation by a man like him.'

'You do not think he will return, then?'

'Never,' said Miss Grafton in a choking voice.

'And I grieve to tell you, Mary, that he will find yonder his happiness destroyed, his mistress lost to him. His honour even has not escaped. What will be left him, then, Mary, equal to your affection? Do you answer, Mary, you who know yourself so well.'

Miss Grafton placed her white hand on Buckingham's arm, and, while Raoul was hurrying away with headlong speed, she sang in dying accents the line from *Romeo and Juliet*:—'I must begone and live, or stay and die.'*

As she finished the last word, Raoul had disappeared. Miss Grafton returned to her own apartment, paler even than death itself. Buckingham availed himself of the arrival of the courier, who had brought the letter to the King, to write to Madame and to the Comte de Guiche. The King had not been mistaken, for at two in the morning the tide was at full flood, and Raoul had embarked for France.

LXXXVI

SAINT-AIGNAN FOLLOWS MALICORNE'S ADVICE

THE King most assiduously followed the progress which was made in La Vallière's portrait; and did so with a care and attention arising as much from a desire that it should resemble her as from the wish that the painter should prolong the period of its completion as much as possible. It was amusing to observe him following the artist's brush, awaiting the completion of a particular plan, or the result of a combination of colours, and suggesting various modifications to the painter, which the latter consented to adopt with the most respectful docility of disposition. And again, when the artist, following Malicorne's advice, was a little late in arriving, and when Saint-Aignan had been obliged to be absent for some time, it was interesting to observe, though no one witnessed them, those moments of silence full of deep expression, which united in one sigh two souls most disposed to understand each other, and who by no means objected to the quiet and meditation they enjoyed together. The minutes fled rapidly by, as if on wings, and as the King drew closer to Louise and bent his burning gaze upon her, a noise was suddenly heard in the ante-room. It was the artist, who had just

arrived; Saint-Aignan, too, had returned, full of apologies; and
the King began to talk and La Vallière to answer him very
hurriedly, their eyes revealing to Saint-Aignan that they had
enjoyed a century of happiness during his absence. In a word,
Malicorne, philosopher that he was, though he knew it not, had
learned how to inspire the King with an appetite in the midst
of plenty, and with desire in the assurance of possession. La
Vallière's fears of interruption had never been realised, and no
one imagined she was absent from her apartment two or three
hours every day; she pretended that her health was very uncertain; those who went to her room always knocked before entering, and Malicorne, the man of so many ingenious inventions,
had constructed an acoustic piece of mechanism, by means of
which La Vallière, when in Saint-Aignan's apartment, was always forewarned of any visits which were paid to the room she
usually inhabited. In this manner, therefore, without leaving
her own room, and having no confidante, she was able to return
to her apartment, thus removing by her appearance, a littler
tardy perhaps, the suspicions of the most determined sceptics.
Malicorne having asked Saint-Aignan the next morning what
news he had to report, the latter had been obliged to confess that
the quarter of an hour's liberty had made the King in most
excellent humour. 'We must double the dose,' replied Malicorne,
'but insensibly so; wait until they seem to wish it.'

They were so desirous for it, however, that on the evening
of the fourth day, at the moment when the painter was packing
up his painting implements, during Saint-Aignan's continued
absence, Saint-Aignan on his return noticed upon La Vallière's
face a shade of disappointment and vexation which she could
not conceal. The King was less reserved, and exhibited his annoyance by a very significant shrug of the shoulders, at which
La Vallière could not help blushing. 'Very good!' thought Saint-
Aignan to himself; 'M. Malicorne will be delighted this evening;'
as he, in fact, was, when it was reported to him.

'It is very evident,' he remarked to the Comte, 'that Mademoiselle de la Vallière hoped that you would be at least ten
minutes later.'

'And the King that I should be half an hour later, dear Monsieur Malicorne.'

'You will be but very indifferently devoted to the King,' replied the latter, 'if you were to refuse His Majesty that half-hour's satisfaction.'

'But the painter?' objected Saint-Aignan.

'I will take care of him,' said Malicorne, 'only I must study faces and circumstances a little before I act; those are my magical inventions and contrivances; and while sorcerers are enabled by means of their astrolabe to take the altitude of the sun, moon, and stars, I am satisfied merely by looking into people's faces,* in order to see if their eyes are encircled with dark lines, and if the mouth describes a convex or concave arc.'

And the cunning Malicorne had every opportunity of watching narrowly and closely, for the very same evening the King accompanied the Queen to Madame's apartments, and made himself so remarked by his serious face and his deep sighs, and looked at La Vallière with such a languishing expression, that Malicorne said to Montalais during the evening: 'To-morrow.' And he went off to the painter's house in the street of the Jardins Saint-Paul* to beg him to postpone the next sitting for a couple of days. Saint-Aignan was not within, when La Vallière, who was now quite familiar with the lower storey, lifted up the trap-door, and descended. The King, as usual, was waiting for her on the staircase, and held a bouquet in his hand; as soon as he saw her he clasped her tenderly in his arms. La Vallière, much moved at the action, looked around the room, but as she saw the King was alone, she did not complain of it. They sat down, the King reclining near the cushions on which Louise was seated, with his head supported by her knees, placed there as in an asylum whence no one could banish him; he gazed ardently upon her, and as if the moment had arrived when nothing could interpose between their two hearts; she, too, gazed with similar passion upon him, and from her eyes, so soft and pure, there emanated a flame, whose rays first kindled and then inflamed the heart of the King, who, trembling with happiness as Louise's hand rested on his head, grew giddy from excess of joy, and momentarily awaited either the painter's or Saint-Aignan's return to break the sweet illusion. But the door remained closed, and neither Saint-Aignan nor the painter appeared, nor did the hangings even move. A deep mysterious silence reigned in the room—a silence which seemed to influence even the birds in their gilded prison. The King, completely overcome, turned round his head and buried his burning lips in La Vallière's hands, who, herself faint with excess of emotion, pressed her trembling hands against her lover's lips. Louis threw himself upon his knees, and as La Vallière did not move her head, the King's forehead being within reach of her lips, she furtively passed her lips across the perfumed locks which caressed her cheeks. The King seized her in his arms, and, unable to resist the temptation, they exchanged their first kiss—that burning kiss, which changes love into a delirium. Suddenly a noise upon the upper floor was heard, which had, in fact, continued, though it had remained unnoticed, for some time; it had at last aroused La Vallière's attention, though but slowly so. As the noise, however, continued, as it forced itself upon the attention, and recalled the poor girl from her dreams of happiness to the sad reality of life, she arose in a state of utter bewilderment, though beautiful in her disorder, saying, 'Some one is waiting, for above——Louis, Louis, do you not hear?'

'Well! and am I not waiting for you, also?' said the King, with infinite tenderness of tone. 'Let others henceforth wait for you.'

But she gently shook her head, as she replied, 'Concealed happiness . . . concealed power . . . my pride should be silent as my heart.'

The noise was again resumed.

'I hear Montalais's voice,' she said, and she hurried up the staircase; the King followed her, unable to let her leave his sight, and covering her hand with his kisses. 'Yes, yes,' repeated La Vallière, who had passed half-way through the opening, 'Yes, it is Montalais who is calling me; something important must have happened.'

'Go then, dearest love,' said the King, 'but return quickly.'

'No, no, not to-day, sire! Adieu! adieu!' she said as she stooped down once more to embrace her lover, and then escaped. Montalais was, in fact, waiting for her, very pale and agitated.

'Quick, quick! he is coming?' she said.

'Who—who is coming?'

'Raoul,' murmured Montalais.

'It is I—I,' said a joyous voice upon the last steps of the grand staircase.

La Vallière uttered a terrible shriek, and threw herself back.

'I am here, dear Louise,' said Raoul, running towards her. 'I knew but too well that you had not ceased to love me.'

La Vallière, with a gesture, partly of extreme terror, and partly as if invoking a curse, attempted to speak, but could only articulate one word. 'No, no!' she said, as she fell into Montalais's arms, murmuring, 'Do not touch me, do not come near me.'

Montalais made a sign to Raoul, who stood almost petrified at the door, and did not even attempt to advance another step into the room. Then, looking towards the side of the room where the screen was, she exclaimed: 'Imprudent girl, she has not even closed the trap-door.'

And she advanced towards the corner of the room to close the screen, and also, behind the screen, the trap-door. But suddenly the King, who had heard Louise's exclamation, darted through the opening, and hurried forward to her assistance. He threw himself on his knees before her, as he overwhelmed Montalais with questions, who hardly knew where she was. At the moment, however, that the King threw himself on his knees, a cry of utter despair rang through the corridor accompanied by the sound of retreating footsteps. The King wished to see who had uttered the cry, and whose were the footsteps he had heard; and it was in vain that Montalais sought to retain him, for Louis, quitting his hold of La Vallière, hurried towards the door, too late, however, for Raoul was already at a distance, and the King saw only a kind of shadow turning the angle of the corridor.

[The story is concluded in *The Man in the Iron Mask*]

LIST OF HISTORICAL CHARACTERS

ANNE OF AUSTRIA: Anne of Austria (1601–66), daughter of Philip III of Spain and a member of the Spanish Habsburg family, married Louis XIII in 1615. She remained aloof from the intrigues of Marie de' Medici, the Queen Regent, but actively opposed Richelieu, who set out to destroy Austro-Spanish influence on French policy. She was loyally supported by her 'Spanish entourage', the members of which were steadily eliminated by Richelieu. After Louis's death in 1643, she ruled as Regent during the minority of Louis XIV, working closely with Mazarin, who was almost certainly her lover and possibly her husband. With his help, she defended the interests of the crown during both the Parliamentary and Aristocratic phases of the Fronde (1648–53). Thereafter, she played a lesser political role and as Queen Mother her influence over Louis declined after he took personal control of government after 1661. She died of breast cancer in 1666.

BAISEMEAUX: François de Montlézun (c.1613–97) joined the King's Musketeers in 1634 in which he served with the historical originals of d'Artagnan, Athos, Porthos, and Aramis. He saw active service in Italy during the 1640s and was appointed Captain of Mazarin's Guards in 1649. In 1655 he became *seigneur* de Besmaux, a family property in the Gers in south-west France, and was named Governor of the Bastille in 1658, a post which he held until his death in 1697, leaving a fortune of 2 million livres.

BEAUFORT: François de Vendôme (1616–69), Duc de Beaufort, grandson of Henri IV and his royal mistress Gabrielle d'Estrées. Jailed at Vincennes in 1643 for plotting with Madame de Chevreuse against Mazarin, he escaped on Whit Sunday 1648. For his role in the defence of Paris against the Parlement's forces under Condé he was acknowledged by the people as 'King of Les Halles'. In 1653 he made his peace with the King and later served with honour in the Mediterranean where he died, at the siege of Candia.

BELLIÈRE: see Plessis-Bellière.

BOILEAU: Nicolas Boileau-Despréaux (1636–1711), poet, critic, and principal theorist of French classicism.

BOUTEVILLE: François de Bouteville, Comte de Montmorency (1600–27), famous duellist who dispatched his last opponent at noon on the Place Royale. He was decapitated for blatantly infringing Richelieu's ban on duelling.

BRIENNE: Henri-Auguste de Loménie (1595–1666), Comte de Brienne. An experienced diplomat, he was appointed by Mazarin in 1643 as secretary of state at the Foreign Office. He sold his office to Hugues de Lionne in 1663.

BRIENNE: Louis-Henri Loménie (1635–98), Comte de Brienne, son of Henri-Auguste. He had entered the Foreign Office in 1651 through the influence of his father: the same year he became a secretary of state. In 1663 Louis XIV requested his resignation. His *Mémoires*, first published in 1720 and reissued in 1828 and 1838, were one of Dumas's sources of information on the background to the period.

BUCKINGHAM: George Villiers (1592–1628), first Duke of Buckingham. *The Three Musketeers* chronicles, in exaggeratedly romantic terms, the course of the impossible, requited love he felt for Anne of Austria. A favourite of Charles I, he acquired great wealth and popularity, and he wielded enormous political power, not always wisely.

BUCKINGHAM: George Villiers (1627–87), second Duke of Buckingham, was, after the assassination of his father, brought up with the children of Charles I. During the Civil War he lost his estates, fought at Worcester with Charles, emigrated, and returned secretly to marry the daughter of Thomas Fairfax to whom his estates had been given. They were returned to him after the Restoration and for 25 years he was the wildest of the rakes at Court. He had his father's charm and unpredictability but not his effectiveness. Thus, when Charles crossed from Scotland into England in 1651 on his way to defeat at Worcester, Buckingham, though very inexperienced, demanded command of the army. When Charles refused, he sulked and refused to change his shirt. One of the rakes in the entourage of Charles II, he was unpredictable, inflammable, and bisexual. Though he continued to exert great influence on the King, his excesses and intrigues led him to see the inside of the Tower on four occasions.

CHALAIS: Anne-Marie de la Trémouille, Mme de Chalais, daughter of the Duc de Noirmoutiers. Sometime mistress of the Comte de Guiche (q.v.).

CHALAIS: Henri de Talleyrand (1599–1626), Comte de Chalais, plotted with Madame de Chevreuse against the life of Richelieu. He failed and in August 1626 was beheaded not by the regular executioner but by an unskilled volunteer who required thirty attempts to complete his task.

CHARLES I: Charles Stuart (1600–49), King of England, was executed at Whitehall on 30 January 1649.

CHÂTILLON: Isabelle Angélique de Montmorency-Bouteville (d. 1695), widow of Gaspard de Coligny (1620–49), Duc de Châtillon, who was killed at the battle of Charenton in 1649. She was well known for her amorous intrigues and may have been mistress in 1651 to Charles II. She remarried in 1664 and became the Duchesse de Mecklembourg.

CHEVREUSE: Claude de Lorraine (1578–1657), Duc de Chevreuse.

CHEVREUSE: Marie-Aimé de Rohan-Bazon (1600–79), widow of the Duc de Luynes, married the Duc de Chevreuse in 1622. She was one of the Queen's 'frivolous' friends and ran through many lovers most of whom, like Chalais (q.v.), she involved in her plots to unseat Richelieu. Louis XIII exiled her but she regularly returned to Court where she continued her intrigues. She abetted Buckingham's plans to invade France in 1628 and was again banished, first to Poitou and later to the château-prison at Loches, 40 km south of Tours. In 1637 she escaped and fled to Spain and thence to England, where she was caught up in the English Civil War and briefly imprisoned on the Isle of Wight. She lived in Belgium until she was allowed to return to France in 1643 by Mazarin, whom she opposed. She was again exiled for her intrigues, and eventually settled in Brussels where she continued to side with the enemies of Mazarin. She returned to France after the Amnesty of Reuil on 12 April 1649. She continued to be active throughout the Fronde, though her scheming partnership with Laigues (q.v.) continued on a reduced scale. Dumas makes her the mother of Raoul.

CINQ-MARS: Henri Coeffier d'Effiat, Marquis de Cinq-Mars, executed in 1642 for conspiring against Richelieu with Madame de Chevreuse.

COLBERT: Jean-Baptiste Colbert (1619–83), a draper's son, was by 1639 an official in the War Office under Le Tellier. In 1651 he entered the service of Mazarin who entrusted him with increasingly important responsibilities and who, on his deathbed (9 March 1661), recommended him to Louis XIV: 'I owe you everything, but I pay my debt to your majesty in giving you Colbert.' In 1661 he became Louis's chief minister and immediately began introducing the reforms which were necessary after the maladministration of Fouquet (q.v.). In 1661 revenues amounted to 82 million livres but took 52 million to collect; within a decade, the figures were 104 and 27 million. Among other measures, Colbert forced the tax-farmers to restore Crown revenues which they had appropriated. His economic policies were accompanied by administrative reforms and a determination to develop every aspect of national life. Dumas did not care for him, and usually portrays him as ruthless and personally uncouth. Even so, he gives a fair estimate of Colbert's achievements in *The Man in the Iron Mask* (World's Classics edition, p. 466).

CONDÉ: Louis de Bourbon (1621–86), Duc d'Enghien, became Prince de Condé on the death of his father in 1646. Known as 'Monsieur le Prince' and 'Condé the Great', he fought with valour at the battles of Rocroy (1643), Nordlingen (1644), and Lens (1648). In the autumn of 1648 he threw his military skills behind the royal cause. Believing he had been insufficiently rewarded for his efforts, he reacted with such arrogance that he alienated both the Queen and Mazarin. In 1650 he was jailed at Vincennes. In 1651 the political situation had changed and Mazarin was forced to release him. He thereupon raised an army to rescue the young King from his advisers. He failed, refused to accept the peace of 1653, went over to Spain and took part in all the campaigns against France. He was rehabilitated in 1659, and retired to his estate at Chantilly. Recalled to service in 1668, he fought his last battle in 1674.

CRÉQUY, MME DE: wife of François Créqui (sic) (d. 1687) who was made director of France's galleys in 1661, and Marshal of France in 1668. Mme de Créqui enjoyed a reputation for great virtue.

DANGEAU: Philippe, Marquis de Dangeau (1638–1720), an assiduous courtier renowned for his wit and author of a detailed *Journal* chronicling life at court from 1684 onwards.

FELTON: John Felton (1595–1628), the Puritan zealot who murdered the Duke of Buckingham at Portsmouth in 1628. In Dumas's version of events (*The Three Musketeers*, chapter 59), Felton was goaded to his act by Milady.

FOUQUET: A protégé of Mazarin, Nicolas Fouquet (1615–80) was still, in 1661, Superintendant of France's finances and the master of vast wealth acquired through abuse of power. He built the magnificent château at Vaux (1658) and was a generous patron of art and literature. He was admired for his munificent style of management, but resented by sections of the court and the bourgeoisie for his unashamed corruption. It has been argued that Louis turned against him out of jealousy for his wealth, but it is more likely that he feared the influence of Fouquet who, in 1658, acquired the Breton island of Belle-Isle from which he might have led a campaign against the throne at a time when Louis had yet to command the obedience of all the provinces of France. A cabal was formed to ruin him. Fouquet was arrested by Charles de Batz (the real d'Artagnan) in September 1661 and, after his trial, was escorted (also by d'Artagnan) to the prison of Pignerolles in the Savoy, where he remained until his death in 1680. Dumas, himself a reckless man who admired lavish style, gives Fouquet a noble and sympathetic persona. It was Fouquet who appointed Aramis Bishop of Vannes and promised him a cardinal's hat. On his instructions, Aramis fortified Belle-Isle, using the skills of Porthos who remained ignorant of his plans. Exploiting his position as Vicar-General of the Jesuits, Aramis was prepared to throw the inexhaustible resources of the Order behind his protector against the wily Colbert who, by means of purloined letters, had amassed enough evidence to convince the King of Fouquet's corruption. Dumas viewed Fouquet as a dashing Cavalier who possessed all the flair and imagination he found lacking in the grim and devious Roundhead, Colbert.

FOUQUET: Basile Fouquet (1622–80), brother of Nicolas, was an *abbé* with devious talents whom Mazarin placed at the head of his secret service. He had a hand in many of the political intrigues of the 1640s and 1650s, and his plotting helped his brother to acquire high office. He turned against Fouquet after about 1657 and quarrelled publicly with him in January 1661. After Fouquet's fall, he was exiled. After Fouquet's trial in 1664, according to Courtilz de Sandras (*Memoirs of d'Artagnan*, iii. 163 ff.), he pretended to be mad to escape a fate similar to his brother's. Fouquet's judgement of him ('a fellow without a heart, without ideas; a devourer of wealth'; *The Vicomte de Bragelonne*, ch. 55) was shared by many.

GRAMONT: Antoine de Gramont (1604–78), Comte de Guiche, later Duc de Gramont, was made Marshal of France in 1641. He was the father of Raoul's friend, the Comte de Guiche (q.v.).

GUICHE: Armand de Gramont (1637–73), Comte de Guiche, a soldier and a man of considerable charm who enjoyed amorous intrigues with both men and women. Dumas makes him Raoul's closest friend. He was part of the entourage of Philippe d'Orléans, whose favourite he was. 'He was the handsomest and most attractive man at court, utterly charming, gallant, bold, courageous, who radiated an air of natural nobility and grandeur. The vanity which resulted from possession of so many good qualities, together with the contemptuous manner which accompanied everything he did, detracted somewhat from his merit, yet it must be admitted that no other courtier possessed as much of that commodity as he. Monsieur had been extremely fond of him since boyhood and had always maintained regular relations with him which were as close as any that can exist between young men' (Mme de La Fayette, *Histoire de Madame Henriette*, p. 449).

GUISE: Claude de Lorraine (1496–1550) was the first of the Ducs de Guise who were politically active in the sixteenth century: François (1519–63), who took Calais from the English, was assassinated by a Protestant, while Henri (1550–88), who had a claim on the French throne, was famously murdered at Blois. Though the family had passed its heyday, Henri de Lorraine (1614–64), Duc de Guise, was prominent at the court of Louis XIV.

HENRI IV: Henri IV (1553–1610), grandfather of Louis XIV, had revived French fortunes abroad and at home ended the religious strife of the sixteenth century.

HENRIETTA: Henrietta Stuart (1644–70), youngest daughter of Charles I and Henrietta Maria and granddaughter of Henri IV of France. She was left at Exeter when her mother fled to France, but her governess, Lady Dalkieth, dressed as a beggar woman, smuggled her to France in 1646 where her mother brought her up as a Catholic. Clever and beautiful, she became Duchesse d'Orléans ('Madame') when she married Philippe, brother to Louis XIV, on 31 March 1661. Philippe's homosexuality and jealousy made their marriage unsuccessful. In 1670 Louis XIV sent her to England where she persuaded Charles II, her brother, to sign the Treaty of Dover. On her return to France, she died of poison.

HENRIETTA MARIA OF ENGLAND: Henrietta Maria (1609–69), daughter of Henri IV and younger sister of Louis XIII, had married Charles of England by proxy in 1625. The marriage had been arranged by Buckingham. After the Rebellion, she parted from Charles in 1644 and escaped to France whence she observed events in England with alarm. She was not well received, especially after the death of Charles I when she lived in near destitution. She remained in France until October 1660, when she returned briefly to London with Henrietta. She spent the years 1662–5 in England (Pepys called her 'a very little, plain old woman') and died of an overdose of opiate in her château at Colombes. Her remains were buried at Saint-Denis.

LA BAUME LE BLANC: Laurent de la Baume le Blanc (1611–51), *seigneur* de la Vallière, soldier and administrator, married Françoise de la Coutelaye in 1640, mother of his three children. See la Vallière and Saint-Rémy.

LA FAYETTE: Marie-Madeleine Pioche de la Vergne (1634–93), Comtesse de la Fayette, separated from her husband and settled in Paris in 1659. She was an intimate of the circle of Henrietta (later Duchesse d'Orléans) and wrote an account of her life, *Histoire de Madame Henriette d'Angleterre* (published posthumously in 1720), on which Dumas drew heavily. She is remembered as a novelist, her masterpiece being *La Princesse de Clèves* (1678), written in a formal, ceremonial style, which shows that duty and happiness are not compatible. She is usually credited as the pioneer of the *roman d'analyse*— the psychological novel—to which the French have remained addicted.

LA FONTAINE: Jean de la Fontaine (1621–95), known primarily as the author of the *Fables* (1668–94) and various collections of *Tales* which appeared between 1664 and his death.

LAIGUES: Geoffroy, Marquis de Laigues (1614–74), former Captain of guards to Gaston d'Orléans, who fought in the campaigns of the 1640s and distinguished himself at the battle of Lens (1648). His association with Madame de Chevreuse (whom he later secretly married) dated from the Fronde (see *Twenty Years After*) in which he played a prominent part.

LAPORTE: Pierre de la Porte (1603–80) entered the service of Anne of Austria in 1621. He enabled her to correspond with the Spanish court and for his 'treasons' was imprisoned by Richelieu in 1637. He returned to favour when Anne became Regent in 1643. He served the Queen loyally and was made Louis XIV's *valet de chambre* in 1645, a position which he used to undermine the influence of Mazarin. His *Memoirs*, first published in 1755, were one of Dumas's major sources.

LA ROCHEFOUCAULD: François (1613–80), Prince de Marcillac, later Duc de la Rochefoucauld, played a prominent role in the Fronde. However, he is best remembered as the author of the cynical *Maximes* (1665) which attribute human motivation to love of self.

LA VALLIÈRE: Françoise-Louise de la Baume le Blanc (1644–1710), later known as the Duchesse de la Vallière, was born near Amboise. She was part of the entourage of the Duchesse d'Orléans at Blois and moved with her to Paris after the death of Gaston d'Orléans (q.v.). In 1661 the Duchesse de Choisy proposed her as lady-of-honour to Henrietta d'Orléans with a pension of 100 livres and the privilege of living at the Tuileries. There she caught the attention of the King. She was his mistress between 1661 and 1667 and bore him four children. Reckoned to be no great beauty, she was tall and slim, had blue eyes and poor teeth. Contemporaries noted that she limped slightly, but danced well. She attracted Louis by the sweetness of her face and manners. After being replaced by Madame de Montespan, she retired from court life in 1670 and took the veil in 1674.

LA VIEUVILLE: Charles (1582–1653), Marquis de la Vieuville, was briefly Superintendant of Royal Finances in 1623 when he introduced fiscal reforms which antagonized the nobility. He was arrested on the orders of Richelieu in 1624. He later served during the Regency of Anne of Austria and again became Superintendant of Finances in 1651.

LIONNE: Hugues de Lionne (1611–71), Minister of State and Secretary for Foreign Affairs, who concluded the Treaty of the Pyrenees with Spain in 1659.

LONGUEVILLE: Anne-Geneviève de Bourbon-Condé (1619–79), Duchesse de Longueville. She was the sister of Condé (q.v.) and mistress of la Rochefoucauld (q.v.) during the Fronde.

LORET: Jean Loret (1600–65), the author of a weekly verse gazette which commented on public events and people. He supported Fouquet and, after his arrest, spoke in his defence. For his pains, Colbert stopped his small pension. However, Fouquet, from prison, arranged for a sum of money to be paid to him anonymously.

LORRAINE: Philippe (1643–1702), called the Chevalier de Lorraine because it was assumed that he would join the Order of the Knights of Malta. Later known as Prince Philippe, he was for many years the favourite of Philippe d'Orléans who ensured he was given military and ecclesiastical preferment.

LOUIS XIII: Louis de Bourbon (1601–43), 'Louis the Just'. He became king of France and Navarre in 1610 on the assassination of his father, Henri IV. He survived the revolt led by his mother the Regent, Marie de' Medici, and appointed Richelieu as his Prime Minister in 1624.

LOUIS XIV: Louis de Bourbon (1638–1715), the Sun King.

LUYNES: Charles (1578–1621), Marquis d'Albert, Duc de Luynes was an intimate of Louis XIII. He was instrumental in turning the King against the Queen Regent's ambitious adviser, Concini, in 1617. Subsequently, he acquired high office as Constable of Normandy. But in 1621 he failed to halt the Protestants at Montauban and, growing increasingly unpopular, he was disgraced. In 1617 he married Marie de Rohan, the future Duchesse de Chevreuse (q.v.).

LUYNES: Louis-Charles d'Albert (1620–90), Duc de Luynes, son of Madame de Chevreuse by her first marriage.

MALICORNE: Germain Texier (1626–94), Baron de Malicorne. Dumas makes him the son of a lawyer, an intriguer with lofty ambitions. In fact, Malicorne was a squire of the Duc de Guise by 1648 and already the lover of Mlle de Pons. In 1665 he married a daughter of Saint-Rémy (q.v.) by his first marriage.

MANCINI: the family name of Mazarin's numerous nieces and nephews. Hortense (1646–99) married the Duc de la Meilleraie, a great-nephew of Richelieu: the couple took the title of Duc and Duchesse de Richelieu. Louis fell in love with Marie (1640–1715) in 1658 but instead made a political marriage with the Infanta of Spain. Olympe (1639–1708) married the Duc de Soissons in 1657 and later became Louis's mistress.

MANICAMP: Louis de Madallan de Lesparre (c.1628–1708) fought his first campaign in 1646 and served under Condé at Lens (1648) and elsewhere. His *seigneurerie* at Manicamp in the Soissonnais was made into a *comté* in 1693 and his son, Roger-Constant (1691–1723), was known as the Comte de Manicamp. However, of the historical Louis de

Madallan (who lost an arm at Charenton in 1652), Dumas retains only the name.

MARIA-THERESA: Maria-Theresa of Austria (1638–83), daughter of Philip IV (1605–65) of Spain. Through an alliance promoted by Mazarin, she married Louis XIV at St Jean-de-Luz on 6 June 1660. Of a retiring disposition, she suffered considerably through the King's infidelities first with Madame and then with La Vallière.

MARILLAC: Louis de Marillac (1573–1632) was arrested for intriguing against Richelieu and executed at the Place de Grève.

MAZARIN: The Italian-born Giulio Mazarini (1602–61), a soldier and diplomat in the service of the Pope who sent him to France to negotiate with Richelieu in 1630. Richelieu retained him to defend French interests in Italy. He was present at the French court as papal legate in 1634, became Richelieu's protégé, and in 1639, on entering the service of the King of France, was naturalized French. In 1641 he was made cardinal through the influence of Richelieu who, shortly before his death, recommended him as his successor. Though personally unpopular, he made himself indispensable to the Queen Regent. Mazarin was her lover and may (as Dumas believed) have been secretly married to her: though a cardinal, he was not an ordained priest. His power aroused the envy of the nobility, his demands for increased taxes alienated the middle class, and his foreign origins were a focus for popular resentment. He was generally considered to be excessively avaricious and self-serving: estimates of his private fortune on his death range from 13 to 40 million livres. His diplomatic skills were very great. He furthered French interests in southern Germany by the Treaty of Westphalia which ended the Thirty Years War in 1648 and secured the alliance of Cromwell in 1654. At home, he survived the Fronde and so strengthened the French throne that Louis XIV's creation of the modern French nation owed a great deal to him. He brokered the marriage of Louis XIV with the Spanish Infanta in 1660. He died at the Château de Vincennes on 9 March 1661, more, it was reported, a philosopher than a Christian, though the priest who attended his last moments affirmed that he died in the true faith.

MICHON, MARIE: the name by which Madame de Chevreuse is known in *The Three Musketeers*.

MONK: George Monk (1608–70) was a career soldier who had seen active service on the Continent. After signing the Covenant, he served under Cromwell and in 1654 was made governor of Scotland. When political disorder peaked in the autumn of 1659, he decided to intervene. On 1 January 1660 he crossed the Tweed with 6,000 men and in five weeks reached London unopposed. He kept his motives secret and allied himself with no party. His own preference for the return of the Stuarts was confirmed by the rising tide of popular opinion. On 23 May 1660 he was at Dover to meet Charles who made him Duke of Albemarle and gave him the highest offices in the state. He withdrew soon after from political life but continued to serve Charles as a naval commander in engagements against the Dutch.

'MONSIEUR': the court title of the King's brother: it was given to Gaston d'Orléans until his death in 1660 and thereafter to Philippe d'Anjou, who succeeded him as Duke of Orléans.

'MONSIEUR LE PRINCE': that is, Condé.

MONTALAIS: Nicole-Anne-Constance de Montalais, whom Dumas calls 'Aure', was lady-in-waiting at the court of Gaston d'Orléans at Blois, and a companion to Louise de la Vallière. In 1661 she was attached to the retinue of Henriette, Duchesse d'Orléans, to whom she was presented by Mlle de Montpensier. She shared the apartments of Louise de la Vallière at the Tuileries and received her confidences, which she broke to further her own schemes. She had a taste for intrigue and was involved in the 'Spanish letter' affair of 1662, a plot to inform the Queen of Louis's secret liaison with La Vallière.

MONTESPAN: Françoise-Athénaïs de Rochechouart de Mortemart (1641–1707) was born at the château de Tonnay-Charente. A maid-of-honour at the wedding of Philippe d'Orléans and Henrietta in March 1661, she married the complaisant Duc de Montespan et d'Antin in 1663. As Mme de Montespan, she was to oust Louise de la Vallière from the affections of Louis XIV by 1667.

MONTMORENCY: Henri, Duc de Montmorency, was executed for treason in 1632.

MOTTEVILLE: Françoise Bertaut (1621–89) married Nicolas Langlois, *seigneur* de Motteville, in 1639, by which time she was a trusted member of the Queen's 'Spanish' entourage. Her *Memoirs*, first published in 1723 and reprinted in 1824 and 1838, were extensively used by Dumas for the background to the period.

NAVAILLES: Suzanne de Baudéan (d. 1700), Duchesse de Navailles, married Philippe de Montaut de Bénac, Duc de Navailles, in 1651. In 1661 he was governor of Le Havre. She was appointed lady-in-waiting to the Queen but was disgraced in 1664.

ORLÉANS: Gaston-Jean-Baptiste de France, Duc d'Orléans (1608–60), younger brother of Louis XIII, known as 'Monsieur', had regularly participated in the intrigues mounted against Richelieu. On the accession of Louis XIV in 1643, he was appointed Lieutenant-Governor of the Kingdom. He supported Anne of Austria during the first Fronde but after the second was exiled to Blois in 1652. He was reconciled with Louis at the end of 1659 and received him at Chambord and Blois in January 1660. In *The Man in the Iron Mask* (World's Classics edition, p. 190), Aramis judged him to be 'void of courage and honesty', a verdict echoed by contemporaries like Retz who remarked that Orléans 'had everything a gentleman should have, except courage'.

ORLÉANS: Henri d'Orléans (1595–1663) was the husband of Madame de Longueville, Condé's sister.

ORLÉANS: Marguerite de Lorraine (1613–72), Duchesse d'Orléans, wife of Gaston, known as 'Madame' and, after his death, as the 'Dowager Madame'.

ORLÉANS: Philippe d' (1640–71), second son of Louis XIII and Anne of Austria, and brother to Louis XIV. He was Duc d'Anjou until the death of Gaston, his uncle, in February 1660 when he inherited the title and was thereafter known as 'Monsieur'. He married Henrietta of England on 31 March 1661. His homosexuality ensured that the marriage was not a happy one.

PHILIPPE: see Orléans, Philippe d'.

PLESSIS-BELLIÈRE: Suzanne de Bruc (1608–1705), wife of Jacques de Rougé, Marquis de Plessis-Bellière (1603–54), who died in action at Naples. She remained close to Fouquet throughout the 1650s. It was she, not Mme Fouquet, who organized the superintendant's cultural gatherings which could be serious but were often playful: when her parrot died in 1653 Fouquet and his entourage wrote verses to mark its passing.

RICHELIEU: Armand-Jean du Plessis (1585–1642) was Bishop of Luçon before being appointed cardinal in 1622. He was named Head of the Royal Council in 1624 and became the most powerful man in France during the reign of Louis XIII. An admirer of Machiavelli, he played a crucial role in maintaining France as a great international power and in creating the highly centralized state which Louis XIV was to inherit and further strengthen. It was against the wily and ruthless 'Red Duke' (so called because of his cardinal's robes and his Dukedom of Richelieu) that d'Artagnan and his comrades had waged an epic struggle of wits in *The Three Musketeers*.

SAINT-AIGNAN: François de Beauvillier (1610–87), Comte de Saint-Aignan, a former governor of the Touraine. He was elected to the French Academy in 1663. He was part of the military establishment at the court of Gaston d'Orléans at Blois before becoming First Gentleman to the King's Bedchamber. Though considerably older than Louis (he had three daughters who were abbesses), he became the purveyor of pleasures to his Majesty.

SAINT-RÉMY, MME DE: Françoise le Prévôt de la Coutelaye, who became Mme de Saint-Rémy on her third marriage in 1655. Her first husband was Besnard, Councillor at the Parlement of Rennes. Her second, Laurent de la Baume le Blanc (q.v.), was the lord of the manor of La Vallière at Reugny, 10 km. west of Amboise, and owner of a town house at Tours, where their daughter Louise was born on 6 August 1644. Her second husband died in 1651. In 1655 she married Saint-Rémy, First Chamberlain to Gaston d'Orléans. After Gaston died in 1660, she moved to Paris with Saint-Rémy (q.v.).

SAINT-RÉMY: Jacques Couravel, Marquis de Saint-Rémy, was appointed principal chamberlain to Gaston d'Orléans at Blois on 6 March 1655, the year in which he married Louise's mother, Françoise de la Coutelaye. After Gaston's death in February 1660, he moved to Paris where he continued in his functions in the household of Philippe, the new Duc d'Orléans.

SCUDÉRY: Georges de Scudéry (1601–67), author, with his sister Madeleine (1608–1701), of two influential novels in the 'precious' style: *Artamène, ou le Grand Cyrus* (1649–53) and *Clélie* (1654–60).

THOU: François-Auguste de Thou (1607–42) was decapitated with his friend Cinq-Mars (q.v.) for plotting against Richelieu.

TONNAY-CHARENTE: see Montespan.

TREMBLAY: Charles le Clerc du Tremblay, brother of François (q.v.), surrendered to parliamentary forces on 12 January 1649 and was replaced as governor of the Bastille by Pierre Broussel.

TREMBLAY: François le Clerc du Tremblay (1577–1638) was known as 'le père Joseph' but also as 'l'éminence grise' because of his monkish robes and shadowy power. He became chief adviser and confidant to Richelieu, whom he first met in 1611.

TRÉVILLE: Arnaud-Jean du Peyrer (1598–1672), Comte de Troisvilles (pronounced and usually written Tréville), was a Gascon career soldier like d'Artagnan. His courage and loyalty were admired by Louis XIII who appointed him Captain-Lieutenant of his Musketeers in 1634. In 1642 he was exiled for his opposition to Richelieu, and when Mazarin disbanded the Musketeers in 1646 he retired to Foix as its governor. According to *The Three Musketeers*, which makes the main characters about ten years older than their historical counterparts, it was in Tréville's office in 1625 that Dumas, following Courtilz de Sandras's pseudo-*Memoirs of d'Artagnan* (i. 13), arranged the first meeting between d'Artagnan, Athos, Porthos, and Aramis.

VALENTINOIS: Catherine-Charlotte de Gramont (1639–78), sister to the Comte de Guiche, married Louis de Grimaldi, Duke de Valentinois, Prince of Monaco, in 1660. She was not reckoned to be chaste, even by the broadest standards. Mme de Sévigné speaks of her often as the Princesse de Monaco.

VALOT: Antoine Valot (1594–1671), court physician to Louis XIV.

VANEL: Anne-Marguerite Vanel was the daughter of Claude Vanel (d. 1687), a magistrate in the Paris *parlement* and later controller of finances to Philippe, Duc d'Orléans. She was the wife of Jean Coiffier, who became a member of the Royal Audit Office in 1654. According to Courtilz's *Vie de Colbert* she was 'a dainty and extremely pretty young woman with a lively and very witty turn of mind'. In the late 1650s she became Fouquet's mistress, subsequently transferring her affections to Colbert who, wearying of her high spirits, passed her on to his brother.

VENDÔME: see Beaufort.

VILLEROY: François de Neufville (1644–1730), Duc de Villeroy and Marshal of France, a prominent figure at Court who later commanded Louis's armies: he was defeated at Romillies in 1706. He was designated by Louis XIV as governor of the young Louis XV. His father, Nicolas de Neufville (1597–1685), Marquis de Villeroy and also a Marshal of France, had been Louis XIV's governor.

WARDES: François-René Crespin du Bec (1620–88), Marquis de Vardes, captain of the Cent-Suisses, well known for his intrigues. He was bold, scheming, and a consummate liar, though Mme de Motteville nevertheless found him 'charming' (*Memoirs*, Paris, 1847, iv. 279). His wife, Nicolaï, died in 1660, an event which scarcely interrupted the flow of liaisons and plots. Implicated in the 'Spanish letter' affair of 1662, he was banished to Aigues-Mortes, of which he had been appointed Governor in 1660, where he remained for seventeen years.

EXPLANATORY NOTES

[The symbol † indicates that fuller information will be found in the List of Historical Characters.]

7 *Raoul and the Comte de la Fère*: Raoul, Vicomte de Bragelonne, is the son of the Comte de la Fère, a family title to which Athos reverted after the adventures described in *The Three Musketeers*, which ended in 1628. On Raoul, see note to p. 185. For Athos, see note to p. 176.

with the Queen-Mother: in the last chapter of *The Vicomte de Bragelonne*, the Queen Mother, Anne of Austria†, persuaded the 2nd Duke of Buckingham†, who loves Henrietta of England†, now Duchesse d'Orléans, that personal honour and the future relations between France and England would be best served by his return to England. By Dumas's chronology, a few weeks only have passed since Henrietta married Philippe, Duc d'Orléans†, on 31 March 1661.

sister-in-law a present: 'Madame' was the courtesy title given to the wife of the Duc d'Orléans who, as the King's oldest brother, was always known as 'Monsieur'. 'Madame'—Henrietta, sister of Charles II—was thus Louis XIV's sister-in-law and the 'various goods' were silks for which Lyons was famous.

M. Colbert and M. Fouquet: in the spring of 1661, the two most powerful royal ministers. See List of Historical Characters.

Blois: 18 km. south-west of Paris on the Loire. In 1628, at the end of *The Three Musketeers* (World's Classics edition, p. 663), Athos retired to 'a small property in the Roussillon'. Subsequently, a 'near-relative' named Bragelonne left him the estate of La Fère (*Twenty Years After*, World's Classics edn., p. 352), a half-hour's gallop from Blois and at a distance of three gunshots from La Vallière, a fifteenth-century manor near Reugny, 10 km. north-west of Amboise: see *Twenty Years After* (World's Classics edn., p. 129). There was no estate of La Fère or Bragelonne.

ask me for something: Athos may reasonably expect any request he makes to be favourably received. His standing at court is extremely high after the crucial role which he, abetted by d'Artagnan, played in restoring Charles II to the throne of England: see *The Vicomte de Bragelonne*, chs 24–33.

8 *de la Vallière*: Louise de la Vallière† was the daughter of Laurent la Baume le Blanc†, *seigneur* de la Vallière. After his death, his widow, Françoise, married the Marquis de Saint-Rémy†, principal chamberlain to Gaston d'Orléans†.

dowager Madame's household: Marguerite de Lorraine, wife of Gaston d'Orléans, was known as the 'Dowager Madame' after her husband's death in 1660.

Princess's maids of honour: the Princess is Henrietta, Duchesse d'Orléans. The story of how she secured the appointment is related in *The Vicomte de Bragelonne*, chs 77–81.

not very pretty: Louise was not considered a great beauty and she walked with a slight limp, the result of a badly set broken leg. She was known especially for the sweetness of her character. Mme de Sévigné described her as 'a little violet hidden in the grass'.

9 *the credit of the family*: though a Marquis, Saint-Rémy was of unremarkable stock. Even though, after Gaston's death, he continued as principal chamberlain to the Dowager Madame, he was, in seventeenth-century terms, no more than a superior servant.

devotion to your Majesty: though Athos has wearied of the politics of court and the intrigues of ministers, he remains faithful to a noble, chivalric concept of service to the monarchy. He had attempted to rescue Charles I and defend the interests of the young Louis (in *Twenty Years After*) and had helped restore the English monarchy (in *The Vicomte de Bragelonne*) not because he hoped for preferment but out of loyalty to the principle of kingly rule. It is this philosophy which he has instilled in Raoul.

young as I am: Louis XIV, born in 1638, is now 23 and at a turning point. His capable First Minister, Mazarin, died on 9 March 1661 and, free of interference, Louis will choose (on 4 May) to take personal charge of the affairs of France. The absolutism of his reign is already detectable in his decisive manner.

10 *gloomy and melancholy*: Raoul has already received an intimation that Louise does not love him as deeply as he loves her. See *The Vicomte de Bragelonne*, ch. 89.

12 *d'Artagnan*: as Lieutenant of the Royal Musketeers, d'Artagnan occupied quarters in the Louvre, the Royal Palace. His duty required him to remain near the King. However, with the money given as a reward for his part in restoring the English monarchy, he has acquired a house in town which he rents out: see *The Vicomte de Bragelonne*, chs 52 and 61.

Guiche's livery: Armand de Gramont, Comte de Guiche†, Raoul's closest friend.

13 *de Wardes*: in the pseudo-*Memoirs of d'Artagnan* (i, chs 6–7), Courtilz de Sandras tells how an English noblewoman, called simply 'Milédi', becomes infatuated with the wealthy Marquis de Wardes, 'one of the handsomest noblemen of the court'. He is identified (iii. 54–9) as the brother of Antoine, Comte de Moret, who was killed at the siege of Gravelines in 1658. De Wardes became a favourite of Louis XIV and might have gone far had he not fallen under the influence of the Comtesse de Soissons. From these and other details, it is clear that Courtilz had in mind François-René Crespin du Bec, Marquis de Vardes, who serves as the basis for two distinct characters in the saga. In *The Three Musketeers*, the treacherous de Wardes (aged 25 in 1627) is a loyal servant of Richelieu and a cousin to the Rochefort who insulted d'Artagnan at Meung. He stands in the path of d'Artagnan as he speeds to England to retrieve the diamond studs given by Buckingham to the Queen and is left for dead at Calais in chapter 20. In fact, the historical de Wardes† was 7 years old at the time and his villainy premature. But in the last of the three Musketeer chronicles, the same historical figure reappears as his own son and plays a role much closer to his real, intriguing self.

Manicamp: Dumas turns the historical Manicamp†, a minor noble, into an essential part of the entourage of the Comte de Guiche. Though he is poor, he scorns money and exhibits an aristocratic nonchalance which endears him to Guiche. In Romantic terms, he is a dandy who hides great shrewdness under a veneer of laconic banter.

affair of the barricade: see *The Vicomte de Bragelonne*, ch. 87, where de Wardes insults Raoul and provokes him to a duel.

14 *my whole being*: in *The Vicomte de Bragelonne* (ch. 84), Guiche organized the reception of Princess Henrietta of England at Le Havre in February 1661 on her journey to Paris where she would marry Philippe, Duc d'Orléans. Guiche promptly fell in love with her.

15 *Duke of Buckingham*: according to one of Dumas's main sources for the sentimental history of Louis XIV's court, Madame de La Fayette's *Histoire d'Henriette d'Angleterre* (1720), Buckingham was first 'extremely attached' to the Princess Maria, Henrietta's sister. After her death in December 1660, 'the Duke fell so passionately in love with [Henrietta] that it might be said that he took leave of

his senses' (Mme de La Fayette, *Œuvres complètes* (ed. Roger Duchêne, Paris, 1990), p. 448). Buckingham was included in the party which escorted Henrietta from London on her way to France in January 1661. Pepys reports (11 January) that their departure from Portsmouth was delayed when a storm blew the ship on to a sand bar and Henrietta fell 'sick of the meazles'. He also records (7 February) that Buckingham and Sandwich fell out at Le Havre 'at cards'. Mme de La Fayette (op. cit., pp. 449–50) gives these events a more dramatic turn. When the royal party reached Portsmouth, Buckingham, unable to 'bring himself to be parted from the Princess of England, asked permission of the King [Charles II] to journey to France'. When her ship grounded and Henrietta fell ill, he 'behaved like a madman plunged into despair during those moments when he believed her very life was threatened. At the last, when she was well enough to brave the sea and make towards Le Havre, he became so excessively jealous of the attentions which the English Admiral [Sandwich] showed for the Princess that he would grow angry with him for no reason, and the Queen [Henrietta Maria], fearing lest some serious disorder should result, commanded the Duke of Buckingham to proceed directly to Paris while she remained some while in Le Havre to allow her daughter to regain her strength. When she was completely well again, she travelled to Paris. Monsieur [Philippe d'Orléans] sallied forth to meet her with all the attentions imaginable and continued until his marriage to show her a consideration which lacked nothing except love. But the miracle which lit a flame in the heart of this Prince was within the reach of no woman of flesh and blood. The Comte de Guiche was at that time his favourite.' Even so, Buckingham's attentiveness was plain even before the marriage was celebrated: 'Monsieur soon became aware of it and it was on this occasion that Madame Henrietta first became acquainted with his constitutional jealousy of which he was later to give her so many proofs. She observed his downcast looks and, as she cared nothing for the Duke of Buckingham who, although most charming had all too often known what it is not to be loved, she spoke to her mother the Queen who made it her business to straighten Monsieur's crooked thoughts and make him realize that the Duke's love was an absurd matter of no consequence. This did not displease Monsieur, yet he was not entirely satisfied. He spoke of it to his mother the Queen [Anne of Austria] who felt some sympathy for the passion of the Duke which reminded her of the love which his father had long ago shown to her. She insisted that the matter should not be made public but took the view that the Duke should be given to understand, when he had continued at the French court some while longer, that his presence was necessary in England. And this was what was decided and acted upon.' Dumas followed this account closely in *The Vicomte de Bragelonne*: Anne allays the fears of Monsieur in ch. 91 and persuades Buckingham to leave France in ch. 92.

16 *meet him at Vincennes*: that is, challenge Buckingham to a duel in the Bois de Vincennes, which lay outside the city walls.

a mission: Buckingham was charged with escorting Henrietta to Paris, where she was to be married.

close to the Bastille: the fort of Vincennes housed part of the Royal Administration but was also a secure jail which held prisoners of State from the thirteenth century until the French Revolution. It was located a few miles from the Bastille, a fortified gaol built in the fourteenth century, which was constructed in the old city wall, at the Porte Saint-Antoine in the east of Paris. It was extended at various times and, as we shall see (see note to p. 59), was equipped with eight towers each five storeys high. Prisoners entered a courtyard overlooked by the Governor's quarters (the 'Cour du Gouvernement') and passed through a guarded portcullis before being taken to a dungeon or, in the case of prisoners of rank, to a room in one of the towers. The Bastille held many notable historical and literary prisoners and eventually came to symbolize the repressive character of the *ancien régime*.

the Palais Royal: Cardinal Richelieu had acquired land near the Louvre, then the Royal Palace, and on it built a residence, completed in 1636, which was known as the 'Palais Cardinal'. In 1639 he gave it to Louis XIII, and thereafter it was known as the Palais Royal.

17 *the father*: that is, George Villiers, first Duke of Buckingham, who plays a dashing role in *The Three Musketeers* as the melancholy lover of Anne of Austria. The 'older courtiers' here express an opinion not shared by the English who had been alarmed by the first Duke's recklessness and feared the influence of the second on the fledgling King Charles II.

Belle-Isle: Belle-Isle, a large island off Saint-Nazaire, in Quiberon Bay. It had belonged to the Abbey de Sainte-Croix at Quimperlé before passing into the Gondi family. It was bought in 1658 by Fouquet[†] on instructions from Mazarin. Fouquet, considering it a safe refuge against any reversal of his fortunes, fortified it with 200 cannon. In *The Vicomte de Bragelonne*, he had commissioned Aramis to plan the fortifications and the work was supervised by Porthos (chs 68–72). When d'Artagnan discovers the secret plot, Fouquet forestalls Colbert, who fears that Belle-Isle might be used as a base for a campaign of opposition to the throne, and makes a gift of the island to the King (ch. 74). In fact, Fouquet never offered Belle-Isle to Louis XIV. After Fouquet's arrest on 5 September 1661, royal troops were sent there and the garrison promptly surrendered. Fouquet's grandson, the Marshal de Belle-Isle, gave the island to Louis XV in exchange for the Comté de Gisors in 1718.

17 *captain of the musketeers*: actually Captain-Lieutenant. The Musketeers, then numbering 100 men, had been formed in 1622 as Louis XIII's personal bodyguard. The Captain was the King, day-to-day command being exercised by a Captain-Lieutenant, a post held between 1634 and 1646 by Tréville†. In that year, the Musketeers were disbanded by Mazarin who re-formed the force in 1657 when he appointed his nephew, the largely absentee Duke de Nemours, as Captain-Lieutenant. They were then a company 150 strong, were paid 35 *sous* a day and wore a sky-blue surtout decorated with a silver cross. They were known as 'Grey Musketeers' after the colour of their horses. A second company of 'Black' Musketeers was created in 1660. Both followed the King and saw service in the siege wars of the period. Dumas's d'Artagnan received his commission in the Musketeers from Richelieu in 1628 at the end of *The Three Musketeers* but had not progressed beyond the rank of lieutenant by 1649 (*Twenty Years After* (World's Classics edition), p. 29). For his part in bringing the first phase of the Fronde to a satisfactory close, Anne of Austria had named him Captain-Lieutenant (ibid., p. 769). However, Mazarin had rescinded his appointment 'as soon as peace was made' after the conclusion of the second phase in 1652: see *The Vicomte de Bragelonne* (ch. 14), where a rather bitter d'Artagnan resigns his commission. He remained briefly a free agent until Louis recalled him in ch. 53 where he offered to make him 'Captain-General' to report on the situation at Belle-Isle. This d'Artagnan accepted and he is now at last officially commander of the Musketeers.

18 *good terms with me*: after the death of Mazarin (9 March 1661), Louis, abetted by Colbert, resolved to end Fouquet's corrupt reign as finance minister and began by attacking his lax direction of the 'farming' of taxes: 'tax-farmers' bought an entitlement to collect taxes, proceeded to raise more money than was contracted for and kept the difference. It was a system open to abuse. In reality, Louis would not have dared to challenge the powerful Fouquet openly,

but Dumas relates (*The Vicomte de Bragelonne*, chs 49–64) how the King set up Courts to try two corrupt tax-farmers, d'Eymeris and Lyodot (both inventions of Dumas). Fouquet attempted to rescue them but his efforts were frustrated by d'Artagnan who drove off the mob and ensured that the men were duly hanged (ch. 62). Although Fouquet therefore has no reason to like d'Artagnan, he decides that it is better to have him as a friend than as an enemy and, forestalling Colbert, rewards him handsomely for his services to the Crown. D'Artagnan, whose experience of life makes him suspicious, nevertheless concluded that Fouquet was a man of chivalry and honour, the antithesis of the avaricious accountant, Colbert.

19 *the Queen-Mother, the young Queen*: that is, Anne of Austria[†] (wife of Louis XIII and mother of Louis XIV), and Maria-Theresa[†], Queen of France since June 1660.

red and perfumed lips: with such indirect indications Dumas establishes the more than ambivalent sexuality of 'Monsieur' (the court title of Philippe, Duc d'Orléans).

20 *my departure*: see note to p. 7.

appreciates true gentlemen: Dumas ranked Charles II of England among life's cavaliers with the first Duke of Buckingham, Fouquet, and the Musketeers and set them against life's roundheads: Richelieu, Mazarin, and Colbert.

dweller in the East: there are many instances of sleepers who wake, from Epimenides to Rip-Van-Winkle. Claude Schopp (*Les Mousquetaires*, 1991, ii. 593 n.) suggests Dumas has in mind Hasan Badr al-Din, the victim of an elaborate plot by the father of his bride who wishes to be certain that he has consummated his marriage. He is carried off by two genies (one of whom is shot down by Allah by means of a shooting star) and abandoned at Damascus. He protests that the previous night he 'lay in Cairo' but the crowd tells him he is mad. His trials continue and he believes that for ten years he has been a pastry-cook in Damascus. When he is released from his dream and restored to his wife Sitt al-Husn, he wonders 'whether he was awake, next whether he was asleep, and lastly whether he was mad': see *The Thousand and One Nights* (tr. Mardrus and Mathers, Routledge & Kegan Paul, 1964, nights 21–24). Dumas greatly admired the verve and invention of *The Arabian Nights*, first translated into French between 1704 and 1715 by the Orientalist Antoine Galland (1646–1715).

21 *the Chevalier de Lorraine*: Philippe de Lorraine†, a member of the entourage of the Duc d'Orléans and, like his patron, homosexual. Dumas gives him a disruptive role to play.

23 *of your father*: see *The Vicomte de Bragelonne*, ch. 87, where de Wardes claims that d'Artagnan 'was guilty of a cowardly act towards my father'.

24 *of the darkness*: a reference to events in ch. 35 of *The Three Musketeers*, in which d'Artagnan, with the help of Kitty, the maid, and under cover of darkness, is welcomed into the bed of Milady who was expecting de Wardes senior. The episode was based on Courtilz de Sandras's pseudo-*Memoirs of d'Artagnan* (tr. Ralph Nevill, London, 1899, i, chs 6–7) where 'Milédi' was in love with de Wardes but was tricked by d'Artagnan.

25 *married in England*: according to Courtilz (ibid.), d'Artagnan encountered an Englishwoman, known only as 'Milédi', in Paris in 1643, where she was part of the entourage of the Queen of England: her hatred of him began when she took exception to his anti-British sentiments. Dumas developed the character into a figure of great power and mystery. Her true identity is never revealed, but in *The Three Musketeers*, she is known at various times as Anne de Breuil, Lady Clarick, and Charlotte Backson. Athos knows all about her because she was his wife until, on disovering that she bore the brand of thief and harlot, he repudiated her. Subsequently, she married (bigamously) the fictitious Lord de Winter, Baron of Sheffield, who was already dead, poisoned by her, when d'Artagnan first encountered her in 1626. Clearly, de Wardes is entirely ignorant of the circumstances of his father's extra-marital adventures.

your father's murderer: after failing to kill her most persistent adversary on several occasions (most memorably by means of a gift of poisoned wine sent to the Musketeers at the siege of La Rochelle in 1628: *The Three Musketeers*, ch. 42), Milady had embarked for England where she was apprehended and detained by her brother-in-law. Using all her feminine wiles, she persuaded her gaoler, the puritan John Felton†, to do her will: he duly murdered the Duke of Buckingham at Portsmouth on 23 August 1628 (ibid., chs 50–9).

26 *death of King Charles I*: de Wardes was badly wounded during his treacherous attack on d'Artagnan at Calais in 1626 during the affair of the Queen's diamond studs (*The Three Musketeers*, ch. 20). He had lived long enough to tell his young son that he hated

the man who had slain him, even though he had met him only once. D'Artagnan seems to confuse his English adventure in 1626 with his return to France twenty years later when, in spite of the heroic efforts of the Musketeers to save him (see *Twenty Years After*, chs 63–70), Charles I was executed on 30 January 1649.

27 *which forbid it*: duels had been outlawed during the reign of Henri III (1574–89). Louis XIII renewed the ban in 1617 and in the following decade a number of high-ranking duellists were decapitated. Richelieu enforced the ban as did Louis XIV and his successors in the next century. The ban was justified on a number of grounds. The Crown could not afford to lose good fighting men in petty squabbles but, more importantly, the duelling code was based on an ideal of aristocratic honour which not only transcended royal authority but directly challenged it. Even so, duelling—a form of natural justice which took precedence over the King's law—outlived the *ancien régime* and continued in France in various forms until the end of the nineteenth century.

28 *M. Baisemeaux de Montlezun*: François de Montlézun, *seigneur* de Besmaux (or Baisemeaux†), became Governor of the Bastille in 1658 and remained in office until his death in 1697.

31 *tired enough*: in fact, it took d'Artagnan 'three seconds' to wound de Wardes three times and not much longer, as his opponent attempted to surprise him with his dagger, to pin him 'to the earth with a fourth wound through the body' (*The Three Musketeers*, World's Classics edition, p. 192).

32 *at La Rochelle*: at the siege in 1628. See *The Three Musketeers*, chs 41–46.

Grimaud: Athos's loyal, taciturn servant since the beginning of the Musketeer saga.

33 *the Cardinal's time*: d'Artagnan and Baisemeaux may be 'acquaint-ances of five-and-thirty years' standing', as we soon learn, but Baisemeaux did not become a Musketeer until 1634, and could not therefore have taken part in the rivalry between the King's Mus-keteers and Cardinal Richelieu's Guards of which so much is made in *The Three Musketeers*.

34 *my income*: as with most public offices during the *ancien régime*, the governorship of the Bastille was bought and sold like any other property. Fortunes were made out of the difference between the expenses of the office and the income they could be made to generate. The Governor of the Bastille was paid 50 livres a day for royal prisoners, 30 for aristocrats and generals, from 15 to 5 for

detainees of lesser social standing, and 3 livres for poets, tradesmen, bailiffs' clerks, etc. Baisemeaux purchased the post in 1658
for 40,000 livres (well short of the 150,000 later quoted by Dumas)
and, when he died in 1697, he was worth 2 million livres. The
franc was introduced only after the Revolution of 1789. Until
then, its equivalent was the *livre tournois*. The *pistole* was worth 10
livres and the *louis* 24.

35 *you are sixty*: born around 1613, Baisemeaux is not quite 50, which
makes him at least five years younger than d'Artagnan.

at Montlézun: Montlézun was the family name. His estate, acquired in 1655, was at Baisemeaux in the Gers.

12,000 francs a year: d'Artagnan's estimate seems high. In 1660,
musketeers were paid 35 *sous* a day. More generally, a sub-
lieutenant's pay was 1,000 livres and a full colonel received 6,000.
The 20,000 d'Artagnan was offered by Fouquet in *The Vicomte de
Bragelonne* (ch. 63) was quite exceptional.

from the King himself: see *The Vicomte de Bragelonne*, ch. 53.

Messrs Tremblay and Louvière: when the Fronde began in 1648, the
Governor of the Bastille was Charles le Clerc du Tremblay[†] who
capitulated to the *frondeurs* in January 1649. He was replaced by
Pierre Broussel, a respected member of the Paris *parlement*, whose
arrest in August 1648 had triggered the unrest. Broussel's functions as governor were carried out by his son Jérôme, *seigneur* de
Louvières.

36 *sprung from the barricades*: i.e. the Fronde. As the King's first
minister, Mazarin[†] controlled the buying and selling of public
offices.

Aramis: Henri d'Aramitz was an obscure Musketeer mentioned
(along with Armand de Sillègue d'Athos d'Autevielle and Isaac de
Portau) in the first chapter of Courtilz's pseudo-*Memoirs of
d'Artagnan*. In *The Three Musketeers*, Aramis was already considering becoming a Lazarist brother. But d'Artagnan finds him in a
Jesuit monastery in *Twenty Years After* (chs 9–10) where he is
known as the abbé d'Herblay. He was appointed Bishop of Vannes
by Fouquet in April 1661 (*The Vicomte de Bragelonne*, ch. 17) and,
as we shall see, he is set to rise even higher.

37 *150,000 francs, then?*: i.e. 5,000 *pistoles*, or 50,000 livres per year for
three years.

Noisy-le-Sec: d'Artagnan too had vainly sought Aramis at the Jesuit
monastery at Noisy-le-Sec, 6 km. north-east of Paris, in *Twenty*

Years After (ch. 9). He had also failed to find him at Melun in *The Vicomte de Bragelonne* (ch. 17), but finally caught up with him at Vannes (ibid., chs 71–73).

40 *the Queens*: i.e. the Queen Mother (Anne of Austria) and Queen Maria-Theresa. Also present a few lines below is Madame Henrietta Maria, wife of the late Charles I, currently the English Queen Mother, then in Paris following the marriage of her daughter ('grand-daughter of Henri IV') to Philippe d'Orléans.

Nestor: king of Pylos, oldest of the Greek princes who besieged Troy, known for his wisdom and renowned for the speech he delivered to the assembled chiefs at the beginning of the *Iliad* (Bk. 1). Homer rated his 'honey-tongued' eloquence as superior even to that of Ulysses.

for a ballet: Henrietta (now 'Madame') had been smuggled to her mother in France in 1646 at the age of 2 and had been brought up on the fringes of the French court. Mme de Motteville records (*Mémoires*, iv. 255) that Louis refused to dance with her at a ball given in the winter of 1655, saying that 'he did not care for little girls'. He had even asked his brother, Philippe, why he was so eager to marry 'a bag of bones' (Mlle de Montpensier, *Mémoires*, Paris, 1824–5, iii. 421). But Henrietta made a great impact on the French court. 'What are called grace and charm informed her whole person, her actions and her mind, and never was princess so well fitted to be loved by women and adored by men' (Mme de La Fayette, op. cit., p. 448).

41 *Montalais*: Nicole-Anne-Constance de Montalais[†], referred to by Dumas as 'Aure'.

43 *Porthos*: after his exhausting ride from Vannes with a despatch from Aramis to Fouquet (see *The Vicomte de Bragelonne*, chs 73–74), Porthos has been rebuilding his strength.

44 *new application for funds*: Fouquet has already provided the King with 2.5 million livres to pay for the wedding of Philippe d'Orléans and Henrietta (*The Vicomte de Bragelonne*, ch. 75). He knows that he will maintain his position (which guarantees his freedom) only for as long as he can supply the King with money. Colbert is of course anxious to bankrupt his coffers and bring him down.

45 *investigation of the accounts*: see note to p. 18.

Cardinal: that is, Richelieu had been not only the effective ruler of France in the reign of Louis XIII but had also been a prince of the Church.

Belle-Isle: which he had given to the King. See note to p. 17.

47 *Marie Michon*: the name adopted by Mme de Chevreuse†, Aramis's secret contact at court in *The Three Musketeers*.

deeds and titles: Aramis provided Baisemeaux with money to purchase the governorship, but retains the legal papers proving his entitlement until the debt is repaid.

48 *gate of the Bastille*: the Bastille was situated in the parish of Saint-Paul-des-Champs: its cemetery (opened in 631 and in use until 1791) was the designated burial-ground for its prisoners. Travelling east from the Louvre along the Rue Saint-Antoine, Aramis passes the church on his right, then comes to the Rue du Petit-Musc which ran down the western wall of the Arsenal to the Seine, before halting at the Porte Saint-Antoine at the junction of the Rue Saint-Antoine and the Rue des Tournelles, where the Bastille was situated.

53 *'Grey Eminence'*: François le Clerc du Tremblay†, brother of Charles, former governor of the Bastille.

Sixty: the Bastille could accommodate up to 80 prisoners but averaged 40 inmates during the reign of Louis XIV. On the daily tariff, see note to p. 34.

56 *Mazarinades*: the name given to the large number of pamphlets, songs, and other lampoons directed against Mazarin both at the time of the Fronde and afterwards. As Claude Schopp has noted (*Les Mousquetaires*, ii. 627 n.), the prison register has no record of a prisoner of this name, though it does mention a book-binder named Marsolier.

57 *Seldon*: one of Dumas's occasional characters based on a mention in Courtilz's *L'Inquisition française ou l'Histoire de la Bastille* (Paris, 1715) of a 'schoolboy of twelve or thirteen' who was jailed in about 1674 for writing satirical verses against the Jesuits. In *The Man in the Iron Mask* (World's Classics edition, pp. 236, 295), Seldon is Irish or 'Scotch'.

Marchiali: the burial register of the Bastille at 19 November 1703 records the death of 'Marchioly, aged forty-five, or thereabouts', the name being subsequently changed to 'M. de Marchiel'. Dumas was not alone, however, in writing 'Marchiali', a name which shelters the identity of the prisoner who wore the famous mask. For a review of the many attempts to establish the true identity of 'Marchiali', see the Introduction to *The Man in the Iron Mask* (World's Classics edition, pp. xvii–xxii).

58 *Volnay*: one of the best-known Beaune wines.

59 *towers of the Bastille*: on each of its longest sides, the Bastille had four towers, each five storeys high. Prisoners were accommodated in them and also in underground dungeons according to rank. The Tour de la Bertaudière was situated in the south-west corner.

Seven or eight years, nearly: that is, since 1653 or 1654. In capitalizing on the perennial fascination with the mysterious masked prisoner, Dumas advances the chronology by several decades.

63 *at Belle-Isle*: see *The Vicomte de Bragelonne*, chs 69–70.

64 *loved by them*: in *The Three Musketeers*, Aramis (born, we now learn, in 1606) wrote verses, including a poem made up of lines of one syllable. He was also the lover of Mme de Chevreuse ('Marie Michon'). In *Twenty Years After*, he had been loved by Mme de Longueville.

71 *to resemble him*: the mystery will not be revealed until *The Man in the Iron Mask* (World's Classics edition, p. 34) where the valet of the preceding pages is identified as La Porte[†], the nurse as Mme Péronne, and the veiled lady as Anne of Austria.

the letter 'M': for Marchiali.

72 *Mme de Bellière's door*: Suzanne de Bruc (whom Dumas calls Eliza), Marquise de Plessis-Bellière[†].

Madame Vanel: Anne-Marguerite Vanel[†], a former mistress of Fouquet.

Bellière: perhaps in Brittany. The family had connections with Nantes.

73 *twenty-eight years old*: the Marquise was in fact 53. Her husband was killed in battle in Italy in 1654.

74 *Danaë's tower*: an oracle foretold that Danaë, daughter of King Acrisios of Argos, would produce a son who would kill his grandfather. Acrisios, determined to prevent any such unfortunate occurrence, shut her up in an inaccessible tower made of brass. However, Zeus, assuming the form of a shower of gold, seduced her. The result was Perseus who survived and, while demonstrating his skill at quoits, inadvertently killed a bystander who turned out to be his grandfather.

75 *Jupiter*: in Roman mythology, the equivalent of the Greek god Zeus.

Buckingham: Marguerite means, of course, Fouquet.

de Chalais and de Thou: both Chalais[†] and de Thou[†] were decapitated by unskilled executioners: it took thirty blows of the axe to sever Chalais's head from his body in 1626.

76 *Saint-Mandé*: now part of Paris's eastern suburb, Saint-Mandé, in the Bois de Vincennes, was in 1661 a small rural community dominated by the country house where Fouquet's literary entourage and political associates met regularly.

77 *on M. Colbert*: shortly before his death on 9 March 1661, Mazarin had recommended Colbert to Louis. The young King, however, had already decided to rule France himself. His decision to remove Fouquet would be taken on 4 May.

   M. Fouquet's honour: see note to p. 17.

78 *these friends are dead*: i.e. d'Eymeris and Lyodot: see note to p. 18.

   Egeria: a secret, trusted adviser. In Roman mythology, Egeria was a wood-nymph from whom Numa Pompilius (761–714 BC) received counsel on how to frame wise laws. They met in a grove near Aricia.

   great strides: though hardly an impartial observer, Mme Vanel's observations on both Fouquet (see note to p. 44) and Colbert will be vindicated by history.

80 *without a heart*: Dumas means no more than a dubious attraction of opposites based on the 'atomic' system of Democritus (born *c*.470 or 460 BC) who argued that all things, from material phenomena to thought and even the gods, were accretions of atoms impelled by a primary motion which brought them into contact with each other. Epicurus (341–270 BC) refined this philosophy, concluding that the visible world is the result of collisions of atoms: even the soul is made of subtle particles. Such views have little place in the thought of René Descartes (1596–1650) who argued that truth is to be sought in a 'Method' which he defined as a process of rational deduction from the most incontrovertible truth, rising from the simple to the complex. He was a materialist only in the sense that he believed that the body was a machine, but affirmed that it was somehow linked to a soul capable of thought and will. The expression *atomes crochus* now means no more than a natural affinity.

   French gold: a frequent and well-founded charge which Dumas substantiates in *The Vicomte de Bragelonne*, chs 10, 45–48.

81 *M. Faucheux*: one of Dumas's invented characters.

82 *from Messieurs de Guise*: on the Duchess and the Guise family, see the List of Historical Characters.

83 *balas rubies*: a type of spinel ruby, pale rose-red or even orange in colour.

my father and mother: yet Dumas will later make her the daughter of 'Lord Grafton': see p. 654.

85 *two hours*: earlier (*The Vicomte de Bragelonne*, ch. 47), Fouquet, using his English horses, had covered the 50 km. separating his house at Vaux-le-Vicomte and the Louvre in an hour and a half.

it will be remembered: in *The Vicomte de Bragelonne* (ch. 54), Mme de Bellière uses a house connected by a secret passage to Fouquet's residence at Saint-Mandé to warn him that Louis and Colbert have begun to move against the tax-farmers who support him. She summoned him by means of an ingeniously contrived bell. Dumas, never a man to waste a secret tunnel, confuses Fouquet's house at Saint-Mandé with his town house at the present no. 374, Rue St Honoré, which was joined by a passageway to no. 263 opposite, and was used for stores, kitchens, and stables.

87 *gained a victory*: Mme de Bellière's assessment of the honourable, chivalric Fouquet was shared by Dumas who, before the end of the paragraph, will present him as an archetypal Romantic hero, fine, feverish, and melancholic.

88 *other creatures*: Dumas's view of women was very much a reflection of his times, which classified them according to a set of fixed images: the *femme fatale* (Milady, Montalais), the innocent maiden (Louise), Woman-as-Mother (Anne of Austria), and the woman of experience, of whom Mme de Bellière is an example. For other comments on women, see pp. 124, 181, 333, 449, 598.

92 *his departure*: in the middle of April 1661.

the Queen-Mother: 'Monsieur and Madame' are Philippe d'Orléans and his bride of two weeks' standing, Henrietta, daughter of Charles I and of Henrietta Maria (the 'Queen-Dowager'). The Queen is Maria-Theresa, wife of Louis XIV, and the Queen-Mother, Anne of Austria.

93 *almost a Frenchman*: Buckingham† had spent much of his adolescence in France.

94 *recently adopted daughter*: that is, 'Madame'.

96 *Port-Royal*: originally a convent, founded in 1204 near Chevreuse, Port-Royal transferred to the capital in 1625. By 1636 it was already moving towards Jansenism, an austere doctrine of divine grace declared heretical in 1713. Among the Port-Royal faithful were a number of the century's most gifted moral philosophers and logicians, including Pascal. Racine was a pupil of the school which they ran, as was de Wardes, it seems, unless Dumas simply

refers to the influential *Logique de Port-Royal*, an essay on the 'art of thinking', which appeared in 1662. Port-Royal taught a method of rational argument based on Cartesian principles (see note to p. 80). It was closed by Louis XIV in 1709 and the building demolished in 1710.

99 *any interference*: that is, to pursue his passion for Madame. But Dumas simplifies. At this point (mid-April 1661), according to Mme de La Fayette (op. cit., p. 449), Guiche was in love not with Henrietta but with Mme de Chalais†, whose response was lukewarm: 'He sought her out, followed her wherever she went . . . if he were not truly loved he was not hated either, and she looked upon his love without anger.' Guiche then turned his attention to Louise de la Vallière until the King began to find her attractive, upon which Guiche, 'who was not sufficiently in love to challenge so formidable a rival, gave her up and even quarrelled with her, using her very rudely' (ibid., p. 453). It was not until Madame realized that Louise had captivated the King (towards the end of July) that she became receptive to the attentions of Guiche.

100 *for Madame's society*: 'After remaining some time in Paris, Monsieur and Madame removed to Fontainebleau [19 April, where Louis and Maria-Theresa had preceded them]. Madame took thither good cheer and amusement. The King realized, now that he saw her at closer quarters, how unjust he had been in not finding her the most beautiful woman in the world. He became very attached to her and was extremely attentive . . . This was around the middle of the summer' (Mme de La Fayette, op. cit., p. 451).

Fontainebleau: south-west of Paris, near Melun. The famous château was built in the sixteenth century for François I and was situated in an extensive forest, a favourite hunting-ground of the kings of France.

101 *Châtillon*: like Mme de La Fayette herself (op. cit., p. 451), Mme de Châtillon† was a maid-of-honour to Madame. Subsequently she was one of the many conquests of Charles II.

and Mademoiselle de Tonnay-Charente: see List of Historical Characters. Malicorne† and Montalais†, both social climbers, have been in league since *The Vicomte de Bragelonne*.

102 *Spanish seguedillas*: popular songs and dances. Both Maria-Theresa and Anne of Austria were Spanish.

105 *by delaying the explanation*: also a part of Dumas's battery of narrative techniques.

109 *Epicurean philosophers*: Epicurus taught that pleasure is the greatest human good and that the ideal life is one from which all anxieties are banished. It was this philosophical cultivation of the mind—and not simple hedonism—which attracted the 'Epicureans', a group of intellectuals sympathetic to Fouquet. Interest in such ideas had been revived by Gassendi, a free-thinker, who published a life of Epicurus in 1647.

111 *as his emblem*: Louis chose (in 1662, a year later than events recounted here) to be known as the Sun King not merely because the sun and stars were an image of his court but also, he said, because the sun shines its light upon all, does good unceasingly, and is unwavering in its course.

113 *abruptly*: though Guiche spent much time in Henrietta's company at Fontainebleau, Monsieur's jealous outburst occurred later that summer than Dumas's narrative requires. Events unfolded as follows: 'At this juncture [when Maria-Theresa realized that Louis's affections were elsewhere engaged], there were persistent rumours that the Comte de Guiche was in love [with Henrietta]. Monsieur was soon apprised and showed him a great deal of hostility. The Comte de Guiche, either on account of his proud nature or out of countenance on seeing Monsieur informed of a thing of which he would have preferred him to remain ignorant, had a stormy interview with him and quarrelled as though they had been equals. The matter became public knowledge and the Comte withdrew from court. On the day the rumour broke, Madame remained in her room and saw no one. Not knowing what had happened, she gave orders that only those who were to rehearse [a ballet] with her should be admitted, and the Comte de Guiche was of this number. The King answered with a smile saying that she was unaware that there were persons who ought to be excused, then proceeded to tell her of what had passed between Monsieur and the Comte de Guiche. The matter thus became public knowledge and the Marshal de Gramont, father of the Comte de Guiche, despatched his son to Paris and ordered him not to return to Fontainebleau' (Mme de La Fayette, op. cit., p. 455).

115 *tranquil future for her*: her optimism will be short-lived as Louis increasingly takes control of domestic and foreign policy in the 1660s which will see reform at home and war abroad.

poor young man: that is, Buckingham, the son of the man she once had loved, for whom she feels a certain maternal responsibility. To placate Philippe, she had sent Buckingham home to England in the last chapter of *The Vicomte de Bragelonne*.

119 *a fortnight*: Anne is mistaken. Monsieur married Henrietta on 31 March whereas events are situated well into the period spent by the court at Fontainebleau (19 April to the beginning of August).

121 *1662*: read '1661'.

123 *my father*: Charles I, beheaded on 30 January 1649.

125 *any woman*: not because he 'loves himself too much' but because, as Dumas reminds us again, he is homosexually inclined.

128 *displease you*: see note to p. 40.

131 *for Buckingham*: see note to p. 115.

   a year past: Dumas postdates Louis's assumption of power. After the death of Mazarin on 9 March, Louis decided to rule personally, though it was not until May that he felt sure enough of himself to begin the process of ousting Fouquet. It is now past mid-summer, for rehearsals are beginning for the *Ballet of the Seasons* (music by Lully and libretto by Benserade) which was performed at Fontainebleau on 26 July 1661.

136 *Pomona*: Etruscan goddess of fruit, fruit-trees, and gardens, and wife of Springtime. The allusion becomes clearer when we learn that Louis danced the role of Spring.

   Egypan: a kind of troll, half-man and half-goat, which lived in hills and pounced upon the unwary traveller.

137 *son of the Marshal de Gramont*: that is, Guiche.

139 *glad to see you*: in fact, it was Guiche's father who ordered him to leave Fontainebleau: see note to p. 113.

   Madame de Noailles: Anne-Louise Boyer (1632–97), Duchesse de Noailles.

140 *Garamanths . . . and Patagonians*: the Garamantes were known to classical authors as a people of the African interior who lived like brute creation. The Scythians were barbarians who occupied regions north and north-east of the Black Sea, the furthermost parts of which were uninhabited because of the coldness of the climate. The Hyperboreans were reckoned to be the most northerly people; they lived beyond Boreas (the home of the north wind) which Virgil located beneath the North Pole. The Caucasians lived on Caucasus, an immensely high mountain situated between the Euxine and Caspian seas. The Patagonians were an austral people who inhabited an area of what is now southern Argentina, at the tip of South America.

142 *installed at Fontainebleau*: Louis and Maria-Theresa left Paris for Fontainebleau in the middle of April. However, according to Dumas's narrative, it is now July.

Moret: Moret-sur-Loing, 10 km. south-east of Fontainebleau.

bathing in the Seine: 'it was mid-summer. Madame was in the habit of going to bathe each day, setting out by coach, because of the heat, and returning on horseback, followed by all the ladies dressed in the most gallant costumes and wearing innumerable feathers in their hair, escorted by the King and the youth of the court. After supping, they climbed into carriages and, to the sound of violins, spent part of the night being driven along the canal' (Mme de La Fayette. op. cit., p. 451).

145 *Vulaines*: Vulaines-sur-Seine, 5 km. east of Fontainebleau.

bathing Dianas: Diana persuaded Jupiter, her father, to agree that she would never marry. He gave her a quiver of arrows and a retinue of nymphs and made her queen of the woods. Surprised while bathing by Acteon, she turned him into a stag which was promptly eaten by his own dogs. Diana was represented wearing a chlamys, a short tunic, pinned at the shoulder, which allowed her knee to be seen.

147 *Oreades*: in Greek mythology, nymphs of woods and grottoes.

149 *Saint-Aignan*: Louis had made Saint-Aignan[†] First Gentleman to his Bedchamber.

150 *formal style of gardening*: the seventeenth century admired the disciplined, geometric garden, best exemplified in the work of André Le Nôtre (1613–1700), designer of the parks of Vaux-le-Vicomte and Versailles, where nasturtiums and flowering broom were quite out of place. The 'picturesque and the fanciful' would not appeal greatly until the second half of the eighteenth century, when the less formal, more 'natural' style of the 'English garden' suited pre-Romantic sensibilities.

155 *with some one else*: by the end of June, Louis's attentiveness to Madame was causing concern to both the French and English Queen Mothers. 'The rumours reached such a pitch, and the Queen Mother [Anne of Austria] and Monsieur broached the question so openly with the King and Madame, that they at last began to open their eyes and perhaps reflect on matters on which they had not reflected before. They resolved to put an end to the rumours and, for reasons of their own, agreed between themselves that the King should pay his attentions to some lady of the court.' They considered Mlle de Pons, Mlle de Chemerault, and Louise

de la Vallière, who was then attracting the eye of Guiche. 'In concert with Madame, the King began to pay his respects not merely to one of the three whom they had chosen, but to all three at the same time. But he was not long in making up his mind. His heart spoke for La Vallière . . .' (Mme de La Fayette, op. cit., p. 453). By 20 July at the latest, Anne of Austria learned that Louise was the King's mistress.

156 *Dr Dawley*: there appears to be no trace of Dr Dawley in the entourage of Charles II, whose court physician was the celebrated Dr Scarburgh. His advice is very much in the tradition of the anti-medical satire of Molière.

157 *Montespan*: Mlle de Tonnay-Charente married the Duc de Montespan in 1663. As Mme de Montespan[†], she succeeded Louise as the King's mistress in 1667.

159 *lame*: 'although she was slightly lame, she danced well' (Mlle de Montpensier, *Mémoires*, iv. 394).

Daphné . . . escape Apollo: a nymph who was changed into a laurel bush just as Apollo was about to catch her. Henrietta's remark becomes more pointed when it is remembered that Apollo was the sun god and Louis the Sun King.

162 *Condé*: Condé[†], known as 'Monsieur le Prince' and 'the Great Condé', was one of the century's leading soldiers.

Mme de Scudéry . . . without stopping: in *Clélie* (1654–60), a long pastoral novel by Mlle de Scudéry[†], appears the 'Carte de Tendre' ('Map of Tenderland') which guides lovers through the approved stages along love's way. Louis plans a course which takes him along the river Inclination. Other routes led to the 'Lake of Indifference' and the 'Sea of Aversion'.

163 *celebrated costume*: Louis XIV was portrayed innumerable times in varied courtly, heroic, and symbolic dress. The most celebrated image of his theatrical roles, however, showed him as the Sun in a ballet performed in 1662 which is generally thought to have prompted his decision to be identified henceforth as the Sun King, a device which he adopted that same year.

Villeroy: the Duc de Villeroy[†], a prominent courtier and later military commander.

166 *grove of trees*: the ballet was danced on 26 July 1661. It was, reports Mme de La Fayette (op. cit., p. 454), 'the finest that ever was done, partly owing to the place where it was performed, which was the bank of the lake, and partly on account of the ingenuity which

had been used to bring the staging of the piece from the far end of a long avenue. The theatre was filled by an immense crowd which imperceptibly drew nearer and was illuminated by fauns who danced in front of the stage.'

167 *Mechlin*: Mechlin (or Malines) in Belgium, famous for its distinctive bobbin-lace.

168 *Guiche is here*: Guiche's reappearance is an invention of Dumas. Ordered to leave Fontainebleau by his father (see note to p. 113), he remained in Paris where he made remarks intended 'to persuade the public that they would not be in error if they supposed that he was in love with [Madame]'. His 'offensive vanity' made Henrietta furious (Mme de La Fayette, op. cit., p. 457).

170 *five-and-thirty years of age*: a reflection of Dumas's fascination, echoed by his contemporaries, with the woman of experience best portrayed, perhaps, in Balzac's *La Femme de trente ans* (1831–4).

171 *hamadryads*: nymphs, sisters of the dryads, who inhabited forest-trees and died when the tree died. The nymphs of fruit-trees were called Melides and Hamamelides.

Pomona: see note to p. 136.

174 *a devoted sister*: Madame de Valentinois†.

175 *mutual hopes*: their girlish mood is evoked in chapter 1 of *The Vicomte de Bragelonne*. Like Louise, Montalais had been part of the retinue of the previous Duchesse d'Orléans at Blois in the Loire valley. There were châteaux nearby at Cheverney and Chambord.

177 *Acteon*: see note to p. 145.

178 *Henry II . . . Gabrielle d'Estrées*: Fontainebleau had been a royal residence since the time of François I (1494–1547). Diana de Poitiers (1499–1566) was the mistress of his successor, Henri II (1519–59). Gabrielle d'Estrées (1573–99) was the mistress of Henri IV (1572–1610), by whom she had two sons, César and Alexandre de Vendôme.

179 *M. de Montespan*: whom Françoise-Athénaïs de Tonnay-Charente would marry in 1663. However, Mme de La Fayette notes that she was at this time in love with the Marquis de Noirmoutiers and wished to marry him.

181 *the Stadtholder*: there was no Stadtholder in 1661. William of Nassau had died in 1650 leaving an infant son to inherit his title. The Act of Exclusion (1654) debarred any member of the House of Orange from holding the office, and it was not until the French

invasion of 1672 that William of Orange was proclaimed Stadtholder.

182 *in comedies*: a staple situation of traditional comedy, renewed by Molière and popular until the time of Beaumarchais and beyond.

183 *my idea of love*: Louise's sentiments, which contrast with the sex-as-war approach of her friends, are more in keeping with the idealistic mood of Dumas's romantic times than with the seventeenth century, when Racine presented love as an irresistible passion and Corneille and Mme de La Fayette showed it in conflict with duty.

184 *twelve years*: that is, since 1648: see *Twenty Years After*, ch. 15.

185 *fourteen summers*: Louise was born in 1644 and, by this involved account, Raoul in 1638. Yet the circumstances of his conception as recounted in *The Three Musketeers* (chs 10 and 22) show that he was born in 1633, which allowed him to be just old enough to take part in the battle of Lens with Guiche in 1648 in *Twenty Years After*. In fact, Raoul is as much an invented character as d'Artagnan. Dumas based him on a stray remark by Mme de La Fayette (op. cit., p. 458) who evoked Louise's early life 'at Blois where a man named Bragelonne had been in love with her. A few letters had been exchanged; Mme de Saint-Rémi† had got wind of the affair. In the event, matters did not progress very far.' The man has been identified as Jean de Bragelonne, a Councillor at the *parlement* of Rennes. But it seems more likely that he was related to one of several Bragelonnes in the service of Gaston d'Orléans at Blois: Jérôme (1588–1658), whose son François (1626–1703), *seigneur* de Hauteville, was Captain-Lieutenant of Gendarmes to Gaston; or, as seems most likely, Jacques (d. 1679), Chevalier de Bragelonne, Chief Steward in Gaston's household.

190 *the great Rond-Point*: the central circus (or roundabout) where the park's main drives converged.

199 *a long time ago*: the Comte de la Fère is Athos, who had a hand in rescuing Anne of Austria's studs and in the various struggles with Richelieu and Milady recounted in *The Three Musketeers*. But these events are less fresh in Louis's mind than Athos's role, told in *Twenty Years After*, in the heroic but unsuccessful attempt to save the life of Charles I. More recent still was the contribution Athos had made in restoring Charles II (now Louis's brother-in-law) to the throne of England: see *The Vicomte de Bragelonne*, chs 24–38.

209 *The Blaisois*: that is, the area around Blois.

212 *as we have been together*: Raoul and Guiche had first served together at Lens in 1648 (*Twenty Years After*, World's Classics edition, p. 487). Subsequently they fought at Bléneau in 1652 and at the battle of the Dunes in 1658 when Turenne, besieging Dunkirk, defeated the Spaniards.

213 *in the Empire*: exiled again for attempting to distance Louise from the King, Guiche fought against the Turks in Poland in 1662–3, later for the Dutch against the English, and returned to France in 1669, though he did not reappear at Court until 1671.

221 *tyrant of Samos*: Polycrates ruled Samos, in the Archipelago, from about 536 to 522 BC. He was so fortunate in all his endeavours that Amasis, King of Egypt, advised him to placate the fates by depriving himself of something he valued. Polycrates threw his richest ring into the sea. But when he was offered a fish as a present, it was found to contain the ring. Such good fortune could not last, nor did Polycrates, who was put to death by Oroetes, satrap of Sardis.

Quo non ascendam: Fouquet's motto: 'to what heights can I not aspire?'

224 *'The Frog . . . the Ox'*: in which the frog, to increase its size, puffs itself up until it bursts (*Fables*, i. 3). The *Fables choisies* of La Fontaine† were not published until 1668.

Vaux: the château at Vaux-le-Vicomte, near Melun, was built by Le Vau for Fouquet. The interiors were designed by Le Brun and Mignard and the gardens were laid out by Le Nôtre. Work had begun on it in 1654.

227 *Marquis de la Vallière*: Louise's father was Laurent la Baume le Blanc† and her stepfather, the Marquis de Saint-Rémy†, formerly chamberlain to the household of Gaston d'Orléans at Blois, who continued to exercise the same function in the service of Philippe d'Orléans. Louis had first set eyes on Louise at Blois, when travelling to meet the Spanish Infanta in *The Vicomte de Bragelonne*, ch. 8. He had then greeted her with an 'egotistical cold smile'.

229 *Saint-Mandé*: see note to p. 76.

three months since: Aramis was appointed Bishop of Vannes in April (*The Vicomte de Bragelonne*, ch. 17), though, in reality, the diocese already had an incumbent, Charles de Rosmadec, who had held the post since 1647.

they are savages: Brittany, one of the oldest provinces of France, was an independent duchy until it was joined to the French Crown by the marriage of Charles VIII and Anne of Brittany. It became fully French in 1532 during the reign of François I. However, the Bretons remained geographically, culturally, and linguistically apart, and relations with Paris were often strained, with peasant revolts occurring at intervals, notably in 1675.

230 *river to Belle-Isle*: Aramis's geography is vague. The island lies some 3 leagues (12 km.) south of Quiberon Point which is roughly 9 leagues (46 km.) from Vannes, which stands on the river Rohan. Alternatively, 25 leagues separate Belle-Isle from Saint-Nazaire at the mouth of the Loire.

231 *late in life*: see note to p. 36.

232 *war is probable*: Louis was to prove an ambitious king, intent on enabling France to expand into her 'natural' frontiers in the north-east. After the death of Philip of Spain in 1665, he annexed part of the Spanish Netherlands and in 1672 invaded the Dutch Republic.

234 *toady of the King*: the Marquis de Dangeau† became prominent at Court at a later date than Dumas suggests.

236 *Phillis*: by convention, the name of the shepherdess in pastoral verse, used by poets and playwrights from Virgil (*Eclogues*, III and V) to Milton (who speaks of 'Country messes / Which the neat-handed Phyllis dresses' (*L'Allegro*) and beyond.

238 *maids of honour*: some editions translate the couplet as follows: 'When maids of honour happen to run short, / Lo! Guiche will furnish the entire court'. The second couplet a few lines on is rendered thus: 'Why, there's the birdcage, with a pretty pair, / The charming Montalais and——', though the point is even clearer as 'He baited the birdcage . . .'

Racine . . . La Feuillade: in 1661 Molière (1622–73) had just begun to make his name, but *Andromaque*, which made the reputation of Racine (1639–99), was not staged until 1667. La Feuillade may be Georges d'Aubusson de la Feuillade (1609–97), ambassador to Madrid and Vienna, or his brother François (1625–91) who later became Marshal of France.

239 *Monsieur's household*: chs 77–78 of *The Vicomte de Bragelonne* tell how Malicorne† pays the impecunious dandy Manicamp† to obtain appointments for Montalais and Louise as maids-of-honour to Madame. In reality, it was through the influence of Mme de Choisy, wife of Gaston d'Orléans's notary, that Louise became part of Henrietta's retinue. Dumas presents Malicorne as the ambitious son of a lawyer from Orléans who was legal adviser and banker to the Prince de Condé: see *The Vicomte de Bragelonne*, ch. 79. His

historical model, a minor noble, had already been in the service of aristocratic masters for some fifteen years.

244 *Pythagoras*: Pythagoras (*c*.582–*c*.500 BC), mathematician and philosopher, enjoined his followers to moral abstinence and silence.

Ris or Melun: Ris-Orange near Évry on the Seine is 50 km. from Fontainebleau, and Melun 16 km. along the same road to Paris.

245 *Ariadne*: the name which eluded Saint-Aignan earlier. Ariadne, daughter of Minos, gave Theseus a clue of thread which enabled him to escape from the Cretan Labyrinth after slaying the Minotaur.

Faun . . . Dryad: a faun was a horned, cloven-footed country sprite and the dryad a wood-nymph.

place of residence: see note to p. 239.

249 *used to say*: 'Alas!' Cardinal Mazarin, who was Italian, spoke French with an accent which was eagerly exploited by satirists and duly recorded by Dumas.

254 *Beau Paon*: the inn ('The Fine Peacock') is an invention of Dumas.

256 *Fontainebleau*: Dumas is normally very careful with topographical details. His description of Fontainebleau, however, is entirely invented.

258 *nescio vos*: 'I know you not': the close of the parable of the ten virgins (Matthew 25: 12).

Oedipus: Oedipus saved Thebes by solving the riddle set by the Sphinx: what animal walks upon four feet in the morning, at noon upon two, and in the evening upon three? The answer was Man.

the following: the mysterious travellers are all fictitious.

261 *verba . . . manent*: a Latin proverb.

265 *Franciscan*: the Franciscans were founded in 1208 by Saint Francis of Assisi.

267 *Vicomte de Melun*: perhaps one of the descendants of Charles de Melun, *seigneur* de Normanville, governor of Paris and the Bastille, who was decapitated in 1468: in Dumas's day, the Baron de Brumetz was also Vicomte de Melun. Or perhaps Louis de Melun (1634–71), Marquis de Maupertuis, who became a musketeer at a very early age and went on to have a distinguished military career.

268 *Carmelite order*: the monastic Order of Our Lady of Mount Carmel was founded by Berthold, a pilgrim or crusader from Calabria, in 1156, though a legend attributes its foundation to the prophet Elijah. The order became mendicant in 1247 and its members

were known as White Friars. An order of Carmelite nuns was instituted in 1452.

268 *Jesuits, Augustines, and Cordeliers*: on the Jesuits, see next note. 'Augustinians' was the name of a number of Catholic orders and groups, all claiming to follow a rule for monastic life based on the writings of Saint Augustine. The Cordeliers (so named because of the knotted cord they wore about their waists) were a branch of the Franciscans and acceptance of their rule is generally said to date from the papacy of Leo X (1513–21).

society of Jesus: the Society was founded in 1534 by Ignatius Loyola to convert the infidels of the Middle East. Thwarted by the Turkish occupation of the Holy Land, the Society turned its attention to the new difficulties facing the faith in the wake of the Reformation. In 1539 Loyola proposed a modification which, in addition to the standard vows of chastity, poverty, and obedience, also required members to serve as missionaries wherever the Pope directed them. It was then that they adopted the motto *A.M.D.G.*, *Ad majorem Dei Gloriam* ('To the greater glory of God'). According to its monarchical constitution, authority lay with a Vicar-General, who was elected for life by a congregation of professed members and was advised by a council of six. Accused of laxity and an unsuitable interest in temporal matters, the Jesuits have always attracted a great deal of suspicion and, at various times, were expelled from France.

270 *'The general!'*: Dumas's Franciscan is an invention. A German named Nickel was Vicar-General between 1652 and 1664.

271 *animo . . . viribus impossibile*: 'the spirit is willing but the flesh is weak'.

273 *your own successor!*: this was not the established procedure: see note to p. 268.

274 *the Emperor*: the Holy Roman Emperor, Léopold I (1640–1709), was not 'opposed to the progress of our order' but was wholly under the influence of the Jesuits. His vast powers were rooted in a long and complex history. Charlemagne had restored the Roman Empire and was crowned Emperor by the Pope in 800. After his death, the chaos which ensued was halted by Otho the Great who assumed Charlemagne's title in 962. Until Francis II of Habsburg relinquished the imperial title in 1806, a succession of German princes claimed to exercise the powers of Roman Emperors who called themselves 'Holy' to signify that their expanding empire was Christian. Enlarged by the addition of annexed territories, it

fell to Rodolphe of Habsburg in 1276, an event which initiated its long domination by the Habsburg dynasty through an intricate series of royal marriages.

a revolution: an idea foreign to the seventeenth century but very familiar to the French since 1789.

House of Austria: the Houses of Austria and Spain were joined by marriage in the late fifteenth century. Charles V (1500–58), King of Spain, became Emperor in 1519, ruling Spain and her colonies, Flanders, Austria, and Germany. In 1522 he gave the German territories of the House of Austria to his brother Ferdinand who acquired Bohemia and Hungary by marriage in 1526. Tension remained high between France and Spain, and the House of Austria took the lead as the champion of Catholicism and as a power aiming at universal domination in the Thirty Years War, which ended in the Peace of Westphalia in 1648 and gave Lorraine to France. Hostilities were to continue in the Netherlands, but the House of Austria never recovered its former power.

275 *Coram isto?*: 'in the presence of this man?'

claim to the crown of Spain: this would not, however, prevent Louis asserting the rights of his Queen to the Low Countries and annexing part of the Spanish Netherlands in 1667 to compensate him for her unpaid dowry. He justified his action by reference to the Law of Devolution which awarded inherited property to the female children of a first marriage. Maria-Theresa was the only child of the first marriage of Philip IV (1605–65) to Isabella de Bourbon. Philip was succeeded by Charles II (1661–1700), one of the five children of his second marriage, to Marie-Anne of Austria.

276 *to respect it*: other European countries were indeed to be drawn into the War of Devolution which ended in 1668.

pronto: 'quickly'.

a brother of the Infanta: in the summer of 1661, Philip's only son was Philip-Prosper (1655–61) who died shortly before the birth of his brother, the future Charles II, in November.

277 *expulsion of the Jesuits*: the fortunes of the Jesuits followed a general pattern: brilliant rise, followed by repression and then restoration, a cycle several times repeated in France from which the Jesuits were expelled in 1598, 1762, and 1901 for activities regarded as conspiratorial and subversive. But in 1661, they had less to fear fron Pope Alexander VII than from Pascal's scathing attack on them in his *Provincial Letters* (1656–7).

277 *the Archipelago*: that is, the Aegean Sea.

278 *Harpocrates*: a divinity, reckoned to be the same as Orus, son of Isis, adopted by Greeks and Romans as the god of silence. He is represented holding one finger on his mouth. Sometimes he appears on a lotus-flower, with finger to lips.

279 *jubilee*: a full and general indulgence granted by the pope on certain occasions; a time of celebration.

280 *now dead*: an odd lapse. Mme de Chevreuse is far from dead and will reappear as a plotter. 'Mme de Chevreuse, who still retained some of the very great influence which she had formerly enjoyed over the Queen-Mother, undertook to persuade her to bring Fouquet down. M. de Laigues†, secretly married, so it was said, to Mme de Chevreuse, was furious with the Superintendant. He controlled Mme de Chevreuse' (Mme de La Fayette, op. cit., p. 455).

fifteen years: that is, since 1646. Dumas does not develop the significance of this information. See notes to pp. 57 and 71.

281 *in hoc signo vinces!*: 'by this sign shall ye conquer!'

he shall die: Pope Alexander VII died of natural causes in 1667.

Ravaillac: François Ravaillac (1578–1610) murdered Henri IV at Angoulême in 1610, prompted, as was believed in some quarters, by the Jesuits.

286 *friend of my childhood*: see note to p. 185.

288 *Amadis*: son of Perion, the protagonist of *Amadis de Gaule*, a collection of romances translated from the Spanish and hugely popular in France from the middle of the sixteenth century onwards. Amadis was the flower of chivalry, the model courtly lover.

289 *with King Charles II*: see note to p. 199.

290 *the Walloons*: Raoul had faced the Spaniards at Lens in 1648 and Walloons (and others) at Dunkirk in 1658.

292 *of his pocket*: Manicamp, constantly short of funds, used his influence with Guiche to secure court appointments for Malicorne in *The Vicomte de Bragelonne* (chs 77–81). But while the devious Malicorne uses money in the pursuit of power, the honourable Manicamp needs money to be a gentleman. It is the difference between bourgeois self-interest and the aristocratic code (shared by d'Artagnan) which held that spending money was more important than earning it.

294 *ends in* ame: i.e. to rhyme with Madame.

295 *a cake, for instance*: in the *Aeneid*, the prophetess of Apollo threw Cerberus a soporific confection of honey and drugged corn.

M. de Beautru: perhaps Nicolas Beautru (d. 1661), Comte de Nogent-Beautru and Captain of Guards, who was famed for his wit; or Guillaume Beautru (1584–1665), Comte de Serrant, chamberlain to the late Gaston d'Orléans.

296 *'Who is Malicorne?'*: see note to p. 239.

297 *from Le Havre to Paris*: see *The Vicomte de Bragelonne*, chs 83–8.

with the father: that is, Athos's role in restoring Charles II, brother of Henrietta, to the throne of England.

301 *Mademoiselle de Chalais*: see note to p. 99.

262 *brother and brother-in-law*: i.e. Charles II and Louis XIV.

at Villers-Cotterets: a château, rebuilt during the Renaissance and given by Louis XIV to the Dukes d'Orléans who occupied it until the French Revolution. Villers-Cotterêts, Dumas's birthplace, is 50 km. north-east of Paris.

Gabrielle: see note to p. 178.

305 *King Candaules*: the wife of King Candaules (716–678 BC) incited Gyges to kill her husband, subsequently married him, and ruled the kingdom of Lydia for 28 years.

306 *Molière*: Molière (1622–73) specialized in the comedy of obsessive behaviour.

308 *Naiad*: while dryads were tree-nymphs, the naiads, daughters of Zeus, inhabited fountains and rivers.

309 *of character*: Maria-Theresa was pious and fulfilled her public duties, but preferred a retiring life full of good works. Louis found her tiresome and avoided her.

310 *regency, or of the last reign*: that is, of the court of Louis XIII and, after his death in 1643, of the Regency of Anne of Austria.

312 *de Chatillon . . . de Créquy*: both ladies-in-waiting to Madame. See List of Historical Characters.

313 *King Aquilo*: that is, the north wind, more usually depicted as a chubby-cheeked child in the act of blowing.

314 *M. Loret*: Jean Loret[†], author of *La Muze historique*, a rhymed gazette.

316 *ingeniously constructed conversations*: the vogue of 'Preciosity' had been mercilessly satirized by Molière in *Les Précieuses ridicules* (1659).

317 *Tyrcis*: the characters in the tale which follows are taken, as the fashionable pastoral convention required, from the *Bucolics* and *Eclogues* of Virgil. References to ancient kings and gods (for instance to Apollo, the sun god) are intended to flatter Louis, the Sun King.

319 *Hebe*: goddess of eternal youth until forced to give way to Ganymede, Jupiter's cup-bearer.

320 *Mnemosyne*: goddess of memory and mother of the nine Muses.

321 *'Phillis'*: the portrait which follows is a pastiche on the precious parlour-portrait then fashionable. Later in the century, La Bruyère was to perfect the much older tradition of Theophrastus in his *Caractères* (1688–94).

322 *where Virgil left it*: Bucolics, bk. I.

Europa: daughter of Agenor, King of Phoenicia. Jupiter, enamoured of her great beauty, changed himself into a bull and mingled with her father's herd while Europa and her attendants were gathering flowers in the meadows. She was unwise enough to sit on his back, whereupon he carried her across the sea to Crete.

327 *the Academy*: the French Academy, established by Richelieu in 1635. Saint-Aignan would be one of its forty members by 1663.

329 *Socrates to Montaigne*: an example of Dumas's extravagant touch: both Socrates (470–399 BC) and Montaigne (1533–92) maintained that philosophy was the study of human nature.

331 *terrible passions*: although Racine showed the ravages of passion, Dumas has in mind the wild antics of heroines like Marguerite de Bourgogne, who ordered discarded lovers to be cast from the top of a tower into the Seine. Marguerite was the heroine of *La Tour de Nesle* (1832), one of Dumas's most spectacular melodramas.

of the eighteenth: after the Fronde, the aristocracy was tamed by a code of etiquette which not only encouraged the nobility to spend rather than create wealth, but also militated against seriousness: the ruling class, refusing to be bored, took refuge in badinage which reduced intellectual life to a kind of courtly game. But Dumas's claim that it all began with Henrietta is wide of the mark.

332 *sibyl*: although Plato speaks of only one sibyl (or oracular sooth-sayer), other ancient authors mention up to ten.

333 *treated as a man*: another stage in Louis's emancipation from the power of the Court.

had been removed: Hamlet, v. ii.

343 *first bent upon me*: in May 1660. See *The Vicomte de Bragelonne*, ch. 8.

344 *Virgil alludes to*: the sentiment, though a common one, does not appear to have been expressed anywhere by Virgil.

Hungary water: made of rosemary, sage, and other spice. According to tradition, the recipe was given by a hermit to a Queen of Hungary.

346 *the Belle-Isle affair*: see note to p. 17.

347 *two weeks ago*: no royal troops were sent to Belle-Isle before September, after the arrest of Fouquet.

Sarzeau ... towards Quimper: Sarzeau lies on the Golfe du Morbihan. Quimper is 120 km. north along the Breton coast.

348 *what has become of him?*: Porthos is still recuperating at Fouquet's house at Saint-Mandé after his heroic ride from Vannes. See *The Vicomte de Bragelonne*, chs 73–4.

349 *Milo of Crotona*: a Greek athlete, renowned for feats of strength. In old age, he attempted to split an oak with his bare hands, but the tree closed on his hands and, trapped, he was devoured by wolves.

engineer of Belle-Isle: under Aramis's supervision, Porthos had fortified the island. See *The Vicomte de Bragelonne*, ch. 69.

a Paladin: a knight of the retinue of Charlemagne.

352 *fête at Vaux*: see p. 224.

353 *devoted to me*: Aramis's motives begin to become clearer. Opposed to the policies of Colbert, the advocate of state control and opponent of individualism, he seeks to ensure that the old values of chivalry, faith, and freedom (as represented by Fouquet) will prevail. Even so, the plan he mentions a few lines later to ensure that 'a King' sympathetic to his aims will 'sit on the throne of France' is still mysterious. But alert readers will not have forgotten the masked prisoner who resembles Louis XIV ...

354 *mayor of the palace*: the expression, which dates from Merovingian times, continued in use to signify the highest and most powerful of the King's ministers.

356 *Nocte ... mane*: a gnomic utterance attributed to Virgil: 'it rained all night long; the games will be held tomorrow'.

357 *Lyonne*: Hugues de Lionne[†], secretary for Foreign Affairs.

358 *fête at Vaux?*: 'For some time past, the King had been saying that he would like to go to Vaux, the superintendent's magnificent house. Yet although prudence should have led the latter to prevent

the King's seeing something which was such a blatant example of his misuse of the royal finances, and although the dignity of the King ought to have prevented his calling on a man he was intent on humbling, neither the one nor the other gave thought to such considerations' (Mme de La Fayette, op. cit., p. 456).

359 *Domine non sum dignus*: 'Lord, I am not worthy': a response made in a variety of ceremonies. Claude Schopp (*Les Mousquetaires*, iii. 15 n.) traces the anecdote to Courtilz de Sandras's *Mémoires de M.L.C.D.R. [Monsieur le Comte de Rochefort]* (1678). When still a young man, La Vieuville[†] spoke this traditional response as a reluctant Henri IV conferred a decoration on him. The King replied that he was only too aware of it.

360 *the illness*: Anne's cancer of the breast, which would eventually kill her, did not declare itself until 1664.

Apremont: the Gorges d'Apremont are situated a few miles northwest of Fontainebleau.

their progress: 'The King's attachment to La Vallière grew steadily, and made great progress with her. They kept their distance carefully. He did not see her at Madame's receptions nor during the day's drives, but for the evening's excursion he would get out of the carriage of Madame and take up a position near La Vallière's coach, the window of which was lowered, and, since this took place under cover of the darkness, he was able to speak to her with the greatest of ease' (Mme de La Fayette, op. cit., p. 454).

363 *in a month*: it was held on 17 August 1661.

374 *no longer to be understood*: a clear statement of Dumas's preference for the dashing individualism of the chivalric code against the grubby materialism of his own day.

379 *coquettes*: if his amours with Mme de Chevreuse and Mme de Longueville are typical, Aramis has known only the strong-willed, non-melting variety of womanhood.

383 *in her life*: as Louis XIII's queen, she had plotted against Richelieu in defence of Spanish interests.

advice to the Queen: Mme de Motteville[†] had been a prominent member of Anne's 'Spanish party'. The Queen Mother had always been attended by Spanish ladies who included Doña Molena mentioned here, 'first lady of the bedchamber to the Queen[-Mother]' (Mme de La Fayette. op. cit., p. 462), who was still in her service at the time of her death.

Mme de Chevreuse: another lapse, unless Dumas intends that Anne's memory be at fault. Certainly, her musings about Mme de Chevreuse† are incorrect and will be contradicted as events unfold.

gain them over: Anne judges the new generation very much as Dumas viewed the youth of his day.

386 *in her bosom*: see note to p. 360.

389 *Perhaps*: Montaigne, aware of the inability of the human mind to know anything with certainty, adopted this device in 1576: see *Essais*, bk. II, ch. 12. Rabelais's dying utterance is said to have been: 'I go to seek a great Perhaps.'

391 *Duke de Roquelaure*: Gaston-Jean-Baptiste (1615–83), Duke de Roquelaure.

394 *the Sabines*: the Sabines were an ancient race who, after long resistance, were annexed by Rome in 290 BC. They are best remembered for the invitation issued to them by Romulus to a festival of games during which the defenceless Sabine women were carried off by his followers who thus founded the city of Rome.

396 *Saint-Laurent*: by the middle of the seventeenth century, a fair and market held on a site on the right bank of the Seine, lasting from July until the end of September.

398 *Planchet*: the Rue des Lombards was then known for its apothecaries and confectioners. The street still exists: it crosses the Boulevard Sébastopol and ends at the church of Saint-Merri (formerly Saint-Médéric) in the 4th *arrondissement*. Planchet, d'Artagnan's faithful servant from the start of the saga, had become a grocer: he was the proprietor of 'The Golden Pestle'.

399 *Rue Saint-Médéric*: there was no such street. Dumas intends the cart to turn off the then Rue Saint-Martin, opposite the church of St Merri (a corruption of Médéric), into the Rue des Lombards.

a week: the chronology is again very uncertain, but the reader, having lost touch with d'Artagnan since the very first chapters, will not mind now that he is back.

400 *siege of La Rochelle*: in 1628. See *The Three Musketeers*, chs 41–6.

culverins: an early name for the cannon.

magical leaves: i.e. hashish, already fashionable as a source of 'artificial paradises' for Romantic writers like Baudelaire and Gautier.

401 *like his hare*: 'Maître Corbeau' is the crow in 'The Crow and the Fox' (*Fables*, i. 2) and the hare is from 'The Hare and the Frogs' (ii. 14).

restore King Charles II: see *The Vicomte de Bragelonne*, chs 19–32. Planchet is interested because he had largely financed d'Artagnan's English adventure and had made a rich return on his investment.

401 *Monk to be put in a box*: in *The Vicomte de Bragelonne* (chs 27–8), d'Artagnan had kidnapped General Monk†, shut him in a chest, and ferried him from Newcastle to Holland where he finally pledged his allegiance to Charles II.

403 *dried grape, or raisin*: the Malaga grape is the name given to any variety grown near Malaga. The best-known is the muscadel.

Epicurean philosopher: see note to p. 109.

407 *the fourteenth*: presumably of July, if the time is intended to dove-tail with events at Fontainebleau: see note to p. 363.

408 *at Boulogne*: in fact, Calais. See *The Three Musketeers*, ch. 20.

mordioux: a corruption of 'Mort-de-dieu', an oath consistently placed on d'Artagnan's lips as a reminder of his Gascon origins.

409 *at the Palais Royal*: see above, ch. 3.

410 *Golden Portcullis*: a tavern at the northern end of the Rue du Petit-Musc (see note to p. 48).

Faubourg Saint-Antoine: the Rue Saint-Antoine became the Faubourg Saint-Antoine at the Porte Saint-Antoine which was built in the old city wall next to the Bastille. The soldier is walking in an easterly direction.

a weakness for brandy: d'Artagnan here demonstrates precocious powers of deduction of the kind which Dumas's readers were beginning to find so fascinating in the tales of Edgar Allan Poe, the father of detective fiction.

411 *of the police*: Paris was then an extremely violent city. It was policed by 300 *archers* (foot constables) and 120 mounted men. Responsibility for public order was shared by the Châtelet, the *parlement*, the *Hôtel de Ville*, and the Watch, which both pursued and tried law-breakers. In 1667 enforcement was entrusted to the newly created Lieutenant de Police according to the principle that 'the functions of the courts and the work of the police are frequently incompatible'.

413 *a falsehood*: d'Artagnan was Captain of Musketeers, not of the Guards.

414 *Pierrefonds*: after the adventures recounted in *The Three Musketeers*, Porthos had married the widow of a lawyer and, in time, had acquired titles and lands. Since the end of *Twenty Years After*, he

has been Baron du Vallon de Bracieux de Pierrefonds, the latter being his estate near Villers-Cotterêts, north-east of Paris.

Hermes . . . extended wings: Hermes, Zeus's messenger of good news, is usually represented with a herald's staff and wings at his feet or shoulders: the lips on which a finger is placed normally belong to Harpocrates, god of silence. Iris, messenger of the gods when they intended discord, was associated with the rainbow, a road let down from heaven for her to travel on.

415 *at Belle-Isle*: see *The Vicomte de Bragelonne*, ch. 69.

416 *from Vannes*: see *The Vicomte de Bragelonne*, ch. 73. A reference to Porthos's epic ride which had left him exhausted.

417 *present of Belle-Isle*: see note to p. 17.

419 *demolished the temple*: Judges 16: 26–30.

424 *as you may have seen*: see *The Vicomte de Bragelonne*, chs 70–1.

427 *Mousqueton*: Porthos's servant since the beginning of the saga.

428 *a quartan fever*: a fever which recurs every fourth day.

429 *red . . . black politician*: that is, Richelieu was not afraid of shedding blood, while the wily Mazarin preferred dark plotting.

M. de Marillac . . . and M. de Montmorency: all were executed on the orders of Richelieu: Marillac† (1632), de Thou† (1642), Cinq-Mars† (1642), Chalais† (1626), and Montmorency† (1632) for plotting and treason. Bouteville† (1627) was executed for breaking Richelieu's ban on duelling. The Fronde, a nobles' revolt which turned into a civil war, was the response to Mazarin's policies.

I struck for the King: as did his three companions who all believed that Mazarin's policies best served the monarchy as an institution.

432 *the rind left*: an allusion (which explains the chapter title) to La Fontaine's 'The Rat who Withdrew from the World' (*Fables*, vii. 3): it retired inside a Dutch cheese.

434 *partnership with him*: the 'firm' of d'Artagnan and Planchet was set up in *The Vicomte de Bragelonne* (chs 19–20) to finance the attempt to restore Charles II to the English throne.

435 *at Berry*: Porthos seems to refer to his estate at Bracieux. But while there is indeed a Bracieux 18 km. from Blois in the old province of Berry, Porthos's property is situated east of Paris, 'in the Soissonnais' (*Twenty Years After*, World's Classics edition, p. 245). Later (p. 391) Porthos will speak of his 'little farm at Bracieux; it has twelve acres'. Pierrefonds is also 'in the Soissonnais' (p. 436).

437 *Ivry*: near Évreux, the site of Henri IV's victory over the Catholic League in 1590.

445 *Noisy-le-Sec*: see note to p. 37.

446 *Madame de Chevreuse*: Dumas forgets that he has twice reported the death of Chevreuse.

447 *delights of Capua*: Hannibal took the island in 215 BC and wintered there, 'succumbing', it was said, 'to the delights of Capua'. In French, the expression means wasting precious time on idle pleasures.

448 *for the last fifty years*: this suggests that Porthos is nearing 60.

Samson and Delilah: Judges 16.

450 *Harpagon*: the miser of Molière's *L'Avare* (1668).

451 *United Provinces*: i.e. Holland.

452 *the Pleiades*: the seven daughters of Atlas, reduced to despair by the sufferings of their father, killed themselves and were metamorphosed into the constellation which bears their name.

453 *nom de guerre*: it was usual for younger sons who entered the army to take other names to avoid confusion with older brothers. However, d'Artagnan continued to use his family name and, although Dumas normally thinks of Aramis, Porthos, and Athos as having *noms de guerre*, their names are derived from obscure historical originals. See note to p. 36.

454 *a royal appetite*: Louis XIV was famous for his appetite. One contemporary wrote: 'I have often seen the King consume four full plates of different kinds of soup, an entire pheasant, a partridge, a large dish of salad, two large slices of ham, mutton with gravy and garlic, a whole tray of pastries, and then fruit and hard-boiled eggs' (quoted in Joanna Richardson, *Louis XIV*, London, 1973, p. 89).

457 *Polybius, or Archimedes*: Polybius (*c*.210–*c*.125 BC) was a Greek historian, known better for his ideas on strategy (to which he devoted a treatise) than as an engineer. Using various mechanical principles of his own invention, Archimedes (287–212 BC) defended Syracuse against the besieging Roman army for three years.

when we met: in *The Vicomte de Bragelonne*, ch. 72.

458 *a saying*: 'Nascuntur poetae, fiunt oratores.'

258 pounds: standing 6 feet 4 inches and weighing 18 stone, Porthos would now pass almost unnoticed in a rugby scrum. In the seventeenth century, when the average height was 5 feet 6 inches, he was a giant.

ridiculous part at Belle-Isle: partly for keeping him in the dark about Aramis's plans, but also for leaving him stranded at Vannes. See *The Vicomte de Bragelonne*, ch. 73.

461 *the King will make me all that*: it has long been d'Artagnan's ambition to be appointed Marshal of France. But his loyalty is to the King not to Fouquet, just as he had served Louis XIII and not Richelieu.

arrest a new Condé: Condé† was arrested in 1650 on the order of Mazarin.

462 *the lottery*: Dumas's tale is constructed of large blocks of narrative devoted to interwined stories which run in parallel. After nine chapters featuring d'Artagnan, we now return to Court.

471 *three love-letters a day*: this episode is taken from Mme de La Fayette (op. cit., p. 459) who, however, situates it in November 1661. 'The next day, [Montalais] brought Madame a letter from the Comte de Guiche. Madame refused to read it. A few days later, Madame fell ill. She returned [from Fontainebleau] to Paris in a litter and, as she proceeded thither, Montalais tossed her a bundle of letters from the Comte de Guiche. Madame read them as she journeyed along . . . Madame's youth, the good looks of the Comte de Guiche, but above all the interference of Montalais led the princess into a gallant affair which was to cause her considerable unpleasantness. Monsieur was still jealous of the Comte de Guiche who neverthe-less never ceased his visits to the Tuileries, where Madame was still lodged. She was very ill. He wrote to her three or four times every day. For most of the time, Madame did not read his letters and gave them all into the care of Montalais without enquiring as to what use she made of them. Montalais did not dare keep them in her room; she handed them over to a man with whom she was then in love, named Malicorne.'

Italian vivacity: in Dumas's day, it was still widely believed that Northern nations were cold and phlegmatic (especially the Eng-lish), while Southern peoples were passionate. The reference, a few lines on, to 'Spanish' jealousy is in the same vein. Mérimée had already exploited it in *Carmen* (1847) on which the libretto of Bizet's opera (1875) was based.

477 *treasure of the Hesperides*: three sisters who guarded (with the as-sistance of a sleepless dragon with a hundred heads) the golden apples given to Juno as a wedding present.

absent for a month: really, nearer three. Buckingham had left France in the middle of April and it is now still July: see note to p. 92.

488 *going to fight*: the duel is an invention conjured out of a passing detail recorded by Mme de La Fayette (op. cit., p. 460): 'At that time [early 1662], someone mentioned, within the hearing of the Comte de Guiche who was with Vardes [Dumas's de Wardes], that Madame was far more ill than anyone believed, and that the doctors thought that she would not recover from her sickness. The Comte de Guiche appeared greatly affected by this news; Vardes escorted him away and helped him to conceal his evident distress. The Comte de Guiche admitted to him how things stood between himself and Madame and took him fully into his confidence. Madame disapproved strongly of what the Comte de Guiche had done and would have preferred him to cease seeing Vardes. He told her that he would fight a duel with him to please her, but that he could not break with his friend.'

490 *Saint-Denis*: then a village, outside the city wall, north of Paris, overlooking the plain where the duel was probably fought.

     called Rochin: an invention.

494 *wolves*: in England, the last wolf was killed during the reign of Henry VII, though they persisted in Scotland until the middle of the eighteenth century. In seventeenth-century France, in spite of vigorous hunting and the spread of agriculture, wolves were still common.

498 *fully to realise*: Henri IV, a bluff, decisive man, was committed to making France a unified nation. His lead was followed by Richelieu, first minister to Louis XIII who was, however, constantly opposed by elements of the nobility who refused to submit to the Crown. Mazarin continued the process and the Fronde broke aristocratic power. Louis XIV completed the work of creating a centralized state. He introduced a sophisticated system of etiquette which encouraged courtiers to worry more about status and privilege (the right to be present at the King's *levées* or to sit on a certain kind of stool which symbolized rank) than about the erosion of their former political rights. The process was extended even to language, art, and literature where rules defined taste: thus a tragedy was unacceptable if not subject to the unities of time, place, and action. Conformism, not individualism, shaped the whole of the classical outlook. Dumas detected a similar shift in the France of his day. The heroic tradition of Napoleon had given way to the dull, rule-bound reign of Louis-Philippe (1830–48), and 'fellowship' and 'affability' had been replaced by the new bourgeois spirit of materialism. It is at rare moments like this that the political implications

of the Musketeer saga become clear: Dumas recommended a return to the old chivalric values which he took to have made life worth living before they were swamped by Louis's absolutism and throttled by the deadening hand of Colbert the administrator.

Bourbon family: the Bourbon family goes back to the tenth century but did not become royal until, by way of the kingdom of Navarre, Henri IV was crowned King of France in 1589. The line survived the French Revolution and was restored to power in 1815, but died out on the death of the Comte de Chambord in 1883. The Spanish branch survives and still provides pretenders to the French throne, as does the younger Orleanist branch (begun by Philippe, brother to Louis XIV) which provided a succession of Comtes de Paris. Bourbon kings were vigorous, decisive men, keen on hunting and endowed with strong appetites.

500 *to the palate*: Dumas was a cook of genius. His *Grand dictionnaire de cuisine* was published posthumously.

501 *salt marshes*: the area surrounding the Golfe du Morbihan, on which Vannes is situated, has many salt marshes which had long been systematically exploited. When d'Artagnan was investigating Belle-Isle (*The Vicomte de Bragelonne*, ch. 67), he posed as a merchant looking for suitable salt-works to invest in.

entremets: now a dessert but in the seventeenth century a sweet dish served between courses.

502 *duke and peer*: Porthos has always had a childish affection for honours. Already a baron, his ambition now is fixed on a dukedom.

503 *verses*: the writing of verse (as Dumas notes, it can hardly be called poetry) was a part of the affected, 'precious' etiquette between lovers then in vogue.

Colossus of Rhodes: an enormous statue of Apollo, one of the seven wonders of the ancient world, which stood at the entrance to the Gulf of Rhodes. It was said that ships could sail under its legs.

505 *with respect to duelling*: see note to p. 27.

506 *edicts*: that is, against duelling.

my physician: Antoine Valot†.

510 *close observation*: d'Artagnan's bravura display of deduction anticipates the detective novel which was not to begin its lasting popularity in France until the 1860s.

511 *Gramont*: Gramont† was the family name of the Comte de Guiche.

513 *errare humanum est*: 'to sin is human (to forgive divine)'.

515 *their potatoes*: one of Dumas's cheerful historical blunders. The
potato (long thought in France to cause leprosy and fevers) was
not commonly grown there until the end of the eighteenth century. *Le Siècle* (15 March 1849) explained that *pomme de terre* had
been printed instead of *pomme d'amour* (tomato). But the error has
persisted.

a carbine: a lighter version of the old arquebus which was discharged when the match-holder, released by the trigger, struck the
priming-pan. After the heavier musket (which required a forked
rest) was introduced into the French army in 1575, the various
kinds of arquebus remained in private hands only. Pistols were one
form of hand-culverins which appeared in the middle of the sixteenth century. The flintlock pistol was in general use only by the
end of the seventeenth century.

516 *statue of Silence*: that is, of Harpocrates, god of silence, though his
statue on the Capitol is more famous.

fable of Adonis: a handsome youth of Byblos who was mortally
wounded by a wild boar. He was metamorphosed into an anemone
by Aphrodite.

517 *M. de Saint-Maure*: a name invented for the circumstance.

518 *where are they now?*: another lament by d'Artagnan (and Dumas)
for the passing of a generation of bolder, braver, finer men.

521 *Place de Grève*: the Place de Grève had been a place of execution
since 1310: the guillotine was first used there in April 1792. Called
the Place de l'Hôtel de Ville since 1806, the site is on the right
bank of the Seine, opposite the Pont d'Arcole.

as a model: that is, in dealing severely with duellists.

525 *a Paladin*: see note to p. 349.

529 *Galatea*: a sea-nymph loved by the giant Polyphemus. But she
preferred the shepherd Acis on whom the jealous Polyphemus
crossly dropped a very large rock.

533 *the Hesperides*: see note to p. 477.

538 *Rue du Feurre*: another street which Dumas invents at Fontainebleau.

543 *historiographer*: Mme de La Fayette records that Montalais gave
sensitive documents into the safekeeping of Malicorne: see note to
p. 471.

544 *Fer-à-cheval crescent*: at Fontainebleau, a horseshoe-shaped staircase, built by Jean Cerceau in 1634. It leads from the central
pavilion into the Cour du Cheval Blanc, named after an equestrian

statue of Marcus Aurelius erected during the reign of Charles IX (1560–74). The courtyard came later to be known also as the Cour des Adieux, from Napoleon's farewell to the Old Guard in 1814.

550 *Triumfeminate*: that is, a council of three women. A variant of triumvirate, originally the three-man committee (Pompey, Caesar, and Crassus) which assumed power against the Senate in 60 BC.

551 *Marie*: i.e. Maria-Theresa.

no longer belongs to me: according to Mme de La Fayette, who reports that her suspicions were aroused only in the autumn, 'the young Queen was quite unaware that the King was in love with [La Vallière]; however, she sensed that he was in love with someone and not knowing who to be jealous of, set her thoughts on Madame' (op. cit., p. 459).

with all her heart: the tradition of the openly acknowledged Royal Mistress was already established and was to be further consolidated by Louis XIV and his successor, Louis XV, whose *maîtresses en titre* included Mme de Pompadour and Mme du Barry.

552 *Dauphin without you*: when the Comtes de Viennois sold the Dauphiné (in the French Alps) to Philippe VI (1293–1350), they demanded that the King's oldest son (that is, his heir) be called the Dauphin, which to them was a title like Duke or Count. Maria-Theresa was in fact already pregnant. The first of her six children, known as the Grand Dauphin (1661–1711), was born on 1 November 1661.

553 *an insult*: the Dutch were apprehensive of French territorial ambitions which Louis was to promote actively after 1665 (see note to p. 275). Large numbers of pamphlets and other lampoons ridiculing the pretensions of the 'Sun King' were printed and circulated in Holland which Louis would later use as an excuse for taking a hard line with the Dutch. On the medals, see note to p. 586.

Madame d'Olonne: Catherine-Henriette d'Angennes, Comtesse d'Olonne, married Louis de la Trémouille in 1652 and acquired a reputation for virtue before losing it spectacularly.

casa de usted: 'your house': that is, 'under your own roof'.

Pallas . . . and Achilles: in ancient mythology, Pallas was a name for Minerva, goddess of wisdom. Venus was the goddess of love and Mars god of war. Hector was killed at the siege of Troy by Achilles who was mortally wounded in the heel by an arrow shot by Paris: see the *Iliad* (bk. 12).

555 *one master in France*: the power of the nobility, broken by the Fronde, was further diminished by the strict code of conduct which Louis XIV laid upon his courtiers. Anne here approves of policies inaugurated by Henri IV and vigorously followed by Richelieu and Mazarin who had laid the foundations for a centralized, modern state under an absolute monarch.

562 *He recalled*: Dumas regularly provided readers old and new of his serialized novel with recapitulations of previous events. See note to p. 185 and chapter 1 above.

569 *Swiss Regiments*: Swiss mercenaries served in the armies of various European countries: the last Swiss regiments in France were disbanded in 1830. Here, Dumas refers to the Swiss who formed the Palace Guard, in existence since medieval times.

   so early an hour: Dumas again anticipates events. Mme de La Fayette (op. cit., p. 461) reports that, in the winter of 1661, Madame, prompted by Montalais, made certain insinuations involving Guiche to the King and raised doubts in his mind. Louise 'became troubled and informed him that she was concealing certain important matters from him. Thereupon, the King fell into a terrible rage. She did not reveal what she was hiding; the King withdrew, feeling desperately betrayed by her. They had once agreed that, whatever differences they might have, they would never go to bed without settling them and writing to each other. The night passed without Louise's receiving word from the King and, thinking that her fate was sealed, she lost her head. Early the next morning, she left the Tuileries and took herself off like a mad thing to an obscure little convent at Chaillot.' The flight took place on 24 February 1662.

570 *Chaillot*: a convent of Carmelite canonesses (see note to p. 268), founded at Nanterre in 1639, which had moved to a site at Chaillot just south of what is now the Arc de Triomphe. The two Carmelite convents there were convenient destinations for errant daughters. It was to Chaillot that Mlle de la Motte-Argencourt had been directed by Anne of Austria, who feared her influence over the young and susceptible King. Guiche's sister, Marguerite d'Orléans, had experienced a brief taste of the regime before accepting her fate: marriage to the Duc de Toscane in April 1661.

   instead of descending: that is, Louise heads east, whereas Chaillot, outside the city walls, lay a few miles to the west along the Rue Saint-Honoré.

517 *Place de Grève*: Louise had set out from the Palais Royal (though Mme de La Fayette specifies the Tuileries), turned left along the Rue Saint-Honoré, and right down the Rue du Coq which led to the Louvre roughly on the line of the modern Rue Marengo. She walked along the eastern side of the Louvre (where Claude Perrault (1613–88) had not yet started on the colonnade (built 1667–73)), down the Rue du Petit Bourbon, past the Church of Saint-Germain l'Auxerrois from which she needed only to cross the Place de l'École to reach the river. Still heading east along the Quai de l'École and the Quai de la Mégisserie, she arrives finally at the Place de Grève. Dumas's invariably accurate topographical indications are confirmed by maps of seventeenth-century Paris.

572 *La Rapée*: the fifteenth-century Hôtel de la Rapée, on the road to Charenton on the right bank of the Seine, later gave its name to the Quai de la Rapée which is across the Seine from what is now the Gare d'Austerlitz. D'Artagnan is surprised because Louise is walking in the wrong direction.

I have a house: with the money he received to recompense him for his role in the restoration of Charles II (he had refused money but allowed the King to buy his sword), d'Artagnan had bought a property which he let, for a rent of 375 livres, to an innkeeper. The inn, called 'The Image of Our Lady', faced the Place de Grève but had an exit in the Place Baudoyer, a geographical arrangement which, in spite of Fouquet's planning, had failed to save his supporters d'Eymeris and Lyodot from the gibbet. See *The Vicomte de Bragelonne*, chs 52, 60–62.

575 *in the theatre in London*: *Richard III*, v. iv. But d'Artagnan had previously recalled being taken to the theatre by General Monk to see *Much Ado About Nothing*: see the final paragraph of ch. 65 of *The Vicomte de Bragelonne*.

Barrière de la Conférence: a customs gate, built in 1633, which controlled river traffic. It was situated just to the east of the present Pont de la Concorde on what is now the Quai des Tuileries.

576 *evasions with France*: Dumas advances by several years the worsening relations between France, the Dutch, and Spain: see note to p. 553. But, as he indicates, Mazarin had framed the Treaty of the Pyrenees in such a way that Louis would be able to take advantage, after 1665, of a clause allowing him a legal claim upon part of the Spanish Netherlands.

579 *in India*: the Portuguese were the first to set up regular trading links with India in the sixteenth century, but in the seventeenth,

the Dutch replaced them, operating through an East India Company floated in 1602. An English Company had received its royal charter in 1600 but was forced by the Dutch in 1624 to withdraw from trading in the islands and set up new factories on the continent. The French Compagnie des Indes was formed between 1642 and 1664 and in 1668 it established a factory at Surat. In 1672 the French took St Thomé from the Portuguese, who then still controlled most of the west coast, but the Dutch drove them out. It was not until the eighteenth century, when the French were as strong in India as the English, that battle for control was fully joined.

579 *ties of blood*: Henrietta Maria, sister of Louis XIII, was the wife of Charles I, and mother of Charles II and the Duchesse d'Orléans, sister-in-law to Louis XIV. However, England would not become France's 'natural ally' in Louis's campaign of territorial expansion later in the 1660s.

580 *Batavian pamphlets*: the satirical prints published in the Dutch Republic. The term derives from the Batavi, a Germanic people who, in Roman times, occupied the *Batavorum insula*, an area between the Rhine and the Waal.

      M. le Prince: that is, Condé†. For the other names, see the List of Historical Characters.

581 *Argus*: a prince of Argos who had a hundred eyes, fifty of which were always open. Juno set him to keep watch on Io, of whom she was jealous and had metamorphosed into a heifer. But Mercury beguiled Argus with his flute and, when he was completely asleep, cut off his head.

582 *La Vallière's apartment*: 'And so La Vallière finding in the same chamber where she herself was lodged a young woman in whom she had already confided, now made her confidences complete and, since Montalais had a far readier wit than she, found much pleasure and great relief in doing so.' Montalais had told Louise of Guiche's love for Madame and had sworn her to secrecy. She had kept the secret, thus inadvertently giving Louis cause for his jealous outburst of the previous evening. When she learned that Louise had disappeared, 'Montalais was beside herself' (Mme de La Fayette, op. cit., pp. 458, 461).

583 *Mademoiselle de Mancini*: Marie de Mancini†, with whom Louis was in love before he married the Infanta. See *The Vicomte de Bragelonne*, ch. 13.

586 *stetit sol*: the medal was notorious. It bore the legend *in conspectu meo stetit sol* ('on beholding me the sun stood still'), a text adapted from Joshua 10: 13: 'And the sun stood still, and the moon stayed, until the people had avenged themselves upon their enemies . . .'

Nec pluribus impar: Louis's device: '[a sun] not eclipsed by many suns'.

588 *the fifth*: 'In the morning, the King was informed that no one knew where La Vallière was. The King, who loved her to distraction, was greatly concerned. He went to the Tuileries to find out from Madame where she could be. But Madame knew nothing, being ignorant of the reason for her leaving . . . The King made extensive enquiries and soon discovered where La Vallière had gone. He hastened to the place with an escort of three men. He found her in the outer parlour of the convent . . . She lay prostrate on the floor, weeping and beside herself. The King remained alone with her and, in the course of a long conversation, she admitted to him everything that she had kept concealed. This confession was not enough to grant her his pardon. The King said only as much as needed to be said to oblige her to return, and he sent for a carriage to take her back' (Mme de La Fayette, op. cit., p. 461).

596 *never to leave Thee again!*: Louise's words are prophetic. Abandoned by Louis in 1667, she asked permission to seek permanent retreat. She entered the Carmelite Convent in the Rue Saint-Jacques (not at Chaillot) on 18 April 1674, took her vows on 4 June and remained there as Sister Louise de la Miséricorde until she died, full of piety and years, in 1710.

598 *ascended the staircase*: '[The King] returned to Paris to insist that [Louise] be received by Monsieur who had roundly declared that he was well pleased that she had quitted his household and that he had no intention of taking her back. The King entered the Tuileries by a back stair, went directly into an antechamber and sent for Madame, having no wish to be seen, for he had been weeping. There, he begged Madame to take back La Vallière and told her everything that he had just learned about her and her affairs [with Guiche]. Madame was greatly taken aback, as may be imagined, but could deny nothing. She promised the King that she would break with the Comte de Guiche and agreed to receive La Vallière once more. The King had some difficulty in obtaining this from Madame, but he begged so long, with tears in his eyes, that finally he got what he wanted' (Mme de La Fayette, op. cit., p. 461).

605 *a long poem*: an echo of the famous line of the *Art poétique* (ii. 94) by Boileau†: 'A sonnet without blemish is the equal of a long poem.'

609 *Mortemart family*: to which Mlle Tonnay-Charente† belonged.

612 *middle height*: Louis (like d'Artagnan) was 5 feet 6 inches tall, the average height for a man in the seventeenth century.

623 *tu quoque*: 'you too'. According to Suetonius (*The Twelve Caesars*, I. §82), Caesar's reproach to Brutus was spoken in Greek. The expression is more familiar in English as *Et tu, Brute* (*Julius Caesar*, III. i).

625 *Pylades . . . for Achilles*: Orestes, son of Agamemnon and Clytemnestra, killed his mother with the aid of his sister Electra to avenge the death of his father. His friendship for Pylades, to whom he gave Electra in marriage, was legendary. Patroclus was the friend of Achilles, and fought with him at the siege of Troy. His death at the hands of Hector brought Achilles out of his tent, to which he had withdrawn because he had been slighted by Agamemnon, and set him on the path of revenge (*Iliad*, bks 16 and 17).

628 *Saint-Germain*: i.e. the Renaissance palace of the French kings at Saint-Germain-en-Laye, 20 km. west of Paris.

631 *towards her*: the secret stairway is an invention prompted by a stray remark made by Mme de La Fayette (op. cit., p. 456): 'It was thought that it was [at Vaux-le-Vicomte] that [the King] first saw [Louise] in private, but for some time he had been seeing her in the apartments of the Comte de Saint-Aignan.'

636 *Hampton Court*: on the Thames, 15 miles south-west of London.

638 *seven wise men of Greece*: Solon of Athens ('Know thyself'), Chilo of Sparta ('Consider the end'), Thales of Miletos ('Nothing is certain'), Bias of Priene ('Most men are wicked'), Cleobulos of Lindos ('Follow the golden mean'), Pittacos of Mitylene ('Do not procrastinate'), Periander of Corinth ('All is possible to him who works').

640 *Hero*: priestess of Venus, loved by Leander, who swam the Hellespont nightly to visit her. When he drowned, she too threw herself into the sea.

to paint yours: court-painters were present at Fontainebleau but no portrait of La Vallière dates from the summer of 1661. The best-known are those by Pierre Mignard (1610–95) and Jean Nocret (1618–72), formerly court-painter to Gaston d'Orléans. Both

Mignard and Peter Lely (1618–80) also painted her with her two surviving children. The description of La Vallière two paragraphs further on seems to be based on none of these, but on a large allegorical portrait of the Royal family in 1670, where Madame wears the jet ornaments and pearl-grey gown and holds flowers in both hands. It is reproduced in Joanna Richardson, *Louis XIV* (1973), pp. 86–7.

641 *an Erycina*: a surname given to Venus, derived from Mount Eryx in Sicily, where she had a temple.

Patru . . . Tallemant des Réaux: Olivier Patru (1604–81), a lawyer and friend of Boileau, better known as a speaker than as a teller of tales. The address he gave on his entry to the French Academy in 1640 was so well received that the 'discours de réception' was thereafter required of all newly elected members. Tallemant des Réaux (1619–92) wrote anecdotal memoirs called *Historiettes* which are of great historical interest. They were largely completed by about 1659 but not published until 1834.

644 *his grandfather*: Henri IV†, who was fond of this particular oath.

645 *the Euripus*: a narrow strait between the island of Euboea and the coast of Bœotia (of which Thebes was the capital), swept by a tidal current so irregular that Aristotle is said to have thrown himself into it because he could not find a cause for the phenomenon.

Cocytus: in Epirus, one of the five rivers of hell. The unburied dead wandered its banks for 100 years.

646 *Wolsey*: the Palace was built in 1526 by Cardinal Wolsey who presented it to Henry VIII.

Alhambra: the palace of the Moors in Granada.

Titian . . . Van Dyck: Titian (1477–1576) and Giovanni Antonio Pordenone (1484–1540) were artists of the Venetian school. Antoine Van Dyck (1599–1641), born at Antwerp, painted the celebrated portrait of Charles I to which Dumas refers.

prisoner to Hampton Court: read 1647. After being arrested at Holdenby Castle by Cornet Joyce on 3 June, Charles I was obliged to follow the army. 'The leaders of the army, having established their dominion over the parliament and the city, ventured to bring the king to Hampton-Court; and he lived for some time in that palace, with an appearance of dignity and freedom' (David Hume, *History of England* (1789), x. 81). Wearying of his confinement, Charles escaped on 11 November, but thereafter was held prisoner at Carisbrooke Castle on the Isle of Wight.

648 *Lady Castlemaine*: Barbara Villiers (1641–1709), Countess of Castlemaine and Duchess of Cleveland, a cousin to Buckingham. She became Charles II's mistress in May 1660 immediately after the King's return to England, and by him had a number of children later acknowledged by Royal Warrant.

Lucy Stewart: Dumas merges Lucy Walter (c.1630–58), whom Charles made his mistress at The Hague in 1648, and Frances Stewart (1648–1702), who came to court in 1663, was pursued by the King in 1666, and later became Duchess of Richmond.

Grafton: Mary Grafton is an invention, nor was there yet a Duke of Grafton who was father to her and to Mme de Bellière: see p. 654. Henry Fitzroy (1663–90), second son of Charles II by Barbara Villiers, Lady Castlemaine, was acknowledged by the King, and the duchy of Grafton was created for him. Dumas simply conjures a suitably 'English' name.

649 *son of one*: i.e. Athos.

651 *almost a savage*: Raoul alludes both to his military campaigns in 'many countries' (see note to p. 212) and his adolescence which he had spent largely with Athos on his estate at La Fère, near Blois.

652 *ever since we met in France*: Raoul had cooled the tempers of Buckingham and Guiche at Le Havre, when Henrietta had disembarked in February 1661. See *The Vicomte de Bragelonne*, ch. 85.

653 *past four days*: it is still early July.

654 *Do you know her?*: Madame de Bellière†, née de Bruc, was French, as Dumas noted on p. 83.

655 *used to write to me before*: see note to p. 185.

658 *cartoons by Raphael*: both Charles I and Charles II were collectors of art. Hampton Court already held a rich collection of paintings, including works by the Italian masters, Holbein, Van Dyck, Peter Lely's 'Beauties of the Court of Charles II', and the cartoons of Raphael (1483–1520).

exile, poverty, and misery: the 'fourteen years' span the time between Charles's arrival in France in 1646 and his restoration in May 1660. *The Vicomte de Bragelonne* (chs 6–32) portrays Charles during this time as a poor, lonely outcast. In reality, though he suffered the indignities of a king in exile, he was well attended and travelled extensively in pursuit of his claim to the English throne.

659 *a Helen*: Helen, wife of Menelaus, was carried off by Paris and thus was begun the Trojan War.

662 *a perfect Bœotian*: the people of ancient Bœotia were farmers whose rustic ways were despised by sophisticated Athenians. The term therefore came to mean a person of rude manners and slow intelligence.

663 *his antechamber at Blois*: see *The Vicomte de Bragelonne*, ch. 8.

665 *'Silence gives consent'*: *Qui tacet consentire videtur*. Sayings along these lines exist in most European languages.

egenti cuncta: a Latin tag, not the device of her non-existent 'house'.

667 *or stay and die*: III. v. The words are spoken by Romeo.

669 *people's faces*: as a novelist, Dumas found the art of reading character from faces very useful. A comprehensive system of 'Physiognomy' was codified by Johann Caspar Lavater (1741–1801).

street of the Jardins Saint-Paul: a medieval street but still in existence (4th *arrondissement*), which runs south from the Rue Charlemagne to the Seine just east of the Pont Marie.

THE WORLD'S CLASSICS

A Select List